THE *Black Lotus* SERIES

e.k. blair

ISBN-13: 978-1539052562

Cover Design by E.K. Blair
Editing by Lisa Christman, Adept Edits
Interior design by Angela McLaurin, Fictional Formats
Photography by Erik Schottstaedt

Editor: Lisa Christman, Adept Edits
Photographer: Erik Schottstaedt
Cover Designer: E.K. Blair
Interior Designer: Champagne Formats

ISBN:978-0-9963970-0-1

Editor: Lisa Christman, Adept Edits and Ashley Williams
Photographer: Erik Schottstaedt
Cover Designer: E.K. Blair
Interior Designer: Champagne Formats

ISBN: 9780996397025

bang

THE BLACK LOTUS SERIES

USA TODAY BESTSELLING AUTHOR

e.k. blair

For Cathy

Because life is not a fairytale, but we all need that one person who keeps the dream alive.

You are that person for me.

"I'm afraid I can't explain myself. Because I am not myself, you see?"
-Lewis Carroll

preface

THEY SAY WHEN you take revenge against another you lose your innocence. But I'm not innocent. I haven't been for a very long time. My innocence was stolen from me. Taken was the life I was supposed to have. The soul I was born with. The ruby heart embedded in a life full of hopes and dreams. Gone. Vanished. I never even had a choice. I mourn that life. Mourn the what-ifs. But I'm done. I'm ready to take back what was always meant to be mine. Vengeance is what I seek to reclaim what was viciously ripped from me. So now? Now I plot. Now I take control. Now I don my crown of hatred.

one

(PRESENT)

"HONEY, ARE YOU almost ready?" my husband's voice calls from the other room.

I look at my reflection in the mirror as I slide in my pearl earring, whispering to myself, "Yes."

Straightening my posture and smoothing the slick fabric of my dress, I run my fingers through my long, red hair. A blanket of carmine. Loose waves falling over my bare shoulders. The coolness of the midnight blue silk that clings to the slight curves of my small frame. The stoic good wife. My husband, the beacon of my admiration, or so it seems.

"Stunning."

My eyes shift in the mirror to Bennett as he strolls into my closet and towards the island dresser where I stand. He drags my hair to the side, exposing my neck for his lips to land.

"Mmm," I hum at his touch before turning in his arms to adjust his black bowtie.

His eyes are pinned on me as I focus on his neck, and when I flick my attention up, he gives me a soft smile. I return it. He's striking with his strong bone structure, square jaw, and chestnut hair with the faint flecks of silver. A sign of his thirty-four years and his influential status. A mogul. Owner of the world's largest steel company. He is power. And I the recipient.

"Baldwin is ready with the car," he says before kissing my forehead.

I grab my purse and Bennett helps me with my coat before we take the elevator down. As we walk through the lobby of The Legacy, my home for the past three years, Bennett keeps his hand on the crest of my back, guiding me out into the night's bite of winter.

"Mr. Vanderwal," Baldwin, our driver and good friend to my husband for years, greets with a nod before turning his attention to me, "Mrs."

"Good evening," I say as I slip my hand in his, and he helps me into the back seat of the Land Rover.

Bennett slides in after me and takes my hand in his lap when Baldwin shuts the door and then hops in the front seat. 'Metamorphosis' by Glass, Bennett's favorite, swallows the silence and fills the car. Lifting my free hand up, I place it on the ice-cold window, feeling the dampness and chill as it seeps into my skin.

"I love the snow," I murmur, more to myself than to my husband, but he responds anyway.

"You say that every winter."

Turning to look at him and then down at our linked hands, I release a soft hum before he shifts and says, "So Richard said he stopped by this hotel the other day and mentioned that it would be a good location to hold our New Year's Eve party this year."

"What's the name?"

"Lotus."

"Interesting," I note before asking, "This is McKinnon's new hotel, right?"

"His son's, actually. I've yet to meet him."

"Hmm."

Giving my hand a light squeeze, he questions, "What's that look for?"

"McKinnon can be, well . . ."

"An ass?"

I smile and agree, "Yes. I just never knew he had any children, that's all."

Driving through the Saturday evening traffic in the loop of Chicago, we finally pull up to the newly built boutique hotel that will cater to the city's elite. We tend to find ourselves at a monotonous number of events such as this. With Bennett's status, not only in this city, but worldwide, his presence is of an accord that is sought after for publicity and other reasons. But Bennett has found himself in several business dealings with Calum McKinnon over the years, so tonight's event wasn't one that we could skip out on.

When Baldwin opens the door and helps me down, I right myself and adjust my long dress before being led through the glass doors and inside the lobby of Lotus. While Bennett leaves my side to check our coats, I take in the decorum of guests and bite the inside of my cheek. I know I'm with the wealthiest man here, but my nerves tend to stain my gut, wondering if these people can see right through me.

I'm greeted with a glass of champagne and the eyes of a few women that serve on some of the charity boards that I sit on.

"You ready, honey?"

My husband wraps his arm around my hip and guides us over to the first of many interactions we will have. I gloss on my smile, raise my chin, and play the part. The part I have played since I met Bennett.

He's a loving husband, always has been. Firm in his business, but so very gentle with me, as if I'm breakable. Maybe I used to be, but not anymore. I'm as strong as they come. Weakness derives from the soul. Most everyone has one, which gives a woman like me leverage. Leverage to play people to my liking, and so I do.

"Nina!" I hear my name being drawn out by one of my *friends.*

"Jacqueline, don't you look lovely," I say as she leans in to kiss my cheek.

"Well, I can't even compete with you. Gorgeous as always," she says before turning her attention to Bennett and blushing as she says hello. I'm sure she just soaked her panties as well. She's a desperate flirt. Her husband is a sorry excuse for a man. But that husband is a business partner with Bennett, so I put up with his misogynistic bullshit and feel sorry for the twit that he married. She's been trying to get into my husband's pants since I first met her. I've never said a word because desperation is not something that Bennett is attracted to.

While Jacqueline flirts with my husband, I scan the room. Everyone dressed in their finest, drinking and socializing. I turn away from the mindless people and take in the sleek, modern design of the hotel. A minimalistic fitting but clearly bathed in money. As I float my gaze around the room, I land on a pair of eyes staring at me. Eyes that catch my interest. Standing in a small group, not paying attention to a single person around him, a man—a startlingly attractive man—is watching me. Even as I look at him from across the room, he doesn't divert his lock on me; he merely cocks a small grin before taking a sip out of his highball. When a slender blonde strokes his arm, the contact is lost. Impeccably dressed in a bespoke suit, he has a slightly uncaring look about him. His hair is styled loosely, as if he just ran his hands through the thick locks and said *fuck it*, and his defined jaw is covered in day-old stubble. But that suit . . . yeah, that suit is clearly covering a body that is well maintained. The lines and cuts hug his form, accentuating broad shoulders that V down to slender hips.

"Honey?"

Pulled away from my lingering eye, I turn to my husband's curious look and notice that Jacqueline is no longer by his side.

"What's got your attention?" he asks.

"Oh. I'm just taking everything in. This place is amazing, huh?"

"I was asking about the party, but I guess you were zoned out. So what do you think?"

"Yes, I agree. This would be a great venue and a nice change of scenery," I tell him, and when I do, I see *fuck it* guy approaching. He has an ease with his stride, and the other women in the room see it too.

"You must be Bennett," he says in a silky, rough Scottish brogue that's reminiscent of his father's accent as he reaches out his hand to my husband. "I'm Declan McKinnon. My father speaks very highly of you."

"Good to finally meet you, Declan. I haven't seen Cal here tonight," Bennett says as he shakes *fuck it* guy's hand, who now has a name.

"He's isn't here. He had to fly to Miami to take care of some business."

"That old bastard never stops moving, does he?" Bennett laughs and Declan joins, shaking his head, saying, "Sixty years old and still barking orders to anyone who will listen. Hell, even to those who won't."

When Declan looks over to me, my husband apologizes and says, "Declan, this is my wife, Nina."

Taking my hand, he leans in and kisses my cheek before pulling back and complimenting, "It's a pleasure. I couldn't help but take notice across the room earlier." Looking at Bennett, he adds, "You're a lucky man."

"I tell her that every day."

I wear my smile as a good wife should. I've been doing this for years, numb to the ridiculous accolades these men tend to throw around in their lame attempts at gentlemanly ways. I can see that Declan makes no attempts though. His shoulders are loose. He's relaxed.

"This place is quite an accomplishment. Congratulations," Bennett tells him.

"Thank you. It only took a few years off my life, but," he says as he takes in the surroundings, "she's exactly how I envisioned her," before bringing his eyes back to me.

This guy is outright flirting, and I'm surprised when it slides past Bennett as he continues in conversation.

"I was just telling Nina that your hotel would provide a perfect backdrop for our year-end party that we throw for our friends."

I butt in with a smirk, saying, "It's a once-a-year event where my husband releases the reins, allowing me to create an event to accentuate his financial power, simply to remind everyone who's on top. A penis extender, if you will, and he's due for his annual visit." I tease with a tender femininity that has the boys laughing in amusement at my tart words. I laugh along with them as I shoot my husband a flirty wink.

“She’s got a sweet mouth on her,” Declan says.

“You have no clue,” Bennett responds as he looks down at me with his grin. “But despite what she says, she loves planning this yearly engagement, and I get a thrill out of watching her spend all of my hard-earned money. But we’re in a bind because the venue we selected a few months back is now under renovation and the space won’t be ready in time.”

“When does this event take place?”

“It’s a New Year’s Eve ball,” he answers.

“Sounds like that is doable,” Declan says as he takes out a business card from inside his suit jacket, and instead of handing it to Bennett, he hands it to me, saying, “Since it seems you’re the woman I’ll be answering to, here are my contact numbers.”

Taking the card from between his fingers, I watch as he turns and tells my husband, “I’ll be sure to oversee the planning to ensure that Nina gets everything she requests.”

“Looks like I’ll be writing a big check this year,” my husband jokes. “Well, Declan, it was great to finally put a face to the name, but if you’ll excuse us, I’d like to show off my wife on the dance floor.”

When Bennett leads us to the full dance floor and wraps me in his arms, I take the opportunity to peek over his shoulder to find Declan watching me intently. This guy makes no qualms about his interest, and a pang of elation thrums inside me as my husband slowly moves me with ease.

We continue to spend the evening mingling and visiting with friends and business associates before we retire for the evening and head back to The Legacy. Stepping off the elevator and into the penthouse that Bennett owned when I first met him four years ago, we walk through the darkened living room. The only light is from the moon that’s casting its glow behind the snow-filled clouds outside the floor to ceiling windows that span across the two walls. I enter the master suite behind Bennett, and as I slip off my heels, I look up to see that he has already undone his bowtie and it hangs around the collar of his white tuxedo shirt, which he is now unbuttoning.

His eyes are rapt as they move down my body. I stand there as he slowly approaches and then slides his hands along the length of my sides until he finds himself on his knees in front of me. He runs his hands up my legs through the opening of the slit in my dress, and as soon as his fingers hit my panties, I turn it off.

The steel cage wraps around my heart and before my stomach can turn, I shut down.

Numb.

Vacant.

He drags my panties down my legs and I step out of them before I feel the warmth of his tongue when he slides it along the seam of my pussy, but I am able to keep myself from entertaining the slightest impulse of intimacy. I've been sleeping with my husband for years, but I refuse to allow the pleasure I lead him to believe I'm experiencing.

Why?

I'll tell you why.

Because I hate him.

He thinks, in this moment, that we're making love. His cock fills me slowly as I lie beneath him. Arms laced around his neck. Legs spread open wide, inviting him in deeper as he makes a meal out of my tits. He believes everything I want him to. He always has. But this is merely a game for me. A game he foolishly has fallen into. He never questions my love for him, and now my body writhes underneath his and moans in mock pleasure as he comes hard, jerking his hips into me, telling me how much he loves me, and I give his words right back.

"God, Bennett, I love you so much," I pant.

His head is nestled in the yoke of my neck as he tries to calm his breathing, and when he lifts up, I run my fingers through his hair and over his damp scalp as he looks into my eyes.

"You're so stunning like this."

"Like what?" I question softly.

"Sated."

Idiot.

two

(PRESENT)

ROLLING OVER IN bed, I find myself alone. Nothing new. Bennett's aftershave still lingers in the air, and when I freshen up and walk out into the open-concept living room, I see him sitting at the bar in the kitchen. He reads a file while drinking his coffee. Tying the sash of my silk robe around my waist, I approach him from behind, wrapping my arms around his shoulders, giving him a kiss.

"Good morning," he says with a grin, happy to see me.

"You're up early," I respond as I note his three-piece suit.

Setting the file down, he turns to pull me in between his legs. "I'm leaving for Dubai. Did you forget?"

"Of course not. But you don't leave for another few hours," I tell him and then drop my head, adding in mock sadness, "I wish you would stay."

Kissing my lips, he draws away and strokes his fingers through my long hair, combing it back. "It's only for a few days. Plus, you'll be busy."

"Busy?"

"I need you to start getting everything lined up for the party. It's just over a month away and announcements need to go out soon. Richard isn't going with me, so he'll be around this week if you need anything."

Richard is Jacqueline's husband and Bennett's business partner. He has always rubbed me the wrong way, but I feign my liking for him merely for Bennett.

He wears an ascot for Chrissakes.

"Okay. Well, I'll do some work from here today and then call the hotel to set up a meeting."

As I walk over to fix a cup of hot tea, Bennett gets back to his work before he has to catch his flight. After a while, Baldwin takes his luggage down to the car while we say our goodbyes.

"I'm gonna miss you," I murmur, to which he responds, "Honey, you always say that."

Rubbing up against him, I cover his mouth with mine. "Because I always do."

He smiles.

I smile.

"Call me as soon as you land so that I know you're okay."

"I love you."

I follow him to the elevator and give him one last kiss before he leaves and then make my way to the study to work on the laptop. Getting myself comfortable, I open the lid and type *Declan McKinnon* into the search engine. Link after link floods the screen. I click on one and read:

Declan Alexander McKinnon
Born in Edinburgh, Scotland
Age: 31
Son of Calum McKinnon and the late Lillian McKinnon
MBA studies at The University of St. Andrews in Scotland

I continue to read about his various academic and business accomplishments and recognitions. I've met his father on several occasions and know that the family name is a well-respected one, so I can imagine the pressure on him to keep it as such.

Clicking over to the image search, hundreds of pictures of him grace the screen with a variety of women attached to his arm. Clearly he enjoys his bachelor status, but it seems he is new to the Chicago area.

Without pondering on him too much, I close the internet down and open Bennett's address book to begin working. Because of his notoriety, our extravagant annual event calls to the cravings of egos. For that alone, security and privacy are a necessity.

In lieu of my usual distaste for my husband, I must give him credit for being a self-made man. For building this multi-billion dollar company from the ground up and making the Vanderwal name something to be admired. A name that adorns me when my former was tarnished.

Once I have a rough guest list, I email it to Bennett for his lookover. Walking out of the study, Clara catches my eye. She's busy unloading groceries in the kitchen when I say, "I didn't hear you come in."

"Mrs. Vanderwal, hi," she says sweetly. "Your husband insisted that I come in today since he's going away on business. Is he still here?"

"No, you missed him." Walking over, I step into the kitchen and start helping her put away the food.

"Stop fussing over this," she playfully scolds, and I smile at her when she shoos me out of the kitchen.

I never had a mom, and although Clara is an employee, she fills our home with a warmth that only a woman with a strong maternal sense can do.

"Would you like for me to fix you a cup of tea?"

"No, thank you. I had one earlier."

I take a seat at the bar as she asks, "You hungry?"

Shaking my head, I say, "I think I'm going to hang around here today. Bennett wants me to start working on the ball, so I figure I'll lie around and surf the internet for ideas."

"Is it that time already?"

"Mmm hmm."

"How fast the years go by. When you get to be my age, you better not blink. Ever," she says with a soft smile as she starts to pull out pans to cook.

I walk over to the windows and watch as the snow falls over the city. From up here on the seventy-first floor, I feel like a queen. I take a moment to enjoy the view before I get to work while Clara busies herself in the kitchen, preparing meals for the next few days. Time escapes me and before I know it, the sky is darkening and Clara is saying goodbye.

WHEN I WAKE up the next morning, I take my time getting ready. I wander over to the windows, and as I'm looking down on the busy traffic in the loop on this Monday morning, I take a sip of my tea and then hear my phone ring. I see it's Bennett and answer.

"Hey, honey," I say as I walk over to the sofa and take a seat.

"Hi. I tried calling when I landed yesterday."

"Sorry. I went to bed early."

"That taxing of a day, huh?" he jokes with light laughter.

"Yeah, something like that. Must be this constant snow we're having. Makes me lazy," I tell him. "So how is everything going?"

"Good. Just met with our new client and had a late lunch. I'm heading back to the hotel now to grab a shower before I have to wine and dine these bastards later tonight at dinner, but I wanted to catch you because I missed hearing your voice last night."

"You missed my voice, huh?"

"I missed more than your voice," he flirts.

Letting out a deep breath, I tell him, "I miss having you in bed with me. I'm always lonely without you here. This place is too quiet and too still."

"Didn't Clara stop by yesterday?" he asks.

"She did. You know, you don't have to mollycoddle me. I'm a big girl."

"I like to . . . what did you call it? *Mollycoddle*?" I can hear the chuckle in his voice when he says this, and I play right back in laughter, saying, "Yes. Mollycoddle. For such a worldly man, you should broaden your vocabulary."

"Is that so? Well, maybe when I get back I should show you just how expansive my vocabulary is."

I laugh. If there's one thing Bennett is not, it's a dirty talker, but I give him a flirtatious, "Hmm . . . maybe you should come home early."

"I wish. Although I *am* enjoying the warmer temperatures here. It's nice and sunny."

"If you're trying to make me jealous, it won't work. You know I love the cold and grey. Gives me a reason to cuddle up to your warmth every night."

"So what kept you warm last night?"

"Stuffing my stomach full of Clara's baked ziti and then huddling down deep in the blankets."

"Well, I'll be home soon enough to keep you warm, hun," he says in a smooth voice before asking, "So what's on your agenda today?"

"I was going to give the hotel a call to see if I can set up a meeting to look over the space again."

"We were just there."

"Yeah, but now I want to see it empty, without all of Chicago's upper crust loitering in it."

He laughs at me and then says, "Sweetheart, don't you forget that you are as upper crust as they get."

"And I only have you to thank for that, darling," I tease. "But seriously, I want to see what the space looks like empty and talk to management to find out if they have any new leads on vendors. I'd like to step out of the norm from what we've done the past couple of years."

"As long as it has your hand in it, it will be amazing. Everything you touch turns to perfection. Just look at me."

"Perfection, huh? Well, I can't argue with that ego of yours. I wouldn't change a thing about you."

"And I you," he compliments before saying, "The car just pulled up to the hotel, so I need to let you go."

"Okay. Try not to work too hard. I miss you."

"Miss you too, love. Have a good day."

We hang up and I let out a deep breath. Talking to him like that used to be difficult in the beginning, but now it's as natural as wanting to wipe dog shit off your shoe.

I walk into my closet to pull out the clutch I took to the party the other night. Opening it, I take out the business card that Declan gave me and walk back out to the living room to make the call.

"Lotus," a woman's voice purrs.

"Declan McKinnon, is he available?"

"And who shall I say is calling?"

"Nina Vanderwal."

She puts me on hold for a moment and when the line is picked up, she tells me, "Mr. McKinnon is finishing up a meeting. Would you like me to take a message?"

"Well, I don't want to disturb his schedule, but I will be organizing an event and would like to come see the main ballroom space and discuss vendors."

"Of course. Let me direct you over to our manager," she says before transferring me.

After a brief chat with the hotel manager, we set up a meeting an hour from now. Hanging up the phone, I call Baldwin to have the car ready to drive me over to the hotel. When he arrives, I'm ready as he helps me slip my coat on over my ivory silk top that's tucked into my tailored, black, wool pants.

"Are you ready?" Baldwin asks as I grab my purse.

"Ready."

We ride down on the elevator, and as we walk through the lobby, the car has already been pulled around out front.

"Watch your step," Baldwin says as I maneuver around the small ice patches in my high heels.

When I arrive at Lotus, I walk in and am greeted by the manager who is waiting for me. He leads me into the ballroom, and I take note of the space. The main seating area will easily accommodate the event, and there is an attached lounge that houses various cigars and liquors that are displayed around the dark mahogany room. The bar is broad and masculine, and the woodwork is quite impressive. It's a shame all this was hidden beneath the sea of people that was here at the grand opening. The setting is an intimate one despite the vast size of the room. The dance floor is situated down a small flight of stairs, setting it off from the dining room, creating a less hectic atmosphere for entertaining.

A familiar accent catches me off guard as I'm walking around and taking notes in my memo book.

"How does she look?" His brogue casts through the room, and when I turn to catch his eye, I ask, "Excuse me?"

Scanning the space, he clarifies, "The space, I mean. Looks different empty, doesn't it?"

Turning my head to admire the décor, I say, "Yes. I was just thinking about how much detail I failed to see the other night with all the people here."

He walks over to me, looking polished in his slacks and fitted button-up, sans suit jacket and tie, with a slight grin on his face, and reaches out for my hand and finally greets, "It's good to see you again, Nina."

The way my name is caressed by his accent is without a doubt sexy as hell.

As he brushes his lips over my knuckles, the stubble along his jaw grazing over the soft skin of my hand, I don't respond, but when he keeps his hold a beat too long, I pull away. His smirk remains, as if amused by my reaction.

He casually turns to the man that was showing me around and dismisses him. Turning back to me, he shoves his hands into the pockets of his slacks and asks, "So, what do you think?"

"I think my husband was right; it's the perfect place to host the party."

"Great. Did you need to look around anymore?"

"I think I've gotten my fill for the moment."

He seems humored by something, maybe me, and pulls his hands out of his pockets, placing one on my back as he leads me out of the room.

"Let's go to my office and discuss the details then."

We make our way into his office, and I stand in the center of the oversized room as he walks over to his desk, moving with a relaxed confidence, and grabs the laptop. He nods his head towards the leather couch, saying, "Please, have a seat."

I situate myself and open my planner, flipping through the pages to find my calendar, when I feel his eyes on me.

"Why are you looking at me like that?" I ask when I look up at him, feigning my annoyance.

"Where does one even buy a paper planner anymore?" he teases.

"Lots of places."

"I haven't seen one of those in years. You do know they make these things called tablets now."

Smiling at his banter, I say, "Yes. Every now and then I'm able to crawl out from under my rock to keep up to speed with modern technology, thank you."

He shakes his head and laughs as I watch his smile reach his green eyes and crinkle at the corners.

"Do you even own one?" he asks, still smirking at me.

"No."

He doesn't respond, but his unfaltering look pulls out my answer to his unspoken 'Why?'

"I like privacy. Technology disrupts that. I can burn paper and throw the ashes away as if it never existed. Untraceable." Giving the sly grin back to him, I add, "But you? Don't you think it's foolish that you're putting yourself out there? To be exposed?"

"Is this a riddle?"

I laugh, ignoring his question as I flip through my calendar and confirm, "You have December 31st open, correct?"

Sighing, he shifts and looks at his laptop, saying, "Yes."

"Great. Bennett likes to keep this event small, two hundred or so. Security is important to him—"

"You as well?" he interrupts and I soften my face, smile, and say, "Yes. Me, as well. As I was saying, guests will need to check in, so will your staff provide that amenity?"

"Anything you want."

We spend the next hour discussing ideas for setup and scheduling meetings with a few vendors for the next couple of weeks before I call to have Baldwin pick me up. Declan's well-bred manners sway to the salacious side with the way he kisses me when I leave, gripping my upper arms in his hands and dragging his lips along my cheek before pressing his lips on the shell of my ear, whispering, "Until next time."

three

(PRESENT)

DECLAN CALLED ME two days ago to confirm my meeting with the florist. He recommended the company located in Andersonville that his hotel uses to outfit the lobby, so I agreed. After discussing the masked ball theme with Bennett this morning, he gave me the green light, which made me happy. I can tell he misses me from our phone call—he wasn't quick to hang up—but he'll be returning from Dubai tomorrow evening. Despite his loneliness, he was happy to have acquired the production plant that he set out to buy from the nearly bankrupt company over there.

The drive to Andersonville takes longer than usual with the weather. Winters in Chicago are brutal to the city but a brutality that I enjoy. So as I ride in the backseat, I find myself watching the white snow hit the window and slowly melt to a drizzling cascade down the glass.

Arriving at Marguerite Gardens, I walk into the rustic shop. Brick walls, weathered wooden floors, extravagant floral arrangements set atop the agrarian tables, and *him.* Standing there in charcoal slacks and a light blue button-up, he turns away from the woman he's speaking with and smiles as I walk over to him. Miffed.

"What are you doing here?"

"You made it," Declan announces quietly with what looks like irritation and drops a scant kiss to my hand when he takes it.

"I didn't know you'd be joining me."

"I promised your husband I would oversee everything to ensure you get exactly what you want. So here I am," he states, and then lowers his voice, "ensuring you get exactly what you want."

"Why do you do that?"

"Do what?"

"*That,*" I say. "Your crass flirting."

"Do I make you uncomfortable?"

"Are you trying to make me uncomfortable?"

Completely ignoring my question, he turns around and calls out, "Betty, show us what you have."

The lady he was talking to when I walked in is now situated behind one of the tables.

Declan pulls a chair out for me, and as I take a seat, Betty greets me and says, "So I was informed that we are planning a New Year's Eve party. Do you already have an idea of what you'd like?"

"I believe we are firm on a masquerade theme. I was leaning towards dark oranges and whites."

Betty and I go through a couple of books, taking notes on flowers and arrangement styles while Declan remains quiet in the seat next to me. At the end of our meeting, we decide on various arrangements of rusty orange dahlias, mint and buttercup roses, antique hydrangeas, ranunculus, and aspidistra.

After Betty excuses herself to leave Declan and me, I pull out my phone to text for the car, but before I can start typing, he snatches it out of my hands and says, "I'm starving."

"Good to know," I snap—annoyed—and grab for my phone at the same time he pulls it away and out of reach. "Give me my phone."

"Have lunch with me."

"No, thank you," I say, making a mockery of my politeness.

Taking my hand and pulling me out of my seat as he stands, he says, "It wasn't a question."

His words come out clipped, almost angry, so I don't give him attitude when he picks up my coat and helps me put it on. I'm not sure what to think about this shift in his demeanor. Normally, he's light and flirty, but today he's quiet and stern.

The frigid wind nearly stings my skin when he leads me outside and walks us over to his black Mercedes sports car. Of course *he* would drive a luxury car like this. It fits the mysterious, sexy look about him. I slip down into the cold leather seat and watch as he walks around the front of the car before he opens his door and gets in.

"Where are we going?" I ask.

"Not telling." He says this with no interpretable body language as he pulls out of the parking lot.

"Why?"

"Because you argue too much."

Feeling like a scolded child with his tone, I want to defy him just to piss him off, but instead, I'll play his game. I'll give him the cooperation he wants.

It's time to start testing the waters.

The drive is short and quiet, and I'm surprised when he turns this luxury car into the lot at the Over Easy Café. I can't even hide the smile on my face at the contrast of this picture as he parks in front of the modest diner.

"Is something funny about this?" he asks when he shuts the car off.

Shooting my narrowed eyes at him, I say, "Your mood is really starting to scathe me. I don't know why you're so pissy, but I wish you'd just cut the shit," before opening my door and walking towards the building. When I look back, he's standing there with an almost proud grin on his face. *What the hell?* I can't figure out what this guy wants, sass or obedience.

Once inside, the place is busy with busboys clearing tables and people chatting loudly while eating. We are quickly served with coffee, and when I pick up the menu, Declan finally speaks, saying, "I figured you hadn't eaten in a place like this in a while, so I thought I would take you somewhere low-key. Don't worry; you'll like the food. Order the blueberry crunch pancakes."

His eyes are soft, as well as his voice, when he says this, and I ask, "Why are you suddenly being nice?"

"I'm cutting the shit. Take it while it lasts because I'm not a man who likes to take orders."

And now, I read him clearly.

With a smile, I give him a sliver of obedience when I say, "I'll have the blueberry crunch pancakes then."

After our waitress stops by to take our order and fantasize about riding Declan's cock, she giggles as she walks away.

"Do you get that a lot?" I ask. "Women feeding your ego as you watch them blush in your presence."

"You always dissect everything like that?"

"You always avoid questions like that?"

Leaning his forearms on the table, he says, "No more than you do."

"You realize, unless we're discussing business, we talk in circles, right?"

"Okay then. No circles. Ask me a question," he prompts and then takes a sip of his coffee, waiting with curious eyes. Emerald ones rimmed with his dark lashes. I can't blame our waitress for her reaction. I wonder how many women go home after meeting him to fuck their fingers or vibrator before their pitiful husbands return from work.

Cleaning my thoughts, I ask the most innocent question I can think of, even though I already know the answer. "Where are you from?"

"That's your question?" he laughs, and when I glare at him, he swallows it and says, "Edinburgh."

"Scotland?"

"Do you know of another?"

Smartass.

"I thought you were cutting the shit and being nice," I say as I lean back and pick up my coffee mug.

"Momentary slip. My turn. How long have you been married?"

"A little over three years."

"How long have you been together?"

"Four years. And that was two questions," I lightly nag.

"I'm not good at following rules either," he says and then continues before giving me a chance to speak. "Sounds like a speedy path to the altar."

"What can I say? When Bennett wants something, he wastes no time in claiming it."

When our waitress returns, I watch as she nervously makes eyes with Declan while she serves our food. I laugh and he takes notice, shaking his head.

"See what I mean?" I ask after she walks off.

"Does that bother you?"

"Why would it bother me?" I question and pick up my fork to cut a piece of my pancake.

"Then why even mention it?"

"Circles, Declan. We're doing it again," I say and then take a bite of the granola-filled pancake as he watches.

"Okay, no circles. You have any kids?"

"No."

"Do you want kids?"

"I can't have kids, so it doesn't really matter what I want."

He takes a pause, not expecting that answer, and then asks, "Why can't you have kids?"

"That's none of your business," I tell him and then take another sip of coffee.

"Do you love him?"

Swallowing hard, I clarify, "My husband?"

"Yes."

He takes a bite of his eggs as I straighten my back and look him dead on. "Your assumption that there could be a possibility of more than one answer is offensive."

I notice the slight upward turn of the corner of his mouth, and he holds his stare for a beat before saying, "Funny how you chose not to answer that question, but instead, avoid."

"Of course I love him."

Lie.

"So he's it?"

I hesitate, making sure he takes notice, and then respond with a simple, "Yes," careful to ensure a slight tremble in my voice.

He catches my subtleties as he keeps his eyes pinned on me and I shift, playing uncomfortable, and I'm certain he buys it when he changes the subject. We spend the rest of our meal in idle chitchat about nothing in particular, and as we leave and walk towards his car, my foot hits a patch of ice, unsteadying my balance. Declan's hands are on me fast as I shuffle and land my back against the side of his car. He's close. Chest to chest. Foggy vapors escaping us with each breath. I don't speak or move away. I wonder if he's going to make a play, because I can tell he's thinking about it. But putting thoughts into action takes balls, and I'm hoping he has them.

In a low voice, he urges, "Push me away, Nina," as if he's testing me.

But I'm the one doing the testing; he just doesn't know it. So I respond with, "Why?"

"Because you love your husband."

Pushing my hands against him, I move him away from me as I say, annoyed, "I do love him."

As if no exchange was just made, he opens the door for me to get in.

When we pull onto the main street, he asks, "Where do you live?"

"Why?"

"Because I'm gonna drive you home," he says, turning his head to look at me.

"The Legacy."

The silence between us is noticeable, and I wonder what he's thinking about, but I don't dare ask. He doesn't allow my thoughts to overtake me when he turns on the stereo. I can tell he's using the music to distract himself as he keeps his eyes focused on the road. I'm granted no reprieve as I consider the thoughts that are scrolling through his head right now. But this part is out of my hands because I won't push. The fall has to come of his own accord. I'm merely the fuel that feeds the vehicle; he's the one driving it. And the destination is up to him.

When he pulls up to my building, he shifts the gear into park and looks over at me. He hasn't spoken for the whole drive, and he remains quiet. Wanting to calm any of the ill thoughts he may be having, I lean back against the seat and let out a sigh as I roll my head over to look at him.

Our eyes are locked, his hands still on the steering wheel, and then I say in a soft voice, free from any undertones, "I had a nice time with you." Declan nods, unconvinced, so I give him a little more to coax him, adding, "I don't have many friends."

When I say this, his hands drop slowly to his lap as he turns slightly towards me. He then asks, "What about those two hundred people on the guest list for the event you're planning?"

"If it weren't for Bennett, those people wouldn't give me a second glance. I wouldn't want them to though."

"Why not?"

"Because they're nothing like me."

"How so?"

Lowering my head to focus on my hands, I don't respond immediately.

"Tell me, Nina."

My eyes meet his when I say, with a faint shake of my head, "I guess I'm still trying to figure that out."

"And your husband?" he questions.

"He doesn't know this. He thinks I enjoy the lunch dates with the wives when I really loathe them."

"Then why even bother?"

Letting go of a deep breath, I say, "Because I want to make my husband happy."

He leans over, closer to me, resting his arm on the center console, and asks, "And what about you, Nina? Who wants to make you happy?"

"Bennett makes me happy," I state while his eyes search my face for hints of dishonesty, and I make sure to let a few slip through. Drifting eye contact for a quick second with a couple rapid blinks. Nodding my head as if trying to convince myself of the words. Giving him a small, feeble smile.

I know he buys it when he says with a gentle voice, "Liar."

He's confident in his accusation when I don't deny it, instead, lowering my head and then turning to look out the windshield.

"I should go." Looking over at him, he gives a nod before I open the door and step out.

Walking to the lobby doors, he calls out, "Nina." When I turn around, he's rolled down the passenger window and gives me back my earlier words. "I had a nice time with you too."

I reward him with a smile before walking away.

When I get inside, I drop my purse and coat on the dining room table and call Baldwin to let him know I got a ride home with Declan and that I won't be needing him for the rest of the evening. I then walk over to inspect the kitchen and notice there is fresh fruit in the fridge that wasn't here this morning, letting me know that Clara has already been here and left.

Knowing there won't be anyone else coming or going, I waste no time pulling my coat back on and grabbing the keys to one of the cars before picking up my purse and heading back out.

When I pull out of the parking garage, I make my way to I-55 and start heading south to the one person who has always been there for me. It's been a few weeks since I last saw Pike, and I miss him. I allow myself the excitement of finally being able to see him—my best friend since I was eight years old.

I pull off the interstate and into the town of Justice before turning onto 79th and heading to the trailer park. When I pull up to the mobile home, I park the car, and take out the key I hide in the lipstick case in my purse. The bass of someone's car stereo rattles the windows, and when I unlock the door and step inside, I relax my shoulders, sigh, and walk straight into Pike's arms. I take his warmth, comfort, and everything else only he can offer as he holds me.

With my arms wrapped around him tightly, I breathe, "I've missed you."

"It's been nearly three weeks," he says as he pulls back to look at me, and when he does, I can see he isn't happy. "Where the fuck have you been, Elizabeth?"

four

(PAST)

"ELIZABETH," MY DADDY calls from outside my bedroom door. "Do you need help?"

I struggle against the glittery fabric of my princess dress, trying to find the opening of the sleeve to push my arm through. "No, Daddy," I call out in a heavy breath as I twist and wriggle my arm, finally finding the opening.

"Are you ready?"

I walk over to my toy box and pull out the pink plastic heels that match my sparkly dress. Putting them on, I walk over to my door and open it. I look up at my daddy, holding a small bunch of pink daisies.

"I never get tired of seeing that beautiful smile," he says before taking my hand and kissing the top of it. He then hands me the flowers. "For my princess."

"Thanks, Da—I mean, Prince."

"May I come into your castle?" he asks, and I grab his hand, pulling him into my bedroom—our pretend castle for the afternoon.

"Would you like some tea?" I ask as we walk towards my table by the window that my tea set is on.

"I would love some. My travel from the kingdom was quite long." I watch him sit down on the small chair and giggle as his knees hit his chest.

Daddy and I do this often, have our fairytale tea parties. I don't have a mommy or any brothers and sisters to play with, but that's okay because I get to have him all to myself. He has the prettiest blue eyes, but he tells me mine are prettier.

Setting down the flowers, I pick up the teakettle and pretend to pour him a cup while he eyes the plastic pastries, swirling his finger above them as he decides on the one that he wants.

"Daddy, just pick one."

His eyebrows shoot up in excitement when his hand lands on the yellow cupcake with sprinkles. "Ahh, this one looks delicious," he says before taking his make-believe bite and then licking his fingers.

I scrunch up my face, squealing, "Eww. Princes don't lick their fingers."

"They don't?"

"No. They use napkins."

He looks around, and says, "Well, I don't have a napkin, and I don't want to waste the icing on my fingers."

I exaggerate thinking, tapping my finger on my cheek, and then agree, "You're right. Okay, you can lick your fingers."

We sit in the sunlight of my room and have our fairytale tea, talking about the flying horses we'll ride to the magical forest.

"Did I tell you about Carnegie, the caterpillar I met?" he asks.

"You met a caterpillar?"

"The last time I took my steed to the forest, I did. He had some berries he shared with me and then told me a secret," he says quietly as he sets down his teacup.

"What?!" I exclaim excitedly. "You met a *talking* caterpillar?"

"I did. Do you want to know what he told me?"

"Mmm hmm," I hum, nodding my head energetically.

"Well then, he told me he had been living in the magical forest for years, but that he was once a prince."

"Really? What happened?"

He folds his arms over the tops of his knees and leans his chest against them, saying in a secret whisper, "The kingdom's sorcerer cast a spell on him, turning him into a caterpillar."

"Oh no," I gasp. "Why?"

"Turns out, the king was upset because he told Carnegie to stop sneaking out of his room at night and stealing juice boxes from the fridge, so he had the sorcerer use his magic to turn him into a caterpillar."

"Daddy!"

He has a playful smile on his face. I know he's teasing me since he's been getting on to me about waking up and drinking juice boxes at night. Last night he scared me when he turned on the kitchen light and caught me drinking an apple juice.

"You're not gonna cast a spell on me, are you? I don't wanna be a caterpillar."

"Why not? I could introduce you to Carnegie."

"But I would miss you," I pout.

He reaches out his arms for me. "Come here, baby doll," he says as he turns in the small chair and stretches out his legs. Hoisting me up on his lap, he wraps his big arms around me and makes me giggle when he kisses the tip of my nose. "I'd never cast a spell on you and send you away. You're my little girl, you know that?"

"I thought I was a big girl now that I'm five."

"No matter how big you get, you'll always be my little girl. I love you more than anything."

"Anything? Even more than chocolate?"

I watch him laugh, big smile, lines at the corners of his eyes. "Even more than chocolate."

I place my hand on his cheek, prickly with his stubble, and tell him, "I love you more than chocolate too."

He pecks his lips to mine and then asks, "You wanna know what's sweeter than chocolate?"

"Uh huh."

Before I can leap off his lap, he starts playfully attacking my neck, tickling me as he blows raspberries and then plops us on the floor as I roll around, laughing and squealing. He doesn't stop until the doorbell rings. As I try and catch my breath from all the laughing, he sits up on his knees and orders, "Hop on."

I get off the floor and jump on his back, taking a piggyback ride all the way to the front door.

You've heard the saying, "Beware of what lies on the other side," right? Neither of us could have possibly imagined how our lives would be forever changed when he opened that door. I used to wish that someone would cast a spell on me, forever changing me into a caterpillar. I could've had a good life, living in the mythical forest with Carnegie. Spending our days searching for berries and floating aimlessly on the lily pads in the pond. But instead, I was about to find out the hard truth of life at the age of five. The truth they keep from you as a small child, allowing you to believe that the fairytales are real . . . but they aren't. And neither is magic.

"Cook County P.D.," is all I hear as men come charging into the house.

Chaos. Loud chaos.

"Daddy!" I scream, scared, panicked, clinging my arms around his neck like a vice when a man grabs for me. "DADDY!"

"It's okay, baby," I hear my dad say as another man is talking at the same time.

"You're under arrest."

I don't know what those words mean as ice cold fear runs through me, fisting my daddy's shirt in my hands, unwilling to let go of him.

"It's okay, baby. It's going to be okay," he keeps repeating, but his voice is different and I think he's scared too.

"You need to come with me," the man who's grabbing me says.

"No! Let go!"

I begin kicking my legs when I'm pried off my daddy's back, stretching his shirt because I have my hands clamped so tightly to the fabric as I'm being pulled away.

I see my daddy's eyes—blue eyes—as he turns to look at me. "It's okay," he says calmly, but I don't believe him. "Don't be scared. It's okay."

"No, Daddy!" I cry out as the tears fall. I hold on to his shirt until I am pulled so far back it pops out of my hands.

The moment I am no longer touching the man that sings to me at night, that puts my hair in pigtails, that dances with me while I stand on top of his feet, I'm whisked away. I see my prince drop to his knees as I watch over the man's shoulder who's carrying me away.

"DADDY!" I shriek, throat burning, as they clamp my daddy's hands together behind his back with something. His eyes stay on me, never once pausing as he says, over and over, "I love you, baby. I love you so much, baby girl."

And for the first time ever, I see my daddy cry before the door closes on him and he's gone.

"Let me go! DADDY! NO!" Kicking and swinging, I can't escape this man's hold on me.

"It's okay. Calm down, kiddo," he says, but I won't. I want my daddy.

The man sits down on my father's bed with me still in his arms, fighting. He continues to coax me to calm down, but my screaming and thrashing don't falter until I grow tired. My body is limp as I'm crumpled against his chest.

"Can you tell me your name?" he asks.

I don't speak.

A moment passes and then he says, "I'm Officer Harp. Michael Harp. I'm a policeman. You know what that is, don't you?"

I nod my head against his chest.

"Can you tell me your name?"

Still scared, my voice cracks when I tell him, "Elizabeth."

"Elizabeth. That's a nice name," he says. "I have a daughter whose middle name is Elizabeth. She's much older than you are though."

He continues to talk, but I don't pay attention to what he's saying. I'm so scared and all I want is my daddy. I close my eyes; I can see him on his knees crying. He was scared just like me.

After a while, the door opens and I lift my head to see a chubby woman walking in. I think I've seen her before but I can't remember where. As she gets closer, she says, "Your red hair is beautiful. Has anyone ever told you that?"

"Where's my daddy?"

"That's what I am here to talk to you about," she tells me. "Would you like to join me in the kitchen? We can get a snack or something to drink."

"Umm . . . O-okay," I mumble as the policeman sets me on the floor. When I follow the two of them out of the bedroom and into the kitchen, I look through the house to the front door, but nobody's there anymore.

"Why don't we have a seat?" the woman says, and I walk over to the table and sit down. "Do you want something to drink?"

I nod my head and she prompts, "Can you tell me what you want?"

"Juice box."

Looking over at the policeman, he opens the door to the pantry, and I say, "They're in the fridge."

He walks over, pops the straw in, and sets it in front of me before he leaves the room.

"Confusing day, huh?" she says as she folds her hands together on top of the table. "What's your name?"

"Barbara," she answers but it doesn't help me remember how I know her.

"When's my daddy coming back?"

She takes in a deep breath and then tells me, "That's what I'd like to talk to you about. Your father broke some pretty big rules and just like when you break a rule, what normally happens?"

"I get in trouble."

She nods her head and continues, "Well, your father is in trouble, and he won't be able to come home right now."

"What did he do?"

"I'm not quite sure just yet. But for now, you're going to come with me. I work for the Department of Children and Family Services, which means I'm going to find you a home with really nice people that you will stay with while your father is in trouble and can't be here with you, okay?"

"B-But, I don't want to leave."

"Unfortunately, I can't let you stay here alone. But you can bring some of your things with you. How does that sound?" She says this with a smile, but it doesn't help the churning of my stomach.

Quietly, I slip off of the chair and start walking to my room. I go over to the tea set that's on the table and pick up the pink daisies. My princess flowers. I sit down in the chair that he was sitting in and look over my shoulder to see Barbara walking into the room.

"Do you have a bag?"

I point to the closet and watch as she starts going through my dresser, packing up my clothes. She roams around, going back and forth between my bedroom and the bathroom as I clutch the flowers to my chest.

"You ready to go?" she asks when she steps back into the room, but I don't want to look at her because I don't want to go.

Staring out the window and up into the blue sky, I ask, "When can I come back?"

"I'm not sure," she responds. "Probably not for a while."

Out of the corner of my eye, I see her move across the room and kneel down beside me. As I turn to look at her, she says, "Don't worry. Everything's going to be okay." She looks down at the daisies. "Those are pretty flowers. Do you want to bring them with you?"

Leaving the house, we walk out to her car and I hop into the back seat. As I look out the window, I watch the policeman shut the front door to my house and lock some sort of black box onto the door handle.

"What's that?" I ask Barbara, who's sitting up front.

"What's what, dear?"

"That thing he put on the door."

She looks over to see what I'm talking about and responds, "It's just a lock since we don't have the keys," and then starts driving away while I hold tightly to my flowers.

five

(PAST)

IT'S BEEN THREE years since I was taken away from my home and placed in foster care. Three years since I've seen my dad. I was told he was trafficking guns to South America. I still don't understand everything, but then again, I'm just an eight-year-old kid. A ward of the state of Illinois. Three years and I miss my dad every day. No one will take me to go see him since he's over six hours away, serving his nine-year sentence in Menard Prison.

I sit in my room and wait on my caseworker, Barbara, to come pick me up to take me to my new home. Three years and I'm leaving my fifth home to go to my sixth. The first place I went was in the same town of Northbrook, where I'd lived. But after getting caught sneaking out of my bedroom window a few times during the night, they said they couldn't manage me, and so I left. The same thing has happened at each home I've lived in.

At first I was scared. I cried a lot. I missed my dad and would scream for him, but he never came. I didn't understand then, but I do now. I'm not gonna get to see him until he gets out. I'll be fourteen years old. Fourteen is my new lucky number. I count everything in groups of fourteen just to remind myself that the time will come when I can see him again and we can go back to our life together in our nice house in our nice neighborhood. I miss his smile and the way he smelled. I can't explain it, but sometimes when I'd be at preschool, I can faintly remember lifting my shirt to inhale his scent when I was missing him. The smell of my dad.

Comfort.

Home.

When I hear the doorbell ring, I know it's time. I've been through several home switches before. You'd think I'd be scared, but I'm used to it now. So I grab my bags and head out to the front door. Barbara is standing there talking to Molly, the foster mom that doesn't want to deal with me anymore.

They both turn as I approach and say *hi*.

"You ready, Elizabeth?" Barbara asks.

Nodding my head, I walk past Molly as she places her hand on my shoulder, saying, "Wait."

She kneels down to give me a hug, but I don't return it. I'm sad, but I don't cry; I just wanna leave, so when she lets go, that's what I do.

While I sit in the passenger seat, watching the buildings pass by as Barbara drives, she turns down the radio and says, "Talk to me, kid."

I hate when she calls me *kid*, like I'm not special enough for her to use my name. She only uses it when there are other people around, but alone, I'm *kid*.

"What do you mean?" I ask.

"I've found five good homes for you, and you've managed to get kicked out of every one of them. You keep me busy, you know that?"

I'm not sure if she really wants a response, so I stay quiet before she adds, "You can't keep sneaking out at night. What the hell are you doing out on the streets in the middle of the night anyway?"

"Nothing," I mutter just to say something to appease her. Truth is, I started sneaking out to see if I could find Carnegie. Sounds stupid now, but when I was five, I thought he'd be there, waiting for me to find him. So I would sneak out and walk around, hoping to stumble upon that magical forest. It never happened, and now I'm old enough to know fairytales aren't real, but I still sneak out and look for the forest anyway.

"Well, listen, I couldn't find a home to place you in around here, so you're gonna be in a different town. You're not gonna be seeing me anymore since I don't live there. I'm still going to handle your case, but Lucia will be your contact. She should be doing a visit with you later this week. But a piece of advice—stop causing issues or the next stop will be a group home."

"So I won't see you again?"

She looks over at me, saying, "Probably not, kid."

We've been in the car for almost two hours when we finally exit the highway.

"Welcome to Posen," Barbara says, and it isn't but a couple minutes later when she pulls into a rundown neighborhood.

Chain-link fences run alongside the cracked sidewalks. The homes are old and small, unlike the large brick house I lived in with my dad. Most of these homes have cars parked on their unkempt lawns, chipped paint, and everything about what I'm seeing brings on a well of tears. My stomach knots, and I turn to Barbara, saying, "I don't think I want to live here, Barb."

"Shoulda thought about that when I told you to stop sneaking out at night."

"I promise. I won't do it again. I'll say sorry to Molly," I beg, and when she pulls into the drive of a dirty, old, two-story house that looks like it's barely standing, I start crying. "Please. I don't wanna live here. I wanna go home."

She turns the car off and looks over at me. I feel like I'd do just about anything to convince her to turn the car around and take me back to Northbrook.

"I'm in a bind. You're eight years old with an unstable home history. Now this family has been fostering for years. They are currently fostering a boy a few years older than you," she tells me. "I talked to them just the other day. You'll have your very own room and will go to the same school as their other foster kid."

I keep my mouth shut and listen. I don't want to be here. I wanna run, just open this car door and run as fast as I can. I wonder if she'd be able to catch me.

"You listening?" she asks and refocuses my attention back to her.

I nod my head.

"Come on. I've got a long drive back," she says as she gets out of the car and opens the back door to grab my bags.

With a shaking hand, I open the door and follow her along the weathered driveway to the steps leading up to the front door. The rusted screen door squeaks loudly as she opens it and knocks a few times. I stand there, picking at my nails, praying to God that no one opens the door. That this is all a big mistake and we're at the wrong house.

But it isn't a mistake, and someone does answer the door. A woman, dressed in a homely, long, denim skirt and a light purple sweater, opens the door. I stare at her as Barbara starts to talk. The woman doesn't look scary, but I still feel like bolting. She looks down at me and gives me a soft smile. Her ratty ponytail is attempting to tame her long, brown, frizzy hair.

Stepping aside, she invites us in, and the place smells like stale cigarette smoke. While she leads us through the small living room and back to the kitchen, the two of them continue to talk as I take everything in. Wood-paneled walls, brown carpet, mismatched furniture, and ducks everywhere. *Everywhere.* Ducks on pillows, wooden ducks, ceramic ducks, glass ducks. They line the book shelves, cover the tables, and when I look up, they are even on top of the kitchen cabinets.

"Elizabeth."

It takes me a second to realize that Barbara is saying my name, and when I look over at her, she gives me one of her fake smiles and says, "Mrs. Garrison says that your bedroom is upstairs."

"I hope you like purple," the woman says to me as I look at her purple top and then back up to her face when she says, "You're the first girl we've gotten, so I got a little carried away."

Barbara gives me an annoyed look, nodding her head to encourage me to talk.

"Yeah," I finally say. "Purple is nice."

She smiles and lays her hand over mine. I want to snatch it away, but I don't. I don't do anything that my mind is screaming I should. I just sit.

"Well then, why don't I help you up with your bags before I go?" Barbara says.

The three of us walk up the stairs as they creak beneath our feet and into the purple room. The walls match Mrs. Garrison's sweater, and I watch as she shows me the closet and then the Jack-and-Jill bathroom that adjoins to the other bedroom.

"This seems like a great room, huh?" Barbara says when she plops my bags down on top of the purple twin bed.

"Mmm hmm."

"Well, I have to get back on the road," she tells me, and when she does, I feel the tears hit my cheeks.

Suddenly, I've never felt more alone. Empty.

"There's no need to cry. You're gonna be fine. I know that change can be hard, but you'll be okay. Like I said, Lucia will be out to meet you in a few days, okay?"

"Okay." It's an auto-response because I'm far from okay.

With a light pat on my shoulder, Barbara leaves me behind, standing in the purple room with duck lady.

"Would you like me to help you unpack, dear?" she asks.

"I'll do it."

"Are you hungry? I could fix you a sandwich."

I look up at her through the remaining tears in my eyes and nod my head.

"Great. We normally always eat at the kitchen table, but I'll bring it up to you if you'd like."

"Okay," I say as I start unzipping my bags.

"Elizabeth," she calls from the hall, right outside the bedroom, "I hope you'll like it here. Carl, my husband, worked hard painting this room for you. He's out running a couple errands, but should be home shortly."

When I don't respond, she excuses herself and heads downstairs, leaving me alone to unpack. Next to the bed is a small window that looks out over the front of the house. All the houses are the same aside from the various colors of paint. Everything looks decayed here.

I take my time putting my clothes away and eventually eat the peanut butter sandwich that Bobbi brought me. She told me to call her that rather than Mrs. Garrison.

Aside from a small dresser, desk, and bulletin board, the room is pretty bare. When I walk into the bathroom, the sink counter is already occupied with the other kid's stuff. I wonder if he's like me, how old he is, and if he's nice. I feel like I need a friend more than ever right now. I'm so far from home and so alone.

A loud rumbling from outside calls my attention, and I walk over to look out the window. An old, grey, beat-up pickup truck pulls into the driveway. I watch as an older, fat guy gets out of the driver's seat and starts walking towards the house. Then the boy gets out, but I can't see what he looks like under his baseball cap.

I stay in my room and listen as they walk in, talk to each other, and then I hear the creaking of the stairs. Bobbi is the first one I see, followed by her husband.

"Elizabeth, how's the unpacking going?" she asks.

"Good," I say as I look at the man. He's got a big belly, stains on his shirt, and long, messy hair.

"That's good. This is Carl, my husband," she introduces.

"Elizabeth, is it?" he asks.

Nod.

"You settling in all right?"

Nod.

"You don't talk much, do you?"

Feeling like I need to say something, I mumble, "I'm just tired."

"Well, I'll leave you be then," he says. "Glad to have you here."

Bobbi smiles as Carl walks out and after she asks me how I'm doing and if I need anything, I lie and assure her that I'm fine. She closes the door behind her and as soon as she does, I see the light from the other bedroom flick on through the bathroom. I watch, and when I see the boy with the baseball cap, he turns to look at me.

"Hi," he says as he stands on his end of the bathroom.

"Hi."

Taking off his cap, he tosses it on his bed and runs his hand through his sweaty, dark brown, nearly black hair. He then walks through the bathroom and into my room, looking around.

"This color is sickening," he says, giving me my first real smile in a long time.

"I lied," I tell him. "I told her I like purple, but I don't."

"You been in the system long?"

"Three years."

"Nine for me. I just got here a couple weeks ago."

"Are they nice?" I ask.

He takes a seat on the bed next to me, and he smells like cigarette smoke and soap. "Bobbi hasn't been here much. She just got back in town from some crafting show she did."

"Crafting show?"

"Yeah, she makes wooden duck figurines and crap to sell at fairs, flea markets, and shit, so she's gone a lot. Carl works at the auto mechanic shop down the road." He pauses and then adds, "He drinks a lot."

I don't say anything, and we sit in silence for a moment before he asks, "How old are you?"

"Eight. You?"

"Eleven. Almost twelve. Name?"

"Elizabeth."

"You scared, Elizabeth?"

Looking over at him, I pull my knees to my chest, wrap my arms around them, and nod, whispering, "Yeah."

"It'll be okay. Promise."

I watch as a hint of a smile crosses his face and something about it tells me that I can believe him.

"I'm Pike, by the way."

Six

(PRESENT)

"WHERE THE FUCK have you been, Elizabeth?"

"I'm sorry," I say as Pike loosens his hold on me. "I haven't been able to get away, but I'm here now."

Pike takes a step back, raking one hand through his thick, choppy, dark hair and releases a rough breath through his nose.

"Pike, come on. Don't make me regret coming here. I only have tonight before Bennett comes back home."

"I'm just sick of living in this shithole while you're living your precious life in that fuckin' penthouse. It's been over three years," he bites and then falls back onto the couch.

Looking down at him, I try to soothe his irritation, "I know. I'm sorry, but you knew it would be like this. You knew this wouldn't work if we moved fast."

"Are you even working at it at all, Elizabeth? Because from where I'm standing, it seems you've gotten quite comfortable in your new life."

"Don't be a dick, Pike," I say, raising my voice at him. "You know me better than that. You know I hate that asshole with everything I am."

He leans forward, resting his elbows on his knees with his head dropped. Walking over to him, I sit down on the couch and start rubbing his hardened shoulder, muscles tense out of frustration.

"I'm sorry," he quietly says, and sits back, pulling me with him and holding me.

I need the contact, need his touch. I always have, so I linger in it for a moment with my arm slung around his waist. I hate being away from him, but I know he hates it more. I don't blame him. This is the shittiest place he's lived, but he's paying the owner of this trailer under the table to keep himself off the grid. He's still hustling to get by, and here I am, lying in his arms wearing a goddamn Hermés coat that probably costs more than this crap-hole he lives in.

"It's okay," I assure him. "I'm sorry you're stuck here, but it won't be forever."

"I'm beginning to wonder if it will."

I swing my legs across his lap so that he can cradle me to his chest, and when I get comfortable in this new position, I tell him, "I met someone."

"Yeah?"

"Yeah. I think he's interested."

"You said that about the others. What makes you think this one is different?" he questions.

"I don't know that he is, but it's worth a shot, right?"

He doesn't respond, and when I tilt my head back to look up at him, he locks eyes with me.

"I'm not giving up," I say. "I need you to know that. I'll do whatever it takes to get us that new beginning."

He kisses me, slipping his hand behind my head to hold me close. The familiar taste of his clove cigarettes comforts me the way a blanket would a child. He's my comfort. I've depended on him ever since I was a little girl. He's protected me as an eight-year-old child and continues to, even though I'm now a twenty-eight-year-old woman.

The rough warmth of his tongue slides along mine, slowly, as he pulls back, ending our kiss.

"So who's the unfortunate bastard?"

"His name's Declan McKinnon. Bennett and I were at an event of his when I first met him."

"What kind of event?" he asks.

"It was the opening of his hotel. He had a showy party with all the right names in attendance," I tell him. "I don't know much about him, but I do know that his father is a developer and has a long string of high-end hotels behind his name. I'm not sure how many Declan has his hands in, but that one for sure."

"He seems too high profile," he says as he shifts me off his lap and heads to the kitchen. "Beer?"

"Yeah."

He pops the caps then hands me a bottle when he sits back down next to me.

"I know he's not the ideal choice, and I wasn't even going to mess with him, but he's working with me on an event and we're spending a lot of time together. I dunno . . ." I take a sip of my beer, and then add, "Time will only tell, but I can already see the intrigue. But I just met him, so I'm still trying to figure him out."

"And what do you think so far?"

"I think he's the type of guy who likes to have control. But at the same time, he seems amused when I get snarky with him. I already planted the seed that I'm a person that might need to be saved." I laugh at the memory of being in his car just a couple hours ago. "I'm pretty sure he bought right into it. Stupid fool."

"Has he touched you yet?" he clips.

"No, Pike. I've known the guy for a week; you know I don't work that way. Men like to chase, so I'm gonna make him chase until he can't resist."

"You think he could possibly fall for you?"

"I'm hoping he does," I tell him.

"I do too. I'm sick of living like this, babe. You have no idea," he says as he clutches my face in his hands and looks me over. "Knowing that fuck has his hands on you . . ."

"I don't feel it."

"Don't lie to me."

"I'm not," I say, but I am. I try so hard to not feel Bennett's hands on me. I work at staving off any orgasm with him, and I hate myself when my body isn't strong enough to fight it and he makes me come. It happens every now and then and the bile that rises is a burning reminder of the weakness that still lives inside of me. A weakness I continue to try to kill off, but Pike would be pissed if he knew, so I lie, allowing him to believe that only he has that part of me. The part his eyes are telling me he wants right now.

"Tell me you hate him, Elizabeth," he grits as he crawls on top of me, pushing my back down on the couch.

"I hate him."

With a near growl, he crashes his mouth to mine, and the beer slips out of my hand, clanking against the floor. His tongue invades my mouth, hands grab locks of my hair, body pressing hard against mine. He takes over me, grinding his hard dick between my legs as I start fiddling with the buttons on his jeans. Once undone, I shove them down, past his hips, and he yanks mine down as well. We move quickly and carelessly. He sits back and jerks the pants off one of my legs.

"Show me your tits," he demands, looking down at me.

I pull my top off and unclasp my bra, tossing it aside, and his rough hands are on them quick. He then takes his cock and pulls off a couple hard pumps while he twists one of my nipples between his fingers, sending a shockwave straight to my belly.

"You want me to take it away?"

"Yes," I breathe.

"Say it. Tell me that you need me to take it away."

He continues his torturous attack on my nipple before releasing and moving to the other. Pike knows I need him to numb. He's always allowed me to use him like this. To numb the pain. Numb the past. Numb the present. Fucking Pike is my personal narcotic, and I'm long overdue for a hit. The words are near agony, when I give him what he loves to hear, "You're the only who can make it go away, Pike."

He lowers his head, sucking the abused bud into his mouth.

"Ohh, God, Pike. Fuck me. Just do it," I beg.

He quickly rips his shirt off, revealing the ink splayed across his chest and arms, before shoving my panties to the side and thrusting himself inside me. A volatile transgression as the sounds of our flesh slapping together fill the room. I grab his ass, urging him harder, and he gives it, pounding into me.

Closing my eyes, I drift away to where nothing exists but the pleasure that builds inside. His carnal grunts heat my ear with his breath as he buries his head in the crook of my neck. We fuck filthy, like animals. The denim of his jeans that are shoved below his ass chafe the backs of my thighs while we grind ourselves into each other, my butt off the couch as I meet his thrusts with my own. Greedy.

He grabs my hips as he sits back on his knees, bringing my pussy up to him when he starts slamming into me at a brutal pace.

"Fuck, Pike," I pant as I reach both my arms over my head and grip the arm of the couch.

The swell of his dick inside of me as he gets close causes an eruption of fire, singeing its way through my veins as he makes me come. I go rigid, tensing up to get the most out of the orgasm, grinding my clit against his pelvis. A few seconds later he crashes into me and stills, letting go of a guttural hiss, as he shoots his tranquilizing disease inside of me.

Collapsing his sweaty chest on top of mine, our labored breaths are heavy, and I'm pacified. For as long as I keep my eyes closed so I don't have to see the best friend that I just used, I'm okay.

Pike gives me a sick power that I crave. The power to take control, if even for a moment. Using him to clean me of the rot that contaminates me. And he gets off on being the one who can do that. To be the only person who can take it away, making my body a tomb. But now, as he slips his softening dick out from inside me, his warm cum running between my thighs when I sit up, I'm bathed in degradation, and he knows it. It's always the same.

He pulls me into his arms as he sits back after tugging his pants up. With his hand rubbing my back, I swallow hard as I attempt to control the feelings of shame.

"Why do you still feel this way?" he asks, knowing me all too well.

I don't respond. He's used to my silence after we have sex. What could I say that he doesn't already know? The thing is, I know Pike loves me in a way I don't share. He's my brother and my best friend. But to him, I'm more. He's never come right out and said it, but I know it anyway. It doesn't stop him from fucking other girls, but I know he needs it. Pike has a thing for sex; he likes a lot of it. More than the average person I would assume. It's never bothered me since I don't view sex much differently than one would toilet paper. Using it to wipe away the shit-stain of life, and when you feel clean, you flush it and walk away.

"You don't need to feel like this. I don't care that you use me in this way. I love you, so you can have it. If it makes you feel better, then just take it," he says. "I'd rather you let me do this for you than allowing someone else."

His words make it even worse, so I pull back and shift to slide my leg back into my pants. He watches as I grab the rest of my clothes and walk to the bathroom.

After I clean myself up and put my clothes back on, I walk out to see Pike wiping up the beer I spilled all over the floor.

"Sorry," I say as I stand there, and when he walks past me to throw away the wad of paper towels, he responds, "I don't care about the beer."

"I'm sorry for more than just the beer," I tell him. "I wish I could give you more money."

"I knew what I was signing up for. We both did. It's too risky, so just ignore my bullshit," he says as he walks back to the couch and motions for me to sit next to him. He pulls out a cigarette and lights it, taking in a long drag and then adding, "I just missed you," as the smoke drifts out of his mouth, forming a vaporous cloud in front of his face. "When will you be able to get back here again?"

"More often after the New Year. Bennett has a busy travel schedule, and I'm sure it's gonna be even busier now."

"Why's that?"

"He just bought another production plant earlier this week in Dubai, so I imagine he'll be going back to oversee the new outfit on the place and get it up and running," I explain.

"That's good for us," he laughs and I join him.

"My thoughts exactly," I say through a thick smile that I let wane when I ask, "How've you been?"

"You know how it is. Nothing has changed for me," he tells me. Pike has always found a way to skate by, pulling small cons and such. But he makes most of his money selling drugs. I used to as well. When we got out of the system, we lived with one of his friends that Pike worked for, dealing drugs. Pike was the middleman, putting himself on the street to sell product and made a decent amount of money doing so.

"You need anything?"

"For you to get your head on straight with this one."

"I've got my head on straight, Pike." I hate when he talks to me like that. Like I don't know what the hell I'm doing when I'm the one pulling the biggest con here, putting his skills in the sewer. "My focus has never wavered. But I need you to trust me. I know what I'm doing."

"Just be careful. Hands clean, remember?"

I nod and then grab the remote to turn on the TV. We spend the next few hours hanging out like we used to, but before it gets too late, I know I have to leave and head back into the city.

"With the holidays coming up, don't get mad if I can't get away, okay? I'll try, but until January, it'll be hard."

"I get it. Don't do anything stupid trying to come see me," he says as we stand up and walk to the door.

I grab my coat and slip it on, then turn to give him a long hug. It's hard to leave him, knowing he's here in the shit-hole. He's the only family I have and to not have any contact with him is scary for me since I know how easily family can be taken away. So with my cheek pressed to his chest, I take in his scent and hold on to it while he runs the fingers from both of his hands through my hair and down to my face. Cupping my jaw, he angles me to look up at him. His brown eyes are intense when he asks, "Hard as steel?"

"Yeah," I breathe.

He taught me, at an early age, how to live without emotions. How to wrap that steel cage around my heart, always telling me that no one can ever hurt you if you can't feel. So I don't. Outside of Pike, there's no one I'll give that to because emotions are what make people weak. And I can't afford to make that slip. The heart is a weapon—a self-inflicting weapon—that if not trained properly, can destroy a person.

Seven

(PRESENT)

I WATCH AS Bennett moves around the bedroom, getting dressed in his three-piece suit to go in to the office for the day. He arrived late a couple nights ago and as I presumed, his schedule is now packed with travel after the purchase he just made. Even though he's home now, he's been living at the office before he heads out again at the end of this week.

The chill in the air is getting to me, and I sink down into the bed and further under the covers.

"Do you need me to adjust the thermostat?" Bennett asks me as he nears my side of the bed.

"Are you not cold?"

He sits on the mattress beside me, leans down to kiss my nose, and then smiles.

"What?" I ask as he pulls away.

"Your nose is cold. Come here."

I sit up, and he wraps me in his arms in an attempt to warm me up. Slipping my arms around his waist, under his suit coat, I curl into him.

"I missed this," I breathe. "Having you—here—with me."

"I know. I missed it too," he says, moving back to look into my eyes. "You can always come with me, you know? You don't have to be alone."

"I know, but Declan has already scheduled appointments out with vendors for the party. I'll be busy for the next few weeks."

"How did your visit with the florist go the other day?" he asks.

Running my hand along his silk tie, I tell him, "It went well. I think we got nearly everything picked out."

"Good."

He combs his fingers through my hair and leans in to kiss me. Slow and soft, taking his time. Bennett tends to be overly affectionate after he returns from a trip, and I never deny him, so I shift up to my knees and hold his face in my hands. When he grips my hips, clutching onto the satin of my slip gown, I take over his mouth, urging him on. He pulls me down atop his lap, and his growing cock presses against me as I grind my hips into him.

"God, baby. I can't get enough of you," he mumbles against my neck, between his gentle kisses.

"You want me?"

"I always want you," he tells me. "But you're gonna make me late. I've got a meeting."

Grinning at him, I say, "I'll be fast," before slipping off his lap and onto my knees on the floor beside the bed. Quickly working my hands, I undo his slacks and yank them down. And as he sits on the edge of the bed, I wrap my lips around his dick and suck him off while he moans my name.

Once fully satisfied, he kisses me deeply when I walk him to the door before he leaves.

"I hate that I have to leave when all I want is to make love to you all day."

The ringing of my cell interrupts us, and he waits while I grab it off the kitchen counter and answer.

"Hello?"

"Nina, it's Declan."

"Hi."

"I was wondering if you could stop by the hotel later today. Betty, from Marguerite Gardens, is having a few arrangements delivered for you to look at," he says.

"Um . . . sure. That shouldn't be a problem at all. What time would be good?"

"They should be delivered by noon."

"Okay, I'll swing by later then," I tell him before we hang up.

"Who was that?" Bennett asks when I walk back over to him.

"Declan. The florist is sending over some sample arrangements for me to look at later today, so I'll just take one of the cars to the hotel if Baldwin is going to be with you."

"You sure?"

Lifting up on my toes, I give him a little kiss. "I'm sure."

"I'll call you when I leave the office. How about I take you out for a nice dinner at Everest tonight?"

"Sounds perfect," I say with a smile.

He runs his thumb down my lips and then gives my chin a little pinch, saying, "Have a good day, okay?"

"You too."

As soon as he leaves, I walk into the kitchen to put the kettle on the stove, and while I wait for it to boil, I look over to the dining room table. The extravagant vase of purple roses that Bennett gave me when he got home last night sits in the center of the table. The sight causes a physical reaction inside of me. A twisting in my gut as I grit my teeth. I hate purple. I told him it was my favorite though, so when he gives me flowers, his way of showering me with affection, it only reminds me of everything I hate. Purple walls flash in my mind, and it only reinforces my steel wall. Bennett is everything a husband should be, so it was essential that I create fissures within him. Purple flowers being one of them.

The squealing whistle of the kettle snaps me out of the purple and into the present. I fix my tea and make my way into the bedroom to get ready for the day. Knowing I'm going to be seeing Declan, I want to look nice, so I set my mug down on the center island in my closet and start sorting through my clothes. Selecting a simple black shift dress, I pair it with patent black heels and my white, wool, knee-length coat.

After a slow morning getting ready and taking a phone call from Jacqueline to schedule a lunch date with the girls, I grab my purse and head down to the parking garage. It takes a while to get to the hotel with the hectic lunch traffic in the loop, but when I arrive, the valet takes my car and I make my way back to Declan's office.

When I approach his door, I can hear his voice on the other side. He sounds angry, barking orders with whoever he must be on the phone with because it's only Declan's voice I hear. I wait, and when I notice the conversation has ended, I give the door a couple light taps.

"Come in," he calls.

Opening the door, his focus is on his laptop and nothing else as he's clicking away at the keyboard.

"Bad time?" I question hesitantly, and when he hears my voice, he flicks his eyes my way and swivels his chair away from his computer to face me. "I can come back."

"No," he simply states as he stands up and walks towards me, taking me by the elbow and turning me to walk with him. "This way."

His snippy attitude the other day at the florist was irritating, but for some reason, right now, it doesn't have that effect on me, figuring that whoever he was just speaking to is the culprit of his mood, and not me. I follow him out of his office and down to an opulent private dining room that's currently free of people. He opens the double-etched glass doors and leads me into the dark room, dimly lit by the sparse chandeliers. Towards the back of the dining space, there is a secluded table that's covered in burnt orange and white flowers with dark, rich greenery. Some accented with spiral grapevines and others darkened with blackened moss.

Declan still has a hold on my arm when we walk over to the table.

"I'm impressed," I say, and it's then that he releases me. When I look at him, I notice his jaw flex as he grinds his teeth. His focus is on the table and not me, so it's with a soft voice, I speak. "Declan?" Looking over at me, I ask, "Are you sure this isn't a bad time? I can go."

He relaxes his face and runs his hand behind his neck and down along his lightly stubbled jaw. Releasing a sigh, he says, "Stay."

Nodding my head, I turn away and take a step over to the arrangements and begin studying each one. There are five, each ornate and exquisitely put together. The designs unique and exactly what I had in mind.

I still when I feel Declan's fingers graze the sides of my neck, and as I turn my head to see him standing right behind me, he moves his hands to the collar of my coat, and starts to slip it off my shoulders. Adjusting myself, I allow him to take my coat and watch as he lays it across the back of a chair.

"Thanks," I murmur.

"What do you think?"

Keeping my eyes on him, I don't answer immediately. I want the contact to see how he responds. It doesn't take long for a sexy grin to cross his face.

"They're perfect. I'm not sure how to pick one over the other."

"So take them all," he says.

"Take them all?"

"Why not? Who says you have to choose?"

"Isn't there always a choice?" I ask with an undertone that states we're talking about more than just flowers.

"Not when you're a Vanderwal."

With superficial offense, I say, "Is that what you think? That because of my name I simply take what I want?" He quirks a brow without saying anything, and I add, "Is that what *you* do? Because correct me if I'm wrong, but the McKinnon name sure isn't one that people are not aware of."

"Are we talking personal or business?" he questions.

"Business is personal when it belongs to you, and last time I checked, it's your name that robes this hotel."

He walks over to one of the other tables and takes a seat. Leaning back and resting one of his arms on the table, he says, "Yes. I take what I want."

I stay put, standing by the flowers, and question, "In which case?"

"In all cases. Now stop standing there and sit with me."

"Is this you taking?"

With a smile that he plays so well, he says, "Are you up for grabs?"

"No," I state curtly. "And these games you tend to enjoy playing with me are getting old, and frankly, I don't enjoy being toyed with as if I'm here solely for your entertainment. So again, cut the shit, Declan." I grab my coat and start walking towards the door, hoping he makes the move I'm goading him into.

His hand grips the top of mine as soon as it hits the door handle, and I freeze, keeping my head down.

"Don't go," he says, and I remain silent as he continues to speak. "You're not a toy, Nina, and I apologize if I made you feel that way."

"So what is this?"

"This is me, simply wanting to get to know you," he says, and when I look at him, he adds, "You say you don't have friends, right?"

Turning my head away from him to avoid eye contact, he says, "Everyone deserves a friend, Nina. Even you."

"And you think you're gonna fill that void?" I ask, looking back at him. "What makes you think I need that?"

"Tell me then, who do you talk to about the things you can't with your husband?"

I pull my hand out from under his and move to face him. "Who do *you* talk to?"

Silence.

"You expect me to just put myself out there when I don't know anything about you? And what do you give me in return, huh?" I question.

"The same," he answers. "So let's start now. Before you knocked on my door a few minutes ago, I was on the phone with my father. He was being a fuckin' knob as always, ridiculing me for decisions I'm making that he doesn't have a say in, and it drives him crazy to not hold the power in this situation. So there you go, my father's a bastard to me."

His eyes are sharp as he says this, the intensity prevalent, and I feel like I just made progress. But I don't want him pissed right now, so I break the tension, and make him smile when I tease, "A fuckin' *knob*? Is this some Scottish insult you guys throw around because I've never heard anyone call someone a *knob* before?"

"Yeah, darling, it is, but if you prefer something more authentic, I can call him a fannybawbag, but then to the random American, I'd probably just sound like a pussy."

I laugh at his statement, but let it fall off my lips as I look down at my feet and quiet myself.

"What is it, Nina?" he asks, taking note of my shift in mood. When I don't immediately respond, he takes my hand, holding it in his as he walks me over to a table and we sit down. "Tell me something about you."

"I don't know what you're wanting."

"Anything. Just give me a piece," he says, but when he sees me hesitate, he offers, "Tell me why you don't have any friends."

I release a breath, giving him what I know he wants to hear. "Because I'm not from this world. I'm not like those women, and . . ." I stall, taking a moment before adding in a hushed voice, "I'm afraid they'll judge me, so I rather they just fear me because it's easier that way." When I say the words, the truth that lies within them surprises me.

"So you hide?"

"I suppose."

"Are you lonely?"

"Do I seem lonely?" I question.

"In this moment? Yes."

Deflecting, I turn it on him, asking, "And what about you? Are you lonely?"

"I moved here from New York when we broke ground on this place. I've been so wrapped up with getting everything fit for opening, so yeah, I've become lonely."

"When did you leave Scotland?" I ask.

"I used to spend my summers here in the States when I was in university back home. I'd come here and work for my father, learning the ins and outs of the business, but I didn't officially pack up and leave until after I graduated with my master's," he tells me. "That was seven years ago."

"Do you miss it?"

"Scotland?"

With a nod of my head, he answers flatly, "Yes," before asking, "Where are you from?"

"Kansas."

"What brought you out here?"

I shift in my seat, marking my discomfort with answering, but before I can speak, my cell rings from inside my purse that's lying on the table. Picking it up, I see it's Bennett, and answer the call.

"Bennett, hi," I say so Declan knows who I'm talking to.

"Just checking in. My meeting wrapped up a lot earlier than I expected, and I was hoping to see you," he says sweetly.

"You just saw me."

"So is this your way of saying you're too busy?"

"No, I'm never too busy for you. Are you still at the office?" I ask as I cast a quick glance over at Declan and see the irritation in his eyes.

Good. Get jealous.

"Yeah. Are you hungry? I can have something delivered."

"That sounds great, honey," I tell him, playing up the sweetness just to pluck on Declan's nerves, and I can tell it's working by the tensed muscles in his neck and his set jaw. "I'm on my way now, okay?"

"All right. I love you."

"Love you too."

Looking at Declan, I tell him, "I have to go meet Bennett."

"Yeah, I heard," he says, clipping his words.

I run my hand over his clenched fist that rests on the table, and say, "Thanks."

"For what?"

"Talking to me." Staring into his eyes, I tell him again, "Thank you," so he can hear the sincerity in my words.

His hand relaxes under mine, and he flips it so that he's now holding mine, and with a smile, says, "Let me walk you out."

As he helps me with my coat, I finally feel like I've found the match I've been looking for. There have been a few men before Declan, but none that ever gave me the promise I feel he may have, so I let him hold on to my hand for a moment longer than I should as he walks me out to the valet who is waiting with my car.

I slip into the driver's seat and Declan peers down, reminding me, "Friday is your appointment with the caterer. Four o'clock."

"I've got it on my calendar."

"You mean that paper calendar that doesn't provide you with notifications or reminder alerts?" he teases.

Laughing at his dig, I say, "Yeah, that one. But apparently that's all I need since you tend to do the reminding for me."

"I'll see you Friday then?"

"You'll see me Friday," I affirm before he closes my door, and I start driving over to the Willis Tower to meet my husband for a late lunch, all the while, feeling optimistic for the first time in a long time.

eight (PAST)

I SIT BY myself on the front steps of the school, waiting for Pike to meet me so that we can go home. He's in trouble with one of his teachers again and has detention, so I take the hour to get all my tears out so that he doesn't see me cry. Apparently I've lost track of time when I hear the metal doors bang open and pop my head up to see Pike walking down the steps. Quickly, I wipe my face, but he sees the tears anyway.

"Why're you crying?" he asks, but I don't say anything as I stand up and shrug my backpack on over my shoulders. "Elizabeth? What happened?"

"Nothing. Can we go now?"

"No. Not until you tell me why you're upset."

Hanging my head down, I kick a couple pebbles on the sidewalk, telling him, "The kids in my class make fun of me."

"What did they say?" he asks in a hard voice.

"Doesn't matter," I tell him. I've been at this school for a few months now. Long enough to hit a growth spurt and no longer fit into the clothes my last foster family bought me, so now I'm stuck wearing clothes that Bobbi gets from thrift stores, and the other kids pick on me for the way I look.

"It matters to me," he states, and when I look up at him, I say, "They call me names. Saying I look like I get my clothes from a garbage can." I can feel the tears fall again as I continue, "They call me names to my face and then whisper and laugh at me."

"Those kids are ass wipes."

"I have no friends, Pike," I say, crying. "I'm all alone, and I wanna go home. I miss my dad, and I wanna go home."

In a second, he has me in his arms, and I wet his shirt with my tears. Every night I pray to a God I'm not sure even exists that I'll wake up from this nightmare, but I'm still here. I'm almost nine years old and I haven't seen my dad, heard his voice, felt his hugs—nothing—in nearly four years. I have a case worker who has only seen me twice since I've been here, and both times I cry and beg for her to take me to my dad, but she won't. He's too far away. I'm starting to believe that I'll never get him back because waiting until I'm fourteen seems like forever.

"I'm sorry," Pike eventually says as we stand on the sidewalk hugging. "But you're not alone. You have me."

He's right. He's the only one I have, but he's a twelve-year-old boy, and next year he'll be at the middle school, leaving me here alone. Alone with kids that don't like me.

When he draws back and looks down at me, I cringe at the greenish tint left over from the black eye Carl gave him the other day. I learned fast that when Bobbi is around, Carl is semi-pleasant, but the moment she leaves, he starts drinking. I try to hide and be invisible when he drinks because he's scary to be around. He yells a lot, and if Pike and I make too much noise, he gets really mad and usually hits us.

My first slap came a week after I got here. Bobbi left for the weekend and Carl was downstairs watching TV while I was upstairs. I found a radio on the top shelf of the closet in my room and was standing on a chair to get it down, but I slipped, causing the chair to tip over and the radio to crash to the floor. Carl busted through my door and saw the broken radio. Before I knew what was happening, he had yanked me up by the arm and slapped me across the face. The burning sting held to the skin of my cheek as I cried into my pillow afterward.

Pike and I take our time walking home, but when we get to our street, Bobbi's car is gone, and only Carl's truck is in front of the house. My stomach sinks. It's the weekend, so I'm sure it'll just be the three of us. Bobbi never tells us when she's leaving, but lately, it seems to be all the time. She's never home anymore.

"Just go straight to your room," Pike tells me as we walk to the front door. "I'll grab you a snack and bring it up."

"Okay."

But that wouldn't happen. Instead, I was about to be introduced to a black hole that would claim another piece of my faith in human decency.

"Where the hell have you kids been?" Carl yells at us when we walk in, and the gravel in his voice makes me cling to Pike's arm in fear.

"I had detention. I told Elizabeth to wait for me so she wouldn't have to walk home alone," Pike explains.

"You think I have all the goddamn time in the world to be wondering where you shits are?" he shouts and then grabs Pike by his shirt, ripping him out from my hold on his arm and shoving him away from me. He then gets in my face, stinking of beer and cigarettes.

"And you . . ." he spits as I start to cry, which does nothing but piss him off even more. "Fuck! Why are you always fuckin' crying? I'm not gonna spend another weekend here with you listening to this shit." When he lifts his dirty shirt and starts to unbuckle his belt, the chills of fear run rampant, spiking through my veins.

Pike bolts off the floor and goes after Carl, but it only takes one hit to knock Pike back, and Carl has his hand locked around my wrist as I scream and thrash. Suddenly, he has me lifted off the ground with a firm hold around my waist.

"Let me go!" I scream. "Stop! Let me go!"

I hear a crash, and when I look up through my tears, I see I've kicked over a couple of Bobbi's ducks and have broken them.

"You little shit!" he yells, but it's blended with Pike's screams as well, and I panic. Sheer panic.

Screaming, crying, kicking, and the next thing I know, I'm being shoved into the small hallway closet. Carl throws me hard against the floor and then pulls me up by my wrists, using his belt to tie me up to the lower garment bar. Everything is a chaotic blur. Everyone is yelling, and the terror in my body is making it hard for me to breathe through my shrieking cries for help. I hear Pike, and I hold on to his voice when Carl's fist smashes into my face.

SLAM.

LOCK.

Darkness.

"No! Let me out!" I cry. "Pike, help me! Let me out! Please!"

I can hear the beating Pike is getting now. Grunting. Heaving. Screaming. I twist and yank my wrists, trying to free myself, but the leather is biting into my skin, and I'm only hurting myself. The side of my face where he hit me pulses in beats of hot pain, and I fall onto my bottom with my arms pulled above my head and cry. I cry for what feels like years in the darkness.

My body grows tired and weak. Arms cold and tingly. I stand up, wedging myself between the wall and the garment rod, and I can feel the warmth flowing back through my arms to my hands. I try wriggling my fingers around to grab on to the strap of leather, but it's too dark to see anything and my fingers are too small. What would I do anyway? Unstrap myself and walk out of here? Carl would kill me, so what's the point in trying?

I listen to the faint sound of the TV in the living room as my head starts to droop. I'm so sleepy, but my arms hurt too bad when I sit, and I can't sleep standing up. Not sure what to do, I remain wedged against the wall while I keep jerking out of sleep when my head falls. My mind is a haze. I try resting myself in the corner, but can't find any comfortable position. Soon enough, I hear the sounds of the TV shut off and listen as Carl walks out of the room.

Oh my God. He's not gonna let me out.

Tears fall, burning my skin on the way down my face, and I can only assume that Carl split my skin when he punched me, but nothing can stop them from falling down my cheeks.

WAKING UP, MY arms are freezing. I must have fallen because I'm now sitting on the floor. I have no idea if it's night or day, and the urge to go to the bathroom is overwhelming. When I stand up to relieve the pain in my arms, I press my legs together to keep myself from peeing. I begin to cry, wondering what I'm supposed to do, but in that very moment, I hear Pike on the other side of the door.

"Elizabeth?" he whispers.

"Pike?" I whimper.

"Shh. Carl is sleeping."

Trying to choke back my cries to stay quiet, I strain my words, "Please, Pike. Get me out."

"I can't," he says. "The lock on this door works from the inside."

"What?"

"Without the key, it can only be unlocked from inside," he tells me.

"He's got my hands tied. I can't move, and I can't see anything," I say, beginning to panic, and he hears it.

"Don't cry, okay? I'm here," he tries assuring me.

My body begins to twitch as I clamp my legs tighter. "Pike?"

"Yeah?"

"I have to pee," I tell him. "Really bad."

"Fuck," I hear in a muffled voice.

It's then the pain and urgency take over, and I feel the warmth seep out, spreading through the fabric of my pants and trickling down my leg. Mortified. Embarrassed. I slip to the floor and begin weeping as quietly as I can.

"Are you okay?" he asks, but I don't answer, I just continue to cry.

PIKE STAYED WITH me on the other side of the door for hours last night, talking to me, trying to keep me company. I must have fallen asleep again because I don't remember him leaving. The TV is now on, so I know Carl is awake. My stomach has been growling, but I'm too scared to call out to him.

The time passes slowly, and I try to keep myself distracted by daydreaming, pretending I'm anywhere but here. I imagine I'm with my father, and we're riding together on his white steed he used to tell me he had when we would play make-believe. We ride through the countryside and find ourselves in that magical forest. Carnegie is there, and we go hunting for berries. Some berries give us special powers, and some are just delicious to eat. When rain falls, we hunt for mushroom tops to hide under until the storm passes, and we meet fairy butterflies that fill the air with glitter as they fly.

My thoughts get interrupted often with the pain that surges through my hands and arms. I'm so tired but can't find a way to get any real sleep, and now with my stomach knotting up from hunger, I find myself constantly shifting from sitting to standing.

"ELIZABETH?"

Pike's voice brings me out of a light sleep, and I try to bend and flex my wrists as the leather cuts into my skin. "What time is it?" I ask.

"It's Saturday night. Almost midnight," he tells me.

"I'm hungry."

"Hold on."

I move to my feet to soothe my arms. I feel so gross with my pants soaked in my own pee. It stinks, and I know Carl is going to be pissed whenever he decides to let me out, which hopefully will be tomorrow since I have school on Monday. Plus, Bobbi should be coming home soon. At least I hope she is.

I hear Pike sliding something under the door. I lower to my knees, but didn't think this through, because my hands are bound.

"Pike, I can't get whatever you slipped under the door."

"Shit. I'm sorry, I didn't even think," he whispers. "Is there any way you can lean your head down to get it with your mouth?"

"No. The bar is too high."

"Use your foot and try to push it back out," he instructs. "I don't want

Carl to know I was trying to sneak you food."

I shuffle my foot around, but can't feel anything, so I just start sliding it against the floor and towards the door, hoping by chance I get it out. After a second, I hear, "Got it."

"What was it?"

"Just a tortilla," he says. "I heard Carl talking to Bobbi. She's gonna be home tomorrow afternoon."

"I feel sick."

"What's going on?"

"I'm just so tired and hungry," I tell him. "My arms hurt really bad. He's got his belt pulled so tight around my wrists."

"He's a sick fuck."

"Pike?"

"Yeah?"

"Please don't leave me. You're all I have." The tears return, and I let them come without fighting it. I feel so hopeless.

"I'm not leaving you. You're my sister. We're not blood, but you're my sister." His words hit my heart, knowing he's all the family I have. "Did I ever tell you about the time I fell off the roof at my last foster home?"

"No."

I sit back down and listen as Pike tells me story after story. He even tells me about his mom, that she was a drug addict and that's how he wound up in foster care when he was only two years old. Hours pass and he never stops talking to me, keeping me company until I drift off into a fit of restless sleep.

WHEN I HEAR someone messing with the door handle, I swiftly move to my feet, wedging against the wall. Light pierces my eyes, and I immediately close them.

"What the fuck is that smell?" Carl snarls as I slowly try to open my eyes against the stabbing light.

His hands start undoing the belt around my wrists. You'd think I'd be happy to be getting out of this closet, but I'm so tired that all I feel is numb.

"Did you piss yourself?" he asks with anger, and when I nod my head, he yells, "You better clean this shit up."

The belt is finally off, and my hands are free. I grip my one wrist in my hand and stand there, scared to move, until he tells me to get out. Before I can go upstairs, he makes me clean the floor where I had been going to the bathroom. I finally look at my wrists to see they're covered in blood from the broken skin where the leather was cutting into me.

When I get upstairs, Pike is sitting on my bed, but I'm too embarrassed, so I ignore him and go straight to the bathroom, shutting the door, and stripping out of my soiled clothes. Before I get into the shower, I look in the mirror to see the black eye Carl gave me. I step into the spray of water and fall apart.

After I finish my shower, I wrap up in a towel and go back into my room. Pike is still on my bed, so I grab some clothes and go back to the bathroom to get dressed. Coming out, I finally look at the bruises on his face as he reaches his hand out. I walk over to the bed, take it, and let him pull me down and hold me. I stay in his arms, the only comfort I feel life has to offer me right now, and close my eyes.

I was locked in that closet for two days with nothing—nothing but Pike, who snuck down each night to talk to me through the door so that I wouldn't be alone. Knowing that he would do that for me makes me want to hug him harder, so I do.

"Thank you," I mumble against his chest.

"What for?"

"Staying with me at night."

"Like I said, no matter what, you're my sister," he says, and I respond with, "And you're my brother."

nine

(PRESENT)

BENNETT LEAVES TODAY to go back to Dubai to start an overhaul on the production plant, gutting it and replacing everything with the same equipment that is used at the other plant he has here in the States. When I told him that I was meeting with the caterers today, he had his assistant call and hold his plane so he could go with me. The idea of having him and Declan in the same room causes my nerves to go a bit haywire. Especially when I just saw Declan for coffee yesterday.

He continues to press me about Bennett, and I'm confident with my performance as he seems to be under the assumption I'm not all that happy and that I'm only keeping up the façade for the sake of appearance. But I don't want there to be any awkward exchanges today when we meet up with him at his hotel, so this is where it turns tricky. I'd like to keep both men apart from each other, so the added fact that Bennett is linked with Cal, Declan's father, isn't optimal. It was never in my plan to target a man like Declan, but so far, he's the one that has taken the bait. I just need to be careful with handling this situation. One little slip could be disastrous, and I've invested too much time to make a fatal error.

"Are you ready, honey?" Bennett asks as he walks into the living room where I'm sitting.

I stand, straighten my pencil skirt, and walk over to him. "Yes. I just need to grab my coat."

"We'll drive so that you'll have the car with you when you leave. Baldwin will pick me up to take me to the airport."

"I hope it wasn't too much trouble to delay the charter," I say as I slip on my coat and grab my purse.

"No trouble at all. I just hate that I have to be gone again with it being so close to Christmas."

We leave the apartment and head down on the elevator.

"By the way," he says. "I spoke with my parents. They want us over Christmas Eve for a dinner party they're hosting."

I cringe inside at the thought of spending time with those assholes, but I smile anyway, saying, "Okay. I've been meaning to call your mother, I've just been a little scattered with everything else going. And now you're leaving again."

He takes my face in his hands and kisses my cheek. "It's only temporary."

"I know."

"It'll be busy for a while, but once everything is up and running, it'll slow back down."

The elevator opens and we make our way to the parking garage. We take the Land Rover, and when we pull out, we're greeted by more snow.

"It's supposed to get bad later," Bennett says.

"I'll be sure to get home before it does."

"I can hire another driver if you need me to."

Cocking my head at him, I smile, saying, "I survived before without a driver, Bennett. I'll be fine."

Baldwin will be accompanying Bennett on his trip this time, so he won't be around to drive me. One less person I have to worry about.

"With me gone so much and this brutal winter we've been having, it worries me knowing you're driving around in this mess."

Laying my hand on his thigh, I assure him, "I'll be fine. You worry too much."

He takes my hand in his, kissing my knuckles, and says, "I just don't want anything to happen to you. I can't help but worry when I'll be a world away."

I lace my fingers with his and relish in the fact that this new purchase will have him so far away for a longer span of time, allowing me to work on Declan. It couldn't be a better situation. With Bennett and Baldwin gone, I'll be able to come and go as I please without having to explain.

When we pull up to Lotus, the valet opens my door and helps me out.

"Watch your step, miss."

"Thank you," I say before Bennett walks around to take my hand and lead me inside.

I show him to the private dining room that Declan had the flowers in earlier this week, and when we walk in, Declan is there talking to the chef.

"Nina," he says with a smile, and my nerves float to the top of my stomach. He takes my hand, giving me a chaste kiss on the cheek, and then greets my husband. “Bennett,” he says with a firm handshake. “It’s good to see you again.”

“I hear my wife is keeping you busy.”

“She knows what she likes,” Declan chuckles and Bennett joins him. “But she hasn’t fired me, so I guess I’m doing something right.”

“Don’t get too high on yourself just yet,” I add with the sass I know Bennett loves but, at times, can irritate the hell out of Declan. He takes it well, never losing his grin. I want to make him jealous, but it’s a fine line with Bennett here, so I’ll make sure to gauge Declan’s body language and not push him too far.

Declan introduces us to Marco, the chef I’m considering for the party, and we then take a seat at one of the tables.

“So, Bennett, Nina tells me you’ve been slammed with work lately.”

“That’s a massive understatement, and to be happening this time of year is less than ideal,” Bennett says and then reaches over to hold my hand that’s resting on the table. “Fortunately for me, I have an understanding wife.”

Just as I give him a smile, we are presented with a sculpted Caprese salad.

“So how did you get into steel production?” Declan asks, and I remain quiet as they talk.

“At the time, I was acquiring and renovating vacant buildings when I came across a manufacturing plant that was going bankrupt. I was able to purchase it at a bargain, keeping the owner from going into insolvency. I flipped the place, and next thing I knew, we were up and running, gaining a solid client base.”

“From the ground up,” Declan states.

“Just like your father,” Bennett adds.

I watch Declan’s jaw flex as he grinds his teeth. He takes a sip of his wine and then says, “You two must be proud of yourselves,” with a condescending tone, possibly taking Bennett’s remark as a stab against the fact that Declan is, in a sense, riding on his father’s coattails by going into the family business. But I know Bennett, and no such suggestion was meant on his part.

Bennett notes Declan’s insinuation, and deflects, turning to me, asking, “Are you going to see Jacqueline tomorrow? I thought Richard mentioned something to me about it.”

“Mmm hmm.” I wipe my mouth, and add, “The girls want to make a day at Neiman’s, and I need to find a dress for the party.”

"I thought you couldn't stand them," Declan butts in, and I immediately heat in anger that not only is he being grossly inappropriate in exploiting something *he thought* I was revealing in confidence to a friend, but I also don't need him raising any red flags with Bennett.

I widen my eyes, letting him know he crossed a line, when Bennett questions, confused, "You don't like them?"

"Um, no. I mean . . . Declan just meant that . . ." *fuck*, "Well, I voiced to Declan that sometimes they can be a tad overbearing. That's all." Looking into his eyes, I have to wonder if he's upset that I would reveal something like that to Declan. Something that has nothing to do with the business we are supposed to be conducting while we're together, so I cover myself, adding, "I had run into one of Jacqueline's friends at the florist when Declan and I were there. She was being a little snippy, so I loosely made that statement to him. I possibly spoke out of frustration. I like the girls, but you know how it can be when you get us all in one room."

He buys it, saying, "I'll never pretend to understand the mind of a woman," with light laughter, and I smile with him.

"Me neither," I tease. "And I'm one of them." Taking my fork and stabbing a basil leaf, I mumble with a grin, "Snarky bitches," before taking a bite.

Bennett laughs at my crudeness as I give Declan a disapproving glare.

We get halfway through the second course with building tension from Declan when Bennett gets a call from Richard that he has to take. He excuses himself and steps outside of the room, walking down the hall, and when he's out of sight, I turn and snap, "Your games aren't funny. I was under the assumption that the few pieces I gave you, pieces *you* asked for, would remain private and not for you to use when you felt someone was stepping on your dick."

He leans to the side, grabs the arm of my chair, and abruptly yanks it towards him, quietly gritting, "Your smart mouth is unbecoming, Nina, so watch how you speak to me. And no one *steps on my dick*, especially your husband—the man you say you love but doesn't seem to know shit about you."

"You think you're cute?"

"Do I look like a man who gives a shit about being cute?"

Narrowing my eyes, I tell him, "You look like a man who's jealous, but you shouldn't even be going there with me."

"Why's that?"

"Because I'm a married woman, and your juvenile accusations are insulting. You don't know anything about my husband and what he does or doesn't know about me."

"You're a liar," he accuses.

"Excuse me?"

He leans in closer, mere inches away from my face, and says, "I think you like making me jealous. Am I right?"

In a soft voice that I make sure comes out shaky, I respond simply, "No."

"I don't believe you."

"What do you want from me?"

"Bullshit aside?"

"Bullshit aside, Declan. What do you want?"

His eyes are near daggers when he answers, "You."

Perfect answer, idiot.

I stand up, throwing my napkin on the table and turn to go find Bennett, although I have no intentions of leaving this room, and Declan doesn't fail when he grabs my arm and jerks me around, pulling me flush against him. He looks down at me, and I shift my eyes away.

"Look at me," he demands, and when I don't he grabs my chin and pulls it around to face him. "I said look at me, Nina."

"You're an ass."

"And you've got a filthy mouth," he says before taking a taste, sealing his lips with mine. He isn't gentle, and his stubble grazes roughly against me as he wraps his hand around the back of my neck. His grip on me is firm, and I make sure he feels me respond to him for a brief moment when I move my lips with his before forcefully pushing him away.

His grin is arrogant as he takes a step back, putting distance between us.

"What do you think you're doing?" I bite harshly.

"Testing you."

"You're an insolent prick."

"Then why did you kiss me back?" he questions. "Don't lie to me either because I felt it."

"You didn't feel anything, and neither did I." Walking back over to the table, I pull my chair back and sit down, saying as I keep my eyes forward, "Don't ever do that again."

Seconds later, Declan returns to his seat in front of me, and with perfect timing, Bennett comes back in. This situation is bordering on dangerous, so I'm relieved when Bennett says, "I apologize about that, but it seems I'm going to have to leave earlier than expected."

"What?" I ask.

"I'm sorry, honey. The charter is ready to go. There was miscommunication about the reschedule, and we have to head out."

"Now?"

He holds his hand out to me, and I take it as I stand up. "Declan," he says when he turns to look at Declan who is now standing as well. "Sorry to run like this. It was good seeing you again."

Declan doesn't speak, but instead gives him a curt nod as they shake hands.

"If you'll excuse us for a moment," Bennett says as he wraps his arm around my shoulders and starts leading us out. Looking over my shoulder, I watch as Declan remains standing, keeping his eyes on us as we walk out of the room.

God, he's so transparent.

I walk with Bennett to the lobby, and when he stops in front of the doors, I play the sad wife. Slipping my arms around his waist, I lay my head on his chest and hold on to him.

"I don't want you to go."

His lips fall on the top of my head, giving a kiss, and then he responds, "I know. I'll get back here as soon as I can."

I look up at him, and he takes my lips, the lips that Declan just had, and he kisses me. Long, slow, soft. He keeps the connection for a moment before pulling away and looking down at me. "You're so beautiful."

"Don't."

"Don't what?" he questions.

"Say sweet things that'll make me miss you even more."

He smiles, and when I glance out the front, I see Baldwin pulling up. With a heavy sigh, I turn back to Bennett as he says, "I've gotta go."

"Okay," I respond with hesitation as I nod my head.

"I'll call you as soon as I get there," he tells me and then teases, "Use this time to buy me lots of Christmas gifts."

"I'll spoil you rotten," I laugh.

"You already spoil me rotten."

With one more kiss, we say goodbye, and I watch as the car pulls away, happy that he's finally gone.

ten

(PRESENT)

WITH MY HUSBAND on his way to the airport to spend the next two weeks on the other side of the world, I get my game face on and head back to Declan, who's still in the dining room.

"What was that about?" he questions when I walk back in and sit down.

"Just saying goodbye."

"Are you sad?"

Shifting in my seat, I say, "Can we not talk about this?"

Declan doesn't push his questions anymore, staying quiet for the most part, aside from safe chitchat as we finish our meal. We discuss the catering and visit with Marco for a while, and after I hire him to cater the party, we open a bottle of wine while we spend a lengthy amount of time selecting the menu offerings. Once business is handled and the foods are selected, Marco excuses himself and I follow Declan to the lobby to have the valet pull my car around.

"Oh no," I breathe as I look out front. "How long were we talking with Marco?" It's a white out with snow falling hard and already piling high, making it impossible for me to leave.

"A few hours," Declan responds. "You can't drive in this, Nina."

"No, I know," I say and then shake my head, adding, "It's just . . . I told Bennett I would leave before the storm hit."

"We lost track of time. Nobody's fault. You can stay here."

"I don't have anything with me," I say and Declan lets out a quiet laugh. "What?"

"Nina, you're standing in one of the most exclusive hotels in the city. I'll get you whatever you need."

"Anything?"

Smiling at me, he says, "Come on," as he leads me back to his office.

He then gets on the phone telling whoever is on the other end to prepare a penthouse suite with all amenities and to bring him the key.

When he hangs up, I tell him, "You didn't have to do that. I don't need the penthouse."

"You'll be next to me. This way you won't be tempted to sneak out and play in the elevators," he jokes as if I'm some teenager.

"Next to you?" I question.

"I occupy one of the penthouses."

"You live here?"

"No," he replies. "I have a loft in River North, but I house a room here as well for when I'm too tired to drive home, or in this case, get stuck in a blizzard."

"River North? I would've thought you lived here in the loop."

"Too pretentious for me. No offense."

"Says the man who drives a pretentious car," I tease with a smile, and suddenly, all the tension and frustration from earlier seems to let up as we lightly poke fun at each other.

"Well, I can't argue the car, but it's nice to leave the loop at the end of the day and escape to a place that's a bit more low-key."

He says this and I think back to the breakfast diner he took me to the other week. Declan definitely looks the part and has the name that follows, but I wonder how much of it is really him. River North is full of wealth these days, but he's right, it's not pretentious.

After a while, when one of the staff delivers my room key, I follow Declan as he shows me to my room. Only two suites occupy the top floor, which is only accessible by the occupants—Declan and myself.

"This is you," he says as he walks me over to the left side of the elevator banks.

"Thank you."

"I'm on the other side," he tells me. "So if you need anything . . ."

"I'll be fine," I assure.

"Dinner later?"

"I'm pretty full from Marco's meal," I say. "I think I'll make it an early night."

As I turn to unlock the door, he adds, "Like I said, if you need anything, let me know."

"Night, Declan," I say and then walk into the room, letting the door shut behind me.

Looking around, the walls are solid floor to ceiling windows showcasing the twinkling lights of the city that's now covered in a blanket of snow. The space is large, with an open-concept living room, dining room, and kitchen. All of which are furnished in sleek upholstery and rich leather. I note the fireplace that is situated in a smaller sitting area that's set off from the rest of the room in a sunken section a couple steps down. I make my way into the bedroom that's lined with the same panoramic windows. I lay my coat and purse down on the plush white linens and go into the bathroom. I laugh at the extremities Declan's staff went to when I see every toiletry you could possibly need, plus a two-piece set of pajamas folded inside a shopping bag from Roslyn Boutique. Picking them up, I note the designer. The length that this hotel went to is no doubt a simple favor to myself. Lotus is known for its exclusivity and privacy for its patrons. Not anyone can just walk in and book a room.

After settling in, changing into the pajamas, and making a cup of hot tea, I sit on the floor with my legs crossed, knees pressed against the cold window as I watch the snow fall down on the city below. I think about how to use this night to my advantage with Declan. I know I should find my way to his room, and start to go through a variety of reasons for why I would go knocking on his door.

Time passes as I get lost in thought, and when I look over to the clock sitting on one of the end tables, it reads 10:23 pm. Setting my mug on the floor beside me, my mind drifts to Pike, and I can't help the guilt that passes through as I think about him in that cold, dilapidated trailer while I'm sitting on top of the city. The click of a door steers me away from Pike, and when I turn to look over my shoulder, I see Declan.

"What are you doing on the floor in the dark?" he asks as he walks across the large living room towards me.

"Do you make it a habit of breaking in to your guests' hotel rooms?"

With a grin, he says, "Technically, I didn't break in." He holds up a key card before dropping it on the coffee table when he walks past it.

"You could have knocked."

He steps next to me as I sit on the floor, and I have to tilt my head back to look up at him. He stands with his hands in the pockets of his slacks as he looks out the window.

"I love the snow," he murmurs, and without thinking, I agree, "I do too."

He looks down at me, his face shadowed in the darkened room. "Are you okay?" he asks, concerned for some reason.

"Why?"

"Because I come to check on you and you're on the floor pressed up against the window without a single light on. Seems sad."

I turn my attention back to the city below when I respond, "I like watching the snow fall."

He sits down next to me, his knee touching mine. I allow a few moments of silence to pass before saying, "Thank you."

"For?"

"The room," I tell him. "It's beautiful."

"It's just a room, Nina," he says, downplaying the scale of his hotel as he keeps his focus on the snow.

"Lotus," I say, acknowledging the name of the hotel. "Interesting choice. Why Lotus?"

"There's something about a beautiful, nearly flawless flower, emerging from muddled water."

"Hmm." I pause before stating, "Self-reflection," inferring that the meaning strikes a chord with himself.

Tilting his head to look at me, his breath feathering my cheek, he says, "Is this you trying to dissect me?"

"Is there something lying beneath that I should be looking for?"

"Everyone has something beneath that they're hiding." He peers into me. At least that's what he wants me to believe, but I'm not permeable. I soften anyway, giving him the sense that he's actually having an effect on me. I blink a few times and shift myself, cueing him that I'm nervous, and then he asks, "So what is it? Tell me what you think you've found."

Taking in a deep breath, I release it with my theory. "You have a distaste for the business that owns your name."

He doesn't move, and I add, "Or maybe your distaste is for your father."

"Interesting. Why bring him up?"

I smile and say, "Come on. We've both met the man. He's a bastard; you said it yourself the other day."

Declan laughs under his breath, saying "You're not delicate with your words, are you?"

"Did I give you the impression that I'm delicate?"

With a soft hum, he gives me an inquisitive look, and then asks, "What about *your* father?"

He catches me slightly off guard. A pinprick in the one soft spot that I've never been able to harden.

You want to know my weakness?

Well, there it is.

I miss my father.

Shifting the focus, I redirect, saying, "We're not talking about me, remember?"

"Of course."

"Do you even get along with him?"

"As well as anyone else does," he answers.

"That's a very political answer."

With his hand, he brushes my cheek slightly as he takes a lock of my hair and tucks it behind my ear, saying, "Whether or not you're in politics, everything is political. We all save face for others to perceive us in the best light. Nothing is real until you break down the walls and reveal the ugliness."

"Ugliness," I repeat as I look at him.

"The truest part of a person is always the ugliest. And with your evasiveness, I would bet that you're pretty damn ugly beneath all that gloss."

He keeps a straight face as he says this, and the truth behind his words irritates me. I know I'm ugly. Uglier than most. I'm tarnished and decrepit, but I'll be damned if I ever let him or anyone else see the wretched heart that beats inside of me.

"You're an asshole," I bite.

"Baby, I've been called a lot worse, so if you're trying to offend me, you'll have to do better than that."

With a glare, I say, "I don't get you and your insults. I thought you wanted to be my friend."

He moves in closer to me, and with a low voice, murmurs, "I don't want to be your friend, Nina."

Taking a hard swallow, I feign nervousness, whispering, "You should go," as he continues to move himself toward me, and then over me, forcing me to lie back on the floor with both his hands braced on either side of me. "Declan, this is wrong," I breathe.

"Why?"

"You know why."

"Tell me you love your husband," his voice taunting.

"I love my husband."

"Tell me you don't want me," he says, eyes pinned to mine.

"I don't want you."

My breathing increases and grows heavy when he lowers himself onto his elbow and starts running his one hand down the center of my sternum, between my breasts, adding quietly, "Tell me you're not lying to me."

"I'm not lying to you."

Then, with his legs intertwined with mine, he slips his hand down my pants, under my panties, parting the lips of my pussy and dragging his finger through my heat. He smiles cagily down at me when he feels how wet I am and then quickly removes his hand, bringing it to my lips and shoving his finger into my mouth, telling me, "Taste your lies, Nina."

His breath bathes me with his words, and I give in, allowing my tongue, for a brief and noticeable moment, to wrap around his finger, giving him the obedience I know he craves, but inside, I'm mortified and disgusted. I hate that my body would react this way—growing wet for this man. Pulling away and jerking my head to the side, I don't look at him, but soon feel his nose gliding along my exposed neck, hearing him inhale my scent.

"Declan . . ."

"Hmm . . .?"

I roll my head back, and look straight up at him. "Get the fuck off of me."

When he doesn't move right away, I fist my hands, and flip the switch on him, weakly slamming them against his chest, allowing the look of guilt to wash over my face. "Get off of me now, Declan."

He moves back and sits on his heels as I rise off of my back and scoot away from him, muttering, "Please, just go. Just leave me alone."

"Nina . . ."

"You can't do this to me. I'm not *that* person."

He reaches out for me, saying, with apology in his voice, "I don't want to upset you; you just make it hard for me to control myself when I'm around you."

"Why are you doing this?"

"Because I like you. Because I know you're not happy. I can see you hiding, and I don't want you to do that around me."

"I'm not hiding," I affirm sternly.

"Okay then," he releases in frustration. "You want me to accept that when we both know it's a lie?"

"I'm not hiding," I repeat, and with that, he stands and walks away and out the door.

Fucking, Christ!

A part of me wants to squeal in victory, knowing I've got this guy by the balls, and the other part feels like it needs a drink because he's so goddamn deluged with intensity. I've come across a few guys in the past year, but none have shown this level of interest. They all fizzled before anything could ever get started, so the elation that I feel with Declan gives me the power I need to move forward.

I NOW FIND myself tossing and turning in bed, unable to sleep because my mind won't seem to quiet down. It's past one in the morning when I decide the night with Declan isn't over just yet. He wants to believe that I'm lying to him about my contentment with Bennett, so I'll give him reason enough to confirm his assumption. Throwing the covers off of me, I walk through the room and out the door. This floor is private, so I go ahead and walk past the elevator bank and down to Declan's room. Standing in front of his door, I take a deep breath, and allow my mind to go to a place that'll put me in the state I need to be in when he opens the door and looks at me. He needs to believe I'm harboring a deep pain inside, so I drift back twenty-three years. I'm being ripped out of my father's arms, watching him fall to his knees as he's cuffed. I can see the tears falling down his face, and when I feel my cheeks heat in the pain, the tears puddle in my eyes. I knock.

Lights.

Camera.

Action.

The door opens, and I look up to see Declan standing in nothing but a pair of pajama bottoms that hang on his narrow hips that angle down from his broad, sculpted chest. My tears are heavy, but they don't spill over. He takes one step towards me and pulls me into his arms, his cheek pressed to the top of my head, holding me tight. No words are spoken when he brings me inside his room and shuts the door.

I keep my arms around his waist as he walks me back to his room and over to his bed. Cradling my face in his hands, I look up at him, and his eyes are noticeably worried.

"Stay."

With a nod of my head, he pulls the sheets back, and I crawl into his warm bed. He follows, scooping me into his arms. His body pressed against mine, my head resting on his chest, I take the comfort I need in this moment. My mind isn't with Declan or Bennett or this whole fucked up scenario, it's with my dad. I opened that gate for one second to trick Declan and now I'm five years old—scared and lost.

The first tear drops, and I fucking hate that I'm exposing this weakness. It's one thing to manufacture pain for the sake of deception, but my father is very much real, and it hurts. I don't want to think too much, so as Declan comforts me from what he believes is Bennett, I take the consoling for my father.

Neither of us says a word as I silently fight to contain the few weeps that break free, all the while Declan's hold is firm and strong around me. I weave my legs with his and eventually allow myself to drift to sleep.

eleven

(PRESENT)

STANDING IN FRONT of the windows, I look down and watch as the snowplows make their way through the city, clearing the streets. I left Declan's room early this morning while he was still sleeping. I wanted to build the mystery and chase, and waking up in his arms would make it too easy for him, and from what I've learned about men, easy leads to a shallow investment. I need Declan to be fully immerged if I have any chance at this working out, so I quietly slipped out of his room.

I laugh when I hear the knock on my door since last night he took it upon himself to just barge in on me with no warning. But it isn't Declan standing on the other side; it's room service.

"Mr. McKinnon ordered breakfast for you this morning," he says as he wheels in a white-clothed cart with a French press and a platter of fresh fruit and crullers.

"When was this request made?" I ask.

"Maybe an hour or so ago, Mrs. Vanderwal," he says. "May I pour you a cup?"

"No, thanks."

"Would you like anything else?"

"It seems Mr. McKinnon has covered all his bases this morning. Thank you though," I tell him before he turns to leave. The pit of my stomach pinches and this display should please me, but instead, irritation swarms. I should have never connected to his comfort last night. It was a foolish move on my part, and now I'm pissed at myself.

I leave the food and coffee and head to the shower to clean up. Not having any other clothes besides what I wore yesterday and the pajamas, I slip back into my dress and press a little powder on my face from the compact in my purse and then dry my hair.

Bennett calls in the late morning, worried about me getting stuck in the storm yesterday, but I assure him that I'm fine and should be home later today now that the city streets have been plowed. We talk for a while, and when I hear another knock, it's then that we say our goodbyes and hang up.

As I open the door, Declan walks right in, looking more put together than me in his tailored suit, white button-up left open at the neck, and no tie.

"What, no breaking and entering today?" I say, my words laced with the remaining irritation from earlier.

"I left the key on your coffee table last night," he responds as he walks over to the food cart. "You haven't touched anything."

"I don't need you catering to me, assuming you know what I like to eat or that it's your right to even make assumptions about me," I snap while I walk into the kitchen to put the kettle on.

"So, we're back to steely-bitch Nina?"

Turning to look at him, I say, "I'm going to have a cup of tea and then I'd like my car to be ready so I can go home."

"It's still snowing."

"The plows already came through."

He walks over to the kitchen and stands by the bar, asking, "What happened to you this morning? I woke up and you were gone."

"Your ego bruised?" I say with a condescending grin that pisses him off.

Rounding the bar, he backs me against the countertop, and hisses, "Now it's time for *you* to cut the shit." The kettle starts to squeal, and before I can turn to get it, he reaches over and slams it on the other burner, startling me, and flips the knob off. Caging me in with his arms, his tone is hard when he says, "Your games are starting to piss me off, and I don't like being played."

"And what about your games, Declan? The ones you've been playing since the night I met you?"

"Did I not apologize to you?" he questions. "Don't forget that *you* came to *me* last night."

"Moment of weakness. Won't happen again. So if you were hoping—"

"God, you're fucking aggravating."

"The feeling's mutual," I say as I move to push him back, and when he keeps his stance and doesn't budge, I bark, "Let me out."

"No."

Pushing my hands against his hardened chest, I get pissed. "I'm serious, Declan. Back up!"

"No."

"Let me go!"

"Not until you stop bullshitting me. Stop lying, and tell me why you came to me last night."

Pressing my chest against his, I narrow my eyes, saying, "I already told you. Moment of weakness."

He grabs me above the elbows, biting down hard before saying, "And I told you not to lie."

I fist my hands, jerking my body away from him, and he lets go of me. He stays back while I walk across the room, putting space between us, and go over to the windows.

"You think I get off on encroaching on a married woman?" he asks.

Wrapping my arms around myself, I keep my back to him.

"You think I'm an asshole?" he continues. "Join the club. I'm a fucking ass, but I can't help how you make me feel when you're around."

I can feel the heat of him as he moves in behind me. His hands find my shoulders, and he gently tugs to turn me to face him, but I cast my eyes downward.

"Tell me I'm not alone here, or tell me I am because the moment I think I can read you, you flip on me." When I look up at him, his eyes hold hope in my response. "Tell me why you came to me last night."

"Because . . ." I begin, but let it linger.

"Tell me."

"Because I didn't want to be alone."

"Why?"

"Declan . . ." I hesitate.

"Why, Nina?"

Lowering my head, my voice cracks perfectly when I say, "Because I'm lonely." He runs his hands from my shoulders, up my neck, and to my cheeks, angling me up to him. As I look into his eyes, I add, "Whether he's here or not, I'm lonely."

"And when *I'm* here?" he questions.

"I don't feel so alone."

He releases a breath and drops his forehead to mine as I grip my hands around his wrists.

"I'm sorry," he says. "I was a dick to you yesterday."

"I wasn't very nice either."

He lifts his head, telling me, "Don't leave. Stay. Let me make it up to you."

"I can't. I need to go home."

"Why?"

With a light laugh, I say, "Well, for one, I need to change into some clean clothes."

"So go home and change. I'll pick you up."

"What are we gonna do?" I ask.

"When's the last time you had any fun?" I shrug my shoulders and he says, "So let's have some fun."

A COUPLE HOURS later, I'm back home. Declan called a little bit ago, saying he was on his way and to be sure I was dressed warm. So I've made sure to comply since the temperatures are no less than frigid as the snow continues to fall.

When the doorman calls to let me know Declan is here, I grab my wool coat, scarf, gloves, and knit hat. I see Declan standing in the lobby as the elevator doors open, and it's the first time I've seen him dressed down in a pair of dark wash jeans and grey sweater under his black wool coat. He looks sharp, and when he turns towards me, his smile grows.

"You ready?" he asks as we walk towards each other.

"I'm not sure," I respond warily. "I don't know what we're doing."

"Come on."

I follow him out the front doors and see his car parked along the street, but he leads me in the opposite direction.

"We're not driving?"

"No."

I slip on my ivory knit hat and wrap my scarf a couple more times around my neck while he watches with a smile and then holds his hand out for me. I don't take it at the risk of someone seeing me, so when I begin to walk, he places his hand on the small of my back as he leads us across the street to Millennium Park.

"You know it's closed, right?" I ask when he leads us to the ice rink. "The snow's too thick."

"It's closed for everyone in the city, but you."

"What?"

"Mr. McKinnon," a young man greets as we approach the rink.

"Walter, thanks for doing this," Declan says as they shake hands.

"Any time, man," he responds and then looks at me, asking, "You ready?"

"We're skating?"

Declan laughs, and Walter says, "That's the deal we made. You ever been?"

Slightly embarrassed, I tell him, "Actually . . . no. I haven't."

"Never?" Declan asks, and when I shake my head, he says, "But you live here in the park." When I shrug my shoulders, he jokes, "This oughta be fun," and I smile at his mischievous grin.

After we grab our skates, Walter opens the gate to the rink, and I grab ahold of the metal railing as Declan steps out onto the ice with ease.

"Take my hand," he instructs, seeing my nervousness.

"This is embarrassing," I tell him.

"Good."

"Good?"

"You're always so uptight, Nina," he says. "Come on, take my hand."

"I'm gonna fall on my ass."

He glides over to me, holding out both of his hands, and tells me, "Let go of the railing and take my hands."

Placing one hand in his, I step onto the ice before letting go of the railing and giving him my other hand. It doesn't take but a second before my balance falters, and I fall into his chest. He grips my waist, laughing, and says, "Relax. You're too stiff."

"It's freezing out here, and you've got me on ice. I can't relax," I grumble.

"Stop bitching." He then takes my hands again and begins skating backwards while gliding me forward. "Try moving your feet."

"Uh uh. I'll fall."

With a grin on his face, he asks, "Why are you so stubborn?"

"Are you serious? I could ask you the same question."

"Just for today, why don't you try trusting me?"

As he continues to hold my hands and pull me around the rink while he skates backwards with total control, I question, "Is that what you like? Having someone that just obeys you and never voices their opinion?"

"No, Nina. It's not about obeying, it's about trusting; something I don't think you do too easily."

"Trust can be costly," I argue.

"Or it can be comforting."

He keeps his eyes steady on me when I finally give in, and with a sigh, agree, "Okay, fine. One day."

His smile is cocky, and I shake my head at him, asking, "How did you get the rink to open for us?"

"Walter did some work for me at the hotel during construction. So I called him, slipped him a few bills, and here we are."

"Is everything that easy for you?"

"No," he says with a piercing look. "Some things I have to work for."

He says this and I drop my eyes to cut the tension building, and when I do, I lose my balance, tripping over my toes. I grab on to his coat as I fall hard on my hip, pulling him down with me. He hovers over me, laughing, while I'm flat on my back.

"My ass is getting wet," I say as I try to sit up, but he doesn't allow me with his body lying on top of mine.

His fingers run through my hair, and he murmurs, "Your red hair is beautiful with the snow in it."

A shiver runs through me from the chill of the ice, and he moves away, getting steady on his feet before helping me up.

"You done?"

I give him a nod, and he helps me off the ice and over to a bench. When we sit down, he pulls my feet onto his lap and starts to untie the laces on my skates. Slipping them off my feet, he runs his thumbs firmly up the arch of my foot, kneading along the way before repeating the same on my other foot. I watch him as he does this, and he never pulls his attention away from my eyes. The adoration he exudes is palpable, and it's a shame that it's wasted on someone like me, but I'll take it and use it to my benefit.

We get our shoes on and thank Walter before we rush back towards my building. Walking over to his car, he pulls his keys out and opens the passenger door.

"Get in."

"Where are we going?"

"It's my one day for you to trust me," he says. "Get in."

I move past him and slip down into the leather seat of his Mercedes before he closes the door. When he gets in, he starts the car and pulls out onto the scarce streets of the city. I keep quiet during the drive as we head north on Michigan Avenue towards River North. Looking over at him, he turns his head to me, questioning, "What?"

"Are you taking me to your place?"

He shoots me a wink, and when I open my mouth to speak, he shuts me down, reminding, "One day, Nina."

Turning into the building's garage on Superior, we head inside and onto the elevator. He slips a key into the punch pad before hitting P.

"You nervous about being here?" he asks as we ascend to the top floor.

"Should I be?"

Stepping over to me, he takes my hand as the doors slide open, and we step off the elevator and into an impressive living space. He has the whole top floor to himself, and as I look across the massive living room with multiple bucket accents in the vaulted ceiling, I note the architectural detailing of the modern design. Near solid glass walls that look out over the city, and against the far wall, an enormous Archlinea chef's kitchen.

Noticing the stainless steel staircase, I ask, "What's up there?"

"A private rooftop deck."

"This place is amazing," I say as I step further into the loft. For as impressive and spacious as it is, it's warm and comfortable, a feeling I appreciate because it's so far from how my place feels.

"Coffee?" he asks.

"Please." Taking off my coat and scarf, I lay my things on one of the couches and walk over to the couch that's closest to the large walk-in fireplace.

Declan soon joins me, handing me a mug and then turning the fireplace on before sitting next to me.

"How long have you lived here?"

"Since I moved to Chicago around two years ago."

"It's a big place for just one person."

"Says the woman who lives in the penthouse of The Legacy," he remarks with a smirk, and I laugh.

"That was my husband's place since before I met him," I defend.

"You like it there?"

"I've grown to," I answer. "It's only me there most of the time with Bennett working and traveling so much."

He doesn't respond as he takes a sip of his coffee and then sets it down on the end table. Turning to me, he says, "I want to know about you."

"What do you wanna know?"

"What did you study in college? Did you work before you married? I want to know who you are aside from his wife," he says as he angles his body to face me.

I cradle the mug in my hands, drawing in the heat, and answer, "I was studying Art History at the University of Kansas when my parents died during my third year."

"How did they die?" he asks. He doesn't respond the way most people do when you mention death. He never says *I'm sorry*, apologizing for something he had nothing to do with, and I appreciate that, even though I'm feeding him lies.

"Tornado came through and landed on top of the house I grew up in. They were found under the rubble a few days after," I tell him. "I was an only child, so when I found out they had been pulling loans and a second mortgage on the house to pay my college tuition, there was no money. I had to drop my enrollment for the next semester and never went back."

"What did you do?"

Bringing my legs up and folding them in front of me, I respond, "I was all alone, so I did what I had to do to get by. I worked various jobs to barely meet my rent and pay my bills."

"So how did you wind up here in Chicago?" he asks.

"After a few years, I was just depressed and going nowhere. All my friends had since graduated and were moving on with their lives while I was stuck. I needed a change, so I packed up what little I had and drove here. No reason, really," I say. "I had just enough money to put a deposit down on a small studio apartment and got a job with a catering company. I used to work these fancy parties, and as stupid as it sounds, even though I was nothing but the help, I used to pretend that I was part of that world. The part that didn't have a care in the world, being able to wear pretty dresses and drink expensive champagne. A world I would never be a part of until I was hired to work a party for Bennett Vanderwal."

"That's how you met him?"

"Pathetic, huh? Kinda makes me look like a gold digger, but it wasn't like that at all," I tell him. "For the first time in a long time, I didn't feel so lost. And when he looked at me, he didn't see the poor girl from Kansas who ran to escape her miserable life."

I tell Declan this lie and the look on his face is that of sorrow, but the life he feels bad about me having is a life I would've done almost anything to have. God, if he knew the truth about how I grew up, he'd run. It's not a story anyone in their right mind would ever want to hear. It's the type of story that people want to believe doesn't really exist because it's too hard to stomach. It's too dark of a place for people to even consider being reality.

"And now?"

Looking down at my mug, I watch the ribbons of steam float off the coffee and dissolve in the air when I answer with false trepidation, "And now I realize that I *am* that poor girl who ran. The girl he never saw me as. It's like I woke up one day and suddenly realized that I don't really fit in to all of this.

That I'm no longer sure of my place in this world."

Declan moves to take the mug out of my hands and sets it down on the table as he closes the space between us. Taking my hands in his, he asks, "Do you love him?"

With diffidence, I nod my head, murmuring, "Yes."

When he cocks his head in question, I add, "He loves me. He takes care of me."

"But you feel alone," he states.

"Don't."

"Don't what?"

"Make me speak badly of him," I respond.

"I don't want that. All I want is for you to speak honestly to me."

"That's what I'm doing, but . . ." Dropping my head, I hesitate, and he urges, "But . . .?"

"It feels wrong to talk to you like this."

"Did it feel wrong when you were in bed with me last night?" he questions.

"Yes."

His voice is low and intent, asking, "When did it feel wrong? When you got into my bed or when you snuck out of it?"

I take a moment and swallow hard before answering, "When I snuck out."

His hand finds its way into my hair, threading through the tresses, and then he guides it to my cheek with his other hand still holding mine. With a faint voice, he says, "I want to kiss you right now."

Reaching my hand up to the one he has on my face, I hold on to his wrist, close my eyes, and weakly plead, "Don't."

"Why?"

"Because I don't want you to."

"Why?"

I open my eyes to him and say, "Because it's wrong."

"Then why doesn't it feel that way?"

"Maybe it doesn't now, but eventually it will."

He drops his hand from me and sits back. I hold him off because right now he's merely hungry and I need him starving—ravenous. I need him to fall hard for me. Harder than I believe he's capable of right now. So I'll keep him at bay for a bit longer because it seems to be working.

twelve

(PRESENT)

BENNETT CONTINUES TO call me every day to check in as usual. He misses me. Nothing new. Let him miss me. Let Declan miss me too. Both men, eating out of the palm of my deceitful hand. Mortal puppets. Foolish puppets.

The drive to Justice is a long one because of all the snow on the roads. From the scenic display of Christmas in the city, to the muted slum of the ghetto—I miss Pike no matter where I am. I take my key when I park my car and let myself in. The sounds of a woman moaning, almost theatrically, filter through the trailer from the bedroom. The squeaking metal from the bedframe composes the rhythm at which Pike fucks her. The curdling inside my gut is sickening, and I go back out to my car to wait for the chick to leave.

If you think I'm jealous, you're wrong. I don't care who Pike fucks. I don't care who anyone fucks. To me, sex is disgusting. It's a means to an end. If you're not miserable, I don't see the point. My body used to reject the act, rousing me to vomit afterward. Hell, sometimes I would throw up during sex. I've been able to sequester the nausea, but the dirtiness of the act remains.

With Bennett, I've become numb and vacant when we have sex. I used to be overcome with hatred when he'd find his way inside of me, but I shut that off quickly, and now the illusion that what we have isn't just sex, but making love, is one that he has never questioned.

Yeah, I'm a good actress.

I watch as the snow collects on the windshield, and with the screech of a door, I turn to the trailer to see a pathetic-looking woman walking down the steps with her ratty, purple fur coat wrapped around her. She probably thinks she looks trendy, but she just looks like a skank.

When she gets into her rusted Buick, I turn to see Pike standing, arms braced on the sides of the door frame, pants unbuttoned, no shirt, and tattoos on full display. He smiles as he looks at me, and when I get out of the car, he asks, "Been here long?"

"Not too long."

He steps aside as I walk in, and the door slams shut.

"I didn't expect to see you so soon."

"Bennett's out of town. Will be for another week," I explain and set my coat and purse down on the edge of the couch.

He lights a cigarette, and when he takes a drag, I step over and hug him. He folds me in his arms and I get a whiff of perfume. Pushing back from him, he questions, "What is it?"

"I can smell her cheap drug store perfume on you."

He laughs at me and shakes his head. "What's got you so pissy?"

Sighing, I turn to walk over to the couch, and as I sit, I release a heavy breath, saying, "I'm just tired."

"I guess," he mumbles when he joins me on the couch. "So, how's it going with the guy?"

"Declan? Good. Really good."

"Where are you at with him?" he asks.

"I'm working him," I say. "He's jealous of Bennett."

"That's it? Come on, Elizabeth, clue me in."

"We've been spending time together. What do you want me to say? He likes me; it's evident. We spent the day together yesterday."

"What did you guys do?"

"He took me ice-skating," I say with a slip of a smile, and his face contorts before he snaps, "What the fuck?"

"What?" My voice is pitchy with defense.

"You're shitting me, right? You're out ice-skating like a goddamn kid when you're supposed to be seducing this ass wipe. And while you're off screwing around, I'm living in this shitfest."

His tone sparks my temper. Standing up, I turn to look down at him, and piss my words, saying, "Fuck you, Pike. You don't know shit about what I'm doing, so just sit tight, fuck the trash that walks in here, and let me handle myself."

"Handle yourself?" he sneers. "Tick tock, tick tock."

"You wanna speed this shit up? You're tired of waiting? Then hire one of your thuggish street friends to take care of it and spare me my own time," I lash out.

"You're taking too much of that time."

Walking across the room, I clench my hands at my sides and take a deep breath before turning back to him. "Just remember that we *both* agreed to keep our hands clean in this. We hire someone, we have a direct link to our plan. The deal was that we would never speak the words, that we would simply goad a person into it. You think you could do a better job?"

He stubs his cigarette out in the tray on the coffee table and then stands, saying, "Not unless they prefer dick over pussy."

"God, Pike," I seethe as I fist my hair, and when I drop my hands to my sides, I tell him, "I'm so sick of fighting with you. It's all we seem to do lately, and I'm done with it."

"Perks of an older brother," he says with a pompous smile.

Mumbling under my breath, "I guess," I grip my hands on my hips and look over at him.

He stands there staring at me, and I can't help but laugh at his demeanor, full of ego. "You really do drive me crazy," I tell him.

"I know."

With a shake of my head, I add, "And you need to stop doubting me. It pisses me off."

"I know," he repeats with surrender. "Come here."

With a childish groan, I make my way over to him and stubbornly take his hug, and then tease, "Seriously, her cheap perfume is making my nose burn."

"You're so high and mighty now, huh? Don't forget where you come from."

"How could I?"

We stand there for a long while as I get the comfort from him that I've been missing since the last time I saw him before I finally speak again. "I have a good feeling about him, Pike."

"Hmm."

"He's already falling. He doesn't hide it well."

"I worry about you," he says, and I lean my head back to look at him, questioning, "Why?"

"Because I know how hard it is on you being with Bennett. I worry about how it's going to affect you when you start adding this other guy in."

I know that Pike is genuine in his feelings for me. We're family, and I get that he worries. He always has. But I remind him, "Hard as steel, right?"

With a nod of his head, he keeps his arm around my shoulders as we walk back to his bedroom. It's routine at this point—our sex. We do it every time I come and see him, reminding me of the one person I can trust in this world, the one person who has always taken care of me.

His pants are still unbuttoned, so with a tug, he drops them to his ankles and steps out. I lie back on the bed—the bed he just fucked another girl in, but I couldn't care less. My body is entirely worthless, so I give it freely without much thought. Undoing my pants, I watch as he pumps his dick a couple times, and when he reaches to check if I'm ready, he feels how dry I am. I want the sex with him, but most of the time, I struggle to get wet. It didn't seem to be a problem when Declan felt me up the other night, but more often than not, I need a little help.

Pike pushes my knees wider and spits his saliva on me, wetting me, and runs his fingers through my folds to spread it. When I give him a nod, he holds himself and pushes inside of me. Pinching my eyes shut, I grip my arms around him as he fucks me, clearing my head and wiping away the stains of Bennett, and now, Declan.

RETURNING HOME, CLARA is in the kitchen cooking. I unwrap the scarf from around my neck and walk over to the kitchen to greet her.

"Clara, hi," I say as I look on the stove to see what she's making.

"There you are. I feel like we keep missing each other."

"Smells good," I say, eyeing the skillet of beef stroganoff.

With a warm smile, she responds, "I figured you could use some comfort food with the nasty winter we've been having."

I open the fridge to pull out ginger soda, saying, "It's perfect. I haven't eaten all day, actually."

Turning to me, she spots my drink and asks, "Is your stomach upset?"

"A little."

I always tend to feel a little queasy after my visits with Pike. The after sex blues followed by the upsetting goodbye. It tends to have this effect on my stomach when I leave, turning back into the emotionless machine I've been forced to become ever since I was a little kid.

"There's a package from Mr. Vanderwal in the living room. It was delivered earlier today when you were out," she says, and when I walk over, I see the large, white box wrapped in a gold satin ribbon.

My stomach churns, and I down another gulp of my ginger soda.

I pick up the lightweight box and untie the ribbon, letting it drop to the sides. Inside lies a masquerade mask. Black, laser-cut metal, which gives it an almost evil, seductive feel. The black, double-faced satin ties hang as

I pick it up out of the box. It's probably more perfect than anything I could have found on my own and that annoys me, the fact that he can be so good at nearly all he does. I look in the box for a note, but there isn't one, so I turn and ask Clara, "Was there a note or anything with this?"

"No, dear," she answers over her shoulder from the kitchen and then my cell rings.

Cringing when I see who the caller is, I answer with charm, "Jacqueline, hello."

"Where have you been?" She's huffy in her question.

"What do you mean?"

"Neiman's? Shopping? Yesterday?"

I completely let it slip from my mind that I was supposed to meet the girls yesterday. I was so distracted with spending the night at the hotel and then hanging out with Declan that it didn't occur to me that instead of being with him, I should have been at Neiman's.

"I'm so sorry; I must have forgotten. You're not upset with me, are you?"

"I'm not, but Catherine was running her mouth about how you've been acting like a bitch towards her."

And this is the shit I hate about these women. I have absolutely nothing in common with any one of them. They have way too much time on their hands that they seem to enjoy filling with petty drama. They're all spoiled and entitled, yet I'm forced to grin and bear it, and so I respond, "I don't even speak to Catherine outside of when we're all together."

"Exactly. She thinks that you think you're better than her."

I am. As sick as I may be, I'm still better than the shallow depths of them.

"Jacqueline, you know I don't enjoy the gossip, so if there isn't anything else, I should get going."

"I was hoping we could get together soon. It's been a while—the gathering at Lotus, I believe," she says.

"Of course. I'll check my calendar and call you," I reply before we say our goodbyes.

Walking over to Clara, I smile as she moves around the kitchen. I wonder for a moment what my life would have been like if I'd had a mom. For one, I wouldn't have ever gone into foster care after my father's arrest. I never met my mom. I don't know anything about what happened to her since the only one who could have explained it to me was my father, and I was so young when he went to prison.

I've seen a few pictures to know I got my red hair from her. She wore it in a short bob, where mine is long with just a hint of waves. She was pretty. I used to imagine her living with my dad and me when I was tied up in that closet. She'd smile and kiss my father while I cringed but secretly loved watching them like that. She would hold me at night, rocking me while my dad sang to me. He always sang to me at night. I'll never forget the sound of his voice as I would fall asleep.

The top of my nose tingles at the thought of him, and I don't even realize how tight I have my teeth clamped shut when Clara asks, "Are you okay?"

Unlocking my teeth to answer, an ache shoots through my gums at the release. "Will you stay for dinner?"

Her warm smile penetrates my mournful thoughts, and I smile back at her when she says, "I'd love to." She turns to pull a couple plates down as she inquires, "Now tell me, what did that lovely husband of yours send you?"

"A very beautiful mask for the masquerade."

"Have you gotten a dress yet?"

She fixes our plates as we begin to talk about all the details of the party I've been working on. We eat and talk and laugh, and for a moment, I pretend she's my mom.

But only for a moment.

thirteen

(PAST)

TOMORROW'S MY BIRTHDAY. You'd think I'd be excited about turning ten years old, but it's just another reminder that life isn't going to get any better. I used to go to bed at night thinking that tomorrow would be a new day, a hopeful wish on stars. But stars don't grant wishes. I've lived in this house with Pike for almost two years, and I now know that tomorrow is nothing but a repeat of the day before and stars are nothing but burning rocks.

I wonder if I'll even be let out of this closet for my birthday. Unlikely. This is where I have spent nearly every weekend since the day Carl first tied me up a year and a half ago. When I told Bobbi what had happened, her response was, "Well, what did you do to provoke him?" Yeah, turns out, she doesn't give a shit about me or Pike. We're nothing more than her paycheck. A means to get by, to pay her bills and put food on the table, food I rarely get to eat since I'm always locked up with my hands bound.

I feel like I live in the dark more than I do the light. Pike sneaks down every night to talk to me. There's not been a single night that he hasn't spent with me outside of this door. I quickly learned to train myself to sleep during the days so that I could be awake when Pike would visit me. I didn't ever want to be alone and without him.

Carl likes to slap me around before tying me to the garment rod, and there is now a padlock on the outside of the door. I'd tell my caseworker, but I'm terrified of losing Pike. And there's no guarantee that the next home would be any better; at least here, I have my brother. So when my crappy-ass caseworker does decide to show up, which is about once every few months, I keep my mouth shut.

Shifting up to my feet, I allow the blood to drain back down my arms. I pee as I wait on Pike. The filth of spending days peeing on myself doesn't even faze me anymore. It used to embarrass me, but now, it's second nature.

"Elizabeth," I hear Pike whisper, and I'm relieved that I finally have him here with me—my distraction.

"Hey."

"Are you okay?"

"I don't even know why you still ask me that question," I reply.

"Sorry," he says. "Happy birthday. It's after midnight, so it's officially your birthday."

"Wish me a happy birthday when I turn fourteen," I tell him.

"Just four more years."

"It feels more like four hundred," I say in defeat. I'm starting to feel like I'm never going to escape this hell and see my dad. I don't believe life can be that good.

"Well, it's not four hundred, it's only four," Pike tells me.

I situate myself back onto the floor with my hands bound above my head, and ask, "Since it's my birthday, can I pick the game tonight?"

"Go for it."

"Umm . . . how about food, but it has to be junk food," I say. Pike and I play alphabet games with each other. One of us will pick a theme and whatever letter our words ends with has to be the beginning letter to the word the other person has to come up with. If you can't think of a word, you lose. It was Pike's idea to start playing these games. I used to just sit and cry when he would come to me at night, so this was his way of keeping my mind occupied.

"Okay, junk food," he starts. "AirHeads."

"Swedish Fish."

"Happy Meal."

"That's not a food, Pike. It's a meal," I laugh.

He tries defending his play, saying, "Yeah, and what is a meal made of? Food."

"But it's not an actual food because you can choose what you want in it."

"Yeah, but no matter what you choose, it's still junk."

Pike is nothing but serious in his argument, which makes me laugh. Our connection with one another is strong. He's everything a brother should be: protective, caring, annoying, and everything else I could have imagined a sibling would be.

"Uh uh. You can't use that as a game play," I tell him.

I can hear the irritation in his sigh before he says, "Fine. Ho Hos."

"Those are so good."

With a chuckle, he agrees, "I know."

We continue with the game, and eventually, I win, making sure I rub it in since he's beaten me the last two times we've played.

After a while, Pike has to go back to his room and I'm alone once more. Resting my head back against the wall, I shut my eyes and try to relax enough to at least drift a little, if not actually fall asleep.

I startle awake when light hits me. Opening my eyes, I quickly clamp them back shut from the pain of being in the dark for the past three days. Who knew light could be so painful? But it is. It always takes a couple hours for my eyes to adjust.

I can smell Carl along with the stench of my urine, and I'm shocked when he starts to unlatch the leather belt he uses to bind me. He has holes poked all the way down so that he can fasten me tightly and not have to worry about me working my hands free. My arms are like noodles as they fall to my sides. Warmth slowly flows back into my hands, and the tingling begins to run through the length of my lifeless limbs.

"God, you smell like shit, kid," he grumbles, and I crawl to my knees, squinting to find the bottle of bleach he keeps stored in the corner of the closet. It's now routine, that as soon as I'm untied, I'm to clean the floor with bleach.

When I get upstairs, I head into the shower to wash myself. I didn't think I'd be getting out until tomorrow, so I'm determined to stay quiet and invisible so that Carl doesn't change his mind and toss me back into that black hole again.

After I'm cleaned up, I return to my bedroom to see Pike lying in my bed. He's always here to comfort me when I get out of the closet. Walking over to him, I crawl into his arms and let him hold me.

"I have something for you," he whispers, and when I lift my head from his chest, I ask, "What is it?"

"A birthday present."

I let my head fall back down on him and sigh, "You shouldn't have bothered."

"Well, I did, so be polite and pretend you're happy."

Sitting up, I cross my legs as Pike quickly runs into his room and then returns with a plastic grocery sack. He hands it to me and sits back down on my bed. Inside is a doll with bright red hair made out of yarn. A smile finds its way to my lips, and he says, "Her hair reminded me of you."

No doubt, Pike stole this from some store, but I don't care. This will be the only gift I get this birthday, and I love him for giving it to me since there are very few things I can call my own.

"I love you, Pike," I say, looking at him as he sits there with an almost worried expression when he asks, "You don't think it's stupid?"

"No. It's perfect, and I love it."

He reaches out to hug me, and I cuddle into his embrace with the doll pressed between us as he says, "I just didn't want you to be sad today."

"I'm sad every day, but it would be worse if I didn't have you."

"Pike!" we hear Carl yell from downstairs. "Get down here."

My stomach twists when I see Pike's face go to stone. He hates the man as much as I do.

"One sec."

When Pike sits up, I ask, "Did you do something?" wondering why Carl sounds so pissed.

"Does he need a reason?" is all he says when he sulks out of my room, and I feel sick when I follow him out and stand at the top of the stairs as he walks down.

Carl grips the back of Pike's neck and tugs him in close, saying, "Basement, you little shit."

His head drops, and when Carl opens the door that leads to the basement, Pike descends down the stairs. I hate that he's always down there. He told me that Carl takes him there to knock him around, and I hate that I can't do anything to protect him. Every time he goes to the basement, I just sit and wait for him to return, and when he does, he won't even look at me. It's like he's mad at me. I asked him once if he was, but he swore that he could never be upset with me. It's so different with us, because when I'm let out of the closet, Pike is always there to hold me. But when Pike comes up from the basement, he wants nothing to do with me. He avoids me and hides in his room. It's awful when all I want to do is hug him to make him feel better like he does for me, but he won't let me.

I lie on my bed, slip on my headphones, and hold my new doll while I listen to music, trying to drown out the pain that fills my chest. Closing my eyes, I eventually grow tired and start to nod off when, suddenly, my doll is snatched out of my arms. Opening my eyes, I see Carl hovering over me. As I slip off my headphones, he snarls, "Get your ass in the basement."

Too scared to even question him, I trail behind him as fear chills my body. When he opens the door to the basement, my legs shake beneath me as I step down the stairs. I've never been down here before, and the panic has never been so fierce when I see Pike standing in nothing but a pair of boxers, his clothes crumpled on the floor next to him.

The look on Pike's face scares me. He's never looked at me like this, like he's scared too. But Pike is never scared. I stand a few feet away from him and nervously turn my head back and see a dirty mattress lying on the cement floor. Turning back to Pike, my eyes wide, my heart pounding, my tears pricking, I hear Carl ask, "How old are you today?"

I face him as he sits in a metal folding chair that sits in the corner.

In a weak voice that trembles, I answer, "Umm . . . t-ten."

He doesn't respond, only slowly nods his head and takes a long moment before adding, "You scared?"

I take a quick look at Pike, whose eyes are pinned to the floor, and then back at Carl and nod yes.

His next words changed my life forever. It was my tenth birthday, and I was old enough to know better than to believe in fairytales. I knew that Prince Charming, flying steeds, and talking caterpillars didn't really exist, but what happened next made me realize that monsters did. And I just so happened to be living with one.

A

Real

Life

Monster.

With a low, stern voice, his demand comes. "Take your clothes off."

My heart slams down into the pit of my stomach as my body shivers. I'm frozen. I can't respond, so I just stand there. The air is still until Carl repeats harder, "Take your clothes off. All of them."

I snap my head over to Pike, and he's now looking straight at me. I know I should be terrified by the tears on his cheeks and the look of sorrow in his eyes. Without even blinking, I feel my own tears roll out effortlessly. Shaking my head in confusion, Pike gives me a nod that tells me I need to obey.

My jittery hands slowly go to the hem of my shirt, and when I grip the fabric, a pained cry rips out from my constricted throat. It echoes off the concrete walls and floor. Pinching my eyes shut, I slip my shirt off and over my head and then hold it over my chest, even though I haven't grown breasts yet.

"Pants," he orders.

I don't look at him. My eyes remain closed as I unzip my jeans and push them down my legs and step out, still clinging the shirt to me.

"Drop it."

The ice in his voice frightens me, so I open my fingers and let it drop to the ground.

"Good girl," he says and I can hear the smile that wears his words. "Now your underwear."

God, if you're real, please help me.

Stepping out of my underwear, I attempt to cover myself with my arms and hands as I stand there. And when I finally open my eyes, that's when Carl speaks.

"Have you ever seen a dick before?" he asks as he opens his fly and tugs his pants down. His is the first I have ever seen and my throat burns with the bile that creeps up.

"You ever touched one before?"

My tears are heavy, and I can't hold back the sobs any more, pleading, "Please don't hurt me. I'll do anything."

"Anything?"

My cries are loud when he makes his demand, "This is what I want. You're gonna let Pike fuck you while I watch. You do that for me, I won't lay a hand on you."

I shake my head vigorously, not understanding what he means, and when I look over at Pike, he stands for a moment before taking the two steps towards me, quietly saying in a choked voice, "You don't want him touching you."

My head won't stop shaking, and I can't stop crying as I try to stammer out, "I d-don't know what he w-wants."

He releases a defeated sigh when he tells me, "He wants us to have sex." When he reads my confusion, he asks, "You know what that is?"

"I th-think so. I mean . . . I d-don't, umm . . ." I can't get my words out through the terror that's stabbing me from the inside. I've heard of sex. I know of sex. I just don't understand what it is exactly.

"On the mattress!" Carl's voice booms, causing me to startle.

In a hushed voice, Pike begs, "Please don't be scared of me," as he takes my hand and walks us over to the stained mattress on the floor.

"Lie on your back," he says, all his words in whispers so that only I can hear. He takes off his underwear before lying on top of me and my helpless cries fill the room. He lowers his mouth to my ear and quietly talks to me, saying, "It's gonna be okay. Don't even look at him. You don't have to look at me, but please promise me you won't look at him."

I nod my head against the side of his head so that he can feel my response.

His last words to me before I lose every last piece of hope that somehow life will be okay are, "I'm so sorry, Elizabeth."

fourteen

(PAST)

MY LIFE CONTINUES to be a wasteland. It's simply pointless to even try to see the good in anything anymore. I'm now twelve years old. The only hope I've been clinging to is that in two years, I'll get my dad back. But that hope turned to ash and dust when my caseworker stopped by yesterday.

"Only two more years," I said, and with a confused look, she asked, "What happens in two years?"

"I get my dad back," I told her. "I can go home."

She seemed annoyed when she shook her head and sighed, "That's not how it works."

"What do you mean?"

"The state terminated his rights to you. When he gets out, you don't get to go back home. He's not allowed to have any contact with you."

My face heated in pure white anger when she added, "This is your home—here—with Carl and Bobbi."

I walked away from her at that point. The hopelessness and defeat were too much for me to hide and I didn't want her to see me upset. She's a piece of shit, this world is a piece of shit, my life is a piece of shit. I used to pray to God to help me, but he never did, so he's a piece of shit too, leaving me in this nightmare. Me—living in the darkness, bound up with leather belts, scars imbedding their home in the frail skin of my wrists. Me—humiliated and degraded—having sex with my brother while Carl beats off as if we're his own personal porn show. It's my living hell.

I used to cry all the time after being forced to have sex with my brother, the horror that started on my tenth birthday. When it was over that first time, I locked myself in my room, screaming and crying into my pillow. I'll never forget that day; it's burned its memory inside of me. A day that I truly felt my innocence being stripped away.

Putting my clothes back on, Carl laughs at me and I run up the stairs and into my bedroom, locking the door behind me. I feel disgusting and when I fall onto the bed, I take the red-headed doll Pike gave me earlier and with all the force I have, throw it against the wall, releasing a violent sob as I do. I can't stop the tears or the ache that fills me. I'm nothing but tears and snot and drool—ugly—and the salts from my eyes eventually start making the skin of my cheeks sting. My body wears out, after first being tied up in the closet for the past three days, and now the depth of my breakdown. With swollen eyes, I'm finally unshackled from this misery as I drift off into my dreams.

When I wake up, Pike is sitting in bed next to me. I look up at him as his back rests against the headboard. His eyes are sad and bloodshot, and I'm mortified. I can't even look at him. I don't want him to see me, so I close my eyes and roll over, away from him.

His voice is soft and strained when he says to my back, "I'm so sorry."

I cry. It only takes a second for this heavy weighted pain to claim me—to own me. My body heaves in an unsteady rhythm, and he doesn't touch me like he normally does when I cry.

Time passes as my cries weaken into shallow whimpers that hiccup out of me, and then he speaks again, "Please look at me. Tell me you don't hate me."

I shake my head, keeping my body turned away from him when I feel him scoot down and lie behind me. His head presses against my back, and I hear him sniff before he starts talking to me quietly, making his confessions. "You're not alone. I haven't been telling you the truth. Carl doesn't just hit me when I'm down in the basement with him." He chokes back a whimper, and when I hear it, the tightening in my throat becomes painful. "He makes me do sick things to him." His voice cuts off; he's crying, and I can't stand it. I roll over and his eyes are shut, but his hands find my face as he rests them on my cheeks.

When his eyes open, he says, "Please don't hate me. Don't let him destroy what we have. Don't give him that power to rip us apart from each other." He takes in a shaky breath. "You tell me all the time that I'm all you have, but it goes both ways. I have nothing but you. You're my only family, Elizabeth. Please don't let him take you away from me."

Wrapping my arms around his back, I bury my face in his neck as we both cry together. In this world, a world I'm beginning to learn is a cold and dark place, I fear being alone. I need Pike, and knowing that he needs me too, pushes me to finally speak. I never thought I'd be saying these things, but suddenly I become an open book when I start blubbering against the damp skin of his neck.

"I don't hate you; I love you. But you hurt me. It hurt really bad."

"I'm sorry."

"And now I'm sad and scared and embarrassed and so alone."

"I am too," he admits.

"I'm scared I'm gonna lose you."

"I won't ever leave. I swear."

Pike never has left my side. Even though we don't attend the same school, he has planted himself in my life as a threat to others. I still get teased, but not as much. The summer is nearing an end, and I'm going to be at the middle school this year with Pike at the high school. I wish I could be with him. The only times I feel even a remote amount of relief from the never-ending suffering is when I'm with him. Somehow, he makes it possible for me to breathe in this clandestine world the two of us live in.

If anyone knew that Pike and I were having sex, they would freak, but to us, it's become just another facet of our lives. It used to scare me, used to make me cry, but I've learned to numb myself down in that basement. We have sex long enough for Carl to get off and then we escape to our rooms. Bobbi knows what goes on down there, but she chooses to ignore it as she makes her cheap-ass crafts and collects her stupid ducks.

I'm ready to go back to school because it means I don't have to constantly live in that God-forsaken closet. Now that I'll be back in school, I know I'll only have to go into the blackness on the weekends. I'd endure almost anything to keep Pike, so I've never mentioned a word of what goes on inside of that house for fear that I'd be taken away—away from Pike. If I didn't have him, I'd have no one, and no guarantee that I wouldn't be placed in another abusive home, only to find myself all alone. So I stay, and my silence eats away at the little bits of goodness that are left in me.

I'VE BEEN IN bed all day with a bad stomachache. I've been tossing and turning, trying to distract myself from the pain by listening to my music, but I'm miserable. I jerk up and sit when I feel something warm between my legs. Rushing to the bathroom, I cringe when I see blood on my underwear. I sit on the toilet, pee, and then clean myself, wadding a handful of toilet paper up and shoving it in the crotch of the clean pair of underwear I put on. Embarrassed, I know I need to get some money to go to the drug store, but there's only one person to ask, and I really don't want to. With my hand on his bathroom door handle that leads into his bedroom, I close my eyes and swallow an awkward breath as I rotate the knob and wait for the click.

Peeking in, he's lying on his bed, reading a sports magazine.

Timidly, I quietly call out, "Umm . . . Pike?"

He looks up at me as he lowers the magazine to his chest. "What's up?"

With my head down, I stammer, "I . . . umm, I need a few dollars."

"I just gave you money the other day," he complains.

"I know, but I . . ." I briefly look up at him and then move my eyes away when I let him know, against the heat of my face, mumbling, "I think . . . I think I just started my period."

"Oh," he responds, caught off guard with what I just told him. "Umm, yeah. I mean, sure," he rattles as he gets off the bed and walks over to his dresser.

God, this is so embarrassing.

"How much?"

"I don't . . . I don't know."

When I see his feet appear next to me, I hesitantly look up at him. He hands me a ten-dollar bill and asks, "Want me to walk with you?"

I shake my head and then duck back into the bathroom.

When I return from the store, I shove the bag of maxi pads in my dresser and then go set Pike's change next to his sink. I really don't think I can face him right now. My stomach still hurts, so I decide to crawl back into bed. I close my eyes and roll to the side when I hear Pike walk into the bathroom.

"You okay?" he asks.

"Mmm hmm."

"Is that what the stomachache is all about?"

I really wish he would stop asking so many questions. He has no idea how much I just want to disappear right now, but I answer anyway, saying, "I don't know," because I honestly have no clue. Bobbi wouldn't sign the permission slip for the sex ed the fifth graders went to last year, and I have nobody to talk to, so his guess is as good as mine.

The bed dips, and when I look over my shoulder, he's lying down, reading the same magazine from earlier. I turn my head back and smile at the fact that, no matter what, he's always here for me.

After a while, a couple of Pike's buddies stop by. He hops in their car and takes off for a while, leaving me at the house all by myself. I go down and rummage around the kitchen. I fix myself a sandwich, and when I sit down to eat it, I hear the screen door squeak open and then slam shut. Leaning over in my chair, I see Carl. He's so gross with his greasy shirt that's barely covering his fat, pot-bellied stomach. I sit back and continue eating as he strolls in and grabs a beer from the fridge.

"Where's your brother?" he asks before taking a swig.

"Don't know. He left with a couple friends."

Not wanting to be in the same room as him, I shove the rest of the sandwich in my mouth and rush upstairs. It's then that I hear Pike return, and when he gets upstairs, I go to his room and watch as he pulls out a wad of money and shoves it in his dresser.

"Where'd you get that money?"

"Shh, I don't want anyone knowing I have this, okay?"

Lowering my voice, I ask again, "How did you get it?"

"I've been working for a few months, trying to save money so that I'm not on the streets when I turn eighteen."

"Working? You were gone for thirty minutes."

He comes to stand in front of me and whispers, "If I tell you, you can't say anything to anyone."

"Pike, I don't talk to anyone but you."

"I've been running drugs for a guy I know."

My eyes widen, and I ask, "What do you mean *running*?"

"Selling," he states.

"Are you crazy? What if you get caught?"

"I'm not gonna get caught. Relax."

"What are the two of you doing up there?" Carl hollers from downstairs.

"Nothing," Pike shouts.

"Good, then get your fucking asses down to the basement."

"Fuuuck," Pike sighs and then holds my hand.

For a moment, I feel the drowning of my heart, but this is nothing new. We are down in that basement at least once a week, if not more. Pike has really helped me learn how to numb myself from what goes on down there, so I take in a deep breath and hold it for a second before slowly releasing it.

"You okay?" he asks, and when I nod, he gives my hand a soft squeeze before we make our way down.

I never know what Carl will have us do, so when I get down there, my stomach turns at the thought of me being on my period. Pulling back on Pike's hand, he turns to me, but before I can mutter anything, Carl speaks.

"Clothes off and fuck her on the bed," he barks at Pike.

He lets go of my hand and starts to strip while I remain standing, not wanting to do this while I'm bleeding.

"I said *clothes off*!"

"I-I . . ."

Pike looks at me, and I start to shake my head quickly, not wanting this to happen, and he gives me an urging eye.

"What the fuck is going on?" Carl yells as he stands in front of me.

I'm scared as hell when I open my mouth and stammer, "P-please, I . . . I started my period."

The hungry grin that grows on his face is sickening. He takes a few steps back, and then asks, "You're bleeding?"

I give him a nod.

"Okay then," he says as he sits down on the chair. "Take off your clothes and lay on the bed."

"What?" I breathe out.

"Don't worry, Pike's gonna fuck you in the ass."

"What?!" Pike's voice is that of shock, and I begin to panic.

My hands turn jittery and I start apologizing, "No. I'm s-sorry. It's fine, we can have sex."

"I like my idea better, now take off your fucking clothes and get on your hands and knees."

"What the fuck? I can't do that," Pike says as I start removing my clothes.

It's as if my blood is running dry because all I feel is cold ice running through me. I swallow hard, and then terror floods through when Carl lurches out of the chair and grabs Pike by the neck, seething, "The way you shits are trying to defy me right now is pissing me the fuck off."

Pike grunts loudly when Carl's fist hammers into his jaw, nearly knocking him over.

"Do what I fucking tell you or she's gonna get locked in the closet for the rest of the week after I beat the shit out of both of you!"

My legs are jelly, barely able to support me on my knees as I prop myself up on my hands. Suddenly, I forget how to go numb, and my body begins to quiver as I start crying, scared of what's about to happen.

I let my head hang down as I feel Pike behind me. Nothing happens though. All I can hear is his heavy breathing. I stay in this position for a while longer and eventually turn my head to see Pike stroking his penis with an almost pained look on his face. He then lets go of himself and puffs out a heavy breath, saying, "I can't do this. I can't even get hard."

Sitting back on my heels, I feel relieved, but that feeling is immediately snatched away, and sheer horror invades when Carl growls angrily. He knocks over his chair when he stands, metal clanking against the concrete, and suddenly the flow of life stops.

Slow motion.

Carl walks straight towards me, yanking his belt out from the loops of his pants. My heart goes frigid, pounding in solid hard beats that vibrate through my whole body. Pounding so hard I can hear it. His eyes are filled with a murderous glare, and Pike's screams penetrate me as he charges Carl and slams his fist into the side of his face.

I can't breathe, but somehow I'm screaming when Carl turns and knocks Pike straight to the ground with one single punch, followed by ruthless kicks to his side. Pike writhes in agony as he heaves, "Don't you fuckin' touch her!" over and over and over until his voice is no longer audible and his eyes glaze over.

When Carl looks back at me, he unzips his pants and adrenaline kicks in. I'm on my feet fast, bolting to the stairs. After a couple steps, I'm brought to my knees as a piercing sting slices through my back.

THWACK!

A shrill wail rips out of me, and I look over my shoulder just in time to see the leather belt he's holding come flying down at me.

THWACK!

Arching my back in pure agony, I scream out as tears spring from my eyes. The leather belt bites my flesh again and again before he forces me on all fours, pushes my face down to the cold cement, and rapes me from behind.

fifteen

(PAST)

AFTER CARL'S ATTACK, Pike doesn't come into my room for a while. All I want to do is die, just put myself out of this misery. I don't even know how to understand what just happened down there. It all came so fast, and I've never experienced that much pain in my life. The pain in my back seemed to disappear when he started raping the one part of my body I never expected.

And now, I lay on my stomach with my face buried into my pillow as I try to muffle my sobs. My top is still off because of the stinging of my back. I'm too scared to look at it to see what he's done to me.

"Oh my God," I faintly hear through my cries, and when I lift my head, I see Pike looking down at me. He's horrified, but I don't ask why because I'm so humiliated.

He kneels beside my bed with a painful groan and lays his hand on my arm, stroking it with his trembling thumb. The side of his face is swollen and badly bruised.

"Tell me what I can do." His voice is worried and his eyes are nothing but a display of his pity.

I can't even think about speaking as my tears soak into my pillow.

He takes my hand, folds his fingers through mine, and holds it tightly, and the touch alone makes me cry harder.

"I'm so fucking sorry," he says with his eyes welled with tears.

My hand is clenched around his and I don't let go for a long time. Eventually, Pike kisses my knuckles, and moves to stand.

"I'll be right back," he says and then goes into the bathroom. When he returns, he's holding a wet towel. "I don't want to hurt you, but your back is covered in dried blood. Just lay still, okay?"

I nod as he gently lays the warm, wet towel on my back. My muscles cinch up, and I whimper as my flesh stings. He presses his hand down on the towel, and I cry out, "Oww."

"I'm sorry."

"W-what does it look like?" I ask, but also scared to know.

"You have a couple nasty gashes and a lot of welts."

"It hurts."

He sighs and holds my hand as he carefully starts cleaning the blood off my back.

"One day, I promise you, that fucker is gonna pay for this," he grits out and all I can do is nod my head as I start thinking about what it would feel like to kill him.

How sick am I? A twelve-year-old girl fantasizing about killing someone.

What's happening to me?

A FEW WEEKS have passed and school has started back up. Carl hasn't touched me since that day, but it was only three days later when I was back in the basement, forced into giving Pike a blowjob. Afterwards, I was tied up in the closet and left there for another two days.

Pike and I now sit out on the curb in front of the house. Bobbi is inside watching TV and Carl is still at work. Summer is coming to an end and the smell of autumn is in the air. You know that smell, the smell of death. I don't know why, but I love it. Leaves falling to their grave on the chilled, damp streets, eventually to be covered in ice and snow when winter hits.

I listen to Pike as he rambles on about some girl who's an upper classman at his school that keeps following him around. It doesn't surprise me. I've always thought Pike was cute, and now that he's almost sixteen, he's even cuter, not that I have a crush on him or anything; it's just a fact. But nobody knows how pathetic the two of us are. Sometimes I get curious as to how someone would react if they knew. I mean, could you imagine that girl asking Pike to tell her something about himself, and his response was, *I'm almost sixteen, and, oh yeah, I have sex with my twelve-year-old sister.* Yeah, people would definitely think we're sick.

"Isn't that your caseworker's car?" Pike questions, and when I turn to look down the street, sure enough, it's Lucia's car.

"What's she doing here?" I can't stand my caseworker. She only stops by to check in on me a few times a year, so the fact that she was just here a month ago makes me a little anxious.

She pulls her car along the curb as Pike and I stand.

"What are you two doing out here?" she asks, and Pike tells her in a shit-mocking tone, "Oh, you know, just enjoying the lush scenery of this picture-perfect neighborhood that you thought would provide a nice backdrop for a wholesome upbringing."

Lucia sends Pike a glare before saying, "You mind giving Elizabeth and I a moment to speak?"

"I'll be in my room," he tells me as he heads inside the house, leaving Lucia and me standing on the front lawn.

"Why don't we have a seat?" she suggests, and we walk over to the front porch steps.

"What are you doing here?"

"I got some news that I needed to come talk to you about."

"Am I being moved?" I ask, nervous of her response because I can't live without Pike. The thought alone pricks my eyes with tears.

"No. It's about your dad," she says.

Pulling on that one tiny piece of hope in my heart that I've been able to hang on to, I ask, "Is he getting out early? Will I be able to see him?"

She shakes her head, and when I see her face drop, she takes that hope right along with it, saying, "I'm sorry. Your father's dead."

And that's the moment when you realize that hopes and dreams are as fucked up as the fairytales.

I drop my head and watch my tears drop like heavy weights to the dirty concrete below my feet. They spread and seep into the porous ground where I'm sure they'll find their home in hell. But they won't be alone for long because my heart feels unbearably heavy too, like it could drop right out of me at any moment.

I wanna scream. I wanna kick and hit something. I wanna stomp my feet like a toddler and throw the most soul-ripping tantrum a girl my age could, yelling at the world and to anyone who'll listen how I hate all of them. I want to scream so hard that blood comes out. I wanna do it all, but I don't. It's a war inside me, but I hide it well. What's the point of exposing it? It's not like it's going to make a difference. No one is coming to rescue me. So instead, I sit on these steps and quietly cry.

I have a million questions swarming, finally asking, "How?"

"It seems there was a fight that broke out with some of the inmates and your father was stabbed. The place went on lockdown and by the time the guards were able to get to him, it was too late."

"Why? I mean, I-I . . ." I can barely speak as the sobs start breaking through my façade, causing my body to wrack in heaving tremors. "Are you sure it was him? I mean, what if they made a mistake?"

"There's no mistake, Elizabeth," she says softly. "I'm so sorry."

"But I don't have any other family. I mean, w-what happens n-now?"

"Nothing changes."

Glaring over at her, I say, "Everything changes." I turn my head back down and begin crying, covering my eyes with my hands. The instinct to run is fierce, but I have nowhere to go, and that pisses me off. I don't wanna be stuck here. I don't want this life. All I want is my dad. So with that, I stand and spit my words at my worthless caseworker, "I fucking hate you! I hate everything about you! You don't give a shit about me or my dad! You're just a stupid bitch!" I go inside the house, slamming the door as hard as I can behind me and run upstairs. But I don't go to my room; I go to Pike's. I'm loud, bawling like a baby when I walk in. He immediately pops off the bed and is in front of me in a second, asking, "What's wrong? What happened?"

Falling into his chest, he bands his arms tightly around me while I release the most wretched sobs of my life. I fist his shirt in my hands so tightly it feels as if I could break my own fingers, but I like the pain. I need the pain. I need something—anything—to distract me from the most unbearable pain of all.

It can't be real.

He can't really be dead.

He just can't be.

"Elizabeth," Pike says, and I feel like I'm gonna throw up the emptiness that fills me because if he's gone, I'm gone.

I don't even realize we've walked across the room until I open my eyes and we're lying down.

"What did she say?" he asks.

"I hate her, Pike. I hate everyone," I choke out around the pain.

"Tell me."

My words hurt as they come out, "M-my dad. She said he's dead, Pike. That someone stabbed him, and he died." Saying the words cuts deep, and the hold that Pike has on me suddenly becomes a thousand times stronger.

"Shit," he murmurs under his breath before I cry, "It isn't true. It can't be."

Hearing it from Lucia, I felt numb, but now, with Pike—my safety—the emotions overpower me. I'm drowning and I can't breathe. All I can do is scream and cry, and so I do, just like a helpless baby, never letting go of my grip on Pike's shirt. It's as if his shirt is my lifeline, and if I let go, I'll free-fall into nothingness.

And now I lie here, crumbling into a million pieces. I'll never be whole again. I'll never forgive the world for this.

I want my dad.

Now.

I want the rough whiskers of his face scratching me when he gives kisses, I want his smooth voice singing to me again, I want his touch, his hold, his love, his healing, his smile, stories, tickles, laughs, eyes, hands, smell—everything. I wanna be saved.

I want my prince.

Pike tucks me under his chin, kissing the top of my head every now and then. Eventually the noise in the room begins to fade as I tire and quiet down. My body feels so heavy and my head pounds, making it hurt to open my eyes. Pike continuously runs his hand up and down my back in an attempt to soothe me, but nothing can dull this agony.

Into the quiet room, I whisper, "Do you ever think about dying?"

"Sometimes," he responds softly.

"Does it scare you?"

"No. You?"

"Not anymore," I tell him, and then ask, "Do you think my dad was scared?"

"No," he says without any hesitation.

"How do you know?"

"Because, if he's dead, then he'll always get to be with you. Knowing he'd finally get to see you again, I doubt he was scared."

His words bring on a slew of silent tears that soak into his shirt. "It's not fair, Pike."

"No, it's not. You deserve everything that's good in this world, and I swear to you that I will fight to give you that. One day, when we're out of this mess, I'll find a way to make you happy."

"I don't believe in happiness," I weep. "I don't believe in anything anymore."

He brushes my hair back and scoots down to look me in the eyes. "Believe in *me*."

His dark eyes are stern, and I realize, that in this moment, he's my only chance at survival. Pike has always done his best to protect me; he's always cared about me. From the first day I got here, he's been my brother. It was instant. And now, I have no other choice but to believe in everything he says because he's my only constant.

When he leans in and kisses my forehead, I don't even think when I nuzzle in and kiss his neck. He keeps his lips on my forehead and doesn't move, but his hands find my cheeks as he holds me close. Before I know it, his lips are on mine in an unmoving kiss. I grip on to his wrists, and in a blur, in an unnoticeable moment, our mouths move together.

I've never kissed Pike before—never even thought about it—but somehow, this feels right. He's the first boy I've ever kissed. We've been having sex for two years, so you wouldn't think kissing him would feel like anything at all, but it does. Out of nowhere, he's taken my mind away from everything bad as I focus on only him. It's like I can finally breathe.

Rolling on top of me, he reaches back to take his shirt off, and I sit up to remove mine as well. When we're stripped down to nothing, he pulls the sheets over us, and I'm tucked in warm with him. Everything about this feels different than the hundreds of times we've done this before. It's always cold and dirty, with Carl watching us the whole time.

"Don't go there," Pike says, knocking me from my thoughts.

"Where?"

"Don't think about him. He has nothing to do with this. We're not on that mattress down there; we're here in my bed. You're safe."

"Just us?" I ask.

"Just us," he says as he pushes himself inside of me, and for the first time, I find the magic that I gave up believing in. It turns out Pike had it all along, because in this moment, I don't feel any more pain or hurt.

It's just us, and I'm safe.

sixteen

(PAST)

MY TEETH CHATTER as I walk home from school. I wound up getting in trouble for fighting a girl who was making fun of me today, landing me in afterschool suspension for the next two weeks. Pike has been working more and more, so we haven't been walking home together much lately, and he refuses to let me tag along with him. He says he doesn't want me getting mixed up with his friends, but he always makes sure he's home before Carl gets there so I won't be alone with him.

Life hasn't changed that much. I'm fourteen—a little taller, filling out more, my hair has grown a few more waves than it used to have, and I have more scars on my wrists. It looks like I've been trying to slit them, but six years of being belted up in a tiny closet will do that to you. I hide them well though, wearing long sleeves that fall past my wrists that I often tug further down.

Since learning about my dad's death two years ago, I've grown pretty numb to everything around me. I feel like a living, breathing machine most of the time. I'm able to turn myself off and on pretty easily. For the most part, I'm in off mode, frozen and void. I only allow Pike to see me on. He's my only release, the only one I show my true self to. Since that afternoon, the afternoon I learned that I would never see my father again, Pike and I have continued to sleep together, privately, in his bed. I've found myself becoming selfish with him, using him to take away all the bad. It's so hard to explain, but when I'm with him like that, I feel like I'm washed clean. Once I realized what I was doing, I was honest and told him. The guilt was overpowering me, and when I explained my feelings to him, I thought he'd be mad, but he wasn't. He told me to take whatever I needed to take from him. I still feel the guilt though. The shame of using him so selfishly eats at me after we're done and I grow quiet, often crying. Pike soothes me as best as he can, holding me, assuring me that it's okay—that everything's okay.

I'm a mess, but that's to be expected with the harsh introduction I received to this crazy, fucked up life. I'm fourteen—too young to be this bitter and angry. For a while, when I would see a child with their parent, I'd wish for that parent to die. I wanted every kid to feel the pain I was feeling because it wasn't fair to me.

Life's cruel, and I'm its bitch.

I'm Carl's bitch too. Lately he's been fucking me, wanting Pike to watch. He made me promise to never look at Carl, so I always keep my eyes locked on Pike's no matter who I'm fucking that day.

My first orgasm came about a year ago. Carl was jerking off in the corner while Pike and I were having sex. It had never happened before, so when what was always such a sickening act turned into pleasure, it scared the crap out of me. I couldn't face Pike afterwards; I was too ashamed. When I finally unlocked my bathroom door a few hours later, he came in and talked to me about it. It was humiliating, having my brother explain to me what had happened. He told me it was a natural part of sex, but I didn't like it. It made me feel dirty and embarrassed. And now, knowing it could happen again, I fight hard to prevent it. Pike knows this, so when we're alone in his bed, he tries to get off fast so that he doesn't accidentally make me feel it again. It's weird, because I like having sex with Pike when we're alone, but at the same time, it scares me because I don't want it to feel good—it shouldn't feel good. But I want to be with him because it's with him that I don't feel the misery and the ugliness. He takes it all away, and even if it's only for a moment, I feel free.

When I turn the corner, I see Pike sitting on the curb smoking a cigarette. "Pike!" I shout from down the street, and he looks over to me then stands up.

"Where the hell have you been?" he asks, pissed.

"I got in a fight and now I have afterschool suspension."

Taking a drag from his cigarette, the smoke drifts lazily out of his mouth when he gets all big-brother-protective, saying, "Tell me what happened."

"That girl I've been telling you about, you know, the one who's been making my life hell? She just kept running her mouth in the cafeteria, calling me names. I couldn't take it anymore, so I lost it."

"What'd you do?"

"She was sitting at the end of the same table as me, so I chucked my apple at her and it hit her in the head. Before I knew it, we were out of our seats and I had her on the ground."

"No shit?" he says with a mild, pleased grin on his face. "Well, I don't see a mark on you, so I take it you won?"

"It wasn't a competition, Pike," I say, still feeling like the loser the kids at school tell me I am.

"What's wrong? You kicked her ass; you should feel good."

"You're such a boy," I sigh, dropping my head. When he drapes his arm around my shoulder, I add, "I hate it there. I have no friends."

"They're bitches, Elizabeth. Young, stupid bitches."

"*I'm* young and stupid."

Pike tosses his cigarette before we walk inside the house. "Young, yes. Stupid, no," he says as we go upstairs. "You only have a couple months left there. Next year, you'll be with me again."

"Right," I scoff. "You'll be a senior and I'll be the freshman freak."

He plops down on the bed, folding his arms behind his head, responding, "Nothing about you says *freak*. Trust me. Those girls are just jealous because you're prettier than them."

His words heat my neck, but at the same time fill something inside of me. The last time anyone ever said I was pretty, I was five, and it came from my dad. He would always tell me I was beautiful and pretty, saying I had the most gorgeous red hair. Looks are shallow, I know that, but I didn't realize how much I needed to hear that until just now.

"What's wrong?" he asks, noticing the sadness behind my eyes. "Come here."

I walk over and sit down next to him.

"What's wrong?" he repeats.

"I feel ugly inside," I admit.

"Don't," he states as he sits up next to me. "There's nothing about you that's ugly."

"Really, Pike?" I question with ridicule.

Annoyed with my tone, he defends, "Nobody knows us. Nobody knows. It's you allowing what other people might think or say that makes you feel that way."

"It's what I feel, Pike," I argue in a pitched voice.

"You have the power to change that. How you feel is how you *allow* yourself to feel."

"So, it's my fault? My fault that I feel this way?"

"Feel sad. Feel angry. Hate whoever you want. Blame whoever you want, but don't, for one second, think that you're any less than what you are. You're not ugly or dirty or whatever else you're thinking." His tone is hard and stern when he says this, but in an instant, he softens it, saying, "There isn't anything I wouldn't do for you. You still believe in me?"

I nod.

"Good. Because it won't always be like this."

"No?"

"No."

"Tell me, Pike. What's it gonna be like? Tell me the fairytale," I voice with a slip of mockery.

"I'm gonna make you believe in the fairytale again."

I laugh softly at his determined words, and he smiles at me.

We spend the next hour goofing around and getting our homework done. Carl got home a while ago, but he hasn't said a word to us, which is a relief, and now the smells of food cooking fill the house. Bobbi hardly ever cooks. More like never.

"You think we're gonna get any of that?" Pike asks, referring to whatever it is she's making in the kitchen.

"Doubtful," I respond with a roll of my eyes, and we both smile at each other.

"Pike," Bobbi calls from downstairs after the doorbell rings.

"Be back," he says.

I stay on his bed, and when I hear the front door shut, I turn to look out the window to see Pike and his caseworker on the front lawn talking. Whatever is being said, Pike is visibly pissed, raking a strong hand through his hair. His muffled yells are distorted and I can't make out what he's saying. When he turns his head and looks up to the window, my stomach drops hard. The expression on his face tells me I should be worried, and I am. I jump off the bed when he walks back to the house. He runs up the stairs, meeting me at the door. With his hands on my shoulders, he pushes me back into the room and closes the door behind him.

"What's going on?" I question as the panic rises.

Looking down, he shakes his head, and then pulls me tightly in his arms, hugging me.

And now I'm freaking out.

"Pike, what's happening? You're scaring me."

"I'm so sorry," he says, and I know it's bad. He only says that when something bad is about to happen. He doesn't let go of me as we stand there, holding on to each other.

I didn't think life could get any worse for me, but it could—and it would. I've always battled with the idea of hope. Hope had always failed me, but for some reason, I kept holding on to a tiny piece of it. I was scared to know what the world would be like if I didn't have it. But Pike's next words to me would stab me from the inside—white horror—filling me with the blood of life's harsh reality. A reality that would spit its gritty words in my face, telling me, "Hope is for the ignorant, little girl. Give it up."

Taking his arms from around me, he cups my cheeks, takes out the knife, and stabs me to the core with his words.

"You're gonna be okay, Elizabeth."

My whole body shakes, my voice trembling in confusion, "What?"

Pressing his forehead against mine, I hold his wrists in a death grip as he says, "I'm leaving."

He just siphoned all the air from my lungs with those two words, and I turn cold, shaking my head vigorously against his.

"I have to go. They're placing me in a group home."

"No."

"I'm so sorry," he painfully breathes.

"No." My word, a wretched plea.

Pike presses a hard kiss to my forehead, and I cry out, "No!" as his back shakes against my hands. "No!"

"It's done. Apparently Carl made a call. He wants me out."

"Don't go. You can't go."

"I don't have a choice," he says, and when he pulls back, I see the fear in his eyes, and I know it's all for me. We both know what'll happen without him here. I'll be all alone for Carl to do with as he pleases.

"You can't leave me here. You can't leave me with him," I desperately plea.

He takes a step back, fisting his hair, gritting under his breath, "Fuuuuck." He paces as I stand in shock, crying. Eventually, he turns back to me and affirms, "Fourteen is still gonna be your year. Your dad won't be coming back for you, but I will."

"Don't do that," I tell him. "Don't you dare give me hope."

His eyes are burning, dark coals when he says, "I swear to you. I'll give you that fairytale. Let me age out. I'll come back for you."

"A year? Pike, don't leave me here with him for a year!"

"We can't run away now. Think about it—two of us go missing—it's too risky. But just one—you—we could get away. Less than one year, you'll be free from here. One year alone and out at fourteen; you can do it," he tells me while I cry in fear of what life is going to be like without him. "You're so fucking strong," he asserts. "I *will* come back for you."

I sling my arms around his neck, and continue to beg him not to leave me. I'm terrified I'll never see him again, my only friend, my only family—my brother. Who's going to protect me?

"I have to pack," he whispers.

"Now?"

"My caseworker is downstairs waiting on me."

"Oh my God," I mutter to myself. I can't believe this is happening. My heart feels like a wrecking ball inside my chest, pounding away at my pathetic life. I wander over to Pike's bed and sit down, gripping the edge of the mattress with my hands, and watch as he starts shoving clothes into his duffle bag. The tears simply fall from my eyes with no effort. I lost my dad with the faith that I would see him again, and now I'm losing Pike with the knowledge that life doesn't guarantee you anything, no matter how badly you want it.

Once his bag is zipped, he kneels down in front of me with his hands on my knees. He's a blurry vision, muddled through the tears that separate us. "You're all I have," he says. "You're it. I won't lose you, and you won't lose me."

"Please." It's a vague plea—a plea for anything, really.

"I need you to listen to me, okay?" He takes his thumbs and wipes the tears from my eyes. "*Really* listen to me."

I nod.

"I'm with you," he assures. "When you're in that closet, I'm with you. When you're in that basement, I'm with you. I'm always with you, okay? But I need you to make me a promise. I need you to promise me that you'll turn yourself off. Just shut it off. He can't hurt you if you don't feel. The people who get hurt in life are the ones who allow themselves to feel."

My tears grow heavy, plunking to their death in a free-fall, landing on my knees. Looking down at him, without much thought, I kiss him. We've never kissed outside of his bed when we're having sex, but I kiss him now because I don't know what else to do. He holds me tight, kissing me back as I cry against his lips, refusing to let go of him.

When our mouths part, he looks into my eyes, saying, "I love you."

"I love you too."

He stands, grabs his bag, and promises, "I'll come back for you."

And just like that, as if I ever had a choice in the matter, my brother, my only lifeline, walks away from me.

And I'm all alone.

Seventeen

(PAST)

I DON'T NEED to tell you what happened next.

You already know.

Life without Pike was worse than the swamps of hell. Alone. Desolate. A life no one wants to believe is real—but is. I became dark inside. No. That's not true. I became colorless. You couldn't have painted a portrait of me because I no longer existed. To exist, you have to have life and I was merely a robot—a machine—tell me what you wanted and I'd do it, paralyzed to emotions and consequences.

Fuck you, life.

I hate you.

The moment Pike walked out the door, Bobbi came up to my room. I was crying, begging her to use the phone when the threat came. She told me that she knew about Pike and I having sex, and if I told anyone or attempted to leave, she would tell Social Services and I would be placed under mental evaluation in a state hospital. She also told me that Pike would be arrested and sent to jail for statutory rape of a minor since seventeen is the legal age of consent in the state of Illinois. So that was it; I kept my mouth shut.

I haven't heard from Pike since he left a little over three months ago. He's gone, probably happier, and left me to fend for myself. I don't blame him. *Run away, Pike. Run far from me and this life.* I've come to accept that he wouldn't be coming back for me. I had my first freak out after the first month, missing him, wondering if it was all a lie and whether I'd ever see him again. That first month was really the only time he would have been able to see me. I was still in school, but as soon as summer hit, I was rarely let out of the closet. No longer did I have Pike to talk me through the nights; I had no one.

School started up again last week. I was so anxious, nervous to see Pike now that we would both be in high school. Would he grab me and hug me, or would he look right through me as if I no longer existed? But I didn't have to worry so much because he wasn't there. I searched the halls and then wound up going to the office only to find out that he transferred to another school. They wouldn't tell me where though. Walking out of the office that day, I thought to myself, *Maybe this is where you give up, Elizabeth. Maybe this is where you realize life's fate for you. Maybe this is where you finally stop fighting for something that was never meant to be.*

That was last week, and I still haven't made any decisions about those thoughts. And so I resume my mechanical life. Wake up, go to school, go home, be fucked by my greasy, fat foster dad, shower, homework, bed. Bed is always a variable; it's either bed or leather restraints and locked in the closet. Despite the disgust, I'm hyperaware of my appearance. I've been lucky so far to avoid the puberty pimples; my skin is soft and flawless from the neck up. Beneath my clothes is a different story—various colors of new and healing bruises, welts, and cuts. My wrists look like I've had a few failed suicide attempts. My red hair is bright and full of lazy, loose waves that fall past my slender shoulders. My face, it deceives everyone because no one would ever guess the horror that lives beneath. But no matter how ugly I feel, I try to take care of myself.

When the final bell rings, I shove my books into my backpack and walk through the halls. I have no friends here; maybe it's my fault, or maybe it's theirs. I keep to myself. I never speak unless called on by a teacher, and even with that, I never say more than necessary. My grades are good, not that I have any aspirations after I graduate. I'm sure I'll be flipping burgers somewhere or turning tricks, giving out blowjobs depending on how much money I want to make.

Cynical?

Yeah, I am.

I move slowly, letting everyone pass, bumping into me as they rush out of this school and into their freedom. But this is my freedom—here at school and away from home. So I take my time, and when I finally walk out the metal double doors, I tighten my coat around me and start heading home. Before I can make it off school grounds, a black, vintage Mustang pulls alongside me, and I think I'm imagining things when I hear his familiar voice.

"Elizabeth, thank God."

Pike gets out of the car and has me in his arms fast. The comfort is overwhelming, and it doesn't take long before I'm weeping into his shirt.

“Fuck, I’ve missed you,” he breathes in my hair, and I nod against his chest. “Are you okay?”

I pull back and look up at him, ignoring his question, asking, “Where have you been?”

“I didn’t know how to find you. I tried sneaking by the house a few times this summer, but you were never there.”

“I was there,” I tell him. “He kept me locked up for most of the summer. He knew about us . . . that we were . . . you know. It pissed him off and he said that’s why he got rid of you.”

“Shit.”

And then the crying starts as I deflate and say, “I thought you gave up on me.”

“Never.”

He then turns to the car, and when I peek around him, I see the driver. He’s older, maybe in his twenties, with tattoos down his arms.

“Come with me. We can talk,” Pike says as he looks back at me.

“Can’t be gone long. Carl normally gets home around five.”

“Don’t worry. I’ll have you back in time,” he tells me and then opens the door to crawl into the back seat before holding his hand out for me. “This is Matt, by the way,” Pike introduces, “He’s a good buddy of mine.”

“Hey,” Matt says, giving me a nod in the rearview mirror before pulling back out onto the street.

“Hey.” My voice, barely a whisper when Pike pulls me into his arms.

“Talk to me.”

I keep my eyes on Matt, not wanting to speak in front of this stranger.

“Don’t worry about him,” Pike tells me. “He’s cool.”

“I was scared I would never see you again,” I admit quietly.

“I told you to believe in me. I’m not leaving you. The place I’m staying has strict rules. Basically school and then back by eight o’clock curfew.”

“What’s it like?” I ask. “The group home, I mean.”

“It’s okay. You’re not there, so I spend most of my time worrying about you.”

“This cool, man?” Matt says when he pulls into the back lot of a run-down strip mall.

“Yeah. Just give us an hour,” Pike tells him as he parks the car and then gets out.

“Where’s he going?”

“Just giving us some alone time. I want to talk to you. I wanna know if you’re okay.”

I shake my head and a few tears slip out. “It’s awful, Pike. It’s so bad.”

“You’re gonna be okay.”

I shake my head again.

“I know you don’t see it, but you’re a strong girl. You *will* be okay.”

“He does horrible things to me. Things he never did before,” I reveal. He cradles me to his chest and kisses the top of my head as I hold on to him, adding, “And now you’re not there to take it away.”

Moving my head up to him, he kisses me, resting his lips on mine and I go soft in his hold. He shifts and moves over me, lying me down on my back against the cold leather seat.

“What are you doing?” I mumble against his kisses.

“Taking it away.”

“But your friend . . .”

With his hand on the button of my pants, he says, “He won’t be back for a while.” He pops the button, looking down at me, and then asks, “Is this okay?”

I nod as I murmur, “Yes. Just take it away.”

And he does, right there in the back seat of his friend’s car. Pike cleans me of the past three months, fading away all the filth Carl left behind and covers it with the goodness of himself.

PIKE HAS CONTINUED to pick me up after school for the past seven months, but only once or twice a week. He’s mostly with Matt, but every now and then, Matt loans him his car and Pike and I can be alone. I love those times. I found out that Pike and Matt work together, running drugs on the street. After I met him, it didn’t take long for Matt to question Pike about fucking a fourteen-year-old in the back of his car every week. I had never seen Pike so pissed and defensive, threatening Matt that he’d knock the shit out of him if he ever questioned him again.

Matt is slime and gives me the creeps. He eyes me constantly, like he’s waiting for his chance to get into my pants as well. I don’t say anything to Pike about it, but I don’t trust the guy.

Every time I see Pike, he has a new tattoo. I hate that he’s marking himself up so much. Kinda like, with each tattoo, he’s taking away a piece of the Pike I know and replacing it with a new Pike—a Pike I only get to see once a week in the back seat of that Mustang while we have sex. We don’t have a lot of time to talk, so it feels as if I pretty much use him to escape. It’s overwhelming now, the emotions afterward. I've started crying a lot when we're done. It worries Pike. He tries to talk to me, and I've tried explaining how it's starting to make me feel guilty, but he assures me it's okay. So after sex, I cry and Pike holds me, doing what he can to make me feel better.

But Pike hasn't come around in two weeks. He told me to give him time to sort out his plans for when he turns eighteen, and I've been trying to be patient. His birthday was last week, and I've been on pins and needles, anxious to get the hell away from Carl and Bobbi. Carl has been getting more violent with me lately, punching me during sex and spitting in my face. He fisted me across my face last night, giving me a black eye before tossing me on my stomach and taking me from behind. He doesn't do that all too often, only when he's really pissed about something. But last night got really bad, and he lost control. I kept my mouth shut and let my mind drift as far away as it could, waiting for it all to be over. He still has that same mattress. It's now stained in blood, vomit, sweat, and Carl's urine.

This is why I'm so anxious for Pike to come get me.

So after I apply more ointment to the split skin of my black eye, I sit on my bed and stare out the window, looking for Matt's black Mustang. Soon I grow tired as I peer into the darkness outside. Disappointed, I sulk down under my covers and stare at the purple walls for a few minutes before turning out the light and drifting off to sleep.

A weight on my arm causes my eyes to pop open. Startled in the blackness, my heart pounding, I hear a soothing, "Shh."

"Pike?" I whisper as I sit up and reach out for him.

His hand runs down my cheek as he softly breathes, "You still believe in me?"

"Yes."

Pike tosses the sheets off of me, and the adrenaline kicks in. Like a million bees swarming in my chest, my heart pumps as Pike and I move fast, tossing my clothes and few belongings into a bag. Everything blurs in a speedy haze, and I almost feel like I'm going to be sick. My stomach is in knots with fear and excitement that I'm seconds away from being free from the hell I have been living for the past six years.

When Pike zips the bag and throws it over his shoulder, he takes my hand in his. I can see his smile grow in the shadows of the moonlight, and I can't help myself when I lean in and kiss him, giving him every piece of my heart for this gift he's giving me. My fairytale, rescuing me from the evil monster that lurks in the dungeon.

"I love you so much, Pike."

"I love you too," he quietly murmurs. "You ready?"

"Yeah."

With my hand in his, he walks me over to the window he'd crawled in and slips out before helping me out. We teeter along the roof to the edge where Pike tosses the bag down to Matt who is waiting on the front lawn. He quickly runs to the car, tossing the bag in while Pike jumps off the roof and into the grass below. You'd think I'd be scared to jump, but I would jump ten stories down into a pile of varmints if it meant escaping from here. So when Pike holds his arms out, I jump, leaping into whatever life awaits me on the other side.

Once in the car, Matt drives us away as I stare back at that shitty, white house that has kept me caged since I was eight. I've spent nearly half my life locked in that tiny closet and forced down into that basement. The car finally turns, and when the house vanishes, I fall into Pike's chest and begin sobbing like a baby.

Free. Relieved. Saved.

Pike swore fourteen was still going to be my year. I wanted to believe him, but I always doubted. Nothing has ever worked out for me, nothing until now. My cries are loud, but nobody speaks, and eventually, after time passes, I curl up in Pike's lap and close my eyes while Matt continues to drive into the night.

eighteen

(PRESENT)

CHRISTMAS HAS PASSED and Bennett has been home for the past couple of weeks. With the holidays, time has been consumed, leaving little interaction with Declan. We did meet up for coffee before Bennett returned from Dubai. The encounter was more pleasant than our usual tension. We just talked, and he told me about living in Scotland and falling into his father's business. I almost feel bad for manipulating him so much—almost. My purpose is clear, and no one will stand in the way of me righting the wrong.

To appease Jacqueline, I agreed to meet up with her for lunch with a couple of the other girls. So when Baldwin drops me off at Le Sardine, a local French bistro in the west loop, I see the girls already sitting at one of the white, linen-covered tables.

"There she is," Jacqueline says as I approach and take a seat.

"Sorry I'm late. I had to take a few calls."

"Are you all set for New Year's Eve?" Marcia asks as I take a sip of the water that's set for me.

"I believe so. I'm just happy Bennett is here. A part of me was worried he'd have to go back out of town."

"Please. He'd never miss this event, or a chance to show you off," Jacqueline says. "The man is crazy about you. I'm a little jealous."

Who is she kidding? Jacqueline is innately jealous and does a shit job at covering her attraction to my husband, but I give a charming smile, responding with, "I'm just happy he's back home."

Marcia's attention goes to the front of the restaurant, and when I turn to see what's caught her eye, I tense for just a moment.

"He is so fuckable," she says under her breath, causing Jacqueline to blurt out, "Marcia! My God."

"What?" she defends. "Look at him and tell me you wouldn't let him do things to you."

I watch as Declan talks to the hostess as Jacqueline responds, "You're married."

"I don't care. It's worth the risk, right?"

"Ask Nina."

Turning my attention back, I question, "Ask me what?"

"About *him*," Jacqueline says as she nods her head towards Declan.

"What makes you think I know anything?"

"Don't be coy. He owns the hotel you're planning the party at," she states.

"Doesn't mean I know him personally," I defend. "But from what I do know, he seems like a nice man." As I say this, Declan catches my eye, and with a slight smile, walks back towards the kitchen. Scooting my chair out, I politely excuse myself, saying, "With that being said, I'll be right back."

"Where are you going?" Marcia asks.

"To go say hello," I tell her as I drop my napkin on the table and walk to the back of the restaurant.

When he turns to see me, I smile, and slide up next to him along the cold granite countertop that divides the dining room from the kitchen. "You following me?" I question with flirtation.

"Do you want me to follow you?"

Taking a pause, I turn on my game and respond, "Maybe."

His smile meets his eyes.

"I haven't heard from you in a while," I say.

"I figured you were busy with family affairs. Didn't know you were wanting to hear from me," he says, flirting right back.

"I enjoyed our coffee date," I tell him. "I like talking to you. Just missed it, that's all."

"Is that all you missed?"

"Declan," I softly nag.

"Yeah, I know. You're married."

Needing to break him, I softly whisper, "I miss spending time with you."

His eyes hesitate for a second, and then he grips my elbow, causing me to instinctively look over my shoulder to see that, for the moment, the girls aren't looking at us. Declan quickly pulls me back to a private hallway that leads to the restrooms.

"What are you doing?" I ask and tug against his hold, but he has me pinned against a wall before I can say anything else.

His face is close to mine as we stare at each other. My heart pounds in fear that someone will see us, and he reads my anxiety, saying, "No one can see us."

"What are you doing?" I ask again.

"What are *you* doing?"

"Nothing."

"You're flirting with me, Nina. You're leading me on."

"I'm not."

His eyes roll down to my mouth, and then he speaks in a soft, guttural tone, saying, "Don't fucking lie to me."

"I don't know what you want me to say," I whisper.

"What are you feeling?" he questions, pressing his body into mine, pushing my back flat against the wall. "Tell me what you're feeling . . ."

Pressing.

". . . right . . ."

Closer.

". . . now."

"I love my husband."

"Is that you telling me or you trying to convince yourself?"

Releasing a fractured breath, I see the darkness in his eyes, and I make my move, saying, "I don't know."

His hand comes to meet my neck, almost forcefully, wrapping his fingers and thumb around its slender form, pinning my head back to the wall in a possessive, yet soft, chokehold. Taking a moment, he simply looks into my eyes and I finally see the hunger before he kisses me, sucking the breath straight from my womb. Lips crashing, heavy breaths, all the while, keeping me in his firm grip. His aggressiveness spurs me to grab on to his dress shirt, clenching the crisp fabric in my hands while he takes over. Sinking his tongue into my mouth, I taste the ice of his breath, or maybe it's my soul I taste. I lure him in further as I slide my tongue along his, and when I do this, he quietly growls into my mouth, causing a slight vibration between us.

Abruptly, he pulls away, keeping his powerful hand around my neck as he takes a step back. He stares; he doesn't speak, he just stares, examining my reaction. But my reaction is calculated, pulled straight from my playbook.

Quaking, aroused breaths.

Making the rise and fall of my chest visible to him.

Letting out an erotic but nervous hum.

Relaxing my muscles and sinking into the hold he has on me.

"Say it," he demands.

I shake my head, denying his request, and when I do, the tips of his fingers increase the pressure around my neck.

"Tell me how you feel," he urges.

I quicken my breathing and am able to push the deceit out in the form of a tear. Slowly spilling over, I feel the wetness linger down my cheek, but before it drips off my jaw, Declan's tongue licks it away. The tender touch surprises me, and when I drop my head, he finally releases his hold on me and cradles my face, tilting it up to look at him.

His eyes soften, and I give him the words I know he wants, saying quietly, "I don't know what the word is for what I feel for you, but I feel it."

"Do you want it?"

With slight mock-hesitation, it's game on when I respond, "Yes."

The corner of his mouth lifts, and this time, he's gentle when he moves me to kiss him. His lips are soft as they press into mine, but he keeps it short, and then says, "Come to the hotel after you're done here."

"Okay," I answer without any question, and then he's gone, walking away from me. I take a moment to compose myself before returning to the table, and when I walk back out into the restaurant, I do a quick glance and notice that Declan has already left.

"And where were you?" Marcia asks with gossipy intent.

"Restroom."

"With?" she presses.

Narrowing my eyes, I tell her, "You're insinuations are vastly inappropriate and offensive. If you're wanting dirty gossip, you're going to have to find it elsewhere."

"I'm sorry. I wasn't trying to insinuate anything," she says, back-stepping.

I pick up the menu, mind still on Declan, while Jacqueline and Marcia fall back into whatever conversation they were having before I returned. We spend the rest of our lunch in idle chitchat, and then Jacqueline goes on her usual rants about our other so-called friends. I sit, playing along, nodding my head to feign my interest in what's being said.

After the bill is paid, we exchange cheek kisses before leaving. Baldwin is parked out front, waiting on me, and when he opens the car door, he asks, "Good lunch?"

"Lovely," I respond sarcastically, and when he gets into the front seat, he looks at me through the rearview mirror with a pondering look that I have to smile at and then admit, "Okay, maybe lovely isn't the right word."

He laughs and pulls out into traffic.

"I need to stop by Lotus before we go home. Seems my signature is needed on a few invoices and I want to see that the room is set up properly."

"Of course."

Pulling up to the hotel, I get out of the car and walk in, heading straight back to Declan's office. He sits behind his desk, and when I step in, he stands up, saying, "Close the door."

I do.

He strides right up to me, takes my face in his hands, and kisses me, never breaking his fluid movements. Slipping my arms around him, I kiss him back. Excitement rushes through me, or maybe it's the adrenaline of finally knowing this is happening. The plan that Pike and I set out to accomplish over four years ago. All this time, and finally, it's happening. I want to throw myself at Declan, but I have to be smart, remember the game, and not lose focus of what I need to do. So I control the endorphins and pull away.

"What is it?" he questions.

"I'm just . . ."

"Just what?"

Taking a moment, I respond, "Scared."

"Of me?"

I shake my head with his hands still on my face, holding me.

"Of this?"

"Yes." With a drop of my head, I lay my forehead against his chest, adding, "I'm married. I don't know what I'm doing."

"You're married, yes. But are you happy?"

Looking up into his eyes, I say, "I'm not sure what I am. All I know is that this feels good. You feel good."

The intensity in his eyes reveals the pleasure he's taking in my candid words, and I take advantage when I slip my hand around the back of his neck and pull his lips down to mine, showing him that it's him I want—because truth be told, he *is* what I want, what I need.

"Come see me," he says when we break our connection.

"When?"

"Tonight."

"I can't. I have a dinner," I tell him.

"I want you to come see me."

Taking a step back, out of his hold, I hesitate, saying, "I don't know."

His jaw twitches in what I can assume is frustration or anger. "Don't waver, Nina."

"That's so easy for you to say, isn't it?" I nearly snap. "Because you're not the one who is about to fall into a situation that will turn you into a person who acts in Machiavellian schemes. I am."

"I am too. I know what I want. And even if it comes with the manipulation right now, I still want it."

"I don't know," I say in a heavy sigh. "I'm not that kind of person, Declan. I'm faithful and good. This—kissing you—it's already hurting me. But . . ."

"Say it," he demands.

"But it's already filling something in me I didn't know was even empty until you. I just . . . I just need a little time to think about this."

"I'm not a patient man, Nina."

"I know. But please, just . . ."

He steps to me, gripping my arms tightly in his hands, and says, "We both know what you want here. You're lying to yourself right now if you say it's Bennett or else you wouldn't have come here."

"Stop."

"No."

Tugging my arms away, his grip tightens and I see the beginnings of a smirk.

"Declan, stop. Let go."

"No," he says in a hardened voice. "I don't play games, and this is you, playing with me."

"I'm not playing, Declan. This isn't a game; this is my life, a life I've made with my husband, and right now, I'm really confused. Just let me think," I tell him.

His hands let go of me and he walks to the door, opening it. I watch him, trying to read past his glare as he states, "Then go think," before he silently dismisses me from the room.

I don't worry too much about the fact that I just pissed him off. All is fair in love and war, right? So I straighten myself and walk to the door, stopping to look at him with soft eyes, and then leave. This will never work properly if I go to him; he needs to come to me. So I'll make him jealous. I'll make him attack.

nineteen

(PRESENT)

RETURNING HOME FROM running a few last minute errands before the party tonight, I hear the annoying chuckle of Richard, Bennett's business partner, coming from the office. I toss my shopping bags on the dining room table before heading into the kitchen.

"Honey, is that you?" Bennett calls out from across the house.

"Yes, dear."

I grab a bottle of chilled Chardonnay from the wine fridge and begin opening it as the boys round the corner. Smiling up at Bennett as he moves in behind me, I turn my head so that he can take a kiss.

"What are the two of you discussing?" I ask.

"Just a couple of merger opportunities, that's all."

Setting the bottle down, I respond, "I didn't know you were interested in something like that."

"We're not," Richard blurts out. "We're not entertaining any of the offers."

I turn to face Bennett, and he doesn't even seem to acknowledge Richard as his eyes are focused on me with a slight smile. It isn't until I raise up on my toes to give my husband a kiss that Richard speaks again, saying, "Jacqueline mentioned you girls having lunch yesterday. Said you had the attention of another man."

He's such an asshole.

"Who?" Bennett asks.

"Declan," I tell him and then step away to face Richard, adding, "He's the owner of the hotel the party is being held at tonight, but I'm sure that small detail was left out of whatever gossip was being slung around about me. I'm sure you're well aware of maintaining good graces with people you do business with, am I right?"

"No need to get defensive, honey," Bennett says.

"Not defensive, just cankered with offhanded suggestions," I defend while eyeing Richard.

His wink peeves me as he says, "Well, you know how women can be."

Mustering up the most gracious smile I can, I say, "As charming as this little interaction has been, you must excuse me while I get ready for the party." I turn to Bennett, give him a kiss along his jaw, and whisper suggestively, "Join me in the bathroom," before walking away and saying to Richard, "I look forward to seeing both you and your wife tonight."

Whatever Jacqueline's intentions were when she decided to tell her husband about my run-in with Declan, I know I need to play it off as nothing to Bennett and be on my best behavior tonight so that he isn't the least bit tipped off about what I'm doing. So when he walks into the bathroom after a few minutes, I turn to face him, and silently strip off my clothes as he watches. His growing erection is noticeable through his slacks as I sit myself up on the sink counter and spread my legs open, inviting him to take what he wants.

I watch him loosen his tie, and when he starts working the buttons on his shirt, I lick my fingers and drag them down to my clit, rubbing soft circles. I think about anything but Bennett, working hard in my imagination, attempting to get myself wet. Leaning my head back against the mirror, I prop my feet up on the ledge and close my eyes. When the vision of Declan hovering over me with his hand inside my panties in his hotel the other night flashes in my head, my eyes pop open.

Fuck. I can't think about him.

In an instant, Bennett is crouched down in front of me, hands spreading me open wider before dipping his tongue inside me. I continue massaging myself as he laps me up like I'm the only one who can quench his thirst. He sickens me, and as soon as I feel the swirl of hate manifest, I turn every part of me off and simply go through the movements I know he likes. I'm a well-oiled machine at this point, flawless in my performance.

He has no idea that I'm the poison in his bones, making my home in his soul. I've crept under his skin, and he never suspected a thing other than everything I've wanted him to, but he's made my life a hell, and payback is a wicked bitch that comes in the form of me. I'm the devil seeped within the cracks of him. What he doesn't know is that it's because of him that I am what I am, and he's fallen into the cobwebs of my lies like a fool. I guess I should love him for that, because when he least suspects it, he's going to give me everything I've been seeking—vengeance.

"WOULD YOU MIND zipping me up?" I call out to Bennett from inside my closet.

I stand in front of my floor-length framed mirror that rests against one of the walls. The strapless black satin gown is adorned with a scattered crystal beaded bodice that fades down into the slim, silky black skirt that falls to the floor. When Bennett walks up from behind, his smile is wide when he catches the zipper and slowly drags it up the center of my back.

"You're beautiful," he tells me before dropping kisses along my bare shoulder.

"Bennett, that tickles," I giggle as I shimmy away. I look at his reflection in the mirror as he laughs and then ask, "Can you help tie my sash?"

Looking down at the wide, burnt orange, satin sash that's draped around my waist and down my hips, he shakes his head, holding the two ends and says, "What do I do with this?"

"For such a smart boy, you think you could manage a simple tie," I tease. Giving a wink, I straighten my posture and instruct, "Just a loose knot. I'd like it to hang slack a little below my waist."

As he works the fabric, my mind goes back to Declan. I haven't spoken to him since yesterday, but I know he'll be at the party tonight. He's growing impatient with me, which is good, but just as before when Bennett and Declan were together, my nerves are heightened. I don't mind if Bennett suspects that I might be having an affair, but to have him suspicious this early on could be fatal. I need to make sure that Bennett is none the wiser and to simply assume that through the time spent together planning this event, we have become nothing more than friends and that the only intimacy I crave is that of my husband.

"How's that?" he asks as he steps away.

I turn and look over my shoulder at the back of my dress and smile. "It's perfect. Thank you."

He wraps his arms around me and draws me in close. He's clad in his black tux and bowtie—classic Bennett. Looking into his eyes, I softly sigh and relax in his embrace, whispering, "I miss you."

"You have me, honey. I'm right here."

"For now. But I still miss you, like I can never get close enough to you for it to be enough," I tell him, my words nothing but maladies for my liking.

"God, do you have any clue what that does to me?"

"Hmm . . . tell me."

"If I tell you, I'm going to unknot that sash and peel this gown off of you."

My smile grows, and he kisses the corner of my mouth, always careful not to smudge my lipgloss. We spend a few moments holding each other before we slip on our coats and head down to the car.

When we pull up to the hotel, Baldwin parks in front and Bennett grabs the box with my mask. He opens it and pulls out the black, laser-cut metal mask and says, "Where did you find this? It's really unique."

His comment catches me off guard because I assumed it was a gift from him, but then it dawns on me that the reason there was no card or note was because it's from Declan.

"Oh," I say, taking a second before lying, "I found it online and ordered it."

"Come here," he says as he leans in. Gently placing it on my face, he loops the ribbon behind my head and secures it in a bow.

I can't believe Declan did this and never said anything. "Does it look okay?" I ask.

"You're perfect."

I hold out my hand for his mask—a golden etched mask with large contrasting burnt orange and deep red swirls of flame. When I have it tied in place, I softly press my lips to his.

"Let's go," he says. "I want everyone to see how beautiful you look tonight."

Laughing at his words, I remark, "Arm candy?"

"You're so much more than candy."

He takes my hand as we walk in, fashionably late, to the already busy room. I stop for a moment to take everything in: the dark room is flanked with fire-burning rustic lanterns lining the walls, lavish orange and red flowers and greenery filling the tables, people dressed in their finest gowns and tuxes, and masks that reflect the theme—devils, harlequins, studded black leather, and of course my own black metal mask.

"I didn't think you could top yourself, but this is amazing, honey," Bennett tells me.

The room is busy with friends, my husband's colleagues, waiters serving various drinks and hors d'oeuvres, the band playing, and people dancing and mingling.

"Shall we?" Bennett says as he leads me into the dark, fire-lit room.

It isn't long before we are mixed in with the crowd and greeting our guests. I quickly snatch a flute of champagne off a silver tray. Taking a sip, I hear Jacqueline from behind me, "Nina, I'm impressed."

When I turn to face her, I respond, "You say that as if you had doubts." My words come out a little tart, but she doesn't seem to take offense.

"Never. You always put on the best events," she says. "You look amazing, by the way. I love the orange."

"Thank you. I had the pleasure of seeing your husband earlier today. Seems he and my husband couldn't take a day off from business."

"Boys will be boys," she says, and then adds with a smirk, "Especially when it comes to money and slinging their power around."

We both laugh at the honesty of her statement when I feel Bennett's arm wrap around my shoulder. "What are you girls laughing about?"

"Do you really need to ask?" I tease.

"Do you think you could pull yourself away from gossiping about me so that I can take you for a spin on the dance floor?"

"But talking about the quandaries of the men in our lives is so much fun," I mock with a grin.

"I can only imagine," he states before giving Jacqueline a nod and complimenting, "You look lovely this evening, Jacqueline."

"As do you, Bennett," her response laced in her usual flirtation. "If you'll excuse me, I should probably go find Richard."

When she walks away, Bennett leads us down to the crowded dance floor, and I finally spot Declan out of the corner of my eye. He stands in a small group, looking sharp in a black tux, but with no tie and the top couple buttons open. His eyes are covered in a gold and black diamond checkered harlequin mask, but I know it's him by the day-old stubble on his strong jaw. When Bennett holds me close, I watch Declan over his shoulder as we move around the dance floor. His eyes finally find mine at the same time a slinky brunette slides up next to him and he wraps his arms around her waist. His eyes never stray from mine as she whispers something into his ear and I see the smile grow on his face, pleased by whatever she's saying.

My stomach coils, not from jealousy, because I don't get jealous, but from the fear of knowing that I could've fucked myself by playing too hard to get with him. Maybe I read him wrong and the push and pull act I've been playing with him was more of a turn off than a turn on. Or maybe he's just trying to make me jealous to get me to finally make a move with him. No matter which of the two scenarios it may be, I only have one option in this and that's to play him at his own game.

So as Declan flirts with the woman on his arm, eyes still pinned to mine, I let my eyes fall shut as I run my nose along Bennett's jaw until my lips meet his in a tender kiss. With one hand behind his neck, I bury my fingers in his hair as I continue to kiss him.

Drawing back slightly, Bennett runs his knuckles down my cheek with soft eyes before he pulls me back into his arms. When I look over to Declan, he isn't paying me any attention; instead, he's sipping on whatever is in his double old-fashioned as he grazes his fingers slowly up and down the woman's bare arm.

The thick cloud of defeat begins to wash over me and not even the best actress in the world could stave off the mood shift that flicks inside of my stomach. It's a sick feeling that chokes me in a painful clench of knowing that this may not ever happen for me. That more years of my life were spent wasted on a quest that will come to naught.

I spend the next couple of hours focusing on Bennett, trying to distract me from myself, swallowing down the shit mood, but it still manifests in my gut—a never-ending reminder. But no one is wise to my inner-workings as we stroll through the room, visiting, toasting to the new year that is upon us, laughing, drinking, smiling, bragging, complimenting, faking . . .

And then I become the biggest fake of all when Bennett spots Declan and calls out for him.

"Bennett," he drawls in his ever-present brogue. "Good to see you again."

"Same here. This is quite an event."

"Well, you and I both know it's only because of Nina here," he says as he gives me an approving nod.

With a hint of a smile, I loop my arm through Bennett's as I return the nod.

"Catherine," he says to his date, "I'd like you to meet Mr. Vanderwal and his *wife*, Nina."

I can't ignore the needle he uses to stab the word *wife*, but I keep myself in check as I extend my hand to her for a gracious shake.

"It's a pleasure," I say.

"This is a wonderful party."

"Well, I'm glad you're enjoying yourself," I tell her and then turn to Bennett. Reaching up to affectionately cup his cheek, I excuse myself, saying, "Do you think I could get a few minutes? I'm a little warm and not feeling too well."

"Are you okay?"

"I'll be fine. I just need a little breather. I'll be back shortly," I tell him and then give him a loving kiss in front of Declan, taking my time in an indecent display of affection. Lucky for me, I know Bennett, and he loves to make a show out of me, so I use that with the intent of making myself somehow feel better about this colossal failure I've created.

The emptiness inside of me swells as I make my way out of the room and down the hall towards Declan's office where I know there's a private bathroom. I just need to be alone to pull myself together from the swarming thoughts that are flooding my head right now.

Another knife in a faltered dream.

I walk over to the large, leather ottoman that sits in the center of the plush powder room. Heat creeps its way up my neck as thoughts of Pike enter, and I reach back to pull the ribbon loose on my mask. The cool air meets my skin as I drop the mask to the floor. I allow myself this rare moment of weakness as I sit here, but it's interrupted when I hear the door open and look over my shoulder to see Declan.

I don't speak as I watch him lock the door behind him. And then he faces me. His jaw is set tight as he takes his mask off, giving me a clear view of his darkened eyes, nearly black.

"I'm done with the fucking games here," he barks as he walks over to me.

I stay quiet, slightly confused about this situation, as he continues, "You, making a spectacle in front of me with that man we both know you're not happy with. Is this you trying to make me jealous?"

He stands over me, looking down, when I snap, "I should be asking you the same question."

"Shut your mouth, Nina," he demands sternly.

He's pissed—jealous.

I'm suddenly revived, but the games are over. I'll give him exactly what I know he wants, my submission to his demanding request. He startles me when he abruptly grabs ahold of my arms and forcefully yanks me up to my feet and spins me around in his arms so that we're both facing the mirror. With one hand clenched around my arm, his other grabs my jaw, forcing me to look at our reflection.

"Look at me."

I do.

"You want me?"

Nerves crash inside of me, accelerating my breathing, but I don't respond.

"Answer me!"

"Yes." My voice, hoarse in its attempt to speak.

"Say it," he snaps as he releases my face and slips his hand down to my throat, gripping it firmly, forcing my head back. "Say it!"

"I want you."

As soon as the words are out, he pushes me down quickly, and before I know it, he has my dress lifted, exposing my backside. My hands grab on to the edge of the sink to brace myself as he yanks my panties to the side.

"Look at me," he instructs in a hard voice, and I do as he says, lifting my head to meet his eyes in the mirror. "I don't have a soft touch, Nina."

I nod my head and see him nodding as well in our mutual understanding of his words as he unhooks his belt and begins to unfasten his slacks. I shut down, taking my mind far away from what's about to happen.

"Stick your ass out for me."

I do, and without any warning, he slams inside of me, locking our bodies, causing a pained whimper to bleed out from my lips. With his hands on my hips, he hunches his shoulders over me, pinning me over the sink as he thrusts his cock in me over and over in a pounding feat of control, and I give it to him as I hold on tightly.

"Look at me," he snarls in my ear. His eyes are hooded in primal need as I watch him fuck me from behind. I fight the heat that I can feel boiling inside of me, grinding my teeth as I try to ignore the slapping of his balls against my clit with each volatile thrust. But unlike Bennett, Declan forces me to stay in the moment with him when he says, "Tell me how bad you want me."

I quickly shake my head, not wanting to speak.

"Tell me, Nina."

"Mmm mmm."

My denial is punished in an erotic agony that shoots through my core and up my spine when Declan painfully pinches my clit between his fingers, causing me to scream out and jerk my body away from him, but he bands his one arm around my waist, locking me still in his hold. He doesn't let up as he hisses in my ear, "Tell me," never once faltering as he continues to pump in and out of me.

"Please," I shriek as tears prick the back of my eyes when he pinches harder, pulling on my most sensitive part. My head drops as I release another pained cry before finally giving him the words, "I want you."

"Louder!"

"I want you. Please." My words, more a plea than anything else, spur him to go harder, pounding inside of me at a violent pace. His assault erupts quickly as he comes, spurting his hot sperm inside of me with a powerful grunt.

I stand there, legs quivering beneath me while Declan has his face buried in my neck. His dick is still rock hard inside of me when he finally lifts his head, but I keep mine down, confused about what just happened. Wondering if that was him wanting me as his or if that was nothing more than a punishment for playing games with him.

When he pulls out of me, he drops my dress down, covering me up. His breaths are labored, as are mine, and when I right myself, I catch a glimpse of him shoving his dick inside of his pants, and then I look away.

"Don't do that," he says, and I turn around to face him. "Don't look away from me."

I don't say anything because I have no clue what to say in this moment, but he breaks the silence after his shirt is tucked in and his belt is buckled. Taking a couple steps towards me, I grip the edge of the sink as he scolds, "Don't ever try to make me jealous again, do you hear me?"

"Yes," I murmur.

"Now go back to your husband, but don't you forget whose cum is inside of you right now," he says before taking my chin between his fingers and giving me a hard kiss, then turning and walking out of the bathroom, leaving me standing here, a fucked up mess.

I turn around and look at myself in the mirror, working quickly to pull myself together before returning to the party. Taking in a few slow, deep breaths to calm my racing heart, I smooth my hair and blot the sweat from my forehead with a towel. I don't have time to think about what just happened because I've been in here for long enough, and I need to get back to Bennett. I give myself another glance over to make sure everything is in place before I pick my mask up from the floor and walk out.

When I make my way back to the party, I scan the room for Declan but he's nowhere to be seen.

"You feeling better?" Bennett asks, causing me to jump. "Are you okay?"

"Yeah, you just snuck up on me," I breathe.

His eyes roam over my face before he asks, "Why did you take your mask off?"

"I was hot," I tell him. "Would you put it back on for me?"

When I hand it over to him, I turn around, and as he's tying it back on, I spot Declan's date, but she's alone. Taking one more look over the room, I still don't see him.

"There," he says and then wraps his arm around my shoulder. "Let's go find a quiet spot and sit down for a little bit."

"I'm fine. Really," I assure. "Dance with me."

He smiles and we spend the rest of the evening dancing and enjoying our night. After the countdown to midnight, we ring in the New Year with champagne toasts and lots of kissing, but with Declan nowhere in sight, it seems he must have ditched the party after fucking me in the bathroom. It isn't until we get home that I lie in bed and replay everything that happened with Declan. Putting all the pieces of him together, I'm fairly certain that what happened was him staking his claim, albeit in a primitive and territorial fashion.

With Bennett going to Miami in a couple of days, I plan to lay low and focus my attention on him before I seek out Declan. That is, if he doesn't seek me out first.

twenty (PRESENT)

"HONEY."

"Yeah?" I say as I grab a few more dress shirts from Bennett's closet and walk back out into the bedroom to pack them in his garment bag.

"I wanted to talk to you about Baldwin. I'll need to continue taking him with me for my trips to Dubai. I just want to make sure you're okay with that."

"We discussed this before, and I told you I'm fine. But why do you need to take him with you?" I ask.

"The laws there are strict, and I like having him to keep an eye on everything," he explains. "It's just safer that I'm not alone."

After zipping up his bag, I walk over to him and ask as I wrap my arms around his waist, "Should I be more worried about you?"

"No. I don't want you to worry about a thing, which is why Baldwin will be traveling with me."

"Just you saying that already has me worried."

"It's just, last I was there, a situation arose with a couple who shared a cab that was staying at the same hotel as me. It made me realize how much I didn't know about the laws there," he tells me and then leads me over to one of the chairs that sit next to the windows.

"What happened?" I ask as he takes a seat and pulls me down on his lap.

"They were friends sharing a cab and they got arrested. According to the driver, they were holding hands and kissed, which I found out was against the law unless you're married. The bellman who brought my bags to the room told me that they would most likely go to prison for the indiscretion. So, I just want the added security measures around me while I'm there on the jobsite, that's all."

Shaking my head, I remark, "That's crazy."

"I know I had mentioned you coming with me, but I don't think that would be a good idea. I'd worry too much, so I think it's best that you stay put here, where I know you're safe." He runs his hand through my hair, adding, "I wouldn't know what to do with myself if anything ever happened to you."

"Baby, nothing's going to happen to me. I'll stay here and wait for you," I tell him and then add with a smile, "impatiently."

He laughs and brings me in for a kiss.

"So what are your plans for the next few days while I'm gone?" he questions.

"I need to stop by the Tribune Tower to meet with Mr. Bernstein about that social piece I was approached about writing."

"Did you decide to do it then?"

"I think so. I mean, it'll be great exposure for the charities we work with. I figured we could use this opportunity to get the word out about some of the smaller foundations we are affiliated with," I explain. "I know I'm not a writer or anything, but I can try, right?"

"I'm proud of you, you know that? Plus, you'll have an editor, but I have no doubt that you're fully capable of writing a great article."

"Well, the least it will do is keep me busy while you're gone."

"Three days. It's only three days," he says with a grin.

"Yeah. Three days and then you leave a few days after that," I tell him with a soft poke to his ribs, which causes him to laugh and nuzzle his head into the crook of my neck, giving me a couple nips.

We continue to talk and be close until Baldwin calls with the car, and Bennett and I say our goodbyes for the next few days while he's in Miami on business. Once he's gone, I go to check my phone, wondering if Declan has tried contacting me, but I have no new messages. It's been several days since the incident in the bathroom at the New Year's Eve party, and I haven't had any contact with him since. But now that Bennett is gone, I make the decision to drive over to his loft.

I distract myself when Clara comes over, helping her in the kitchen, preparing meals for the week. We share a glass of wine, and I fill her in on the party and we talk about her daughter's wedding that is coming up in a few months. When everything is prepped, labeled, and placed in the freezer, she says goodnight and I take a quick shower to freshen up.

I dress casually, leaving my thick, red hair in loose waves and dabbing on a touch of makeup. I prep myself on the drive over to River North with how I plan on approaching Declan, needing to play heavily on his emotions to pull him into what he will assume is just your everyday affair. So I listen to a few songs that aid me in my doleful mood, and as I pull up to Declan's building a little after nine, I breathe a sigh of relief when I look up to the very top to see the lights on in his place.

Giving myself a last look in the rearview mirror, I walk into the building and buzz for Declan on the intercom.

"Who is it?" his voice questions through the speaker.

"It's me," I say softly.

I have to wait a few silent moments before his voice responds, "I'll be right down."

Since you need a card to get to his floor, I wait for him by the elevator. When it finally opens, and Declan steps out towards me, I do as I planned and simply stand there, staring at him, willing the tears to bathe my eyes, until he finally speaks, "What are you doing here?"

With a subtle shrug of my shoulders, my voice trembles when I respond, "I don't know."

He closes the space between us, cupping my cheeks in his hands, but I don't give him a chance to say anything when my vision blurs with unshed tears and I weakly say, "I want to be mad at you. For what you did the other night. But . . . for some reason I can't bring myself to hate you." My head falls to his chest, and he holds me tight in his arms when I add, "I just . . . I'm scared, but I want to be here with you."

He presses his lips to the top of my head, and with me tucked in his arms, he moves us to the elevator and holds me the whole way up to his loft. When the doors open, he leads me across the room and over to the same couch we sat on the other week, next to the already burning fireplace. I curl up next to him, resting my head on his shoulder when he finally breaks the silence, saying, "The last thing I want is for you to hate me, Nina."

"Then what was that in the bathroom?"

"Me."

Lifting my head, I see the creases in his forehead, but his look is solid when he says, "I won't apologize."

With a faint nod of my head, I whisper, "Okay."

"Like I told you, I don't have the softest touch. I don't want you to mistake that for a lack of feeling, because I won't deny that I already feel strongly about you."

"I'm scared."

"I know," he states softly.

"Do you?"

His thumb runs along my cheekbone when he says, "I won't ever do anything to hurt you."

"But . . . Bennett . . ."

"He doesn't need to know anything until you're ready to say something. He doesn't exist here, here in my home. It's just you and me," he tells me before his lips touch mine in a soft kiss. A very un-Declan-like kiss. He's gentle, and when I reach up to touch his face, he grabs my wrist in his hand and hoists me on top of his lap. My legs straddle his hips, and his erection is evident as it presses between my legs.

His hands quickly find my breasts, and he squeezes them achingly hard as I sink my fingers into his hair, fisting it in my hands. When I tug at the roots, he growls in my mouth and lifts up my top. I raise my arms in an invitation, which he accepts as he pulls off my sweater. And in a fluid movement, he stands up with my body clung to his, legs wrapped around his hips, and he walks us down the hall and into his master suite.

The room is dark, lit only by the lights of the city below. My back falls against the soft bedding when he lays us down. His mouth is all over me, dragging down my neck, over the swell of my breasts, to the dip of my navel. He unhooks my pants and slips them off my legs, along with my shoes. I look up at him as he stands over me, peering down as I lie here in my bra and panties. Slowly, he starts working the buttons on his shirt before tossing it across the room. His shoulders and arms are roped in muscle. His smooth chest is nothing but hardened, accentuated slabs that define his broad build and narrow to a deep-cut V, sinking down into his pants.

He starts to undo his leather belt, and when he slips it from the loops of his slacks, he grips it firmly in both of his hands as if he's about to make use of it. Suddenly I run cold, and ask hesitantly as I sit up, "What're you gonna do?"

"Don't ask me questions, Nina."

My eyes lock on the leather belt, and I begin to feel nauseous at the thought of it, at the thought of being tied up in a closet for days, at the thought of being beaten and the snapping of leather as it slices into the skin of my back, at the thought of being choked with a leather belt while forced to suck my foster dad's dick. I can't tear my eyes away from the tight hold he has on his belt and the spiraled veins in his arms. All I can hear is the pounding of my heart in my ears, and I take a hard swallow.

"Look at me," he says, and I can't hide the fear that I'm sure is splayed across my face. "I meant what I said, I'll never hurt you, but I'm not like most guys."

I nod. I don't know what else to do because I can't lose him when I've finally come this far.

"I like control. Do you understand what that means?" he questions in an even tone as I shift my attention to his eyes.

"I don't want you to hurt me."

He steps between my legs and touches my face. "This isn't about pain, Nina. This is about trust. Do you trust me?"

I don't trust anyone, but I give him the word anyway. "Yes."

"Do you?"

"Yes."

"Good girl."

Those two words, I've heard them so many times from that piece of shit, Carl. He'd always say them to me when I would make him come. No one has ever said those words to me since him, until right now. And I know this is going to destroy me, but what other choice do I have? So I play the part and give him a soft smile when all I want to do is vomit.

"God, you're so beautiful," he breathes and then leans down to kiss me, sliding his tongue past my lips, tasting me deeply. He reaches around and unclasps my bra with ease. It's then that he kneels between my thighs, running his hands over my knees and up my legs while he sucks my pert nipple into his hot mouth. His tongue swirls around before he bares his teeth, pulling more of my breast into his mouth and biting down, making me whimper as his teeth sink in to the supple flesh.

In a quick move, he thrusts my legs wide open and drops his head to my center, taking my pussy in his mouth, licking me through the lace of my panties and then grazing his teeth along my mound as he pulls away to take a lingering look before standing up.

"Do you have any idea how sweet you taste or what it's like for me to look at you like this?"

"Declan," I sigh at the same time he tells me, "Lie back."

I do as he instructs and he takes my hip, flipping me over onto my stomach. In forceful movements, he grabs my arms, bringing them behind my back, and I feel the cool leather binding around them, above my elbows, in a painful restraint. With a sharp jerk of the belt, my shoulder blades pinch together, and all the slack disappears as the leather bites into my skin in an unrelenting vice, which there is no getting out of as he loops the belt and then fastens it. My heart trills in my throat, and my heavy breathing is prevalent. But it's when I begin releasing panicked noises into the sheets that a ribbon of breath heats my ear as he presses his lips to its shell and gives me a quiet, "Shhh, baby. Trust me."

He brushes my hair back as I lie there with the side of my face resting on the bed. I give him a nod, but everything in me is telling me that this is going to be too much. And then he's off the bed, grabbing my hips and lifting my ass up in the air, propping me on my knees with my chest still on the mattress. He yanks my panties down to my knees, and then his hands spread my ass open before his mouth is on my bare pussy. The wetness of his tongue gently laps over my clit while his hands roughly squeeze my butt, and when he wraps his lips around my nub and sucks, he brings a hard hand down, smacking my ass. I yelp in pain, lying there like some animal, helpless at the hands of someone else, and I'm taken back to the fucking basement I never wanted to think about, but I'm there, on that filthy mattress being humiliated by my foster dad.

My eyes squeeze shut, and I will every ounce of effort to disengage, to think about anything other than what's happening, but Declan makes it impossible when he slips his tongue inside of my pussy as he drags his fingers along the crease of my ass, forcing me to tense up. He then takes that hand, reaches under me, and grabs my breast, pinching my nipple between his fingers as he continues to fuck me with his mouth. I try to focus on the ache in my arms, but he grasps my attention when he takes his mouth off my pussy, grabs ahold of the belt, and pulls me back, lifting my chest off the bed, so that I'm now sitting on my heels. Turning my head to him, he offers me his mouth, saying, "Taste yourself," and then kisses me, caressing my tongue with his.

I want to scream for him to stop because I don't want to be doing this with him, but I don't. I force myself to think about what I'm using him for, what I need him to do for me. The words *you can do this, you can do this* repeat over and over in my head, but there's an intensity with Declan that I haven't experienced with a man before. It's easy to shut down with Bennett, but Declan has a power that keeps me in the moment, making the escape near impossible.

Pulling away from our kiss, he says, "Tell me what you want. Ask for it."

"I want you," I lie.

"What do you want me to do?"

"Fuck me."

"Ask me," he demands and the request irks the shit out of me, but I swallow the irritation.

"Will you please fuck me, Declan?"

Rounding his hand over my butt and down between my legs, he sinks his finger inside of my pussy, asking, "You want it here?" with his face pressed to the side of mine, his chest against my back.

"Yes."

"I want to hear you say it," he requests, and I just wish he would stop fucking talking so I can at least attempt to go numb.

"Please, Declan. Just fuck me. I want you inside of me. I want to feel you in my pussy. I want all of you filling me up," I tell him, giving him all the words I feel he wants to hear so that we can get this over with.

And with that, I hear his pants hit the floor from behind me as I sit on my knees, waiting for his next move, and then it comes.

His hand grabs a fist of my hair as he shoves my face back down into the mattress. Letting go, he widens my knees, ass up, and then gives my pussy one last lick before he buries himself balls deep into my core, forcing me to slip forward on the bed. He quickly grabs my wrists that are stationed at the small of my back and holds them firmly with one hand while the other fists the belt.

I turn my head face down in the bed, and do what I can to disengage, but his voice keeps penetrating me as he talks, forcing me to tell him that I want him, that I want this, that I like this, that it feels good. I can't escape. I'm in the moment. I'm never in the moment, but right now, I'm in the goddamn moment, and the churning of my stomach begins to rouse into a disgusting rumble of bile I pray stays down.

"Let go, Nina. Stop fighting me," he says, as if he knows I'm trying with everything I have not to come. My body is so tense; I'm an idiot to think he can't feel it. He'll know if I fake it, but I keep fighting anyway. "Don't fight me," he hisses, his accent thickening as his desire grows. He then reaches around, dragging the wetness up to my clit, and starts massaging in slow, torturous circles. He has no idea he's destroying everything inside of me.

I hold my breath and bite down hard. I can't deny him what he's demanding. He'll ask too many questions, questions I can't ever answer for him, so I give in and allow him to give me the repulsive pleasure I hate to feel. It builds along with the bile, and when his cock swells inside of me with his oncoming release, I break. And out of nowhere, he makes a tender gesture when he laces his fingers with mine and holds my hand while I come. The orgasm takes over my body in ripples of fiery explosions that shoot through every inch of me. I can't suppress the moans that rip out of me, humiliating me, and then they're joined with Declan's as his orgasm mirrors mine. The feel of his cock throbbing inside of me as my walls spasm around him prolongs the release I wish would stop, but it quakes through me, holding me hostage to the man behind me. Our hands locked tightly together the whole time, as if he knows how hard this is for me and this is his way of offering a gentle support.

A second later, he lets go of me, and with fast hands, releases his belt from my arms, and they drop lifelessly to the bed as his body collapses on top of mine. I can't look at him. I can't even open my eyes. As my orgasm fades away, the pleasure between my legs remains as a reminder as to what just happened. I have to pull my shit together—fast—as Declan shifts to my side and brings me into his arms.

I tuck my knees up, and when I do, he cradles me in his hold, humming into my ear. I focus on his sounds to calm my racing heart and queasy gut. Taking in slow, deep breaths, I wonder how I'm going to get through sex with him again. I'm too exposed—too alive—too hot—too ripe—too present. I want to cry, but I don't, so I lay my head on Declan's chest and selfishly take the comfort he's offering because I don't have any other options here. He holds me, soothing me with the lull of his hums as I listen to his steadying heartbeat.

"Talk to me," he requests.

"I don't feel like talking."

"I need you to talk to me. Tell me why you were fighting me."

"I wasn't," I try to deny.

Turning on his side to face me, he wraps his hand behind my knee and drapes my leg over his hip, bringing us closer, when he says, "I felt you, Nina. I need you to talk to me. Did I scare you?"

Yes.

"No."

"Did I hurt you?"

Yes.

"No."

"Then what?" he asks softly with worry etched in the lines of his face.

Trying to relieve whatever is running through his head, I wrap my arms around his neck, hug him close, and tell him, "You're just really intense, and I guess . . . yeah . . . maybe you scared me a little."

"I'm sorry," he says, shifting his forehead to rest against mine. "Look at me."

When I open my eyes, his are peering into mine, noses together, so close.

"I *never* want to scare you. I *never* want to hurt you. I only want to be close with you, but this is the only way I know how to be."

"You don't have to apologize for who you are," I faintly breathe. "This. Being here in your arms. I've never felt more safe. So just hold me, okay?"

And he does, for a long time, while I try to get my head straight. We just hold each other, and then after a while, he takes my hand, and licks my palm before kissing it and then presses it to his chest.

"You consume me, you know that?"

I shake my head, saying, "I assumed I annoy you most of the time."

"You do," he laughs. "Your smart mouth irritates me, but it's also something I love about you. You don't take my shit, and I like that. But at the same time, I need you to be able to take my shit. I'm demanding and stubborn; that's not something I'm willing to change because I thrive on control."

"Why?"

He releases a deep breath, telling me, "Let's not talk about why. Not tonight."

"One day?"

"One day, darling," he says as he pulls me in closer to his naked body. "Can you stay with me tonight?"

"Mmm hmm. Bennett's in Miami for a few days. I'm yours until he gets back."

Leaning his head back to look me dead on, his voice is acid when he says, "No."

"No?"

"You're mine regardless of where he is. Here or not. I don't play well with others."

I hesitate for a second and then say, "It's not that simple. He's not like he appears, Declan."

"What does that mean?"

"It's just . . . It's not easy."

When he shakes his head in confusion, I repeat on a hush, "It's just not that easy."

His lips lightly brush over mine in a sweeping kiss, and I can taste the ice of his breath when he whispers, "I don't expect anything with you to be easy, but that's not enough to stop me from having you."

And with those words, I kiss him, allowing him to feast on my sugary poison. He may have a power over me in bed, one that will no doubt cause me suffering, but in the end, I'll take the pain because I know I'll be able to destroy him enough to save myself, to give me everything that was stolen from me when I was five years old.

twenty-one
(PRESENT)

WAKING UP IN Declan's bed the following day was peaceful. Peaceful in every morbid way. His hands were all over me while his face made its home between my legs before he pulled me on top of his lap. He had my arms crossed behind my back while he held each of my hands, locking my arms from moving as I fucked him. And again, he held my hands while I came. If I'm being honest, I feel like I need that support from him, because what he makes me feel during sex is sheer torment and anxiety. I don't want sex to feel good. It shouldn't feel good. But he doesn't give me any other choice, so I lied to him, telling him that Clara was going to be at my place and that I needed to be there so she wouldn't worry or question my whereabouts. I just needed to get away from him.

As soon as I get home, I take a scalding hot shower, washing every part of me, but nothing can clean me the way Pike can. I feel myself breaking and stop the fight long enough to let it out. Never in my life have I ever wanted to feel what Declan makes me feel. As images from last night and this morning run through my head, the tears surface as my stomach convulses in bubbles of putrid disgust. Unable to hold it down, I quickly step out of the shower, fall to my knees over the toilet, and vomit uncontrollably. It's a painful mixture of saliva, puke, and tears. Visions of Declan, Carl, leather, flesh, cum, that filthy mattress, the smell of that basement, the smell of Declan, my vicious hate for Bennett, my loneliness of missing Pike, my father's headstone. Everything consumes me. I hear it, smell it, see it, feel it, and then another forceful expulsion barrels its way up my throat and into the toilet.

In this moment, I hate my life. I hate everything about this shithole of a life I so desperately want to free myself from. Sobs achingly rip out of me, and as I fall back onto the cold slate floor, I lie there, wet and naked, the smell of my vomit filling the room. And when I close my eyes, I see my dad.

"Princess, what are you doing?" he mumbles in a sleepy voice as I crawl under the covers with him.

"I'm scared."

He helps me pull the blanket over myself and then cuddles me in his arms, saying, "Nothing will ever hurt you. I'll always protect you. Now, tell me what scared you."

"I can't remember. I just woke up and I was scared."

"Bad dream?"

I nod my head against his chest and snuggle underneath the covers of his bed, asking, "Can I sleep with you tonight, Daddy?"

"You don't want to go back to your own bed?"

"No. I just want you."

His large arms band around me tighter. "How can I say no to that?" he says and then kisses my forehead, the stubble on his face pricking my skin, causing me to giggle.

"Daddy! That tickles," I squeal and as soon as the words are out, he's laughing and nuzzling his face in my neck, pretending to eat me. The both of us laugh loudly in the dark room, rolling around his big bed.

I start pinching his sides, and he rolls onto his back with a huge smile and chuckles, "You win. You win. I give up."

"You never give up," I tell him, and he responds, "Sometimes a man needs to know when to let a lady a win. Now give me a kiss right here."

He points to his cheek as he speaks, and I lean in and kiss his unshaven face, feeling the prickling pokes on the soft skin of my lips.

"Come here," he says, and I lie back down in his arms as he kisses the top of my head. "Close your eyes now. There's nothing to be scared of. I'll never let anyone hurt you. You're always going to be safe."

"I love you, Daddy."

"I love you so much more, Princess. Come find me in your dreams."

The vision fades and I roll to my side, curling into a ball, and cry for all the things he promised me that never happened. I was never safe, and this world hurt me beyond what I ever thought a human could be hurt. All because of Bennett. And now I lie here in his bathroom, our bathroom. He's my husband. We share a home, a bed, a life. I knew what I was doing when I embedded myself into his world, but after what just happened with Declan, I wanna run. Run so far that I never have to look back and remember any of this. Run all the way back in time. Back to Northbrook, back to the house I used to live in, through the front door, into my bedroom where my father still waits for me at my little table, with pink daisies, to join him for our princess tea party. Maybe if I cry hard enough, the world will take pity on me, shift off its axis and make all my dreams come true.

I want my daddy.

After all these years, I just want my daddy.

A COUPLE HOURS pass, and I now sit in the living room as I watch another snow-filled day. My body aches, and I'm tired after my meltdown. I know better than to let those feelings bleed through. It's been a long time since I've cried like that and allowed myself to feel sorry for the life I wound up with. So now I sit here and gain control as the fire ignites inside of me. The fire I let fizzle out earlier. I feel its embers in the molten heat of my veins. A resurgence of what I'm doing here. This is about regaining what was stolen from me. Taking back what was mine to be had before my father was ripped away from me and murdered in prison. I can handle Declan; I just had a moment of weakness last night, but now, I have rectified that steel wall.

Fuck Declan.

Fuck Bennett.

This is about righting the wrong.

This is revenge, and I'm ready.

Without wasting any more time, I grab my coat and keys and head down to the garage to go to Justice. I need to see Pike.

When I pull up to his trailer, I see Matt's car. I'll never forget that night when Pike crawled through my bedroom window in the middle of the night. Matt was there too. Pike held me while I cried for hours in the back seat of Matt's car as he drove us to northern Illinois where he had rented a rundown apartment with Pike. The three of us lived together for a few years until Pike and I got a place of our own.

I never went back to school. I was a runaway, but I didn't let that define me as a complete failure. Pike gave me money to buy a few home schooling kits that got me through high school. Doing it on my own doesn't take away from the fact that I'm just as knowledgeable as any other graduate, diploma or not. I've always loved school and learning new things. I would look through the course catalogues from the local university and buy the textbooks for the classes I was interested in and read them on my own. Pike has always teased me, but I wasn't going to let the reality that I was a high school dropout plague me.

Until I was of age, I couldn't risk getting a job either, so I helped Pike, weighing and bagging the product Matt would bring in. Because of the people they dealt with, I was always by Pike's side. It was safer running the streets with him than to be left alone in the apartment.

But I've never liked Matt despite Pike's friendship with him. I had to fight him off a few times when he would get drunk and try to get into my pants. But it was him that stood by my side on that fateful night, the night he and Pike gave me one of the greatest gifts I could've asked for. Matt and Pike gave me payback in the form of death. The first stroke of revenge as the both of them stood by my side as I lit the match, killing both Carl and Bobbi in the ink of night. I was only fifteen when I discovered the sweet taste of vengeance as their pleading screams were engulfed in the flames of hell.

So to see him here, now, irritates me because no matter how much I dislike him, I'll always be indebted for that one precious gift he allowed me. And when I shut off the car and walk inside, Matt sneers, knowing everything about what I'm doing with Bennett, "Well, well, well, what drug in the shit-stain on high society living?"

"It's an amazing thing to see."

"What is?" he asks.

"The way your vocabulary has matured through the years," I give him as I slip off my coat and then look over to Pike, saying, "I need to talk to you."

"Dude, get lost," he tells Matt.

"What the fuck?"

"Don't start that shit, you know Elizabeth has a hard enough time getting out here to see me," he tells Matt as he stands up and walks over to me.

I give Pike a hug and watch as Matt grabs his coat and starts heading for the door. "Call me when she leaves."

"Yeah, man. Talk to you later."

Matt looks back over his shoulder at me when he gets to the door and then leaves. I wrap my arms more tightly around Pike and nearly smother him.

"Whoa. What's going on?" he says as he holds me.

"I really missed you," I tell him thickly.

"Is everything okay? Did something happen?" he asks as then we walk over to the couch and sit down.

"I fucked Declan last night."

The concern on Pike's face isn't surprising. Aside from Carl, Pike is the only guy I've ever had sex with, until Bennett. But Bennett is nothing compared to Declan.

"Shit," he sighs. "Are you okay?"

"He tied me up with his belt," I reveal to him.

"What the fuck?"

"It's how he is. He's forceful. He actually fucked me at the New Year's party. That was the first time. It was a dirty fuck in a bathroom."

"Wait. Go back," he says, confused.

"I was trying to make him jealous at the party, apparently it worked. He followed me into the bathroom and we had sex. I didn't see him or talk to him until I went to his place yesterday. Bennett is in Miami, so I wound up spending the night with Declan. Sex with him is awful. It's impossible to drown out what's going on because he's so demanding throughout. I left this morning to go home because I was feeling disgusted."

"Come here," he breathes as he tugs me into his arms. We sit for a moment and then he asks, "So what are you thinking?"

"I can't walk away. He's the right guy, I know it."

"How can you be sure?"

Shaking my head, I say, "I don't know. I just feel it. I can't explain; it's just how I feel."

"I don't know," he says, doubting my words.

Feeling a little annoyed, I question, "What?"

"Do you think he's capable?"

"That's not a question anyone can really answer, but yeah, I think he could be."

"What if he finds out?"

"He won't."

Eyeing me, he presses, "Don't be so sure about that. Confidence is a dangerous thing to have."

Turning out of his arms, I sit back and exhaust, "Fine. What if he finds out? I don't know, Pike. What would it matter? No crime would've been committed."

"What about Bennett? If Declan finds out or isn't capable, are you going to be able to do it?"

I laugh in frustration, turn to face Pike, and say, "The way you doubt me makes you look stupid. I love my father, and he paid the ultimate price when he was murdered." With a stern look, I seethe, "If you don't think I'm capable, you don't know me."

"I do know you. Better than anyone else. But we're talking about killing someone, Elizabeth."

"I know what we're talking about, Pike. I've been living this game for four years. I share a bed with that son of a bitch," I snap.

Pike rakes his hands through his hair, exasperated, and says on a heavy breath as he leans back, "I know. God, I know. It's just, it's been such a long time. You just kinda get used to the life you're living, you know?"

"Yeah," I say softly. "I know. It's the same for me, but I guess I'm a little more distracted than you are, considering my role. But I feel it's finally happening. This is what we still want, right?"

"I promised you I would do whatever it took to make your life better. I'm not changing my mind on that. That fucker is gonna pay for what he did to your life."

Nodding my head, my smile grows at the thought of paying Bennett back for all the shit that has happened to me. For the death of my father, for all the destruction he and his parents caused. I'll revel in the only thing that will remain after Bennett is gone—money and power. Ruining Declan's life along the way to my salvation is something that's simply unavoidable if Pike and I want to keep our hands clean in this. So that's it; we move forward with the plan.

This is the moment Pike and I have been waiting years for. We take the evening to discuss plans and timing, and agree that I'll come back in a few days after Bennett leaves for Dubai. After we talk, Pike cleanses me, and then I'm back on the road. Back to gain my retribution.

twenty-two

(PRESENT)

AFTER MY MEETING with Mr. Bernstein at Chicago Magazine this afternoon, I've been working on the social piece that they want to publish next month in the February issue. The magazine is featuring a few "It" couples for their Valentine's edition, and wanted to highlight Bennett and me by having me write the piece myself. I was instructed to write about how we keep the spark alive while noting the many pots we have our fingers in, such as the charities and foundations we work with and support. Bennett seemed excited when I called him a couple hours ago to tell him about the details of the piece and my meeting with Mr. Bernstein and the editor that was assigned to me.

When I wrap up my work, I start getting ready. Declan finally caved and texted me after a mere twenty-four hours. It didn't surprise me he couldn't wait any longer. The text was short and clipped, straight to the point, and I agreed to stop by. Although I'm nervous about sex with Declan again, I try to focus my attention on other things, but it still lingers in the back of my mind. After I'm dressed, I head out and drive to Declan's place. When the elevator opens, he's already wearing a smile as he steps out, holding his key card out for me.

"Here," he says.

"What's this for?"

"To save me the hassle of having to come down here to get you every time you want to come by. Take it."

With a flirtatious smile, I say, "So, I'm a hassle?"

"You? Never."

As we ride up in the elevator, he steps in front of me, pushing me up against the mirrored wall, and kisses me. With his hands around my neck, he controls every movement of the kiss as his tongue parts my lips so that he can take more. Our bodies are pressed together, and the heat of him overcomes me, so that when he finally pulls back, I feel a little flushed.

"Missed you," he states as he looks down at me.

"Did you?"

"Always."

He takes my hand when the doors open, and I can smell food cooking in the kitchen. I follow him as he leads me to the bar and pulls out a stool for me.

"What's all this?" I ask as I take a seat.

"Dinner."

"You cook?" I ask with a smirk as he grabs a bottle of wine and begins to pour me a glass of Pinot Noir.

"Why do you look so surprised?"

Shaking my head, I take a small sip before saying, "I guess I don't really know much about you, so I'm sure there's a lot about you that'll surprise me."

He smiles at my words as he walks into the kitchen and begins chopping a few vegetables.

"What are you making us?"

"Champagne almond chicken, roasted vegetables, and new potatoes."

"Sounds amazing," I tell him as I continue to sip my wine and watch him move with ease around his kitchen. "Who taught you how to cook?"

"My mum. I can remember back to when I was little and she used to drag a chair in front of the stove for me to stand on. I would watch her and help her when she needed something stirred up. Eventually she started having me crack eggs and doing other simple tasks," he tells me as he scoops the veggies up and drops them into a steel bowl. "And as I got older, she and I would cook these elaborate meals."

"She sounds like a wonderful mom."

"She was."

"Was?" I ask, and when I do, he looks up at me, and says, "Another day," the same words he used when I asked him why he needed to control everything.

"What about you?" he asks me. "Do you like cooking?"

"I never learned."

"Your mum never taught you?" he questions.

I shake my head, knowing the truth of never having a mom, but Declan only knows of the lies I've told him about my family, so I tell him, "No. She worked a lot and wasn't around much. I do like to watch Clara cook when she comes over to prepare meals. Every now and then she lets me help out, but not often. I pretty much do what your mom allowed you to do on that chair. I only stir things and sniff around."

I watch the creases deepen at the corners of Declan's eyes when he looks at me and laughs.

"I've asked Bennett to cut back on her schedule, that I'd like to do more around the house, but he refuses. Clara has worked for him for a long time, and he likes knowing she's there."

Declan looks at me for a few moments when I stop talking, and then finally breaks the silence when he says, "Come here," and motions for me to join him.

"Why?" I ask suspiciously.

"Because I'm going to teach you how to cook, darling."

I smile, hop off the barstool, and walk over to join him. He reaches over and grabs a head of garlic, setting it on top of the chopping block, and then hands me a knife.

"I roasted that earlier. Garlic is always better when you roast it beforehand," he explains as I look at him and nod. "Peel off two cloves and then lay the knife flat on top."

I do as he says, plucking off a couple cloves. Declan stands behind me and holds his hands over mine, laying the knife flat on top of one of the cloves, and then grabbing the wrist of my other arm.

"Now, make a fist and slam it on top of the knife to mash the garlic," he instructs.

With his hand on my wrist, I make a fist and bang it down on the knife, smashing the garlic beneath.

"Perfect," he murmurs over my ear. "Do the same thing with the other clove."

He keeps his hands on mine as I repeat the process. He then helps me prepare the sauce for the chicken, toasting the almonds and chopping up the shallots and mushrooms. Once I've poured in the champagne, he helps me line the dish with the chicken and pour the sauce over top.

"Would you turn the oven on? It'll automatically set at 350, so just put it on bake."

"Okay," I say as I walk over to the oven and turn it on.

I watch Declan finish up, and when the oven beeps, he slides in the dish and sets the timer for thirty minutes.

"What are you smiling at?" he asks as he steps in front of me.

"You."

"Why's that?"

Reaching out to wrap my arms around his waist, I tell him, "I like you like this," my words coming from a place of honesty.

"Like what?" he questions as he steps even closer, running his hands through my hair and tilting my head up to him.

"Just like this. You, laid back in your jeans and t-shirt, teaching me to do something new. I like sweet Declan," I say softly as I peer up into his emerald eyes.

"You're saying I'm not always sweet?"

I begin to laugh and then respond, "Most of the time you're an asshole."

His head falls back in a burst of laughter, and the sound causes me to laugh harder. His smile is wide when he looks back down, giving my words back to me, admitting, "I like you like this too."

"I'm afraid to even ask," I tease.

"Don't ever be afraid," he says before adding, "You're soft. You don't show it often, but when you do, I like it."

His words immediately straighten my face as he runs his hand down my cheek, telling me, "I like it when you're soft with me."

"It's not easy for me."

"I know, but I want that from you."

He's oblivious to the fact that I intend on using his words to create the perfect venom to bite him with. So with a gentle nod of understanding, I slip my arms around his neck as he dips his head to kiss me. His hands grip my ass and he pulls me off the floor and into his arms. Looping my legs around him, he takes me over to the couch and sits us down with me on top of him. We continue to kiss, his taste of need spilling into my mouth. Hard, fast, soft, slow, licking, biting, sucking, it's all there in the heat of him as time falters in the moment. But we both snap our heads back when the fire alarm sets off and the smell of burning food takes center stage.

"Fuck," Declan breathes in mild amusement as he looks over my shoulder, and when I turn to see the smoke-filled kitchen, I jump off his lap and rush over to find pillowed clouds of smoke billowing from the oven.

"Shit!" I squeak out and immediately open the oven door, only to be blinded by the rushing mound of smoke.

Declan moves next to me and reaches in with oven mitts to pull out the black, charred chicken. My look of mortification for somehow ruining dinner is contrasted by his laughter, which ticks me off. He tosses the dish on top of the stove and then runs over to open a few of the sliding glass doors to air the place out and then goes to shut off the screeching smoke alarm.

"What did I do wrong?" I ask when he returns to the kitchen, and when

I see he's still laughing, I snap, "Cut the shit and stop laughing at me."

He leans over the stove, looking at the oven setting. "Shit, Nina," he chuckles.

"What?" I huff.

"You turned the oven to broil instead of bake."

Embarrassment builds inside of me, and I don't say anything as I back up to the counter behind me and stare across at the meal I incinerated.

"Well," he says when he turns to face me. "Looks like you weren't kidding when you said you couldn't cook."

"I'm so sorry, Declan."

"Don't be. It's fine," he assures, running his hands down the length of my arms.

"Stop."

"Stop what?"

"Grinning at me like that. It's embarrassing."

"Why?" he questions. "Because you're not perfect?"

I narrow my eyes at him, saying, "There are things I can cook perfectly."

"Is that so? Now you've piqued my interest."

"Out!" I demand as I start pushing against him. "I'll fix this. Just give me a few minutes."

He turns back, saying sweetly, "You don't have to fix anything. All the delivery menus are in the drawer by the fridge."

"No. You've given me something to prove to you, so I'm going to prove it," I tell him. "Just . . . get rid of the charred chicken please."

"Okay then," he chuckles, and when his dinner is disposed of, I start rummaging around the kitchen to find the few items I need.

Truth is, I was honest with him. I have no idea how to cook. Once Pike and I were on our own, we barely had enough money to pay rent in the gutter apartments we lived in. Hell, half the time we would wind up being evicted. We scraped by our whole lives, finding liquor to be a better investment than affording a safe place to live. At least when you're drunk, you can escape the realities of life.

So as I stand over the pan on the stove with a spatula in my hand, I look over my shoulder to see Declan closing the sliding doors. I'd be lying to myself if I said I wasn't attracted to him, because I am. It's a shame we couldn't have met in a different lifetime, but to dwell on the never-be's is nothing but an endless path of disappointment because this *is* the only life in which we will meet.

Plating our dinner, one of the few things I can cook, I walk over to the dining room table and set the plates down.

"Would you grab the wine?" I call out to Declan, and when he walks over to the table with the bottle, I smile up at him as he looks at his plate and laughs.

His eyes flick to mine, noting, "You look extremely proud of yourself, and I haven't even tasted it yet."

"Because I know there's no way you're not going to like it," I remark as he takes his seat and places the napkin in his lap.

"From the girl who teased me about taking her to the Over Easy Café," he says as he picks up the grilled cheese and takes a bite. I take a sip of my wine, and then he finally admits, "Best grilled cheese of my life."

We both laugh as I pick up my sandwich and begin eating with him. It's been a long time since I've felt comfortable like this. It's different with Pike, probably because he knows every disgusting piece of me, but Declan looks at me as if I'm something clean and good. It's all a lie, but for the moment, the lie makes me feel happy and maybe a little bit whole. So we sit here, in his multi-million dollar penthouse and enjoy our dinner of grilled cheese and Pinot Noir.

After dinner, I help Declan with the dishes. We clean the kitchen up, and when everything is back in place, I notice the burnt smell still lingering. Taking a lock of my hair, I sniff it while Declan watches.

"What are you doing?" he asks.

"My hair, it reeks of smoke."

"What about mine?" he says, walking over to me and ducking his head down.

Running my fingers through his thick hair, I tell him, "Yeah, yours does too."

He then takes my hand and leads me down the hall and into his bedroom. Flicking on one of the lamps, he walks us into the large bathroom, which houses a massive, marbled, doorless shower with a large, seamless pane of glass on one side. His and hers sinks line two of the walls in dark cabinetry with tailored, white, apron-front sinks. And along the wall of windows is an extra-large, sleek, rectangular jacuzzi tub that is sunken down. The room is modern and masculine, just like the rest of the loft.

Focusing back on Declan, he's running a bath, and when he turns to me, he stands in the middle of the room.

"Take off your clothes, Nina."

"A bath?" I question.

He reaches over his head, pulls off his shirt, and tosses it aside, saying,

"Yeah, a bath," as he walks over to me and grabs the hem of my top. "Lift your arms."

He removes my shirt and then slips my pants down my legs. I hold on to his shoulder as I step out, and with him knelt before me, I look at him as he slowly drags my panties down. When he has them off of me, he runs his hands up my legs to the center of my tiny V. With one hand sliding up between my legs, he splays it over my pussy and lower belly, holding it in place as he looks into my eyes. "So beautiful."

His accent fucks those two words. No one has ever looked at me the way he does, and it spurs an awkwardness inside of me because if he only knew what this body has been through, he'd be repulsed by the sight.

After we take off the rest of our clothes, he holds my hand as I step down into the tub filled with hot water. When Declan gets in, I situate myself between his legs, resting my back against his chest as I lie back into him. His arms wrap and cross around my breasts as he holds me close, and the warmth of both him and the water take me over. Releasing a heavy sigh, I close my eyes, and sink further into his hold as my body relaxes.

"Tell me what you're thinking," he murmurs from behind me.

"Mmm."

His chest vibrates in silent laughter before saying, "That's all I get? *Mmm?*"

"I'm relaxing."

He drags my hair off my one shoulder and starts kissing my damp neck, pressing his lips into my sensitive skin, causing me to shiver with goosebumps, which I know appeases him when he quietly chuckles.

We remain like this for a while, just taking in the warmth of the bath, nearly melting into each other.

"Should I be worried?" Declan says, breaking the long span of silence.

"About what?" I ask, my eyes still closed as I rest the side of my face against his chest.

"That I've been fucking you without a condom."

"I told you before, I can't get pregnant," I remind him.

He remains silent for a moment before responding, "Tell me why."

Taking in a deep breath, I shift up and slightly turn to the side so I can look at him when I say, "I have stage three endometriosis."

"I don't . . ." he begins with confusion written all over his face, so I explain, "It's basically where you have abnormal cell growth outside of the uterus. So the chances of me getting pregnant are pretty much non-existent."

"Baby, I'm . . ." he starts, shaking his head, and he's clearly more uncomfortable about it than I am. "When did you find this out?"

"In my early twenties," I tell him. "I started having painful periods around that time. They became worse and worse until the pain got so bad that I was taken to the hospital because I didn't know what else to do. They started running a bunch of tests and after a few months they finally figured out what was wrong."

"Is there anything they can do?"

"No. When you have it, you have it. There's no cure or anything."

"And the pain?" he questions with apparent concern.

"I've experimented with a few hormone treatments for pain, but the side effects were pretty bad, so I had to stop. I only take prescription pain pills, but it doesn't help that much."

He runs his fingers through my hair and then cradles his other hand to my face when he says, "God, baby, I'm sorry. I don't know what to say."

"It's fine," I try assuring him. "This isn't anything new to me. I've known this for years. It's okay."

"Do you want children?"

Shrugging my shoulders, I respond, "Does it even matter what I want? I mean, it's not like life is giving me a choice here."

"Of course it matters."

"I won't ever be a mom, so there's no point in tossing dead wishes into the air." I've done enough of that. I can remember Pike sitting next to me when the doctor told me that I wouldn't be able to have children. It was never anything I had even thought about until he told me that I couldn't. I cried for days while Pike held me. As if I was mourning the death of something that never was mine to lose. But that was over six years ago, and I've come to the realization that I'd probably be a shitty mom anyway. What would I be able to give a child? Before marrying Bennett, Pike and I survived by dealing drugs and barely scraping by. It's not a life I want, so why the hell would I want it for my kid?

"You can still be a mum, you know?" Declan says, his words coming out gently.

Not wanting to be rude and completely shut him out, I give him a weak grin and softly request, "Can we talk about something else please?"

"I'm sorry."

"It's okay. It's just not something I talk about often, so . . ."

"You don't have to say anything else," he assures before giving me a kiss and wrapping me back up in his arms.

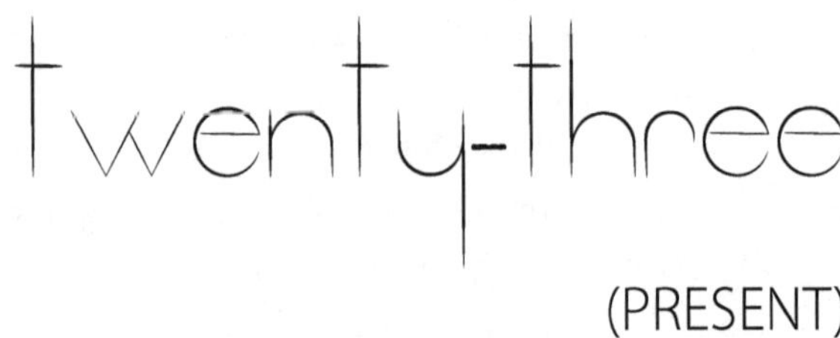

(PRESENT)

I ENDED UP leaving Declan the other night after our bath. Bennett was returning from Miami the following day and I wanted to be home in case he arrived early. I've been careful about my communication with Declan while my husband is home. We talk mostly through email because those are easily deleted unlike phone records that are logged and recorded. I would prefer to not even send emails, but Declan insists on talking to me throughout the day.

While Bennett is in the shower, I sit in the study to find that I already have an email waiting for me.

> ***FROM: D. McKinnon***
> ***TO: Nina Vanderwal***
> ***SENT: Jan. 10, 1:23pm***
> ***SUBJECT: Want You***
>
> ***When does he leave? I want to see you.***
>
> ***-D***

I quickly reply while I still hear the water running from Bennett's shower.

> ***FROM: Nina Vanderwal***
> ***TO: D. McKinnon***
> ***SENT: Jan. 10, 1:58pm***
> ***SUBJECT: Re: Want You***
> ***Some people find it polite to start with a greeting, even if***

it's as small as a simple 'Hello.' But to answer your question, he leaves around 3:30pm.

-Nina

His response is almost immediate.

FROM: D. McKinnon
TO: Nina Vanderwal
SENT: Jan. 10, 2:00pm
SUBJECT: Greeting as suggested- HELLO.

Meet me at the hotel?

-D

FROM: Nina Vanderwal
TO: D. McKinnon
SENT: Jan. 10, 2:01pm
SUBJECT: Re: Greeting as suggested- HELLO.

We need to work on your social etiquette. Greetings in the subject line are rude as well. I can be there at 4:00pm.

-Nina

FROM: D. McKinnon
TO: Nina Vanderwal
SENT: Jan. 10, 2:04pm
SUBJECT: Etiquette Reject

4:00 then. Come to my room. I'll leave an elevator key for you at the front desk.

-D

FROM: Nina Vanderwal
TO: D. McKinnon
SENT: Jan. 10, 2:05pm
SUBJECT: Cheap

Why do I feel like a prostitute or worse, a booty call?

-Nina

FROM: D. McKinnon
TO: Nina Vanderwal
SENT: Jan. 10, 2:06pm
SUBJECT: Cheap?

Booty call? What the hell is that? Regardless, you know damn well you are so much more than either of those. But I'm not going to sweeten it up for you; I need you, and I'm growing impatient and harder with each minute I don't have your body all over mine. 4:00!!

-D

I laugh at the realization that he doesn't pick up on the American slang as I delete the emails from my inbox and then delete out of my trash. Closing the laptop lid, I make my way into the bedroom where Bennett is walking out of the bathroom, covered in only a towel. I smile as I walk over to his suitcase.

"What's that smirk all about?" he questions as he approaches.

"You."

"What about me?"

"Walking around here wet, wearing only a towel, is a mean thing to do to your wife," I tease.

"Why's that?"

"Because you're leaving me for a couple of weeks, and this is the lasting vision you're giving me."

"And what about what I gave you a couple hours ago?" he says, referring to the long sex session we had earlier.

"That will give me something to think about when I'm lying in bed at night . . . lonely."

"You better call me when you're feeling lonely," he says suggestively, sparking me to laugh.

"Stop that. You need to go get ready before you start running late," I nag. "I'll finish packing for you."

"Whatever you say, boss," he jokes before kissing me chastely and then walking back into the bathroom.

I gather the rest of his things from his closet and make sure he has everything he needs packed up. Bennett and Baldwin will be in Dubai for the next two weeks, along with Richard. They will be working on hiring a team while the renovations are still underway. I shifted around Clara's schedule to allow myself more freedom to come and go without her eyes on me.

When Bennett finally comes out of the bathroom about a half hour later, I decide to give him a proper good wife farewell. Maybe it's my conscience weighing on me, or maybe it's knowing I want to keep him from getting suspicious of me, but no matter what, I need to do whatever I can to make him think that what we have together is solid. So as I walk towards him, I reach under my arm and start unzipping the side zipper of my dress. He stays put, staring at me as I stroll across the room. When I'm standing in front of him, he slips his hands under the straps on my shoulders and allows the dress to fall to the floor around my feet.

"I just want you," I tell him, "One more time before you go."

"However many times you need, I'll give it to you."

And he does. Maybe I'm overcompensating, but I feel it's needed as we lose all track of time. Once I've led him to believe that I'm fully sated, we pull ourselves together and regroup. I take a glance at the clock to see it's already four and that I should be at Declan's hotel. When Baldwin walks in to help Bennett with his luggage, I grab my coat from the closet and slip it on.

"Where are you headed?" Bennett asks, and I quickly lie, "I told Marcia I would meet her for a coffee when you left. But now you've made me late," I flirt with a wink.

"I believe you made *me* late, Mrs. Vanderwal."

"Are you complaining?"

"Not at all, and please feel free to make me even later if it suits you."

I catch Baldwin smiling as he overhears our conversation and turn to Bennett, accusing, "You're a perv."

"Only for you," he laughs. "I'm going to miss you."

We say our goodbyes on the elevator down to the lobby. Bennett seems genuinely sad to be leaving me while I'm anxious to get to Declan, knowing

I'm running really late. I keep it hidden though as I take my time playing the loving wife who's already missing her husband who hasn't even left yet. But when he does, and we exchange our gentle kisses, Bennett walks out to the car where Baldwin is waiting and I head down to the parking garage.

When I arrive at Lotus, I leave my car with the valet before walking in and picking up the keycard Declan left for me at the front desk. As I step out onto the top floor, I use the keycard to let myself in to Declan's penthouse room.

"Where the fuck have you been?" he immediately shouts when I walk in, and the gravel in his voice startles me.

"I'm sorry."

"Where have you been for the past hour?"

He stands across the room as he barks his words at me. Wearing a tailored suit and tie, he looks powerful in his firm stance, and his narrowed eyes and clamped jaw are evidence that he's beyond pissed.

"Declan, I'm sorry," I say softly. "Bennett was running late and didn't leave until now. I got here as soon as I could."

He begins to make his way over to me, hands clenched in fists to his sides, stating, "I don't like not knowing where you are. You say four o'clock, you better be in front of me at four o'clock."

I open my mouth to speak, but nothing comes out. If I argue, I'm just gonna piss him off even more. His hand comes out to grip me under my chin. With his face hovering over mine, he admits, "I was worried something happened to you."

"I'm s-sorry," I breathe.

Dropping his forehead to mine, he closes his eyes for a moment as he takes in a deep intake of air through his nose. My body jumps when his fingers suddenly pierce into my jaw, and I can feel every bit of tension in his body as he opens his eyes and takes a small step back with my face still in his grip. His eyes are venomous, causing my heart to pound as a small whimper sounds from my throat.

"His smell is all over you," he seethes in disgust.

"I-I . . ."

"Did you fuck him before you came here?" his voice grinds out from his clenched jaw, but I don't lie when I whisper on a shaky breath, "Yes."

His hand falls from my chin as he looks at me in pure anger.

"On the bed," he barks. "And take that fucking dress off, I don't want to smell him when I'm fucking you."

"Declan, please."

"Get on the fucking bed! NOW!"

The bite to his words has me in a panic, worrying about what he's going to do, but I don't hesitate when I start moving across the room and into the bedroom. Quickly removing my dress, I sit on the edge of the bed and wait in the darkness for Declan. It takes him a while, but eventually he appears in the doorway. His shirt is now off, and his slacks hang on his hips with his belt clutched in one hand. The sour taste of bile burns the back of my throat, and I close my eyes, begging, "Declan, please."

"Don't talk, Nina."

I keep my eyes closed out of fear and urge on the disconnect, willing the fire of revenge to consume me so Declan won't have this power over me. I know he's right in front of me; I can feel the heat of him soaking into my skin.

"I'm not stupid to think you wouldn't have sex with that man, but I expect you to come to me clean, do you understand?"

With a quick nod of my head, he snaps, "Answer me!"

"Yes."

"Open your eyes, and answer me."

When I open my eyes, I notice the strained muscles in his arms and shoulders as I murmur, "Yes."

"Were you trying to make me jealous?"

"No," I quickly blurt out in defense. "I didn't . . . I didn't think, Declan. I'm sorry."

He moves to sit down next to me, saying, "I'm going to punish you now. Not because I want to hurt you, but because I don't want you to forget."

"Please," I say as I shake my head, and when he looks at me, it's dejection that I see in his eyes.

"I don't ever want to smell him on you again."

"I promise."

"Lay your chest across my lap," he instructs in an even voice.

I reach my hand over, placing it on his knee, giving it a soft squeeze, before obeying his request and laying myself across his thighs. When I close my eyes, I hear the clank of his metal belt buckle as it hits the floor, and in a few movements, he takes his tie out of his pants pocket, and wraps my wrists in the cool silk, knotting the fabric tightly.

His hand begins to caress my exposed ass in nothing but a lace thong, and then his hand is gone. Tensing up, I wait for the impending strike, and when it finally comes in a merciless slap against my flesh, I yelp out in a bleeding squeal as the pain radiates through my skin.

In the next second comes another vicious blow as he grunts with force.

And another.

Another.

Smack.

Smack.

Smack.

"Aaagh," I cry out in fiery pain. The sting of his firm hand hitting me chokes me up with each punishing slap. My arms strain against his silk tie, and his hands grab my hips, throwing me forcefully on my back, landing in the center of the bed. Smiling cagily at me, exultant in debasing me. Like a raging animal, he rips my panties down my legs, forces my thighs open, and strikes my pussy with an excruciating slap.

I scream out in pain as tears spring to my eyes. His soft tongue is immediately on my now burning flesh, licking me in a slow lap over my seam. The contrast of his touches has a maniacal effect on me, evoking vulnerable whimpers. I feel everything he's doing, but I'm also outside of my body, no longer in control of any part of me. Emotions take over—fear, pleasure, pain, satisfaction, sadness, comfort. They conflict and collide in a volatile war inside of me, taking me over as I fall powerless to Declan, lying here as he kisses and licks through my folds the same way he does my mouth. He then slips his hand under my back, finding my hand and holding it tightly as my mind begins to swirl in a kaleidoscope of colors and lights, and I give in to the goodness of it all, losing myself as he wraps his mouth around the sensitive bundle of nerves while he pumps his finger inside of me.

To ward off the pleasure in his touch is a doomed feat as I lie here, restrained, weak to everything he's giving me until I feel the wet heat between my legs as I crash into fragments of pure warmth as it trills through my core and down my limbs. A glittering fire sparking inside of my veins, taking my body captive as I writhe under his touch, our hands clenched together.

All I can think in this moment is that this man is obscene.

He doesn't give me a chance to gather all the pieces he just broke me into when he jerks me up and pushes me to sit on my heels as he stands on his knees before me. Fisting my hair in each of his hands, he yanks my head back, looks down at me, demanding, "Suck my cock with that sweet mouth of yours," before forcing my head down, but I take him willingly into my mouth. He doesn't give me any control as he tugs my hair, bobbing me up and down the length of him. I begin to fight his demanding ways, pushing my head back against his hands, wanting to move more slowly, but he's much stronger than me with my hands bound behind my back.

"Don't fight me, Nina," he grunts, but I want to. I want to fight him and he feels it, yelling in scolding grit, "Yield to me!"

But I don't and he pulls my hair harder, biting on his sulfurous voice, "Yield to it. Trust me, baby."

The whisper of his pleading demands seep out through the cracks of his words. He doesn't know I hear it, but I do, and something about it makes me turn it over to him, giving him the control he so desperately needs for some reason. He moves me along the heat of his large cock as I let my tongue glide along the silky smooth flesh. The sounds spurring from him are nothing but primal lust, and when I feel him thicken in my mouth, he throws me back on the bed, straddles his knees on either side of me, pulling off a couple of hard pumps, right before he shoots his cum onto my stomach and tits. His eyes are pinned to mine as he spreads himself on me while he continues to jerk himself off. I watch him—he's beautifully brutal with his merciless touch.

He keeps my arms tied behind me as he lies down next to me and pulls me into his hold, hugging me against his strong body. I'm completely vulnerable to him, naked and restrained, but I'm not scared. He punished me, yes, but he'd never really hurt me. He keeps telling me to trust him, and I can at least trust knowing that I'm safe with him, so with my hands bound, my body goes limp, molding to his as he holds on to me.

We lie there together, his cum drying on my skin, as he combs his fingers through my hair, saying, "I only want to smell myself on you," before he reaches behind me and unknots his tie.

As soon as my hands are free, I sling my arms around his neck, needing the comfort and not quite knowing how to react after what just happened between us. He cradles the back of my head, pressing his lips to my ear, whispering, "I've got you, darling." And when I nod my head against his as I cling to him, he strengthens his hold on me as he breathes into my skin, "I adore you."

My emotions are all over the place, and I don't know what to do with the feelings that overcome me. It's a sickening delight. I hate that he enjoys this with me, that he looks at me the way he does. But I really hate that I can't escape with him. He doesn't allow me that freedom and it scares the shit out of me. My heart continues to race as I lie here, and he feels it, keeping me close to him and giving me a soft, "Shhh," in my ear. He holds me in his arms in a nurturing way, but Declan is far more primal than nurturing, yet somehow he's able to blur those lines in moments like this.

"I missed you," he eventually tells me.

"I missed you too," I sigh. "But he's gone, so I'm all yours."

"I don't just want you to be mine when he's gone, Nina. I want it all the time."

"It's complicated, but I'm here with you, and I just want you now. No Bennett, please," I urge.

Declan moves to kiss me, keeping his touches soft and affectionate, as we slowly move together. And with his lips against mine, he mumbles, "How are you feeling? Did I hurt you?"

"No."

"I need you to know that I will always protect you," he says, his words reminiscent of my father's when I was younger, and when I pull away to look in Declan's eyes, I can see the truth behind them.

"I know," I tell him. "Trust comes hard for me, but I'm trying."

"Love that."

I smile at my manipulations as they come so easily with him. It's like I don't even have to think or try; I just speak and he's putty in my hands. Eventually we fall asleep before waking a couple hours later. Declan orders up some food, and I lie, telling him that I need to be home because Bennett wanted to video chat later and he would know if I wasn't at our place. Declan is frustrated but we agree that we will get together tomorrow and spend these next two weeks together as much as possible. Truth is, I have to go to Pike tonight.

Before I leave, Declan installs an app on my cell phone that will allow us to text without anything being tracked by phone records. His possessive ways make me laugh, but I'm curious to know why he is the way that he is.

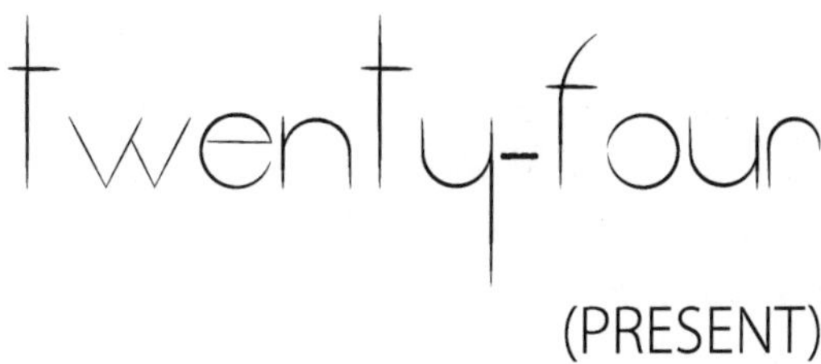

twenty-four

(PRESENT)

IT'S NEARING MIDNIGHT and my stomach is in knots when I pull up to Pike's trailer. I turn the car off and sit for a moment; the sounds of the sharp wind blowing over the snow-covered ground fill the silence. My nerves keep multiplying the longer I sit here. I've known that this day would eventually come, but the realness that it's finally here pangs in my gut.

When I get out of the car and walk inside the trailer, Pike doesn't say a word when he comes over to me. My face is stone as I stand there.

"Hey," he says in a gentle voice.

"Hey."

"So . . .?"

"So . . ." I begin and then tell him with a nod, "This is it."

"Are you sure?"

"Yes."

Pike places his hands hesitantly along my jaw, asking, "So we're doing this?"

"Yes." My voice trembles, but I muster up my strength, resisting all the emotions I feel swarming around the two of us.

"Are you scared?"

I nod my head, giving him my honest answer through my hardened façade, and he nods along with me, letting me know I'm not alone, but we both know it's up to me to pull this off.

"Don't be scared. Remember what we're doing this for," he tells me, his eyes burning with intensity. "This is for your father. This is for you and everything you were stripped of. You wanted a new life; we're almost there, Elizabeth. Can you taste it? The fairytale?"

"Yeah," I breathe.

"So we fight the monsters first," he says and then softly presses his lips to mine, and when he pulls away, I slip off my coat and toss it aside before looking up at Pike, swallowing hard, telling him, "I'm ready."

"Say it again."

"I'm ready."

"Close your eyes," he instructs, and I do.

I stand here and feel the warmth of Pike's hand brush down the side of my cheek as he whispers to me, "This is for you," before taking his comforting hand away.

My heart crashes inside my chest as I wait, and then it comes, Pike's hard fist barreling into the side of my face and over my eye. A blast of pain singeing across my cheek and down my nose as my body collapses to the floor. Pike then grabs ahold of my wrist, moving my hand that's covering my eye away from my face and hammers down another powerful fist across my cheek. My screams are strained as I cry them out, and Pike instantly covers my body with his, holding me in his arms and cradling my head against his chest as I cry in agony. My face is hot, tingling as I feel the immediate swelling.

Pike continues to hold me, rocking me back and forth, reminding me over and over why we are doing this, but he doesn't need to convince me; I know why I'm doing this. As my tears dry, the pounding of an oncoming headache dulls out the piercing throbs down my face.

I don't even need to say anything when Pike picks me up off the floor and carries me to his bed.

"I'll be right back," he says and then walks out of the room, only to return a few moments later with a glass of water and two Tylenol. "Here. Take these."

Swallowing the pills, I set the glass down and lay my head back on the pillows.

"How bad does it hurt?" Pike asks.

"I have a really bad headache."

"Your eye?"

"It all hurts, but it's okay. I don't want you to feel bad or apologize," I tell him as he lies down next to me. "How does it look?" I ask.

He reaches out to touch the tender skin, and I flinch back at the pain.

"Sorry," he mutters. "It's really swollen and pink right now. It's starting to bruise. You'll have a nasty black eye for sure by the time you wake up tomorrow."

I nod and can't help the evil smile that creeps along my lips and then turns into laughter. Pike hesitates before allowing his smile to appear, and when I see it, I roll onto my back as my laughter grows louder. Clutching my belly, I feel deranged, like somehow I'm on top of the world, celebrating our devilish game, and basking in the glory of my growing black eye.

The past few years have been spent bonding a marriage to look like nothing other than a happy couple who is completely devoted and in love with one another. It seemed as if getting to this point of destruction would never come, but here it is in the grasp of our fingertips. And now the emotions of stress, loneliness, doubt, and determination come to fruition as they spill out of me in this crazy display of morbid laughter.

When we start to calm down and compose ourselves, I roll over to face Pike, asking, "Am I crazy?"

"Aren't we all a little crazy?"

Smiling, I say, "A simple *no* would suffice."

"No."

I straighten my expression, and when Pike turns his head to look at me, I remind him, "I love you."

"I know you do."

"No," I say. "You've never wavered on me. After all these years, you've always been my constant, from the moment we met when I was eight years old. You're the best brother anyone could ever have, and I really love you."

Turning on his side, his fingers feather along my swollen cheekbone as he leans in and kisses me, running his tongue along my bottom lip. I pull him in closer, tangling my legs with his as he shifts on top of me. We begin to undress each other, and I'm ready to take what only Pike has been able to give me. Moving my naked body with his, I reach down to grab his hardened dick and then guide it inside of me. And finally, I'm able to escape from everything around me.

WAKING UP IN my bed the next morning, the side of my face throbs in heated rhythm with my heartbeat. I haven't put ice on it to help with the swelling because I need it to look as bad as possible. I know Pike felt like shit last night after hitting me the way he did—the way he had to—but I tried assuring him that I'm okay.

As I walk across the room and into the bathroom, I look at my reflection in the mirror. Pike was right, there's a nasty black and blue bruise around my eye and along the crest of my cheek. I reach up to touch the swollen flesh and wince. The bruise is tender and the side of my face looks horrific.

It's perfect.

I go ahead and take a quick shower and get dressed, slipping on a pair of jeans and a long cashmere sweater, dabbing on just a light touch of powder and lipgloss. The chime of my phone comes as I expected with Declan's text.

Miss you.

I type my response.

Miss you too.

Come to my place. I need to touch you.

My devious smile grows while I type out my next text.

I can't. I'm not feeling well.

You okay?

Just sick.

I'll come pick you up and bring you here.

He responds just as I predicted, so I continue to goad him to me with my replies.

Thanks, but I'm just going to stay here today.

You avoiding me?

No. I just don't feel good.

Then let me take care of you.

As I'm typing out my next text, the phone begins ringing in my hand, displaying Declan's name on the screen.

"Why are you calling me?" I ask when I answer.

"Why are you avoiding me?"

"I'm not. I told you; I'm not feeling well."

"So instead of lying in your bed, lie in my bed. I'm coming to pick you up. Pack a bag," he insists in a calm tone, but I resist, telling him, "Declan, no."

He lets go of a sigh and then questions, "What's going on?"

I pause, and with an uneven voice, lacking confidence, I murmur, "Nothing. Just . . . just nothing."

"You're lying to me."

"Declan, please."

"I'm on my way," he snaps, hanging up before I can respond.

He'll be here shortly, and I've no time to waste getting excited. I have to look the part, so I focus my attention on the one thing that always destroys me—my dad. I sit on one of the couches in the living room, stare out at the grey, snow-filled day, and let my mind drift to him, to my childhood, to everything that hurts me. I think about pink daisies, and the feel of my father's whiskers poking me with his kisses. And then I think about the first time I went to his grave, coming face to face with the reality that he was really dead.

After a while, I'm not even thinking about Declan. I'm solely consumed with pain and sadness as I cry into my hands. My throat knots as the misery takes over, but the jerk of reality comes when the house phone rings, and I know Declan is here.

"Hello?" I say when I answer the call.

"Mrs. Vanderwal, this is Manuel. I have a Mr. McKinnon here to see you."

"Um, yes. Go ahead and send him up, please."

"Will do. Good day, miss."

I hang up the phone as a few more tears seep out, and I let them linger on my skin as I wait for the knock, and when it comes, I look at my splotchy face, bloodshot eyes, and bruises in the hallway mirror before walking over, ducking my head down, and slowly inching the door open, saying, "Declan, you shouldn't be here."

"Let me in, Nina."

Turning my face away from him, I walk into the living room as he follows from behind.

"What's going on?" he questions, and when I don't respond, he grabs my arm and turns me around. "Fucking Christ," he says with a horrified look on his face when he sees my black eye. "What the hell happened?"

Covering my face with my hands, I begin to cry again. It's easy to do with my current state of mind. He doesn't miss a beat when he pulls me into his arms and holds me while I quietly weep, wetting his shirt with my tears.

"Darling, what happened?"

"Bennett was here when I got home last night," I lie.

Gripping my shoulders, he pulls away to look down at me, his eyes filled with venom when he asks, "He did this?"

The tears drip off my chin, and I slowly nod as I watch his face turn to pure rage, his grip on my arms tightening.

"I'm gonna fucking kill that bastard," he growls. "Go pack your bags. You're coming with me."

"Declan—"

"Now, Nina. I can't even fuckin' think straight. Go pack your shit. You're not staying here," he snaps, and I don't say anything else when I turn to walk into my bedroom and to my closet. I begin to quickly pack my bags, and as I walk back out, Declan is pacing the room. When he looks up at me, he rushes over, takes the bags out of my hands, and tucks me under his arm.

"Where's your coat?" he quietly asks, and when I point to the foyer closet, he wastes no time. He pulls out my coat, slips it over my arms, and then hands me my purse. I quickly put my sunglasses on before we walk out the door.

He doesn't speak as we take the elevator down and head outside to his car. He tosses the bags in the trunk and then we are on our way to his place. His grip on the steering wheel is firm, knuckles white, muscles flexed. With his focus on the road, I watch his jaw clenching as he grinds his teeth.

When we finally make it to his place, his silence remains as we walk into his loft. With my hand in his, he leads me back to his bedroom. Tossing my bags onto the floor, he sits me down on his bed and gently removes my sunglasses. His eyes look over my face, examining my swollen cheek and black eye. I flinch when he touches it, and he whispers a quick apology before reaffirming, "I'm serious, Nina. I want to kill him for doing this to you."

"It's not that bad," I mumble as I drop my head.

"Have you fuckin' seen your face?! It's pretty fuckin' bad!" He takes a moment and a few deep breaths before softening his voice, "I'm sorry. I don't want to yell at you. Just . . . Why don't you lie down? I'll be right back, okay?"

"Okay."

Declan leaves the room, and when he returns with an ice pack, he takes a seat next to me on the bed where I'm lying down and gently places it over the side of my face. Wincing at the contact, I close my eyes and place my hand over his as he holds it in place.

"Tell me what happened," he whispers as he looks down at me.

"When I got home last night, he was there. I had told him that I was spending the afternoon with a friend, but he found out I was lying and delayed his flight until early this morning," I explain, and when a few tears seep out and roll down my temples, I continue, "He was mad, and just . . ."

"Hit you?"

I nod, and he asks, "He's done this before?"

When I nod again I see the muscles in his neck strain. Sitting up, I lean back against the headboard and begin to cry, telling him, "I'm so scared, Declan. If he ever found out about us, I don't—"

"He won't find out," he jumps in.

"He could."

"He won't."

"He's not what people think."

"How long has this been going on?" he asks.

"Shortly after we married. It didn't start out so bad, but now . . ."

"Come here," he says as he shifts to my side and drapes his arm around me, drawing me into his hold. He kisses the top of my head before saying, "I can't let you go back to him."

"I have to."

"You don't have to do anything, Nina."

"It's not that simple. I'm terrified of what he'll do because he's capable of anything," I tell him as the remaining tears roll down my face. "This black eye is minor compared to . . ."

"To what? Christ, Nina, it looks like someone beat the shit out of you with a fucking bat. You have no idea what I want to do to that fucker right now. Just thinking about him having his hands on you is paralyzing."

The rage in his voice is unyielding, and his eyes are dilated in fury.

"I'm sorry. I didn't want you to see—"

"*You*? The *real* you?" He closes his eyes for a second, pinching the bridge of his nose, and then looks at me with sincerity. "Don't ever hide from me. Not a single goddamn thing."

I don't respond, but he isn't waiting for me to when he wraps his arm around my waist and shifts us down into the sheets. My eyes close as he drops delicate kisses on my battered cheek and over my eye. With his lips against my skin, he breathes his words, saying, "It kills me to know this about you."

"I don't want you to hurt for me."

"I'll always hurt for you. I *want* to hurt for you, to take it away from you so that I can bear it for the both of us," he whispers and then seals his lips with mine in a passionate kiss. But he can't take my pain away. Nobody can. Pike tries, but it never lasts longer than a brief moment. My pain is threaded within the fibers of my existence. Here to stay. A reminder that we all come in different forms of decrepit.

Declan drags his lips away from mine, saying, "Open your eyes."

Blinking them open, I stare up into his green emeralds when he tells me, "Leave him."

"It's not that simple."

"Leave him."

"It's not easy like that," I say, needing him to understand that I can't just walk away, but he moves past my words, telling me, "I don't want easy. I want *you*."

"I . . ."

"Tell me what you feel for me," he says as he parts my legs and settles himself between my thighs.

"I don't know if there's a word for it, because it's strong, but it can't be love."

"Why not?" he says, his cock growing harder with each word spoken.

"Because I've only known you a couple of months. It's crazy to think about how much I already feel for you. I feel crazy for having the feelings I have for you."

"Why?"

"Because I hardly know you."

"You know me," he states as he rocks his hips, pressing his erection into me.

"Do I?"

"I adore you. Do you need to know anything else?"

My breathing grows unsteady as he continues to grind himself against me.

"Open up to me. Tell me how you feel. Give me the words," he insists.

"I don't know," I release on a staggered voice.

"You do. You're just scared."

"Let me be scared then," I request, but he turns it down, saying, "I won't ever let you be scared, baby."

He reaches back and pulls off his shirt before sitting on his haunches and telling me, "Undo my pants."

Sitting up, I slip the leather strap of his belt out of the buckle, and unzip his slacks. He watches me as I reach my hand inside of his boxers and take his stiff cock in my hand, curving my fingers around the thick shaft. Without taking our eyes away from each other, I begin to stroke along the velvet smooth skin sheathing his rock hard erection. When his breathing begins to falter, he grabs ahold of the end of his belt and pulls it free from his pants.

"Take your hands off me and put them above your head."

I lie down on my back and place my hands where I was told. He pulls my top off and unclasps my bra, tossing it to the floor before lacing his belt through the slats in the headboard, tying my wrists together, and securing them in an unrelenting bind.

"Tell me how you feel right now."

As we look deeply into each other, I reveal softly, "Safe," and there's a part of me that doesn't believe that word is a lie.

"Say it again."

"Safe."

Leaning down, he brushes his soft lips along my bruises. "Always." He then begins running his warm lips down between my breasts, taking them both in his hands when he peers up to me. "Always safe with me."

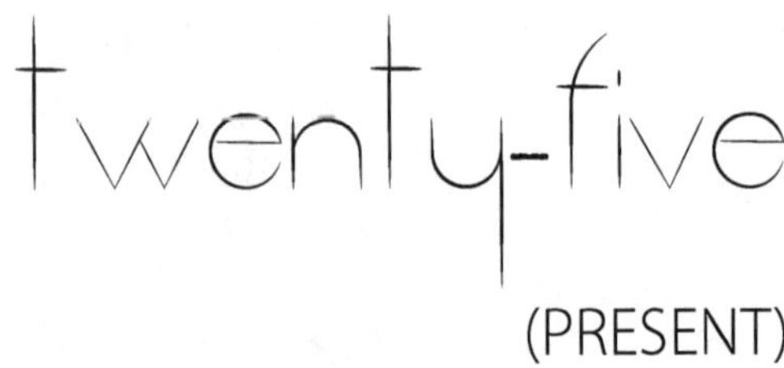

twenty-five

(PRESENT)

THE SHOCK OF cold touching my skin jolts me awake.

"It's just me, darling," Declan soothes as he presses an ice pack to my cheek. "I didn't want to wake you, but your bruises look to be swelling."

I stare up at him as he takes care of me and just watch as he examines my face.

"You okay?"

"Sleepy," I mumble as I move to sit up.

Declan releases a soft growl when the sheet drops to my waist, exposing my naked breasts.

"You're obscene," I tease with a grin and then pull the sheet up to cover me, but he yanks it away.

"Don't cover yourself; you're too beautiful."

"What about you? You expect me to be naked while you're fully clothed?" I argue weakly with a smile.

Dropping the ice pack onto the pillow, he stands beside the bed and looks down at me, saying, "You want me naked?" and when I nod, biting my lip, he tells me, "Then undress me."

"Now, not only are you obscene, but obnoxious."

"You love it," he states with a devious smirk.

"Mmm . . . maybe."

"Say it. Tell me you love it," he urges.

"No," I squeak out in laughter, and with a stern tone, he retorts, "Don't ever tell me no."

"No," I repeat with a flirty wink.

He crawls back into bed and over the top of me with a sexy growl. "Bad girl."

"I thought I was a good girl?"

"Only when you listen well," he responds as he lies next to me. "Come closer. Wrap yourself on me."

And I do, rolling over, draping my arm across his chest and wrapping my leg around him as he bands his arms around me.

"You feel so good like this," he releases on a heavy sigh.

"Like what?"

"Covering me like you want me."

"You think I want you?"

"I can't seem to figure out what you want," he exhales. "I hate that you won't let me inside your head."

I don't respond to his statement as we continue to hold each other, and after a while, he breaks the silence, saying, "Why do you hide yourself from me?"

"Does it look like I'm hiding from you?" I tease with a grin as I lie here naked.

With a straight face, he lays his hand over my heart and says, "You're hiding *this* from me."

"How do you know that?"

"Because I can see glimpses of it at times. Of whatever pain is inside. Do you ever let yourself feel that? The pain?"

"Why would anyone want to feel pain?" I whisper. "Showing that exposes vulnerability, and vulnerability is your soul's weakness."

"People are weak, Nina. It's just fact."

"I don't want to be weak."

"You're only human," he says. "You bleed like everyone else, but you hide it."

"And what about you? You like to control nearly every facet of your life. You wouldn't do that if you weren't attempting to bury something."

"You're right," he willingly admits. "I need control to deal with pain, but trust me when I tell you this, I *feel* that pain. I can temper it, but it's always there." And then he hits my one tender spot when he asks, "You miss your parents?" and everything inside of me runs towards my dad.

"Yeah," I whisper on a pained breath as I feel my father's presence ache inside of my chest. And when the tears prick and my nose tingles, I close my eyes.

Declan sees right through me though. "Open your eyes."

But I don't.

I keep them closed, saying with honesty, "You want me to show you my pain, but I don't know how to do that," and when I open my eyes, the tears spill out.

"You're doing it right now."

Pointing at my dampened cheeks, I state, "This is weakness."

With his hands cradling my head, he contradicts my words, saying, "This . . . this is strength," before licking the salt of my pain.

I hold on to his wrists as he rests his head against mine in this soft moment. I feel like I use Declan so much for this, for this comfort I've never really had before. He gives it in a way that's different from Pike, and it feels good. Peaceful. I know my time is limited with Declan, so I might as well take what I can while I have him.

And in an unusual reaction for me, I reach down to the hem of his shirt and lift it up, peeling it away and dropping it to the floor. He takes my face in his large hands again and holds me still as he looks down at me, and I swear he can see inside of me.

I begin to unbutton his pants, and when he's finally naked with me, he drops his head to my chest, grazing the stubble of his jaw lightly over my nipple. The friction is replaced with the smooth softness of his tongue. I feel it between my legs when he sucks the pert bud into his mouth as he continues to caress me with his tongue.

His touches are soft, not like his usual display of dominance over me, and in this moment, I need the softness. So as I nestle my fingers into his thick hair, I move his head to look up at me and breathe, "Don't tie me up. Not this time."

He's never *not* restrained me or been forceful in his touch, so when he gives me a nod, I'm a bit surprised. This is the first time he's allowed me to touch him during sex, and in this moment of uncharacteristic fragility, I let my hands wander along the deep cut lines of his muscular body as it hovers over mine. We move at a relaxed pace, his hand skimming over every curve of my body.

When he positions himself between my legs, he holds his cock in his hand and runs the head of it up through my folds to my clit and slowly back down, saying, "I'm gonna make your heart beat," as he pushes himself inside of me, filling me entirely as my eyes fall shut.

He fucks me with slow, deepening strokes. There's no friction, no tension. It's just the two of us moving in this tender rhythm.

"Open your eyes. Connect with me."

I do, and he never takes his focus away from me. He's never felt so real as he does right now, in this very moment. The collusion on my part festers guilt inside of me, but it shouldn't. I shouldn't be this live wire that I am right now, gripping on to the broad knots of muscle that run along his arms. I shouldn't be feeling the pleasure that he's slowly building to fruition inside of me. I shouldn't be allowing him to do this to me, allowing me to do this to myself. It's too ripe, too much life.

I'm getting lost between reality and fantasy, and I need to pull pack. I didn't think Declan would be able to drive me so high like he's doing, moving as slowly as he is, so I close my eyes in a weak attempt to fight it away. To fight away the foreign emotions that are brewing inside.

You will not feel.

You will not feel.

You will not feel.

"Oh, God," I moan without any filter of control.

"Let yourself go with me," he urges when he takes my hand in his, lacing his fingers with mine as I begin to tremble into a shattering explosion of colorless light.

Clinging my free arm around him, he never lets go of my hand. Holding him tightly against me, my body writhes and bows up into his as I ride out the wave of ecstasy, coming hard around his cock. When I look up at him, I see the grimace in his face as he continues to move inside of me and then pulls out.

"What are you doing?" I ask, knowing he didn't come.

He lies on top of me, bracing himself on his elbows with his face over mine.

"Why?" I breathe out on an uneven whisper.

"Because that was for you."

Don't let yourself feel.

Don't let yourself feel.

My cycle of words slowly dies inside of my tightening chest. The thickness of my throat makes it hard and painful to breathe, and I know he sees it when he gently squeezes my hand that he's still holding and says, "Don't hide. If you need to cry, it's okay."

Immediately, with his words, the liquid heat fills my eyes, blurring my vision of his face into a prismatic swirling of watercolors before they finally spill out and run down the sides of my face. He rolls us to our sides, never letting go of my hand, as I quietly weep into the warmth of his skin.

We stay in bed for most of the morning. Declan cooks us a late breakfast while I take a shower and get ready. The smell of eggs is in the air when I walk into the living area and over to Declan who's standing over the stove.

"Smells good," I say as I slide up next to him and watch as he folds the egg of the omelet over a mixture of tomatoes and spinach.

"You hungry?"

"Starved," I answer before he leans down to give me a kiss filled with eagerness as his tongue invades my mouth. He doesn't stop fucking my mouth with his until the scent of burning egg wafts through the air.

"Fuck," he says, pulling the pan off the stove and onto the unlit burner, making me laugh as I move over and start opening and closing cabinets. "What are you looking for?"

"A mug."

He walks over, opening the door to one of the cabinets and pulls down a mug for me, saying, "There's coffee in the French press," as he nods to the glass carafe on the counter.

"Thanks, but I prefer tea in the mornings."

He smiles, and then gets the kettle on for me. While I wait for it to boil, I spot my purse lying on the foyer table, and when I pull my cell out, I have two missed calls from Bennett. When I look at the time, I count the hours and realize that it's a little after eight in the evening for him. It's not like me to miss his calls, but with this new turn of events, my mind has been elsewhere.

Knowing I have to call him and check in, I walk back over to the kitchen with my cell in my hand.

"I need to make a call. Would you mind if I stepped out?" I ask gently, careful not to rock the boat too much.

But he doesn't give it a second thought when he responds, "Of course. My office is down that hall across the room," as he points in the opposite direction of where his bedroom is.

"Thanks. I won't be too long."

Walking into his office, it's nearly as large as his massive bedroom, with rich, wooden bookshelves that line the back wall and up to the ceiling. His desk sits in the middle of the room. A dignified piece of mahogany accented by a large, leather chair with antique brass nailhead trim. I don't sit at his desk, perching instead on the tufted black leather Chesterfield sofa that sits over by the bookshelves. I take in the musk of rich leather and look around. Everything in this room is covered in Declan's masculinity.

I quickly swipe the screen of my phone and call Bennett. He picks up, immediately saying, "Honey, I've been worried."

"I'm so sorry. My phone was on silent and in my purse."

"What have you been doing all morning?"

"Writing. I've been working on that article," I lie. "Seems I'm not a natural. I've been cooped up in the office and lost track of time. I'm sorry I missed your call and made you worry."

"I don't want you to apologize. It's fine. I just miss you, that's all," he says sweetly, not even questioning my deceit. Knowing how fooled I have both of these men makes me smile, and I play into the good feelings, returning the sweetness, "I miss you too. Tell me about your day."

"I had to fire a couple men on the project. It's been stressful."

"What happened?"

"Deadlines weren't being met by the contractor, oversights to code specifications, and other issues I'd rather not discuss right now," he explains, the note of frustration and exhaustion evident in his voice.

"I wish I was there. I'm sorry you had such a rough day. Is there anything I can do on my end to help you with anything?"

"Just tell me how much you love me."

"Bennett . . ." I say, leaving his name lingering between us.

"What, honey?" he murmurs softly.

"I miss you, and I love you so much. I hate it when you're not here, when I don't have you next to me. It's . . ." I trail off when I realize Declan is standing in the double door entry to the room. His scowl is murderous as he glares at me from across the room, causing my spine to straighten as I sit up. He's irate, there's no doubt, but I'm playing my ace at this point. To one man, I'm his loving and devoted wife. And to the other, I'm an abused woman who's trapped in a marriage to a terribly violent and powerful man.

Bennett pulls me back to him when he picks up my lost words and questions, "It's what, honey?"

With my eyes on Declan, I answer my husband, "It's lonely," and my words aren't taken well by Declan as I watch his jaw grind and then set.

"I feel it too," he responds as I drop my head to avoid Declan's scowl.

Needing to end the call before Declan loses his shit on me, I say, "Honey, can we talk later?"

"Yeah, no problem. I'm actually in the car with Baldwin. We are meeting the project manager and one of his architects for dinner."

"Okay, well, I hope you have a good evening. I'll call you later tonight before I go to bed."

"I love you."

With my head still down, I return his words, "I love you too, Bennett."

When I hang up, I slowly raise my eyes to see Declan walking towards me. He stands in front of me as I look up at him, but he doesn't sit, he just exudes his authority while staring down at me, jaw still locked.

"Dec—"

"Don't talk," he snaps, cutting me off, but I don't take his order when I state softy, "He's still my husband."

"And those words you said to him?"

"They're just words," I whisper in a mock cowardly tone.

"You miss him?" he asks, keeping his words clipped and tight.

"No."

"You love him?"

"No."

"Are you lonely?"

"No," I tell him firmly.

His tension looms as he stands here, unmoving as time passes in silence. He eventually breaks it when his rough voice admits, "I want to punish you for calling that dickfuck in my home, but . . ."

His voice trails as he closes his eyes and puffs out a hard breath through his nose, his lips pressed firmly together. I give him a moment and then he slowly shakes his head as he drops down to his knees in front of me. His hands grip my hips and his head falls to my knees before he looks up, but he isn't looking into my eyes; he's looking at my bruises.

I open my mouth to speak at the same time he does, but I let him go first.

"You have no idea how hard it is for me to keep my shit under control, knowing what's going on. And then finding you in here, talking to *him* . . . I wanna throw my fist into the fucking wall." He takes his hand and cups the side of my tender face. "But then I look at this," he says, referring to the bruises, "and I'm afraid I'll scare you."

"I don't scare that easily," I breathe.

"I think you lie about that. I think you want me to believe that. Maybe even *you* want to believe that, but it's all a lie. It's you . . . trying to convince yourself."

I take a hard swallow, nervous, that even through all my shit, he seems to read me pretty damn well. As much as I want to deny what he's saying, if you cut me deep enough, I believe there's truth to how he sees me. I hate that about him.

"I want you," he states matter-of-factly, and I nod. "I can't refute my feelings, even though a part of me wants to because I know I can't have you, but I want you. I want to have you, I want you mine, I want to own you."

Closing my eyes, I rest my forehead against his as my body slacks forward. Declan holds me, adding, "I want all of you, and it fucking hurts to know I can't have that. But I don't want to stay away from you either."

"I don't know what to do because . . ."

"What, baby?"

I draw my head back slightly to look at him when I explain, "There's a reason we got married so quickly. I didn't see it at the time, but . . . shortly after we were married I saw his obsession with me." I urge on the emotion when I feel the constricting of my throat. My words strain as I say, "He'll never let me go. And if he knew about you, he'd ruin you. He's powerful enough to do that."

"Let him ruin me."

"But it's me," I tell him on shaky words.

He peers his worried eyes into me, and I choke back a faint whimper, when he asks, "What are you afraid of?"

I take a pause before finally speaking the words that bring a flare of protectiveness to his eyes.

"He'll kill me."

twenty-six

(PRESENT)

DECLAN WAS BEYOND furious about me coming back home yesterday. I've spent the better part of the last two weeks staying at his place, only coming home a couple of times when I knew Clara would be here. I made my case to him though, making it clear that it has to be this way and that Bennett could never know about us. Spending as much time together as we have been, I see Declan falling hard for me. He's honest about how he feels about me and us and makes no apologies about it. For a man who exercises his power and authority, not only with me but with nearly everyone I see him come in contact with, he masks a vulnerability that I can see him trying to hide.

The bruises on my face were pretty much nonexistent when Bennett arrived home this morning. We spent hours in bed together, making up for the two weeks he was away. He wasn't happy when I had to leave to drop off my article that I was able to finish on the days Declan went to work, leaving me with nothing but time while I hid out at his place. It's not like I could really go out with my face looking as bad as it did. But Bennett understood, and even suggested that I take a little time for myself since he was starting to feel the jet lag of the nine-hour time difference from Dubai.

While Bennett's at home, Baldwin takes me over to North Michigan Avenue where I spend most of the day strolling in and out of the various stores, doing some much-needed shopping. I stop by Neiman's to pick out a few dress shirts for Bennett and a couple of ties. Before calling Baldwin to return with the car, I decide to make one last stop. Bearing the single digit temperatures outside, I loop my scarf a couple of times around my neck and head down to La Perla.

I learned while staying with Declan that he has an affinity for lingerie. Since I need to continue to draw him in deeper, I'll do whatever I can. When

I walk in, my stomach instantly rumbles. Being in stores like this makes me feel dirty and gross. Always has. I know I have a fucked up sense of sexuality; I'm not blind to the effects my childhood has on me. Just thinking about adorning a body that I find repulsive—a body that has no value to me—disgusts me. But this isn't for me or my liking, it's for Declan's.

Browsing through the insanely expensive selection of silks and laces, I pick out a few silk culottes that are embellished with hand-embroidered lace. For as kinky as Declan is in the bedroom, he prefers when I wear things delicate and feminine, so I'm sure he'll like these French knickers. I add a few pairs of lace panties and bras before a sales lady approaches, offering, "Would you like for me to start you a fitting room?"

"No. I'd like to go ahead and purchase these," I tell her, feeling like I need to get out of here before my mounting nausea suffocates me.

After I make my purchases and shove the ivory bag down into my larger Neiman's one, I text Baldwin for the car and tell him to meet me at the Starbucks that's down the street. The last thing I need is for him to know I was buying lingerie.

Baldwin is noticeably quiet as he drives the few minutes it takes to get back home. When I get off the elevator, I'm surprised to see Jacqueline with her baby on her hip walking through my living room.

"Jacqueline, what a pleasant surprise," I greet as she approaches me with Bennett striding along behind her.

"Well, Richard would rather sleep and let me take care of his business than doing it himself," she says, and when Bennett kisses my cheek and takes the shopping bags from my hands, he explains, "I needed to sign off on a few files Richard had that need to be faxed off ASAP."

"I see," I mumble, and then turn to Jacqueline and her son. "He's growing fast."

"I know. It's amazing, isn't it?"

"I suppose," I respond, not caring to discuss the charms of motherhood.

"Well, I better get going. Richard is going to be hungry when he wakes, so . . ."

That guy is such a lazy bastard. Always has been. He treats Jacqueline more as a servant to his needs than a wife. Pitiful woman puts up with it too, but that's her choice.

"It's a shame you can't stay longer. I've been so tied up lately, but we should see about a lunch date," I say, pretending I truly care about our plastic friendship.

"That sounds great. I'll call you," she replies and then looks to Bennett, saying, "I'm sorry Richard couldn't come himself."

"No worries, Jacqueline. We will see you later," he says as he walks her to the door to see her out.

They exchange goodbyes and then Bennett is back to me, taking me in his arms. "Did you have a good time shopping?"

"I did. Have you been working this whole time?"

"No. She just stopped by a few minutes ago," he tells me. "I took a short nap and unpacked."

"You? Unpacked?" I tease. "I'm impressed."

"So little faith in me," he responds with laughter and then dips his head to kiss me. "By the way, Cal made a call to my office while I was gone. Seems he heard about the refitting in Dubai and is curious about investment options."

"Oh," I remark, wondering if Declan knows his father is interested in investing with Bennett's company.

"He wants a meeting, but isn't able to get out of New York because of his tight schedule, so I'm going to fly out there for a few days. I want you to come with me."

"Of course. When would that be?"

"In a couple of weeks. I have to run back down to Miami for a few days beforehand."

"Miami?" I question, letting him see my frustration. "I didn't see that on your schedule."

"The realtor called while you were shopping. We finally came to negotiations on the property sale."

"Finally."

Bennett has a number of properties, a beachfront in Miami being one of them. He's had it for years, but since I've known him, he's never used it. Although he travels there for business, he stays in hotels since the house is out of the way.

"So . . . New York?"

Smiling, I respond, "Sounds perfect. Hopefully it's not all business; I'd like to be able to have some time with just you."

"I'll make sure of it, but for now, I've made reservations for dinner tonight."

"I better go get cleaned up then. I think I'll go soak in a hot bath for a while."

"Want company?" he asks in a smooth tone, and I nod before kissing his jaw.

We spend the rest of the day together, and after an extravagant meal, we head home and it isn't long before Bennett crashes from not only the rich food, but the time change as well. I lie there in bed next to him and simply stare. I faintly remember him as a child. His face is clear to me only because I've seen plenty of his childhood pictures at his parents' house.

He sleeps peacefully as I recall playing with him in my backyard. I don't remember much, but he used to push me on my swing set. I would tell him to push me higher, push me into the clouds, and he would give me a giant push and then run under the swing as I went up. One time he didn't make it, and I came crashing down on him. He said it didn't hurt him, but I could tell that it did.

We were never good friends, just neighbors who would sometimes play together if we were both outside at the same time. He was older and already in elementary school. Soon after I started kindergarten, I was taken away and never saw him again. That was until Pike found him several years ago. When I saw him again, he had just turned thirty. Nothing about him looked the same to me, not until his mother showed me some old photo albums. That's when I started remembering more of our time together as young kids.

And now I lie here, thinking about the part he played in the nightmare that became my life and the hate begins to fester. I want to kill him. But more than that, I want to make him suffer. I want to yell and scream, tell him who I really am. Tell him how he ruined my life, and how because of him, my father is now dead. I want him to know the destruction he caused for opening his foolish mouth. It takes a lot of effort not to clench my fist right now and beat the living fuck out of his face.

Suddenly, a muted glow casts along the ceiling and I turn my head to see there's a notification on my cell phone. Rolling over, I look to see Declan has sent me a text. I grab the phone and quietly slip out of bed to make my way to the other side of the apartment and into the office before reading his text.

Miss you.

I sit down at the desk and type back.

Same here.

Are you okay? I can't stop worrying about you. I fucking hate it.

I'm fine. You don't need to worry about me.

Don't ever tell me not to worry.

When I notice it's after two in the morning, I respond.

Why are you up so late?

I told you. I can't stop thinking about you and if you're okay. I got used to having you in my bed and now all I can picture is you lying next to him.

I don't know what to say. What do you want me to say?

That you feel what I feel.

I do.

Tell me.

I _____ you.

What does that mean?

There's not a single word I can think of that could properly describe how I feel about you, but I feel it and it's powerful.

So you _____ me, huh?

Yeah.

I _____ you too. I want to see you. Tomorrow.

Okay. I can get away during the day.

Come to 31st Street Harbor. Dock-K. Slip-47.

You have a boat?

Yes. What time can you be there?

10am.

10am. Don't be late.

I shake my head at his need for control and grin as I message him back.

Trust me, I won't. My ass and pussy are both still mad at you.

Ass, maybe, but there is no way your pussy could still be mad with the number of orgasms I have given it since.

You think so?

I know so. I'm getting hard just thinking about your divine pussy wrapped snug around my cock.

His crass words come as no surprise to me. Declan has a filthy mouth that he's let loose a few times. He's so blunt and honest in bed, never feeling the need to be modest with his words in any fashion.

Mmmm.

I'm serious. I have to control my thoughts because as soon as I think about you I get rock hard.

I'll be sure to take extra special care of you tomorrow. I can't have you walking around like that. The women already stare at you as it is, fantasizing about riding that cock.

Nobody is riding this but you.

I laugh and give him a taste of his possessive words and type my response.

MY cock!

Fuck. You're killing me. I'm going to bury it so deep inside of you tomorrow.

I'm not going to want to let you go. I already miss you terribly.

Love that. My girl.

Your girl.

It takes him a while to respond as I sit here in the darkened room until he finally sends his next text.

Did you fuck him today?

Declan, you can't ask me that.

Make sure you're clean and don't fuck him before you come see me tomorrow.

His request makes his jealousy crystal clear. I'll tell him whatever makes him feel better, but I won't stop fucking Bennett. I have to keep my charade up with him too.

Please don't treat me like that.

I'm serious. I'll lose my shit if I smell him on you.

You won't. Now stop being a dick and be nice to me.

Getting feisty?

I shake my head with a smile.

Always feisty.

I know. We need to work on that.

I'm not subservient!!!

You could be. ;)

Now you're just trying to get a rise out of me. I get your little game, McK-

innon. Push me till I defy you so that you can get your jollies by 'teaching me a lesson.'

You've got me all figured out, don't you?

Does that bother you? That I can read you?

No. I love that you can read me. Now I just have to figure out how to read you.

Hmm. . .Maybe I like being a mystery.

I think we both know that I can see past your walls pretty well. Hide all you want, darling, but I'll always find you.

You think so?

I know so. When I want something, I do what it takes to get it.

So, McKinnon, tell me. What is it that you want?

You. You already know that, but I like that you asked me anyway just so you could get the affirmation you were apparently seeking, which tells me all I need to know.

And what's that?

That you want me too.

Possibly.

Don't be coy. You don't need to play that game with me because you already have my full interest. I get that you're scared, but you don't need to be with me.

You sure about that?

There's no doubt. What about you?

I take a moment and think about how I want to respond to his question. I don't want to be too blunt and just say *yes*.

I'm afraid.

Of what?

Afraid that you'll hurt me.

Never.

Don't say never because you're very capable.

If you're afraid, I'll hold you.

And what if I freak out?

I'll hold you tighter.

It's now that I realize I have a huge smile splayed across my face that has been there for most of this conversation. Regardless of the truth as to what is going on, Declan is fun to talk to. He always has been. Despite the evil I'm playing and the lies I've told him, I feel like I have a friend. I'm playing him just as I am with Bennett, but I despise Bennett whereas Declan was never a person I had any disparaging feelings towards. The only fault is that he's the unlucky bastard that fell for me.

You better have a good grip.

No one will ever hold you tighter.

I could stay up all night talking to you, but I have a date tomorrow morning that I cannot be late for.

Why's that?

This time, I opt for sweet words over the flirty, tart ones I typically use with him.

He tends to worry about me when I run late. He gets upset. But I really like this guy, so I want to be sure that I'm rested and on time so that he knows I care about him enough to not cause him worry.

I adore you.

I ____ you.

10am?

10am. Night.

Night, darling.

When I make my way back into the bedroom, Bennett is still in the same position, sound asleep. It only takes a second for my ill feelings to return, so when I slip into bed, I roll to the side so I don't have to look at him. And with my thoughts returning to the conversation I just had with Declan, I quickly ease myself to sleep.

twenty-seven

(PRESENT)

"DID YOU HAVE any trouble finding it?" Declan asks as I step aboard his luxury performance yacht.

"Dock K. Slip 47. Just where you said she'd be," I say with a shiver as the biting wind gusts off the water.

"Let's go inside."

I follow Declan into the saloon that's fitted with a white, linen sofa and chairs that surround a large, wooden table.

"Quick tour?" he suggests as he takes my hand, and I give him an agreeing smile as he leads me through the galley and down the stairs. After showing me the starboard cabin and en-suite, along with the guest cabin and bathroom, he leads me down to the owner's stateroom and master en-suite. The room is sleek with rich, cherry wood, a small seating area to the side, and a large bed in the center.

Declan doesn't waste a second when he turns me in his arms and kisses me. Relaxing into the kiss, I let him move me to his liking, and when he finally pulls his tongue out of my mouth, I grin.

"What's so funny?"

With jest, I say, "No conversation?"

Running his hands possessively down my neck and over my tits, he squeezes them in his hands before responding, "We'll talk after I've had my cock inside you."

He then grabs my hips, lifts me up, and tosses me on the bed. He climbs on top of me and between my legs with a breathy groan as I grab his face and kiss him again. Our lips crash, and we're a blur of quick moving hands, fumbling off each other's clothes. When he slips my shift dress over my head, tossing it aside, I know my shopping trip was worth it when his eyes flare as he takes in my French knickers and matching bra.

With both of us up on our knees, he pauses as his eyes roam over me, taking me in. It's awkward to have a man look at me the way Declan does, with intense want and desire.

"Do you have any idea how beautiful you are?" he says softly, taking his hands and slowly running them down my ribs and stopping on my hips where he gently tugs the silk of my panties.

"Stop," I whisper, wanting to deny his words.

"Stop what?"

"When you say things like that . . ." I start, dropping my head to break the intense eye contact, "it makes me uncomfortable." I look back up into his eyes, adding, "I don't know how to respond."

"I don't need any response, darling. But you shouldn't be uncomfortable, not with me. I love looking at you. I love the way you look naked, your flawless, milky skin," he says as he starts to slowly move his hands over me. "Your perfect tits," he continues, unclasping my bra and slipping it down my arms. "Your pink nipples. It fucking makes me so hard when I see them tighten up just for me." And then he covers my one bud with his mouth, sucking it in and swirling his tongue around before moving over to my other breast to do the same.

I run my fingers through his silky hair, and he lays me back. He begins to lightly trail the tips of his fingers down, over the swell of my breasts, and along the very sensitive skin of my abdomen, sending a shiver up my body.

"And then there's this," he says smooth and low as he hooks his fingers under the waist of my panties and slips them off. "Open your legs for me."

I do, spreading them apart and exposing my bare pussy to him. As he watches me, he releases a guttural moan. He sits between my legs, and with his hands on my knees, taking in the sight of me, he says, "Touch yourself."

Wetting my finger in my mouth, I keep my eyes on him as I reach down and slip it between my lips, dragging my slick arousal up to my clit and begin rubbing slow circles. I watch as Declan's eyes dilate in molten, black lust. He shifts to remove his bottoms and then moves back between my bent knees before he takes himself in his hand and begins pumping his thick cock over me. The sight alone causes me to grow even wetter, which surprises me. I've always struggled in the past, but with Declan it's different. My body always responds to him, even when I try to fight it.

"Dip your finger inside and give me a taste," he demands, and I do, sinking my finger inside the heat of my pussy and then reaching up to offer it to him. He grabs ahold of my wrist and lowers his head, sucking my finger into his mouth. "Fuck, I need you."

He leans over and grabs his discarded necktie.

"Do you trust me?" he asks as he looks down at me and I give him a nod.

I'm used to Declan's need to restrain and control me. There's only been that one time we had sex when I asked him not to that he didn't, but that's been the only time.

"Say it."

"I trust you, Declan," I tell him as he wraps the tie around my head, covering my eyes in a makeshift blindfold.

"Lift your head," he whispers and then knots it in place, leaving me in darkness.

It's now that I feel my heart begin to race. After spending most of my childhood locked in a darkened closet, I have been claustrophobic. I hear movement, and feel Declan getting off the bed, only to return a few seconds later.

"I'm going to tie you up, okay?" he says and I can feel the heat of his body above me as I lie here. He takes my hands and holds them together as I feel a prickly, coarse rope being looped around my wrists. As he continues to secure my wrists and tie me to the headboard, he tells me, "This is a natural fiber rope. It's all I have, so if you fight the restraint you'll hurt yourself. Understand?"

"Yes," I respond and when he's done I try adjusting my wrists, only to have the coarse fibers poke into my skin.

"I'll be right back," he says and then the bed shifts, followed by the click of the door closing.

He's gone, and the darkness begins to consume me. The only noise I can hear is the lapping of the water against the boat. My wrists begin to rub against the brittle rope as I shift around. My breathing picks up, but soon becomes labored with my increasing heartbeat. Suddenly, I feel the room caving in on me, swallowing me up as the air grows thick. I plant my feet flat on the bed; I can't seem to sit still anymore. And then I smell it. That familiar smell of Carl's cigarettes.

"Declan?" I murmur, but all I hear now is the muffled TV on the other side of the closet door. Confusion begins to swarm, and my head grows unbearably turbulent with the increasing smell of cigarettes.

Fear and confusion take over when I realize I'm naked. Carl has never locked me up naked before, and I begin jerking my hands, trying to break free. My entire body goes numb and tingly as I start thrashing around, desperate to find light and escape. Nothing feels real as my head floats, and I hear the echoes of screaming. The pressure of the walls caving in on me is so heavy, collapsing on my chest. I struggle to breathe, yanking and jerking, doing everything I can in my sheer panic to get loose.

Someone grabs my hands, and light filters in. Opening my eyes, I realize the pressure on my chest is a man and the screams are coming from me. Tugging my arms violently to get away, I shriek, "Let me go!"

"Hold still, Nina. Calm down."

Who the fuck is Nina and who is this guy? Where am I? Where's Carl?

"Get off me!" I wail through my burning screams. As soon as my arms are free, I bolt, leaping quickly off the bed only to be tackled down.

"Nina, breathe!" the man shouts as he pins me in his grip. I struggle to fight my way off of his lap, but he keeps his firm hold on me from behind.

"Let go!"

"Breathe, baby. Please, just breathe."

He holds me tight as he continues to talk, slowly bringing me back into my body. The fog in my head filters out, and I begin to remember where I am. Finding my way out of the tunnel I felt I was just in, reality appears, and I realize I must have been hallucinating. The pounding of my heart shakes me, and when I look down, I'm covered in blood, sparking another spike of panic.

"Oh my God." My trembling voice is barely audible.

"It's okay, baby. You're okay," Declan soothes.

"There's blood."

"Shhh, baby. It's okay," he whispers. "Just breathe with me."

I slack into his arms, my back snug against his front, and focus on the rise and fall of his chest as I try to parallel my breathing with his. After a few moments, he lays me down as he sits over me.

I lie here, embarrassed about what just happened and the fact that Declan saw it. He reaches over to pull a blanket up, covering my exposed body. His eyes are heavy with worry as he looks over me. He takes my wrists in his hands, and that's when I notice the source of all the blood.

"We should clean you up." His words come out gentle. "There's a first aid kit in the bathroom," he tells me, and when I nod, he gets up to retrieve it.

I sit up, leaning my back against the headboard, wondering what the hell just happened. I used to have panic attacks like that back when I was a teenager, after I had run away. But that was so long ago. I feel numb, like I'm in a daze. Declan will surely question me about this, but I'm too disoriented to even stress about it.

He returns, sitting in front of me, and starts cleaning the blood from my hands and arms with a warm towel.

"Does it hurt?" he asks and I keep my focus on his hands as they tend to my abrasions.

I give a shake of my head, not wanting to speak right now, as he continues to clean and then bandage the cuts with a little gauze. Once he's done, he sets everything aside and moves to sit next to me, cradling me against his chest.

He holds me for a few minutes before asking, "What happened?"

"I'm sorry."

"Fuck, I'm the one who needs to be apologizing, not you. I should have never left you alone like that."

"Where did you go?" I ask.

"To lock the door out to the cockpit," he tells me, and then draws back to look down at me, running his hand through my hair, combing it back. "Tell me why you panicked."

Taking a deep breath, I decide to just be honest with him aside from a few details. "I'm claustrophobic. I guess with the blindfold and not being able to move, I just . . . I felt like I was suffocating."

"You looked at me as if you didn't know who I was though."

I close my eyes and sink back into his chest. "I don't know. I felt like I was hallucinating."

He kisses the top of my head, and when I look up at him, he plants another kiss on my forehead. The scruff on his face pricks my skin, and for a split second, it feels like my father. I close my eyes again, overwhelmed with the emotions that keep stacking up on me, and freely reveal, "Your stubble reminds me of my dad."

He cuddles me up tighter as words start to fall from my lips without much thought as I tell him, "He used to always kiss my forehead the same way you do." A few moments pass before I add, "I like that you do that."

"Were the two of you close?"

The tightening of my throat makes it hurt to speak when I simply breathe out a trembling, "Yeah."

I choke back the tears that threaten as he rests his cheek on the top of my head. Time is idle between us, and when I feel the wave of sadness creep away, I finally ask Declan, "Why do you do it?"

"Do what?"

"Tie me up. Have you always done that to women?"

He moves his head from mine when I look up to see his face. He gives a nod and then turns his eyes to me.

"Why?"

"Control."

"Will you talk to me about it?" I quietly ask, and his vulnerable words take me back when he admits, "I've never talked to anyone about it before."

"Why not?"

"Because it's painful." And I can see it written in the lines of his face.

I run my hand along his jaw, urging him to look at me when I ask, "Do you think you could tell me? Help me understand you better."

The green in his eyes is bright, brighter than usual, a sign of the unshed tears that threaten him.

"Come closer to me," he says and I do, nuzzling my head in the dip of the center of his chest. I listen to his heartbeat for a few seconds before he starts to speak. "My father used to travel a lot when I was younger. He always made sure I knew I was the man of the house and that it was my job as a man to take care of my mum. I always did. When I was fifteen, my dad had come here to the States on business. My mother was in the den, reading, while I was watching a movie in my parents' room. The door was open, so I was able to see her curled up in my father's old, leather chair he liked so much. She would always complain about how hideous it looked, but when he'd leave, it's where she would always sit and read. She loved it but for some reason got a kick out of nagging my father about it."

I laugh under my breath, and murmur, "Funny."

"She was," he responds. "She had so much life in her and never let the stresses get her down." He takes a pause, and I can feel the muscles in his arms flex around me before he continues. "That night, I had fallen asleep on their bed when I heard a loud commotion that woke me up. My mother's screams were terrifying, and when I lifted my head to look out into the den, I saw a man with a gun pointed to her head."

That was the last thing I ever expected him to say, and when I look up, his jaw grinds down. Declan lowers his head to look at me, and I see the shame in his eyes as he says, "I was a coward."

Shaking my head, I ask, "Why?"

"Because when I saw that gun, I crawled and hid under the bed."

"Declan . . ."

"I could still see them though. My mum was crying and begging for her life while I did nothing to protect her. I didn't even try to help her," he reveals as tears rim his eyes. "I just laid there like a pussy, too scared to move, and watched as that man pulled the trigger and shot my mother in the head."

"Jesus."

Declan's face is tight as he tries to keep his pain under control, but the glimmer of a tear finds its way down his face. I reach up and run my thumb along the wet trail as he watches me, and then out of nowhere, I feel the heat of my own tear as it falls. I realize in that moment that we share a similar pain. Both of our parents were murdered, taken away from us, and we never had a choice in the matter.

"I'm so sorry," my heart whispers, because I genuinely feel his ache.

"That was my mum," his voice cracks, "and I did nothing."

"You were just a kid."

He shakes his head, unwilling to accept that as an excuse, and I know enough to realize that no one would be able to convince him otherwise, so I don't try.

"My father blames me for her death. He always has."

"That's ridiculous."

"Is it?"

"Yes," I state firmly. "What if you had run to protect her and you were the one who got shot? Your mother would have suffered, mourning the loss of her only child. It's a morbid thought, I know, but which would you prefer? A life of mourning or a quick death?"

He cradles my face in his hands, and I see his throat flex as he takes a hard swallow before he finally speaks, his voice holding only notes of seriousness, "I need control. I need to know that I hold the power so that nothing happens without my say. And with you, I've never felt like I needed that control more."

I slip my hands over his as they remain on my face. "Things are going to happen, Declan. That's the shit part of life, that we don't get a say in anything." The reality of these words prick at my heart, knowing the ugly truth all too well. "The world will never ask us what we want. It doesn't care what we want. Bad things are going to happen, but it'll never stop this world from spinning. And what happened to your mother . . . that had nothing to do with you."

"I can rationalize that, but it feels like a lie," he tells me.

"And what about your dad?"

"He reminds me every chance he gets that I'll never be enough. That I failed as a man. So I've spent my whole life busting my ass to prove him wrong. But you were right."

"About what?"

"What you said at the hotel that night. That I hate the name that owns me. You're right. The fact that I fell right into my father's business and didn't create my own success, it's just another piece of arson for him to use on me."

"But Lotus is all yours. Your father doesn't have a hand in it," I remind him.

"He doesn't need his hand in it to own entitlement. It shares the McKinnon name."

"I need to tell you something," I say, wanting him to be privy to the information I just found out about his dad. "Your father is looking to possibly invest with my husband's company. Bennett is going to New York to meet with him and I'm going too."

"When?"

"Later next week."

I can tell that he's pissed with the idea of mixing business with Bennett, and understandably so. He pulls me into his arms, tucking my head under his chin as he sits back, and lets go of a heavy sigh. "I want you far away from that man," he grits.

"I know, but I also know him and what he's capable of."

His arms are tense around me as I nestle my head against his hard chest. "It fucking kills me to sit at home and wonder if he's laying a hand on you. Do you have any idea what that does to me? I feel like a worthless bastard for sending you back to him."

"Don't. You're not."

He takes my hand and pulls it up to his lips and kisses the bandage around my wrist, before looking at me, saying, "I'm a bastard for *this*."

"I should have told you when you blindfolded me that I was feeling panicky."

"I need you to always be honest with me, especially during sex. It worries me that I could be hurting you."

When I nod my head, he leans down and gives me a tender kiss, sucking gently on my bottom lip before pulling away. He keeps his head close, nose against mine, and with my eyes still closed, he breathes in a low rasp, "I love you."

The tremolo of my heart excites me, to know that he's feeling this way, but it also hurts, because he's become someone I like. I hate that I'm about to destroy this person for my own benefit, but it needs to be done. I almost feel guilty knowing that he's having these feelings for me that I don't share, but that's part of the game. That's part of revenge. I've never felt bad for Bennett, but Declan is a good guy. It's a shame that I have to do this to him, but I do.

I open my eyes and look into his, running my fingers behind his neck and up into his hair, giving the sentiment in return, only mine is laced in candied poison when I say, “I love you too.”

twenty-eight

(PRESENT)

THE ABRASIONS ON my wrists healed quickly. Luckily Bennett had left for Miami the morning after my freak out, so I was able to hide my wrists from him for that one night by simply wearing one of his long-sleeved t-shirts and telling him that I was feeling sick. We always have sex before he goes out of town, but because he thought I wasn't feeling well, I was able to keep the scabs hidden from him as we just cuddled together in bed.

I spent the few days he was gone with Declan. He continues to grow closer to me, opening up more and telling me about what it was like for him to grow up after his mother had died. His father treated him like a piece of shit, always belittling him, giving him a sense of worthlessness that he now overcompensates for in his aggressions.

I've met Cal on several occasions and have always thought him bastardly. But with everything Declan has told me, it makes my stomach turn knowing that I have to put on my good graces while in his company tonight. We arrived in New York two days ago, and even though Bennett has had a couple meetings with him, I haven't been present.

Tonight, Cal has invited us to his home for dinner. So while Bennett was in meetings today, I spent my time shopping for a new dress to wear this evening. Nothing fancy, just a feminine, navy shift dress with a lace overlay that I have paired with nude pumps. Bennett looks his usual, wearing a tailored suit and tie, and when the door opens, a woman who can't be much older than me greets us.

"Welcome," she says warmly, looking polished in her ivory slacks and purple, silk top, the color making me cringe. Her raven hair is pulled back into a bun at the nape of her neck. "You must be Bennett and Nina. Thank you for joining us for dinner. Cal speaks highly of the both of you. I'm Camilla, by the way."

Bennett shakes her hand and greets her with a kiss on the cheek before she extends her hand to me, which I take in a polite shake as we exchange pleasantries.

"This is a lovely home, Camilla," I remark as we step into the foyer.

"Thank you. We just finished a remodel. For the past few months we've been living in a construction site," she says in playful displeasure.

I snicker at her mock exasperation, and she turns to me with a smile and adds, "You have no idea how many filthy ass cracks I had to look at during the process."

We both laugh at her crass words as she leads us through the impressive house.

"Cal, the Vanderwals are here," she announces as we walk into a large home office which looks to double as a library as well, but I immediately stumble when I see Declan standing next to his father in front of the large, wood-burning fireplace.

"Bennett," Cal calls out as he walks over to us, but my eyes remain locked on Declan.

What the fuck is he doing here?

My neck heats in anxiety, almost instantly, as I stand arm in arm with my husband. Declan's eyes are dark as he looks at me with Bennett, and I give him the best *"What the hell are you doing here?"* look I can muster without drawing attention to myself.

"Nina," Cal greets, snapping me out of my nonverbal exchange with his son, and when I turn my attention to the silver-haired man, I smile.

"Mr. McKinnon, it's so good to see you again. It's been far too long."

"Enough formalities. Call me Cal and do an old man a favor," he says, opening his arms to me for an embrace. As I give him a hug, I look over his shoulder to Declan who is taking a long sip out of his brandy glass. When Cal draws back with a pleased grin, he looks to Bennett, saying, "You're one lucky man."

"I couldn't agree with you more," Bennett remarks. "She's stunning."

My eyes turn to Declan as my husband speaks his doting words. His face has a hard set to it as he begins to walk over, and in a powerful tone, he speaks to Bennett with his eyes remaining on me, "Entirely stunning. Yet somehow she married you."

I narrow my eyes at him before he looks to Bennett. His jealousy, if he doesn't get it under wraps, could ignite danger in this delicate situation, but Bennett takes it as manly banter and responds, "Indeed. Maybe it was a moment of weakness when she said yes to my proposal, which is why we married within months. I couldn't risk losing her when she finally came to her senses."

As awkward as it is, I have to keep the jig up as his wife, so I turn to him, laughing in false amusement, giving him a taste of the sass he enjoys so much. "Please, I had already figured you for another helpless man in need of a woman's influence before we ever said our 'I do's.'"

"And yet you still married me," he laughs.

"Smart woman," Cal boasts.

"And why's that?" I ask slyly.

"Well," he starts as he steps towards Bennett, clapping his hand on to my husband's shoulder, "most men only strive to be half of what he has become, and they still fail. I can only admire a man who works hard for everything he has. No handouts taken."

I note the underlying passive aggressive statement. That he's implying Declan is of the latter. His remark irritates me, and the need to speak up and defend the guy I feel is becoming a friend of mine pangs at me, so I snap in haste, "If nobody took those handouts, Cal, then everything would simply be left to die. Is that what you want to see? The death of everything you've worked so hard for? Or rather, you could take pride in the person who gives a shit enough to step in to ensure your dream continues to thrive. Seems you've got priorities a tad misappropriated and you should start respecting those that don't follow in your macho *do-for-yourself* attitude."

The look on Cal's face is of priceless shock that I would speak so bluntly to him. The two of us just look at each other when Bennett finally speaks. "Honey—"

"Don't," I snap, interrupting him. "Don't defend his way of thinking. It's sophomoric."

"You'll have to excuse her. She's a feisty one," he remarks, trying to lighten the tension I just created.

When I look over to Declan, the air suddenly feels a little too thick to breathe.

"I can appreciate fire," Cal responds, giving me a wink, which irks me.

"Camilla," I say, turning my attention to her while she stands stoically at Cal's side, keeping a tight lip this whole time. "Could you show me to the powder room?"

After she gives me directions to the restroom, I excuse myself from the group for a much needed breather. Closing the door behind me, I lean against it and drop my head. I'm not sure what I was thinking, making a fool out of myself back there for a guy that's nothing more than a con to me.

"He's more than a con," the voice inside my head tells me. But the fact is, no matter how I identify with Declan, he is, at the end of the day, a con that I'm working. The fact that I can relate to him on certain levels isn't ideal, but it doesn't change the bottom line either. I need to pull my shit together, be the loving wife right now, and deal with Declan later. Preferably back in Chicago.

The turning of the door handle against my back causes me to startle and jump away.

"What the hell are you doing?" I seethe under my breath when Declan steps in, closing and locking the door behind him. "Why are you even here?"

He completely ignores my questioning and starts on his own, asking, "Why do you look at him like you do?"

"What?"

We keep our voices to a minimal whisper even though we are both hostile with inflection.

"The way you look at him, Nina. Don't fucking pretend with me."

"Declan, let me make this clear. He's. My. Husband."

He steps forward, caging me against the wall with his hands, eyes menacing, as he hisses through his Scottish brogue that's growing heavier the more irate he becomes, "Don't feed me shit right now. Tell me, how can you look at him like you do? That cocksucker fucking hits you."

"Because if I treat him like shit, what the hell do you think is going to be my punishment?" And in my moment of rage, I spit out my next words, "I'll give you a hint, the same thing you do when you punish me."

And the dreadful look of remorse that takes over his face makes me instantly regret saying that. For implying that Declan would be a man of such a vile nature.

"I'm sorry," I quickly recant, softening my tone. "I didn't mean th—"

He covers my mouth with his hand, stopping my words, and I feel like shit for what I just inferred. He's never touched me out of hate. I know Declan honestly cares about me, and I care about him. So when guilt fills his eyes, I grab his wrist and pull his hand away, whispering, "That was unjust. You're nothing like him. I know that. I was just caught up and angry."

"You're right."

"No, Declan. I'm wrong. You punish me out of love. It's not the same. I'm sorry I implied it was," I tell him. "You don't hurt me like he does. With him, it's nothing but fear, but with you . . . when I'm with you, it's the only time I ever truly feel safe."

"My mind is fucking with me here. Especially when I see the way you look at him. When I see the way he touches you. Do you have any idea what that shit does to me when all I want is *you*?"

Taking his face in my hands, I affirm with fervor, "I love you, Declan. You. Not him. He's not a choice for me, you are."

"Say it again."

"I love you," I lie. "Only you."

"This can't last forever, you know? Me on the side while I sit at home knowing you're fucking that piece of shit."

"I know. But right now . . . Declan, he's in the other room. We have to go back. We can talk about this back in Chicago. He leaves for Dubai in a couple days."

His lips collide with mine, taking me in an instant, filling my mouth with his tongue. He's urgent and needy, hands on my tits, groping them firmly. I grip his shoulders when he presses his hips into me.

"You feel that? What you do to me?"

"Yes," I breathe as he grinds his erection against me.

"Hike it up," he demands, and I quickly grab the hem of my dress, pulling it up as he swiftly undoes his pants. With his hands firmly on my ass, he hoists me up against the wall, reaches between us, and yanks my panties to the side before thrusting his cock urgently inside of me. "So wet, baby. Always ready for me," he grunts, and the truth of his words hurts as I wonder why my body betrays me like it does for him.

His overwhelming aura has my mind losing focus as he pounds into me, a beautifully brutal display of his love. With my arms tightly wrapped around his shoulders, I hang on, burying my head in the crook of his neck while he fucks me mercilessly against the wall. The small room is filled with our labored breaths and the familiar smell of our sex.

This is Declan's arcane display of his primal need to mark me before sending me back to my husband. He's possessive and makes no apologies about it.

"Put your fingers in my mouth and then touch yourself," he instructs and I do, pushing two of my fingers past his lips so he can wet them for me before I slip my hand between us and start rubbing my already slick bundle of nerves.

"Ohh, God," I exhale.

"That's it. Make yourself cream all over my cock."

"Declan . . ."

"Do it," he commands as he hungrily slams inside of me, hitting me just right that I fall into a suspended reality.

My pussy pulses in waves of pleasure around his cock as I lose my breath in release.

"Fuck, yeah," he growls as he shoots his hot cum inside of me, claiming me as his. He drops his head to my chest as he begins to slow but still pumping small thrusts inside of me.

I let my head fall back against the wall, and when he looks up at me, his request is clear when he says, "Give it to me," and I slip my fingers back into his mouth so he can taste my arousal.

When he lowers me back down, holding on to me as I steady myself on my feet, his cum slowly seeps out of me, wetting my panties as I slip them back in place. We don't speak as we rush to pull ourselves together. I check myself in the mirror, swipe my fingers under my eyes, and then run them through my hair in an attempt to smooth it down. When Declan has his pants back on, he wraps his arms around me from behind and kisses me tenderly under my ear, moving his lips along the delicate skin, telling me, "I love you. So fucking much."

My heart is racing, not just from the abrupt sex, but also from the fear of knowing Bennett is in the other room. I turn in his arms, slightly out of breath, and soothe him the best that I can before I walk out of here and return to my husband.

"I love you too. If I had my way, I'd hide away with you in here forever."

He presses his lips into my neck, and then unlocks the door. "You go ahead. Give me a few minutes."

I run my hand along his jaw, taking in the feel of his whiskers and giving him a soft smile before leaving.

"There you are. I was about to come looking for you," Bennett says when I walk back to where I had left him.

I walk over to where he sits on the couch and take a seat next to him. "I'm sorry. Just needed a moment."

"Everything okay?"

"Yes," I say, and then turn to Cal, who's sitting with Camilla on the adjacent couch. "I apologize for my uncouth outburst. I don't know what came over me."

"No need to apologize. You have a spicy bite to you, nothing wrong with that," he says and then nods to Camilla, adding, "You should hear this one when she gets a fire under her ass."

"Calum!" she squeals, slapping his knee as he starts to laugh.

Bennett and I join the amusement in their exchange when Declan walks in. He quickly glances my way, scowling when he sees Bennett's arm wrapped around me as I'm cuddled up next to him.

"There you are, son. Where the hell have you been?" Cal questions in annoyance.

"Had to take a call," he answers. "I hate to do this, but I'm going to have to call it a night here. Father, it was good seeing you," he says as he walks over to say his goodbyes to Cal and Camilla before turning in my direction. Bennett stands to shake Declan's hand, totally unaware that he was just inside of me. I stand, nervously, next to Bennett, and when the two are finished saying their quick and stale goodbye, Declan takes my hand in his, bringing it up to his lips for a chaste kiss.

"Nina, always a pleasure."

"Likewise," I respond as casually as I can, and when he drops my hand, I watch as he turns to leave.

The rest of the evening passes by easily, but I can't help but wonder about Declan. I shouldn't be wasting my time worrying about how he's feeling, but I can't shake it off. After we leave and get back to the hotel, I pull out my phone and open up the text app that he had installed on my phone while Bennett showers.

Where are you?

His response comes quick.

Out.

His clipped text agitates me, but at the same time hurts me to know I've upset him.

I'm so sorry about tonight.

It was my mistake for being there.

I stare at the screen, not sure what I should type next, but it soon vibrates with another message from him.

Are you okay?

No. I miss you.

I miss you too, darling.

When I hear the water to the shower turn off, I quickly type out my next text.

I have to go. I love you though. I need you to know that.

I do know. I love you too.

I shut off my phone after I read his last text and slip it back inside of my purse. When Bennett comes to bed, his hands are all over me. And even though I was just with Declan, I don't deny Bennett. So as we have sex, I numb myself to him. I act out the motions as I always do, but inside, I turn every part of me off. The only thought I allow to float through my head is one that brings me a dark sense of satisfaction, knowing that this man I hate so much has his dick covered in another man's cum as he fucks me.

twenty-nine

(PRESENT)

"NOT MY FACE this time."

"Why?"

"Because Bennett will be back in a week. I can't have any leftover bruises that are on my face," I tell Pike.

"Okay, yeah. Your back then?"

With a nod, I nervously agree.

"You scared?" he asks.

"A little. My face hurt for a couple days after what we did. I'm okay though," I tell him. "Just do it." I turn away from Pike and tense up, waiting for the blow, but I'm greeted first by his caring touch as he runs his hands soothingly up and down my arms. But the waiting is just causing my anxiety to escalate. "Please, Pike. Now."

The knuckles of his fist hammer into me along my shoulder blade in a puncture of violent pain that shoots down the length of my arm. The force of the blow knocks me forward, and I fall to my knees, catching myself on my hands as I cringe against the pain.

Pike quickly instructs, "On your side," I immediately lie down when he strikes again.

"Ooow!" I scream as he kicks his booted foot into the same shoulder blade, followed by another excruciating blow, and then another. "PIKE!" I shriek in utter agony as I arch my back and roll on the floor, heaving through my breathless cries.

Pike drops beside me and brushes the hair away from my face as I writhe against the throbbing pain. He scoops me into his lap and holds me firmly against him while he whispers in my ear, "Just breathe. Calm down and just breathe," over and over as he rocks me in a lulling sway.

"It hurts to breathe," I strain. It hurts to talk too, like someone is stepping on my lungs.

"Talk to me."

"There's so much pressure in my chest and back."

He picks me up off the floor and carries me in his arms to his bed where he lays me down on my back.

"Take slow, deep breaths, okay?" he says, and I try to steady my trembling breathing into smooth inhales and exhales. "That's it. Just try to relax."

I lie here for quite a while until the pain starts to dull into a continuous heated ache. After I take a few Tylenol, I shift to my side, bringing my shoulder off the bed to relieve some of the pressure. Pike spoons in behind me and lifts my top to bare my shoulder.

"Fuck," he murmurs.

"What?"

"This looks really bad."

"That's the point, right?" I groan.

"Yeah," he says. "This just already looks nasty."

He gently plants a few kisses around my back where I hurt, and then drags his hand over my side and up my stomach. I push his hand away when he runs it over my breast.

"Not tonight," I tell him.

"What's going on?" he questions. I never turn down sex with Pike. It's always been something I've needed. He's my painkiller, taking away the ick in me, but for some reason, I don't feel like I need it this time.

"I don't know," I tell him honestly. "I just . . . I'm okay. I don't know why I feel this way, but I do."

"Come here," he says as he gently helps me roll over to face him. "What's going on?"

I see the confusion in him, but I feel it too. I've always been transparent with Pike, so I shrug and try to explain, "I don't know. Everything has just been so crazy lately. Maybe I'm just distracted, but I feel like I'm okay to not have sex with you right now."

"Are you sure? Because I worry about you. *This* worries me about you."

"I'm okay," I try to assure him.

"You've always needed me."

"I still need you, Pike. I'm always going to need you," I tell him and then give him a kiss.

We both linger in it for a moment before he pulls back and asks, "So how much longer do you think?"

"He's pretty firm on having me to himself," I explain. "He despises Bennett, so I don't think this will stretch out too long. It's hard to say though, but he's really intense. I think if he's triggered at just the right moment, he would snap."

"So you think he has it in him to kill Bennett?"

Swallowing hard, I think about what I know about Declan and answer honestly, "Yeah." But the thought makes my gut twist, knowing that I'm about to ruin this man's life by luring him into becoming a murderer. Pike and I always agreed from the start that we would make sure the blame lies elsewhere. It's the only way to ensure we remain safe and can move on to our new life of wealth and satisfaction. With Bennett alone, this was so easy, but now having Declan involved has made it a little difficult for me to keep my focus.

IT'S BEEN HALF an hour since Declan went up to the rooftop deck. When I got here and he was helping me take my coat off, I flinched in pain. He'd demanded to see my back and when I showed him the black and purple bruises that cover most of my upper back, he lost his shit. I've never seen him so furious before. He then apologized and said he needed some space to calm down. He grabbed his coat and went up to his private deck and has been there ever since, leaving me here on his couch waiting for him. But the temperatures are in the negatives, and I'm worried.

I go ahead and shrug my coat on before walking up the stairs to the door that leads outside. I spot him through the window, sitting on one of the wicker chairs. He has his face hidden in his hands, leaning over with his elbows resting on his knees as the snow falls over him.

I feel like shit.

What the fuck is wrong with me?

Pull your shit together; you've got a job to do.

My guilty conscience doesn't abate. I care about Declan, and I don't want to hurt him, but I have to. I have to make him feel this to drive him to kill Bennett. I just wasn't prepared to feel this way. When I notice his shivering hands, I open the door and walk over to him. He doesn't move as I kneel down in front of him, bracing my hands on his knees.

"Declan." My voice is soft as I speak to him. "It's freezing out here. You're going to make yourself sick."

He lifts his head and moves his hands to my face. "I'm already sick. Seeing what he did to you was all it took."

"Don't let him ruin our time together," I tell him and then stand up, taking his hands in mine. "Come inside with me."

We go back in and head downstairs to his bedroom. Declan doesn't speak as he walks into his closet to strip out of his cold, damp clothes and returns to me wearing nothing but long pajama bottoms. He lies down on the bed, slipping under the covers.

"Take your clothes off and come to me," he says.

I stand in front of him as he watches me undress. The expression on his face is difficult to read as I drop my clothes to the floor. When I slip my panties off, I pull the sheets back and crawl in next to him.

We hold each other close, his body freezing against my warm skin.

"You feel so good," he murmurs into my hair while his deft hands roam over my naked body.

The need to comfort him is strong, so I wrap myself around him to warm him up. When he shifts me on top of him, I lay my chest against his, skin against skin, and he's instantly hard. Without thinking, our bodies begin to slowly move together, and I lift my head to kiss him. I want to take his pain away. The pain I inflicted. His soft lips feather against mine in light brushing kisses—sensual kisses—taking our time to simply feel each other.

He lifts my head with his hands, and I look down into the honesty of his green eyes. He doesn't say anything—he doesn't even need to—I can hear him clearly in the solitude of silence between us. He really does love me. I nod my head, letting him know that I know his thoughts, that I'm here with him.

The way he's touching me right now and with the stillness of the room, it would be so easy for me to escape, but I don't want to. I want to be here. Be in the moment—with him. I let myself drift to a place I've never been. Lost in Declan as he sits up and gently nips the bud of my nipple, hardening it to a peak before moving to the next to show the same loving attention. He savors me, and I like it.

"You're so beautiful," he whispers over my breasts.

Gripping fistfuls of his hair in my hands, I hold him close to me while he lifts his hips and shifts his pants down, and I don't even want to wait. I rise up on my knees as he holds himself beneath me and descend down over heat of his rock hard cock. Our moans blend as he fills me completely, his arms banded around my waist, hugging me, his cheek to my breast.

Neither one of us moves for a while as we hold each other, and when he eventually loosens his arms, he lays back and looks up at me. "I want to watch you take me."

Declan, giving up control and handing it over to me. So with his words, I slowly rise up along his cock, and when I feel the ridge of the tip slip out, I take my time and fall back down over him, sucking him inside of my warmth. It's like my body just naturally craves him, needing him. I place my hands on his chest and continue to work the length of him while he watches me. He runs his hands up my thighs and over my stomach to my tits, handling me gently, caressing me.

I move my hands to his wrists and hold on to them as my eyes fall shut. I've never felt this with any other man. But it's not just now in this moment, it's every single time I'm with him. He always has a way of keeping me connected to him, never allowing my mind to drift, never allowing my body to go numb. I used to fight for that with him. But now? Now I don't even try.

Declan begins to move his hips beneath me, our bodies so in sync. There's a pressure in my chest, a foreign ache inside of me, and it begins to swell. My emotions swarm in confusion. Questions fill my head; each of them hitting the softest parts of me, parts I'm just now realizing exist within me.

Why doesn't this feel dirty?

Why am I not trying to escape?

Why do I let him see the weak in me?

Why do I hurt?

Why am I suddenly doubting everything I thought I knew?

Why can't I breathe?

And when my eyes open, I feel everything I never thought I was worthy of.

I love him.

A hard hit to my heart and I feel like I'm choking.

I really love him.

I see it, a shooting star above, exploding into a million flittering pieces of diamond dust. Shimmering flecks trickling over me, and when I look down, I see them landing on Declan's golden chest. A splattering of crystals, each holding their own prism of sparkles as they glitter against his skin, and then he reaches his hand up to my cheek. Still holding on to his wrists, he wipes my damp cheek.

"Baby," he whispers, but I don't speak. The ache in my chest is too restricting. We don't stop moving as my tears continue to drop to his chest. And when it becomes too much, the realization that I'm falling in love with the one person I should have remained disconnected from, I choke out a painful sob.

Declan quickly pulls me down to him and I break, weeping into his neck as he hugs me against him. This has never felt okay—exposing this vulnerability that has always hidden itself inside of me—but until Declan, I never felt safe enough to expose it. I've always been safe with him. How could I've been so blind to not see what's been happening between us?

He's still deep inside of me, but we're no longer moving as he pets me. His hands gently running the length of my back, his fingers combing through my hair, while I find myself completely overcome with emotions I've never felt before. A deep connection with someone I should have kept at a distance, but somehow, he found his way inside of me.

"Talk to me," he says, and I slightly lift my head to look at him when I say the words I've said so many times, but this time, I truly mean them.

"I love you, Declan."

"I know, darling."

Dropping my forehead to his, I run my hand along his stubbled jaw, needing the soothing prickles against my hand. "I mean . . . I *really* love you."

My confession causes his heart to pick up. I can feel it pounding against my chest. He kisses me slow and deep, tasting me, before he pulls back to speak. "This is what I've been waiting for."

"What?"

Sliding his hand between our bodies, he presses it against my chest, over my rapidly beating heart. "*This.*"

"You have it. It's been yours."

"I haven't truly felt it until right now," he says, and then I move my hand between us and rest it over his heart as well. It thumps into my palm as he tells me, "All I want is you. I'll do whatever it takes, but I need you to know that you're completely safe with me. I'll never hurt you; I only want to love you."

Knowing the web of lies I've created, I know that this will never come forth to culmination with him the way I want it to. I've created a hopeless situation in a place I never expected to find hope. But I did, and it rests inside of this man—a man I've allowed my heart to fall for. The realness is too much, knowing that all I'll come out of this with is all I've ever had—the heartbreak of life's cruel hand. And yet I don't want to fight it anymore, because I feel the same way he does.

He carefully rolls me onto my back and pushes himself deep inside of me, being gentle to not hurt my bruised back.

"Tell me you feel that," he says as he looks down at me and I nod. He pulls back, sliding his thick cock out of me before thrusting inside of me even deeper. "Tell me you feel how much I love you."

"I feel it."

He continues to fuck me with a powerful, slow force, each penetration going deeper and deeper. I grab on to his arms for support, his muscles flexing as his body tenses up with every intense stroke of our bare flesh as my body begins to climb with his.

When the heat ripples through me, I begin to shudder beneath him. He drops his head to mine, his cock grows even harder, thickening inside of me, pressing against my walls as they begin to constrict around his shaft, and I come hard.

"Oh, fuck," he growls, losing control of himself as he pounds into me.

My moans grow louder with each pulse of sheer euphoria that shoots through me. I wrap my legs around his hips, clamping my pussy around him, milking his cock, craving every drop of his sperm that fills me up. I've never felt so loved, but it consumes me in this moment as I surrender everything that I am and hand it over to Declan. I need him to spread his feral scent all over me as he takes me as his to do with as he likes, because I want to be a part of him.

He pins his eyes on me, and I know he can see the hunger in me when he starts fucking me even harder, refusing to stop even though he just came. His pupils are dilated black, flaring in possessive need when he hisses, "You're mine."

"Yes."

Thrust. Thrust.

"I own you."

Thrust.

"Completely," I breathe in submission.

Thrust.

"My property."

Thrust.

"Yes," I mewl in ecstasy as I come again, spiraling away into shrills of sensuous pleasure. He's a beast on top of me, and when he spreads my legs wide open, pressing my knees into the mattress, he slams his hips down, burying his cock inside of me to the root. With a carnal groan, I feel a warm stream of fluid flood inside of me and spill out between our connected bodies.

"Declan," I release on a faint breath—shocked as he fills me with his urine—claiming and marking me as his in the most animalistic way.

He releases my knees and quickly slips his arms under my back, holding me close before rolling us to our sides. My breathing is staggered as we stare at each other. Maybe I should be disgusted by what he just did, considering the things Carl used to do to me, but I'm not. I'm safe—safe enough to hand myself over to him entirely and know that he will take care of me—never hurt me. I love him, and I feel this intrinsic need to be as intimately close to him as I can possibly get.

"You belong to me," he eventually says as our bodies calm down, still connected, and bathed in his scent.

"Yes."

He threads his fingers through my hair, asking, "Your back? Did I hurt you?"

I shake my head slightly, responding, "You settled me. Everything you want from me is exactly what I want to give you. You don't even have to take it. Just have it because it's yours." I give my sincere words and watch as he digests them. His face softens peacefully, and when it does, I take his lips in the most loving kiss I've ever given.

Without selfishness.

Without expectations.

Without malicious undertones.

I give him the purest piece of my heart that I have remaining and hand it over in the most honest way I can despite all the evil that surrounds me. In this moment of time that I have with him, I want to love him and give him the best parts of me I can find. I want to feel this—the part of life that's good, the part of life I never thought I'd feel. I want to give every last bit of what I'm feeling right now to Declan because somehow, in some magical way, he makes life feel like it's worth living.

thirty

(PRESENT)

A RICH, INTOXICATING fragrance fills my senses as I stir awake. Rolling over in Declan's bed, I'm alone, aside from the dozens of pure white lotus flowers that are spread over the bed and myself. Containing my smile would be a feat, so I don't even bother. The heady mixture of fruit, rain, and earth wafts through the room as I take in the beauty of the delicate blooms—Declan's favorite flower.

Turning my head, I see a folded piece of paper sitting on his nightstand. I reach out and sit up, unfolding the paper to read his hand-written note.

Nina,

I tried to shower you in something that was just as pure and beautiful as you, but I fell short. The lotus was the best I could do, but they don't even come close to the perfection I see every time I look at you. I know I said we'd spend the day together, but I have to run into the office for a little while. Call me when you wake up. I miss your sweet voice already.

No one could possibly love you more.

-D

The phone is already ringing by the time I finish reading as I wait for him to answer.

"Good morning," he says.

"When did you do this?"

"Secrets, darling," he teases, and I can picture his smile now, lines crinkling at the corners of his eyes.

"Keep your secrets then, as long as I continue to benefit," I joke right back.

"I adore you."

"When are you coming home?" I ask and his responding growl makes me laugh. "What's that all about?"

"Fucking makes me hard that you call my place *home*."

"You're bad," I giggle.

"You have no idea."

"I think I do."

"No," he says and then pauses before he continues, "I don't think you could ever know how deep you run through me."

It's been nearly two weeks since I finally allowed myself to recognize that I love Declan. I spend every moment I can with him, and even with Bennett in the picture, we've connected in a way I didn't think two people ever could.

"Finish up your work and come home. I want you to show me how deep you can run through *me*."

"Christ. You're not helping my dick by saying shit like that. I'm going to be walking around with a semi and blue balls for the rest of the day."

I laugh, telling him, "Good. Motivation for you to hurry up and get back here."

"I'll call you when I leave. I want you naked and on your knees, waiting for me. I'll let you pick out the belt because I'm going to have my way with you," he demands in a low voice, causing a delightful ache between my legs.

"I want the one you're wearing so that every time you look at it today, you'll think about me naked and on my knees," I say, flirting with mild laughter.

"Bad girl."

"I love you."

"Love you," he says before we hang up.

I lie back down in the sheets, staring at the flowers and dreading tomorrow when Bennett comes back and I have to go to my other home. I love being here with Declan. For the first time, I feel happy.

Truly happy.

Truth is, I'm confused.

Really confused.

Happy and confused.

I hate what I've done here with Declan—lying and manipulating. I want to be honest with him about who I am. I want him to know me, Elizabeth, not Nina. But there's no way to do that. I've set the ball in motion, and I'm not sure how to stop it. I don't think it can be, but I want it to be. I just want to freeze time, cast a spell and make the past disappear so that I can start fresh with Declan. Give him the real me. But I fucked myself. Life has fucked me—it always has. And now I must forsake the one thing I want to be greedy with because what I want most of all is just more time with him.

I pick up one of the white flowers known for their birth in muddy waters only to grow and bloom into a flawless spread of purity. I wish for a moment that this flower could resemble me. That maybe I could be one of the lucky ones to truly get a new beginning. I've never felt as clean as I do with Declan. Not even Pike can clean me the way Declan does. But the reality is, my new beginning will still be filled with rot. Destroying the life of two men—one innocent and one who deserves the destruction—to live a life of retribution. Only that retribution will forever be tainted by the memory of what this will undoubtedly do to Declan.

I brush the soft petals along my lips, close my eyes, and picture my dad. My purity. My salvation. My prince. I wonder if my father sent Declan to me. If this is his gift to me. The good after all the bad. Declan used to scare me. He used to remind me of Carl with his forceful nature, his leather belts, and his affinity for tying me up. But when I started to see beyond that to the core of who he is, he reminds me of my dad. Because I can now look at Declan and see that, he too, is my purity, my salvation, my prince. Even down to the creases in the corners of his eyes when he smiles and the stubble along his face. My dad used to sing to me, and now I have Declan who hums gently into my ear when I'm scared or sad. The ways he soothes me is reminiscent of the things my father used to do.

I try not to think about having to go back to sharing a bed with Bennett. This whole thing with Declan, and the knowing that I can never truly have him, is just another reason to hate Bennett even more.

Needing to move and distract myself. I gather all the flowers and take them to the kitchen. Grabbing a stack of white bowls from the cabinet, I fill them with water and place the blooms down in them to float aimlessly and scatter the bowls throughout the loft.

Their scent envelops every room by the time I have taken a shower and gotten cleaned up and dressed for the day. I decide to go ahead and call Bennett since it's after five o'clock there and he should be heading back to his hotel with Baldwin. Our call is the typical, and after we talk for almost an hour, we hang up.

Things are going to get tricky for a while because Bennett informs me that his schedule is about to free up on his travel, meaning he's going to be home on a more steady basis. The thought of having to leave Declan's bed to spend the nights with Bennett is depressing. I didn't know I needed the comfort as much as I do, and Declan gives it to me perfectly and in a way that Pike could never completely fill for me.

Not wanting to dwell on having to leave tomorrow, I busy myself and decide to surprise Declan by attempting to cook for him. I go to the office and start surfing the internet for an easy, burn-proof recipe. His scent is encased within his leather chair, and I can't fight the sadness that finds my heart as I sit at his desk, in his office, surrounded by everything Declan. I find a pasta dish that seems like something I can manage and quickly print it off so that I can get out of here because I desperately need some fresh air.

I bundle up and make my way to the market. Needing the assistance of one of the workers to find a few of the ingredients, I check my list, and when everything I need is in my basket, I make my purchases and head out.

"Surprised to see you on this side of town," I hear a familiar voice call out, and when I close the trunk, I'm greeted by Richard's snide smile. My heart jumps, and being caught off guard ignites a fire up my neck. Thank God for winter and concealing scarves.

I quickly collect myself, going into my well-crafted act, saying, "Richard. I could say the same about you. What brings you to River North, or, better yet, a grocery store of all places?" turning the question around on him.

"My attorney's office is here. Had a meeting I just got out of and needed to pick up some formula for the baby."

"Aren't you supposed to be in Dubai with Bennett?"

"Had to come back early," he snips before going back to his original question, "What are you doing here?"

"I've been cooped up for far too many days and needed a drive, so I thought I'd spend a few hours roaming some of the galleries," I tell him, figuring it was a good enough lie considering River North is known for its trendy array of art galleries.

"And yet here you are, buying groceries," he snarks. "Finally figuring out what it means to be a housewife?"

God, he's such a womanizing dick.

"As if any of my doings are your business, but since you seem so concerned with my takings on of wifely duties, yes, I thought I'd try my hand at cooking since I'm growing tired of Clara's freezer meals."

"Hmph," he remarks, eyeing me suspiciously.

His doubting look pisses me off, and when I move to walk around him and open up the car door, I ask, "Is there anything else you'd like to question me about?"

"Jacqueline said she's stopped by your building a couple times since

Bennett's been gone. Said you haven't been around much."

"Tell Jacqueline that I have a life and things to do, and if she'd like to schedule time together, then she best call or text me instead of making random drop-ins only to find that I have other obligations that call me away from home," I snap, trying to cover for my lack of presence on my side of town.

He nods with a look of spite before commenting, "I'll be sure to relay your friendly message."

"You do that, Richard."

Getting into the car and closing the door, my heart pounds with anxiety, wondering what the fuck Richard is really doing on this side of town, because I already know that we share the same attorney, and he isn't located in River North.

I drive back towards Declan's loft, all the while looking in my rearview mirror to make sure Richard hasn't followed me. When I'm sure that no one is watching, I turn into the parking garage and park in one of Declan's assigned spots. Turning the car off, I lean my head back, pissed at myself for being so careless. But that quickly morphs into being pissed that I have to be so guarded. That I've created such elaborate lies that they can't simply be washed away. I'm in way too deep for any possibility of that.

I think about Pike and everything he's sacrificed for me. Everything he's given up for the past few years while I work this con. And as I sit here and start to doubt what we're doing, the guilt of what that would do to Pike surfaces. I can't pull out of this that easily anyway. I'm married. If I walked away—disappeared—Bennett would come looking for me. He loves me too much and it would devastate him to lose me. But it's not Bennett that I care about—it's Declan. And how do I find my way out of this without revealing all of my wicked deceit to him. No one would be able to look past it or forgive me for what I have already done. The only option I see right now is to keep doing what I'm doing and cherish every last second I have with him before Pike and I flee.

I GIVE THE sauce a quick stir after Declan calls to let me know he's on his way. So far, I've managed not to set the smoke alarm off in my quest to cook dinner. I walk over to the wine cage and select a nice white to go with dinner and place it in the fridge to chill.

When Declan arrives a while later, I laugh at the shocked expression on his face as he enters the loft and sees me in the kitchen.

"What are you up to?" he says inquisitively.

"What does it look like?"

"Well, you should be naked and on your knees, but instead, you're cooking. Which I hope you've alerted the fire department to be on standby," he chuckles as he rounds the bar, moving close to give me a hug.

I swat his arm, saying, "I'll have you know that I've yet to burn anything."

"Is that so?" he mocks as he grabs my wrist and yanks me with force against his chest, giving me a sexy smirk.

"Yes. That's so."

His mouth instantly finds my neck, licking its way up to my ear where he gently nibbles on the lobe, causing a rush of goosebumps along my arms. I shiver in his hold, and he growls in pride at my body's response to him. I sling my arms around his broad shoulders when he reaches behind my thighs and lifts me up, setting me on top of the counter. With my legs wrapped around him, I feel his cock harden against me as he stands between my legs.

"Just know, next time I say I want you on your knees, you better be on your knees. I won't punish you for your disobedience though, because I love that you cooked for me," he says after kissing me thoroughly.

"Do you?"

He begins to laugh against my lips before saying, "Clearly my cock approves and is eager to thank you," which causes me to burst out laughing right along with him.

"You're such a dork."

"A dork, huh?"

"Yeah."

"No one has called me that since the fifth grade," he teases, and I giggle when I respond, "Well, maybe not to your face."

He buries his head in my neck, biting me and growling at my snarky remark, but it only turns me on. With my ankles crossed behind him, I urge his hips into me, needing the friction against my heat.

"Needy," he remarks.

"You have no idea."

He leans over, flipping off all the switches on the stove, and then hikes up the skirt of my dress. Leaning down between my legs, I hear him inhale deeply through his nose, scenting me.

"Fuck, I love the way you smell when your body readies itself for me," he says before violently ripping my panties right off of me, the lacy fabric shredded as they hang from my one thigh.

My hands take fistfuls of Declan's hair as he kneels before me, spreading my legs wider. I look down at him as he takes in the sight of me.

"You're so fucking beautiful," he says as he flicks his eyes up to mine. He then takes his fingers and sinks them between the lips of my already wet pussy, adding, "This . . ."

"Mmmm."

"This is so fucking beautiful," he says before plunging a finger inside of me.

My hands tighten around the locks of his hair as I release a heady moan. He keeps his eyes on mine while he slowly fucks me with his finger, peering up at me in raging heat.

"You like having me inside of you?"

"Yes," I answer.

"This is mine."

I moan in approval when he takes his thumb and starts pressing smooth circles over my swollen clit. He then crooks his finger to reach the most sensitive spot inside of me, causing my body to lose control as he sparks the live wire that's burning in me. But it's when his hot mouth covers me that I come undone, allowing him to possess me however he chooses.

With the flat pad of his tongue, he massages my clit in tender strokes before baring his teeth and with their razor edge, clamps down and bites me.

"Shit," I hiss as my body jerks away in pain, but he grabs my hips and keeps me in his mouth with a forceful grip. He quickly replaces his teeth with his tongue again, soothing the infliction, blurring the lines between pleasure and pain.

The gentleness that follows the torture makes me crave more of the loving abuse, and he knows it when he pulls away, urging, "Tell me you want it."

"Give it to me."

"Tell me what you want."

"You know what I want."

"Say it," he commands.

"Bite me."

"Ask me," he says. "Beg for it."

Pushing my hips towards his face, I nearly whimper in the desire that flushes through my veins, "Please, Declan. Bite me, and then take the pain away. I wanna feel it."

With a low groan, he's pleased with my request, approving, "Good girl," before unzipping his pants to free his massive erection, solid and hard.

"Your girl," I breathe as he takes me in his mouth again.

I can't keep my eyes off of him, watching him beat off while he blissfully fucks me with his tongue.

thirty-one
(PRESENT)

BENNETT HAS BEEN home for a couple of weeks now, making it difficult for me to see Declan. I have to come up with random excuses to get away and go to him. So I lie, telling him that Chicago Magazine wants another piece from me and that I've been meeting my editor for coffee and office meetings to discuss article topics, or that I'm spending the day at the spa, or going shopping. Whatever I can come up with, I tell him. Declan and I have been spending most of our time on his yacht. When I'm with him, nothing else exists—I'm happy and content. I know I've made a huge mistake and the more time I spend with him leaving my heart unguarded, the deeper I'm falling in love. But I can't help myself. He's intense, overwhelming, addictive, and utterly all-consuming. When I'm not with him, I want to be. These days, I can barely go an hour without wanting to talk to him. That's how much I crave him.

I've been putting off seeing Pike for these very reasons. I'm scared to tell him the truth about what's going on between Declan and me, so for the first time, I'm going to have to lie to him. It's been almost a month since I last saw him, so while Bennett is at work, and Declan is in meetings all day to discuss acquiring a piece of land in London for new construction, I take a risk and drive out to Justice to touch base with Pike. I normally wait until Bennett is out of town, but under the circumstances, I feel like I need to check in.

The place smells of his clove cigarettes, a scent that is so familiar to me, one that I find comfort in. But the smell that brings me the most comfort now is one of sweet, earthy rain—the smell of lotus blooms.

"Four weeks, Elizabeth," Pike's monotone voice says as he sits on the couch. His irritation doesn't come as a surprise as I walk over and sit down next to him.

"I'm sorry. Bennett's been home. He's not traveling as much right now," I try explaining, but he doesn't seem to be in any mood to hear my excuses.

"Just tell me what's going on."

"Pike."

"Tell me you're making progress with that guy."

"His name's Declan, and I'm trying. It's just taking a little longer than I expected," I tell him, lying because the only reason it's taking longer is because I want more time with him.

He looks over at me, fed up, asking, "What the hell does that mean? Last I saw you, you said he was in deep and didn't seem to have much doubt about this taking up a whole lot of time."

"I don't know," I say. "I think I was just wound up with excitement, but I don't feel like he's ready yet."

"How did he react to the last bruises I gave you?"

"He was pissed. I wound up staying with him the whole time Bennett was away."

He nods, stubbing out his cigarette. "So what do you think it's gonna take?"

"I'm not sure."

"How long is Bennett gone this time?" he asks.

"He's not. He's still here in town. It's just been a while since I saw you."

"So you needed me to take care of you," he says, wrapping his arm around my shoulder, assuming I came for sex. But I don't need that from him anymore. And as screwed up as it sounds, considering I'm married, the thought of having sex with Pike would make me feel like I was being unfaithful to Declan. It's a fucked up idea, but the feeling is there regardless.

"No. I just wanted to check in. I didn't want you worrying," I tell him and watch as his eyes narrow.

"What the fuck is going on? What aren't you telling me?" he snaps.

"Nothing."

"For nearly sixteen years you've always needed me for sex, and now, all of a sudden, you don't."

"Nobody said that I don't still need you, Pike."

"You didn't need me the last time you were here, and now today," he says suspiciously as he pulls his arm away from me. I don't speak as he stands up and takes a few steps across the room before turning back to face me. "You say you think Declan needs more time, that he's not ready. But now you've got me wondering if it's you that's not ready."

I stand up, defending instantly, "You don't think I'm ready to see Bennett dead? To see that asshole buried six feet under where he belongs?"

"I'm not talking about Bennett. I don't doubt that you want those things. I'm talking about Declan."

I try covering my nervousness with irritation when I cross my arms and bite my words, "Stop goading me and just say whatever it is you want to say."

He takes a moment, looking at me intently as if he's trying to read me, and then questions in a condescending tone, "You don't love the guy, do you?"

"What?! No!" I blurt out, but I know he doesn't buy it when he cocks his head.

"Then tell me why you don't need me."

"Pike. Don't."

"You're just fooling yourself, you know?" he says. "Don't forget, you're nothing but a lie to him."

But I don't need Pike to tell me what I already know.

"Stop."

But he doesn't. He just keeps talking, saying, "So when he says that he loves you, he doesn't really mean it. He's only in love with this fictional character you've created, *Nina*."

"Pike, I'm serious," I yell, losing my temper. "Cut the shit!"

"You and I both know that if he truly knew you, he wouldn't be saying those words."

"Fuck you!"

"No! Fuck you!" he shouts in hate. "We had a fucking plan here. And here you are, falling for the goddamn con!"

His words stab me, throwing the truth I want to deny in my face. Wishing that his words were nothing but lies, but they're not, and it pisses me off, so I shout back at him, "I'm not like you! I have cracks, and I can't always shut off my feelings like you do, settling for the life you were given. Don't forget I was given this life too!"

He flinches when I sling my words at him, and I'm taken aback by the softer tone of his voice when he responds, "So that's what you really think? That I don't feel? That I don't mourn the loss of the life I should've had? That I don't wonder about or miss the parents I never knew?" He takes a slow step towards me, his jaw flexing, hardening his voice as he continues, "You had a dad that you knew. You had it all. I never had a goddamn thing. But that's why people like you and me fight, because it gives us something to live for when we have nothing left. I thought we shared that."

The look on his face and the pain in his voice cut me deeply. I love Pike. I always have, and to see him hurt, because of me, isn't an easy thing to witness.

I move closer to him, telling him, "We do share that."

He cups my cheeks in his hands, assuring me, "We can do this. You and I can do this together. Don't let go of that because some guy makes you feel something. The real question you need to be asking yourself is: what does Elizabeth make him feel?"

He's right. Declan says he loves me, but what he loves isn't real. Not completely anyway. I allow him to see the real emotions in me, but he thinks I'm Nina, the girl from Kansas. If he knew Elizabeth, there's no way he would feel the same way about me. There's no denying how I feel about him, but Pike is right, I don't truly have the confirmation of how he feels about me—the real me.

I can't speak as I stand here and soak in his words, but he soon breaks the silence, pleading softly, "Don't leave me alone in this."

I wrap my arms around his waist, wanting to comfort him. Pike rarely exposes himself like this to me, so when he does, it's hard for me to deal with. Pike is my rock. My backbone when I feel weak. We stand here and hold each other when I tell him, "I'll never leave you, Pike."

"When I tell you that I love you, I mean it. I love *you—Elizabeth*," he says. "That's something you will never have to question."

And I believe him, but Pike has always loved me in a way I don't share. His love has always bordered on an intimate level, whereas I love him like a brother. But when you grow up like we have, in a world where there is no black and white, it's hard to clearly distinguish the grey, and right and wrong no longer exist. I've never questioned him about his feelings towards me, he makes it clear, and I've never corrected his assumption of my feelings. But the feelings I know he wants from me aren't for him; they're for a man who believes I'm real, only I'm not. I'm nothing more than his poison paradise.

THE MOMENT I see Declan, all of Pike's words from earlier disappear. I watch Declan as he fixes my cup of tea in the galley of his boat, and after he adds a tiny splash of milk, he turns to hand me the mug.

"I've been wanting to ask you something," he says as he leads me down into his stateroom. I crawl up onto his bed, folding my legs in front of me and cradling the hot mug, and when he sprawls out, resting his back against the headboard, he reaches out, saying, "Give me your hand."

I offer him one of my hands and he turns it over, dragging a finger over my wrist. "These," he whispers, referring to the faint white lines that mar the inside of my wrist. They're barely even visible anymore, so I'm a little surprised that he's noticed them. Not even Bennett has.

Declan brings my wrist to his lips and presses them against the tiny reminders of being tied up and locked away as a child. The touch is soft, a sweetness that melts me. "Tell me how you got these?" he asks, and I want to tell him. For some reason, I want him to know the ugliness in me. Instead, I avoid because I don't want to lie to him if I don't have to.

I slowly shake my head, letting him know that I don't want to tell him, so instead he asks, "Did it hurt to get them?"

I don't answer right away as I look into his eyes, eyes that show his concern for me, his love and his caring nature that he's made me privy to.

"Yes," I eventually respond, and he kisses the scars again.

"Can I talk to you about something?"

"What's that?" I question before taking a sip of my hot tea.

"I want you to leave Bennett," he states matter-of-factly.

"Declan, I told you, I can't."

"I have an estate in Scotland," he reveals, "in the countryside of Edinburgh. Come with me. We can disappear."

"He'll find me."

"I'll hire security to watch his moves. We'll know if he purchases a plane ticket. We'll know everything he does. I won't let him get close to you."

The lengths this man is willing to go to for me are tempting. Bennett might try to find me, but he'd never hurt me like I've led Declan to believe. I immediately start thinking about what it would be like to run away with him. To leave everything behind and start a new life with Declan, far from my past. He'd never need to know because there'd be nothing to threaten the truth from revealing itself. But then I think of Pike. I can't disappear on him. He's my family. It's a nice fantasy, but it isn't reality.

"I can't just vanish," I tell him.

He takes my mug and sets it on the bedside table before taking both my hands in his. "Why not?"

"Because . . ." I shake my head, feigning my overwhelming reaction to his offer. "I mean, you're asking me to leave behind everything I know. To walk away and never look back."

"What is there that you'd want to look back for?"

"I don't . . . I don't know."

"We could have a life," he says softly.

"But . . . what about your job?"

"I own the hotel; I don't run it. This was simply a home base for me while it was under construction. Soon, if the deal goes through, I'll be working on the London property."

I hesitate, dropping my head with a defeated sigh. "I don't know."

"You love me, right?"

Lifting my eyes to meet his, I nod, answering, "Completely."

"Look, I know what I'm asking of you. And get that you're scared, but I know what I want, and that's a life with you. I'll do whatever it takes to get that." He moves his hands to my hips and pulls me onto his, my legs straddled on either side of him as he looks up at me. "I never thought I could love anyone the way I love you, but it's painful, knowing I can't keep you safe when you aren't with me. It makes me feel like a piece of worthless shit when I send you home to that bastard."

"You're not worthless," I tell him as I run my hands through his hair. "But what you're asking is a lot for me."

"I know."

"I want what you want, but it all comes with a price."

"I'll do anything to have you. I'll risk it all."

His words should make me happy, but instead, they hurt. I could easily lie to him right now, tell him that Bennett rapes me or some other fucked up shit, and I know Declan would lose his temper and kill the son of a bitch right now, but I don't. I don't want to lose him even though I know I will. It's inevitable, but I feel like I'm a little child, clinging to what makes me happy, desperate not to lose it.

My thoughts rake at my heart, pricking tears that begin to puddle in my eyes.

"Baby, don't cry."

The pressure inside my chest causes an ache throughout my body. I'm grieving the loss of what's sitting in front of me, and it cuts through me allowing the misery to bleed out. Tears fall as Declan watches in silence. He bands his arms around me while my body heaves in breathless cries.

"Tell me what you're feeling," he urges, and when I open my mouth to speak, the words tumble effortlessly from my lips.

"I hate this. I hate every moment I'm not with you. You're all that I want, and I hate life for not being fair to us. And I'm scared. I'm scared of everything, but I'm mostly scared of losing you. You're the one good thing that's ever come along for me. Somehow, in this fucked up world, you have a way of making all the ugly disappear."

"You're not going to lose me," he states in a stern voice.

"Then why does it feel like it's slipping away?" I weep.

"It's not. I promise you, it's not. You're just scared, but you have me now. I'll take all that fear away, every piece of it that you carry around. I'll take it away. I'll give you everything you deserve from this life. I'll do what I can to make up for all your suffering."

I let his words soak into the darkest parts of me, the parts that no longer believe in hope, but somehow, his words awaken what was once lost. If walking away from Bennett, leaving the plan behind and sparing his life, would mean a life with Declan, I'd do it. But I'm so torn up about where that would leave Pike. I feel like I'm in a no-win situation. No matter what I do, someone will get hurt. I want to be selfish. I want to keep Declan as my own. I want the fairytale, but once again, I'm having to face the fact that those are simply saved for books. Sometimes, for some people, there's no such thing as a happily-ever-after.

Through the tears, I kiss him, needing the closeness. Like a wound, I need Declan to kiss it away and dry my tears. I don't let up as our lips tangle in a turbulent desire for healing, a desire that we're both seeking in this very moment. He flips me over onto my back, pinning my wrists above my head with his strong hands. Kneeing my legs apart, he pulls his tongue out of my mouth long enough for me to give him my obedient words of submission.

"Take me, Declan. However you want me, you can have me. I just need you inside of me right now."

And with that, he flips me on my stomach, ties my arms painfully behind my back, and with my ass in the air, he fucks me in a rage of fire. He's rough and in control, pulling my hair, slapping my ass and thighs, and then, like all the times before, holds my hands tightly in his as my body peaks and explodes into a violent orgasm that only he's been able to do for me. But he doesn't stop there. After he unties me, he rolls me to my back, drapes my legs over his shoulders, and feasts on my pussy with slow, loving ease, taking his time as he works my body to perfection until I come for him again. And when I'm done, he sits up on his knees and jerks off, spurting his cum all over my chest, covering me in his scent.

When my heart settles, I grow tired as I lie safely in Declan's strong embrace. The warmth of his chest and his arms around my body soothe me into a lull, and I release a sleepy hum as I begin to drift. Declan then shifts to his side, adjusting us so that we're lying face to face.

"I'm so tired," I murmur while Declan lazily strokes his fingers up and down the length of my spine, soothing me into a near tranquil state.

"Tell me what you dream about," he asks, looking at me as we lie together.

"Why do you want to know what I dream about?"

"Because you're beautiful when you sleep. It's the only time you look truly peaceful."

I release a soft hum when he urges, "Tell me."

"Carnegie." The truth slips out before I even think about it.

"What?"

I take a second, and then decide to give him this piece of the real me, revealing, "He's a caterpillar who lives in a magical forest. Well, actually, he's a prince, but his father had the kingdom's sorcerer turn him into a caterpillar."

"And why's that?" he asks, brushing a lock of my hair behind my shoulder.

"Because the king was upset that his son kept sneaking out of bed at night to steal juice from the kitchen."

"Is that so?" he teasingly questions, but when I don't give him any hint of a smile in return, he drops it as he scans my face.

"I'm a caterpillar too; Carnegie's my friend." The words hurt coming out as I begin fighting the razor of pain that's carving its way through my heart, exposing the blood through my eyes.

"Why are you crying?" he asks as he watches the tears slip out.

"Because it's a lie."

"What is?"

"Dreams. They're nothing but lies trying to trick me into believing life could really be like that."

"Sounds more like a fairytale than a lie."

"*Fairytale* is nothing but a fancy word for a lie used to deceive little kids," I tell him. "A false perception of reality used to give them hope in a hopeless world."

The look in his eyes causes me to close mine so I don't have to see the sadness he's feeling for me. Reality is a fucked-up head-trip that I've numbed myself to, but my dad, I've never been able to control the emotion when it comes to him. He's always been my one and only soft spot—until now—until Declan.

"Do you wish you were a caterpillar?" he asks as I feel the warmth of his thumb dragging across my cheekbones, collecting my tears.

"Yes."

Declan's arms envelop me, and I curl into him when he whispers, "Then go to sleep, darling," before kissing the top of my head and tucking it under his chin. "Go be a caterpillar."

thirty-two

(PRESENT)

ANOTHER THREE WEEKS have gone by since I've seen Pike. Bennett has been home for the most part, and whenever I can find time to slip away, I'm with Declan. I've been skirting around giving him a definitive answer on going to Scotland with him, but he's starting to grow irritated with my avoidance.

The bitter cold of snowy winter has finally let up, even though the city never seems to get above fifty, even on a good day. A gust of wind picks up, nearly blowing the door right out of my hand as I open it up and head inside the building where Dr. Leemont's office is located.

I've suffered from excruciatingly painful periods for around ten years; they are what led me to seek medical help, which resulted in my endometriosis diagnosis. About six months ago, I decided to try hormone therapy again to help with the pain but had to quit after a few months due to complications with side effects. Since December, the pain has been much more tolerable but the past few days have been nothing but razor sharp aches and pain, rendering me bed-ridden, practically unable to move.

Bennett's been a worried mess, taking off work to stay home, doing whatever he can to comfort me. The soonest I could get in to see the doctor was this morning, which really upset him because he had to go to Miami for business. He was supposed to head out a few days ago, but he refused to leave my side and pushed back all of his meetings, but he couldn't delay the trip any longer and wound up leaving late last night.

After signing in, leaving a urine sample for the nurse, and giving blood for the lab, I strip down, covering myself with the provided robe, and wait on the exam table for the doctor. As soon as I told Bennett about my diagnosis, he found Dr. Leemont, ensuring she was the best gynecologist in the state. I've been seeing her for over three years now, and when she finally walks in and I see her familiar smile, I release a heavy sigh, hoping she can do something for this pain.

"Nina, it's good to see you, although I hear you are dealing with some discomfort," she says as she walks across the exam room with her electronic notepad and sits down on a stool by the desk.

"Yes," I respond. "For the past few days."

As she looks at her notepad, she says, "Okay, so I see it's been about four months since you came off the hormones, correct?"

"Yes. Around late November, if I recall correctly."

"That's what I'm showing here on your chart," she remarks and then looks up at me, asking, "Have you experienced any other pain or cramping since coming off the pills?"

"A little, but it's been minor. Nothing that a few painkillers can't take care of."

"And do you recall your last menstrual cycle?"

"Umm, well, it would have been right before I started on the hormones. So . . . back in August or September," I tell her.

"What you are probably experiencing is the last of the hormones leaving your system," she starts saying when a nurse walks in.

"I have Mrs. Vanderwal's labs."

They both step out of the room, and when Dr. Leemont returns, holding the papers, she walks over to the desk and leans against it. She shifts her eyes from the papers to me, saying in a hushed voice, "You're pregnant."

The deflating of my lungs turns me cold in incredulity. "What did you say?"

"According to the urine and blood sample, you're pregnant."

Disbelief—that's all that courses through me right now as I can't seem to generate any other thought or feeling. I sit here and stare at the doctor for a moment when fear and confusion start to filter in.

"How?" I ask while each thump of my heart pumps bursts of anxiety through my blood. "I mean, there has to be a mistake because I can't have kids. I can't get pregnant." My voice is almost unrecognizable as the words fall out of me in a trembling stagger.

Dr. Leemont hands me a tissue, and it's then that I realize I'm crying. She takes a seat on her stool and rolls over next to me, placing her hand on my knee. "I can't imagine the shock you must be feeling right now," she says as I look at her, utterly confused, shaking my head. "Sometimes these things have a way of happening. Is it rare and typically unheard of without having to undergo surgery to remove the lesions? Yes."

"But I haven't even had a period."

"Well, the first ovulation you must have had probably ended up being the time you got pregnant, resulting in the missed period and the absence of one since," she explains, and then the realization that I've been having sex with three different men sends me into a complete panic as I go completely numb and freeze up inside.

Holy fuck! What have I gotten myself into?

"I want to be upfront with you though," she says, her voice remaining calm and soothing, a perfect contradiction of the chaos running through my entire being right now. "Because of the lesions on your uterus, the likelihood of you carrying this baby to term might be lower. This will be a high-risk pregnancy because of that."

Another wave of confusion hits me when her words spark a swell of sadness in me.

What the hell is wrong with me? This should make me happy, right? I can't have a baby, so if my body naturally expels it, then problem solved. So why does the thought of that happening make me sad?

When I don't respond, she asks, "Do you need a moment?"

"A moment?"

She gives me a nod, saying, "Yes. I'd like to go ahead and run an ultrasound to see how far along you are and get a few measurements of the baby."

"Baby," I whisper, repeating her foreign word.

"But if you need a moment—"

"No. I'm fine," I say, interrupting her.

"Okay then. I'll have my nurse call one of the ultrasound techs. She has a mobile station, so you won't have to switch rooms."

Dr. Leemont adjusts the table, allowing me to lie down while we wait. My heart pounds hard against my chest and the sound is all I can hear as I try to sort this all out in my head. I can't grasp on to a single coherent thought as they all tumble into each other in a maniacal collision, aside from the one piece that remains untouched and clear as day: I'm pregnant.

The door opens and a young tech wheels in the large machine. She introduces herself, but I remain quiet as I watch her set everything up while she and Dr. Leemont go over my labs.

Once she's set up and I lie down, she opens the front of my gown and squirts a warm blob of gel on my stomach. Pressing the wand down, she tells me, "Since we don't know how far along you are, I'd like to see if we can get a good view of the baby externally. Normally we do an internal exam, but I'd like to try this out first."

"Okay," I breathe as I keep my eyes glued to the monitor screen.

She begins clicking away on her keyboard while she presses the wand firmly onto my lower abdomen, almost painfully, but then she says, "There we go," and my heart stops. "See that?" she asks as she points to the white peanut on the screen, and as soon as she makes the slightest adjustment to the wand, she freezes the screen.

"Oh my God."

"Let me get a couple measurements to see how far along you are," she says, but *holy shit,* I can clearly see a head and a belly. Not a tiny blip you often hear about that doesn't look like anything. I clearly see a baby: head, belly, and four tiny nubs for its arms and legs. She doesn't even need to dissect the image for me because it's unmistakable. Never has reality hit me so hard with a truth that's undeniable.

"Nine weeks, five days," she says, and then looks at me with a smile before she turns to look at her conception calendar on the monitor. "New Year's baby, it looks like."

I can't speak. All I can think right now is Bennett, Declan, and Pike. I haven't had sex with Pike in over a month, but nine weeks ago, I was having sex with all three of them. God, I'm a sick human being, carrying a baby that could belong to any one of them.

"I'm showing October tenth for a due date," she tells me, and then she presses a button and a loud *woosh woosh woosh woosh* comes through the speakers at a rapid rate.

"What's that?"

"Your baby's heartbeat."

"Oh my God," I whisper again. A heartbeat? It's so real. So alive. Hearing that fast heartbeat inside of me is almost too much as I lie here, trying not to completely lose it.

"Good and strong," she says before turning the sound off and when it disappears, I close my eyes and replay the soothing sound in my head. How is this happening?

When she's done, I sit up and cover myself back up with the gown while she prints me off a few photos and hands them to me, saying a happy, "Congratulations."

But knowing my situation, and knowing what Dr. Leemont said about me being high-risk, there's nothing to be congratulating me about. She hands me the pictures, and both she and the doctor step out of the room so that I can get dressed, but I don't. I just sit here and look down at one of the pictures, a picture that shows a top view: head, belly, and four nubs. A weird laugh slips out through my tears when I compare the baby to a marshmallow.

My hand goes to my belly. I wouldn't even believe it if I didn't just see it with my own two eyes.

A baby. My baby.

I never thought I wanted one. Never thought it was even a possibility. But now that I have one, I don't know how I feel because I'm feeling so much. I'm scared and ashamed, but under that, I feel an overwhelming sense of protectiveness for it. Never have I had anything that was solely mine, and knowing what a fucked up world this is, I'm comforted by the fact that this baby is safe inside of me.

After I'm dressed and have made my next appointment, I head outside. As soon as the cold air hits me, I'm scared to resume my life—resume the lies.

A baby.

What does this mean for me? Will it even survive to see a moment of this world? Do I want it to? The questions multiply as I stand here on the sidewalk, people moving about, cabs honking their horns, life. The wind kicks up and I begin to cry, exposing myself to these strangers around me, but nobody stops to notice. Turmoil is a dark cloud that finds its home over me right now.

I leave my car and walk. I don't know where I'm going, but I need to move. Time passes as I wander the streets of the loop, all the while, crying. Do I tell Bennett? Is this something I can hide from him? If he knew, he'd assume it was his. What if it is? God, I can't have him in my life. But could I kill him? The father of our baby?

Yes. I could. I'd have to because the thought of having to share this with him makes me sick to my stomach. The thought of having to look at his face, the thought of giving him a baby, giving him happiness and joy, it's all sickening.

I desperately need someone to help me. To come and hold me, tell me it's going to be okay. Someone to take care of me, hold my hand, and take away all my anguish. I'm sick of always feeling so alone.

I step off the curb and start crossing the street when I hear a horn blasting. I startle and jerk my head around to see through my blurred vision, a car, heading straight towards me, and I freeze.

"NINA!" a man's voice screams in a panic.

I close my eyes, more tears falling down my cheeks when something crashes into me. I'm no longer on my feet, I'm being carried, and when I finally touch the ground, I know I'm safe by the smell.

Declan.

"Are you okay?" he asks as I open my eyes to look up at him and then at my surroundings. I'm in the lobby of his hotel.

"What happened?" I whisper as I look out of the glass doors to see the street, busy with cars.

"I was in my office when I happened to see you walking. I went outside to catch you when you stepped out into oncoming traffic. What the hell were you thinking?"

"I don't . . ." my voice trembles, and then, like a porcelain doll falling to its death, I shatter. Falling into his arms, the sobs begin ripping out of me.

He quickly scoops me off my feet, cradling me in his arms, as he rushes me out of the lobby and into the elevator. He doesn't say anything as I cry against him with my arms clinging around his neck. He holds me like a child and it comforts me in a way only he can do, whispering, "Shhh, baby. I've got you," softly in my ear.

The elevator opens and he carries me into his penthouse room and sets me down on the couch as he crouches down in front of me. When I drop my head into my hands, he pulls them away, and I can't stop the tears from falling as I look down at him. His face is covered in worry and I know there's no way I could keep this from him because I need him so badly right now. He's the one I want reassuring me. He's the only one I want—always. So when he asks, "Baby, what's wrong? You're scaring me," I don't hesitate for a single moment when I tell him, "I'm pregnant."

I watch as his face falls in a painful expression that breaks my heart. His eyes close, forehead creased in agony when he pleads, "Please tell me it isn't his." The crack in his voice matches the one in my heart, and I give him what I know he wants, what I want, what I wish for—the fairytale that never will be—saying, "It isn't his."

His eyes open and tears fall. "How do you know?"

"Because I had just started sleeping with you and had backed away from Bennett that month. He was out of town a lot, so he didn't question my avoidance." My words, complete lies.

"But I thought you couldn't get pregnant?"

"I know," I cry out. "This was never supposed to happen. It shouldn't have happened, but it did, and I'm so scared."

"Don't cry," he breathes as he moves to sit next to me on the couch and pulls me into his arms. "When did you find out?"

"Just now. I just left the doctor's office. That's why I was walking around.

I just needed to walk."

"You scared the shit out of me. That car almost hit you."

"I'm sorry."

"I need you to talk to me. Explain how this happened."

I lean back, pulling away from his hold and let out a heavy breath before telling him, "I've been in a lot of pain the past few days, so I went to see my doctor. I had been testing out a hormone therapy to help with the pain, but had to stop. The doctor told me the pain is showing up because it takes a while for the hormones to leave the system."

"Why didn't you tell me you were having pains?" he questions.

"Because you worry easily, and I knew it was probably nothing more than what I've always dealt with."

"I worry because I love you. I want to know what's going on with you. I don't want you keeping anything from me," he says, facing me and taking my hands in his, resting them on his lap. "So what did the doctor say?"

"Nothing. She took a look at my labs and that's when she told me I was pregnant." My voice falters on that last word as I begin to cry again.

Declan takes my face in his hands and assures me, "It's going to be okay. I know you're scared right now, but I'm not going anywhere."

"She told me that the baby probably wouldn't make it through the pregnancy though."

"Why?"

"Because I have too many lesions. She said they would keep a close eye on me. I have another appointment in two weeks."

"I'll go with you."

"You can't, Declan," I tell him. "Bennett is the one that found me this doctor. She knows he's my husband."

He grinds his teeth, causing his jaw to flex before hissing his words, "That's my fucking baby, right?"

"Yes."

"Did you tell him you're pregnant?"

"No," I respond, and then drop my head, admitting, "I'm scared, Declan. I'm scared for him to know." I look up, trying to contain the new slew of tears that threaten when I say, "I can't tell him. He can't know."

"He's going to find out, but you're not telling him without me by your side," he says, and the reality of this situation is starting to really hit me. "I know you're scared, but you're going to have to leave him."

"Declan—"

"You're leaving him," he demands.

"Just give me a little time."

"Fuck, Nina. All I've been doing is giving you time."

"I know. I'm sorry, but it isn't that easy. I'll leave him; I will," I say, trying to convince him, but I can no longer distinguish between truth and lies. I don't know what the fuck I'm doing. I'm just panicking at this point when all I really want to do is run away with Declan. For us to go to Scotland, have a baby, and leave this nightmare of a life behind.

"I don't want him fucking touching you anymore, do you understand me? You have my baby inside of you now. That fucker's not going to touch you," he bites with gravel in his voice and I don't even flinch when I agree. "Did he leave yet?"

"Late last night," I tell him. "He's gone for the rest of this week."

He nods his head, and I let my body slack into his, resting the top of my head to his chest. His hands come around the back of my neck and into my hair as I mumble, "I really am scared, Declan."

"I know, darling. I'm going to take care of you though," he says, and when I draw back and lift my head, he places his hand on my flat stomach, adding, "I'm going to take care of both of you."

His words make me smile. I run my hand over his, and I want to believe with everything I have that this baby is his.

"I heard its heartbeat," I murmur and his voice is barely an audible whisper when he asks, "You did?"

"Yeah. It's fast," I tell him. "They gave me a picture too."

I reach over to my purse and pull out the marshmallow photo and hand it to Declan. He stares down at it, and I watch his eyes gloss over in tears. He doesn't try to hide his emotions as he gets lost in the image.

"I didn't think it would look this real, with arms and legs," he chokes out around his tears.

"I'm almost ten weeks, so we missed the stage of the baby looking like a blob," I say as I let go of a sad laugh.

"Ten weeks?"

"I'm due in October," I tell him, and he finally looks up from the photo. His cheeks are damp, and I move to my knees, cup my hands along his jaw, and in the same loving way he does with me, I gently lick his tears away.

thirty-three

(PRESENT)

TODAY IS THE last day I have with Declan before I have to leave. Bennett returns this evening and I've been a wreck all morning. I'm scared and nervous that Bennett will know I'm pregnant, that somehow he'll be able to tell. But I'm also sad, because for these past few days since telling Declan, I've allowed myself to believe that this baby is his and that we're going to make this work. It's all a lie though. I don't know what I'm going to do, but whatever it is, I want to do it with Declan. I don't even want to imagine going back to a life where he doesn't exist for me.

I've never come across anyone like him. His intensity is entirely consuming, and when I'm not with him, all I can think about are ways I can sneak around to get to him. It's like he's the oxygen I need to survive, and when he's gone I'm suffocating. I don't know if love is supposed to feel this way, but it's all I know, and it's all with him.

"How are you feeling, darling?" Declan asks as he walks into the bathroom.

"Better. The heating pad just can't do what a hot bath can."

"You've been in here a long time."

Sinking down into the hot water, I look up at Declan as he stands over me and admire him. His square jaw, covered in day old stubble, the hard lines of his chest that are noticeable through his shirt, the roped muscles of his shoulders and arms. He's a beautiful man, casual in his dark jeans and bare feet, and suddenly, I'm mourning the loss of him as he blurs on the other side of the tears that flood my eyes.

Squatting down on the balls of his feet, he crosses his arms over his knees, asking, "What's wrong?" softly, his brows pinching in worriment.

"I don't want to leave." My voice is a mere whisper as I close my eyes to shield the tears from falling. I've never exposed this vulnerable side to another person as I find myself doing with Declan. I've always prided myself on how well I can cast the iron around me. Stoic and poised; the envy of everyone. But with him? It took something I didn't think I had in me.

Trust.

Somehow . . . somewhere along the way, he got me to trust him, and in the wake of that, I let him in. He now occupies a part of me that I had only reserved for Pike, but Pike only filled parts of that for me. It's Declan who fills me entirely, breaking the elasticity, filling me completely and running over to occupy the other vacant pieces inside of me.

The water laps around me, and I open my eyes to see Declan, naked, stepping down into the large tub. I move forward as he situates himself behind me, wrapping me up in his arms as I sink into his embrace. He slowly combs his fingers through my wet hair, and I release a faint hum in approval for the soothing touch. I run my hands down his strong legs that I'm tucked between and close my eyes again.

"Lean forward," he says, and when I do, he starts to gently massage my lower back. "How's that feel?"

"Really good," I tell him. I've been suffering from searing stomach and back cramps, the same cramps that led me to the doctor earlier this week. Declan became really concerned the other night when he woke up to find me sleeping in the bath tub, filled shallow with hot water. He made me call the doctor to see if she could prescribe painkillers, but since I'm pregnant there isn't anything that wouldn't be harmful to the baby. So I've been spending most of my time soaking in hot baths since it seems to be the only thing that gives me any real relief. The doctor said that this type of cramping is pretty common during an endometriosis pregnancy.

"I hate that you're leaving when you're hurting so much," he says while he kneads his fingers along my back.

"I don't want to go."

"Don't. Stay. I'm not going to be able to function knowing you're with him."

Drawing my knees to my chest, I wrap my arms around my legs, making my request, "Talk to me." I need him to do something to distract me from my sadness.

"What do you want me to tell you?"

"Tell me about your home in Scotland. What's it like there?"

He pulls me back against his chest, grabs a washcloth, and starts dipping it in the water and wringing it out over my shoulders and neck.

"It's rainy most of the time," he begins, and I close my eyes, resting my cheek on his pec and listen as he speaks. "But the green, sprawling hills make up for the lack of sunshine. The countryside is amazing."

"Is that where your house is? In the countryside?"

He drags the washcloth around my neck and down to my breasts, answering, "Yes. It's south of Edinburgh in the Galashiels."

"What does it look like?" I ask, my eyes closed while he continues to soothe me with his voice and touch.

"The estate is called Brunswickhill. It was built in the mid-late nineteenth century, a neo-classical Victorian mansion, but was completely renovated before I took ownership a few years ago."

"You were here though."

"I know."

"Have you ever stayed a night there?"

"No. I hired someone to furnish the place, but I've never actually stayed there yet," he tells me.

"So why did you buy it?" I ask.

"Because after my father sold his house to take permanent residence in New York, I felt I didn't have any more roots there aside from my mother," he tells me.

I open my eyes and look up at him when I ask, "Is that where she's buried?"

"Yeah, it is," he murmurs.

"You bought the place to stay connected to her?"

He nods as he looks down at me, and then kisses my forehead before he continues, "You'd love it there. It's on six acres, so it's peaceful and quiet with a great view of the Tweed River."

"Tell me more."

"There's a huge garden and a Victorian grotto built entirely out of clinker under this huge glazed dome."

"Are there lots of flowers?"

He drops the washcloth and bands his arms around me, tucking my head under his chin, sighing, "Yeah, darling. Tons of red and purple ones."

"Purple?" I question, my mind suddenly seeing the purple walls of my childhood.

"Mmm hmm."

"I don't like purple," I mutter softly, and he doesn't let a second pass before saying, "Then we'll rip them out."

I laugh under my breath and then he inquires, "You've never told me what your favorite flower is."

I take a moment even though I already know the answer, but the thought alone grips my throat, tightening it as I reveal to him, "Daisies. I like pink ones."

"Daisies?" he questions in surprise. "Such a simple flower. I would have thought something lavish."

"Why's that?"

"You just seem like a girl who likes nice things, that's all," he responds casually as he leans back, pulling me with him as we recline.

"Daisies are nice. Simple and nice, which is why I like them."

"I want to know everything you like."

"Is that so?" I lightly tease, and when he kisses my temple, he says, "Tell me a few things you like."

"Mmmm," I hum before revealing, "I like tea, and I like cupcakes with sprinkles. Apple juice, but only when it's in a small juice box. And I like daisies."

"Pink daisies," he clarifies, and I nod, repeating, "Pink daisies."

"What else do you like?"

I tilt my head to the side so that I can see him when I say, "I like the way your stubbled jaw feels when you kiss me."

"Why's that?"

"It makes me think of how a prince's kiss would feel."

His smile grows as he questions, "Aren't princes clean-shaven?"

Reaching up, I run my hand around the back of his neck, saying, "Not in my dreams," before pulling him down to kiss me. His lips move gently with mine, eventually taking his tongue to open me up, tasting me deeply. I savor the ice of his mouth, gliding my tongue along his.

He takes my hips and eases me around to slide over his lap, my legs straddled around him. His cock is instantly hard, and the need for closeness takes over, so I lift up, and with my hand on his massive erection, guide him inside of me. His eyes close as I slowly descend down around him and hold myself still. Neither of us moves as we cling to each other—hugging—flesh against flesh.

"Tell me what you want," he breathes against my breasts as he starts planting soft kisses down the swell and over my nipple, tightening it to a stiff peak.

"This."

"Tell me," he urges.

"Just this. I just need to feel you inside of me right now," I respond, giving him my honest words, because I desperately need to be as close to him as possible right now.

"I am inside of you," he says, loosening his arms and slipping his hand between our bodies, resting it on my stomach. "This is *me* inside of *you*."

My eyes well as I nod, needing to believe that it is a part of him growing inside of me and not Bennett or Pike. I want it to be him because all I want is simply *him*. My tears fall as I gaze into his beautiful, green eyes. Eyes filled with adoration for me and I adore him just as much. I love him. And now I'm doubting everything because all I can see are the rolling hills of Scotland, a nineteenth-century estate, and Declan with our baby in his arms.

The pain of what it would mean to destroy everything good in this man and turn him into a murderer for the sake of this sick game Pike and I schemed up shreds my heart. I tried to stay focused, I tried to shut myself off from feeling anything towards Declan, I tried to stick to the plan. But I can't do it. This isn't a game; this is a man's life. A good man's life. A man that I deeply love.

I can't ruin him and turn him into a monster. If sparing Bennett's life, even though I want him to suffer for what he did to my life, means that Declan's life won't be destroyed, I'll do it.

Killing Bennett isn't worth sacrificing Declan.

My tears grow, spilling over and down my face as I whisper, "I love you. All I want is you. You and me and this baby."

His cock thickens inside of me with each word I speak, but he doesn't urge me to move as we remain connected, locked together intimately. I know what I must do, and it won't be easy. Pike has given up so much these past few years while I've been married to Bennett. But I can't do it. I won't do that to Declan. Truth is, I don't have to kill Bennett to get my fairytale—my second chance—because that fairytale is right here in my arms. This is the happiness I've been missing all my life.

So I'll go to Pike and tell him it's over. Tell him I'll play it out, divorce Bennett, and fold my cards. I'll live the rest of my life as Nina, the girl from Kansas, if that means I won't lose Declan. I'll bury my past.

"I want to own every part of you," he groans as his eyes flare in heat, his fingers pressing into my skin as he grips my ass.

"You already do."

"Grab my shoulders and move," he commands, and I obey, lifting up along the shaft of his cock before gliding back down.

I continue to work the length of him, my pussy snug around him, gripping him in needy ecstasy as the water laps around our bodies. He handles one of my breasts in his hand, tugging on my hardened nipple as he drags his tongue over my other breast before fiercely sucking me into his mouth. With his teeth bared, he scrapes them along the delicate skin and then bites down with force. Screaming out in a seething aura of pleasure and pain, I ride his cock, rolling my hips over him. The warm water swirls over my swollen clit with each of my thrusts, driving me towards my peak.

Declan continues to work my tits, laving me with his tongue, feasting like I'm his last meal and he needs me to survive. He then grabs my hips, jerking me to pound against him as he shoves his cock deeper inside of me, hitting that bundle of nerves that only he's done, and I can't hold on. Dropping my head back, he quickly finds my hand, interlacing our fingers and squeezing it tightly. I pulse and spasm around him as the colorless light of my exploding orgasm blinds me. When I writhe against him, he wraps his free arm around my waist and roughly pins my body down over his cock. He throbs inside of me, growing and contracting with each pump of cum he shoots inside of me.

"Fuck," he moans in a sensual brute as we both come together.

Holding me close to him, my body begins to tremble in fiery aftershocks. I'm wrapped all around Declan when he eventually pulls his head back. Our breaths are erratic and labored as we try to find our way back down.

In a staggered voice, Declan pants, "I want to make you into everything you've ever dreamed of being."

And with those words, I don't need any convincing.

Fuck Bennett.

Fuck the revenge.

Fuck it all.

I have everything I'll ever want right here inside of this beautiful man.

thirty-four

(PRESENT)

I HAVEN'T GONE to see Pike yet. I know I have to, but I've been afraid about how he's going to react to the news that I want out of this. Bennett has been back in town for the past few days, and I find myself caring less and less about playing his wife. For me, it's over, but I feel I can't walk out until I talk to Pike.

I've seen Declan every day since Bennett has returned, and to say he's growing impatient with me is a severe understatement. My excuses are wearing thin, so I finish getting ready to drive out and tell Pike the new plan—the plan that will, for the first time, leave him without me by his side.

The guilt is insurmountable at this point. How do you tell the man, who is probably in love with you, and the one who has been your protector for the past twenty years, that it's no longer the two of you? That you've fallen in love and want to be with that other person? Pike and I have always been together, always honest with each other, until now. I told him I didn't love Declan, but I knew he could see right through me. See deeper than even I could at that point. I knew I cared for Declan, that he was a friend that I was being drawn to, but I hadn't yet realized that I had already fallen for him. Pike already knew though; that's how connected we are.

The house phone rings as I throw on my sweater, and when I answer, it's Manuel from downstairs.

"Mrs. Vanderwal, I'm sorry to disturb you, but there's a gentleman here saying he's a cousin of yours."

"What?" I question, wondering who the hell is down there, and then I hear the unmistakable voice of Pike, arguing, "Dude, just let me go up."

"Yes, please, Manuel," I quickly interject as rampant fear streaks through me. "Go ahead and send him up."

My nerves crash, confounded as to why the hell Pike would come here.

Never has he come here. We agreed from the start that our paths would never cross outside of Justice, so as I pace the foyer, waiting for his knock, I try to grapple with my thoughts and compose myself, all the while knowing what I must tell him.

When the knock comes, I open the door, grab his arm, and yank him inside, snapping, "What the fuck are you doing here?"

But his eyes don't meet mine, instead they scan around the room, taking in my home of the past four years. "Holy shit," he murmurs. "So this is where you've been while I'm rotting away in that shit tank?"

"Pike, what are you doing here? Are you crazy? What if Bennett was home?"

"Relax, Elizabeth. I've been sitting outside all morning waiting for that shit-stain to leave," he says, walking past me and into the dining room. "So . . ." he starts, letting the word linger as he drags a finger down the length of the cherry wood dining table, ". . . where the fuck have you been for the past month?" His words scrape out in frustration.

"I-I'm sorry. I ju—"

"Cut the shit. You told me Bennett was going to be out of town this past week, yet you never once came by to see me. Why is that?"

"Pike, please," I say on a shaky voice as chills run down my trembling arms, scared shitless with what I'm about to reveal.

"Please? What the fuck is going on with you, Elizabeth?!" he shouts, his voice booming through the open space as he slams his fist against the table. "You used to run to me the second Bennett left, you used to beg for my dick, but now, when you do finally decide to show your face, you rush out the door."

"Why are you screaming at me?!" I yell.

"Because you've got a job to do and it isn't getting done!" He walks the edge of the table and back over to me, but when he gets close, I take a step back. "Why isn't it getting done?"

My pulse races as I stutter out the words I've been afraid to say to him. "B-Because . . ."

"Because why?" he hisses as he glares at me.

Swallowing hard, I force out the words, "Because I want out."

His jaw locks and he begins a rhythmic clenching and unclenching of his hands, fisting them at his sides. He takes a moment before he breaks the silence, seething, "What do you mean *you want out*?"

"Pike, please don't flip out on me," I say, trying to keep my voice calm.

"What do you mean *you want out*?"

"I can't . . . I can't do this anymore." My face grows hot with the tears that threaten.

"It's Declan, isn't it?"

"I'm so sorry, Pike. I never thought—"

"You're nothing to him but an illusion, Elizabeth," he says, cutting me off.

"I love him."

My confession sparks a fury in his eyes, and when he takes another step towards me, I take another back, pissing him off.

"So, what now? You think he loves you back?"

"Yes," I breathe.

"You're full of shit. You have no idea what you're saying. You're so wrapped up in this lie that you're buying into this false reality. But it's *false*, Elizabeth. It's not real."

"It is."

"It isn't. You are not Nina. Can't you see that?"

"And what's Elizabeth? Huh? I mean . . . who is she really? Is she me?" I question as the levies break and the tears fall down my cheeks. "Because she doesn't feel like me. Because she was never supposed to be me!" My words now cries, pleading cries. "She only existed because of Bennett!"

"That's right, Elizabeth!!" he barks furiously. "Bennett! Feel that fucking hate! He's the reason for all of this! Don't lose sight of what he did to your life! To your father's life!"

And my fury parallels his, except that fury is robed in a mass of sadness and desperation when I shriek, "I know! God, I know, but I can't do it. I can't destroy Declan like that."

"Fuck Declan! He's the pawn. He's always been the pawn, and you, the queen."

"But sometimes the queen falls."

"Not you," he says sternly as his hands grip my shoulders that tremor under my emotions. "I'm not gonna let you fall."

"I already fell, Pike. I want out. I'll finish this; I'll divorce Bennett, and no one will ever have to know about this."

His fingers tighten around my shoulders, painfully. "You don't love him," he whispers, and I hear every morsel of pain he's trying to hide, but I can't lie.

"I do love him," I say under my breath, and as soon as he drops his head, he lifts it right back up. The look in his eyes turns to cold stone, and he takes a couple steps back, releasing his hands from me.

His sudden shift in demeanor rattles me as I watch him start to subtly shake his head before questioning, "Are you not telling me something?"

"What do you mean?"

"I mean the fact that your hand hasn't left your stomach for the past few minutes," he says, and when I look down, I see that I've got my hand right where he said it was—an unconscious act of protecting what's inside—and suddenly, all the blood drains out of me, leaving me utterly terrified as I watch the viperous hate surface in his eyes.

You've heard of Newton's first law of motion, right? The one that states that an object in motion will remain in motion unless acted upon by an unbalanced force? It's a science that can't be negated, and with the game in full speed, I'm about to learn the catastrophic consequences of that law.

"Pike," I soothe, needing him to calm down.

"Tell me that I'm losing my mind right now. That I'm not thinking clearly. That I'm not—"

Holding my hand up in front of me, I try coaxing my words as I speak slowly, "Please, Pike. I need you to just—"

And then he loses it, exploding like a grenade, screaming in sulfur, "Tell me you are not fucking pregnant!!"

"Pike!" I yell as he grabs my arms violently.

His face—raging red, spitting his words, "What the fuck have you done?"

"Nothing! Let go of me," I yell, panicked, jerking to break free of his hold on me.

"Tell me!"

"Yes!" I immediately shout back, and he releases his grip.

He turns away from me, raking his hands angrily through his hair, as I stand here, nervously awaiting his next move. He keeps his back to me when he continues to talk, "You're fucking pregnant. Jesus Christ. And it can't be mine because you haven't been fucking me."

I don't correct him because he assumes that I'm not as far along as I actually am. This baby could very well be his.

He turns back, and the look in his eyes scares the living shit out of me. I don't see Pike behind them, only a monstrous version of what could be my brother. And when he starts moving towards me—body tense—the shrill of horror stabs me.

"This is over right now. I've spent too many years for you to fuck this up."

"What do you mean?" I ask as I start backing away from him.

And then my world goes into a paradox of raging fast slow motion.

His arm rises with a tight fist.

My arms wrap around my stomach.

Fist barreling down.

My eyes squeezing shut and coiling away.

A collision of knuckles against jaw.

Blow after blow, he's relentless as I fall lifelessly to the ground. The light begins to fade as my screams lull me into the blackness. My lungs cave with every fatal kick to my stomach, and there's nothing I can do as I lie here defenseless to this monster above me. A beating fire of pain ruptures inside, paralyzing me to a corpse as I feel everything breaking inside of me. My screams turn breathless and everything vanishes as Pike grunts like a wild beast, hammering his booted foot over and over and over into the womb that carries the purest part of me.

Black ink bleeds over me as I drift into nothingness. I'm a hollow tomb. Looking up, I see a dark sky, flickering with diamonds. Thousands of them. There's no more pain—there's nothing in this solitude of pure, deathly silence as I lie here and stare into the endless black hole.

Wishes.

I could make an infinite amount of them with all the stars that shine down upon me. But I'm not lying on the ground. I don't feel anything as I float in negative space.

Where am I?

How did I get here?

And then I see him. My old friend. He never changes and that constant nurtures the despair that has always followed me. His green and yellow accordion body slinks over to me, and it's then that I realize how small I am because he appears to be the same size as me.

"I've missed you," he says in his eloquent English accent.

"I've missed you too, Carnegie."

"Where have you been?"

"In hell."

"Is that why you came back?" he asks.

"I don't even know how I got here," I tell him, and he smiles, saying, "Maybe someone knew you needed a little break from hell," as he gives a nod up to the heavens.

"Maybe," I whisper and roll over onto my belly. It's then I see where I am. Large, green blades of grass standing high above the mass of earth beneath. Gigantic trees that border a sea of dark water. Brilliantly massive blooms are illuminated by the full moon above, casting its glow on the array of colorful, exotic flowers; pink, orange, yellow—but no purple in sight. And when my eyes shift down, I take in a breath of awe when I realize why Carnegie doesn't look so tiny. My body, a tube, roped in pink and black, and when I look back at Carnegie, he laughs, "It's spectacular, isn't it?"

"I'm a caterpillar!" I say in wonderment. "Carnegie, do you see this?!"

"I do."

And then it all comes together. I finally made it. I'm here . . . in the magical forest . . . and I'm a caterpillar, floating in a pond that seems like an ocean because I'm so tiny. I begin laughing as we float on our lily pad raft.

"It's good to see you smiling," he says as I scoot around the large, green leaf, reveling in my new form.

Meandering around, I respond, "It's been a while since I've felt this free."

"May I ask you a question?"

Giggling after I round my body into a ball, discovering I can roll, I take a few seconds to play around before acknowledging his request, answering, "Of course," as I straighten my body and inch over towards him.

"Why do you feel like you're in hell?"

His question dulls my zealousness, and when I flatten my body against the lily pad, I tell him, "It's always been hell, Carnegie. But lately, it's become overwhelming."

"What happened?"

"It's a long story."

"Look around," he says. "I've got nothing but time."

"I'm sure, but to relive everything isn't something I wish to do."

"Then tell me what happened last."

I blink and then look up at the black sky, glittered in stars, and tell him, "I fell in love."

"Ahh, love," he says as if he's wise in that spectrum, so I ask, "You ever been in love?"

"Me?" he questions and looks out over the water. "No. I was turned into a caterpillar before ever having the chance to experience such an emotion. But I wonder why it's hell you feel."

"The love is the only part of this story that isn't hell."

"Tell me what it feels like. Love."

A few fireflies above catch my attention, and as I watch them making skittering dashes of swirling light, I answer, "Amazing. It's like an urgency that can never be sated because you can't get enough. One day, you're walking through life, thinking you're satisfied, well, as satisfied as you can be, and then, when you finally feel the click and get your first taste of love, you realize you've been starving your whole life but never knew it. And that one person is all you need to truly feel alive."

"And you found that?"

Giving Carnegie my attention again, I reply, "Yeah. I never knew what it felt like to breathe until I met him."

"So what's hell?" he asks.

"The man I'm married to."

"The one who allows you to breathe?"

"No, the one who slipped the noose around my throat and caused me a life of suffering," I tell him as his beady eyes widen.

"I'm confused."

"I married my enemy," I begin to explain. "And the man I wound up falling in love with was someone who I was supposed to trick into killing my husband."

"Why do you want your husband dead?"

"Because when I was five, I was ripped away from my dad. He was arrested and went to prison where he was eventually murdered, and I went to a horrendous foster home."

"What does your husband have to do with that?"

"Everything," I say as we continue to float around the smooth water. Releasing a deep breath, I begin telling him the story of my father's arrest and how Pike was determined to find answers for me when we were older.

"It took a while, but after going through my father's police records and Pike blackmailing his old caseworker for my file, we finally found out that it all started with a child abuse claim. We kept digging because my father was the kindest man I knew and had never laid a hand on me. And then we found it. A call was made to DCFS from the Vanderwal family."

"Who are they?"

"I'll give you one clue," I say. "When I married my husband, Bennett, I took his name."

"Vanderwal," he concludes. "But why go after him if it was his parents who made the claim?"

"Because in that file was an interview. The interview was with Bennett."

"It was *his* claim?"

"Yes," I reply as I feel the hate begin to boil inside of me.

"What did it say?"

"He had been walking home from a friend's house one afternoon, and when he passed my house, he heard fighting and screaming coming from inside. He saw my dad through the window hitting someone, but he couldn't see the other person. He assumed it was me that was getting hit, so he went home, told his parents, and the call to DCFS was made."

"Who was it that your father was hitting?"

"I couldn't have been home that afternoon because I would have heard it. I was probably still at preschool or something. But looking back, with the information I have now, it was most likely someone he was doing business with. Maybe a deal gone bad; who knows?" I tell him. "The thing is, the state did their investigation. but they couldn't find any signs of abuse or neglect. However, it was noted that the caseworker noticed *suspicious activity* at the house while performing random drive-by's, so a request for further investigation was handed over to the police department who uncovered the gun trafficking. And that was it, he was arrested, and I never saw him again."

Those last words choke me up, the pain of that last image of my father. It's never faded for me; my father, on his knees, the tears running down his cheeks, his words, trying to convince me that everything would be okay.

When Carnegie begins to move closer to me, finding a new spot on the lily pad, I'm pulled from the sad memory, and he questions, "So why did you marry him?"

"I felt this burning desire to avenge my father's murder, to make Bennett pay for all the abuse I suffered in foster care, for everything that was stolen from me.

My innocence.

My faith.

My childhood.

My trust.

My father.

My future.

Everything.

"Bennett is the reason there was a magnifying glass put on my father. It was Bennett who opened his mouth, made a false claim, and destroyed two lives, yet he goes on, happy, healthy, making his life into a glorious success. That was supposed to be my life. But because of him, he took it all away from me and I wound up being raped, molested, bound up in a closet, left for days to shit and piss all over myself. That's the life Bennett gave me.

"I wanted to make him pay for what he did. I wanted revenge."

"But you fell in love," he states, and I whisper my confirmation, "I fell in love."

"And now?"

"And now all I want is to spare destroying Declan. I still want to kill Bennett. I still want to make him pay, but not if it costs the good soul of the man I love."

"Let me ask you something. How old was Bennett when he told his parents he thought you were being abused?"

"Eleven."

Carnegie takes a moment before saying, "Just a kid. A young, innocent kid who saw something that probably scared him, thinking you were the one being hit, and his first reaction was to help."

"But he didn't help, and my dad wound up dead," I defend.

"He was just a kid trying to do the right thing," he counters, but instead of growing frustrated, the tranquility of being in this place with Carnegie keeps my frustrations at bay. "Can I ask you something else?"

I nod.

"What responsibility does your father hold in all of this?"

"My father was a good man," I declare.

"I'm not taking that away from him. But everyone has two sides, and your father was a gun trafficker, was he not?"

Taking a moment, I concur, "Yeah. He was. But he never hurt anyone."

"But he knew the illegal guns would hurt someone. He may not have been the one to pull the actual trigger, but in a way, he *did* pull that trigger," he says before adding, "And it wouldn't have mattered what Bennett ever said, the fact is, if your dad hadn't been dealing in something illegal, Bennett's claim would have been dropped and nothing would have ever happened."

"I know what you're trying to do. You're trying to be the voice of reason, but I've never claimed to be a rational or reasonable person."

"Have you ever had a voice of reason?" he questions.

"I've only ever had Pike, and he's just as screwed up as I am, if not more. We're sick people; I know this. But when you grow up like we did, you can't expect sanity," I say. "My father was good. He didn't deserve the life that was dealt to him after what Bennett did. I didn't deserve it either. The thing is, there will always be someone next in line after my father. The gun trafficking doesn't stop, so what's the point? The world isn't suddenly good now that my father isn't here."

"So you plot to kill?"

"I used to fantasize about what it would feel like to kill when I was a kid," I admit. "The thought brought me a sense of satisfaction and elated me.

Relief. Freedom. Peace. To eliminate the *truly* bad, removing it so that you no longer have to exist in a world where it does."

"You can't live like that. Killing and holding on to the past."

"I'm not holding on to it, I'm trying to let it go."

"You haven't let it go. Instead, you married it, and now it's controlling every aspect of your life. You met a man you love, but Bennett has power over that because he's your husband and you were forced to fill this other man with lies . . . because of Bennett—because of the past you are refusing to let go of."

His words hit me hard. But how do you let go of a wound that is cut so deep there's no chance of it ever healing, at least not without an ugly scar to remind you of it? So I simply ask, "How do I let go?"

"It's easy, really. You find what makes you happy, and you walk towards it, leaving the past behind," he tells me. "So what you need to ask yourself is, *what makes you happy*?"

"Declan." My answer comes without any second thought or hesitation.

"Then go to him. Go find him and don't look back. Soon the happiness will be enough to weaken the control the past has on you, and it won't hurt as badly as it does right now."

"But I'm here. How do I get back?" I ask and watch as he makes his way to the edge of the leaf, and when we pass a log floating in the water, he slides onto it when the bark meets the lily pad.

"Carnegie, wait! How do I get back?" I ask as I begin to drift away from the log.

"There are signs everywhere. You just have to look for them," he tells me. "Come back and visit me, okay?"

"I do. Every night in my dreams."

"Those are dreams though."

"Is this not a dream?" I ask, suddenly very confused about what this is, and his response doesn't help when he says, "This is your awakening," before scooting his spiraled body down the length of the log and eventually disappearing into the forest.

I continue to float aimlessly around the pond, staring up into the sky, thinking about everything Carnegie said to me. He's right; I need to walk away from my past if I don't want it to follow me.

Hours pass as I enjoy the serene tranquility of my surroundings, and when I see the shimmer of the sun rising through the trees in the distance, its sparkling rays light up the murky water. It's then that I see my sign. Green bulbs that stick out of the water begin to open, hundreds of them. One by one, lotus flowers bloom, spreading their pure white petals over the muddled water. They're beautiful, and when I float into the blooms, I have to squint against the bright light that the sun's glow is creating in this fragrant, white paradise.

thirty-five

(PRESENT)

DARKNESS.

Nothing but black as I lie here awake, although I'm not awake. I can feel a warm hand stroking my arm as I inhale a familiar smell.

Bennett.

My body aches, throbbing in a dulled pain, but when I try to move, I can't. When I try to open my eyes, I can't. But I can feel Bennett's touch. I can smell him. I can hear the steady beeping of a machine that alerts me to the fact that I'm in a hospital.

The last thing I remember is lying helplessly on my dining room floor while Pike threw kick after violent kick to my stomach.

My stomach!

My baby!

I can't wake up. But do I even want to? I already miss Carnegie. Do I really want to wake up to find the horror that's waiting for me? What happened with Pike? Why did he do it?

"Mr. Vanderwal," a soft, female voice says, but I can't see anything as I lie here in my comatose state.

"Finally," he says with an urgency to his voice. "What's going on? Is she going to be okay?"

"She's stabilized, but she had a lot of internal bleeding. Unfortunately, there was a fetomaternal hemorrhage and by the time she arrived here by ambulance, she had already lost the baby."

No! God, no!

With all the strength I have, I try to move, I try to do anything, but nothing happens. I'm stuck, unable to get out a cry, a scream, a movement, something to release the torment that is beginning to flood inside of me.

"Baby?" Bennett questions. "What baby?"

Oh, God.

"Your wife was pregnant."

"No. There must be some mistake. My wife has endometriosis. She can't get pregnant," he refutes.

"I'm so sorry. I know this is a difficult time, but according to her OB/GYN file that was faxed over, it seems the pregnancy was confirmed last week. I have noted that an ultrasound was performed, indicating at that time, she was nearly ten weeks pregnant."

I don't hear a response from Bennett, and I can only imagine his shock right now.

Bennett, speak. Say something.

"I'll give you some time," she says. "I'll be back to check in. If you need anything, just hit the call button, okay?"

"Yeah," he responds on a breath, and when I hear the door click, he removes his hand from my arm, and the room is silent.

I can't even think about Bennett, all I can think about is my baby. The baby that Pike took away from me. The baby that Pike killed. He knew exactly what he was doing, beating my stomach as violently as he did.

I hate him.

I thrash around like a maniac inside, trying to free myself, but my body doesn't respond. I'm paralyzed in this bed.

"She's in the hospital," Bennett says, but I don't hear anyone else in the room.

"I need you to get here now," he demands. "Bring everything you have on her."

He has to be on the phone, but what the hell is he talking about? Who is he talking to and what do they have on me? *Fuck.* What's going on? I need to get out of here. I need to find Declan. I can't breathe. Oh my God, I'm panicking and I can't breathe. Machines start to go off, filling the room with loud beeps.

"Nurse!" Bennett yells, and moments later, a cold fluid swims through my veins and I drift out peacefully.

"WHAT THE HELL happened?" I hear a man's voice say. It sounds familiar, but my head is so fuzzy as I come out of a deep sleep.

"I got a call from Clara. She had come to the penthouse and found Nina beaten and unconscious. I don't know what happened. I've spoken to the police and they're investigating," Bennett says. "Tell me what you know."

"You wanna do this here?" the man questions.

"Yeah."

"Her name's not Nina."

Oh no. No, no, no, no.

"What are you talking about?" Bennett asks.

"Her name is Elizabeth Archer. A runaway foster kid," he reveals. "It's all in the file."

"Archer? Sounds familiar."

It should, you asshole.

"Her father was arrested for international gun trafficking," the man says.

"I know her."

"Looks like she came straight for you. Piece of advice . . . call your lawyer."

"As soon as you can, I want surveillance set up," Bennett demands, but there's no need. I'm done with him, and the only thing I'm guilty of is identity theft.

"The affair you originally suspected, she's having one. Name is Declan McKinnon."

"Fuck," he hisses. "What is she up to?"

"Here's the file. Everything's in it." There's a long pause before the guy speaks again, saying, "I'll get security set up. Everything should be in place tomorrow or the next day."

The door clicks and I know I'm alone with Bennett, and that freaks me out, because I no longer have control. He's not a stupid man. If he hasn't already figured it out, it won't be long before he does.

Fuck! Why can't I wake up?

"Elizabeth," he whispers, and I can tell it just clicked by his acknowledging tone. "I always wondered what happened to you."

Bullshit.

"Rick," he says, speaking our attorney's name. "Things could be better. Look, I have something that can't wait. When can you see me?"

What's he going to do? Shit. As much as I hate Pike right now, I need him.

"No, that works. I'll leave right now."

I listen to the movements around the room when a female voice says, "I need to change a couple of her bandages."

"That's fine. I was just leaving," Bennett responds. "Here's my card. I want you to call me the second she wakes up, and I mean *the second*."

He leaves, and I continue to lie here in my comatose state, unable to react to anything. I don't know what I'm doing or what's going to happen to me. I need to run, to go find Pike. I hate that I still need him, but things are headed south, and fast.

I KNOW HE'S here. I can smell lotus blooms, and with that alone, the pinching angst that's been festering relents and I feel safe. His hand is on my belly, another combing through my hair, and I will myself to open my eyes. To move, to do anything to let him know I can feel him. My body hurts so badly as my muscles start to flex and shift.

That's it. Come on; wake up. Wake up.

"Nina?" he says, his voice is sad, but I need to hear it. I need that voice to pull me out of this darkness.

"Can you hear me?" he asks, grabbing my hand, and finally, I can feel my fingers move. "Baby, please wake up. Just open your eyes. Show me you're still with me."

I cling to his words, and light finally filters in. My eyes blink, responding to my body's request.

"Thank God," he sighs in relief as my blurred vision begins to clear. He leans over me, kissing my forehead, and I reach up, grabbing for any part of him.

"I'm here, darling," he assure as I clench on to his shirt, and his hand covers mine. "I'm here," he continues to soothe, and when I try to speak, I gag. "Shh, relax. You have a breathing tube down your throat. Just relax, okay?"

I nod, taking in a few deep breaths, allowing his soft, whispered accent to calm me, and notice the single, white lotus flower that's lying on the bed beside me.

"I'm sorry I wasn't here sooner. When I didn't hear from you, I called all over until I found you here."

I reach up and touch the tube coming out of my mouth and shake my head, needing to tell him that when I leave here, I'm going home with him. I need him to know it's over with Bennett and that it's him I want, but he takes my hand away, reading me well, saying, "It's fine. You don't need to say anything." His eyes are hard and serious when he says, "You'll never go back to that bastard again. You're coming home with me. I should have never let you leave my place the other night."

I nod, agreeing with everything he's saying.

"He's never going to touch you again."

I place my hand over the one he still has on my belly and the emptiness is too much as I begin to cry. He keeps his eyes on my stomach, fisting my hospital gown in his hand. His face pinches, as if he's trying to brace himself for the worst when he finally asks, his voice coming out hoarse, "Please tell me our baby is okay."

And when he finally brings his eyes to mine, I can already feel the salts eating away at my flesh as they spill out. He drops his head and releases a God-awful sob, and I do what I can to give him comfort as I run my fingers deep into his hair, gripping it tightly in my hand as he rests his head on my stomach. Seeing him in this much pain, this strong man who is always in so much control, is unbearable.

His shoulders hunch over and heave as he silently breaks. I want to be swallowed up by anything, just to be taken far away from this life, but I want to take Declan with me. I'll always want him with me, and when he lifts his head, I notice the blackness of his eyes. His jaw grinds and I watch the muscles along his arms constricting. I begin to shake my head as I witness his transformation—the one I had been leading him to make. My heart slams against my broken ribs, and when I grab ahold of his wrists, he snaps, "I'm going to kill that motherfucker."

No, no, no!

I shake my head, and he moves quickly to kiss the corner of my mouth, looking me in the eyes, forcing his words deep inside of me, saying, "That was our baby. My baby."

Frantically, I cling my arms around him, needing him to stay with me, but he pulls back, telling me, "I'm not losing you. I love you too much, but that fucker is going to pay."

I start clawing at the tube in my mouth, yanking it out of my throat, but begin gagging and choking as I watch him walk out of the room.

Declan, NO! You're not a monster; don't do this! Come back!

I thrash my body up, and I shriek through my gagging when the pain from my broken ribs shoots through me like a virulent fire. The machines are going wild, beeping and flashing, and two nurses rush into the room as I try ripping the tubes and wires away from me.

DECLAN!!!

"Hold still. You need to calm down," the nurse scolds, but I can't. He's going to kill him. He can't kill him.

He can't.

Choking against the breathing tube, I'm pinned down as the one nurse removes it, and once it's out, I wail in utter pain, scratching out a dreadful cry, "Declan!! NO! Stop him!"

"Who?"

"Please!" I belt out, but I'm still pinned down, and when I see the syringe, I freak. "No! Don't! Please!!"

And in an instant, I'm a boulder, sinking like a thousand pounds, deep into the bed. I fight the drifting and weep, body and voice growing weaker with every passing second. I cry, powerless to stop what is bound to happen. I can't lose the Declan I know, the Declan I love, because if he does this, he'll never be the same. And in the end, I'll have no one to blame but myself.

What have I done?

When I can't hang on any longer, I slip under into a desolate sedation.

Alone.

thirty-six
(PRESENT)

TWO DAYS LATER

WHEN I WOKE from my sedation, only a few hours had passed. And when the police came to inform me that my husband had been murdered in our home—shot two times in the head—I needed to be sedated again. Knowing what Declan had done—for me—pushed me over the edge.

Guilt . . .

I haven't heard from him or seen him. I miss him. I worry about him. I'm scared for him. I haven't called him because I'm scared to draw any attention, but I've texted him using the app on my phone that he gave me. There's been no response though. Pike has been missing too. So here I am, having no idea what to do, and I'm all alone in a life I no longer want.

I couldn't go home when I was discharged from the hospital this morning; I was too scared of what I would see. The police told me that one of the building's residents made the call to 911 after hearing gunshots. There was no sign of forced entry though, and the police confiscated Bennett's computer and files, among other things, as they move forward in the investigation.

So now I sit here in a hotel room, staring out the window, looking down on a city full of people, but I've never felt so isolated.

Where's Declan? Why hasn't he come for me?

I've been doing nothing but crying. People assume I'm mourning the loss of Bennett, but I'm not. The sick part of me is content with his death. My tears are for my baby and Declan. Never have I been so close to my fairytale ending, and now I hang by a thread while I wait for any type of contact from Declan. I've been looking for signs, signs that Carnegie told me were everywhere, but I can't see beyond the pain of what I have lost so far and the birth of hatred for my brother. The one who promised me that he would always protect me and would fight forever to give me happiness. And then the moment I come within reach of that, he rips it away. I don't know if I could ever forgive him for what he did, because now, all I can do is wish for his death. At the same time, a part of me needs him. To know I still have someone here on this Earth.

What if I lost it all? What if nobody comes for me?

The misery that thought produces overpowers all the aches my body feels from Pike's beating. I couldn't believe what he did to me when I finally saw my reflection in the mirror. My first instinct was to cover my face, but then I realized I have no one to hide from. It's only me.

A pounding on the door startles me, and when I rush over to look through the peephole, my stomach sinks and coils in fear but also relief.

"Pike," I breathe when I open the door and wrap my arms around him, crying hard for all the fucked up emotions I feel for him. Love and hate, it's a bitter mixture.

He kicks the door closed and holds me close before pulling back. His face is white in horror, hands shaking as he runs them through his hair.

"What's going on? How did you find me?"

"I went to see you at the hospital, but you weren't there, and when you weren't at home, I started calling everywhere looking for Nina Vanderwal." His voice is panicked as he speaks. "We have a huge problem."

"What do you mean?"

Pike paces back and forth like a maniac, telling me, "Declan knows."

"Knows what?"

He turns to face me, on the verge of completely losing it, when he says, "About you. He knows your name. He's knows you're Elizabeth."

"What?! How?" I go stiff, and my first thought is that I've already lost him. Pike doesn't give me much time to think though as he continues.

"I don't know, but when I was driving home earlier this morning, that fucker was waiting for me at the trailer."

"Shit! What did he say?"

"Nothing. I saw him, knew exactly who it was, and drove off, never stopping. I went straight to Matt's place and he said that some guy with an accent had called him the day before asking questions about you and me."

"Oh my God," I say, unable to catch my breath. "How does he know?"

"Don't know, but you've gotta get rid of him. He knows too much. He could already be on his way to the police."

"No," I blurt out, trying to scramble my thoughts together. "He wouldn't do that, would he? I mean, he's the one who killed Bennett."

"Are you willing to put your trust in a man you've only known for a few months, a man you conned, a man you drove to murder someone? This is no joke. You could go to prison if this got uncovered."

The rampant fear running through me causes me to go lightheaded and I have to sit down. I can't even think straight as I stare at the floor, trying to think of all the ways he could've found out. But the dagger here is how I deceived him and what he must be thinking, coming to the realization that he probably just killed a man for nothing but a lie—because that's exactly what he just did.

"Elizabeth, you can't sit here and wait. You have to go find him."

"And do what?" I question as I look up at him.

He stands next to the couch where I sit, and with determination in his eyes, he says, "You have to kill him."

"No." I snap, jumping off the couch, and the pain from my ribs twinges and causes me to stumble. Pike just stands there, unmoving as he watches me. And with my hand clenched around my side, I argue, "No. I'm not doing that."

"You don't have a choice! Are you not hearing me? He knows about us."

"I can't kill him, Pike. I won't do it."

"Cut the shit and wake up! You're not understanding what this could do to you," he shouts.

"I love him."

"You don't. And in the end, you're gonna see that you just got caught up in this fantasy. A fantasy that you and I both created for you. But it's not your life."

"It was my life! And then you came in and took it all away!" I yell, losing my cool and letting my emotions take over. "I do love him, and he loves me. I was finally going to have everything I've ever wanted. We were making plans for us, for our baby, and you destroyed it all! I hate you! I fucking hate you, Pike!"

He doesn't flinch at my words as he stands here. "We had a plan and that plan affected both of us. Bennett needed to die—for you! If I didn't do what I did, to push Declan over the edge, Bennett would still be alive and you'd never be able to forgive yourself for letting him go without any consequences for what he did to you." He takes a step towards me, and his condescending tone on his next words do nothing but fuel my hate, not only for him, but for everything my life is. "Do I need to remind you about how Carl would rape you, piss on that mattress, and force you to lay in it while he pounded his filthy dick inside of you?"

"Fuck you!" I shriek as I start throwing fists into him, frantically beating him in the swarm of pure, seething fire.

He quickly grabs my wrists, forcing me down to the couch, and with his face in mine, hisses, "Either you kill him or I will."

"Pike, no! Maybe he won't do anything at all. Maybe he's scared and will keep his mouth shut," my words tumbling out, giving him weak reason after weak reason, but I'm desperate.

"A scared man wouldn't have shown up to my place alone," he says before letting go of me and walking to the door.

I lurch off the couch and throw my body against him, trying to knock him down, but in a flash, he turns and strikes his fist against my already battered face. The force of his punch sends me stumbling back and falling down. By the time I can get up on my feet, he's gone.

"Shit!"

Adrenaline pumps its fury into my system, numbing all of my body's pains as I run to the bedroom and grab my keys. Running out of the room, I waste no time with the elevator as I make a mad dash down the stairs, flight after flight after flight, until I finally make it to the lobby. My throat burns with each breath as I run to my car. Pike is nowhere in sight, and when I pull out of the garage, I have two choices: Lotus or River North. I make the quick decision to try Declan's loft first, praying to anyone who will listen to me that he's there and Pike isn't. I fly through the busy streets, running stop signs and ignoring the red lights I hit.

"Fuck!" I bite out when I drive by Pike's car parked a block down from Declan's building.

Slamming on my brakes when I reach the front of the building, pain pierces my battered body as I run like hell, fumbling with the keycard Declan gave me, and when the elevator opens, I pound the button for his floor over and over as my body quakes in dread and anxiety.

"Come on, come on, come on. COME THE FUCK ON!" I scream with each floor we pass, and as soon as I hit the top floor, two rapid gunshots fire, echoing as the doors slide open.

Speaking isn't even a possibility as I run out and into Declan's living room where I see Pike charging through the loft and then look down at a massive puddle of blood pooling underneath the lifeless body of my prince.

A disgustingly vulgar shriek rips straight from the core of my heart as I run to Declan, falling to my knees in his blood. Touching his face, I try to take in the beauty of this perfectly sculpted man as I wail painfully over him.

"I've got it," I hear Pike say as he rushes back into the room, shoving a file inside of his jacket. Pike's hands are on me quick, pulling me back as I fight against him, screaming and crying. "We have to go!" he urges in a panic.

But I can't speak; the agony is choking me into screeching cries filled with sharp gravel.

"Come on! We have to go. NOW!"

I cover Delcan's body with mine, sealing my lips to his in a breathless kiss as the life drains out of him.

And then . . .

The touch is lost.

Pike has his arms banded around my chest as he lifts me off the floor and starts running.

"Let me go!" I scream, wincing against the pain of my injuries, as I thrash my arms, kicking, trying helplessly to fight my way out of his grip.

"We have to go before the cops get here."

Pike slams through a door, and when we get into the stairwell, he sets me down and pins me against the wall, keeping his hands locked on me.

"Listen to me," he says in a whispered grunt. "Pull yourself together before we both wind up in prison."

"You killed him!" I cry, my words bleeding through the jagged fractures of my heart.

"To save us. I killed him to save us," he defends. "You need to calm down and focus. Look into my eyes and focus."

I do.

"You with me?" he asks.

I don't respond when he adds, "I need you with me, okay? I'm all you have. Listen to me. I need you to do exactly what I say." His words are frantically rushed. "Get in your car. Go home, pack a couple bags, and meet me at the trailer. Don't answer the phone. Don't speak to anyone. Got it?"

"What are we going to do?"

"We're running. Don't fuck around, Elizabeth. Now come on, we have to go!"

And he's right, if we don't get out of here now, our lives will be over. So in a mindless rush of fight or flight, I thoughtlessly fly down the stairs, covered in Declan's blood as I flee towards a freedom I'm not sure even exists.

But I run anyway.

My hands clench the steering wheel, covered in the crimson life of the one man I thought could save me from me. But maybe people like me aren't supposed to be saved. Maybe I'm just destined to bear the weight of the demons that lurk among the good.

When I arrive back at the penthouse, walking through the door as only one, no longer having my beacon of hope growing inside of me, I begin to wonder: *What's the point?* I couldn't even protect the baby that was supposed to be safe from this world. Life's cruel joke of finally giving me something pure and holy, just to have it ripped away from me in an instant.

I don't waste any time though, running straight to the bedroom, the smell of Bennett everywhere. I wonder if he's watching me right now, laughing at the downfall, enjoying my suffering. The bile rises, and I begin slinging clothes in a mad haze into a bag, not even paying attention to what I'm throwing in. Simply moving for the sake of moving, but the actions are entirely thoughtless as the bitterness of my tears leak out and eat through my skin, burning their way back into me. Like a metaphor, reminding me that no matter what I do, I won't ever escape this pain because the moment my body tries to release it, it soaks it right back up.

Fucking life. I hate you.

The world is nothing but a whirlwind of colors and flashing lights, swirling around me as I run back down to my car, not knowing what the next move is—where I go from here—what life holds for me now. Tossing my bag into the back of my car, I look over to the Rover next to it—Bennett's car. And I think, if Bennett is laughing at me right now, does he deserve to be?

Probably so.

I don't know how anyone could be more pathetic than I am right now.

Maybe I'll show him how pathetic I can be; give him another reason to laugh at me.

I punch the security code on the door panel keypad and unlock the car. Opening the passenger door, I flip down the glove box and pull out the pistol that is always kept in there. I lock everything back up and toss the gun in the seat next to me as I pull out and head to Justice.

My thoughts are only on Declan as I drive, swerving around cars to get to a future I'm not sure wants me anymore. All I see are vibrant, green eyes, his beautiful smile that reached them, creating a fan of wrinkles in the corners. The contours of his shoulders and arms, the shoulders I would cling to and the arms he would soothe me with. His touch was unlike any other. Strong, comforting, warm, healing. His soul giving me a hope that maybe I could find happiness, and when I finally realized I had, and that it all rested inside of his heart, albeit tortured itself, he was able to give me something no one else has ever been able to do—something to look forward to.

I pull up to Pike's trailer, a place I used to find solace because I knew he was always on the other side of that door. Now I fear what's waiting for me behind it. But maybe it's the fear I need to find my freedom.

Slipping the gun into the back waistband of my pants, I head inside.

"Finally. I was beginning to worry," he says as he walks over to the window and peers out. "Anyone see you or follow you?"

"No one saw me," I murmur as I fight the need to fall to the floor and sob like a baby. Instead I stand, mournfully numb.

"Why the fuck are you still covered in his blood?! For fuck's sake, Elizabeth! Go clean that shit off of you."

Looking down at my hands, they continue to shake; the life of Declan, crusted in now splintering pieces of browning carmine. I walk, almost robotically to the bathroom and close the door. My image, reflected in the mirror, is frightening. Bruises and a split lip remain from Pike's beating, but the ugliness is adorned with Declan's blood. It's smeared across my lips and chin, the remainders of our kiss. The kiss of death. Sticking out my tongue, I lick it off, getting one last taste of that life, of that death. My death.

I turn the faucet on, but I can't bring myself to wash off the blood. To take the lasting elements and watch them go down the drain of this filthy sink. Maybe I'm twisted, but the thought of licking every last drop of his dried blood off of me, like an animal, delights me. Taking him and making a home for him deep inside of me.

So I walk out, back into the living room where Pike has his bags tossed on the floor. He turns to look at me, cocking his head, and giving me a look of sympathy as he walks over to me.

"You can do this," he says softly, taking his hands and stroking my upper arms. I'm not sure how I'm even breathing at this point with the noose that's strangling me, slowly inching its way up, and any second, my neck will snap with a delicious sound, taking me to Wonderland.

"I love you. You know that, right?" he says gently.

"Yeah," I sigh. I know he does. But Pike is a vile human, just like me, and the love we have for each other is infected with a sickness that only we know. "I love you too."

"I need you to clean yourself before we leave."

"I don't want to," I whimper like a child.

"I know. But it's over. And we don't have time to think about how it feels right now. More than ever, I need you to shut yourself off long enough to get the hell out of here."

"Where are we going?"

"Out of the country. I don't know. But we have to go somewhere long enough for us to figure this shit out."

I shake my head, dropping it, feeling the tears drip off my cheeks. They sink down into the dirty carpet by my feet, and I know I can't go on like this.

"I can't do this, Pike. I can't."

"You can. You're just scared. We've gotten through so much, and we will get through this. Just trust me."

A tingle runs up my arms and drifts slowly down into my chest as I awaken. "I don't know if I can do that anymore."

Pike steps back, dropping his hands, saying, "What does that mean?"

"I don't want to run."

He paces across the room, and I feel it. The end. And it fucking kills me because I do love Pike. I always have.

"They'll come after you, you know?" he threatens.

"No, they won't. I didn't do anything," I refute. "You did it all."

"Is that what you think? That your hands are the ones that are clean in this?" he says, growing irritated with me as his eyes turn to daggers. "I'm the invisible link here. It's you that they'll be after. The wife. The *unfaithful* wife. You had a motive too."

"And what's that?"

He pauses, taking a moment while a sly grin starts to spread across his face. "Your baby."

The mere mention causes a physical reaction inside of me as my heart picks up its pace, rapidly beating inside of me.

"That's right. The police probably already know. The lies you told will become truths because it's what you led everyone to believe."

"Why are you doing this to me?"

"You're doing this. You're the selfish one who's willing to drop everything because you can't do it anymore. What about me? You wanna leave me?"

"I don't know what it is I want because you took all those choices away from me."

"I'm not letting you leave me," he demands. "I've given you too much."

"All you've been doing is taking."

"I gave you my goddamn life!" he screams, clenching his fist and punching it right through the paneled wall. My body trembles in fear when he bores his eyes into me, seething, "I gave you everything. I love you. I always have."

And this is it. My moment of clarity. I'll never get that new beginning because you can't start a new life—a new beginning—when the past is right beside you. And Pike? He's not going anywhere. He'll never leave me, and he'll never let me leave. But I'm not sure I could ever truly walk away from him because when you cut through all the shit, I love him. I love my brother so much.

"I love you, Elizabeth," he says, lowering his voice, almost pleading.

"I know you do."

"You can't leave me. You know I hold too much over you," he threatens.

"I know," I weep, the tears flooding over and down my face as I reach behind me and welcome the feel of ice, cold steel in the palm of my hand.

"Elizabeth, please. Don't give up on me—on us."

"I'm so sorry, Pike. We'll never be apart from each other. Our hearts will always be linked."

And when the look of desperation in his eyes morphs into horror, widening as he watches me bring my arm around, he panics, "What are you doing?"

I release a breathless cry.

"I love you, Pike."

(BANG)

from the author

Listen to *Bang*'s Playlist (http://open.spotify.com/user/1264681839/playlist/2QCPRpGKrc18XPcD9sucy3)

Need to talk to someone about *Bang*? There is a discussion group on Facebook for those who have finished reading.

Discuss *Bang* (https://www.facebook.com/groups/bangdiscussion/)

acknowledgements

SO MUCH WORK was put into this book before I ever sat down and wrote the first word. The planning and plotting took months and months, and to see how this story morphed into what it is now is an amazing thing. The people involved with the creation of this book have been absolutely wonderful even though they have repeatedly questioned my sanity along the way.

Gina, you were the first person I ever told about the idea of this story that I was calling "Bang" because I just didn't know what else to call it. We laughed at the name so many times as we worked closely together creating the cast of characters. I must thank you for Declan; the idea of him was brilliant, and you gave me a great base to build on. Thank you for spending hours on the phone with me, listening to one crazy idea after another. You are my partner in crime, and I love that I can continue to shock you.

Cathy, how can I possibly thank you properly? The hours we spent nailing down the details of this story, the plotting, creating, planning, and developing. You are a priceless asset to me that I do not take for granted. I know I gave you a few moments were you probably thought I was crazy, but you cheered me on nonetheless. You are my ever-constant support and everything a parent and friend should be, and I love you beyond what you could ever imagine. I look forward to working on the following books in this series with you!

Lisa, my editor, thank you for taking my words and making them shine. You are tough on me, but I will forever run to you because it's the toughness I need. I truly feel like I have hit the jackpot with you. I don't know how any other editor could do what you do for me with each and every book. Thank you for caring about not only my words and my story, but for caring about me. I love you; there's nothing more I can say.

My husband, your undying support is beyond amazing and allows me to keep doing what I love. I don't know how to thank you enough, love.

Luna, my bright moon in the dark sky above, my motivator, my cheerleader, my fighter, my friend. Working on this book together and the conversations that it sparked between us have been quite interesting. We have gone from laughing to crying, all the while forming a friendship along the way. Thank you for opening yourself up to this story, for the hard discussions we had while I was writing, for all of your words of encouragement. But above all, thank you for your honesty, even when you knew the words would be hard for me to hear. You are the fire I need by my side.

V, I love our early morning conversations and the way you laugh at me when I tell you my darkest ideas. Discussing my characters with you is always fun for me. You can always find a way to put a smile on my face no matter how discouraged I may be. Thank you for being my best friend through all these years.

My fans, I owe it all to you. For each and every one of you who read my stories, thank you. Bloggers, there are too many of you to mention, but I cannot thank you enough for all the time you spend reading, reviewing, and promoting my work. Your dedication means the world to me. My betas, thank you for all of your hard work. I absolutely couldn't do this without you.

"There is nothing predictable or safe on these pages."
-Jay Crownover,
New York Times
bestselling author

echo

THE BLACK LOTUS SERIES

e.k. blair

NEW YORK TIMES BESTSELLING AUTHOR

For My Fans

"You would have to be half mad to dream me up."
-Lewis Carroll

(BENNETT)

I DIDN'T EVEN take another second after I found out about Nina. Elizabeth. My wife. Jesus, what the hell is going on? The only thoughts in my head since hearing the truth an hour ago are confusion and fear and getting my ass to my attorney's office. I don't know what Nina is up to. Shit, I don't know anything right now. I haven't even had a chance to look at the dossier because I had to make sure that the only other person I care about, aside from Nina, would be taken care of no matter what. My mind is spinning and thoughts are beginning to swarm now that I've made it back to The Legacy.

Pulling into the garage, I park in my spot, grab the file, and rush inside. It's like a thousand hammers beating inside of my chest as I push through the doors, raking my hand through my hair.

"Mr. Vanderwal!"

I stumble in my step when I hear Manuel call my name from across the lobby.

"Mr. Vanderwal," he repeats as he stands up from behind the desk. "I have something for you."

Ice swims through my veins when he picks up a small manila envelope and begins walking over to me.

"Who delivered this?"

"Said her name was Mrs. Brooks and that it was urgent. She was extremely persistent that you open it right away," he says with an outstretched hand, and I take the envelope.

"Thanks." Giving a quick nod, I make my way to the elevators. I recognize Jacqueline's handwriting on the envelope and wonder why she didn't just call me. When the doors open and I step into the penthouse I've been sharing with my wife, the panic manifests into an insurgent need to understand what's going on.

Tossing my coat aside, I head straight to my office and close the door behind me. I take a seat and immediately open the dossier to find a few photos taken of Nina walking out of what looks to be a residential building, most likely McKinnon's. The thought turns my stomach to think about what she's been doing with him all this time I've been away on business in Dubai.

My suspicions started at the masquerade ball. Something was off with her. I could sense it. Her emotions were all over the place—it was evident in her eyes, yet she played it off well and I never really questioned. When travel picked up and I was away for longer spans of time, I grew lonely and thought she might be feeling the same. There was an instance I arranged to have her favorite meal from Cité delivered to her only to find out from the restaurant manager that it was undeliverable because she wasn't home. After I called Richard, I found out that Jacqueline had mentioned Nina not being around as often as she used to. The red flags were there, so I admit, I had her followed. It didn't feel right, but I couldn't bear the thought of losing her. I needed to know, and now that I do and that it was Declan, I want to kill that son of a bitch.

More pictures of Nina, now with *him*. His hand holding hers. Her smiling up at him. His hand in her red hair. Her arms around his waist. A hug. A kiss. Hand on her ass. Hand on his face. Her body pressed against his, all while standing among the busy city traffic.

Fuck!

That's my goddamn wife! The woman I love beyond my own life. What the fuck is she doing? And when I flip to the next piece of information in the file, I'm reminded that she's not Nina when I see a picture of her. She's young—really young. A scanned page from a yearbook with her school photo and name printed right beneath.

Elizabeth Archer.

In ink, there's a note that reads:

Freshman year.

Bremen High School. Posen, Illinois.

Jesus. How did she wind up in Posen?

My eyes are fixed on the grainy black and white photo. She isn't smiling, but she's beautiful. I see the woman I married, and when I close my eyes, I can see *her*—Elizabeth.

And now I feel it.

Guilt.

I set the file down and lean back in my chair while I attempt to grasp on to reality, but my emotions are too conflicting. I can't even think straight.

My wife isn't who she's pretended to be since the day I met her. But why? What does she want? I should hate her, be furious, be in a state of rage. Instead, I feel like driving back to the hospital so I can touch her, see her, hold her, and ask her why, and tell her that whatever it is, I'll fix it for her because I love her.

God, I love her.

What the hell is wrong with me? I should be enraged. Right?

I take a moment and close my eyes when I feel the pulsing of a headache beginning to form. Loosening my tie, I open my eyes and they land on the manila envelope. With curiosity, I open it up to find a flash drive along with a note that reads:

Bennett,

I don't want to say too much, but after overhearing a very strange phone call Richard was having the other night, I've been worried. I wanted to call you since I knew it had something to do with the company, but after finding this flash drive, I got scared. I don't exactly understand what's going on, but I fear it could be really bad. Please look at this ASAP.

Jacqueline

Opening the lid to my laptop, I plug in the flash drive and click on the only file that pops up. It appears to be the company's financial spreadsheet, but the numbers are way off the normal spectrum. I scroll through the information, and when I hit the bottom, I see the account name and panic ignites.

"Oh my God."

My eyes widen as I lean in closer to the screen because I can't believe what I'm seeing. My stomach lurches when I notice faint noises on the other side of the door. Before I even have a second to think, the door flies opens, smashing into the wall.

The man's face is a blur behind the stainless steel barrel of a pistol that's aimed right at me. Chills spark throughout my body, causing my lungs to collapse as I desperately try to speak, but he speaks first.

"You won't ever fucking touch her again," he snarls as he moves towards me with his arm straight out in front of him, marking his target.

I quickly stand on weak legs, holding my hands up in surrender, and plead through my crashing panic, "Declan, don't do th—"

(BANG)

one

(bang)

CRIMSON SOAKS THROUGH the white cotton, spreading its death through the fibers of his shirt as he stands there, wide-eyed. My body goes numb as I watch him slowly stumble backwards. The weight of the pistol becomes too much for my delicate fingers to hold, and the gun slips out of my hand, falling to the floor with a thump at the same time Pike does.

I'm frozen as I stand here, looking down at my brother. His body begins to spasm, his eyes never blinking, and the gurgling sounds in his throat turn violent as he starts choking on his own blood.

I don't move to help him; instead, as if I'm watching a horror movie, I become a voyeur.

This isn't real. This is a dream; it isn't real.

The terror in his eyes is chilling as they glaze over, dilate, and stare into negative space.

His body stills, paralyzed to the ground, and then silence takes over. It's in this moment that I begin to feel the warmth of blood flowing through my veins, and I move. Inching slowly towards Pike, my trembling body kneels next to him, but I'm too scared to touch him.

Is this real?

Simply observing, I note a tinge of blue blooming on his lips. I sit. The world unmoving. My mind drifts to a faraway place where nothing exists. It's pure and empty and free from emotion. I settle in this solitary space, breathing in white noise, when suddenly the body next to me convulses. A retching of coagulated blood splutters out of Pike's mouth as his stomach contracts in alarming pulses, and then instantly stops. My heart pounds in an unsteady rhythm as I watch Pike's body soften into the floor beneath him. And when there is no more life, I wake up, snapping out of my trance as reality barrels into me.

Holy shit!

Grabbing his arm, I panic, jerking him. "Pike?" Shaking his arm, I murmur in fear, "Pike, wake up. Pike, come on." I move to hover over his lifeless body, gripping his shoulders and shaking him profusely, begging louder, "Wake up. Wake up! This isn't funny." Tears burn my eyes, and I choke on my own words. "Wake up, Pike! I'm so sorry. Oh my God, I'm so sorry. Please, wake up!"

His eyes are still wide open, but there's no movement. They're frozen, locked in place, and utterly black.

What have I done?

Pain stabs my lungs as I throw my head up to the heavens and release the most God-awful severing cry, but there's no sound that comes out of me. The agony is too much, so I wail in a torturous breathlessness. My heart, splintering, ripping apart, takes on a new meaning of misery, creating an emotion that never existed before this very moment, but it's too much. I can't bear it, but I feel its birth inside of me.

Looking back down, I no longer see the man I hated only moments ago. Instead, I see the boy who desperately loved me his whole life, and I crumple over, shifting his arm so that I'm able to nestle in the crook against his chest. He's still warm, and like I've done my whole life, I selfishly take comfort from him. I'm nothing but rot, using Pike, even in his death, in an attempt to soothe myself. I wrap myself around him and cry, breathing him into my soul. His shirt is a soggy combination of blood and sweat, yet I can still smell the ever-familiar fumes of his clove cigarettes as I close my eyes.

"You're gonna be okay."

His whispered voice startles me, and I pop up to look down at him. He's alive, blinking, and I see his lips moving when he speaks again.

"Don't cry, Elizabeth. I'm still here."

"Oh my God, Pike!" I murmur in disbelief.

"It's gonna be okay," he assures again, and I cry, "How?"

"Because I love you, and I believe in you. You're a fighter. A warrior."

"I'm so sorry. I didn't mean to shoot you. God, I'm losing control, but I can't lose you."

A hint of a smile appears on his lips. *"You'll never lose me. You're my sister. I've never loved anyone as much as you. All I ever wanted in this world is for you to be happy. You're a survivor."*

"What do I do?"

"Run."

"What?" I question with a slight shake of my head, and when my eyes meet his again, cold, black orbs greet me. "Pike?" Pinching my eyes closed, I open them back up, but the vision remains. He's dead, and I'm losing it.

His words sink in. He's right. I'm a fighter; he taught me how. So with that, I feel my spine straighten, and I take in a couple slow, calculated breaths. I lean down and capture his lips, taking my second kiss of death today. When I pull away, I drop my fingertips to his brows and gently run them down his face, closing his eyelids so that he can sleep peacefully. Wrapping both Pike and Declan safely in the steel cage around my heart, I swallow hard as I shift to stand. Today I lost the two pieces of my black, black heart, but now I have no other choice than to save myself.

I move quickly around the trailer, stripping out of my bloody clothes and changing into a pair of Pike's sleep pants and an old t-shirt. I need the smell of him on me because I'm scared to be alone. Gathering my belongings, I make sure to grab the file Pike took from Declan's before I wipe my fingerprints from various surfaces. Looking back at Pike, who lies dead in a puddle of darkened blood, I release a silent goodbye and thank him for saving me by giving me every piece of him. My body fights hard against the boiling pain that's begging to erupt, and I shove the thoughts away that it should be me lying there—dead. At least then I would be with Declan.

Declan.

Fuck, I'm not strong enough to do this.

My chest heaves and the cage weakens as I shut the door on my past and walk into the unknown future with Bennett's gun tucked into my bag.

As I pull out of the trailer park and onto the main street, my cheeks are coated with tears.

I'm lost.

Alone.

All I can do is go back to my phony life because what other choice do I have? Three men—men that are all linked to me—have been murdered. Bennett, Declan, and Pike. I try to get focused so I can create a plan on what to do when my gut twists in fear as I see Matt's car pass me by, going in the direction I just came from.

Shit!

I could turn around, catch him, explain what happened, but then I hear Pike's voice urging, *"Don't stop driving."*

So I don't.

Shadows of the city pass by as I make it back home and pull into the parking garage.

Wiping down the gun and placing it back in Bennett's car—one bullet short—I rush into the quiet building and up to the penthouse, undetected.

I take a quiet step across the threshold, and when the door slams behind me, I collapse to the floor. And this time, when I wail, my voice erupts in a fiery sob that burns in my soul. Vulgar cries, ripping through the cords of my throat as they expel into the hopeless air, echo off the walls and evaporate into silence. Tears mix with the dried blood of Pike and Declan, dripping from my chin, and fall lifelessly to the tile beneath me. When I see the swirled, translucent red, I let go of my voice and choke on my breath. I'm lost in the splatterings of my pain merged with all that's left of my loves.

Who do I ache for more?

And like the animal I am, with hands braced on the chilling floor, I lean forward on my knees, and I lick the blood.

My salt.

Their metal.

My heart's elixir.

Peeling off Pike's clothes while I make my way to the bathroom, I stare at the blood that's dried on my body, and with no control, I begin to lick that too.

Fingers, hands, arms, knees.

I take it all, loving Declan and Pike, making a home for them in the depths of my body, deep inside. Everything's a haze; my only goal is to consume every last piece of vitality.

And I cry.

Eyes burning.

Lungs aching.

Hope disintegrating.

I'm all powdered ash, so hold your breath before a drift of air picks me up and carries me away to nullity.

"NINA."

Tension aches in my muscles as I stir awake. When I roll over and open my tear-stung eyes, I notice Clara, the housekeeper and cook moving around the room.

"It's nearly noon. You've been sleeping all morning." She speaks in a gentle voice before pulling the drapes back.

Light flashes, burning my eyes, and I jerk my head away, squinting against the sun's rays that pierce the room.

Clara walks around the bed and takes a seat next to me, stroking her fingers through my tangled hair, and the touch awakens the swollen wound in my heart that only sleep can soothe. Tears leak out onto my pillow, and I close my tired eyes.

"You should eat, dear. It might help you feel better."

I shake my head. Food can't heal this. I'm not sure anything can. I've lost everything. My baby, Declan, Pike . . . everything that mattered to me. And for what? Everyone is dead and there's nothing gained. Nothing but misery. The constricting around my heart makes each breath unbearable, and I desperately want to drift away. More than drift, I just want Declan to hold me. To anchor me by wrapping his warm arms around me, cocooning me into his chest, and filling my lungs with his scent—his life.

The one man who showed me what it was to be loved . . . truly loved . . . in the purest form is gone. Gone at the hands of my brother . . . my other love, my protector.

"Maybe a shower?" Clara suggests, but I don't respond. I just keep my eyes closed.

It isn't but a moment until I hear her sniff. When I peek my eyes open, I watch as she brushes the tears away from her cheeks. I shift my body against the tender bruising that remains from Pike's brutal beating a few days ago, the beating that killed my baby and led to the deaths of my husband, my lover, my brother, and my own soul. Clara looks over to me when I sit up and wince.

"I'm sorry. I don't mean to cry."

I don't say anything as I watch her try to recompose her poise through the sorrow she feels. I feel it too but for entirely different reasons. So I pull on my mask and continue my role, saying, "It feels so lonely without him. I keep thinking he's just away on another trip and he'll be walking through the door any minute."

She nods while her tears continue to fall and then looks to me. "I'm worried about you."

I am too.

"I'll be okay."

"Bennett wouldn't want you to be suffering like this."

What she doesn't know, what nobody knows, is that I'm not suffering for Bennett. I'm not the harrowed widow mourning over her husband. No. I'm mourning over the man I was cheating on my husband with and my brother that no one knew anything about. My hidden life. My clandestine existence.

"How could I possibly not suffer, Clara? He was my husband," I choke out. "How am I supposed to live without him when he was my reason for waking up every day?"

"Because the world doesn't wait on us. It keeps moving and expects us to move right along with it."

"I'm not sure how to move right now."

"Well," Clara begins, resting her hand on my knee. "You can start by taking a shower and trying to eat something." Her eyes are sad and filled with concern. When I nod my head, a small smile breaks upon her lips, and she gives my knee a gentle squeeze before getting up to leave the room. Turning back to me, she adds, "Oh, while you were sleeping, your attorney called. He'd like to schedule a time to meet with you to go over Bennett's will."

This was the moment I had been working years for. The moment Pike and I dreamed about. This was supposed to be the moment that brought me victory and happiness. The money. The power. Payback and retribution. And now it means nothing without Pike by my side. I married Bennett to destroy him, but it didn't make anything better—it's just worse.

"I'll give him a call after lunch," I respond before Clara walks out and closes the door behind her.

Getting ready is a blur. I make the movements but then can't remember how I got from point A to point B. Clara is in the kitchen, cleaning up after lunch while I sift through the sheaf of messages from all the calls I've missed since Bennett's death. I'm sure it's all over the news, but I can't bring myself to turn on the TV for fear I'll hear something about Declan. I'd crumble for sure.

I have messages from everyone. I know I need to contact Bennett's parents, and also Jacqueline, since I can see she has been calling excessively. God, the last thing I want to do is deal with these people, and as I'm about to walk away, the phone rings. I let Clara answer it as I head back to bed.

"Nina, it's the funeral home," she calls. "They are needing approval on a few final details."

Drained of energy, I respond, "I'm sorry. I just can't," before dropping my head and walking out of the room.

What the hell do I care about Bennett's funeral? Toss him in the lake for all I care. The bastard continues to ruin everything, even in his death. The anguish wells up into my throat as I fall onto the bed and cry into my pillow.

I fucking hate that man. I hate him for everything he was. Misplaced aggression or not, that asshole took everything away from me.

I cry like mad, trying to expel some of this misery, but I can't sit still. I lurch off the bed, and in a haze, find myself in Bennett's closet, ransacking everything. Ripping clothes from the hangers, thrashing shoes across the room, grunting with each volatile purge until I'm against the wall, slamming my palm into the drywall over and over and over. I beg for the infliction of pain, but the only pain I feel is in my heart. So I clench my fist and pound harder and harder and harder and harder . . .

"Nina! Stop!"

Harder and harder and harder and harder and . . .

"MRS. VANDERWAL, THANK you for coming in. I'm so sorry for your loss. Your husband was a good friend."

"Thank you, Rick," I respond as I stand in front of our attorney's desk and shake his hand.

"Please," he says, gesturing to the chair, "Have a seat."

I look at the man I've known since my engagement to Bennett four years ago as he sits down and pulls out a file of paperwork.

"I wanted to visit with you personally so that we can go over the terms of your husband's will and estate. I know this is a difficult time for you right now, but the day of Bennett's death, he stopped by to visit me."

I nod my head, recalling the phone call that was made in my hospital room. It was the last time Bennett was with me, when he found out that I wasn't really Nina, but Elizabeth, and that I'd been sneaking around with Declan.

Declan.

My throat tightens at the thought of him, but I push it down to focus on Rick as he continues to speak.

"A few amendments were made to the will," he tells me, pulling out a sealed, white envelope from the file. "He instructed me to open and read this to you privately upon his death."

Forcing out a tear, I sit and stare—nervous—but I play it as calm as I can.

"He must have known," he states blankly.

"I don't understand how any of this is happening." My voice quivers around the words, and Rick hands me a tissue.

"Have the police said anything to you?"

"No. But they took almost everything from our home office. The last I heard is they think it's business related."

"Money will make people do sick things," he says, and the chill that streams under my skin causes a sinister reaction inside of me.

He has no clue how close to home his words are hitting right now as I sit and wait to hear my reward for this game of revenge I've played over the past few years.

I dab my eyes with the tissue, and he asks, "Do you need a moment?"

I shake my head, and he takes his letter opener, slicing it through the lip of the envelope. Unfolding the paper, he takes a moment, and I watch as his eyes skitter across whatever is written. Rick clears his throat and shifts in his seat before reading aloud Bennett's words.

My beautiful Nina,

I'm so conflicted writing this letter. The moment I met you, I knew the man I wanted to be. The type of man worthy enough to stand by your side because you are beyond magnificent.

But the conflict there is that you were never the woman I thought you were. I'm pissed at you. I know the woman that lies beneath the fallacy. The fallacy I fell deeply in love with. I don't pretend to have the answers for what you've done, but don't worry, my dear. Don't be scared, because I never told a soul. I'll take my friend, that little girl with the red pigtails, to my grave. Whatever it is that you wanted from me, I hope you found it. I hope that you can forgive me for what happened to you. I don't know the details; all I do know is that I feel responsible.

You weren't the only one who was dishonest though. I lied to you too. There is no easy way to say this, so here it is:

I have a son.

His name is Alexander Brooks.

The utter shock at those words knocks me back, and I'm disgusted at myself for not being able to see what was right under my nose. He was fucking Jacqueline behind my back. My loving husband and my so-called friend.

She was the biggest mistake of my life. It only happened once. The details aren't important, because I've regretted that moment since before it happened. Because it was you I wanted. It's always been you. I laid my hand on her that one time but never again after. Never did I want to because all I wanted was to be covered in you. To be covered in your love that I felt was so real, but I learned today that it wasn't real. Nothing is real, and I don't know what to believe.

What I do know is that I cannot trust anything. I have instructed that this letter only be read in a private setting between legal counsel and you, Nina. It is with this letter that I claim my paternity to Alexander Brooks. A DNA test was conducted shortly after his birth and can be found in a safety deposit box, which I leave to the hereby mentioned custodian, Attorney Rick Parker of Buchanan & Parker. I further move to amend my will to ensure Alexander Brooks is the sole heir to all business assets of Linq Steel Co. and that Nina Vanderwal be sole heir to all personal assets upon my death.

All monies gained from Linq Steel Co., including all materials of the business estate, will be deposited into a trust fund under Alexander's name, which the trustee, Rick Parker, will oversee until Alexander reaches the age of 21.

Rick Parker will notify Jacqueline Brooks in a private meeting to go over the terms of this amended will, and I please beg of you, for the sake of my son, that none of this information leave the parties involved.

Nina, I lied about one more thing. When I said in my vows that I would love you till death do us part, I wasn't being honest, because I doubt death would be enough to make me stop loving you.

Bennett Vanderwal

That bastard. And here I thought I was a good actress, but it was *them.* They fooled me—played me. They were deceivers just as I was—just as I continue to be. I always knew Jacqueline wanted to fuck my husband, I just never knew she actually had. So now I sit here, stoic. I want to laugh at the circuitous nature of it all—the incessant game that continues to reveal hidden secrets, but ironically, they're now someone else's secrets.

Rick sets the letter down and leans forward, pinching the bridge of his nose. Releasing a heavy breath, his eyes finally meet mine. "Did you know?"

I shake my head.

He shifts in his seat, regaining his composure, but I can see his discomfort slicing through his weak façade. "Well, then . . . as you're probably aware, the majority of his assets are named under the business. That's not to say that you won't be left with a considerable inheritance though."

Feigning irritation, my words bite when I state, "It isn't the money I care about."

"Of course not. I apologize. I didn't mean to insinuate that—"

"It's fine. I'm a little overwhelmed with everything right now. So if we're through . . . "

"Yes," he responds, standing and walking around his desk. He holds his hand out for me and I take it as I stand up.

"Thank you."

Rick leads me out of his office, and when I step onto the elevator, he sticks his arm out, preventing the door from closing and offers, "I'm so sorry you had to find out about Bennett like this."

"Well, I guess nobody's perfect, are they?"

"No. I suppose not."

He drops his arm, allowing the doors to shut as he gives me a nod of sympathy, but I would only need it if I cared for the two people that I just found out have been betraying me. Only I don't. His son can have the business assets, because honestly, the money feels tainted now. I'll take it, find a way to start a new life, but that money will always be marked in Declan's blood—my heart's blood. Bennett's death was never worth the life of Declan. Nothing is worth the life of the man who owned every piece of me.

MINUTES TURN HOURS turn days.

A monotonous routine of depression follows me everywhere I go. The razor sharp agony of my bleeding heart aches painfully for Declan. I miss him. Sometimes I think if I cry hard enough, he'll come back. As if life would be that giving.

No.

Life is a piece of shit.

It gave me a taste—one taste of sweetness—before ripping it away from me. The moment I decided to believe in hope, to believe in goodness, it was taken, only to remind me that I'm all alone in this world. But for once, I wanted to believe. I wanted to dig deep to find the good in me so that I could give it to him, however small of a piece it was.

I don my ink, bathed in black, to mourn my loves, but it isn't their funerals I attend, it's *his*. I don't even have to pretend for family and friends because the depth of my heartache runs deep inside of me, only it runs for Declan and Pike, not Bennett, whose funeral I am preparing to leave for.

I've stayed far away from any news on Declan and Pike; their funerals have come and gone, I'm sure. But to show my face would be foolish. I can't link myself to them if I expect suspicion to remain off of me. After all, I'm the spider's silk that webs this whole game together.

Smoothing the wax of deep red lipstick along my lips, I remember how warm they felt pressed against Declan. His sweetness burned into them. Sometimes I couldn't control my love for him, needing more, I'd bruise myself. Driven by pure desire.

I stand back, observing what's left behind. Soft waves of red hair fall over my thinned shoulders, eyes sunken in from the sorrow that eats away at me, but with a few eye drops, my blues beam bright and I'm reminded of my daddy's eyes that shone the brightest of them all. Loss is all around me;

it's all my life has ever been. I run my hands down the smooth black fabric of my shift dress and right myself for my husband's funeral because this is a loss that I welcome with a full heart. Bennett is one of my few victories, albeit bittersweet.

The day is frigid and covered in grey. A light mist falls down on the cold earth as I drive across town to the cemetery where Bennett's parents own family plots. I go alone—the black widow. Everything is black, including the limos and town cars that line the winding street, skirting its way through the immaculate grounds of Bennett's final resting place.

As I park the car, I take a moment to breathe before I notice Baldwin walking my way, carrying a large umbrella over his head. I haven't seen him since I let him go last week. Bennett is gone, and it's time to start eliminating the remnants of him entirely, including his staff. I always liked Baldwin—I liked Clara as well—but after I let go of Baldwin, I said goodbye to her too. They both understood as I explained my reasoning. Clara was the hardest because a small part of me always felt connected to her as a mother figure to me, even though she was never mine to claim.

"Mrs. Vanderwal," Baldwin acknowledges when he opens my door and takes my hand to help me out of the car.

"Thank you," I murmur, eyes guarded behind my dark sunglasses.

His eyes are soft, full of concern, and I can tell he wants to say something, so I give him a smile filled with sorrow and he nods in shared pain, only mine is deceitful.

I loop my arm through his as he leads me over to the burial plot where Bennett's casket is perched above ground, flanked by numerous sprays of fragrant flowers and weeping loved ones. I join them as tears roll freely down my face and drip slowly from my jaw. This asshole they mourn is the pure hate that festers in me. And these tears aren't for him—they're *because* of him.

As I'm led to the last empty chair, next to Bennett's mother, my eyes meet Jacqueline's over his casket. I want to smile at that pathetic woman, but I don't, and she quickly looks away from me, shifting in awkwardness. She knows I know. The attorney called me the other day to tell me that he met with her to discuss Bennett's will and trust for their bastard child.

I sit.

Time passes.

Words of hope and the glory and abundance of God wane on.

Life is a gift, the priest praises.

Bullshit.

The sounds of rain trickling down and people crying dissipate the longer I sit. Many stop and offer me their condolences as I cry and pretend the words that were just spoken here were really meant for Declan and Pike. I sit and reflect on them, honoring their lives today, not *his.* So I nod and quietly thank each person as they one-by-one turn their backs and walk away, emptying the cemetery.

Richard and Jacqueline stop, and in a very out of character move on Richard's part, he gives me a hug, albeit short and tense. Looking over to the betrayer, she tilts her head in unspoken sorrow before opening her arms to me. I take her offering for appearance's sake.

"I'm terribly sorry," she whispers her multi-layered sympathies.

I pull back, keeping the interaction short.

"Thank you for being here."

"Call if you need anything," she says, which I'm sure is more for keeping her husband aloof than it is sincerity for me.

I nod and then Jacqueline walks off with Richard without saying another word.

Only a few people linger when my heart catches at the sight of Callum, Declan's father. I've been purposefully hiding from everything Declan because my heart just can't take the pain, but when Cal's eyes meet mine, I stand and walk toward him.

The endearment he always held for me is no longer there, only the stone face of a man who has just lost his son.

"Cal," I whisper, approaching him as he stands under a large tree. He doesn't speak. "I didn't expect to see you here."

"Your husband was a man I always admired. You know that."

I nod and nearly choke on my own fractured heart when I respond on broken breath, "Your son . . . I am so sorry."

I attempt to keep myself as poised as possible, as one would expect of a business associate. Because to Cal, that's all I was to Declan. He's oblivious to the fact that we were so in love, wanting a life to call our own, and sharing the dream of having a baby together—a baby that once lived in my now rotting womb.

"Life isn't fair, darling," he tells me in his thick Scottish accent, and within it, I can hear Declan's brogue. I drop my head and hold on as tightly as I can to his voice, never wanting to lose it, when Cal's hand cups my cheek. Looking up into his eyes, his face is blurred from the welling of agony in my eyes. He slowly drags his thumb over my skin and collects my tears as he tilts his head and says, "Funny isn't it?"

I blink a few times at his curious words before he continues, "Both men . . . murdered in their own homes within days of each other, and police are coming up blank as to who's responsible."

His words release a violent chill up my spine, and before I can form a cohesive thought, he kisses my forehead and walks away. I watch his back as the rain falls over him and drop to my knees in the mud. He's the last one to leave and I'm alone, hands bracing and sinking into the soggy ground, screaming silently, but it's so loud inside my head.

three

IT'S BEEN TWO weeks since Bennett's funeral, since I looked into the eyes of my love's father. I'm alone and I'm drowning. There's no one left in the world for me, and the only place I find any semblance of peace is in my dreams—so I sleep. I used to always dream of Carnegie, the prince-turned-caterpillar my father once told me about when I was a little girl, but lately, when I close my eyes, it's Declan I see. I dream about what our life could have been: living in Scotland in the estate he used to tell me about, having a baby together, loving each other. The vision covers me in warmth, but the moment my eyes open, I am greeted with the dank coldness of my reality, reminded once again that fairytales are shit-filled lies.

Pulling out another suitcase from the closet, I continue to pack up my clothes. I can't stay in Chicago. This isn't my life—not the one I want because what I want doesn't exist anymore. It's simply another fallen star that I was wishing upon. What I want is the dream, so I decided yesterday that I would go get a glimpse of that dream, of the what-could-have-been, of the what-*should*-have-been. Because the dream is all I have left of him, and I want to see it. I *need* to see it, to know it was real. So I'm leaving for Scotland. I don't know what I'm doing, but I can't stay here any longer.

I continue to move about the penthouse until the phone rings.

"Mrs. Vanderwal?" Manuel says when I answer. "Mrs. Jacqueline Brooks is here to see you. Shall I send her up?"

"Oh," I murmur, not expecting any visitors today. "Um, yes. Please."

I hang up, wondering what it is she's wanting. We haven't really spoken since the paternity of her son was revealed, but what is there to even say? It's not like she was ever truly my friend, just someone I pretended to like for the satisfaction of Bennett.

I open the door when I hear the knock and am greeted by Jacqueline holding Alexander in her arms.

"Jacqueline, please, come in."

Her eyes barely meet mine as she steps inside and slowly walks to the center of the room before stopping and turning around to face me. We both stand here for a moment while I watch her tears well up.

"I'm so sorry," she says on a shaky breath, and I shift my eyes to look at her baby. When he becomes restless in her arms, she sets him down on the floor and he focuses on the stuffed frog he's holding.

Walking closer, I kneel down in front of him and our eyes lock. I take this moment to observe his features, and beneath the pudge, I see Bennett. I never cared enough to ever look at this child in the past, but I should've because it's glaringly obvious. He's right there within this little boy, and my stomach knots. My teeth grind when I feel the heat in my blood surging with a need to slam my fist into this baby's face. My palms are actually tingling with desire, begging my fingers to ball so that I can hammer my knuckles into Bennett's legacy. I hate this child because he is the one thing that carries the life of the man that destroyed mine.

Alexander reaches up with a smile and touches my cheek, and I have to swallow back the sour bile of loathing. It takes great strength to pull back and not knock this little shit across the room.

When I stand, Jacqueline breathes in shame, "Nina . . . I'm sorry."

"Why?" I ask with no influx of emotion.

"For hurting you."

But I'm not hurt, so I simply respond, "Everybody has secrets, everybody lies, and everybody cheats their way through life for self-fulfillment. We wouldn't do it if we felt sorry; we do it because it's our human right to seek happiness."

My words take her by surprise, and when I ask, "Did fucking my husband make you happy?" she takes a deep breath as more tears fall and answers, "Yes."

I nod my head when she adds, "But it didn't make me happy to know I was hurting you."

"People are bound to get hurt in our journey for happiness. If fucking my husband made you happy, don't ever be sorry for that."

She tilts her head with a look of pity.

"Don't worry about me," I continue. "You didn't break me. You can't break something that was already broken."

"He never loved me," she confesses abruptly. "He never wanted me. I took advantage of him when he had too much to drink. I knew it made him sick to look at me after what happened, but he kept up his pleasantries for the sake of Alex. He merely put up with me because he refused to turn his back on his son."

Jacqueline grows more upset with each word while I stand and listen. Her voice cracks in heartbreak when she adds, "But it was always you he loved."

Releasing a heavy sigh, I give her a weak smile, shaking my head, and saying, "I guess in the end, it doesn't really matter. All we are left with is ourselves."

She wipes her cheeks and takes a couple deep breaths in an attempt to compose herself before reaching down to pick up Alexander, and then asks, "So what now?"

"That's a good question, one that I need to find the answer to, but I won't find it here."

"You're leaving?"

"Yes," I say with a nod.

"Where to? For how long?"

"I don't know," I tell her, not wanting her to know, and when I give her son one last look-over, I turn my attention back to her. "You aren't the only one with secrets. We all have them."

She gives me a slight nod and starts moving towards the door. I follow and say goodbye to the woman who blindly found herself tangled in my game of lies. But she'll go back to her husband, Richard, who believes that baby is his, and continue to live her life while I get myself ready to go see what could have been mine. If only . . .

"I'm sorry, Elizabeth."

My heart catches at the sound of his voice as I close the door, and when I turn to look over my shoulder, I see his face, and suddenly I'm soothed. He stands right by me, dark hair, sad eyes.

"Why?"

Pike hangs his head, shoving his hands into his pants pockets, and I can see the tension in his muscles under his ink-covered arms.

"I took that away from you," he says as he raises his eyes to me.

"Took what?"

"What she has. What you deserved."

"Maybe you did me a favor," I respond. "I would've been a shitty mom anyway."

Shaking his head, he counters, *"No. You would have been a great mom."* Pike takes in an uneven breath, and I can feel his regret with each word, *"I'm sorry I took that away from you."*

Truth is, I don't know what kind of mom I would've been, but I was willing to take the role with Declan by my side. I trusted him to keep me together. Trusted that his love would be enough to make me better. But I'm not better, and without him, I'm nothing.

Empty.

"It's life, right?" I say with a defeated shrug of my shoulders.

"Not the life I wanted for you," he says, stepping closer to me. *"All I ever wanted was to give you a better life. All I wanted was to rip that lock off that door when you were little and cut you free from that fucking closet. I wanted to take away all the times I was forced to rape you. I wanted to take away all your beatings, all your hurt. But I fucked up."*

With no need for my steel cage with him, I let my tears fall, and I cry because that's all I ever wanted . . . for my life to disappear. I want to forget all the horror.

"I never meant to destroy you like this."

"I know."

"I panicked. I got scared, and I lost it," he tries to explain through his strained voice that threatens to break.

"I miss you, so much, Pike. I don't even know how to live any more. I have no one. Not one person on this Earth," I cry and then crumple to my knees. But he's right there with me on the floor, hand on my back, as I heave and sob, "What do I do?"

"You live."

"How?"

"You breathe. You fight. You take everything that was meant to be yours in this life because you deserve all of it."

"I'm just so tired of fighting for nothing," I tell him.

Taking my face in his hands, he wipes my tears, saying, *"You're not alone. I'm here. Do you feel me?"*

"Yes."

"It's not for nothing. Never stop fighting."

I close my eyes and relax my cheek into his hand, taking in his touch and truly feeling him. With a deep breath, I inhale his words and search for comfort in them, search for any shred of strength. Strength to breathe, to move, to open my eyes, and when I do, he's gone.

Looking around the room, there's no trace of Pike, no movement, no smell, no sound. Sitting back on my heels, I observe the penthouse, the illusory world I've created, and I hear his faint whisper, *"This was your creation, and you were strong enough to master it."*

And he's right.

I was strong.

But that's when I had something to fight for. That fire in me is gone. Only ash and embers remain. Echoes and shadows. Darkness and death.

Pike is right though; I need to move. If I'm going to live, I need to remind myself that there is good in this life. Even if the good comes in miniscule drips, I have to believe the pain is worth those moments, because I've experienced it. It was real and alive and I would go through this agony all over again just to feel the love of Declan for one more second. I never thought the world could be that good, but it was.

For that moment . . .

It was so good.

Picking myself up off the floor, I steady on my feet before grabbing my coat and keys. As much as I've been avoiding the reality of Declan's absence, I need to face it. To remember that it was real and it's worth this pain.

I pull my car out onto Michigan Avenue and start heading north. The city is alive and moving all around me. I ignore the excitement and smiles and keep straight to River North. Turning onto Superior, I slow down. Suddenly, I feel cold and my clammy hands grip the steering wheel more tightly. There's a sick churning in the pit of my gut as I roll the car along the curb in front of Declan's building.

Shutting the car off, I sit for a moment in the stillness. The only sound is the pounding of my heart as it beats through my chest. This used to be my solace. My little piece of heaven located at the top of this building. When I get out of the car, I look up and see the greenery on his rooftop courtyard, but I know that's the only life up there. His name is no longer on the intercom system in the lobby, only the number for the realtor that is listed to sell his penthouse.

The coolness of the steel on my fingertip hollows me even more, and the masochist in me begs to push the button.

So I do.

I buzz his floor, knowing that this time, his sweet voice won't be greeting me. Instead, it's my phone.

Pulling my cell out, I look at the screen but don't recognize the number. As I take a few steps back toward my car, I answer, "Hello?"

"Miss me?"

It takes a moment to snap out of my thoughts of Declan to recognize the voice on the other end of the call, and a surge of panic flashes through my system. Quickly composing myself, I answer steadily, "What do you want, Matt?"

"We need to talk."

"About?"

"Do I really need to say it?" he taunts, and I don't need a reminder to know that when I passed him in my car the day I shot and killed Pike, he was heading straight to his trailer. Words aren't needed; we both know what I did.

"When?"

"Tomorrow."

"I can't," I tell him as I get back into my car and shut the door.

"You have something better to do?"

"As if my doings are any of your business, but yes. I'm leaving town, so if you'd like to talk, it would need to be done today," I bite in irritation. Matt has always been a source of friction for me. I've put up with him because of his friendship with Pike, but he's always given me the creeps. Still, there's a part of me that's grateful for him, because it was him that gave me one of the greatest gifts, and he gave it from a pure heart.

Probably his only moment of selflessness.

Matt was the one that gave me my first taste of revenge when he set the stage for me to murder my foster parents. My payback for the years of abuse. So as much as I despise Matt, a part of me is thankful for him.

"Thirty minutes? Tribune Tower?" he suggests.

"Fine."

Hanging up, I toss the phone over to the passenger seat. Hearing his voice makes me even more anxious to leave this town. To run far away from this place and from everything I know.

I start heading back towards Michigan Avenue, and once I've parked the car, I walk over towards the Tribune Tower. The streets and sidewalks are flooded with businessmen and tourists. Making my way through the crowds, I cross the street and wait for Matt.

My attention is on a street performer who's playing an old Otis Rush number I recognize on the saxophone. As people walk past him, dropping dollar bills and coins into his open sax case on the ground, I get lost in the smooth melody. I watch the man, and wonder about him. He's old and grey, dressed in tatters of worn clothes. His dark skin is aged with deep wrinkles, and even though his knuckles are worn and ashy, they move with grace along the keys. By looks alone, you'd think he was lonely and sad, but the sway of his head as he plays is a sure sign of happiness. But how does one, who appears to have nothing, find joy? I want to ask him how, but I stumble on my feet when I'm knocked off balance, only to find that I'm now in Matt's arms. He grabs me from behind and turns me around to face him. With a hand on my back and the other holding my hand, he moves me in a slow dance to the music.

His sly grin rakes at me, knowing the pleasure he's taking in having me this close to him. If it weren't for the mass of people around us, I'd push him off of me. The last thing I need is to cause a scene, so I allow him to lead me to his liking while keeping my eyes downcast.

"Don't look so miserable, Elizabeth. People are watching us."

Biting down, I muster up a weak smile and raise my head to meet his eyes. They're dilated dope black, but that's nothing new. It amazes me that this druggie I've known since I was a freshman in high school hasn't wound up overdosing.

Pulling me in closer, he rests his cheek against the side of my head, whispering in my ear, "You miss him?"

Yes.

I don't answer as I focus to keep my composure in front of him, but inside I can feel my wounds ripping deeper.

His hand wraps further around me, tugging me in close while we continue to dance on the bustling sidewalk in front of the Tribune Tower.

"If you're worried, don't be," he continues softly. "I took care of it."

When I pull my head back to look at him, confused by what he means, he adds, "I made it look like a deal gone bad. Cops questioned me, and I confirmed their suspicions."

"Why?" I ask, wondering why he would want to protect me.

"To ensure your loyalty."

A fury of heat ignites my neck with the realization that this punk sleaze was able to undermine and trap me to him.

"What do you want?"

"I'm not ready to collect on my investment right now," he responds with a grin I want to knock off his face.

"You're a sick fuck," I sling at him. "Using Pike for nothing more than a transaction."

"You're one to accuse of using. I watched you use him since we were kids."

"You don't know anything about our relationship," I snap in defense.

"I know that he loved you and sacrificed everything for you."

"And here you are, pissing on the both of us."

"You should be thanking me for keeping your ass out of prison," he throws back at me, and then mocks, "What was Pike anyway? Number three? Four?"

"Fuck you. He was my brother."

Gripping me tighter, the saxophone continues to fill the air around us as Matt dips me and seethes under his breath, "No. Fuck you, Elizabeth. He was my best friend and you killed him, and for what, I have no fucking clue because he never did anything but give you everything you ever wanted."

He then pulls me back up, and I feel like I'm about to explode in hate at this piece of shit who doesn't know a goddamn thing about the truth of me and my brother. He has no idea what the two of us endured and how it fucked us up for life.

When Matt kisses my hand, I realize that the music has stopped.

"Don't stray too far, kitty. Remember your place in this equation. I'll let you know when I'm ready to recoup the debt you owe me," he jeers before turning his back to me and walking away.

I watch as he disappears into the sea of people, thankful that he has no clue I'm about to hop on a plane to Scotland. If he thinks he can use me as a pawn, I won't do anything to dismantle that thought, because pride is a faulty wire that will ultimately burn you.

THE CRACKLING OF the fire fills the room. Darkened in the dead of night, the only light coming from the nearly extinct embers. I've been hiding away in my home office all week, panicked and on the search for anything to weave my way out of this fucking mess.

Knocking back two Xanax and a hit of whiskey, I pick up the phone. My fingers tap incessantly against the bocote desktop as the ringing pierces my ears in this silence that's consumed me.

"Hello?"

"It's me."

"Everything okay?"

Rolling back in my chair, away from the desk, I pinch the bridge of my nose and bite against the oncoming headache. "She's on her way to Scotland."

"How do you know?"

"Because I'm still hacked into her accounts. I just thought you should know."

"Thanks," is all he says before hanging up on me.

five

I GRIP THE ratty, red-headed doll more tightly while everyone sleeps around me, forty thousand feet above soil as the giver of my doll lies six feet under. While I was packing, I found the gift Pike had given me on my tenth birthday stuffed in a box in my closet. I remember him being embarrassed about the doll, having stolen it, but I loved it. And I loved him for being the one person who truly cared about me at a time when I was so alone. This doll was the only good memory of that birthday, because shortly after he gave it to me, I was forced to face the demon in the basement. The demon that would utterly destroy me and mold me into the monster I am today.

"Would you like something to drink, dear?" the flight attendant asks softly.

"No, thank you."

With my mind racing, I can't settle down to sleep. I keep replaying these past few months in my head. Over and over. I miss Pike, but it doesn't even compare to the ache of losing Declan. I hate that in his last hours his perception of me was tarnished. All I wanted was for him to believe I was good and pure, the way he always saw me, but in the end, he discovered it was a lie.

That dossier touched the hands of the men in my life, but it was Declan's hands that hurt the most. It took me a while to open up that file to see what exactly was in it, but when I did, there's no denying the facts from fiction. Declan knew I was a liar, a foster kid, a con artist. It kills me to think about how he must've felt when he realized the truth about me, because all I wanted was to love him, comfort him, and make him feel safe with me.

Who am I kidding though?

I could never love the way a man like that should be loved, but I was willing to try.

"*Tell me what you're feeling,*" I remember him saying as I allow my mind to drift back.

"I hate this," I said. *"I hate every moment I'm not with you. You're all that I want, and I hate life for not being fair to us. And I'm scared. I'm scared of everything, but I'm mostly scared of losing you. You're the one good thing that's ever come along for me. Somehow, in this fucked up world, you have a way of making all the ugly disappear."*

"You're not going to lose me."

"Then why does it feel like it's slipping away?"

"It's not. I promise you, it's not. You're just scared, but you have me now. I'll take all that fear away, every piece of it that you carry around. I'll take it away. I'll give you everything you deserve from this life. I'll do what I can to make up for all your suffering."

I couldn't ever dream of a better man existing, and I never wanted to fall in love with him, but I did. It was wicked and vicious and utterly beautiful, and it was mine. For a moment, he was mine.

And now . . .

He's dead.

And so am I.

His blood is deep inside of me—I made sure of its home—but it isn't enough to save me. Nothing is enough, and the anguish is boundless. There's no release, no cleansing, no Pike to take it all away. I've lost my vice to relieve the ache, to give me my escape, to numb me. It's overpowering, a red river of loathing, a debilitating and suffocating stabbing in the core of my very essence.

It breeds inside of me and my body chills in anxiety. A shrill ring echoes in my ears.

Bleeding, screaming, a tourniquet around ventricles pleading for relief.

Memories of his words strangle me, a noose tightening around my neck.

"We could have a life." "You love me, right?" "I know what I want, and that's a life with you. I'll do whatever it takes to get that."

I can't breathe.

"Excuse me," I stutter breathlessly as I stumble in a rush to the lavatory.

Locking the door behind me, I brace my hands on the sink and stare into my hollow eyes. I attempt to inhale slowly, but my body doesn't allow it. A sheen of sweat coats my pale face, drained of blood, and the hunger inside of me needs to be fed. I need to expel it before it kills me.

My fist takes a life of its own, balling up and slamming itself into my sternum.

Again.

Again.

Knuckles pounding against frail bone, and with every infliction, the ringing in my ears dulls and my lungs begin to fill with much-needed air. I punch myself again and again and again, over and over, busting capillaries with each violent blow. Warmth spreads through my wounded flesh, and when my cheeks heat with tears, I fall back onto the toilet, my hands pressed against the wall of the tiny bathroom as I pant from exertion. My mind clears, but I'm confused by what just happened and why it brought me relief—pleasure, really. The tormenting sadness is gone, freed by the pain I just unleashed on myself.

That was the moment I discovered my new drug. It no longer came in the comfort of Pike or Declan. No. It came from the devil's hand—my hand—and in that moment, I felt a sense of power in my ability to stave off the misery with a blissful brutality that births an endorphined high.

Sighing in refreshed relief, I stand and right myself in front of the mirror before lifting the hem of my top to see the destruction on my body. When I observe the blood pooling beneath my skin, swelling in pink glory, I smile in pride. Contusions mar my skin in reward, and I'm pacified.

This is pain I can deal with. No longer do I have anyone to lean on to alleviate this discord inside of me. All I have is myself. So with a sickening delight, I enjoy my moment of assuagement before returning to my seat to cradle my doll.

LANDING, CUSTOMS, BAGGAGE claim, and rental car. Here I sit in the parking lot, on the other side of the world from where I just came from.

Alone with no plan, no direction.

I sit awkwardly on the right side of the car, wondering if I'll be able to drive without killing myself or someone else. *No time like the present.*

"Here we go," I murmur to myself and then shift the car to pull out of the parking space.

As I leave the airport and start driving through Edinburgh, the scenery astounds me. Declan wasn't lying when he said the landscapes were breathtaking. Freezing rain falls from the dark, grey sky over the Old World city. Stone buildings from another lifetime line the streets, and I'm in awe of the historic beauty. Horns honking pull me away from the sights, and I quickly yank the steering wheel when I realize I'm entering a round-a-bout the wrong way.

"Shit," I screech while waving my hand in apology to the other drivers I nearly sideswiped. Driving on the opposite side of the car, opposite side of the street, has me tense and thrown off.

Turning out of the circle of death, I resume cautiously until I find a place to stop to get a bite to eat. I'm drained from traveling, and when I walk into the quiet restaurant, the hostess sits me at a table towards the back of the small dining room.

"Water?" the woman asks, hair the same shade of red as my own, piled up in a bun on top of her head.

"Please."

"Flat, sparkling, or tap?"

"Flat," I answer and then watch as she walks away, dazed in my unfamiliar surroundings.

These people are clueless to the world I just left behind, to the people I destroyed, to the beast I am. They sit, chatting quietly, very different from the loud and boisterous American manners, and I settle in the hushed atmosphere, looking over the menu.

"Here you go," the waitress says in her thick Scottish accent as she sets the carafe of water on the table after pouring a glass for me. "What can I get for you, lassie?"

Unsure of the menu choices, I tell her, "Something warm and savory."

"You're American?"

I smile and nod, and she then suggests, "Rumbledthumps."

"What?"

"Traditional Scottish dish. Will warm you up from the cold weather."

It takes a few extra seconds to decipher her words through her accent. I never had difficulty understanding Declan, but this woman's native tongue is coated much heavier than what I'm used to hearing.

"Thank you," I respond, handing her the menu, and after I take a long drink of water, I pull out my phone to attempt to get a game plan together.

Once I gain access to the internet, I type in the name of the estate Declan told me about. I remember him telling me it was outside of Edinburgh, but I can't remember where exactly. All I know is, I need to see the house. I need to know it's real. I need to see what could have been mine if only I'd run with him when he asked me to.

Pulling up the search engine, I type in:

Brunswickhill Estate Edinburgh Scotland

It takes only a few seconds for the property to pop up on several different realty websites. I click on the first link, and when a picture of the estate pops up, my stomach sinks. Sitting here, I don't breathe as I stare at the home Declan begged me to live in with him. I swipe the screen with my finger to view the other pictures. One by one, I see what was so close to being my life—my fairytale. It's just as he described: a Victorian mansion set within immaculate grounds covered in lush greens, flowers, trees, and the grotto. I recall Declan telling me how much I would love the grotto that's built from clinker.

Why didn't I run with him when he asked?

Scrolling down the page, I note the realtor as being Knight Frank.

After taking a few minutes to read the online brochure of the estate and looking through the rest of the photos, my food arrives. I take small bites of the potato dish, trying to find comfort in the richness, but my knotted stomach makes it difficult to enjoy. Beneath my skin, wounds slowly split.

Setting the fork down, I start searching online for the public records on the house. It takes a little while, but I finally find what I've been trying so hard to hide from. But it's here in black and white, right under my fingertips. The words informing that the bank seized the estate, and the date this occurred was only a few short weeks after Pike killed Declan. I can still taste his blood from when I took my last kiss.

I read further to find that it didn't take long for the place to resell to a private buyer using an undisclosed trust. I've come to know through Bennett that this isn't an uncommon occurrence among the wealthy. But regardless of the new ownership, I still want to see it. I mark the address and pull up the directions to find it's located about an hour away in Galashiels. Taking one last bite of food, I get the attention of the waitress so that I can pay and be on my way.

Six

"SLEEP WELL?"

"Yes," I reply to Isla, the innkeeper, as I pour myself a cup of hot water from the kettle sitting out in the main dining room.

As I was driving through town last night, I came across this little bed and breakfast and figured it would be a nice place for me to stay while I'm here. Isla greeted me when I arrived, and despite being halfway across the world in a foreign country, something about her demeanor set me at ease. She welcomed me, settled me into my modest room, and quickly excused herself, which I was grateful for. I was beyond exhausted and fell asleep as soon as my head hit the pillow.

"So what brings you to Gala?" she asks.

Dipping a teabag into the mug of water, I'm not sure how to answer. I'm so used to lying and hiding my real self that honesty seems alien. Truth is, I'm not even sure I remember the real me anymore. And then I wonder if I ever truly did. I've been faking it for so long. The last time I remember really feeling in place within this world was when I was five years old. It's like the second my father was stolen from me, so was my identity. And when he died, that identity did too, and all I was left with was a shell of what used to be me. I tried filling the emptiness with hopes and dreams, but that was a waste of time. Then I turned to Pike, using him to fill me with voidance and comfort.

And then there was Declan.

"Are you okay?" Isla questions with concern in her eyes, pulling me out of my thoughts.

"Mmm hmm," is all I can manage around the agonizing block in my throat. After taking a slow sip of my hot tea, a desperate need to find myself takes over, and I do something I haven't done in a very long time.

I tell the truth.

"I lost someone close to me. I came here to feel closer to him."

"Oh, dear," she sighs. "I'm so sorry to hear that."

Her aged eyes are filled with sympathy. Through look alone, she speaks in silence, and I can see understanding and a pain of her own.

"I apologize for being too honest. I didn't mean to make you feel uncomfortable."

"Nonsense. If a woman my age can't handle a little honesty . . . well . . . she hasn't truly lived then."

"I suppose." And she's right. Hell, I feel like I've lived a thousand years on this earth. I doubt you could say anything that would shock me at this point. I bet there isn't a pain that exists that I haven't felt.

"Will you be staying long . . . ?" she begins and then falters her words. "I'm so sorry, hun. It was late when you arrived and your name is failing me right now."

It was in that moment, with that elderly lady who seemed to have answers to questions I had yet to discover, where I made a choice. I thought I had nothing left to lose, but that wasn't fact. You see, somewhere deep inside of me was that five-year-old girl. She held the identity I lost so long ago, and I wanted it back.

"Elizabeth," I tell her. "And I'm not quite sure how long I'll be staying."

"Well, Elizabeth, it's nice to have you here. I won't take up any more of your time. If you need anything, please let me know, okay?"

"Thank you."

I take my tea and head upstairs to my room to unpack and freshen up. After I'm dressed and have settled my belongings in their proper places, I look at myself in the easel mirror that's set in the corner of the room. Ivory slacks, taupe cashmere sweater, nude pumps. Clothes I acquired while living my con. They scream Nina, but I'm at a loss as to what is Elizabeth. Who is she really? It's been so long since I've been her. I feel like I left her that fated day when my father was arrested. I've lived most of my life in a tomb, hiding from the afflictions of this world, until I became Nina.

And now, I'm a hollow illusion—a druxy dressed in gossamer.

I tuck a lock of my wavy red hair behind my ear before grabbing my keys.

With the address to Brunswickhill punched into the car's navigation, I follow the highlighted route that weaves me through the narrow streets up a winding hill. It doesn't take long to hit Abbotsford Road, and I know I'm close.

But not to *him*, only to his ghost.

My eyes sting with unshed tears as I round the bend and see the green sign on the stone gate wall that reads *Brunswickhill.* I'm locked on the sign as my chin trembles and my soul bleeds from the inside, filling me with the poison I feed from.

It's real.

This place—the place he wanted to give me—it's really real.

Pulling the car off the side of the road, I don't realize how tightly my fingers are wrapped around the steering wheel until I let go and feel the ache. When I step out of the car in front of the wrought iron gate that hides my could-have-been palace, the phantom of death hangs over me.

Loss is consuming.

Emptiness is overwhelming.

Sadness is everlasting.

My feet move on their own—closer. I breathe deeply, praying for the scent of him to fill my lungs that don't deserve it, but crave it. It's nothing but sharp ice though. Frigid as my hands grip the cold metal of the gate, tears begin to fall from my already-swollen eyes.

The fissures of my heart begin to rip and shred—burning, stinging, piercing agony erupting. My knuckles whiten as my grip strengthens, and the misery and regret explode in a vile rage. Jerking my hands, shaking the gates, I lose myself in a maniacal outburst. I scream into the bleak clouds, scream so hard it feels like razors slicing through my larynx, and I welcome the pain, pleading for it to cut more deeply.

Slamming the gate back and forth, metal clanging, ice severing my flesh, I sob. I make it hurt coming out. Bitterly cold tears stain my face as my body takes on a life of its own.

I want him back.

How hard do I have to cry to get him back?

Why did this happen to me? To him? To us?

I just want him back.

"Come back!" My voice, shrilling in the air. "Please! Just come back!"

Thrashing around, drowning in wails, my body tires. My hands are frozen, continuing to cling to the bars of the gate as I fall to my knees. I feel my core chipping away while my body heaves. Desperate to catch my breath against my pounding heart, I close my eyes and lean against the wrought iron. Soon, my deep gasps turn into childlike, desolate whimpers.

I just want someone to hold me. To touch me and tell me it's going to be okay. That *I'm* going to be okay. I want my brother, my daddy, my love—I'll take anyone just to get some relief. So I sit here on the cold concrete and cry—alone.

Snow drifts down, weightlessly, falling over me as time passes. The whistling wind through the trees awakens me to the dropping temperatures, and I don't even know how long I've been sitting here when I look up and through the gates. Wiping my tears, I stammer to my feet and try to get a better look at the property, but it's hidden behind the trees. On the other side of the gate, the drive winds up a hill and through a mass of snow-covered trees, and beyond that is a mystery.

But I know.

He told me all about the house, the grounds, the flowers, the glass conservatory.

I look around to find a way in, but the gates and stone wall are nearly nine feet high, and there's no way of climbing over.

What's the point anyway? It's not like anything's waiting for me on the other side. I'm not even sure why I'm still here, and when I look down at my reddened, almost maroon hands, bloodied from the ice cuts, I know it's time to go.

"DEAR, ARE YOU all right?"

"Just slipped on some ice while shopping," I lie as Isla notices my dirty, wet slacks from where I spent most of the day sitting on the snowy ground. I know I look ghastly, and the part of me that's trained itself well wants to poise up, but the weakness in me begs to slump its shoulders and take the embrace I know Isla would be willing to give. I don't know which way to go.

"You're a terrible liar, lassie," she says as she takes my hand and leads me over to the dining room table and sits me down.

She rushes into the kitchen and quickly returns with the kettle as well as a cup and saucer. I watch as her frail hands pour the hot water and dunk in a tea bag before setting it down in front of me.

I don't refute her accusation that I'm a liar. I'm too emotionally drained to play games, and then she remarks, "Your eyes look like they hurt."

And they do.

I've cried more in these past few weeks than I have in my whole life. Pike taught me how to shut off my emotions, act like a machine so that no one could hurt me, and he taught me well. But the strength it takes to turn it all off is beyond what I feel I'm capable of at the moment.

My eyes are a constant shade of pink, and the salt from my tears has burned through the tender skin that surrounds them. Makeup only irritates it and stings, so I go easy with the powder in my feeble attempt to look as presentable as possible.

But I have to wonder why I'm even concerned about how I present myself. I'm thousands of miles away from America. I'm no longer pretending or fighting because I've already lost.

I don't want to be Nina anymore. I don't want the stupid life of Mrs. Vanderwal. It's over. There's nothing left of it because everyone is gone. Maybe, just maybe, I can stop fighting, stop the lies, stop fearing and hiding. For the first time since I was eight years old and left to decay in Posen, maybe now I can finally breathe. I just wish I knew how. It's been almost twenty-one years of suffocating, and when I look over at Isla and see the years marked in the wrinkles of her face, I give her a little more truth.

"I went to the home he used to own."

She reaches across the table and places her hand on my arm. "You said you lost him. What happened? Did he leave you?"

"Yes," I choke out, trying to hold back my tears. "He died."

"Bless you, dear. I'm so sorry."

Swallowing hard, we both sit for a while before she breaks the silence and tells me, "I lost my husband eight years ago. Nothing can compare to the pain of losing the man you give your spirit to. When you put everything you have—everything you are—into the one who promises to take care of you, you become transparent and utterly vulnerable to that person. And when he's taken away, so are you, and yet here you remain, left to continue living your life as if you have something to live for."

"Then why go on living?"

"Well," she starts, looking over to the fireplace mantel where a menagerie of picture frames line the wooden structure. "For me it was for my family. My children. It took a while, but eventually I found the strength to pull myself together and live for them."

I scan the array of family portraits and candid snapshots, and when I turn back to Isla, she smiles, asking, "Do you have children?"

Her question hits me hard. I'm not sure how to answer because it wasn't that long ago that I did have a child. A baby. A tiny baby growing in my womb, and now that womb is empty. So, I keep my answer simple, "I don't have any family. It's only me."

"Your parents?"

Shaking my head, I repeat, "Just me."

Instead of telling me how sorry she is about this fact, she does her best to encourage. "You're so young. You have time in this life. For me, I was an old woman when my husband passed on, but you . . . you have youth on your side. You live for that. You're beautiful; you'll fall in love again, and you have time to create your own family."

"I don't think I'm strong enough to fall in love again." I'm also unworthy and undeserving of love after everything I've done.

"Maybe not now. It takes time for wounds to heal, but there will come a time when you'll be strong enough."

I'm smart enough to know that not all wounds heal, but I nod and give a weak smile before standing up. "I should get out of these wet clothes," I say and excuse myself from the room.

After a hot shower, I tend to the cuts on my hands and then wonder why I even bothered to do so as I pick up a bottle of sleeping pills from my toiletry bag. The pills lightly pad against each other as I roll the bottle in my hand. I keep wishing for some sort of relief, some comfort, but it's been here the whole time. Right here in this bottle.

What's the point of life when life has nothing but vile hate for you?

My body is numb, a casket of waste. I feel nothing in this moment as I consider my escape. I don't want this life anymore. I never wanted it.

I'm outside of my body, standing next to a pathetic woman whose bones now protrude through colorless skin because she refuses to take care of herself. I look at her, slowly deteriorating. She stops rolling the bottle of pills in her hand and stares into the translucent orange before popping the lid off.

"Do it," I encourage. *"Put yourself out of your misery."*

I know she hears me as she moves gracefully, pouring the pills in her hand and then lifts her head, staring across the room at nothing in particular.

"Just do it, Elizabeth. Everything you want is waiting for you. They're all waiting for you."

And then she does it; holding her hand to her mouth, she dumps the pills in and takes a long drink of water from the glass on the bedside table. I walk over to her when she lies back on the bed and run my fingers through her hair, soothing her the way a parent would a child. I meet her craving for tender affection. She looks peaceful in the stillness of the room, breathing in a soft, rhythmic pattern. I notice tears puddling in her blue eyes, but she doesn't cry, and I know she's ready.

"I just can't do it anymore," she whispers to herself and then closes her eyes as she lets go of the fight.

Sometimes, for some people, the fairytale only exists in death.

Seven

WHEN I OPENED my eyes and found myself in the same room I fell asleep in, I had to laugh at how pathetic I was. I couldn't even kill myself; instead I just gave myself one hell of a nap. And there I was, greeted by another day after a lousy botched suicide attempt.

Everything inside of me was paralyzed, yet my body still moved.

Did you know it was possible to have feelings with no emotions?

You can, and I'm proof of it.

I performed the same actions of the previous day with detachment, and it wasn't long until I found myself back at Brunswickhill. I spent hours there, sitting outside of the gates and crying for my lost love.

And the next day, I returned.

And the day after that.

And the day after that.

And even the day after that.

It's a pathetic routine I refuse to break, because for some reason, as upsetting as it is to be at the estate, it allows me to feel connected to Declan. And I need that connection because I don't have anything else to hold on to. So I cling to the forlorn fairytale that never will be.

It's a little over a week that I've been coming here, spending my days crying, pleading, bargaining with a God I don't even believe in to bring him back. Isla now looks at me with pity every evening when I return to shower and sleep. We don't speak much, but it's mostly on my part. I've allowed the wall I spent my whole life building around my heart to crumble to dust, and I've never felt weaker than I do now. Not even when I was being molested by my brother when I was just a child. Or when I was bound up in the closet and locked away for days on end.

No.

This is much worse.

I drive in silence over to Abbotsford Road, and when I round the bend,

I slow the car down as I see the new owners pulling up to the gate. They haven't been around since I've been coming here. Chills run through me as I drive past the gate and follow the winding road until my car is out of their sight. I'm hardly thinking as I follow my body's movements, quickly parking the car and hopping out. Walking back to the gate, I catch the taillights of the SUV as it enters the private drive and I rush to the gates to slip through before they close completely.

Curiosity gets to me, but it's more than that. It's a feeling of ownership, as if this place is mine, because once upon a time ago, it was going to be mine, but time wasn't on my side back then. It still isn't.

I step off the drive and into the snow that covers the ground beneath. I duck behind the trees to remain unseen and start exploring the grounds. Steep hills are covered in bushes and trees that the cold weather has consumed to a barren state. If I close my eyes, I can picture the lush greens and colorful flowers that would come to life under the warm sun. The beauty is still visible though. Everything looks pure and virgin, coated in the fluffy, white powder.

Looking up, I can see the house perched at the top of the hill. My heart grows heavy, sinking down into my gut as I peer up through the trees to see the stonework of what was supposed to be my palace. I continue to weave deeper into the trees, wandering about when I come across a small, man-made, pebbled creek that winds down one of the small hills. It's covered in frozen water and there's a small wooden bench at the bottom where it rounds out into a tiny pond.

And now it hits me . . .

Taking a slow spin to take in my surroundings, nestled within this beautiful place, I realize this resembles what I've spent my life dreaming about. A small forest. Carnegie's magical forest. The thought brings me a warmth of comfort along with a cleaver to my chest because now I feel I've lost even more.

Time passes as I explore, getting lost in my head with fantasies of what could have been and memories of what was. When I get closer to the top of the hill, I can see the front of the house between the branches. It doesn't look like any home I've seen. It's grand and dignified, adorned in large pieces of stone that embody this three-story structure. A massive, tiered fountain stands proud at the center of the circle drive. It's covered in snow, but it doesn't take away from the beauty.

Shrubs line the perimeter of the house, but there are several gaping holes in the hedge, missing bushes that have probably died in the frost and been removed. Everything is so pristine except for the mess of randomly missing shrubs. I take a few steps to try and get a closer look at a small building sitting off to the side of the house when I hear a door close, startling me. Quickly turning, I stagger on my feet, moving deeper into the trees to hide.

A car starts.

"Shit," I murmur under my breath, and I know I have to quickly get back down to the base of the property without being seen.

I see the black SUV making its way down the drive, and I rush towards the gate, trying to keep my balance. There's no way I'll be able to scale the wall to get out if that gate closes, but there are hidden patches of ice I'm trying to watch out for, slowing me down.

Grabbing on to tree trunks for balance as I make my way down, I notice the SUV stop from the corner of my eye, and in a panic to get to my car, I make a run for it. I'm close to the gate, and I take a look behind me to see the SUV moving again. When I turn my head back around, I stumble, crouching over to duck under a massive branch hanging too low. My shoe catches on a patch of ice, knocking me off balance. Taking a huge step to get my slipping feet back under me, I plow down several feet, falling hard onto my stomach on the drive. My palms sting as I try to catch my fall on the icy gravel.

Not wanting to get caught trespassing on private property, I do my best to hop up to my feet.

"Hey!" a man shouts at me, but my pounding heart that beats in my ears muffles him.

I slow my step and stop, cursing myself for being so foolish. Turning around, the man's car door is open, and when he steps out, my lungs fill to the brink of their elasticity. Everything that's been working so hard at keeping me alive soothes, and my hands fly to cover my mouth in utter shock and elation.

Oh my God.

Confusion and fear and anxiety swarm through my veins.

Everything stops.

Time stands still.

I can't move, can't blink, can't breathe.

My eyes scan his figure as the seconds falter between us.

This isn't real. You've been out in the cold for too long. You're upset and hallucinating, Elizabeth. It isn't real.

But he moves.

He's alive! Oh, thank God, he's alive, but how?

Something between a gasp and a cry rips out of me. I can't help the thankful smile that grows on my lips that are hidden behind my hands, and I prepare to run to him. He's alive and on solid ground, not buried in the dirt of the earth like I've believed this entire time. He's whole and beautiful, and I need to cover him in my warmth just as much as I need him to cover me. To heal this suffering that's been gnawing through my flesh and bone, straight into the fibers of my cells.

I breathe in holy relief as he steps away from the SUV.

"What the fuck are you doing here?!"

I drop my hands, stunned beyond what I can comprehend as his harsh tone slays every piece of hope my foolish heart just resurrected.

"You're real?" I question, but my words are barely audible under my panted breath. My pulse is turbulent, and I'm not sure if what I'm seeing really exists.

"You left me to die, you manipulative bitch!"

"No!"

No!!

My brain races to defend, to take away the hate that is utterly obvious in his eyes. His words are suffused in it, leaving them to poison me. A menace to once was.

"You lied." His words come quick as rage boils behind his glare.

"No!" I grapple with words that I can't seem to find in my state of shock. I want to ask him if he's real again, but the venom on his tongue scares me into justifying my actions.

"You cunt!"

"Please, no! It wasn't like tha—"

"What was it like then? Huh? Tell me what is was, *Nina?*" A knowing grin creeps upon his lips—evil—as he takes a step closer, but still much too far for me to touch. "Or is it *Elizabeth?* Who the hell are you?"

"I don't know," I murmur shamefully and then continue, "I don't know who I am. I haven't been me in a very long time." My words are like knives carving pieces out of me. They hurt when I confess, "The only thing I know I am is *yours.*"

"Tell me I wasn't your goddamn pawn!"

"This was never supposed to happen, Declan. Please—"

"What? You turning me into a murderer? That wasn't your plan all along?"

"I love you. Please. You have to understand," I plead against his wrath.

In three quick steps, his hands are on me, gripping my shoulders, swinging me around as if I weigh nothing, slamming me violently against the side of his car.

I can smell him, and suddenly, there's no more pain. His fingers pierce into my flesh, bruising me instantly, and it feels like kisses on my skin. He yanks me closer towards him before smashing me back against the car again, seething through clenched teeth, "You're a sick fuck. Nothing but street trash." He takes in a deep breath, and then adds, "That's right. I know all about you and that punk kid you ran around with."

"It wasn't supposed to end like that," I try convincing. "I fell in love with you."

"End like what? Huh?"

"The way it did."

His hands drop from my shoulders, and before I know it, he's got his hand wrapped around my neck, choking, pinning me against the SUV, and I savor the heat of him against me.

"I killed your husband," he snarls, beautiful breath bathing my face.

"I didn't want that," I gasp on strangled breath.

"What did you want?"

Looking up into his eyes, they're blurred behind my welled tears when I tell him, "You."

"I should kill *you*."

My hands cling to his wrist, urging him to tighten his grip around my throat.

"Do it." My words, an offering of atonement. "I've lost everything, and out of all that, you're the only one I would have given up everything for just to have one last touch." His grip weakens but his hand remains firmly in place, and when I watch our breaths unite in small clouds of vapor between our lips, realization crystallizes.

My God, he's alive.

Letting go of his wrist, I reach up and run my hand along his stubbled jaw, and the comfort in the touch flays me entirely. A disgustingly raw sob erupts from my bleeding heart. I want to crawl inside of his skin and drown myself in his blood. I want to swim in his marrow.

"Don't fucking touch me," he barks, wrenching my hand off of him.

I'm a mess though, unable to contain my emotions as they pour out of me. "I thought you were dead. For weeks I've been mourning you—"

"Get the fuck off my property, bitch."

His words cut me off. I shouldn't be stunned at them, but the snarl in his tone is startling, and I quickly shut my mouth. He then grabs ahold of my jaw, forcing my chin up as he looks down on me, and I don't recognize the devilry in his eyes. He pisses his words, "You're nothing more than a shit-stain, so fuck off. I'm done with you, understand?"

"Please . . . don't."

"Nod your little head and tell me you understand."

The urgency to explain everything to him is powerful, but I know he'd never hear my words with the hatred in him right now, so I obey with a nod. "I understand."

He lets go, not giving me a second look as he turns away and gets back into the SUV. I look at his beautiful face through the windshield. I never want to take my eyes off him, and it kills to know that I have to. He glares at me with daggers as I feel tears running down my cheeks.

"I'm so sorry," I say even though I know he can't hear me and then turn my back on my prince that I so selfishly molded into this monster.

Walking away, I'm confused. There are a million feelings and reactions, and I have no clue which one to grab on to. I don't know how to begin to process the fact that I just saw my angel of death in the flesh. I felt his heat, smelled him, heard him.

It was real.

I see Pike all the time. I even talk to him. But there's never a smell, never a temperature to his touch. It's how I know the difference between hallucinations and reality. But this is real. He's alive, but at what cost? He doesn't resemble the Declan I knew. That man was firm, yes, but he had light in him that shone through his emerald eyes. But this Declan . . . he's hard and cold, and it's all my fault. I knew pushing him to kill Bennett would destroy him, change him, take away his pure spirit.

He looks as worn as I do, his frame more slender, a lack of color in his skin. I ache to touch him, taste him, make him see that this was all a terrible mistake. That loving him was my saving grace. Make him understand how everything changed and changed from a place of honesty I never knew I held inside of me.

How am I supposed to live in the same world as him when he hates me so much?

How do I right the wrongs of my past?

How do I find a hope worth living for when my one hope would rather me dead than alive?

eight

TORMENT IS THE deep well I bathe in daily. It covers me entirely as I sink beneath the surface, feeling its particles soak into the pores of my decrepit skin. Seeping through me, it consumes, wallows, and dwells so I can feel every ounce of its torturous abuse.

Black is the color that stains my insides. Declan used to color me in vibrancy, but that's when he loved me for the lie he believed I was. I'm a sick woman. Deceit paints my rotten soul, and he now sees me for what I am.

How could I destroy a man as wonderful as Declan?

He was a good man, a loving man. His touch was firm yet tender. But now, after seeing him a couple days ago, he's so different. Callous and filled with venom. Worst of all is knowing that I did that to him. I'm the culprit. I'm the cause. I touched him and turned him into a monster.

But even as a monster, I want him. I'll take him in any form I can because I'm so thankful he's alive. That Pike didn't kill him. Glory and joy somehow illuminate this bleak heart of mine and rejoice in the flesh and blood of his existence.

Where do I go now? What do I do when all I want is what I know he'll refuse?

Another touch, kiss, smell, taste. But once I get it, I know I'll want more. It'll never satisfy, never be enough to feed the hunger I have for him. My soul is starved and he's my sacrament.

I want to skin him with my tongue, loving him with every lick.

Alone is where I sit though, here in this bed and breakfast, in this room I've been calling home since I arrived. Too scared to go back to Brunswickhill for fear of what will greet me. Declan isn't a man one can push. He thrives on utter control, so keeping my distance is the only choice I have right now unless I want to throw him over the edge. And I don't. I want him to be able to see that not all of it was a lie, that I did love him, that it was real, and that I didn't want to destroy him the way I wound up doing anyway. I need him to know that, to understand his heart was something I wanted to take care of—I still do.

Hours pass as I sit, staring out the window at the snow-covered hills, wondering what my love is doing. It feels strange to be in a world where he exists and to not know, to not be a part of that world with him when we had become so enmeshed with each other. He was a part of me—still is. He lives within me; I can feel him in my bones—breathing inside of me, keeping me alive.

He is all I have to live for.

I grow impatient and anxious in this room, feeling like a caged animal. I grab my coat and scarf and head down to the car. As I drive the slick streets, I wind up on Abbottsford Road without thinking. It's all I know in this town, it's all I crave. I tell myself I won't stay long, that I'll just drive past, take a quick look. But when I make the sharp turn around the bend, I slow the car down and stop.

Was it all a dream? A hallucination?

Looking at the gate, I wonder if I was *really* on the other side.

Did I just want it so badly that I dreamt it up?

I know I shouldn't be here. I know what I did to him was so awful that seeing me will only make it worse on him. I want to give him that space, the courtesy of staying away because I know that's what he wants. But I'm too selfish. I want him too much, and now that I'm here, the energy collides inside of me. I want to jump over that wall, run up the hill to his front door, break it down, storm the property to find him, hug him, cling, paw, scratch, and ravage him like the animal I am.

Tingles dance up my fingers, into my hands, and up my arms.

I can't sit still.

Hopping out of the car, I rush over to the gates, grab on to them and shake them, screaming at the top of my lungs, "Declan! Please let me talk to you! Declan, please!"

My voice strains as I plead and beg for him. Tears begin to coat my cheeks as I call his name, because simply having it on my tongue and lips feels like a kiss from him. So I scream even louder, a protest of my love, and my voice shrills painfully as I call out, "Declan!" over and over and over again.

I don't stop—I can't.

I'm nothing without him. I'll die without him. He has to forgive me. He just has to. I can't live with him hating me as much as he does. So I fight these gates, screaming and crying and breaking, falling to my knees—absolutely crumbling.

I'm weak as my voice slowly gives out, and I have to catch my breath around my pounding, severing heart. Dropping my head, I weep while the damp ground seeps through the fabric of my pants.

I startle and jump up when the gate begins opening. I turn to see the black Mercedes SUV he was in the other day coming up the road. Desperate to talk to him, I run out in the middle of the street, blocking him. He slows and stops, and with my hands on the freezing hood of his car, emotions overwhelm as I beg, "Declan, please. Please let me talk to you. I love you, Declan."

My words fall out in a blubber of panicky cries as I look at him through the windshield. The car shifts under my hands when he puts it in park and then opens his door. Menacing eyes greet me once again, but I'm frantic for his attention.

"Declan, please, just let me talk to you."

"I thought you understood that I didn't want you coming back here," he snarls in his thick accent, stepping in front of me.

In quick movements, he grabs my arms in both his hands. Faster than what I can fight, Declan drags me over to my car while I cry, "Please, stop. Just give me a few minutes to explain."

"There isn't a goddamn thing you could possibly say to me."

He then yanks me around so I'm facing away from him and slams my front side over against the car, knocking the wind out of me and pinning me down. With my arms bound in his hand behind my back, he presses the side of my face into the hood with his other, needling against the ice. His body hunches over mine and his breath heats my ear as he seethes, "In case I didn't make it clear, I fucking hate you."

"You don't mean that," I whisper, pissing him off even more as he grabs a fist full of my hair and snaps my head back. My neck stretches, sparks of pain shooting through the tendons, and the *chrrrick* of my hair, popping out from the roots, ripping flesh along with it, sears my scalp in pricks of fire. I scream, but he doesn't let go.

"You've got balls, darling. Coming here, knowing one phone call is all it would take for you to be arrested and extradited."

"Why haven't you done it then?" I question through clenched teeth, and he yanks harder, ripping out more hair from my scalp. Gasping in agony, I push him, "Tell me why."

"You think it's because I care for you? You're fucking delusional."

"Then why?"

"Because seeing your face makes me want to kill you. I thought you'd be smart and leave, never come back, yet here you are," he says.

"You won't hurt me."

The sudden force of his hand shocks me, and I scream out in pure white, heated pain. My hand flies to the back of my head, trembling as I touch the bare flesh. Tears fall, and when I turn to look at him, he's holding a chunk of my hair. I can feel the blood trickling down the back of my neck. He stares—no emotion—while my body pangs in agony, but I've dealt with pain and abuse my whole life. I've been beaten, whipped, tied up for days, and one thing I've learned: physical pain is much more tolerable than mental pain.

Bruises fade. Blood dries. Scabs heal.

Sucking in a deep breath, I bring my hand in front of me and it's covered in blood.

"You won't hurt me," I repeat, and it's now that I see the torment in his eyes. There's no doubt he's furious, but there's a void, a hollowness that didn't used to be there.

"You sucked the life right out of me. I don't give a shit about you anymore," he says and then drops the lock of my hair on the ground. "I pray you put a bullet in your head."

I let him go without saying anything as he turns to get back in his car. I bite my tongue, knowing I'll only make him feel worse if I continue to speak. I'll give him a reprieve, but I won't back down. I'll find a way to talk to him, to explain everything. I've manipulated my way around obstacles in the past; I can do it again.

After I watch him drive past me and the gates close behind him, I walk to the side of the road and scoop up a handful of snow. My body tenses in preparation for the pain, and my hand shakes as I reach back. Flinching, I slather the snow on my bloody scalp, and hiss against the sting that singes my head.

I scoop up another handful and pack it against my wound, and once my body stops quaking and numbs, I slip into my car and drive back.

"WHAT HAPPENED?" ISLA questions urgently as I'm walking up the stairs.

"Excuse me?" I respond when I turn around.

Coming up the steps, she looks worried. "There's blood all over your back, lassie."

"Oh, I . . . "

"What's going on? Are you hurting yourself?"

"No," I quickly blurt out.

"Do you need to call someone? The police?"

"No. No, I'm fine," I defend. "It's fine."

Her eyes narrow in annoyance as I avoid her questioning.

"It's not *fine.* Now you tell me what's going on or I'll call the police myself."

"No police. Please," I tell her, and decide to just lie. "It was a clumsy accident. I slipped on some ice and hit my head as I fell."

She gives me a suspicious look before nodding. "You should get yourself checked out by a doctor."

"If it starts to bother me, I will. It looks much worse than it is," I try assuring her.

Once I'm in my room, I head into the bathroom to check out the damage. The blood mats my hair, and the strands are dried to the wound. I peel some of the hair away, and it rips the forming scab causing my head to bleed again. I know I could wet a towel and clean myself up, but I relish the pain. It distracts and takes away from my annihilated heart.

The misery inside of me swells and grows, so I continue ripping the scab apart, pulling my hair, and focusing on that pain instead of my internal pain. I can't release it, but I can mask it, and so I do. When I feel the heat of blood seeping out, there's a release of euphoria that delights me. I savor this momentary distraction and enjoy the blood tickling my skin as it rolls down my neck. It's all I focus on as I sigh in relief and close my eyes.

nine

(CALLUM)

"DON'T FUCK AROUND, inmate. Five minutes," the guard I paid off barks as he shoves the disposable cell phone against my chest.

"I need the card."

"I already programmed the number in the phone," he tells me and then hands me a small, folded up piece of scrap paper. "The verification code."

I nod and he scowls in return. "Make it quick."

Punching in the numbers, I don't have to wait long for the call to go through.

"Hello?" my longtime friend answers. The one I planted in my son's life to ensure I have all my bases covered. A man who presents himself as a loyal entity to Declan, but whose loyalties de facto lie with me.

"I don't have long," I say.

"How the hell are you calling me? I heard you were locked up."

I was arrested before I could make contact with my associate after receiving the call about Nina's whereabouts. Now I sit, here in jail at the Manhattan Detention Complex, waiting for my case to go before the grand jury.

"I have my ways. Look, I don't have time to bullshit. I need you to move the money from the offshore accounts and put it into Declan's foundation."

"No worries," he responds obediently.

"Use his foundation to wash it and make it appear as clean as possible."

"Got it."

"I also need you to keep your eye on Declan. I want him followed. After the shooting, he's been off, if you know what I mean."

"The kid is fucked up, Cal."

"Yeah, well, that's his issue. You need to make sure my issue is the one you're protecting, got it?"

"Wrap it up, inmate," the guard snaps at me.

"That money needs to be moved yesterday."

"I'll handle it," he responds before the phone is snatched from my hand.

ten

EATING ONE OF Isla's Scotch eggs I've come to enjoy and sipping on hot tea, I flip through a local Edinburgh publication. It's been several days since my last run-in with Declan. I've been holed up in my room, crying and feeling defeated. Wondering what to do, where to go, and how to move on in this life.

I was with Pike last night. He lay in bed with me; we haven't done that in such a long time, and I forgot how very comforting it felt. I was finally able to breathe. He spoke to me, soothed me, and in that moment he was real. My head knows it's a phantasm, but my heart refuses, so we talked, cried, and eventually he made me smile.

When I woke this morning, he was gone, but somehow I still feel him here. I remember when we were kids, and even living in the vilest circumstances one could imagine, when I was in his arms, I was okay. He was magical in that way. So was Declan. Both of them loved me and healed me in entirely unique ways.

Pike reminded me of my strength, and I showed him the back of my head, where Declan had ripped out my hair. I told him that I continue to pick at the scab and make myself bleed to feel better, proving to him that I'm weak, that I can't handle the pain anymore, so I create my own. A pain I can control and use to mask the true ache that runs deep inside of me. But he assured me that what I'm doing is a symbol of strength. The fact that I refuse to let my emotions control me, and instead control them, is a testament to my vitality.

I decided to take his words and apply them to Declan. Instead of letting him control me and keep me away, I will take the control to get what I want. I've done it before; I can do it now. Pike is right. I've been allowing myself to crumble and feel as if I'm nothing on my own, but he reminded me that I'm not. That I've always been strong. Reminded me that even though I no longer have him as my vice, I'm powerful enough to create another.

"It's so nice to see you eating," Isla says as she walks out from the kitchen and into the dining room where I sit.

"I've been a little under the weather," I excuse my lack of presence.

She sets down a bowl of mixed berries and eyes the magazine I'm flipping through.

"I found it on the coffee table," I offer. "I was thinking about getting out of town and going into the city for a day trip."

"Have you spent any time in Edinburgh?"

"No. I drove through when I arrived, stopped for a quick meal, and then came here."

"It's a great town," she says and continues to talk, but her voice fades into the distance when I turn the page.

She's muted noise, and everything around me tunnels as I focus on the eyes looking up at me from within the grains of the paper. Dapper as always, in a vested, tailored suit, no tie, and top buttons unfastened. The very essence of Declan, unkempt in a classy way. His face, a couple days unshaven, and I can remember the way the bristles felt against my lips when he kissed me. The way I would find comfort in running my hand along his jaw.

Setting my fork down with ease, my pulse slows in admiration and shock. I hone in and examine every curve and line of his face.

That used to be mine.

No more though.

He loathes my very existence, wishes me dead, prays for it. But that filters out and what remains is the lovingly harsh way his hands felt on my body. The good of Declan takes over my thoughts, and I rush back in time to when he would look at me with his powerful eyes that told so much in the depth of emerald. They would nearly illuminate and brighten when his emotions of adoration were on high, and dull out, blackening when desire and his need to claim and control would ignite. This man is built in impermeable layers, but I was the one he allowed to seep in. I guess the same could be said in reverse because I let him in as well.

Isla's touch on my arm pulls me away from my love.

"Are you okay?"

"I'm sorry," I say with a slight shake of my head.

She nods to the photograph in the magazine. "No need to apologize. With looks like that, you can't help but become distracted."

Laughing, I agree, "Yeah."

"He used to live in Edinburgh before moving to America years back. A perpetual bachelor that the lassies would fawn over."

"You know him?" I question.

"*Of* him," she clarifies. "The McKinnons were a prominent family here, but tragedy struck and they soon found assuage in the US. But recently, Declan, the son, returned."

"Hmm," I hum, feigning nonchalance.

"He lives here in Gala, you know?"

"What happened?"

When she gives me a wondering look, I clarify, "You mentioned a tragedy."

"Oh, yes. Declan's mother was murdered in their home. Callum, his father, soon left, but Declan stayed in Scotland for a while. I think I read somewhere that when Declan finished his studies at University, he moved to the States and went into business with his father. They've both been living in America until Declan's recent return."

I want to correct her, tell her that Declan parted ways with Cal and was making a strong name for himself as an international real estate developer, but I'd rather her not know my link to him.

"He attended St. Andrews at the same time Prince William did," she adds with enthusiasm, but I don't care about the trivial anecdotes she seems to take pride in.

Anxious to be alone, I take my last bite of egg and excuse myself. "Do you mind if I take this with me?" I ask about the magazine.

"Of course not."

"Thank you."

When I close the door to my room, I sit down at the small desk near the window and open the article with Declan's photo. Alone with my love, I run my fingers over his face and pretend it's real. I shut my eyes and try to smell him, but there's nothing except the lingering fragrance of my perfume in the air.

I look back at him and then begin to read the article that the photo accompanies. I feel my smile grow the further I read. And when I discover a charity event where Declan will be the guest of honor, I know this is an opportunity that I must take full advantage of—and I will. I continue to read the piece that boasts about the charities Declan supports and advocates for.

I note the function where he will be honored is being held this Saturday evening at his alma mater, and start scheming.

AFTER READING THE article a couple days ago, I went ahead and made my day trip to Edinburgh, but not after making a few phone calls. The foundation that Declan is being honored for and has become one of the main financial contributors to is one that strives to offer valuable education to under-privileged children. Knowing there will be so many eyes on him at this event, I think it will be the perfect opportunity to talk to him. I doubt he would cause a scene, but rather be forced to be cordial for the good graces of the attendees. He'd have to stand there and listen to me. So I went ahead and became a donor myself, and the sizable check I wrote secured me a seat at the event.

As I stand in front of the full-length mirror here in my hotel room in Saint Andrews, I run my hands down the lace overlay of my navy dress. The thin material hugs my petite form, just barely skimming the floor. I wear my hair down in soft waves to hide the still-grotesque wound on the back of my head. I continue to pick at it daily, and it's grown in size. I don't want it to heal because it's the only physical thing I have to represent Declan. His gift to me, created by his own hands. He gave it to me, and I refuse to let it go. It serves a multitude of purposes: it's my vice, my pain reliever, my trophy, my reminder, my solace. My love, branded into my flesh, and I own it happily.

When I'm satisfied with my appearance, I pick up my invitation and pashmina before heading down to the lobby. The car I called for is already waiting out front, and my heart beats in anticipation as the driver opens the door for me. I've granted myself permission to be vulnerable ever since I woke up in the hospital, exhausted from the emotions I finally allowed to erupt inside of me.

But now . . . now it's time to focus.

I know what I want, and I need to do whatever it takes to get Declan to talk to me, to hear my words, and to understand and believe in what we had. To know it wasn't a lie—not all of it. To know I didn't want him to kill, I didn't want to use him or betray him, but that everything spun out of control so fast I couldn't stop what had already been set into motion.

When we arrive and pass through the gate of Saint Andrews University, I take a moment to admire the historic buildings, aged to refinement. The car jostles along the cobblestone road and slows in front of a building that's adorned with rustic, fire-lit lanterns and a red carpet lined with press photographers. It's foreign that I would attend an event alone and not know a single person, but I refuse to let insecurity taint me.

The car stops and I watch women dressed to the nines in their designer gowns and men in their kilts and fly plaids. I take a hard swallow, straighten my spine, and reach out for the hand of the usher who opens my door.

"Miss," he greets with a nod. "Will you be joined by a companion?"

"No."

"May I escort you?"

"That would be lovely," I accept graciously.

I feign my right to belong and mingle among, what appears to be, the high society of the UK—wealth and prestige. But I'm good at what I do, veiling the disgust that molds me as the vile human I really am.

Looping my arm through his, he introduces in his heavy brogue, "I'm Lachlan."

I look up at his broad, clean-shaven face and smile at the forty-something-year-old man with dark hair distinguished by flakes of silver. Putting on the charm I perfected while married to Bennett, I remark with flirtation, "And where is *your* companion?"

"I'm without as well."

"Really? That surprises me."

"And why's that?"

"Truthfully?" I question, lifting a brow to create amusement, and when he smiles and nods, I'm blunt, telling him, "You're startlingly attractive. I find it hard to believe you're not here with a little tart attached to your arm."

His chuckle is deep and rich when he responds, "Oh, but I do have a beautiful little, what did you call it?—*tart?*—stuck to my arm."

I join in his laughter. "Elizabeth."

"Elizabeth?"

"My name, it's Elizabeth. And I assure you, I'm no tart."

eleven

LACHLAN AND I are all smiles when he leads me into the magnificent ballroom, draped in luxury. The room is masculine, smelling of rich varnish and weathered books, dark mahogany walls, and the finest champagne being served off of polished antique silver trays. As a waiter passes me, I pluck a sparkling flute from the tray.

"Quick on the bevvy. Eager?" Lachlan teases, and I answer with a simple, "Parched," before taking a sip.

But I am eager. Too eager, as I dart my eyes around the room in search of Declan, but all I see are unfamiliar faces.

"Elizabeth," Lachlan starts, pulling my attention back to him. "What brings you here? I attend many of these events, and I've never seen you before."

"I'm from the US. I recently arrived here but have been staying in Galashiels."

"Gala? Interesting. It's such a small town. Most travelers stay in Edinburgh. What's in Gala for you?"

"A good friend of mine," I tell him. "He's supposed to be here tonight actually. Declan McKinnon, have you seen him?"

"That wee bastard?" he belts out.

He must see my confused expression when he explains, "Scottish humor, dear. It's a friendly boast."

"Oh."

I take a sip of my champagne while he adds, "We both attended university here," and then is cut off by a gentleman at the microphone announcing that dinner will be served shortly and to enjoy the band and some dancing.

I scan the room again, which is filled with a mass of people, chatting, drinking, and mingling. Voices are quiet, aside from the random, boisterous comments from the men. Rich with their accents, I must stand out to them as Lachlan introduces me to a few people while everyone makes their way around.

My attention is half-hearted as the time passes. Lachlan accompanies me through the dinner service, and while he's visiting with a few other people seated at our table, I finally spot Declan. He's in the back of the room, at the bar, with a woman on his arm as he converses with a couple men.

I stare.

I can't take my eyes off of him as he stands there in a kilt. Good God, he's perfection. I'm used to seeing him in a dressed down tuxedo at black tie events, but there is nothing dressed down about him right now. Proper in a black jacket, red and black kilt with a matching red and black tartan fly plaid that's slung over his shoulder, and a black leather sporran that hangs low from his hips. Down to his flashes, this man is obscenely beautiful, and I want to rip that wench right off his arm.

I notice he isn't paying much attention to the woman as he drinks from his old-fashioned and continues to talk to the men. I want to jump up and go to him—eager to be in his presence, but I know the reaction I'll get. It's the one I fear, but expect. The one I hate, but deserve.

"Something got your eye?" Lachlan says.

I turn and smile, telling him, "I found my friend."

"Ahh," he sighs as he spots Declan at the bar.

But before I can make a move, a man steps to the podium on the stage and begins talking, starting off with gratitude for the attendance this evening. I watch as Declan makes his way over to the stage while the gentleman continues to address all the attendees.

He's so close, but he's further away than he's ever been, even before we ever met, because his hatred cleaves wounds deeply. And my betrayal spears even deeper.

Declan's name is announced as the quintessential donor to the foundation. His name is praised for his time and devotion to the charity, and the round of applause is loud as the podium is handed over to him and he steps behind it. There's no arguing his humility; I see it in his expression. He feels the attention is undeserved.

He thanks the audience, and I melt into the sound of his voice. His accent, lighter than most others in this room, seduces me as I sit here. I feel exposed, as if people can see how my body is responding to his voice. My stomach trills and my heart quickens in luring excitement. I miss that voice. Miss it whispering softly in my ear, barking his possessive words to me, claiming that I'm his property, growling when he would come. Every sound of his enraptured me the way it's doing right now.

Giving his speech about the importance of proper education for all children, regardless of social and economic stature, I continue to admire the great things he is doing to his outfit. I take in every piece of the man I have been mourning for the past couple months. I can finally look at him without him spitting his enmity at me. So for now, I worship this moment in time where I see my old, confident Declan, speaking gracefully, loving his smile when he chuckles at his small banter.

When his speech comes to an end and he presents his substantial donation to the foundation president and encourages everyone to take out their checkbooks to do the same. He's showered with admiration for his time and efforts with grand applause, which he humbly accepts.

Stepping down from the podium, he shakes hands with the many committee members, and with all eyes on him, I know this is my moment. As conniving as it is, it's the only way I can get his attention without him lashing out.

"Excuse me," I say softly to Lachlan as I stand and set my napkin on my seat.

Keeping my eyes on Declan, I make my way through the people who are now leaving the tables behind to socialize and dance. As I approach, the woman I saw him with earlier is back at his side. She's tall—much taller than my petite stature—with raven hair that's pulled in a sophisticated bun at the nape of her neck. I quickly remind myself of what Declan and I shared not too long ago, and right my posture as I step next to the both of them. When the man in front of me shakes Declan's hand and steps away, green eyes widen in surprise.

"Declan, it's so good to see you again," I croon excitedly, putting on my act in front of the small group that's gathered around him.

He falls in line with me, the way I knew he would, being surrounded by all these people. He chivalrously accepts my hand and a kiss to his cheek.

"What are you doing here?" he questions, with only a mild bite to his tone, but his face is cordial.

"Now, you know charities are dear to me," I tease in mockery with a giggle. "I'd like to make my time in Scotland meaningful."

"And how long is that? Don't you have to get back to the States soon?"

Leaning in closer to him so not everyone can hear, I say, "No. At the moment, time is a little *futile,* if you know what I mean." I then turn to his date, remarking to him while my eyes are fixed on the woman, "Declan, she's stunning."

My words, and the manner in which they are delivered, make her uncomfortable. She fidgets and responds, "I'm sorry, I don't believe we've met. I'm Davina."

"It's a pleasure."

"And you are?"

"An old acquaintance," Declan interrupts, answering for me, and I giggle, adding, "Well, that's putting it modestly."

I can see the tension when he bites his jaw down, so I quickly make my request publically, "I was hoping I could steal you away for a couple minutes. There's something I'd like to talk to you about . . . privately."

"This probably isn't the best time."

"It's okay," Davina tells him with a pleasant smile. "I need to go visit with Beatrice anyway."

Smiling up at Declan, I boast, "Perfect!"

His smile is tight as he walks past me with no eye contact. "Follow me."

I do, keeping up with his quick stride, but when I see he's making his way outside and away from all these people, I grab on to his arm and tug back. "Here is fine."

"I thought you said you wanted privacy."

"This is private enough." I need the crowd to ensure he keeps his emotions in check.

He narrows his eyes and sneers angrily under his breath, "What the hell are you doing here?"

"I needed to see you, to talk to you, and this was the only way I could get you to listen without you losing your shit on me."

Keeping his voice low, his tone is harsh when he says, "What do you want to say to me, huh? *I'm sorry? It's not what you think? Forgive me?* Well, fuck you because there isn't anything I want to hear coming out of your mouth."

"If you'll just let me say my piece, I'll go. If that's what you want, I'll leave—disappear from your life, and you'll never have to think of me again."

Declan grabs my elbow and pulls me closer to him. His face is so close to mine, I can feel the heat of his blood pulsing through his veins. "You think it's that easy? You think I can just shut you out and never think about you again—the woman who deceived me to the point that I . . . " he pauses for a second to make sure no one is close enough to hear his next words, " . . . *took a man's life?* I'll never be able to get rid of you because you're now the demon than lives inside me."

Words slaughter deeply.

The urge to drop to my knees and beg at his feet to forgive me surges through my body. I did this to him. It was me, and the weight of that responsibility is making it near impossible to stay above ground. It's sinking me down to a hell I'm terrified to face.

"Tell me what I can do," I plead. "Because I'd do anything for you, to take any piece of this away from you."

"It's done with. It happened and nothing will take that away, but you . . . continuing to pop up . . . you're just twisting the knife you've put in my back."

"Let me attempt to take it out then."

"That was a lovely speech," an older lady compliments as she walks past us.

Declan quickly thanks her and then turns back to me. "You need to leave."

"No."

"God, you're stubborn."

"Declan, no. I want to explain."

"Not here."

"Then where?"

"Tomorrow," he suggests. "You want to talk privately? Fine, I'll give you that. Come to my house, say whatever it is you need to say, and then leave."

"Okay," I respond with a nod.

"I mean it. You leave Scotland. Go back home."

I continue to nod in agreement with his words, and confirm, "Tomorrow then?"

His jaw clenches. "Yes. And now I want you to excuse yourself from this party."

And I do. Getting what I wanted, I smile, but it doesn't feel entirely victorious for obvious reasons. Retrieving my pashmina and clutch, I say my goodbye to Lachlan and thank him for accompanying me as my escort. He offers to drive me back to the hotel, but I politely decline and accept his flirtatious kiss to my hand before he opens the car door for me.

"It was a pleasure, Elizabeth. I hope to see you around," he tells me, and I return the gesture, saying, "I hope so too."

(DECLAN)

"WHAT WERE YOU doing with that woman?" I ask when Lachlan approaches me at the bar. "How do you know her?"

"I don't. She was alone, and I offered to escort her. Why?"

Taking a hard shot of my Scotch, I bite against the burn. "I want you to follow her."

"Who is she?"

"Just follow her. I want to know what she's spending her days doing."

His chuckle agitates me as he responds, "So now I'm a PI, McKinnon?"

"You want to work for someone else?" I snap, setting my old-fashioned down on the bar with too much force, and repeat harshly, "Follow her."

thirteen

I DON'T WANT to look like I'm trying too hard, so I go for simplicity, wearing a modest cashmere sweater, slacks, and a pair of flats. I keep my makeup light with a touch of sheer gloss on my lips. My hand nervously shakes as I dab on a little concealer under my eyes to cover the evidence of my lack of sleep last night.

When I left the party, I checked out of the hotel, so it was late when I arrived back here at Isla's after the two-hour drive. My mind was racing all night, anxious about seeing Declan today and wondering exactly what I'm going to say. A part of me questions what it is I'm even doing here in Scotland. Confusion is my state of mind, so I don't even attempt to reason my actions, because it's a doomed feat. All I do know is that I'm lost, and Declan is the only thing that's familiar and known.

Slipping on my knee-length, ivory pea coat, I make my way down to my car. I find myself speeding to get to Declan, but I'm worried about what will greet me when I arrive. With white knuckles, I take a few slow, deep breaths as I round the bend in the road and approach the gate. For the first time, I roll up to the intercom box and press the button. There's no answer, but the gates open anyway.

The car moves slowly up the winding road that weaves through tall, snow-covered trees. When I reach the top, I pull in front of what was once promised to be my safe haven of escape. This should've been my home with Declan; instead, he's my lost love, and I, his enemy.

Gravel crunches beneath my feet when I step out of the car. I stand, looking up at the three-story estate that's secluded up here. Majestic and alone at the top of this hill, the only sound is the wind that howls between the trees and the swirling of snow that blows from the bare branches. I look over to the grand fountain and imagine the sound of its trickling water in the summertime.

"What are you doing?"

I turn to the house and see Declan standing at the front door in a pair of tailored slacks and an untucked button-down. My heart's beat immediately responds to him, and I murmur, "Nothing. Just looking at the grounds," while I walk over to him.

He looks down at me as I walk up the steps leading to the front door, and when I get a whiff of his cologne, I want so badly to jump into his arms. To make this all disappear. To go back in time so I can do it all differently. To save him from the cliff of goodness I shoved him off of.

But he doesn't say a word as he gestures with his hand to enter his home.

It takes nearly all my strength to stay on my feet when I step inside the massive entryway. Looking up and around, everything has been remodeled in an elegant, contemporary flair of whites and ivories. The foyer spans the length of the house, and you can see straight to the back where it opens up to the large, glassed atrium. Everything is bright and peaceful, except for the man who walks past me.

I follow as cold darkness leads me into an elaborate sitting room, which has yet to be remodeled. The walls are lined in aged wooden bookshelves that hold hundreds and hundreds of books. So many you can smell the pages and leathered bindings. An antique chandelier hangs over the large seating area of leather wingback chairs and a tufted chesterfield sofa that's identical to the one he had in the office of his loft back in River North.

Declan takes a seat in the center of the couch, offering no welcome when he speaks. "Say what you need to say."

And suddenly, everything I thought about saying last night is gone. I have no words as I look at him. I walk closer, and instead of sitting on the couch with him or on one of the chairs, I sit on the wooden coffee table right in front of him, and when I do, he leans forward, resting his elbows on his knees.

We don't speak for a while; we just look into each other's eyes. Mine filled with pain and sorrow; his filled with chilling anger. Threatening tears prick and burn, but I fight to remain strong, when truthfully, I'm a shattered little girl, yearning to cling to the solace that's right in front of me and never let go.

With a shallow breath, my eyes fall shut, pushing a couple tears down my cheek and I whimper, "I'm so sorry."

I can't bear to look at him in my insurmountable guilt for what I've done. My head drops to my hands as I will for strength, but it doesn't come. That's the thing with Declan, he's always had a way of making it difficult for me to lock up the truth of my emotions. He's the one person who was able to strip down my barricade and make me feel—truly feel.

When I finally open my eyes, he hasn't shifted. His hard face remains, unaffected by my tears.

"Say something," I whisper. "Please."

Creases form along his forehead, and his eyes look to ache, when he finally does speak, asking, "Why did you do it?"

I vow to myself to stop all the lies. To give him transparent truth about everything. If that makes me a savage in his eyes, which it undoubtedly will, then fine. Because if he's going to judge me, I at least want him to do it honestly.

"Revenge," I finally admit.

"I want the truth," he demands.

"I married Bennett with intentions of destroying him," I say, and then pause before adding, "I married him to kill him."

He releases a heavy puff of air in disbelief. "What the fuck is wrong with you?"

"I don't know . . . I don't know."

"Why?"

"What I told you was a lie. The story about me growing up in Kansas and my parents' death. It was all a lie." The guilt has festered long enough, and I crack. My words bleed from the cobwebs of my soul, and I cry as the wounds shred apart. "I don't know how to make it right, but I want to. I never thought I would fall in love with you the way I did." My words spill out through my constricted throat.

"Tell me why," he snarls. "What did he do to you that you'd want him dead?"

"He murdered me. I wanted payback."

Declan's jaw grinds, and I go on, explaining, "I was happy . . . When I was a little girl, I was happy. I lived with my father, and then one day . . . " I choke on the agony of my words. " . . . One day he was taken from me. Arrested. I was only five years old when it happened. It was all Bennett's fault. My dad was sent to prison and I was sent to hell."

I stop when I can't speak anymore and simply cry. Choking in broken gasps of air while Declan just sits here—a stone of a man with eyes of disbelief, confusion, anger. It hurts to look at him, but I do it anyway.

"I never saw my father again, and when I was twelve years old, he died in prison. Killed by another inmate."

"What did Bennett have to do with this?" he interrupts.

"Because . . . it's a long story," I exhaust.

"You owe me the truth."

"He . . . he thought I was being abused by my dad, but it wasn't the truth. He told his parents, and the authorities were called to investigate, but instead they uncovered that he was trafficking guns and arrested him. I know it sounds bad, but he was a good man and I had a good life with him." My cries erupt harder, blubbering, "He wasn't bad, he was perfect and loved me, and Bennett took it all away. In a single moment, he set fire and incinerated everything in my world. That asshole stole my life!"

Shaking his head, Declan mutters, "Doesn't make sense. None of this makes sense."

"It was his fault," I press, but his response is sharp when he moves on, "I don't want to argue your fucked up rationalizations. Tell me . . . what was I?"

"Declan, please . . . "

"Tell me. Tell me what I was!" his voice booms off the walls, demanding to know.

"In the beginning . . . in the beginning you were the pawn," I confess.

"More," he urges.

"Declan, you have to understand that it changed and—"

"More!"

"Okay!" I blurt out and then repeat in a softer, defeated tone, "Okay. Yes, you started as the pawn. I was going to use you to kill Bennett."

"Why not you?"

"Because I was afraid of getting caught if I got my hands too dirty."

His teeth grind as he begins to clench and unclench his fists.

"I'm sorry," I breathe. "But when I got to know you, and we connected so easily, I fell for you. You make me feel something that no one has ever been able to do. No one has ever looked at me the way you do—the way you *did.* I've had a hard life, but—"

"Don't you dare do that. Don't you excuse your fucked ways because of the life you've had."

"I need you to know that what we had, the feelings that I had for you, were genuine. I truly loved you. I still do. I was trying to find a way out of the scam. I was giving it all up so we could be together."

Pinching the bridge of his nose, he takes a moment before speaking. "I need to know something . . . "

"Anything. I'll tell you anything to make this right."

"Was it true? Bennett beating the shit out of you, was that true?" His voice strains on those words, and I hate the witch I am and having to admit,

"No. Bennett never hurt me."

"You fucking bitch!" he scathes through a severed cry.

I see how deeply I've hurt him. It's all over his face and it cuts through his voice. He rests his head on his tightly fisted hands, shaking in horror.

"Tell me what to do. Tell me," I beg, needing to take his anguish away. Needing to make this whole situation just disappear.

"You can't do shit, Nina." And the instant he says my name, he winces, squeezing his eyes shut and then asking, "What the hell do I even call you?"

A muted stillness lengthens between us as we look into each other's eyes—completely demolished. Seconds that feel like hours pass.

And for the first time, although he already knows it from the file, I give him my name.

"Elizabeth Rose Archer."

(DECLAN)

"ELIZABETH ROSE ARCHER," she tells me on soft words after a long span of silence.

How could Satan own such a beautiful name?

I keep my hands fisted tightly so she can't see them shaking, but the roiling fury that runs thick through my blood has me on the verge of detonation. It's all I can do to hold myself together right now. This woman, the one I loved not so long ago, is like gasoline dripping on my burning heart.

Her name was already known to me. I read it in the file I found on her husband's desk after I shot and killed him. Seeing her pictures covered in a spray of his blood destroyed all my trust in the world. It was only a couple hours later after getting home and digging into that file when I soon realized I'd been scammed. Scammed by the only person who had ever been able to seep into my heart so entirely. I've never loved the way I loved her. And to know it was all a lie, the deceit of being played, was more than I could take.

I know I murdered an innocent man, and now, hearing her crazy explanation has my mind so fucked up. How could I have been in love with someone as psychotic as her?

What the fuck is wrong with me?

"Declan, please. Say something. Anything," her tiny voice requests.

My body is a mass of tense muscles I refuse to relax for fear of what I'll do. So I keep myself locked and stern when I speak. "So he never hurt you?"

"No."

"Never mean to you?"

"No. Bennett loved me. He didn't know who I was."

"How'd you get the bruises then?" I ask, remembering how God-awful she would look, covered in horrifically grotesque bruises. Sometimes her skin would split from the swelling and bleed. The battered blood that pooled beneath her skin's surface always stained her body. It fucked me up. Rage and fury for a man I believed was inflicting the abuse, lamenting heartache for the woman I loved, and guilt from not being able to protect her. The emasculating position she put me in, knowing damn well she had me fooled. And now I sit here feeling like a pussy that got manipulated by nothing more than a runaway street kid.

"My brother."

"Brother?"

"He was in on it too. I would go to him to get the bruises."

"It was your brother who beat the shit out of you? On purpose to fool me?"

She nods her head shamefully in response.

"Jesus Christ, you're sick."

I watch while tears drip from her chin and wish they were the acid she filled my heart with so connivingly.

"I know. But—"

"Just stop," I bark. I can't take any more of this shit, but she doesn't stop.

Her words come out in a rush of panic, "When I told you I loved you, when I gave you those words, I meant them. I didn't want to use you, not at that point. I wanted out and to keep you from doing what I initially wanted you to do."

"But you didn't, did you?!"

"Everything spun out of control so fast."

"Were you happy? When you found out Bennett was dead, were you happy?"

"It destroyed me to know I pushed you so far," she counters.

"Answer my fucking question!" I belt out, standing up and searing my eyes into hers as I look down on her. "Did it make you happy?"

Her body trembles when she closes her eyes and admits, "Yes."

"So you got what you wanted?"

"No."

"No?"

She tilts her head back to look up at me, and my bones beg to impale her, to beat the living shit out of her, a punishment she'll never forget. One that would mutilate her for life.

"No. It wasn't what I wanted. It wasn't worth sacrificing you because saving you was all I wanted to do at that point."

I sneer at her ludicrous words. "You wanted to save me so much that you left me in a pool of blood to die?"

Her eyes radiate horror.

"That's right, darling. I was conscious. I felt you, your touch, your kiss. But all it took was for that guy who shot me to say *Go* for you to leave me to die. Was that your idea of saving me?"

"No, Declan," she says through her tears that never stop. "I was scared. It all happened so fast. I didn't know what I was doing. I thought you were dead!"

Her words spit venom, and I can't look at her face any more without hammering my fist into it.

"You fucking left me there to die, you bitch!" I roar, grabbing her arms with force and yanking her up, shaking her as I fume, "Your words are lies. Nothing you say makes any goddamn sense."

Rage takes over and I lose it, slinging her body around and throwing her to the floor. She crumples, falling hard to the ground. I step over, grab the bitch by the sweater and yank her back off the ground as I hunch in her face. She doesn't protest my afflictions; she takes them willingly, the same way she has the past few times I've been rough with her, and I take advantage of her submission.

Her hands clamp around my wrists as I rip her off the floor and shove her away from me.

"Get the fuck out!"

"Please!"

Her voice pierces my ears so harshly I can feel the razor of it in my gut. The pain rings sharply in my head, and I boil over in red-hot revolt, clenching her frail neck in my hand, choking her. My body burns in a pyre of grief and fury as she clings to my arm, and her touch spurs me to plunge my fingers deeper into her flesh, clamping the trachea that lies beneath, cutting off her air supply.

A hoarse gurgle is the only sound she makes as her tear-filled eyes lock to mine. They shine bright from crying, and my tendons yearn to squeeze even tighter. There's so much colliding inside of me, I can feel it in my teeth, so I grit them to keep myself from biting and ripping the skin off her.

I want to kill her. I want to punish her in the worst way possible, but when my arm begins to violently shake, her mouth and eyes instantly pop open wider, and I release my hold.

I can't kill her.

She falls to my feet, gasping and coughing wretchedly as I rake my hands through my hair.

What the hell is happening to me?

The touch of her hands around my ankles gets my attention. Looking down on her, she's resting her cheek on top of one of my loafers. My breathing is heavy as emotions swarm, and it's in the moment she looks up at me, broken at my feet, that I give my final word.

"Leave."

I kick her hands off my legs and walk out of the room, leaving her to show herself out because if I have to look at her for one more second, I won't be able to forgive myself for what I might to do.

This woman has ruined me.

I'm a fucking monster.

Obliterated beyond my own recognition.

And it was all for naught.

fifteen

MAKEUP COVERS MY marred neck as I give myself a once-over before heading out. My body is wounded in delicious bruises and scabs from the man my heart still yearns for. When I look at them, it's like he's still with me—his lingering touch I feen for on my body.

It took me a while to collect myself and leave his home the other day. Hopelessness consumed every inch of existence—it still does. I was weak, curled at his feet, sobbing on his perfectly polished shoes when he kicked me away and left me lying on the ground. My words did nothing but enrage him to the point he lost control. Declan never loses control—he thrives on it, needs it to function. But I could see the chaos swimming in his eyes as they bore down on me while he strangled me.

I didn't panic because I'd gladly take a death upon the hands of true love.

My ticket is booked to fly back to Chicago. I don't want to go, but I also don't want to continue hurting Declan. He's not the same man anymore because of me. His warmth has wasted away—no spark, no light, no love.

Nothing waits for me back in Chicago aside from a penthouse of hidden skeletons. I have no home. There's no one waiting for me anywhere. I figure I'll slip into town, pack up my belongings and leave the state. No longer can I live there because I'm no longer Nina. It doesn't matter where I go though, and that thought is utterly depleting. So, I decide to attempt to escape my pitiful reality and go to Edinburgh for the day to meander around.

I drive in silence, taking in the landscape, and before I know it, I'm in the city. After parking the car, I wrap a scarf around my neck and pull my coat tighter around my body. I begin wandering around the Grassmarket with the Edinburgh Castle towering above. The cobbled, winding streets are lined with a vast array of shops from designer to vintage. I pick up a few things from various stores: soaps, perfumes, a pair of shoes, and an old necklace with a weathered lotus charm. I'm not sure why I bought the lotus necklace, knowing the sadness it'll undoubtedly bring when I look at it, but I just had to buy it regardless. I buy because I don't know what else to do.

My gut is hollow. I'm in a never-ending state of anxiety, and this is my attempt at distracting myself. It's not helping though, so I find a pub to grab a drink, and when I walk into The Fiddler's Arms, I immediately make my way to the bar. The place is filled mostly with men, drinking lagers and whiskey. I spot an empty stool and take a seat.

The bartender places a drink napkin in front of me, saying, "What can I get you?"

Taking a quick look at the tap handles, I don't recognize the names, so I randomly pick one. "Stropramen."

He gives me a nod, begins to fill the mug, and then sets it in front of me. I slip my coat off and hang it on the back of the stool, and then take a long, slow drink in hopes that it dulls out the intensity that's inside of me. I lean forward and close my eyes, focusing on the noise around me, wanting to get lost in it, and when I open my eyes, I spot familiar ones staring back at me from the opposite side of the bar.

A grin grows on Lachlan's face, and he nods to the empty seat next to me in a gesture to join, and I give him a small, inviting smile.

"Fancy seeing you here," he says when he approaches and sits down.

"Wanted to do a little shopping before I head back home," I lie, and my stomach knots at the pathetic deceit.

"You're going back to the States?"

"Yes. Tomorrow."

"Short trip," he remarks.

"I suppose."

He takes a sip of his whiskey and sets the tumbler down when he asks, "Any plans on returning?"

"Doubtful," I reply and take another drink.

I turn to look at Lachlan watching me intently. He's a stately man in his trousers, button down, and tailored sports coat. His hair is lightly gelled and styled to perfection with a dignified part.

His eyes continue to linger on me with a soft expression.

"Why are you looking at me like that?" I peacefully ask.

He takes a moment, and then responds, "You seem down."

"Just worn out. I haven't been sleeping well."

"You left abruptly the other evening after your run-in with Declan," he states. "Perhaps that has something to do with your lack of sleep?"

"Nosey," I accuse with a playful smile.

"Just observant."

"Is that all?"

"You want more?" he lightly chuckles.

"You flirting with me?"

"You're what? Twenty-some odd years younger than me?"

I nod.

"A man like me would be foolish not to flirt with a woman such as you."

"Such as me? And what's that? What am I?"

He takes another sip of his whiskey and then leans in a little closer to me, answering, "Exquisite, my dear."

His flirting isn't meaningful, but more of humorous banter, so I know he doesn't think it rude of me when I begin to laugh.

We both take another sip through our smiles, and he breaks his mock flirtation when he says, "Seriously though, is everything okay? It looked like you and Declan were having a much too dire conversation for a party."

"Just hashing out some unsettled business, that's all. Do you always make it a habit to stick your nose where it doesn't belong?" I tease.

"Always," he boasts, and we both laugh again.

"Well, at least you're honest about it."

"Can I ask you something?"

I nod.

"What brought you here to Scotland?"

I look up at his face, and I don't see any ulterior motives in our exchange other than a man who genuinely wants an honest conversation, so I answer, "Him."

"Him?"

"I came to see Declan. I hadn't spoken to him since he left Chicago, and I guess . . . I guess I just wanted to see him."

"Lovers?"

"Again . . . *nosey.*"

He smirks at my jab.

"Does he have many of those?" I ask.

"Would you feel jealous if I told you *yes?*"

Straightening my neck, I state, "I don't get jealous."

"You're a wicked woman, Elizabeth."

"What makes you say that?"

"In my experience, women who don't get jealous do so because they'd rather get even," he says and then winks.

"Is that what you think of me? That I'm a woman of revenge?" I question in jest, but secretly, I want to know how he truly perceives me.

"You know what my mum always told me?"

"What's that?" I laugh.

"She told me that while the rest of the species are descended from apes, redheads are descended from cats."

"So, I'm a cat?"

"A minx," he notes.

I shake my head, saying, "You neglected to answer my question."

"You mean Declan?"

"Mmm hmm," I hum as I take another drink.

"No."

"No?"

"I've known Declan for a very long time. He will always have a woman on his arm at events, but it's all a show, strictly business. I've only known him to have a couple long-term relationships, but none he was too serious about. I think they were more of convenience than actual love. Declan's a well-guarded man."

Hearing this makes my guilt build heavier, knowing that what he gave me was most likely the first time he had given that to anyone. His love, his heart, his moments of sweet softness. Having this information makes the destruction feel even more malicious.

"He's a shrewd man in business," Lachlan continues. "I can only assume that filters into his personal relationships as well, but perhaps you might have better insight into my assumptions."

"You want me to open up and divulge my personal knowledge of Declan?"

"Did he hurt you?"

"No," I state matter-of-factly, and when he gives me a sly look, I murmur in an honest moment, "I hurt myself."

I refuse to reveal that I also hurt him. I don't want to diminish anyone's perceptions of the powerful, andric man they all know him to be.

"So you *were* lovers?"

"I hate that word."

"Why?"

Turning to face Lachlan, I lean to the side, resting my elbow on the bar top when I say, "It's shallow. That word insinuates a base, sexual relationship rather than intimacy."

"Has anyone ever told you you're gray?"

"You're wanting black and white? As if that even exists. There is no black and white, right or wrong, yes or no."

His eyebrows raise in curiosity, and to lighten the now heavy mood, I tease, "Oh, come on, Lachlan. Surely a man of your age has come to recognize the world for what it is."

"A man of my age?"

"Yes," I respond, smiling, and then laugh as I add, "*Old.*"

"*Old?* Didn't your mother ever tell you to respect your elders?"

"I never had a mother." I catch myself as the words fall so easily and without thinking. I immediately press my lips together and turn in my seat so I'm not directly facing him anymore.

He doesn't make any comment, and the silence is unsettling as we sit here. When I do finally turn my head to look at him, there's a hint of pity on his face. It irks me, but I remain polite because let's face it, besides the elderly lady I'm staying with, this is the first real conversation I've had in a while.

"If you're feeling sorry for me, don't."

He surprises me with his unguarded bluntness when he asks, "What happened to her?"

"You don't beat around the bush, do you?"

"What do I have to lose? You're leaving Scotland; we'll never see each other again."

"Okay, then," I respond as I turn in my seat to face him dead on, and take him up on his offer. What the hell do I care? He's right. After today, I'll never see him again. "I don't know what happened to her. I have no memories of her, so I assume her to be dead. It was always just me and my father."

"You never asked?"

"My father died before I could," I answer directly.

"Have you tried finding her?"

"No."

"Why?"

"What's the point?" I say with a shrug of my shoulders.

"Aren't you curious about where you come from? What if she's not dead like you assume? What if she's been looking for you?"

And when he asks that last question, I start to wonder—hypothetically—if the woman did exist, she wouldn't have had a chance finding me. I was a runaway. An invisible child. And then I was Nina Vanderwal. How would she have ever found me when I've made it impossible?

All I have of my mom is an old photo of her. For a while, I used to think about her a lot, wondering what she was like, if she was anything like me.

"It's never too late, you know?" Lachlan says, and I let his words float in my head.

I've lost everything, but what if . . . what if I haven't? What if there's a chance that I have something left in this life? Is it worth trying to find? Is it worth believing in hope when that dream has failed me countless times? Can I take another disappointment?

Questions.

I have hundreds of them.

Looking back to Lachlan, I want to protect myself, but I'm so lonely. Lonely and in need of comfort, in need of a reason to go on. Because as I stand now, I'm beginning to seriously wonder why I'm still here—moving, breathing, living.

"Why do you care?" I ask the man who shouldn't because I'm not worthy of it.

"There's something about you," he says with all seriousness.

"But you don't know anything about me."

"Doesn't mean that I don't want to," he admits before adding, "All friendships have to start somewhere. Let me help you."

But I've never had friends. I stuck to myself in school while everyone else picked on me. Pike was my only friend, not just from childhood, but also as adults. And let's face it, the so-called friends I had when I married Bennett were just for show.

So I accept his offer, and with reluctance about what I'm agreeing to, I give a small nod.

"Okay then."

sixteen

I'VE BEEN PACKING ever since I got back from Edinburgh. Now that all my belongings are ready to go back to the States, I sit on the floor beside the bed I've been sleeping in for the past few weeks since I arrived here at Isla's. My mind begins to drift back to the conversation I had with Lachlan earlier today. It was weird. A mention of my mother is something that never happens. It's a part of my life that rarely creeps to the surface. But it's there now, and I'm not quite sure how it happened.

There were times in my childhood when I would miss her. But what I was missing wasn't real; it was simply a creation of my imagination. I've never known what it was to have a mom. More than anything, it's always been my dad that I ache for and miss wholeheartedly. But when Lachlan offered to help find my mother, I agreed. I don't know why. My acceptance of his offer came without much thought at all. Maybe I'm just so lonely that I'm willing to grasp on to anything at the moment.

Warmth slips down my neck, extinguishing my train of thought, and when I bring my hand to the front of me, it's bloody with dark flesh under my nails. It's then I realize I've been mindlessly picking at the scab that still remains from Declan. It's grown in size. I reach back and begin to dig my nail into the soft, gummy exposed flesh, and a searing pain slices my scalp.

And finally, my mind is depleted of all thoughts as I go numb.

My eyes fall shut, and I drop my head forward, letting it hang. Fingers that work nimbly find an unpicked edge of a scab, and I grip it between my fingers. A moment passes before I swiftly yank, pulling the scab off along with new, uninfected flesh, enlarging the wound even more. Exhaling a lungful of air, my core tingles in delighted release when I feel a new onslaught of warm, thick blood oozing down the delicate skin of my neck.

Exultation is stolen in an instant when the door to my room opens, and I see Declan's horrified face.

Am I dreaming?

He's frozen for a moment before stepping into the room and closing the door behind him. I don't move as I look up, stunned.

"Christ, what happened?" he gasps, but he isn't looking at me directly.

I follow his focus as my eyes land on my crimson soaked hand that rests on my lap. His legs disappear from my periphery while my vision blurs on my weapon, and then it's gone. Covered in a warm, wet towel.

Touch.

Declan's hand works deftly as he dabs gently, cleaning the blood.

Touch.

My heart's beat reacts, delicate pumps soothe my tormented chest into a lull of lucidity.

Touch.

No longer a hateful, punishing touch; just a touch.

Lifting my eyes to his face that's pinched in puzzlement, he flips my hand palm-up and then over again.

"Where's the blood coming from?"

I don't speak, and when he catches my eyes with his, his voice is fervent, "Nina, where's the blood coming from?"

Don't call me that.

Ache splinters when he calls me Nina, tightening my throat in a menagerie of emotions. A collision so unmanageable, my body doesn't know how to react, so it remains numb and silent as Declan begins to move his hands over me, pulling up the sleeves to my sweater, trying to find the source of the blood.

Lowering my head, I lose myself in skin-to-skin contact, and when his hand finds the back of my head, I go limp, falling into his lap. I lie on the floor, like a baby, with my head on his knees and silently blink out tears. I don't know if they're happy or sad tears. All I know is that they are tears that welcome my answered prayer of solace.

His fingers are tender as they move to nurse me. I rest in a ball, curled at his mercy. His pants dampen beneath my cheek, salting the wool fabric.

If wishes were granted, this would be mine. I wanted to remain in his lap forever. To never lose that feeling because he was everything in that moment. Gentle and loving. Lying there, I felt like a child. Like a little girl being taken care of by her father. And although he wasn't my father, somehow he carried pieces of that man inside of him. It wasn't something he was even aware of, but I was. I saw it and felt it every time I was in the presence of Declan. He held it all: lover, protector, fighter. He was the ultimate fairytale, and I would have done anything to make him my *fairytale.*

"What have you done to yourself?" his voice murmurs above me. "Sit up."

He helps me from his lap, and we sit face to face when he instructs, "Lift your arms," and when I do, he slips the sweater off of me.

Blood stains the back of the top, and he continues to clean me up before spotting my luggage and pulling out a clean shirt that he then puts on me.

Letting go of a deep breath, he sits in front of me while I remain by the side of the bed. Some of my blood colors his knuckles as I watch him drag his hand back through his thick hair. I observe the details of his movements, the way his chest rises and falls with each deep breath he takes, the way a lock of his hair falls over his forehead in dishevelment, the lines of torment that crease his face, the dark lashes that outline and brighten his green eyes that are pinned to mine.

With my trembling hand, I reach up and lightly touch his face with the tips of my fingers. He doesn't flinch or move when I do this, something I thought I'd never be able to do again. And then I mutter my first words on a hushed breath drenched thick in heartbreak, "I thought you were dead."

His throat flexes when he takes a hard swallow. "I know you did," he responds, voice strained.

"Your father . . . " I start, struggling to keep my words alive. "He told me . . . "

"It was a lie."

"Why?"

"I didn't want you looking for me."

Truths are blades. But I deserve every cut that comes my way.

"Your head looks really bad," he notes. "Why? Why are you doing this to yourself?"

I reach back to touch his gift that burns in my flesh, and I'm embarrassed when I answer him with honesty, because I refuse to hide myself from him anymore.

"I didn't want to let it go?"

"It's grotesque, Nina."

"Please. Don't . . . don't call me that."

He drops his head, saying, "I want to hurt you."

"I know."

"My hands itch with the need to rip you apart. I crave it," he confesses and then shifts his eyes back to mine. They're dark and bitter, dilated in vehemence.

"I deserve it."

"You do," he agrees.

Pulling my knees to my chest, I wrap my arms around them, hugging myself.

"Why are you here?"

"I needed to know something . . . " His head drops again, and the utter agony in his voice when he continues wrecks me. "The baby . . . "

A broken whimper forces its way out of me.

"Was it even mine?"

The last thing I want to do is hurt Declan more than what I already have. I want to lie, tell him yes, tell him he was the only one I was sleeping with, convince him of my love.

But I can't.

I don't want to hurt him with the truth, but I also don't want to comfort him with lies.

"I need to know," he urges.

His eyes shine bright with tears I know threaten him, and I cowardly shake my head.

He takes a push back, widening the gap between us, and leans his head against the dresser.

"Why?"

"I wanted it to be," I tell him as I begin to cry from what was stolen from me.

"So it was Bennett's baby?"

"I don't know."

Confusion strikes his face. "What does *that* mean?"

God, I hate this. Hate that I keep deepening the wound. Tears soak my cheeks as I stall.

"What do you mean *you don't know?*" he presses.

"Because . . . b-because . . . "

"Say it."

"There was someone else."

My words ignite a fire within him. His neck is tense, reddening in anger. With elbows on knees and white-knuckled fists clenching hair, I know he's about to blow.

"It's not what you're thinking, Declan," I say in my attempt to explain the fucked up relationship Pike and I had.

"Besides me and Bennett, you were fucking someone else?"

"Yes, but—"

"Then it's exactly what I'm thinking!" he seethes.

"No. It wasn't like that. It wasn't . . . " *God, how the hell do I begin to explain this?* "He was . . . This is going to sound crazy, I know, but it isn't."

"I fucking hate you."

"I love *you!* Not Bennett. Not Pike. *You!*"

"Wait." He pauses for a moment, and then continues, "That name. That guy . . . I went to see him. Found his name in the file your husband had on you."

"Yeah."

"This shit is so fucked up. I can't even get my thoughts straight."

"Pike's my brother," I reveal.

"What the hell is wrong with you?"

"My *foster* bother," I clarify in a rush. "He's my foster brother."

"The same guy that was beating you?"

I nod.

"Do you know how sick this is? How sick *you* are? Fucking three men?"

Wiping my eyes, I move to sit on my knees. "I'm so sorry. I know it sounds messed up."

"*Sounds?* No, Nina, it *is* messed up. You need serious help, you know that?"

I don't bother correcting him when he calls me Nina.

He stands up, looking down on me in fury. "I can't believe I fell for something as disgusting as you."

"It wasn't like that," I say in a panic. "I didn't like him like that. There were no feelings attached. It was the opposite of what you're thinking. I used him so I didn't have to feel. He was a vice. That's all sex was with him. A vice to numb me."

"Numb you from what, Nina?"

"From life!" I cry out. "From everything!"

"Everything? Even me?"

"No. Not you. Once I realized how I felt for you, I never touched him again. I couldn't, because your hands were the only ones I wanted to be touched by. But I was already pregnant; I just didn't know it."

He paces the room, enraged.

"Declan, there's so much you don't know. So much I never told you because I couldn't."

"You could, you were just too selfish."

"Okay, yes. You're right. I was selfish. Selfish and scared. But you loved me, right?"

"I don't know who the fuck you are! Tell me. Tell me who you are because I'm so goddamn confused right now!"

"I don't know," I whimper and then stand with him.

"You do know."

"I don't. I want to know. I'm trying."

"What does that even mean?"

"*I don't know!*"

Pacing a couple more times in determined strides, he finally gives up and walks to the door.

"I can't do this shit anymore."

And then he walks out, not even bothering to close the door behind him.

Sobs explode out of me—loud and vulgar. I don't expect him to understand or to even want to. I'm sick; I know that. I knew I'd never have him again, but it doesn't make the pain any less awful when he walks away from me.

"Elizabeth!" Isla calls out in urgency as she rushes into my room.

I instantly catch myself, swallowing back my sobs and wiping my face. "I'm fine. I'm so sorry for the disruption," I say thickly as I weakly feign composure.

"Stop that!" she scolds as she takes my hand and walks me over to sit on the bed. "Are you okay, lassie?"

"I'm fine. Really."

And with the pitying look on her face, I know she isn't the slightest bit convinced.

"What was the McKinnon boy doing here? You never mentioned knowing him when we were discussing him the other morning."

"I'm sorry, Isla," I state calmly now that my breathing is steadying.

"Sorry?"

"I do know Declan, I just didn't want anyone to know."

Her thumb strokes the top of my hand, looking over me, and finally concludes, "It was him. He's the love you lost." She doesn't question, only states what she's figured out.

I nod and apologize once more for pretending to not know who he was the other day.

"I'm confused though. I thought you told me he died?"

And now I must lie, because I can't possibly tell her the truth.

"I guess it was easier to pretend him dead. The thought of living in a world where he existed without me was much too painful."

With a tilt of her head, her brows tug in sorrow for me.

"I'm sorry I lied to you."

Shaking her head, she affirms, "Don't be. You're heartbroken; it's understandable."

"But it's not excusable."

"It is, dear."

We sit for a while as she continues to hold my hands before adding, "He seemed quite angry."

"He is. But if it's all right with you, I'd rather not discuss it."

"Of course not," she responds. "Is there anything I can do? Anything I can get you?"

"Thank you, but I'm fine."

"Okay then. Well, I'll leave you be. Good night."

"Good night," I say as she walks out of the room and closes the door behind her.

I remain on the bed, unmoving, and alone with my thoughts. Exhaustion presses down on me as I turn my head to the side and eye my luggage.

Maybe I could stay a little longer.

I know I shouldn't. I know I need to need go and erase myself from Declan's life so he can move on and heal. It's a lost cause trying to explain all of this to him. But maybe it doesn't even matter, because in the end, he's right. I'm fucked up and none of this makes any sense.

Seventeen

(DECLAN)

"WHAT ARE YOU doing here?" I ask when I pull up beside Lachlan's car sitting outside the gates to my house.

Holding up a file, he calls out, "Property closing. I need you to sign."

Christ, all I want is to be alone with a bottle of Aberfeldy. To try my best to relax and calm the nerves that Nina has so intensely provoked.

Lachlan pulls in behind me and follows me up to the house. I'm on edge, still unable to even think about what just happened and the things she told me. If I allow myself to go to that place in my head right now, I'll completely lose my shit. So when I get out of the car, I exert control and compose myself.

"You couldn't have emailed this to me?" I complain as we walk inside.

"They won't accept an electronic signature."

Flipping on the lights, I head back to the library to go over the final contract on the property in London I've been contending to acquire.

"You have any plans on selling this place?" Lachlan asks, and when I take a seat on the couch, he sits opposite me in one of the chairs.

"Why?"

"It's pretentious."

"Fucking dobber," I breathe under my breath.

"I heard that, you bastard."

"Good."

I've known Lachlan since our college days. He was working on his PhD while I was working on my master's at Saint Andrews. We were both a part of the OxFam Society and worked on many campaigns together. We've remained linked because of his relationship with my father. When Lachlan was my age, he worked in wealth management at one of the top firms in London, where my dad keeps his investments. Lachlan was his advisor for many years before he opted for a less demanding position and started advising small companies independently.

While I was still living in Chicago, I knew I'd soon be back here. Since I was already involved with purchasing the property in London, my father put in a call, and now Lachlan works solely for me. He handles my business finances and also a children's education foundation I've had for many years now.

"Everything should be as we discussed with the bank," he tells me as I read through the document.

"Looks good." I sign the papers and slip them back in the file. Handing it over to Lachlan, I say, "Life's about to get busy."

"Good thing?"

"Very. After Chicago, I'm ready to dive into this project."

"You ever gonna tell me what the hell happened?"

Standing up, I don't respond. Instead, I walk across the room to the liquor cart, pull the crystal stopper from the decanter, and begin pouring myself a glass of Scotch.

"Declan?"

"Drink?"

"No," he responds. "So, tell me. What happened?"

"Nothing to tell."

I take a sip, relishing the twenty-one-year-old single malt. I allow the smooth smoke of the Scotch to settle on my tongue before swallowing. I appreciate its offering as it makes its way down, heat spreading through my chest.

"She leaves tomorrow, you know?"

"And your point?"

The boyish, smug look on his face grates me, along with the way he relaxes himself into the chair.

"She's stunning."

Tossing back the glass of whiskey, my face pinching against the burn, I set the glass down, and the clank of crystal against glass reveals my frustration.

"Remind me again why I'm friends with you."

"Look, it's apparent there are hurt feelings between the two—"

I stop him mid-sentence, snapping, "What are you, my fucking therapist? Don't pretend to have insight into something you clearly know nothing about."

"I spent the afternoon with her. She's easy to read."

I laugh as I walk back over to the couch. "That woman is anything but easy to read. Trust me. Don't let her fool you. And what the hell are you doing talking to her? I told you to watch her, not befriend her."

The mere idea of Lachlan spending time with her and not knowing what's being said or what their interactions are like rubs a raw spot in me. To not know, and the fact that it bothers me so much, it's infuriating. It's the way she was able to claw her way inside of me and burrow into the one vacant spot no one has ever been able to find makes me hate her even more. She's a cherub of martyrdom, and I, her willing victim. Willing because, as much as I want to, I can't let the red-headed sadist go. I doubt I'll ever be able to because of the mark she's left on me. I'm the unhealed remnant left in her destructive wake.

"She wants me to find her mother," he eventually tells me, cutting the silence.

My eyes dart to his. "What?"

"I offered."

Why the fuck is she giving parts of her truth to him that she hasn't given me?

"Isn't that fantastic!" My cynical words come out loudly. "Do me a favor, try obeying my orders next time. *Follow* her and cut the friendly shit."

"No need to follow. Like I said, she leaves tomorrow," he informs as he pushes himself off from the chair. Standing in front of me, he shrugs on his coat and grabs the file. "I'll deliver the documents."

Leaning forward, I prop my elbows on my knees as I listen to his loafers echo down the foyer.

"I want to know when you find her mother!" I holler.

"Will do," he calls back before the sound of the door closing grants me much needed isolation.

Slumping down into the couch, I rest my head and stare up at the ceiling, replaying the evening. Everything about it is a Gordian knot. And not just the words that were spoken, but the wound I gave her that she's successfully mutilated. I remember ripping the hair from her scalp and the pleasure it gave me to punish her. But her reaction was not what I expected. She didn't as much as yelp at what must have been blisteringly painful. She simply stood there as tears dripped down her face, yet she wasn't crying, not like you would think.

But tonight, when I walked in on her and saw the blood, my only reaction was to help her. Taking care of her and cleaning her up makes me sick, now that I think about it, but in the moment, all the turmoil faded. It was when she started to speak that it all came crashing back. It flooded the room, drowning me in its weight when she told me she didn't know if the baby was mine.

That fucking baby.

All I wanted was that baby. I never knew I wanted one so badly until she told me she was pregnant. Instantly, my soul split and begged to have a son or daughter fill me. I would close my eyes and dream about it.

The news birthed a surge of overwhelming protectiveness inside of me, and I would have done anything for the two of them the moment she told me she lost the baby.

And I did.

It happened all too fast.

Walking away from Nina as she fought the nurse's restraints . . . Speeding through the traffic . . . Grabbing my pistol from the car's console . . . The chill of the metal against my back as I tucked it in my pants . . . Pulling into The Legacy's garage . . . Back entrance . . . Elevator . . . Fury running thick through my veins.

Doors open, I walk.

Foyer, living room, hallway.

Door.

Head and heart pound. Ears ring. Blood boils.

One hand on gun, the other on door.

Open . . . Aim . . . BANG.

I can still smell the gunpowder, see the look of fear in Bennett's eyes, hear him gurgling and choking on his own blood. I killed a man—an innocent man—point-blank. His last words, a plea for me to not do it, still haunt me. But I did it anyway because I thought him to be the man Nina manipulated to me. I believed he killed my baby, and for that, he would die.

But it was a lie.

I shake the visions from my head and walk over to pour myself another glass of Scotch. It's my pathetic attempt to quiet the demons in me.

The conundrum I battle with is the idea that Nina is the vile one, and that somehow I'm good. But I'm not. I'm a killer. She didn't pull that trigger—I did. I don't want to bathe in the same evil as she, but I do.

It was her that screwed with my head, twisting truth with lies, creating me into this monster. But a monster I am, just as she, and I allowed. Whether I intended to or not—I still allowed it.

But it isn't just what I did, it's what she did—or didn't do. Leaving me to die. Not doing anything to help me. Yet tonight, she vowed she loves me and wants to do everything to save me from the path she put me on. How could she say that when she left me with two bullets in my chest, bleeding out on the floor of my loft—bullets fired by her brother?

God, her brother. The brother she was fucking.

All he had to say was *Go* and she went, never coming back for me. I've been lied to and manipulated by many, but her betrayal has debilitated me, ripped my heart out, riven to obliteration. Raping the soul entirely. Who knew her hands could hold so much turpitude?

Everything combined is impossible to digest. The contradictions she throws out do nothing but spur confusion and animosity. My mind craves clarity on the situation, but I doubt I'll ever get that because I doubt her sanity. Yet, the mere mention of her leaving tomorrow evokes a thrum in my chest, and that shit bedevils me the most.

I'VE BEEN TRYING my best to play the part, cooperate with the authorities, and feign my innocence, but shit is looking bad. Cal's been sitting in jail, and it's only a matter of time before they come after me. I can trust that Cal is keeping a tight lip, otherwise, I would've already been arrested. But he knows firsthand what can happen if his loyalty is compromised.

Needless to say, with everything I stand to lose, if they uncovered my involvement in the gun trafficking and my other crimes, they'd fry me. I'm a dead man walking at this point, but I'm not a man who's going to sit back and watch his dynasty collapse. Pawns are beginning to fall, so I need to move fast.

The private charter is set to leave at 3:00am; everyone has been paid off and given the run-down. They know I own their tongues. My new identity is packed in my briefcase, bags are ready to go, and the car should be here shortly.

With a stomach filled with boulders of anxiety, I walk through the dark house to my bedroom where my unknowing wife sleeps. Eeriness looms as I walk into the room. She lies there, peaceful, completely unaware of the world she walks around in daily. Unaware about who I really am. What I really do. But if I'm going to do this, I need my family. There's no other option because they mean everything to me. So with that, I risk it all—because they're worth it—when I sit on the edge of the bed and gently nudge her awake.

She stirs, and when she begins to open her eyes, I take her face in my hands and kiss her. There's no preparing for this life, the one I've chosen to live for nearly thirty years. But never in those thirty years have I been under surveillance like I am now.

"What's wrong, honey?" she questions, pulling away from this uncharacteristic affection.

Remaining as calm, clear, and concise as possible so that she doesn't freak out on me, I say, "I need you to sit up and listen to me very carefully."

"You're scaring me."

"Don't be scared. Everything is going to be okay, but I need you to listen

closely because I don't have much time."

She sits up and gives me a nod with fear-glazed eyes.

I take her hands in mine. "I'm leaving the country," I start when she interrupts me.

"What?"

When I place my fingers over her mouth, I stress, "I need you to not ask questions because I won't be able to answer them. I'm begging you to trust me and know that I will do everything to keep our family together. I love you, but there's a part of this business that isn't legal. I've done some things, and now I run the risk of losing my life." My words are partial truths, but mostly lies because there's no point in laying it all out there. It would only put her in danger.

Her eyes widen and her face creases in confusion as she slowly shakes her head.

"This is what I need from you."

"I don't . . . I-I . . . "

"Take a deep breath, hun," I gently instruct. "You trust me?"

Her nod comes instantly, soothing some of my worry.

"Good. I need you to trust me. Never doubt me or my love, understand?"

"Of course."

"If anyone asks about me, you tell them you don't know where I am. You haven't heard from me or seen me since we got into an argument over my commitment to this marriage. That if you had to guess, I'm simply hiding out in a hotel to avoid coming home."

"Why would I—"

"Trust," I say, cutting her off. "No questions because the more you know, the harder it is for me to protect you."

"Protection from what? F-From who?"

Cupping her cheeks, I affirm, "No one will ever separate us, hurt us, destroy us. I need you to just stay put and lay low. Don't talk to anyone unless you have to. But whatever you say, you do not know where I am."

"W-When will you be back?"

Leaning in to rest my forehead against hers, I whisper, "I don't know."

She then begins to quietly weep with her hands on my cheeks.

"You love me, right?"

"Yes," she responds.

"I need you to know that when I come back, we won't be staying. We'll have to leave the country. It's not something that's negotiable."

"What about our life? Our family and friends?"

"There won't be a life if we stay."

Her body trembles while she clings to me, muffling her cries against my shoulder.

"I don't have much time," I tell her softly, trying not to upset her more.

"What does that mean?"

"I'm leaving now—tonight."

She pulls away, and with broken, tear-filled eyes, she tells me, "You have to give me something. Some assurance that you're going to be okay, that you're going to come back."

"There isn't anything I wouldn't do for our family. I will always protect what's mine. I will *be back."*

And with that, she kisses me with urgency, pulling herself on top of my lap. She tastes like salt as she cries through her loving affection, gripping tightly on to me.

I band my arms around her, reminding, "I love this family more than life."

"I'm so s-scared. I d-don't even know what to think right now," she whimpers, and I wipe her tears.

"I know, hun. I know, and I'm sorry. I never wanted to drag you into this. But I have to go."

"No. Wait," she clips out. "Maybe I can help you. If you just tell me whatever trouble you're in, maybe there's a way out. Something I can do to hel—"

"I promise you, I've calculated everything. Remember what I told you: we argued, and I left."

We have one last kiss when I get the call on the untraceable cell I purchased, letting me know the car is here.

And then I'm gone as the car makes its way to the charter that will take me to Scotland, undetected and off the grid.

nineteen

I'M A SELFISH woman for what I'm about to do, but I can't stop myself. All my luggage is packed in the trunk, but before driving to the airport, I need to say goodbye. I know my words hurt him last night when he came to see me. The more I spoke, the angrier he became and eventually stormed out. But I can't be left with that. I can't have that be our last interaction. I know I'm only thinking of myself right now, but I simply have to see him one last time.

Pulling up to the gate, I push the call button.

"Go home, Nina," his voice says.

"Declan, please. I'm going home. I'm heading to the airport now, I just want to say goodbye. Can you please give me that?"

There's no response, only silence. I wait, and when I'm about to shift to reverse, the gates begin to open. Releasing a sigh of gratitude, I start the drive up the winding road. After I park the car, I take another long look at the house. I try not to think too much about the could-have-been's because they're just never-be's. I still find it odd that the shrubs that line the house are scarce in areas. Big, gaping holes when everything else is pristine, even under all the snow.

"It's freezing out here," Declan calls out to me from the front door where he stands.

"The shrubs look sad," I tell him.

"The shrubs?"

"You're missing a lot of them. Did they die?"

"You could say that," he responds. "Can we get out of the cold?"

Giving him a weak smile, I walk over and enter his home. Declan closes the door and moves past me, and I follow, but today he leads us into the kitchen.

"I was just making some coffee," he says as he pulls the kettle off the stove. "I think the old housekeeper left some tea in the pantry if you'd like a cup."

His politeness is unexpected, catching me off guard.

"Umm, okay. Yeah, that would be nice," I say, stumbling nervously over my words.

I walk around the large center island, and take a seat on one of the barstools. I watch him move about the kitchen, pouring the boiling water into the French press, and then the rest in a teacup for me.

Looking around, I take in the surroundings. The kitchen is tucked away from the openness of the house. It's an eat-in kitchen with a large, farm-style table that sits in front of three, floor-to-ceiling windows that overlook the beautiful grounds. The room is brightly lit from the snow outside, and the windows are slightly fogged over.

"Here you go," he says, and I quickly turn back around to the cup of tea he's set in front of me.

I stare down, watching the ribbons of steam float up and disappear. I'm reminded of the many mornings I would sit at the bar in Declan's loft, sipping on tea while watching him cook breakfast. He always looked so sexy in his long pajama pants and white t-shirt that hugged his broad chest. I could watch this man infinitely and never tire.

The memory of what used to be pangs in my chest as I sit here, and when I look up, I see him standing in front of me on the opposite side of the island.

"Declan," I say on a faint whisper. I let his name linger in the air between us for a moment. "I'm so sorry."

Setting his coffee down, he braces his hands on the granite countertop, letting his head drop. I give him silence, and let it grow as I keep my eyes pinned to the most amazing man I've ever known. His soul knows no boundaries of beauty.

When he finally raises his head and looks at me, I tell him, "If I could go back, I'd do it all differently."

"You can't go back, Nina. And what's done is done."

"I know," I admit with defeat.

"I wish I could go back too, but you can't turn your back on the choices you willingly make, and in that moment, I chose you."

"Do you regret that?" I ask on words that ache.

Before he can answer, his cell phone rings, distracting him from me.

"I have to take this," he says, and I nod as he steps out of the room to answer the call.

I swallow hard past the emotion lodged in my throat. Leaving the tea,

I go stand in front of the windows. The chill from the glass makes me shiver as I watch the snow drifting down weightlessly to the ground. Looking over to the left, I can get just a hint of a glimpse of the grotto, and decide to get a better look from another window in the house.

Slipping off my coat, I lay it over one of the kitchen chairs and make my way out into the main hall of the house. I can hear Declan's voice coming from the library. I wander down the grand hall toward the glass atrium when I pass a set of stairs. With curiosity, I begin to climb the steps that lead to the second floor. With my hand still on the banister, I look up to see the stairs continue to a third floor.

I explore, opening doors and walking down the various corridors that lead to bedrooms, bathrooms, and sitting areas. Everything on this level has been remodeled and finished in greys and stark whites. I then see a massive set of white double doors with intricate carvings in the painted wood. The handles are like ice in my hand when I open the doors to what I discover is Declan's room.

My loss is overwhelming as I look at the large bed that sits in the center of the room. I'll never know the feeling of being wrapped up in those sheets. Declan's right: you can't turn your back on the choices you make, and sadly, I made all the wrong ones and lost him in the process.

I take a step into what feels like forbidden territory and look around the room. Its many windows brighten the space that's painted in a hue of dark grey, which contrasts the white crown moldings, and the fluffy, white down that lies atop the large, black leather, chesterfield sleigh bed. There's a sitting area off to the side with two black armchairs and a chaise, all leather chesterfield as well.

Mindlessly, I walk across the plush carpet and over to the bed. I allow my fingertips to ghost along the white fabric as I mourn the loss of what was once within my reach.

"What are you doing in here?" His words are clipped and irritated.

I look at him over my shoulder before I turn to face him. My mouth opens to speak, but I can't find my words.

"You shouldn't be in here," he tells me.

"I just . . . "

"Just what?" he questions as he starts to slowly make his way over to me in purposeful strides.

"I don't know. I just needed to see this. Your home, this bed . . . *you.*"

"Me?"

"Yes, Declan. *You,*" I say. "I miss you."

"You don't miss me."

"Every day. I do. I miss you every single day."

His jaw ticks, and with darkening eyes, he says, "You miss what I no longer am."

"Don't say that."

"Why? Too much responsibility for you to bear? You want to ignore the fact that your lies altered my life in the most unforgiving way?" His voice grows coarser with each word spoken. "You want to stand there and be forgiven for what you did? Like you're some sort of victim in this?"

"I don't expect forgiveness."

"More lies," he grits through clenched teeth as his hands fist at his sides.

"No."

"Then why do you keep saying you're sorry over and over again?"

He grabs ahold of my shoulders, and my voice stutters, "I-I don't know, b-but I don't expect for you to forgive me for what I've done."

"Then why say it?"

"M-maybe . . . I don't know . . . Maybe hope."

"Hope? For what, Nina? For me? For us?"

"Maybe," I tremble as my emotions grow with his anger.

"You want hope where hope doesn't exist."

Fighting against the sadness is doomed when my chin begins to quiver as I say, "I'll always hope for you."

"After all this, you want me?"

I nod.

"Then tell me," he demands with intent.

My words come easily. "I want you, Declan."

His hands drop from my shoulders and land on his belt. With punishing, black eyes boring down on me, I hear the light clinking of metal as he undoes the buckle. My pulse explodes in a rush of hammering beats that knock hard against my ribs in anticipation. But at the same time, my panicked heart flutters when he yanks the belt out from the loops of his slacks.

I stand here, unmoving, and simply watch him. He takes the back of his hand and runs it down my cheek to my neck and then my shoulder. In a flash quick move, he jerks me around, crossing his forearm over my chest, and pinning my back to his front. My hands grip the sides of his thighs, balancing myself on shaky legs.

"Tell me to stop. Tell me to take my hands off you," he says with his lips pressed to the shell of my ear.

"No."

Fast hands yank my arms behind me, and he binds the belt above my elbows. His restraint is unrelenting, pinching my shoulder blades together. I gasp at the sting of the leather biting into my flesh, and then yelp out when my feet are suddenly kicked out from under me, and I fall hard on my knees. But before I can cry out against the burning pain that's radiating up my thighs, Declan grabs my hair and shoves my head facedown into the bed, making it hard to breathe.

You've heard of the theory of atonement, right? Making a restitution to mend what's been broken. I was willing to be whatever vessel Declan needed me to be so that he could deal with his pain. This was my punishment, my meager attempt to right the wrongs, but what came next would test my limits of love for him. How far would I let his destruction go? At what point would I draw the line? Did I even have limits when it came to Declan? It was in that moment, bound and on my knees, that I would soon find out.

Gasping for air, I scream out when he twists my hair in his hand, ripping open the scab on my scalp. My body tenses as he violently grunts with each movement; he's so different from all the other times in the past. I sense it all around me, the putrid hate.

He lifts off of me and shoves my pants and panties down to my knees, and my heart freezes in terror when he spreads my ass cheeks open and spits on me.

Oh God, no!

His hand grips my shoulder for leverage, and every muscle inside of me constricts when he brutally forces his cock in my ass, ripping me in the most grotesque way. I shriek in sheer agony, my cries bouncing off the walls as he growls with each abusive thrust.

I do everything I can to wrench my body away and fight him, but he's taken away my strength and power. I'm at his mercy, and he's a dark rage of unholy wrath as he takes the one part of me I never wanted to give.

Gone is Declan's control, the awareness of how far he's pushing me.

My screams are muffled when he lays a fierce hand on the back of my head, shoving my face further into the mattress. I wail and gasp, thrashing my body against his merciless pounding. The next thing I know, he shoves his hand into my mouth, all four fingers, prying my jaw open and pulling against my cheek. The fire that sears my flesh and the corner of my mouth is ruthless. It's his way of shutting me up because every attempt I make to scream or cry results in gagging on my own saliva.

Stop! God, please, no! Stop!

With my head turned to the side, drool running out of my mouth and down my cheek, I dart my eyes to look up at Declan, and what I see scares the shit out of me. He's completely depraved, a wild beast attacking me, and the pain multiplies as he shreds me. My body ricochets back and forth as he continues to pound into me. Each thrust is painful, unwanted, and takes me right back to the basement I spent so many years in being raped and molested. My mind can't even process what's happening as a blanket of darkness consumes me.

I close my eyes, praying for this to end, and the next thing I know, I'm taken back to the only other time this has happened. I'm twelve years old, bleeding for the first time, and Carl's pissed because Pike can't get hard to fuck me in the ass. I'm naked, and Carl has my face shoved down on the cold concrete floor. His grunting fills the basement as he rapes me from behind. Blood rolls off my back from the lashings he gave me with his belt. His fat belly slaps against my hips as he rips me open, splitting the tender flesh.

My screams go unanswered.

My body begins to heave and convulse when I come into the present. No longer is Carl raping me, but Declan. The voices in my head are screaming for him to stop as he continues to sodomize me, but it's all I have since he has my jaw wrested open, gagging me, and making it impossible for me to fight back.

"Shut it off, Elizabeth."

My eyes pop open when I hear Pike, and he's here. Tears fall when I look into his consoling eyes. He's right here with me, on his knees beside me. He runs his fingers through my ratty hair and attempts to soothe me.

"Just look at me, okay? I'm here with you. You're not alone, but I need you to turn off your feelings right now."

I fight to relax my body while Pike continues to talk to me and stroke my hair. And soon enough, in a matter of seconds, my muscles slacken and my breathing slows. My eyes are locked to my savior.

"That's it. No one can hurt you if you can't feel," he reminds me. *"I'm here with you, Elizabeth. Just keep your eyes on me. It'll be over soon."*

I nod at his words and trust in them. I keep my focus and never let my eyes stray from his as Declan forces his domination on me. In mere moments, he flexes above me, filling me with his cum. His body hunches over mine as he groans out in pleasure. Or is it anger? Then I notice his hand is no longer shoved in my mouth, but instead, holding my hand.

Why is he doing this?

My head fills with a haze of swirling thoughts and memories that are unrecognizable. I'm dizzy in the wake of what just happened as my head lies in a puddle of saliva, tears, and snot. The mixture, the evidence of my fight, coats the side of my face and cakes in my hair.

"*You're okay,*" Pike assures me . . . and then . . . he's gone.

I don't even get a chance to grieve his loss when Declan pulls his cock out of my ass. I wince against the pain when he does this, but I'm frozen, bent over his bed, unable to move from the shock. I can feel the delicate tissues swell in a blistering heat of rawness.

"Jesus Christ," I hear him pant from behind me, and he quickly releases his belt from my arms.

I remain in place as I listen to his footsteps, followed by the click of the door closing, and it's then I finally take in a breath of air. My body slides off the bed and onto the floor where I lie with my pants and underwear still shoved down around my knees.

Destroyed.

Humiliated.

And in a sick way . . . loved.

twenty

CHILLS WRACK MY clammy body as I lie here on the floor of Declan's room. The room that was supposed to be ours, housing our bond and love for one another.

It was never supposed to be *this.*

But it is.

My thoughts are scattered and confused.

What just happened?

My body trembles in the aftershocks of the trauma it just endured and the memories of my childhood. I fight the vomit that sours the back of my throat as my gut bubbles in disgust.

But you want to know the most fucked up thought running through my head right now?

Here it is . . .

I still ache for him. For his love, his touch, his breath upon my skin.

And then I think about him holding my hand. *He held my hand.* It's nothing new for him—he's always held my hand when we orgasmed. It's his one tender gesture that would remind me, that no matter how rough he chose to be with me, that I could trust in his comfort to always be aware of me and take care of me.

Does he still feel that way?

Bracing my hands on the floor, I push myself up to sit, and my ass stings as I shift. Biting against the pain that shoots through me, I stumble up to my feet. I reach down and pull my pants up. Wobbly on my feet, I walk over to the en suite bathroom, and when I flick on the light, I get a glimpse of my ashen face.

I touch my reflection in the mirror. Somehow, it feels safer than to touch my actual face. There's always a disconnect in one's reflection, and right now, I need that distance. But the reflection I see is *me* at age twelve. I look at me—at her—and my heart begins to pump harder, fiercer, sadder.

Her blue eyes are filled with a pain she hides from the world, and I want so badly to reach through the glass and save her from the life I know she'll endure. I know that deep down she's buried a small light of hope, and it kills me to know it's just a wasted dream. This sweet, little, red-headed girl is destined for a life filled with anguish and despair, and there's nothing I can do to save her. Her future is inevitable, written in the stars, and bound to the solidity that the fairytales she dreams about don't exist. They never did.

Tucking my fingers in a tight fist, I feel the tingles in my palm. Everything clouds around my head in a swarm of shit memories and thoughts.

I'm stronger than this. Don't break; I'm stronger than this pain.

But maybe I'm not strong. I just allowed Declan to fuck me the same way Carl did, and I barely even fought him. I succumbed to him like the trash I am, gave him a piece of my worthless body for his selfish use.

SMASH!

A hundred eyes stare back at me, sad, pitiful, loathing eyes. *My* eyes. The clinking of broken glass falling onto the marbled sink is a song of despair, but it's ruined with my panted breaths. I look into the broken mirror and I hate what I see. I hate what I am. I hate it all. And I want to hate Declan for what he just did, but I can't. I can't, and I hate myself even more for that fact.

I deserved it. I deserve even worse.

If this is his way of punishing me, then I'll suppress the need to fight him. I'll bear it and take it without enmity.

Concentrating on calming myself down, I turn on the faucet and cup my hands under the cold water. My knuckles sting as the water flushes the split skin. It takes my blood and runs red down the drain. I allow the coolness to numb the wound.

After taking a few sips from my hands and rinsing my mouth out, I start opening the drawers and cabinets to find a couple bandages to cover my knuckles. Once I have the band-aids in place, I undo my pants to clean up. Flinching when I wipe myself, I look to see the toilet paper streaked in blood from his assault.

I splash a little water on my face, and finger-comb my hair, before I open the door and take slow steps through the bedroom. I'm timid and nervous about walking out of this room, about facing Declan, about what will happen next. Making my way down the stairs, I don't see him, so I head to the kitchen where I left my coat and the keys to the car.

I stop when I see Declan leaning over the counter. I don't move. I don't make a sound. His back faces me as he's bent over, leaning on his elbows with head in hands. The rise and fall of his shoulders is noticeable as he stands there, slightly disheveled in his tailored slacks and untucked button-up.

When he senses my presence, he shifts his head to look at me and I notice his reddened eyes. The shame is written all over him, staining him in humiliation, but I'm the only one who should feel it. Not him.

He pushes back from the counter and stands up, facing me, and when I take a slow step into the kitchen, I'm overwhelmed with the need to give him honest pieces of me. To open up with truths he's never heard before. To finally let him inside of me.

"Being with you has been difficult," I admit, my words trembling. "It takes me to the extremely dark place of my past."

"Then why me? Why not choose someone else?"

"Because," I choke out as the tears flood my eyes. "B-Because you always held my hand," I weep. "For some reason, that simple touch made it okay. Made me feel safe. I've never had that touch before."

He doesn't respond to my words as he looks at me with tormented eyes.

So I stand here in front of him and tell him the truth as I continue to cry through the shame of who I really am. "On my tenth birthday, my foster dad forced my brother to molest me while he watched and jerked off." Admitting my disgust for the first time in my life suddenly makes it all too real. Tears fall from my cheeks as I bear my disgrace in front of my love. "I was only a kid. I didn't even know what sex was until I was lying underneath Pike on a filthy mattress in the basement."

"Christ," he breathes in horror at my words.

"After that day, I found myself in that basement nearly every day for years. I couldn't believe in heaven or God when I was being forced to do things people want to pretend don't exist. But what happened to me made me believe in evil. And that the devil is real and lives inside the savages of this world."

Declan turns away from me, resting his hands back on the counter and dropping his head. His breath heavy as I add, "My foster dad . . . he had a thing for belts as well. He got off on stripping me naked and whipping me until I bled."

His fists ball tightly at my words.

"You used to frighten me when you'd use your belt on me. All I could think about were all the beatings I was forced to endure as a little girl."

"Stop."

"This is the truth," I sob. "This is what I never wanted you to know about me. I'm ugly and nasty and dirty and—"

"Stop!" he shouts.

I watch the muscles that rope his arms flex with tension. His eyes are pinched shut, and I startle when he slams his one fist into the solid granite with a guttural outburst.

I'm paralyzed, scared to move, completely exposed, and mortified. Never have I opened myself up like this. I never had to with Pike because he was there. A witness. A participant.

With his eyes still closed, he says in acrimony, "Do you have any idea what it's like to love the person you hate?"

Love? God, he can hate me all he wants if he still loves me.

Opening his eyes, he takes a couple steps toward me. "Because I do hate you. More than anything on this earth. I hate you with every pump of blood my heart proffers. I want to punish you in the worst ways, make you suffer and hurt. But God help me . . . I love you."

It's what I've been longing to hear, to know he loves me. But his words are filled with lachrymosity. Whatever may come of us, this love he has for me will always be tinged in venom. But even in the lies of before, it was corrupt. Cursed from the very beginning—and I was the culprit.

"But then . . . " he starts, " . . . you tell me these truths. The truths I wanted from the beginning that you hid from me, and I feel like a bastard for wanting to hurt you, but I *still* want it. I still want to make you suffer."

"I deserve it," I murmur.

"Why did you continue to do it?"

"Do what?"

He struggles for a moment when he clarifies, "Why did you continue to have sex with your brother as an adult?"

Embarrassment heats my neck, and I feel so filthy having to expose this. Hanging my head in shame, I keep my eyes downcast as I answer, "At some point, when we were kids, we started sleeping together in private. In his bed. It wasn't forced, and in those moments, he'd make me feel okay."

"*Okay?*" he questions in confusion, and when I hesitantly move my eyes to look up at him, I say, "I always felt gross and worthless. But something about Pike made me feel clean. He made me feel loved and safe. He was all I had in the world." I begin to choke on my words, telling him, "And he did love me. He always protected me."

"He raped you," Declan spits through gritted teeth.

"No," I defend. "He didn't. He was being molested himself long before. Carl, our foster dad, he forced Pike to do that stuff to me."

"He didn't have to do it. He made the choice."

"He knew if it wasn't him, that Carl would do it himself. I was safer with Pike."

"But Carl . . . did he . . . ?"

I nod. "Yes. It took a while, but eventually he did." And then I admit, "The first time was when I was twelve. He raped me the same way you just did."

Instantly, Declan has his arms around me and I'm crying. He grips the back of my head and cradles me tightly against his chest. His hold is strong and hard but warm. I band my arms around his waist, clinging to him.

He's everywhere, all around me, encasing me in the safety of his touch.

Home.

When I begin to settle my emotions and calm myself, he whispers in my hair, "I'm sorry. I lost control on you."

"It's okay."

"No. It's not okay," he declares when he pulls away to look at me.

"It is. I hurt you. I'm so sorry, Declan. You will never know how sorry I am for what I did to you. I deserve every punishment."

"I don't want to be that man."

"You're not. You're *nothing* like that man," I tell him. "There were times my mind went to that place with you, but you're not like that. I've always felt safe with you. I've always been certain that you'd never really hurt me."

"But I do hurt you. And I like it. And I want more of it."

"Then take it. I'll give it to you. I'll give you anything to make you feel better. If it's my pain and suffering you need, then have it. It's yours."

His hands tighten on me as I speak, and with brows knit together and a locked jaw, he grunts in frustration when he releases me from his hold. Raking a hand through his hair, he growls, "What the fuck is wrong with you? You shouldn't want this. You shouldn't want me. What right-minded person would subject themselves to this?"

"I never claimed to be right-minded. I know I'm screwed up. I know I'm so far beyond damaged I'm irreparable. But I also know that you won't find the same amount of satisfaction in punishing anyone but me."

"Why do it then? Is it to make yourself feel better for what you did?"

"Partly."

"And the other part?"

Taking a few steps over to him, I say, "Because I love you."

"You shouldn't."

"But I do. I never thought anyone could have the power to make me feel as safe and clean as you do. You have the power to make me feel worthy of living. That somewhere out there, life just might have a purpose for me."

"Then why leave me? Why didn't you stay and call the medics? Why did you leave me to die?"

It's in his words I hear the heartbreak I caused.

"I told you. I was scared. Everything was happening so fast, I didn't know what to do. I panicked."

He releases a slow sigh and takes a moment before speaking again. "I'm sure I already know, but I need to hear it from you."

"What is it?"

"I know Pike is dead. And I know he died the same day he shot me."

I swallow hard when he says this, and I already know his question before he asks, "Did you have anything to do with his death?"

My chin begins to quiver, and when I can't hold on to my emotions any longer, my face scrunches as I confess, "I will never forgive myself for what I did. I loved him so much."

"I need to hear you say it," he says sternly.

Fighting back my tears, I take in a deep breath and let go of it slowly before giving him the trembling words, "I'm the one who shot him. I killed him."

"I want to be mad at you. I want to throw it in your face, but that would make me a hypocrite, and it's because of your lies."

"I'm sorry."

"Stop apologizing!" his voice rips when anger takes over. "I don't want to hear anything else from you. Every time we talk, the shit you say . . . it's impossible to understand and digest."

He walks back to the center island, facing away from me as he looks out the windows.

"Get out," he orders on a dead breath.

He's unmoving as I walk around him to pick up my coat and keys, but the struggle is evident within him. I want to say a thousand words, but I know better. So I keep my mouth shut and do as I'm told.

I leave.

twenty-one

“WHAT ARE YOU doing back here, lassie?” Isla questions when I walk through the front door with my luggage.

“I missed my flight. Is it all right if I stay another night?”

“Stay as long as you like,” she says when she walks over and takes one of my bags. “Were you able to reschedule?”

“Not yet. I never even made it to the airport. I’ll have to call the airline tomorrow.”

“Does this have anything to do with the McKinnon boy?” she asks.

Walking into the formal sitting room, I take a seat, answering, “Yes.”

“Heartache is difficult.”

Looking over at her sitting across from me, I give a slight nod. The day has been draining and I feel weak from what happened with Declan. With so many questions swarming in my head, I say, “Can I ask you something?” as I lean back in the chair.

“Of course.”

“Do you believe that people can change?”

She takes a moment and then gently shakes her head a couple times. “No, dear.”

I reflect on her answer as defeat looms overhead.

And then she elaborates, “I believe we are who we are and the essence of what we are built upon is unchangeable. But I believe we can change how we make choices. But just because we can change our behavior doesn’t mean we’ve changed the core of who we are. It’s like someone who’s an alcoholic. They may rehab and make better choices, but I don’t believe that inner voice and craving ever goes away. The change is solely in their choice to not drink, but they still desire it.”

“So, evil is always evil?”

“Yes. And good is always good. But I trust in my faith that we are descendants of rectitude. That each of us, no matter how bad we may think ourselves to be, the core lining of us is threaded in holy fibers."

It's in her words that I'm taken back to my home in Northbrook. The memories of my father and I play in clips of tea parties, nighttime songs, piggyback rides, bedtime stories, and fits of laughter. And Isla is right . . . there was a moment in time I was clothed in nothing but goodness. I was pure and free and honest. But I was just five years old when my light was snuffed out.

The day my dad was taken from me was the day nothing would ever be the same. I lost more than just my light—I lost myself. Lost it entirely. I allowed the world to decay me. But how is anyone supposed to be strong enough to fight back against something so monumental? I was just a little girl. The only person I had in my corner was Pike, but then again, he was just a boy himself. We clung to each other because we were each other's only hope.

I thought I was making all the right choices, but as I look back in the wake of my life, it's filled with nothing but destruction. And now, I'm the only one that remains.

Well, almost.

Declan is still here, but in a sense, he was destroyed as well. His heart still beats, but not like it used to. My choices—my decisions—they're poisonous. I used that poison for power, but it backfired.

"Are you okay?" Isla's voice interjects.

"I made bad choices," I say without thought. The words simply fall from my lips before I can stop them.

"Welcome to life, my dear," she condoles. "I could write a novel with all the mistakes and ill choices I've made in my years. But I've come to realize that's what it's about. Sometimes we have to fall to know how to stand back up. Sometimes we have to hurt people to recognize our flaws and to see that we need to better ourselves."

"Did you ever find that some of your choices were so bad they were unforgivable?" I ask as regret stirs in my veins.

"Yes," she admits with her chin held high. "But even though I knew they were unforgivable, I was still forgiven."

"Who was it that forgave?"

She pauses, and when the corners of her mouth lift in a subtle smile, she answers, "My husband."

"You hurt him?"

"I hurt him terribly."

"Why did he forgive you?" I ask.

"It's called grace. When we love, and when that love comes from the purity of your heart, you give grace. You find compassion and forgive because we're all flawed. We all make mistakes, but love's devotion doesn't cast stones."

I want to believe the love Declan once had for me did come from a pure place. That there's still hope for forgiveness. That there's still a shimmer inside of him that still wants me. Because for me, it's more than a shimmer—it's a raging fire of need and desire I have for him. But after what he did to me today, I don't see this working out. Isla's words are nice and flowery, but flowers eventually wilt and die no matter how much love you give in tending to their needs.

"You look like you could use a distraction," she says before suggesting, "Why don't you settle back into your room, and when you're ready, how would you like to help me prepare dinner?"

"That actually sounds lovely, but unfortunately, I can't cook."

"Everyone can cook. All you need is someone to guide you."

Smiling at her invitation, I accept her offer, and agree, "Okay then. But I'm warning you now, I've been known to incinerate food beyond consumption." I laugh at the memory of the first time Declan tried teaching me to make champagne chicken and I charred the meal. But that laughter is tainted. It's bittersweet. My time with Declan back in Chicago held some of the best moments in my life, even though I was just an illusion of a better version of me.

"If I could teach my daughter how to cook, I can surely teach you," she tells me as we stand.

Picking up my bags, I look over and tease, "But is her cooking any good?"

"She always made the best meals."

"*Made?*" I question her use of the past tense.

"She left this world many years ago."

"How did she die?" I question, knowing all too well the annoyance of the overused *I'm sorry* people give who clearly haven't suffered a death filled with *I'm sorry's.*

"It was a senseless act of violence, but that's part of life, dear," she says, attempting to downsize the ache, but her loss is seen in the gloss of the unshed tears of her eyes. "I'll be in the kitchen," she says and then walks out of the room.

Death is imminent—I know this all too well—but no matter how much we lose, no matter how numb we become, we always feel the pinprick of the vacancy. The parts of our soul that our loved ones take with them when they leave this world are forever left unfilled. They're empty wounds that are always exposed and unable to heal.

As I make my way up to my room, I settle my things in and decide to keep myself busy to block out the thoughts that keep filtering in. Memories of this morning's defilement. The vision of Declan when I looked at him, his villainous eyes, blackened in rage, keeps finding its way into my head. He was a riled beast, taking what he wanted, forcing his power on me.

Shaking the visions away, I quickly rush out of the room to find Isla for the much needed diversion. We spend the rest of the day in the kitchen, and I find myself enjoying my time with her. We cook, share a bottle of wine, and enjoy each other's company, and I'm thankful for the distraction she's able to provide me.

But it's when I excuse myself for the evening and am lying in bed that it all immediately comes rushing back. Declan tying me up, spitting on my ass, smothering my face into the mattress, the pain of his intrusions, the sounds of his wild grunting. I shift in bed, heart pounding, and I feel the burn from his assault, and then it's Carl I see in the darkened room. I can smell the stench of his cigarettes.

Lurching off the bed, I dash to the toilet and vomit. My stomach convulses in heaves as the acidic bile stings my throat, and when I gag, it fills my nose and burns like a bitch. My eyes prick hard with tears, and another bout of puke forces its way out of my gut as my body constricts and hurls over the toilet.

When there's nothing left for my body to expel, I tire and scoot my back against the wall. I wipe the sheen of sweat from my forehead and take in slow breaths. My hands are jittery and my body is broken in a spell of cold sweats. Even if I wanted to shut myself down, I don't think I'd be able to. I don't think I'm strong enough to battle the skeletons I've spent my whole life hiding from. The skeletons that Declan awoke when he forced himself on me earlier today. Only one other person has made me feel that decrepit and filthy, and I burned him to his death. Never did I think Declan would haunt me the same way Carl used to.

WARMTH STIRS ME awake, and as I begin to move, I feel a weight on top of me. Opening my eyes, my body jumps when I see Declan holding himself above me.

"Shh, baby, it's only me," he whispers.

"What are you doing here?"

His eyes pinch shut, and he lets go of a pained breath, saying, "I can't do it. I can't stay away from you."

His words settle my heart, and I don't question him because I need him. Reaching up, I run my hand along his stubbled jaw, and when he drops his head, my body warms in peace as his lips press softly into mine. I can't control the moan that comes out of me, and I wrap my arms tightly around his neck, holding him close.

To have his taste back in my mouth soothes. The world lifts from my shoulders, and finally, I can breathe—*really* breathe. I don't ever want this to end. I need this—need him.

As our bodies begin to move and writhe together, he reaches back and pulls his shirt off. Lowering himself on top of me, he threads his fingers through my hair, saying, "Forgive me for what I did to you earlier. Please forgive me and let me fix it. Let me attempt to take it away."

I place my hand over his bare chest, and I can feel his heart crashing inside of him. I want to calm that heart just as much as he wants to erase what happened in his room, so I nod my head. That's all it takes for him to start slowly undressing me. Slipping my clothes off, along with his, he covers us up under the sheets as our naked bodies rediscover one another.

He allows my hands freedom to roam over his body—an un-Declan-like thing for him to grant me, but I take it. He runs his damp lips down my neck and along my collarbone before taking his tongue and dragging it over my pert nipple. Covering the tight bud with his lips, he sucks with the heat of his mouth, and my body bows in response to the touch.

My hands fist his hair, and he moves to my other breast. His cock is raging hard against me, and his slow movements are making my pussy ache in wetness for him.

"I need you, Declan," I pant in wanton heat.

He pulls back and looks down at me with eyes molten in lust. His hand ghosts down my body, my stomach, and when he reaches my pussy, he sighs as my muscles tremble in anticipation of what I thought I'd never have again.

"Oh, God," I mewl when he delves his fingers into my wet folds. My hands press into his flesh, and I hang on as he begins to pump in and out of me.

I'm on fire, needing more of him, so with a strong hand, I wrap it around his wrist and hold his arm still. When I being to rock my hips and fuck his fingers to my own liking, he growls, and the erotic sound spurs my hips to buck up and fuck him even more fiercely.

"That's my baby," he encourages, and when my moans intensify as my body climbs, he pulls his fingers out of me and quickly pins my arms above my head.

I'm relaxed under his restraining hold. Looking up at him, *this* is the Declan I remember. He's in total control—dominating me with loving affection. With his hand locking my wrists above me, he takes his other hand, fingers glistening in my arousal, and slips them into my mouth. I roll my tongue and suck the taste of my pussy off of him.

He then finds my clit with his wet fingers and gently strokes on the bundle at the same time he pushes his large, strong cock inside of me slowly, so slow it borders on torture. I feel every ridge of his dick until he's buried himself deep in me.

And I'm finally home—safe in the comfort of the only man I ever want to share this with.

He holds himself still inside of me when he says, "You're the only one who's ever made me feel like this."

"Like what?"

Pulling out of me, he thrusts back in, grunting, "Like this," as he fills me deeply.

My body arches off the bed as he elicits carnal moans from deep in my womb, and I spread my thighs even wider for him because I need more.

Dragging his cock out of me again, he slams his hips down into me, while asking, "You feel that?" hitting my sweet spot deep inside.

"Yes," I breathe.

"Tell me," he demands as he drives himself back inside of my body, now pumping in and out with purpose, mending us together.

My eyes falls shut as I let him take me over, giving him my body entirely for him to have and use however he wishes.

"I love you," I release in the breaths of air we now share.

"Tell me again."

My skin tingles in radiant pleasure, warmed in passion.

"I love you, Declan."

I begin to lose myself, bucking my hips to meet each of his thrusts. I can feel his cock growing thicker, harder, hotter. His hold on my wrists tightens, but it only makes me feel safer.

"Open your eyes," I hear him say, and the moment before I do, I smell it—stale cigarettes and piss.

My body locks up when my eyes open and it's Carl looking down at me, fucking me with his disgusting dick and breathing his putrid breath all over me.

JOLTING AWAKE, MY eyes pop open to be greeted by another snow-filled night. Another bad dream possesses my subconscious. This is the third nightmare I've woken from tonight. Gone are the nights of exploring with Carnegie, my caterpillar friend. He's been replaced by morphed scenes of Declan loving me and by dank basements, urine-stenched closets, and the visions of Carl jerking himself off as he watches me.

I take my time to quiet my rapid-beating heart before I lie back down. I focus on the snow that collects on the window. Some of it melts, tuning into trickling rivers that slowly make their way down the glass. I burrow down into the blankets, trying to warm myself, and when I roll over from the moonlit snow, it takes a moment for my eyes to adjust.

It's after I blink a few times that I see him, and I hold my breath, wondering if I'm imagining this—imagining *him.*

twenty-two

HE SITS ON the chair a few feet from the bed I'm lying in, leaning over with his elbows propped on his knees. I know he's really here when he lifts his head and looks at me, the moon illuminating his green eyes. My head remains resting on the pillow, and I breathe in deeply.

Why is he here?

Neither one of us moves or speaks; we simply watch each other in the dark silence. I want to move though. My body begs to crawl onto his lap, to have him dominate every one of my senses. The dream I just woke from felt so real. It's all I want, to be in a place where we can have moments like that together. But the dream turned to a nightmare so quickly, and I know it's because of Declan that it did.

How can I crave this man who now torments me? What is it about him that makes me want to forgive him so easily, to not even question him?

I notice the creases that line his forehead and his brows that cinch in the despair we both feel.

"What are we doing?" His voice, a quiet rasp filled with oppression.

Sitting up, I never take my eyes off of him, but I don't know what to say. I wish I had an answer for him, but I'm just as confused. He has my emotions bouncing all over the place and colliding in a war inside of me.

I lose the contact when he drops his head down into the palms of his hands, and his voice is a soft murmur, "What've I done?" and I don't know if he's talking to me or simply to himself, but I remain quiet as he continues. "What've *you* done? I don't know what's going on here . . . what this is between us . . . what this is inside of me."

"It's a battle between heart and mind," I whisper, and when I do, he looks up at me.

I watch his face tighten in grief, the feeling thickens the room, and it takes him a while to speak again, but when he does, the words are drenched in shame. "Are you all right?"

When I don't answer him, he exhausts on a breath, "That's a stupid question."

"Declan . . . "

"I'm sorry. What I did . . . That wasn't . . . "

"Stop," I tell him when his voice begins to crack.

"What happened to you as a child . . . " His hands clench as he fights with his building emotions. "It fucking breaks me."

"Don't do this."

But he doesn't even acknowledge my words as he goes on, "And then what I did to you . . . I don't know how I lost control like that. Seeing you in that room . . . That was supposed to be *ours*. You don't know how badly I wanted that. How much I wanted to take you away from the husband I thought was . . . "

He lets his words drift, and I want to cry, but I don't. I know he doesn't want to see my tears, so I keep myself focused, but I'm dying on the inside. To sit here and listen to his words that are masking cries of his own is awful. This is a man of abundant discipline and authority, so to hear him so broken down, so weak, it destroys me.

"How do I get past a deceit of this magnitude?" he eventually questions.

"I wish I knew. I wish I could go back. But I can't. I don't even really know how to explain this all. I want to be honest. I want you to know the real me, to know the truth, but it's so hard. Because the truth is so gross and twisted, you probably wouldn't even believe it, because people don't want to believe that life can be that horrifying. I'm a fucked-up human; I know this. I don't know what it is to be a rational person, but you make me want to learn. You make me want to try."

"His eyes were open," he says out of the blue, and I'm confused as to what he's referring to, but then he adds, "After I shot him. I saw photos of you on his desk. I gathered them up along with the file, and when I looked down at Bennett's bloody body, his eyes were still open."

He says this and I remember that Pike's eyes were the same. I'll never forget how haunting they looked.

"He knew who you were."

"I know," I say. "I heard him in the hospital. He was having me followed; he knew you and I were together."

He then stands, walks over to the bed, and sits down next to me. He doesn't touch me, although I wish he would.

"I hurt you today."

"I'm okay," I whisper.

He then looks down at my knuckles that are wrapped in band-aids. "My shattered mirror tells me otherwise."

"Bad memories."

"Did it happen a lot?" he asks on a voice that's barely even a whisper. Like he's afraid his words will break me, and for the first time in a long time, I feel like they possibly could. That I'm not as tough as I used to be.

I give him a nod, but it isn't enough for him when he urges, "I need you to tell me."

I hesitate, licking my lips, wanting to give him the honesty he's asking for but also terrified for him to know.

"Tell me, Nina."

"Please . . . don't, don't call me that."

"I'm sorry," he says, looking away from me. "It's all I know you as."

"Look at me." He does. "This is me. This is what I want you to know."

"Elizabeth," he murmurs, and I nod, affirming, "Yes . . . Elizabeth."

"Tell me then, Elizabeth. Because I need to know you, to figure you out."

"Yes," I respond. "It happened a lot. It was dirty and gross and—"

"What did he do to you?"

I swallow hard, scared to say the words. My hands fidget nervously, and when Declan sees, he covers them in his own.

"I've never told anyone," I confess. "Only Pike knew, and he was there. I didn't have to say a word because he saw it all."

"I told you about my mum, remember?"

"Of course I remember."

"I opened up to you about something I had never spoken about to anyone. I gave you that piece of me. A piece that makes me embarrassed and ashamed."

I remember seeing his tears when he told me he cowered under a bed while he watched a man shoot his mother in the head. A shot that killed her. He thinks himself weak and a pussy—those are the words he used. He made himself vulnerable to me, so I'll give him what he's asking for, something I've never given anyone.

"It started on my tenth birthday with him forcing Pike to have sex with me. He would take us down to the basement. There was a dirty mattress he kept on the floor. He'd watch us while he sat in a chair and jerked himself off. Most of the time he would get up to cum on either Pike or myself." Saying the words turns my stomach, and I can already feel the wave of nausea come over me. "We would be down in that basement at least four times a week. A couple years later was when it switched and Carl started touching me."

I stop and drop my head. I can't bear to look at Declan anymore when I start to feel the filth crawl along my skin. Tears burn the backs of my eyes as I try to keep them at bay, but they come anyway.

"Don't look away from me," he tells me when he tugs my chin up to face him.

With my head up but my eyes closed, I say, "It's humiliating."

"I don't care. I don't want you hiding from me. Look at me and trust me enough to give me this truth."

So I do. I open my eyes, and while tears continue to fall from my eyes and drip off my chin, I tell him everything that happened in that basement. How Carl would rape me, sodomize me, piss on me, beat me, and whip me. How he'd cum on my face and laugh at me while he'd wipe it off with his finger and force me to lick it. How he'd piss on the mattress and shove my face in it, force me to finger his ass while he'd beat himself off. How it didn't take long for him to turn me into a machine because it's what I had to become in order to survive.

I sob as I give him this sick part of me, and explain why I started having sex with Pike by ourselves. Explained how it soothed me and provided an escape for me. I rip myself open and let the rot fall onto Declan's lap as I reveal my twisted childhood to him.

He listens, never interrupting, but encouraging me to go on. His eyes are wide in disbelief and pity, and I know he will never look at me the same way again. He now knows the reality of my pathetic existence. The worthlessness of my body, the one he used to look at in amazement and admiration. He'd call me perfect, beautiful, and flawless.

But now he knows the truth.

This body was never something he should've valued. Anyone would be foolish to value the pile of shit it is. It's simply a capsule—fancy wrapping paper—that conceals everything I'm made of . . . sewage.

"Why didn't you ever say anything?"

"Because I was scared if I did, I'd lose Pike. I feared going to another abusive home and being alone. Pike was all I had; I didn't want to be without him," I try to explain.

"He used you."

"Who? Pike?"

"Yes. If he loved you like you claim he did, he would've pushed you to get help, to get you to a place that was safe."

Shaking my head, I refute, "It doesn't work like that. And he did love me. He gave his whole life to me. I was always safe with him."

Declan bites down hard causing his jaw to tick, and I tell him, "You won't ever change my opinion of Pike. I don't expect you to understand, but we were just kids. We did what we could to survive. Whether you believe it to be right or wrong, what's done is done, and looking back won't change anything."

"I wish I could take it away."

"You can't," I say weakly. "Just like I can't take away the pain in your life. I want to. I want that power more than you know."

Sitting in the darkness, making my confessions and opening myself up, I wonder why Declan remains unmoving by my side. My desire to crawl inside of his head, to know the thoughts he hides in there is strong. His expression is hard to read as he looks at me. The hush in the room is unsettling, yet peaceful. I was starting to wonder if he would ever be able to be in the same room as me without punishing me.

"I should go."

He stands up from the bed, and when he does, I lie down. I watch him turn back to me, and in a sweet gesture, he pulls the covers over my body and then braces his hands on the mattress, hovering over me.

"Stay."

"Why?" I breathe.

"I don't know why. Just don't go back to the States just yet."

He pushes off the bed and walks to the door. I'm sad when he leaves—lonely and empty. His scent looms in the air, and I take a deep breath to capture him in my soul. Lying here in the dark, I feel haunted by the demons I just released.

And now he knows the fallacy of it all.

As for me, I've just sliced through my deepest scar tissue and reopened the wounds of desecration.

I battle with my heart to shut down, to turn into the machine that protects me from that which is destined to destroy me. Between the memories that just rebirthed inside of me and the loss of Declan's presence, the mass of emotions is too much for me to even think about right now.

So I cloak myself in armor and delight in stupor.

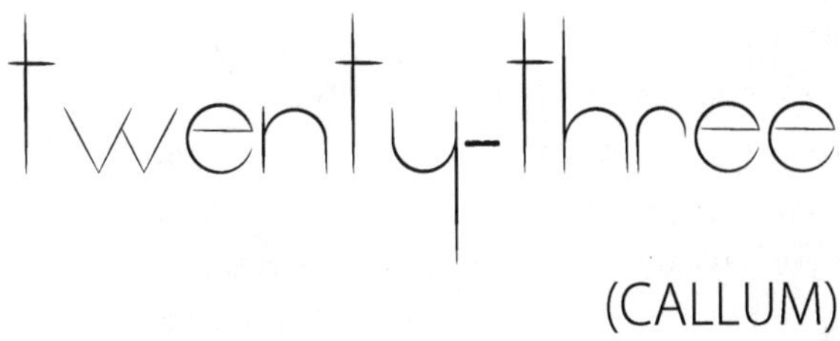

twenty-three

(CALLUM)

I WAS OFFERED a plea deal when my attorney came to see me yesterday. Since my part in all this was simply being a man of the books—the white-collared crook—they want me to rat out the bigger names to the operation. The thing is, I don't have many names. The men that do the runs are worth a lot more to the Feds than I am, but I'm not privy to that side of the business. The one name I *am* privy to is the one I know they want the most.

The king of the cartel.

But to cross paths with him would be a death sentence. I've learned that lesson. So I played dumb, kept his name shrouded in my arsenal. If I nark, I'm a dead man. It's much safer for me in here—locked behind steel and iron.

No one messes with me much. Money buys safety, and I've got an endless source and people on the outside that make sure the steady stream keeps flowing. What isn't available to me is being taken care of by Lachlan, whom I'm now calling.

The guard keeps watch outside of the laundry hall where I now work four days a week, earning a pitiful eleven cents an hour.

"Cal," he greets when he finally answers. "How are you?"

"How the hell do you think I am? Did you take care of the money?"

"Yeah. All done. There was an event recently that was held for the charity, so it was easy to filter into the accounts."

"And Declan?" I ask.

"What about him, sir?"

"Any suspicions from him?"

"No. He's been distracted these days."

"How so?"

"A woman. Elizabeth Archer. She appeared in town recently. He's been having me follow her."

I don't bother to ask why. Time isn't my friend at the moment, but I can only guess that boy will probably forever be fucked up when it comes to trust. He never told me anything about the shooting—who did it or for what reason. But I know it all boils down to Nina Vanderwal. All he told me was to feign his death to her if ever we should cross paths and that he wanted me to keep my distance from him. I agreed, and he disappeared back to Scotland to live in that estate he bought years back. I can't figure that kid out or why he wants to wallow alone in practically the middle of nowhere.

I've yet to have anyone make contact with him, and as far as I know, no one has. He's unaware that I'm sitting in jail for crimes he knows nothing about. Crimes I've been committing since he was a little boy.

"She's staying in town close to him," Lachlan adds.

"In Gala?"

"At the Water Lily."

What the fuck?

"Declan was there?" I ask, wondering if he knows what was kept from him.

"It's where Elizabeth is staying. He was there the other day for a couple hours in the middle of the night and then returned home."

I'm not given the chance to respond when the guard slams the door open and shouts, "Time's up, inmate!"

He snatches the phone from my hands and disconnects the call.

"What the hell happened to five minutes?" I sling in hostility.

"Price influx, bitch. It's gonna cost you more next time."

Grabbing my arm, he leads me out of the laundry room, and even though my bones burn to knock the living shit out of this pussy, I keep myself in check because I can't be getting thrown in the block. I need to continue to have access to that fucking phone or find a way to get my hands on my own.

First thing I need to do is find out who this Elizabeth woman is that has my son going to the Water Lily. So I wait in my cell until rec time and then make my way to the phone bank where I can make my call.

"Cal, baby," Camilla's voice sighs into the phone.

I thank God that the values of this woman are slightly shady to accommodate being involved with a man who's facing up to twenty-five years in a federal prison.

"How are you holding up, love?" I ask.

"I miss you. Trying to take care of everything on my own is drowning me."

"I know. I'm sorry. I need to see you though. I need you here this weekend."

"Of course. You know I never miss a visit. Is everything okay?"

"Yes. I don't want you worrying about me," I tell her. "It's just important that I see you." I urge my words because what I need her to do for me isn't something I can mention on these monitored calls because of the names involved.

"Callum," she softly scolds, "You're in jail. How can I *not* worry about you?"

"Ninety seconds remain."

"Fuck!" Bracing my hand against the cinder block wall, I bark, "Did you send the money into my account?"

"Yes, but you know how slow they are."

"I need you to call about it because I'm all out of time. I won't be able to call you until I get that money."

"I promise, Cal."

"Thirty seconds remain."

"God, I hate this," she cries. "I miss you so much."

"I miss you too. I'll see you in a couple days."

"I'll be there. I love you."

"Love you too."

Walking into the quad, I take a seat in front of the TV that's playing an episode of Jeopardy. I look to my left and watch a couple of illiterates shout out their answers, and I find them to be more entertaining than the actual show.

"Hey, puta."

My body stiffens when the words slither across my ear and the coolness of what I imagine to be a razor blade pierces the flesh of my back.

"I'm talking to you, esé," he says, sitting behind me with his face hovering by the side of mine as he talks quietly into my ear so as to not arouse attention.

"What do you want?" I keep my voice even and hard.

"Your boss wanted me to relay a message for him."

"My boss?"

"That's right. He don't want you actin' a jit. Sayin' things that don't need to be said. Mentioning *names* that don't need mentioning." He digs the blade into my skin, and I bite back against the sting as he sneers, "You don't need to be reminded about your vieja, no?"

I snap my head to look him dead on, and he backs off, slipping the blade down his sock quickly. My blood boils, and the rage that brews inside takes an effort to keep under control.

The guy smiles, dismissing his threats in exchange for a light chuckle, saying, "Whoa, mi amigo. Relax."

"Relax? You mention my *vieja*, and you expect me to relax? I don't need a reminder, and I'm not your amigo. Next time you talk to my boss, you remind him that loyalties lie thick, sometimes in a pool of blood."

He gives a curt nod, taking in my words, and then I add, "You threaten me again, I'll turn you into a prag and stick a brinker on your ass."

He laughs, stands, and before walking away, shakes his head, saying, "You surprise me, blanco." And then, with a smile, adds, "I'll let the boss know we're good."

"You do that."

"I HAD TO lift my bra, Cal!"

"What? Why?"

"Apparently, I look more suspicious than the garbage I was standing in line with," Camilla whispers under her breath and then takes a scan of the room to make sure no one else heard her. "It was utterly degrading."

Sitting at the small table, across from the woman who's loved me for the past year, I'm pissed at the scum that got to see my doll's tits when I haven't had the privilege since they arrested me. She's mortified and angry and completely out of place. She always stands out like a sore thumb when she visits me, dressed in her designer clothes, but that's my Camilla.

"I miss you, love."

"The waiting is killing me. I know it isn't fair for me to say that when you're locked up in here, but I feel like I'm in a constant state of anxiety," she says.

I haven't told her about the plea deal that was put on the table because she'd have me do anything, throw whoever they wanted under the bus, just to get me back.

"The case will be taken to grand jury soon enough. That's the first step. But in the meantime, I need you to do something for me, okay?"

"Okay."

"First, any update on the Vanderwal murder?" I ask since you can't get the guards to turn the TV to any of the news stations.

"The whole company in under investigation, but for what, the public isn't aware of yet." She releases a heavy sigh, leans forward, and grows emotional. "What am I supposed to do, Cal? It's only a matter of time before this all hits the press. Everyone will know; our names will be smeared all over the place."

"My words are safe with you, right?"

"You don't even have to question that. Of course they are. They always have been. I love you and will do anything for you, you know that."

"I just needed to hear it again. This place messes with my head," I tell her, but I know I can trust her. She's unlike any woman I've ever loved. She may be twenty-three years younger than me, but she's a fighter. After my arrest, I came clean to her about the illegal activity I'd been involved with. I told her everything and she didn't disappoint when she offered to tell the authorities whatever it was I wanted her to. This woman would lie, cheat, and steal for me, and I love her even more for that. So as she sits here, prim and proper against the trash of the city's misfits, I smile inside to know she'd probably fight dirtier than most of them, and she'd look simply gorgeous doing it.

"What about his wife? Has she been in the news?"

"No. The coverage is so limited at this point. The police are keeping a tight lip while the case is being investigated."

I give a nod, and then she adds, "Honey?"

"What is it?"

"Have you thought any more on calling your son? Don't you think he should know?"

Clapping my hands together, I rest my forearms on the table. "Not yet."

"I could call him."

I shake my head, saying, "Lachlan mentioned a girl he's been spending time with in Gala. Elizabeth Archer. Can you remember that name?"

"Elizabeth Archer," she repeats. "Yes. Why?"

"I need to know who she is and what interest she has in my son. Lachlan told me she's only been in Scotland for a short time. I couldn't get too much information because the call was cut short."

"Who do you think she is?"

"Don't know. But someone shot Declan within days of Bennett's murder, and he refused to mention who. There's a link in this somewhere; I know it."

"This is so unfair," she voices. "I mean, you never hurt anyone. I don't know why you're sitting here in jail and not the others who are involved.

Why don't you give up their names?"

"You know why, Camilla. We've already talked about it. These aren't the types of people you turn your back on. This business is much bigger than me. And knowing the amounts of money I've been laundering and the lives at stake if someone were to blow the whistle, I'd be killed."

"I know we've talked about it, it's just . . . "

"Look," I say, wanting her to not get wrapped up in the emotions of it all. "For right now, just focus on taking care of yourself. Focus on figuring out who this girl is that's spending time with Declan. I don't want you getting hung up on things that are out of our control right now, all right?"

Nodding, she yields, "All right."

twenty-four

STEPPING FOOT ON foreign soil feels freeing. I'm relieved of the weight I've been bearing on my back, and it's a welcome change to be able to walk around without constantly looking over my shoulder.

I arrived here in Scotland yesterday, and after getting my first night of solid rest in a long time, I woke up this morning, revived.

But now, it's business.

Finding her is my ticket to freedom.

So when I open up my laptop, I start searching with the two names I'm already aware of that she uses: Nina Vanderwal and Elizabeth Archer.

"HELLO?" I ANSWER when my cell rings.

"Elizabeth, it's Lachlan."

His voice disappoints. Ever since Declan came to me and asked me not to leave, I've been hoping to hear from him, but so far, nothing.

"Hi."

"I was wondering if we could get together. I have some information about your mother."

A slight jolt of adrenaline rushes my body. Or is it anxiety? Fear, maybe? I don't know what it is exactly, but it awakens something inside of me, and I ask, "You found her?"

"Yes. Do you have time to meet me?"

"Are you in town?" I ask, knowing he lives over an hour away in Edinburgh.

"I can be. You just tell me what works for you."

"I can come to the city."

"Are you sure?"

"Yeah," I respond. "It'll be nice to have a little change of scenery."

Honestly, I just need a distraction. I spent all of yesterday moping around after having Declan here the night before. The tangled mess of this situation is driving me to madness. Trying to deal with the wound I opened the other night is proving to be too much for me to cope with.

And when one wound opens, so does another.

With the rousing of the shame and disgust of my past that I'd forced to lie dormant for so long, I needed a vice to help me grapple with the war inside of me. So I did what I'm becoming good at, and when the tranquility of blood running down my neck faded, I hammered my fists into my thighs. I wasn't sated until I could finally see the blood pooling beneath my skin. Mutilated alabaster.

I hang up with Lachlan after I jot down his address and grab my scarf and coat. I head out and make the drive to Edinburgh. When I turn onto Merchiston Gardens, I'm greeted with beautiful Victorian homes.

"Did you have any problems finding it?" Lachlan asks when he opens the front door after I pull up to his house.

"I'm in a foreign country," I tease. "I always have problems when I drive here."

He laughs, and as I approach, he remarks with jest, "Well, you appear unscathed, and the car still looks to be in one piece."

"Lucky car," I respond with a wink before stepping into the foyer.

The walls are bathed in rich taupes, ivories, and wines with hardwood floors and large bay windows. The house is airy with lots of natural lighting.

"Lovely home."

Walking past me, I follow Lachlan through the house to a formal sitting area.

"Can I get you a drink?" he offers.

"No, thank you." Slipping off my coat, I drape it over the couch and take a seat with Lachlan sitting adjacent to me. "Impressive."

He laughs, saying, "You're being generous. One could say I was slumming it when compared to the likes of your man's Brunswickhill."

"My man?"

"Isn't he?"

Continuing the light banter, which tends to come easily between the two of us, I say, "Well, for anyone who knows Declan, you're instantly aware that no one stakes claim on him. He operates on the contrary." Crossing my legs, I chuckle, adding, "Total control freak."

"Try working for him."

His words perplex, and I question, "You work for him?" and when he nods, I note, "You failed to mention that."

"You failed to ask."

"Is there anything else I've failed to ask that I should be aware of?"

"Oh, yes," he exaggerates in humor. "But where's the fun in transparency?"

"Man of mystery."

He smiles, and I laugh.

"So, tell me, Lachlan. What is it that you do for Declan?"

"I manage his finances among other things. And what about you?"

"Me?"

"What do you do for a profession?"

His question perturbs, and I deflect, "I prefer to dabble instead of commit to a singular entity."

"Entrepreneur?"

"Isn't that just a fancy word for *unemployed?*"

"Which do you prefer?"

"Honest and straight forward," I tell him. "No reason to dress up the truth because when people realize the crudité is just a veggie platter, they feel cheated and the culprit looks like a fraud."

He laughs, but little does he know, *I'm* the crudité here. I'm a distorted hyperbole. At least that's what I *have* been. I'm trying to shed the guise because I need a solid ground of understanding to figure out who I am. What are the true fibers from which I'm woven?

And then I remember why I'm here, and I wonder, *Am I ready for this? Do I really want to know?* He told me he found her, the mother I've never known, and a multitude of questions begin to rain down: Did she ever love me? Did she love my dad? Why didn't she want me? Did she know my dad was in prison? Did she know I was in foster care? Why didn't she come for me? Why didn't she save me? How could she just dispose of me?

"Are you okay?" Lachlan questions, his voice thick with concern.

I flick my eyes up to him, realizing I let my mind drift and pull me away.

"Yes. I'm sorry." I shift, and leaving the humor behind, I say, "I'm a little uneasy."

"How so?" His voice mellows with the change in mood.

"Wondering if I want to open this door that's been closed my whole life."

"We don't have to do this," he tells me. "If you've changed your mind or you want to wait . . . it's up to you."

"Seems weird," I remark. "Sitting here with you—practically a stranger—and yet you know about my mother when she's nothing more than a question mark for me."

"She doesn't have to be a question mark. But if you're not ready . . . "

"I thought I was. Now I'm not so sure."

He stands up, walks over to the credenza, and picks up a manila envelope. My eyes follow him as he moves to me and sits by my side. Placing the envelope on my lap, he says, "I don't believe there's a right or wrong choice here, but if you do find yourself wanting to open the door to the mystery, it's all in there."

I run my hands along the paper that separates me from my mom, and my apprehension grows. It's the conundrum of whether this envelope holds hope or dejection. Will this lead me to answers or just create more questions? And do I even care? It's not like she means anything to me, *right?*

And then I wonder why I never did care enough to learn about her. Maybe it's because Pike was enough for me to fill that void of family. I mean, he never could fill the void of my father—nobody has the power to do that—but Pike did become my family. He was my protector and comfort, and I didn't feel like I needed anyone else because he was enough.

But now he's gone.

And so is Declan. Even though he keeps me around, he no longer belongs to me. But did he ever?

These few weeks since everything came crashing down, my loneliness has grown to a point of neediness. And now a part of me feels like I need this, whatever it is that's inside of this envelope.

"Tell me, Lachlan, are your parents still alive?" I ask in melancholy, confused about my feelings, wondering if there's anyone else here on this planet that can relate to me.

"Yes."

"Big or small family?"

"Big."

"Close?" I question.

"Yes."

Sad warmth creeps along my cheeks, and I take a moment to push the feeling aside before speaking again. "I never had that."

He doesn't respond, but what is there to say?

"Would you like a distraction?" he offers, and I sigh in exasperation, "Please."

His smile is friendly as it grows, and he takes my hand, guiding me to stand.

Handing me my coat, he says, "Let's get out of here."

He then takes me to Caffé e Cucina where we indulge ourselves with cappuccinos and kouignoù amann, which Lachlan promises I'll enjoy, and the French pastry doesn't disappoint.

We spend a leisurely few hours getting lost in conversation. He tells me stories about his time with Declan at St. Andrews, as well as a few funny tales from his own childhood in Scotland. I ask questions about the culture, as does he about life in the States. It surprises me to find out he's never been to the US. I tease him about eating beans for breakfast, and he teases me about the fact that getting a thirty-two ounce soda, or as he calls it, *fizzy juice,* is a commonality in the States.

Lachlan provides me with a good afternoon, doing exactly as he said he would by giving me a distraction. I haven't spent much time with him overall, but it's nice to feel like I have friend here, someone I can talk to and laugh with. Lachlan makes it easy for me to feel relaxed in his presence, and I enjoy our friendly banter.

But now, the joviality is gone as I sit here, back in my room in Gala. Since I returned, I've been sitting here with this envelope, debating on whether or not I should just throw it away, trash it, burn it. Or should I open it and read it. I asked Lachlan, since he knows what's enclosed, if it was worth me reading. His response was vague, telling me that people find comfort in various ways, and only I could make that decision.

And I did. You see, as much as life had failed me, as much as I wanted to pretend I didn't waste my time on hope anymore—I still hung on to it. And that evening, sitting in my quaint room at the Water Lily Bed & Breakfast in Galashiels of Scotland, I made my decision and allowed that hope to bloom inside of me. I thought that maybe, just maybe, I had a mother out there that wanted me but could never find me. That maybe the envelope held the key to my maternal Godsend. But what I learned next frightened me, and let me tell you, I wasn't a woman who frightened easily.

The first thing I see when I pull out the contents from the envelope is a mugshot of my mom. I recognize her face from the photo I've always had of her. But in this picture, she looks wrecked with a blotchy face and ratty hair. I stare into her eyes, eyes that look like mine. Along with the mugshot are a stack of court documents, a birth certificate, and a contact printout for Elgin Mental Health Center.

The State versus Gweneth Archer catches my eye when I begin to read. Her name's Gweneth. She's always had a face from the one picture I have of her, but I've never known her name until now. I start scanning the court documents, and my stomach begins to twist when I hit certain words. With jittery hands, I flip through the papers. My heart rate picks up in shock and confusion as my eyes dart back and forth, unable to focus on the sentences.

Defendant . . . Child Neglect . . . Abandonment . . . Illegal Sale of a Child . . . Communications Fraud . . .

Disbelief consumes me as I read the words. I grow frantic as I continue to scour through the papers. I will my eyes to focus on the words, but I feel myself on the verge of flipping out.

This can't be real. This can't be true.

Mental Illness . . . Postpartum Depression . . . Manic Depression . . .

I keep reading, and with each word my mind fights to process, I come unhinged. The room begins to tunnel around me, and my chest tightens, making it difficult to breathe.

Prosecutor: *"Mrs. Archer, did you negotiate the sale of your two-month-old daughter, Elizabeth Archer?"*

Defendant: "*Yes.*"

A hysterical explosion of tinnitus ricochets in my head, piercing, shooting an unrelenting blast of pain. My hands clutch tightly to the papers as my vision teeters in and out of focus. I squint, determined to read further, but I'm fading out fast when my eyes scan: *Not Guilty by Reason of Insanity.*

The papers drop, scattering across the floor as my hands shoot up to my ears in an attempt to mute the high-pitched ringing, but it's coming from inside my head. It's splitting my skull as it builds. The welling of every emotion inside of me creates an unbearable pressure, and I need release.

I can't take it.

It's so loud, so painful, too alive, too much.

Oh my God! She sold me.

Shuffling over my own feet, I have no balance as I move across the room. I can't hear anything aside from the squealing in my ears. I stumble and catch myself from falling, gripping on to the closet door handle. Gasping for breath, my eyes blur, and I begin crying—sobbing—wailing—screaming.

She never even wanted me.

Standing in the doorway to the closet, I grab on to the doorframe and hold tightly as I drop my head. My vision diminishes in a wild haze, and it's too much to contain. I can't handle the overwhelming hysteria inside of me anymore.

I can't do it.

I'm going to rupture.

I can't do it.

I can't.

Lifting my head, I dig my nails into the wood, splintering it with my forceful grip. In quick motions, I reel my head back, grit my teeth down, and use every ounce of force inside of me as I violently slam my head into the doorframe. Drawing back, I bear down and do it again, smashing my forehead into the solid wood. My vision bursts in pops of light.

There's a pounding knock on the door, but it sounds miles away.

Thick, warm blood runs down my forehead, over my eyes and nose and cheeks. My body gives out and slides down to the floor. The ringing dampens and my body tingles in gratification as the blood oozes from my gashed head.

I faintly hear the door handle to my room ricketing back and forth, and then there's banging.

"Open the door!"

I can't focus on the voice yelling outside my room as the ringing returns to my ears, and the words I just read run back through my mind. Leaning my head back, my eyes begin to burn with the mixture of my tears, blood, and makeup. The sounds that engulf are out of control and torturous.

The banging grows louder, and I move my eyes to focus on the door.

"Open the fucking door!"

I don't even flinch when I hear the crashing and splitting of wood as the door is being kicked down because I'm too far gone. I'm lost inside myself and nothing feels real anymore.

Another kick, and I watch in a daze as Declan storms over to me.

"Oh my God!" I hear a woman shriek, and I know it's Isla, but I keep my attention solely on Declan.

"Jesus!" he panics when his hands come to my face, but it all seems like a dream.

I can't even feel his touch; my body singes in radiant tingles, but somehow the flesh is utterly numb.

"I need wet towels!" he shouts, and the ringing inside me settles to a low, monotone hum. It's incessant.

"Should I call a medic?"

"No," he snaps at Isla before dabbing the wet towel to my face.

I feel nothing though.

Is my heart even beating?

I know it must be when I finally feel the pressure of touch, but it isn't from Declan. I roll my head to the side, and Pike is here with me. He takes my hand in his and holds it tightly.

"You're here."

"I'm always here."

"Yeah, darling. I'm here. What happened?"

I faintly hear Declan's voice, but it's almost an echo as I concentrate on Pike.

"I miss you so much," I say as I begin to weep through a new slew of tears.

"Talk to me."

"I'm right here, Elizabeth. Don't cry."

"She never wanted me," I choke out.

"Who?"

"Who?"

"My mother. She sold me."

"Fuck her. You never needed her anyway."

"Shh . . . Just breathe, okay?"

"I need someone though. I'm so alone," I say to Pike.

"You're not alone," he insists and then nods his head towards Declan.

I briefly look over, and his hands are still on me, pressing a towel firmly over the top of my head. When I look back to Pike, I admonish, "He doesn't want me. He only pities the pathetic waste he now knows I am."

"Elizabeth, what are you talking about?"

"He cares for you. Why else would he be here right now?"

"How could he care about me after what I did?"

"Love is love. It doesn't just vanish."

"How can you be so sure about that?"

His hand squeezes mine, soothing the chills that now start to wrack me and leans over to whisper softly in my ear, *"Because even though you shot and killed me, I still love you with every little piece of my heart. I still want to give you the world."*

"How can I be sure of what? What are you talking about?" Declan's distant voice questions me, thinking I'm talking to him.

"Is she going to be okay?"

"She's fine! Please go and give us some space, will you?"

I barely hear Declan and Isla, but my eyes never leave my brother's as more tears fall. How can he still love me when I'm so unlovable?

"I'm so sorry," I cry. "I want to take it back so bad, Pike, but I can't! I don't know how."

"Darling, look at me. Who're you talking to?"

"Tell me how, Pike. How do I go back and fix this?"

"You can't."

The finality of my choices, knowing they can't be undone, is a horrendous weight I carry with me now. A weight I doubt I can carry for much longer.

"Elizabeth, look at me! Focus!"

"Look at him, Elizabeth."

"He doesn't love me. It hurts to look at him."

"He hides it, but if you look close enough, you can see his cracks."

"But what about you? I want you to stay. I want you back," I plead like a small child begging for something that's impossible, but I beg anyway.

"You have me inside of you. I can't get any closer than that."

"God dammit, look at me!"

"You're scaring him," he tells me in a calm voice and then urges one last time, *"Look at him, Elizabeth."*

And when I do, one touch is exchanged for another. My hand grows cold as my face warms under Declan's touch, and I begin to sob uncontrollably at the switch.

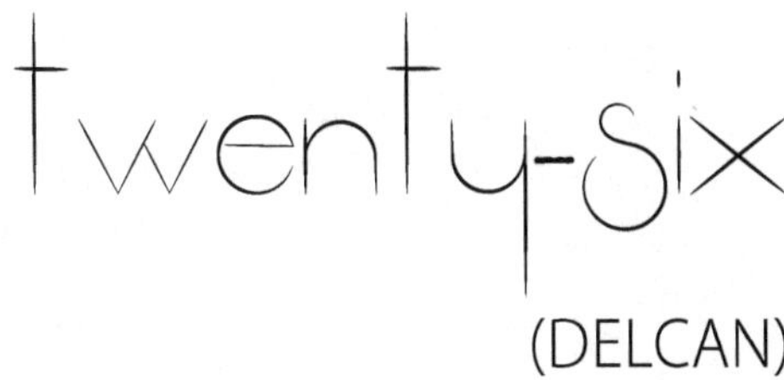

twenty-six

(DELCAN)

"I'M SO SORRY," she wails, but she isn't looking at me. "I want to take it back so bad, Pike, but I can't! I don't know how."

Did she just say Pike? What the fuck is going on?

"Darling, look at me. Who're you talking to?" I ask as I press the now blood-soaked towel on Elizabeth's head, trying to clot the bleeding. But it's as if she doesn't even hear me when she continues to talk to nobody.

"Tell me how, Pike. How do I go back and fix this?"

"Elizabeth, look at me! Focus!" I yell at her, needing to get her to snap out of whatever hallucination she's having.

"He doesn't love me," she goes on. "It hurts to look at him."

Fuck, what's going on with her? She's scaring the shit out of me with her cryptic eyes and this arcane conversation.

"But what about you? I want you to stay. I want you back."

"God dammit, look at me!" I yell again, grabbing her shoulders and shaking her.

Slowly, she finally turns her head and raises her eyes to mine. My hands now cradle her face, and after a couple blinks, she crumples over and starts bawling—completely broken. I hold her as my heart pounds in turbulent beats, confused as shit.

The adrenaline in my system slowly wanes as I sit on the floor with her. Her blood is everywhere, and I still don't have a clue as to what the hell happened in this room before I kicked down the door.

Her body suddenly jolts, hands cup her ears, and her face pinches as she releases a ghastly scream. Horror storms through me, and I grab her shoulders to pull her up.

Her eyes are clenched shut as she cries out, "It's so loud! Make it stop!"

"Make what stop? Tell me what's going on," I urge.

She reaches her hand back behind her, and as I'm trying to get her to open her eyes and calm down, I'm horrified when I catch her clawing at her scalp. She writhes, hissing in an agonizing breath. Urgently, I scramble around her, grabbing her arms to restrain them behind her back. She struggles to get loose, but I tighten my hold when I see the grotesque scab that she's dug her nails into and ripped off.

Fucking Christ, this girl is having a complete breakdown.

"Stop fighting me," I demand harshly.

But she doesn't stop as she cries out, "It's so loud. Let go of me!"

"Breathe. Stop fighting me and just breathe."

I then let go of her arms, but quickly pin them to her sides when I band my arms tightly around her chest, taking control over her. It's harder for her to fight me and jerk around from this position, but she keeps trying. So, I hold her until she begins to tire, all the while, doing my best to keep an even tone as I continue my attempts to soothe her, repeating over and over, "It's okay . . . You're safe . . . Breathe."

When her body weakens, losing the tension, and sinking back into me, I release my firm hold on her. She's quiet and pulls in long, deep breaths. I don't know what the fuck is going on with her, but I do know she's losing her shit. The fact that she's hiding away here and inflicting these attacks on her body is beyond disturbing. One has to wonder if she's suicidal. And the fact that I just caught her having a full conversation with someone that doesn't even exist anymore is insane.

I don't know what to do, but I know I can't leave her alone here. God only knows what she'll attempt next. So, I stand and gather all the papers that are strewn on the floor, then scoop her up into my arms. Her blood is all over me and streaked down her face. Her body folds into me, and I get her the fuck out of here.

"Is she okay? Where are you taking her?" Isla asks in worriment as I make my way to the front door.

"She's fine. I'm taking her to my place."

Walking out into the biting chill of the night, I put her in my SUV. She doesn't speak; she's completely absent. I strap the seatbelt around her and start heading to my house.

While I drive, I pull out my cell and make a call to a friend of mine whose wife is a doctor. I stress to my friend the urgency of the situation, and after he explains what's going on to his wife, she agrees to meet me at the house.

Once we make it back to my place, I carry her in my arms upstairs to get her in the shower and cleaned up. She's totally withdrawn as I begin to remove her clothing. When I have her stripped down, I'm appalled by what I see.

She's covered in a vast array of bruises: blue, purple, green, yellow, brown. They're all over her chest, stomach, and thighs—blotches of muted colors.

"Did you do this to yourself?" I ask, but she doesn't respond. She keeps her eyes downcast and doesn't utter a word. "Look at me."

But she doesn't.

I duck my head to try and catch her eyes, but I get nothing but desolation. Turning on the water, I strip my clothes off as well and then help her into the shower. She stands, unmoving, as I wash her. The water turns red as it runs over our bodies, taking the blood down the drain.

I keep moving to distract myself, but after we're both clean, everything slows. Standing under the hot water, I see a girl I've never seen before. She's severed and lost and weak. She's nothing like the woman I met in Chicago—*Nina.* And I begin to wonder how different these two people truly are.

Who is Elizabeth? Is she anything like Nina? Strong? Snarky? Funny? Smart? Who is this girl standing in front me?

I run my hands over her cheeks and cup her jaw, angling her head up to me. Her eyes shift to mine, and as I look into her, I murmur, "Who are you, Elizabeth?"

She blinks, no expression to her face, and after what feels like hours, she finally responds in chilled words, "I'm nobody."

And as mad as I am at her, as much as I hate her, as much as I want to celebrate her downfall, I have the urge to convince her that she *is* someone. I want to remind her of all the reasons I fell in love with her, but who's to know if those reasons were just products of her deception. I need a ballast of understanding with her, but I don't know if that will ever come.

And what would I even do if I got it?

There's so much I want to say, so many questions, but I know this isn't the moment for any of that. Turning off the water, I grab some towels, tying one around my waist before I get her wrapped up.

I lead her to the bed and sit her down, saying, "Stay here. I'll be right back with some clothes."

I rush to my room to toss on my sleep pants and a t-shirt before returning with a pair of my boxers and a shirt for her. I get her dressed and lay her down in the bed. She remains quiet; I don't even attempt to speak when she rolls onto her side, facing away from me. I know she's got to be physically and emotionally drained, and I want to let her rest, but I also don't trust her to leave her alone right now.

So while I wait for Kyla to arrive, I pick up the envelope that contains the papers I took from Elizabeth's room and take a seat on one of the chairs in the corner of the room by the windows. I pull out the sheaf of documents, and start riffling through them to get them in order before I start to read.

The information contained in the court documents is unsettling, and I can't believe what I'm reading. I spend the next half hour going over her mother's testimony where she admits wanting to terminate the pregnancy when she learned about it, but her husband begged her to keep it for him, so she did. But that after the baby was born, she grew depressed and started having thoughts of harming and even killing Elizabeth when she was an infant. How she felt her husband loved their daughter more than her. And eventually, how she secretly handled the selling of the baby to some guy she met through friends who lived in Kentucky.

The intercom buzzes, alerting someone's at the gate, snapping me out of my engrossed thoughts.

Setting the papers down on the side table, I walk over to the bed and am shocked to see she's still awake as she stares out the window blankly.

"Are you okay?"

No answer.

"I need to run downstairs for a moment," I tell her, but still, no returned response.

Before I walk out of the room, I push the button on the intercom to open the gate and then head downstairs to meet Kyla.

"Thank you for coming on such short notice," I tell her when she enters my home.

"Alick stressed how important it was for you to keep this matter private."

"Yes. The last thing I need is for some reporter to start digging around if it were to be mentioned I was at the hospital with a woman."

Her smile is warm, and when she touches my arm, she says, "You and Alick have been friends for years, and although you and I don't know each other that well, I want you to know that you can trust me."

"Thank you."

"Before I check on the girl—"

"Her name's Elizabeth," I interrupt, my stomach still knotted tightly from reading about her mother.

"Before I examine Elizabeth, can you tell me what happened tonight?"

"I received a call from a friend, letting me know she would be learning something that would probably upset her."

Her brows rise in confusion.

"The details aren't important, but needless to say, she didn't take the news well. After I ended the call with my friend, I rushed over to where she's been staying, wanting to check in on her, and when I arrived, she had locked herself in her room. She was screaming like a maniac and crying. I kicked the door down and she was covered in blood. She must have smashed her head against something. There was blood everywhere. She had calmed a little and began talking. I thought she was talking to me, so I was responding to her, but she wasn't looking at me. And then she mentioned someone else's name," I tell her, not wanting to reveal too much detail. "She must've been hallucinating, and then it was like her whole body was in pain and she started complaining about a ringing in her head."

"Has she had episodes like this before?"

"I'm assuming, but I don't know for sure. When I brought her back here, I put her in the shower, and her whole body is covered in bruises. It's like she's been beating herself. I know she has this wound on her head that she's been picking at."

"Is she on any medications that you know of?"

"No. I don't know."

"It's okay," she assures and then asks to see her.

I lead her up the stairs and into the guest room where I left her. I stand off to the side while Kyla walks around the bed to talk to Elizabeth.

"Hi there. I'm Dr. Allaway. Can you tell me your name?"

I look on, waiting for some sort of movement, but there's no shift when I hear her weak voice answer, "Elizabeth."

"Last name?"

"Archer."

Kyla sets her medical bag on the nightstand and begins asking Elizabeth a series of questions about the evening's events. Kyla helps adjust Elizabeth in bed and sits her up with a stack of pillows behind her back. They begin talking, and Elizabeth's voice sounds hollow as she explains about her mother, and I can tell by what she's saying that she doesn't know the extent of the facts like I do. She probably just read a few words and got herself so worked up, she exploded.

"Was there anyone else in the room with you and Declan?" she questions, knowing I had mentioned witnessing her talking to someone that wasn't there.

I lean against the wall, silent, with my arms crossed over my chest when I catch her eyes glossing over with tears.

She nods, and Kyla asks, "Who else was there?"

"My brother," she answers weakly.

"Can you tell me where your brother is now?"

"I'm not crazy," Elizabeth immediately defends.

"No one said you were. But I need you to be honest with me so that I can help you."

"You can't help me."

"Will you let me try?" she offers. "We don't have to talk about your brother right now if you don't want to, but would you let me take a look at your head?"

Kyla begins to treat the wounds on her forehead and also the one on the back of her head. She then moves to examine the bruises on her body along with taking her vitals. While she does all this, she continues to talk to Elizabeth, and soon she reveals, "Sometimes when I'm really upset or stressed, I see my brother. He talks to me and calms me down."

Once she is finished, she writes a prescription for a mood stabilizer and as I walk her out, she tells me, "I'd like to see her again, but I'd like her to also visit with a psychiatrist. Like I said, I don't know much about this case or the patient's family history, but my first thought is that she's most likely dealing with an untreated depressive episode with some congruent psychosis."

"What does that mean?"

"There's no doubt she is terribly depressed right now, but that coupled with seeing and hearing things that don't exist along with her erratic behaviors raise quite a few red flags. It's actually a good sign though that her hallucinations seem to be related to her distress."

"I've never known her to be this unstable though," I tell her, thinking back to the time we shared in Chicago. She was always so pulled together and witty. Sure she would have these moments of sadness, but nothing like this.

"It's not an entirely uncommon reaction and most often it surfaces under times of extreme stress," she informs. "She also has a slight concussion from her head trauma. Nothing serious, but I would strongly suggest that you make sure you are waking her up every two to three hours, okay?"

"Of course."

"I'll email you a list of doctors I would recommend for her to visit when I get to the office tomorrow."

When she puts her coat on, I hand her back her bag, saying, "I cannot thank you enough for this."

She smiles and gives a nod. "If you need anything else or notice any changes in her, please call me." I watch as she walks to her car, and before she gets in, she reminds, "And get that script filled."

"Drive safely."

Walking back inside, I immediately pull out my cell and call Lachlan.

He picks up on the second ring. "Hello?"

"What the fuck were you thinking calling me *after* you gave her the information on her mother?" I snap.

"Is everything okay?"

"I told you I wanted to know as soon as you knew, not after you met with her. If you're finding it difficult to follow my very simple instructions, maybe you'd be better suited to work for someone who doesn't give a shit about attention to detail."

"It was a complete oversight on my part; I apologize."

"You knew what the fuck was in those court documents, and your *oversight* was in complete negligence."

"Agreed."

"How the hell did you get your hands on those documents with the case involving a minor anyway?" I ask.

"Luckily I know someone who knows someone that I was able to pay off in exchange for papers," he explains, and then asks, "She read them?"

"Yeah, she read them."

"Is she okay?"

"Not of your concern. I think you're forgetting that your priorities are with me. I want you to stop following her because it seems you're sidetracked, and I don't want another *oversight* on your part," I berate and then disconnect the call.

When I turn around, I stop in my tracks when I see Elizabeth standing at the foot of the stairs.

"You were having me followed?"

twenty-seven

"DO YOU BLAME me?" he says after I question him.

And he's right, I can't blame him. How can I expect him not to be suspicious of me?

His face is soured in frustration as he walks towards me. He brushes my shoulder as he passes, saying, "Go to bed," and then heads up the stairs.

"Why am I here?"

He turns and looks down to me. "Because I don't trust you to be alone with yourself." He begins walking back up the stairs, and a few steps later, adds without making any eye contact with me, "The doctor says you have a slight concussion, and I'm to wake you every couple hours. You should get some rest."

"Why are you so cold? You're so on and off," I question, confused by this push and pull he has with me.

"Certainly you don't need reminding, do you?"

I watch as he ascends, and I'm left alone in the silence of his home. His demeanor shifts in a snap, and I can only assume that whoever he was just talking to on the phone is the cause for that sudden snap. I don't worry about being followed because I deserve the distrust.

Making my way back up the stairs, I notice the door to his room is open and quietly pad over. When I look in, he's lying on top of his perfectly made bed. His hands folded behind his head, ankles crossed, and staring up at the ceiling. I'm allowed a moment to absorb him before he senses my presence.

With his body remaining still and his eyes fixed to the ceiling, he says without any inflection, "Get out of my room."

His tone is even, but I can hear the animosity deep within. So I go to the room he's put me in and crawl under the sheets. There's a disconnection inside of me, no doubt due to the extremities of this evening. Maybe I should be embarrassed that Declan saw me coming completely undone like he did, but I'm numb to emotion right now. My body is depleted, and to dissect this whole situation would take more energy than I have. So I roll to my side and stare out of the large windows at the full moon that lights the night's ink and slowly drift away.

WHISPERS CATCH ME, wrapping their sweet timbres around my heart, and gently pull me out of my slumber.

"Elizabeth," his soft rasp calls to me. "Open your eyes."

Fingers comb through my hair, and the touch sends a sparkling shiver through me, warming me from the inside and rousing me awake.

Declan sits on the edge of the bed, hand cupping the side of my head as he looks down upon me. And he's so beautiful, I question if I'm still dreaming.

"Are you feeling okay?"

Exhaustion is all over me, and as much as I want to stay up with him, my eyes drop. I'm able to answer his question with a nod before sleep takes over.

LIGHT FILTERS THROUGH my lids, and when my eyes flutter open, I see Declan moving about the bathroom. When he emerges in the doorway with a glass of water, he flicks the light off, darkening the room. I'm in a haze as his shadow moves closer to me, and when I feel the bed dip, my arm instinctually reaches out for him.

"Here," he says. "Take these."

Dropping a couple painkillers in my hand, I put them in my mouth and then take a sip from the glass of water he gives me. My head falls back to the pillow, weighing a thousand pounds and throbbing with an oncoming headache. I release an appreciative hum at the fact Declan was a step ahead of me in knowing I would need the pain relief. And with my eyes closed, the haze thickens, and I sink into darkness.

GASPING HARD, I'M knocked out of a dead sleep as my body shoots up. Eyes flash open wide and I clutch my chest, panting loudly. My head is clouded with sleep as it strains to catch up to my alert body. Looking around my unfamiliar surroundings, I panic. Everything is disoriented.

"Elizabeth."

My attention flies to the doorway of the room where Declan is standing, and it's then my confusion dissipates into clarity.

"Are you okay?" he questions as he walks over to me and sits down on the bed.

"Yeah," I tremble.

"What happened?"

"I don't know. Bad dream, I guess."

We sit, facing each other, and I notice he's no longer wearing his shirt, and the moment my eyes catch it, I choke on a strangled breath.

It's there, on his chest—my disgrace.

The unmistakable proof.

The reality of my fraudulence.

My focus is locked on what remains from my twisted game. It mars his perfect body.

Two gunshot wounds branded on his left pec, tainting his chest in my scum.

My pulse quickens, and when he looks down to see what has me so shaken, my heart reunites with the anguish from when I thought I'd lost him forever.

My hand lifts, and he doesn't stop me when I reach out and brush my fingertips over the bullet wounds. The raised flesh that hides the deep scar tissue beneath splinters me to the core.

I keep my eyes on his chest as he allows me this touch, and when my chin starts to quiver, I force my words out around the lump lodged in my throat, and the tears slip. "I thought you were dead."

And in an unexpected move, a tender gesture I never thought I'd get again, he cups my face and licks my tears. My hands grip tightly to his wrists as he cradles my cheeks. Closing my eyes, I lean into his mouth as he swallows my salts.

In an unrushed moment, his lick eclipses into a silken kiss that erupts a wondrous rekindling inside of my womb. Whether I believe his emotions to be real or not, I pretend that they are, because I want his love so badly. I want to believe his lips are genuine and they mean exactly what my heart yearns for them to mean.

I calm as we now share the same breath. My hands still cling to his wrists because I need the support of his strength in this moment. Opening my lips with his, he sinks his tongue deep inside of my mouth, claiming and binding us together.

His taste is home—familiar and delicious.

My body begins to swim in bliss when he lays me down on my back, and my legs fall open for him. He's incredibly hard, pressing himself against me. I whimper as his kisses become more intent. His lips begin to move fervently, rapturing my mouth, and I meld to him, allowing him to take take take. I'd give him my last breath if that's what he desired.

He's my body's epitaph.

His intensity grows and we're nothing but wild heartbeats, frantic breaths, bleeding lips, broken souls. We cling, grab, and claw our way to incomprehensible closeness. His mouth finds the curve of my neck, and I writhe in pleasure as he bites me, marking my flesh, breaking through the delicate tissue, bleeding me out for him to taste.

He growls deeply, chest vibrating against mine. Reaching down, he grabs the hem of my shirt and pulls it up, but quickly stops. Bracing himself above me, he looks down at my stomach, and when my eyes move to see what's pulled him away from me, my gut turns. I've mutilated my skin, gifting it with monstrous bruises.

Declan drops his head, the tips of his hair brushing along my stomach. The moment my hands touch his head, he snaps up and pushes himself off of me. I sit up and instantly miss him as I watch his sudden change. His eyes narrow then pinch shut as ache penetrates his face.

What he's able to mend inside of me so quickly, he shatters even faster.

He stands and walks away, depleting the goodness he just filled me with. But before he leaves, he turns back, and says, "You breathe deceitful fumes; I can taste it when we kiss."

And then he's gone, leaving me an empty mess, not wanting to think about the war that's going on inside of him, because that war will always cast back to me, and I can't deal with the responsibility of that burden in this moment. I'm too weak.

WHEN THE SUN begins to shine through the windows, I wake. My head is already throbbing as I stretch and sit up, tired from being woken up all through the night. I had a hard time falling back to sleep after kissing Declan, and when I walk to the bathroom, my darkened eyes confirm.

I rummage around but find no toiletries. All my belongings are back at

Isla's. I shiver from the chill in the house as I make my way to Declan's room, but it's empty.

"What are you doing?" he asks, startling me, and when I turn around, he's walking up the stairs with a mug in each hand.

"I woke up, and . . . I was just looking for you. I wanted to freshen up, but there was nothing in the bathroom."

He hands me one of the mugs, and I'm instantly greeted with a fragrant floral spice from the tea he made for me.

"Umm . . . thanks," I mumble when he moves past me and into his bedroom.

I don't know whether I should follow him, so I stay put, but I don't have to wait long for him to return with his leather toiletry bag I remember from his loft back in Chicago.

"Here," he says as he hands it to me. "You can use my things."

He then walks into my room, and this time, I follow. He takes a seat in the sitting area by the windows, and I go into the bathroom, closing the door behind me. I open his bag, pull out his toothbrush, and take comfort in using it along with his deodorant. I brush my hair, careful not to rip off the bandage the doctor put over the scab on the back of my head.

When I walk out, he's made himself comfortable, looking pulled together in slacks and a crisp, charcoal button-up. But I can see the exhaustion in his eyes as well. I walk over and slip back into bed, covering up in the warm blankets, sitting against the upholstered headboard. I take a sip from my cup of tea and look over to Declan who's flipping through a stack of papers.

"Are those . . . ?"

He raises his head and says, "I wanted to know what upset you, so I took them from your room."

"Did you . . . I mean, have you . . . ?" I fumble with my words as my anxiety picks up, remembering what I read.

"I figured it would be best to talk about this and deal with it head on instead of it taking control over you."

Shaking my head, I tell him, "I don't want to talk about it, Declan."

"Why?"

Putting the tea aside on the nightstand, I wilt down in the bed and give him my honest thoughts. "Because it hurts too much. Because talking won't change it. Because my life is already too screwed up for me to handle."

He sets the papers down on the coffee table in front of him, leans forward, and says, "Ignoring it is only going to make it hurt worse. That's your problem, Ni—Elizabeth." Shaking his head at his near slip, he looks back to me and continues, "You hide everything, and when you do that, you give those things power over you."

"I don't."

"You don't think so?"

"No," I respond, and he releases annoyance in a sigh, saying, "Then explain last night to me."

"That wasn't—"

"Have you looked at yourself lately?" he chides. "A woman who's in control wouldn't be smashing her head into a fucking wall."

"You don't understand," I defend.

"Then please, explain it to me. Make me understand why your body is covered in contusions."

His glare is sharp, pinning his frustrations to me as I sit here awkwardly. Knowing how Declan saw me last night, knowing the things I've revealed to him, I feel denuded of my armor I'm used to hiding behind. I've laid myself bare to this man, but now I want to hide again. I want to throw the façade on and lash my crude words at him. Push him out of the honesty I've been giving him.

But he sees me wanting to avoid when he presses, "I want you to tell me why you're determined to destroy yourself. Tell me why."

Shaking my head, I stutter, "I don't . . . You wouldn't understand . . . I can't . . . "

"Why hide now? Why? Just talk to me. Tell me."

But I doubt he would even understand if I told him. I barely understand it myself. As I continue to avoid answering, he stands up and walks over to me, sitting on the bed in front of me. His closeness, especially after kissing him last night, unsettles me, and I let my fear grow.

With a rigid tone, heavy with his brogue, he says, "Help me figure you out. Tell me why you're hurting yourself."

"I'm not . . . " I begin when I hear the tribulation in the cracks of his stern voice. I give in to his request because I know he deserves it. I owe him whatever it is that he wants. "I'm not hurting myself."

"I don't understand."

"It makes me feel better," I confess. "When I'm hurting, *really hurting,* I hit myself and it takes the hurt away."

"You're wrong. You're just masking the pain; you're not getting rid of it."

"But I don't know how to get rid of it."

"You deal with it. You talk about it and face it and process it."

His words are reminiscent of Carnegie's. He once told me something very similar when I spoke with him about Bennett. But the thing is, to face a pain like that takes a particular type of strength I don't possess.

"But what about you?" I accuse. "You hide."

"I do," he admits freely. "I miss my mum, and I hide from that whole fucked up situation. But it's not eating at me the way you allow things to eat at you. I'm not the one throwing punches at myself, *you are.*"

His words are caustic. They piss me off because they're true. He's right, and I hate that. I hate that I've become transparent to him. Hate that I've allowed that. Gone is the camouflage. I left it behind for atonement, for repentance.

"I don't know how to do this," I concede.

He gives an understanding nod. "I know. I just want you to talk, that's all."

"About my mom?"

"It's a good place to start."

"What's to say? I mean, I'm scared to know too much," I tell him, struggling to not break down.

"Too much? Did you not read through everything?"

"No. I was so upset, that I . . . I just couldn't read it. I couldn't focus."

He insists that I need to know, so I sit and listen to him tell me the documented facts of how and why my mother sold me to some guy she barely knew. And the fabricated story she told my father and the police that I was kidnapped when she left me in my car seat unattended while she went inside a gas station to pay.

He speaks in detail as I sit here like a stone, forcing my feelings away. I keep my breathing as even as I can as I concentrate on restoring my steel cage while he continues to tell me about her mental instability. She had extreme postpartum depression and was later diagnosed with manic depression and deemed insane by the courts, which is why she was sentenced to a state mental hospital instead of prison.

"Say something."

I keep my eyes downcast, afraid if I look at him, I won't be able to hold myself together as well as I'm doing right now. "Is she still there?"

"No. She was released after serving twelve years."

"What?" I blurt out in disbelief, finally looking up to Declan. "But . . . I was still a kid. Why didn't she come for me?"

"She relinquished her parental rights."

My thoughts begin to collide in my head, and when I turn my face away, he catches me. "Don't do that. Don't avoid."

"Why am I so unlovable?"

"Look at me," he demands, and when I do, his face is blurred through my unshed tears. "Your mum was sick. She—"

"What the fuck are you doing?" I scream in disbelief. "Why are you defending her?"

"I'm not defending, I'm being rational."

"You can't rationalize what she did," I throw at him. "She sold me! What if the police had never found me? But she didn't care what happened to me as long as she got what she wanted."

"You don't think it's worth making sense out of? To find any semblance of understanding?"

"Are you kidding me? No! What she did was wrong! People like her don't deserve understanding!"

"You mean people like you?" he throws at me.

"What?"

"How is what she did any different than what you did?"

His assumption that I'm anything like the woman who sold me pisses me off, and I snap, "What the hell is that supposed to mean?"

"I'm talking about *you.* Why did you marry Bennett? Why did you make me fall for you? Why did you lie?"

"It's not the same," I state, refusing to believe I'm of the same vile nature as my mother.

"Because you wanted something to make you feel better. Because you were only thinking of yourself and you didn't care what happened to the people who came in your path or that you destroyed," he answers for me in growing rage.

His words shut me up. I don't want to acknowledge the parallels, but it's there, unmistakably. He just threw it in my face.

"She knew better," I poorly argue.

"So did you," he affirms.

"I can't forgive her for what she did."

"No one is saying you have to. I just want you to face the facts and deal with it. I don't care how you deal with it as long as you do something with the information instead of hiding from it," he says. "And yes, what she did was awful, and it makes no sense, but neither do your actions."

"And neither do *your* actions, Declan," I condemn, and he knows exactly what my words imply.

"No, you're right. I can't make sense out of the things I've done to you. But I do know enough to recognize that ever since I took a man's life, I haven't been the same. I carry an appalling amount of animosity inside of me that I don't know how to deal with."

"So we're all just screwed up?"

"To some degree, yes," he responds. "I don't want to downplay what your mother did, that's not what I'm trying to do. I just want you to face the facts and do something with it."

And I see his point, because it doesn't even take me a second thought to know I don't want to resemble that woman in the slightest. I don't want that hostility living and breeding inside of me anymore. I want to let go of the resentment. I want to let go of the blame. I want to let go of the constant fiending for payback. But sometimes we don't get what we want, and even though I want to be without it, a part of me will probably always want to hang on to it.

twenty-eight

I AIM MY foot to land on the small patch of snow just to hear it crunch under my rain boot. The sound brings me a tiny piece of joy as I walk the grounds. The snow started to melt away yesterday when the sun finally peeked out from behind the heavy blanket of grey clouds. But today is another dank day, cold and damp.

Declan still has me here at his house. He took me back to the Water Lily to pack some of my belongings, but I'm still paying for the room because he told me this arrangement was simply temporary until I was well-rested and feeling better.

This is my second day here, and I've hardly seen Declan. He spends most of his time up on the third floor where his office is. When the sun came out yesterday, he suggested that I soak up the vitamin D, so I decided to enjoy the grotto. I spent hours inside the clinker structure. He has a small round table with two chairs set in the center under the glass ceiling. Even though the temperatures were in the thirties, the sun warmed the room where I sat and daydreamed like a little girl. As if that grotto was my palace, and I, the princess captured, waiting for my prince to save me.

And now, as I walk the grounds, stepping from snow patch to snow patch, I feel myself imagining this fabulous property as my magical forest. Winding through the trees, up small hills, passing flower gardens bedding the blooms that will emerge in the coming months, as well as benches and manmade stone and pebble creeks. I wish for one of the creeks to be the mythical Lethe that Declan and I could drink from to vanish the past into a vapor of vacuity. To eradicate the sufferings of our souls.

It's as if this is the forest I spent my childhood searching for. I used to sneak out of my foster homes during the night in a fit of wanderlust, hoping to find the place my father told me about. The fairytales of kings and queens, flying steeds, and of course, Carnegie—my life-long caterpillar friend who used to fill my dreams. He hasn't come around since that night when I turned into a caterpillar as well. He's been replaced by the corrosive memories of my past, and when I'm lucky enough, empty nights of blank space.

I find a spot up on a hill to perch myself. I sit and my pants dampen, seeping up the melted snow that soaks the earth beneath me, but I don't care because I'm at peace. I fold my legs in front of me and look down on this house that for now, I imagine is my kingdom. And when I close my eyes and lie back on the sodden ground, I believe that the man hiding away in his office at the top of the castle is my prince.

I breathe in the essence of the innocent child-like dream, and I'm five years old all over again. Dressed in my princess gown, I see my father holding the bouquet of pink daisies. His face still a crystal perfect image in my mind. Although twenty-three years have passed, I'm still a little girl, and he's still my handsome daddy who can fix anything with his hugs and kisses.

"You're so beautiful," his voice whispers through the wind, and my eyes flash open when I sit up.

My heart flutters at the realness of his voice, and then I hear it again.

"Where have you been, sweetheart?"

"Daddy?" My voice rings high in optimism through the breeze blowing through the trees above.

"It's me."

Looking around, I see no sign of anyone. I know this isn't real, but I don't care. I let whatever chemical my brain is spilling take me away, and I give into the illusion.

"I miss you," I tell the wind that carries wishes coming true.

"I miss you too. More than you'll ever know," he says, and I smile at the way his voice warms my chest. *"What are you doing out here in the cold?"*

"Escaping."

"Escaping what?"

"Everything," I say. "Being out here and exploring transports me back to a place of happiness. Where evil doesn't exist and innocence isn't lost."

"But what about down there?" I look down to the house as he continues, *"Why can't you find that inside those walls?"*

"Because inside those walls lies the truth. And the truth is . . . evil *does* exist, and innocence is just a fable."

"Life is whatever you want it to be, sweetheart."

"I don't believe that," I tell him. "I don't believe we are stronger than the forces of this world."

"Maybe not, but I'd like to think of my little girl as someone who would

fight for her fairytale."

"I've fought my whole life, Daddy. I'm ready to throw in the towel and give up."

"Who are you talking to?"

Turning my head, I see Declan standing off in the distance.

"I'm not crazy," I instantly defend.

He begins walking towards me. "I didn't say you were."

But if I did what my soul is screaming for me to do, he would. Because right now, the emptiness that refills what my father just warmed makes me want to cry out at the top of my lungs for him to come back. It roils inside of me, panging on the strings of my heart, but I mask it for fear of completely breaking down.

Declan sits next to me, and I deflect, teasing, "You just might destroy those slacks, sitting in the slushy dirt with me."

He looks at me, and his expression is hard to read, but it's almost despondent.

When he doesn't speak, I ask, "Why have you been hiding in your office?"

"Why have you been hiding out here?" he counters.

"I asked first."

Taking a deep breath, he admits, "Honestly . . . It makes me nervous to be around you."

"Why?"

He pulls his knees up and rests his arms over them as he explains, "Because I don't know you. I feel like I know the character you played—I know Nina. She made me comfortable. But you . . . I don't know you, and that makes me nervous."

But before I can speak, he says, "Now it's your turn to answer. Who were you talking to?"

Casting my eyes away from him, I reveal, "My dad," and wait for his response, but what he says next surprises me.

"What did he have to say?"

Shifting my attention back to Declan, he looks sincere in wanting to know, so I give it to him. "He told me I need to be stronger."

"Will you tell me about him?" he asks, and then smirks, adding, "The truth this time."

"What I used to tell you about him, the way he comforted me, the way you two resemble each other, it was all true, Declan. The lie was the Kansas story. Truth is, we lived in Northbrook. He was a great dad. I never had to question his love for me because he gave it endlessly." Thoughts from the past pile up, and I smile when I tell him, "The reason my favorite flower is the pink daisy, is because that's what he would always buy me."

My chest tugs when the memories fall from my eyes and roll down my cheeks.

"We used to have these tea parties. I'd dress up and he'd join me, pretending to eat the little plastic pastries." I wipe my tears, saying, "I never asked about my mom. I never really thought about her because my dad was more than enough. I never felt like I was missing anything."

"You mentioned he went to prison," he says, and I nod.

"Yeah," I respond and sniff before explaining, "He was caught for gun trafficking. I was five when the cops arrested him in front of me. The vision of my dad on his knees, being handcuffed, and promising me that everything would be okay is still so vivid in my mind."

"So what happened?"

Shrugging my shoulders, I resign, "That was it. I never saw him again. I went into foster care and had the shittiest of caseworkers out there. He went to Menard Prison, and I wound up in Posen, which was five hours away."

"Nobody ever took you to go see him?"

"No. My caseworker barely made time to come see me, let alone drive me across the state. But she did make the time to come tell me when my dad had been killed in a knife fight."

"How old were you?"

"Twelve."

He reaches out and takes my hand, turning my palm up. His voice is gentle when he says, "You didn't answer me when I asked you this before, but I need to know." He then drags his thumb over the faint white scars on my wrist. "Tell me how you got these."

My head drops in embarrassment, not wanting to add another layer of disgust on top of everything else he knows about me. With my hand still in his, he takes his other and covers my wrist with it. When I look into his eyes, he urges, "I want you to tell me."

So, I take a hard swallow and muster up what strength I can to confine the pain. It takes me a moment, and after a measured breath, I cut through another wound and allow it to bleed out for Declan. "When I wasn't in the basement, I was in the closet. My foster dad would tie me up with his leather belt to the garment rod in the closet beneath the stairs and lock me up."

"Jesus," he mutters in disbelief. "How long would you . . . ?"

"Every weekend. I'd go in on Friday and come out Sunday. Sometimes

I'd be in there during the weeknights. But during the summers, it was constant. I'd be in there three to five days at a time. He'd let me out long enough to go down in the basement, but then he'd tie me back up and lock the door again."

I feel numb when I tell him this, caging off the emotions I fear. The horror splayed across his face is hard to look at, so I keep my head down, but he picks it up. Moving closer to me, with his hands on my cheeks, he angles me to look up at him. My jaw is locked tight while I continue to hold myself together.

"Why?" he scolds harshly as he holds me in his hands. "Why didn't you tell someone? Why did you let that happen to you?"

His words rankle my nerves, but instead of blowing up at him in a rage, I narrow my eyes, and seethe, "You don't know shit. You had a home, you had a family, you were safe. So don't you dare sit here and question my actions. You don't know fear like I do. I may be fucked in the head, but one thing I do know for sure . . . I didn't *let* those things happen to me. What happened wasn't my fault, so fuck you for blaming me."

I jerk away from him and stand up, but he's quick when he meets my moves and grabs my arm. He pulls me back to him, and when I try yanking out from his hold, he tightens his grip.

"Let go of me!" I yell, but he says nothing as I struggle my arm free. I don't wait another second and start walking down the hill away from him. I don't expect anyone to understand my childhood, but to think a little girl would allow someone to debase her like I was is fucking crazy.

"I'm sorry," his voice hollers down to me, but I keep walking. "Elizabeth, stop!"

I do. I instantly stop the moment I hear his voice break. When I turn to look up at him through the trees, I exhaust in a softer tone, "I was just a little kid."

With hurried steps, he makes his way down, and when he's standing before me, he says, "I'm sorry. My words came out wrong. I'm just angry." He grabs on to me. "I'm so fucking angry when you tell me these things. I feel helpless."

"Why?"

"Because I want to take it away from you. Because somewhere inside my hate for you, a part of me still cares."

Staring up at him, I know better than to leech on to the goodness and hope of what he just said, so I ask, "Which one is it? Do you care more than you hate?"

I watch the tension strain through his eyes, and a moment passes before he answers, "No."

His honesty burns and sinks down inside of me. I question why I'm even here if he hates me so much. I feel like a game to him, but I don't even know what he's gaining from playing with me like this.

Shrugging out of his hold, I take a couple steps back from him before demanding, "Take me back to Isla's."

"No."

"It wasn't a question, Declan. I'm leaving," I tell him and then turn my back and rush towards the house, fuming mad.

I move quickly, doing my best to avoid ice patches, when I hear his heavy footsteps behind me. Looking over my shoulder, he's moving fast, but I'm too angry to face him right now, so I pick up my pace and start running from him.

"Elizabeth, stop!" he shouts from behind me, but I don't, and with each of my strides, my armor cracks.

His words just reminded me how alone I am in this world. Foolish of me to think maybe he wanted me here for the sake of wanting to be near me.

When I finally reach the house, I make my way around the back, but he catches me. His hand locks around my elbow, and when I stumble over my feet, he swings me around to face him and loops his arm around my waist. I cry out when he picks me up, lifting me off the ground.

In a flash, he has my back pressed against the side of the house, his body pinning me to the stone. With him flush against me, both of us panting heavily, I don't fight him as emotions overflow between us.

He doesn't speak, and neither do I, and before I know it, without thinking, my arms wrap around his neck. Our eyes are locked, never straying. He rests his forehead against mine, and my heart beats uncontrollably when he moves his hands to my pants. With our heads pressed together, staring into each other's eyes that reveal the unfamiliar emotions we're both experiencing, his cold fingers press against my stomach as he unzips my pants. He shoves them down, and I fumble, kicking off my rain boot, and working my one leg out of my pants as he unhooks his slacks.

The foggy vapors from our heavy breaths swim between our mouths, and suddenly, his hands wrap behind my knees, lifting me up. I lock my ankles around him, and the instant I feel the heat of his cock against me, a couple tears escape and fall down my cheeks.

He grips himself in his hand and presses into my folds, wetting his dick as he runs his burning tip through the slick warmth of my pussy. My arms cling tightly around him when he barely pushes the head of himself inside, teasing me, tugging at my opening. Clenching my thighs around him, a few more tears fall when he finally pushes himself inside of me.

I moan in carnal heat when he buries himself in my body. My heart leaps at the connection that soothes all the friction away. I'm finally pacified and free. I revel in knowing he has the antidote to clean the rot in me. I'm like the angel of martyrdom and he's the bezoar that purifies.

"Tell me you're not leaving," he says on a heavy voice that edges on violence, and I yield to him, saying, "I won't leave," because I'd do just about anything for him in this moment to keep his touch.

And with my words, he takes my mouth in a savage kiss as he begins fucking me with powerful, deep strokes. His eyes blacken in primal lust as he takes me, driving me back against the wall with each of his urgent thrusts. The sounds of my moans mixed with his heady pants fill the air around us.

His body grows rigid when he moves his hand to my throat, wrapping his fingers around my neck in a light choke. He releases a husky growl, and I can feel his cock strengthen and throb inside of me.

"Touch yourself," he orders, and I obey.

Licking my fingers first, I drag them down to my swollen clit and begin rolling them in soft circles. My eyes swim out of focus as our bodies reunite consensually for the first time in months.

His grip constricts around my throat, depleting the amount of air I'm able to take in, but I don't panic as my body finds comfort in the familiarity of his tender force during sex.

"Put it inside of you so you can feel me," he instructs, and I reach down a little further, my neck pushing against his hand as I slip my finger alongside his cock, sinking it in my pussy at the same time he slams inside of me. I pump my finger in rhythm with him. Touching us in this way, feeling the warmth of our mended bodies, slick in arousal, it's too much.

"Oh, God," I mewl loudly as I feel my walls pulse around my finger and his cock.

"Don't ever walk away from me again," he scolds.

"Never."

"You wanna come?"

"Yes," I strain around the cords of my throat that he continues to hold hostage.

And in his feat of control over me, he orders, "Ask permission."

"Please."

My body rises in a fiery storm amidst the nearly freezing temperature.

"Ask!"

"Please," I repeat in a breathless whimper. "I need it."

"Don't do it. Don't defy me," he warns, and when I reach the brink, I clamp my thighs to his hips with as much strength as I can to slow him down.

Holding on to my breath, I fight with everything in me to ward off the orgasm that's about to erupt.

"That's it," he delights in his power over me.

But I can't hold on. Looking in his eyes, I give in, "Can I come? Please, I need it."

"You want it?" he taunts.

"Yes."

"Fuck yourself faster," he instructs, and I do.

I lose all control and begin fingering myself against his cock that swells inside of me, spurring my explosion.

I come.

Hard and wild.

Every muscle in my body tightens in spasms of euphoria, bucking my hips into Declan, greedy to keep the pleasure going. And then I feel his release. He soaks my finger that's still inside of me, fucking myself while he fills me up. I don't stop moving as his cum seeps out of me, running down my hand.

His teeth grit as he keeps his eyes on me the whole time, and I watch him grunt in pleasure through the shatters of light that fracture my vision into a thousand prismatic flakes of pure ecstasy.

When our bodies slow, he lets go of my neck, and my head falls to his shoulder as I allow my body to slack against his. He holds me for a moment while our hearts calm and we catch our breath.

I wish for frozen time, forgotten sins, and never-ending love.

But I know this isn't love on his part. I'm not sure what it is, but I know it isn't that. I want it to be though, so I keep my head tucked into the crook of his neck, scared to move, because I know the moment I do, reality will resume, and his loathing for me will continue.

I wrap my legs tighter around him, wanting to prolong having him nestled inside of me, but my attempt at pushing time away doesn't last. When I feel Declan pulling out of me, I slip my finger out and wrap my hand around his still hardened cock. But he doesn't allow the contact, taking my wrist and forcing me to let go.

With my feet steady on the ground, I watch as he shoves himself back into his pants. He doesn't utter a word, and his eyes are no longer on me. And then he's gone, turning his back and walking away from me, leaving me with my pants down, covered in his cum, in the bitter cold.

Maybe I should feel used and dirty. Maybe I should hate him. Maybe I should give up and be done. But my heart won't let me. Because in the end, I know I'll always want him any way I can get him.

I'm an epicurean for his pain.

He's my sadist, and I'm his masochist.

We're the reflection of each other's monsters.

twenty-nine

I HAVEN'T SEEN Declan since he walked away from me, leaving me alone in the cold earlier today. But I haven't been looking for him either. I've spent most of the day roaming around the house, taking in the history, the artwork, and exploring the books in the library.

And now, as I lie on the chaise here in the atrium at the back of the house, I gaze up at the black velvet sky peppered with stars through the glass structure. With civilization sparse and the lack of clouds, you can see every star in the sky. Thousands of them, glittering in the obsidian of night, each holding wishes from foolish people and hopeful children. And I can't help myself when I throw my own up to a few of them tonight.

The house is dark, the only noise coming from the wind as it whistles through the bare trees. And with Declan's constant push and pull, he reminds me of the wind. It blows, wrapping itself around me, but as soon as I feel it, it's gone. It's uncatchable, unstoppable, uncontrollable, and as much as I want Declan, all I'm really doing is chasing the wind.

I turn my head to the shadow of Declan who stands in the open doorway. He wears only his long pajama bottoms that hang low on his hips. A warmth surges through me as I admire the deep cuts of his abs and the defined muscles that rope his broad shoulders and arms. He's so beautiful that it pains me to look at him, but I can't stop myself.

"Are you okay?" he says after a long span of silence.

I nod, but it's a lie. I'm not okay. He fucked me like an animal and left me in the cold. One minute he's caring and sweet, and the next, he's transformed—angry and silent, completely shut down and wanting nothing to do with me. And now, here he is, and I wonder what version I'm going to get.

He walks into the room, and I keep my eyes on him as he moves with ease.

"What are you doing out here? Aren't you freezing?"

"I like the cold," I tell him.

"I know you do."

His words make me want to smile, but I refrain. Moving closer, he then sits next to me on the chaise.

"Where've you been all day?" I ask.

"In my office. I came looking for you because I have to leave tomorrow for London."

"Oh."

"I'll be gone for just a couple of days."

"What's in London?"

"Business," he answers, offering no further insight, so I inquire, "Another hotel?"

"Yes. I recently closed on the land. I'm meeting a few different architects tomorrow that I could potentially hire."

"That's really exciting." And when I sit up, I ask, "When will you be taking me back to Isla's?"

"I won't," he says evenly. "I would prefer if you stayed here where I can keep an eye on you."

"An eye on me?"

He then looks away and nods his head in the direction of a small camera that's attached to one of the steel beams that connects the panes of glass.

"They're in all the rooms," he states, and it makes sense that he would have that level of security in a home this massive.

"Declan," I hesitate, feeling awkward about staying here while he's away.

"I don't trust you at Isla's. Twice I've walked in on you hurting yourself."

"But it feels weird to be here if you're not."

"You don't like it here?" he asks, and I instantly respond, "No, it isn't that. I do like it here. It's just . . . "

"Then you'll stay put until I get back."

"I don't understand you," I whisper weakly.

And with my words, he exhales deeply, turning to look away from me, dropping his elbows to his knees.

"Declan, please. Give me something to work with here. Tell me something to help me understand."

He keeps his head forward, and the tension and struggle is all over him. The muscles in his back flex, and I can see the rise and fall of it as his breathing increases. I know it's a reflection of his building emotions, I just wish I knew what they consisted of.

I want to touch him, but I'm afraid it will piss him off and he'll leave again, so I keep my hands in my lap as I simply watch.

When he finally speaks, his voice cracks, along with my heart, as he says, "Your voice . . . the moment I heard your voice after I was shot, I did everything I could to fight my eyes open just so I could see you. I'd already read the file. I already knew you had been lying about everything. But a part of me . . . " His voice slips before he takes a hard swallow and looks over his shoulder to face me, continuing, " . . . a part of me wanted to believe I had gotten it all wrong and that it wasn't a lie. But when he said *Go,* and you did so easily, leaving me to die . . . " His face contorts with the pain he's fighting to hide. " . . . No one has ever made me feel so worthless and disposable."

"I was scared." My words tremble, not knowing what else to say. "I was *so* scared."

"I was too, and you left."

I hold my breath as I stare into his eyes that harbor the scars I inflicted. The burden of guilt that consumes me is paralyzing as I watch him expose the fragile pieces he hides so well. He's a man who is nothing but strength and control, but in this quiet moment, he reveals just how broken he is. Broken and hurt, and it's all because of me.

"When I came here," he starts again, "I wanted nothing to do with you. I wanted you dead, but then I found myself outside with a shovel, digging up the flower bushes that surround the house like a fucking maniac losing my mind."

"Why were you digging them up?"

"Because you told me you hated the color purple, and those shrubs bloom purple flowers in the spring."

And that's the dagger that impales my façade of strength. Tears pool in my eyes, and my body restrains to not completely burst into tears.

"My head has been so fucked up because I can't get you out of it."

"When I was eight years old," I begin, needing to speak because the sound of his voice is too upsetting for me. So, I distract myself and reveal another part of my past. Another denouement for him. "I wound up being moved to a different foster home. The one that would make me believe that monsters were real. I was terrified to the core, and when I was shown the room I'd be sleeping in, all the walls were painted purple." Declan's hand finds my cheek as I continue to talk. "All the years of torture and abuse were stained in purple."

His other hand covers my other cheek, and he holds me. I don't want to lose the touch, but I need more to remedy the sour bile that ripples in my stomach. Mirroring his affections, I cover his cheeks with my hands. A rush of comfort wraps around me as I feel the crackle of his unshaven jaw under my hands. I tug him in and he comes to me willingly, touching his lips to mine. We don't move as we rest peacefully against each other.

The moment fractures when he abruptly pulls away. My hands fall from him as his clutch tightens around my face. I can feel the strain in his hands as their nerves vibrate against my cheeks. His body locks up, the corded muscles banded around his shoulders contract.

"Why?" I breathe. "Why do you turn so cold?"

He grinds his teeth, and his eyes flare disdainfully at me. "Because I don't want to be this close to you. Because I despise you. Because you're a scheming witch."

His tone stabs like an ice pick, and I wonder if it will always be this way with us. If he truly is incapable of allowing himself to ever be vulnerable with me again. Maybe he's destined to be the yearning ache of my heart.

La douleur exquise.

"Then why have me here? Why don't you throw me out, tell me you hate me?"

"I do hate you," he sears.

"So why touch me, kiss me, fuck me?"

"They're my sick cravings," he admits. "The hunger grows worse the more I feed it."

And the scheming witch he just accused me of being comes to life. Because with him, I want to be selfish. I want him to be mine and no one else's.

I know I'm narcissistic when I tilt my head to the side, presenting him with the soft skin of my neck, but I don't care when I invite him to take, saying, "Then feast."

"You don't want me this way."

"I want you in *every* way."

His growl is low, deep within his chest, but far from the heart that beats in deadly ways. He's a degenerate of love, but I want him regardless.

He stands and demands, "Strip. And when I return, I want you on your knees, face down on the floor and ass up."

And he just made me feel like I'm a child and taking orders from Carl. I watch as he walks out of the room, and I begin to question if it was a lie. If I really do want him in any way I can get him. Because right now, I want to barrel my fist into his dick for ordering me to expose myself in a humiliating position on this freezing concrete floor.

As much as I want to spit my acrid words at him, I know the derelict I am.

So I do as commanded.

I strip.

And when I walk to the center of the room, I kneel down. With my knees parted, I lower my bare chest onto the ice-cold floor, whimpering against the scathing chill that bites the tender flesh of my nipples. Stretching my arms in front of me, resting my cheek on the floor, I spread my knees wider, lift my ass in the air, and close my eyes while my heart beats wildly.

Presenting myself in degradation, I wait.

And I wait.

And I wait.

Time passes; I'm not sure how long I've been in this position when the muscles in my legs begin to burn and cramp. My body grows colder with each minute lost with no sign of Declan.

Shivers overtake, and when I can't hold on to this position any longer, I let my body fall to the side. Lying here naked and mortified, I finally blink out the tears as I pull my knees into my chest and quietly weep.

Was this his plan? Was this a punishment? To shame me, knowing he wasn't going to come back for me?

My body turns numb after a while, making it difficult to move my muscles when I attempt to pick myself up off the ground. Slowly, I pull my clothes back on while I vacillate between loneliness, resentment, sadness, and anger. All of it swarms through me, taking my energy, and depleting me to the point where I just want to disappear.

Wrapping the blanket around me, I walk into the kitchen to get a drink, and when I do, I notice a car down at the gate on the intercom monitor. The windows are darkly tinted, so that when I move closer to the black and white screen on the wall, I can't make out the person who's driving. But then the car starts to back up, and when it drives away, I begin to wonder about the life Declan has here in Scotland and the people he surrounds himself with, if any at all. I only know about Lachlan—that's it. I wonder if he's as alone as he appears to be, and who's lurking at the gate in the middle of the night.

I don't even stop to peek in his room as I head to bed. I'm too embarrassed.

Did he ever come back to the atrium and see me exposing my body for him?

I shake the thought away, and when I go into the bathroom, I see he's set the bottle of pills the doctor prescribed me on the sink. I take a pill out and stare at it, wondering if I'm just like her, just like the woman who never wanted me. I wonder who the hell I am. I fear I'll never know if I stay here in this tug of war with the man who hates me.

Flicking the pill from my fingertips, it plops into the toilet water. I know if I leave here and go back to the States, I won't want to do it alone. I need Pike. I'll probably always need him because he's still all I have, and if I take that pill, I risk losing him. And I can't lose him.

"Get out," I seethe when I walk back into the bedroom and see Declan.

"I couldn't do it," he says. "I knew if I went back to you, I'd fuck you and hurt you because I want to punish you. I wouldn't have been able to resist taking all this anger I have out on you."

"I can't do this, Declan," I say in defeat. "I want to. I want to be strong enough because I don't ever want to be without you. But I'm starting to think that being here with you might just hurt worse than not being with you at all."

He walks over and sits on the edge of the bed, dropping his head.

"There too much pain in me. There's so much rage and hate, and I don't know how to get rid of it," I tell him. "I've been fighting my whole life trying to rid myself of these feelings that won't ever go away." I move to sit across the room from him in one of the chairs. "I thought getting rid of Bennett would be what I've been needing. That somehow I would feel better about this life, but . . . " I begin to cry, "I don't feel better. Nothing feels better. And then I killed my brother, and I'm not entirely sure why, but I did, and I carry that with me every day. I plot revenge and I kill and I fight and I still hate this life. I still hurt and it won't go away."

I don't even realize my eyes are closed and I'm bent over sobbing out my words until I feel his hands on my knees. I open my eyes to see him kneeling in front of me.

"But this hurts too," I add. "Being here with you hurts me, and as much as I want to hate you for all the ways you've been humiliating me and punishing me, I'm scared to leave. I'm scared I'll never see you again."

"Was Pike the only one?"

"What?" I question, confused as to what he's asking.

"You said you kill. Was he the only one?"

I hesitantly shake my head and shock streaks his face.

"How many?"

Closing my eyes, I confess, "Three."

"Jesus Christ," he mutters in disbelief. "Who else?"

"My foster parents," I say when I look back down at him, and his shoulders lax a little.

His hands slide past my knees and grip my thighs with his question,

"What happened?"

"Pike and I ran away together, and shortly after, we returned one night with a friend of his, and . . . "

"I want to know everything," he demands harshly. "I want to know how those fuckers died."

"Pike and his friend, Matt, they tied them to the bed and dumped a couple containers of gasoline on them," I say. "I remember standing there, watching them scream and flail around, trying to break free. Matt handed me the match like it was a gift, wrapped in the most delicate silk bow, and it was. When I struck that match and threw it on that bed, it was the greatest gift anyone had ever given me," I cry. "Those sick fucks destroyed every piece of me. But here's the really sick part, as happy as it made me to kill them, it still wasn't enough. It's never enough, Declan, because I'm still so alone. I still feel worthless and disgusting, and all I ever wanted was the one thing Bennett took away from me. I miss my dad."

Declan pulls me out of the chair and onto the floor with him as I lose myself to the emotions I'm so used to caging up. He cradles me in his arms, gathering me up completely, and pressing me tightly against him.

"I miss him so much. It hurts so bad. But then I met you. And it took me a while to see it, to see how I felt about you because I'd never experienced that feeling before. I'd never loved like I did with you, never opened myself up like that. And when I look at you, I see parts of my dad in you. The way you'd comfort me and love me. No one has ever given me that."

"What about Pike?"

"He was my brother. It was different. With you, I finally felt like I had a home. But I knew I had destroyed our love from the beginning. I knew we never had a chance."

"But that didn't stop you."

"I was selfish. I knew that no amount of time with you would suffice to make it easier for me to walk away."

His eyes only take a second to scorn. The flip is instant, like it always is with him, and I know what set him off when he spews, "But you did walk away."

I don't know what else to say, so I plead for penance in the absence of words. And as we sit, his touch on me fades as his animosity breeds. It stirs in the reticence between us, and I know our expiration date is near.

The awareness that we have this death sentence over us makes me want to do two things, but I don't know which one to choose.

Do I run away, or do I stay and watch us die a painful death?

thirty

I'VE BEEN DRIVING around the countryside trying to find the house the old lady at the Water Lily told me about. I was able to track Nina down once I found out she was going by Elizabeth Archer again. Made my life a little easier, and when I found out where she was staying, I was grateful when the owner was forthcoming about where I could find her. She never doubted me when I lied and told her I was Elizabeth's uncle and had been trying to get in contact with her.

I had to laugh to myself because when Bennett had me follow her not so long ago, she was the easiest little thing to trace. And now, exactly as I thought, she's with the same bastard she was with back in Chicago.

But now, I've wasted the light of day because this fucking town isn't very considerate with street signs. I round yet another bend in the road with no houses in sight. I slow down, peering out the window, when my headlights catch a small plaque on a stone wall, and it's then I see gates. Slowing more, the sign reads what I was told it would: Brunswickhill.

"Checkmate," I mutter under my breath as I kill the headlights and pull up to the gate.

Stepping out of the car, I look up the steep hill, but can't see anything in the dark. No lights. Nothing.

"Fuck."

Getting back behind the wheel, I decide to just call it a night. I know that beyond this gate, they are more than likely here. For now, I'm tired as shit, but at least I have my stakeout position. And knowing there's a manhunt back in Illinois, my next steps need to be quick and deadly.

thirty-one

I CAN STILL feel the vibrations that ricocheted though my bones with each gunshot. The two that Pike fired into Declan's chest, and the single blast from the gun I held that took my brother from me. The sound is something I'll never forget. A bang so loud, it knocks your shoulders back, deafening and startling. And when the mark is hit, the ice your heartless heart pumps fills your veins, and you know you'll never be the same again.

Forever changed.

Forever a monster.

Each bullet leaves a soot stain on your soul that you can't get rid of, and you never forget the taste of burnt gunpowder on the back of your tongue. Each life you take brands you for eternity.

I hoped it wouldn't. I hoped the aftereffects would wither away as the echoes did. But if there's one thing I've learned in this life, it's the realization that echoes live forever. I may no longer hear the screaming demons of my past, but they do indeed continue to scream. It's a reminder that you're never truly free.

I don't know where I'm going or what I'm doing, but I don't think this is the place for me. I've been lost in my head all morning. Declan left at sunrise for the airport. When he did, I needed to find comfort and realized I left my doll behind.

I called Isla to tell her I would be stopping by to collect the remainder of my belongings. Since he took the SUV, I take his Mercedes roadster to Isla's.

As I pull up to the charming house that I've stayed at since my arrival several weeks ago, I know, that as much as it hurts, there's nothing here for me in Scotland. I never knew what it was I was looking for when I came here. The last thing I thought I would find was Declan alive, but I did. And maybe that's gift enough, to know he'll go on and that his life wasn't sacrificed because of my deceit.

The key is under the ceramic planter right where Isla said she would leave it. I walk in, and even though I've only been at Declan's for a couple of days, it feels much longer. But then again, each day with him is filled with insurmountable emotions and conversations. It's taken a toll on me, having to face my past and confess the truths I've hidden for so long. The hardest is having to see the pain Declan battles inside of himself—pain that was birthed because of me. I own it; he endures it.

I head upstairs, and after finding my doll, I begin to pack my things and focus on keeping the dread at bay. I wish I had direction, I wish I knew what I'm doing and where I'm going. It's a heavy emotion to carry, to know how alone I really am. But I fight to keep myself numb to all the questions there are no answers for.

I move faster the more my thoughts wander. Flashbacks of what's occurred in this room begin to gnaw, and when I walk over to the bed to grab my phone that I had left behind, I freeze. Below the window, parked in the street, is the same car I saw on Declan's gate monitor last night. Or at least I think it is. So many of the cars here are the same, so I can't be certain, but something in my gut sparks the paranoia.

The car is directly under my view, so all I see is the roof. Hopping off the bed, I rush downstairs, lock the front door, and make my way through the house to see if I can get a better view. Passing the windows, I find myself walking into a room I've never been in before—Isla's room. Pushing the door open, the room is dark with the heavy drapes shut. Barely parting the curtains with my fingers, I peek out, but the car's gone. The street out front is now vacant, aside from my car.

I open the drapes further to get a better look, and sure enough, the car is gone. Shaking my head, I release a pathetic sigh.

You're losing your mind, Elizabeth.

I take in a calming breath, retiring my batty thoughts that have no basis. I turn my back to the window and close my eyes as I laugh at myself. When I open them back up, I take in Isla's room. Scanning around, I walk over to her nightstand to look at the book resting on top. I'm running my fingers along the cover of *Madame Bovary* when I notice a collection of photos on the mantle above the fireplace. I move slowly along, looking at each picture.

"Oh my God."

Picking up the tarnished silver frame, I hold it close as I look in disbelief. I wonder if this is the foolish paranoia that remains from the car outside or if this is exactly what my eyes believe it to be.

How did she get this? Why does she have a picture of him?

He's younger than what I've ever seen him, a little boy, but the eyes are irrefutable. There's no mistaking what I know so well.

It's him.

But why?

The doorbell rings, startling me, and I drop the frame, cracking the glass as it lands on the wooden floor.

"Shit."

Scrambling, I pick up the small frame and tuck it in the back of my pants as I run to see who's at the front door.

Before I make it, there's a loud knocking.

"Elizabeth? You in there?"

Lachlan?

Looking out the window, I see it's him.

"What are you doing here?" I question when I open the door.

"Declan asked that I check in on you, and when no one answered my gate call at his home, I came here."

"He's been gone only a few hours. What trouble could I possibly have gotten myself into in such a short period of time?" I tease, but the cool metal frame in my pants is evidence I smirk at.

"What's so funny?"

"You men need hobbies," I quip as I turn my back and walk towards the stairs.

"I've been worried."

"Have you now?"

"Declan told me you had a hard time with the file," he says.

Embarrassment rouses, but I shut it down quickly. "I'd prefer to never discuss that issue again."

"Of course. My apologies."

"Look, I appreciate you checking in on me, but if you don't mind, I'm just packing the rest of my things to take back to Declan's."

"Are you sure everything's okay?" he presses as if he's privy to something he believes me to be aware of.

Call it intuition, but everything about today has got me on high alert for some unsettling reason.

"Yes, everything is just fine," I say smoothly with a light smile to appease him. "The past couple days have been taxing, as I'm sure you can understand."

He nods, taking my directive to not mention the file.

"You can report back to your boss that the kid in question is taking good care of herself."

I smile at my words, and he laughs in return, agreeing, "Will do."

He turns to leave, but before he shuts the door behind him, he says, "By the way, I've tried calling you a couple times . . . "

"I left my phone here. No one calls me on it, but now that I know I have a babysitter, I'll be sure to charge it up for you," I joke.

He shakes his head at me with a smile and then leaves. I go to the door and lock it behind him before returning to my room. Tossing the rest of my things in my suitcase, I take the photo out of the frame and shove it in my bag. I don't know why she has this picture, but I want it for myself.

When my luggage is loaded into the car, I head back to Brunswickhill after returning the key to the planter. A part of me wants to call Declan to ask why he sent Lachlan to check in on me. He says he hates me, but then I see these hints of the man I knew back in Chicago. The man who was furious if I was more than a minute late. The man who controlled and dominated to ease his worry. But I won't call him because I never know what it is about me that's going to trigger him to push me away.

"What the hell?" I murmur under my breath when I round the bend in the road and see the same car that was at Isla's now sitting outside of Declan's gate.

Slowing the Mercedes, I stop and wait since the other car is blocking my way. My curiosity is piqued, wondering if Declan is still having me followed, and if so, why they are being so blatant about it.

Growing impatient, I honk my horn, and when I do, the driver's door opens. I watch a shiny, black loafer step out onto the street, and a thousand penetrating emotions shoot off inside of me.

What the fuck is he doing here?

Nerves wrack me as I fist the steering wheel tightly in my hands. I watch him approach my car, and for a split second, I consider running him over. But truth is, I have no idea why he's even here.

So without wasting another second, I fall back into the character I know so well and hide myself in Nina's mask. Righting my spine, I forget all about Elizabeth, and open the door.

"How quickly you move on," he taunts as I stand before him.

"Nice to see you too, Richard."

"I doubt you mean that, but thanks anyway."

"What are you doing here in Scotland?"

"I could ask you the same, but I think it's pretty clear."

His words irk me as always, and I bite my response, "Cut the shit, Richard. Tell me why you flew halfway around the world."

His face flattens in a no-nonsense expression when he states, "We need to talk."

"About what?"

"Your husband."

As far as I know, Richard knows nothing about the lies and deception. He only knows me as Nina, Bennett's wife, and now widow. He's been Bennett's business partner from the very beginning, and the two of them were close. Not close enough though because I know Richard is clueless to the fact that Bennett fucked his precious little wife and that the baby Richard believes to be his is, in fact, just a pathetic bastard.

"I haven't been contacted about anything concerning the investigation," I tell him. "Are there any new developments?"

His eyes narrow, and I don't trust the hinting grin on his face. "Don't you think it's a little hard to be in the loop of information when you're operating on a cheap, disposable phone?"

My poker face is strong, but my body numbs, wondering how he knows about my untraceable phone. My words deflect my panic as I say, "Always butting your nose in where it never belongs, aren't you?"

"Like I said, we need to talk."

"Then talk."

"Inside," he states firmly.

"Why not here?"

He grows irritated, fuming loudly, "Because it's fucking cold and my balls don't like it."

He's so damn disgusting.

I hesitate on taking him inside Declan's home, but figure it's safer up there with all the cameras than down here on the street.

"Fine."

He follows me through the gate and up to the house. As I lead him in and to the library, he remarks, "You don't ever slum it, do you?"

"Is there a point to the nonsense you spew?" I sit across from him, and when he takes a seat, I say, "So what is it? What is so important that you needed to travel all this way?"

He leans forward and takes a moment before looking over at me, revealing, "I know who you are."

"Oh yeah, and who's that?"

"No use in playing coy because I know your dirty, little secrets."

His words imply threats, and I don't take well to his evasiveness. "Cut the shit and get to your point."

"He knew. Bennett had me following you when he suspected you were fucking around on him."

"It was you?"

He nods as he leans back, getting much too comfortable for my liking. I think back to the hospital, and I knew the voice sounded familiar when he told Bennett who I really was, but I couldn't pinpoint it with all the drugs they had me on.

"Needless to say, I wasn't surprised when I discovered your affair," he says condescendingly. "What *did* surprise me was when I found out you were nothing but runaway street trash."

"What's your point, Richard?"

"Why did you marry him?"

"Because I loved him," I lie. "Nothing wrong with reinventing yourself to get a fresh start in life."

"Except when the person you reinvented yourself for winds up dead."

"You're an asshole," I sling at him in mock disgust.

"I just have one question . . . who did it? Who did you have off him?"

"I don't know what you're talking about."

"How convenient, but I don't think the cops would buy it if I turned over all the information I have on you."

"You're so cute," I sneer, pissing him off. "You think your threats have an effect on me? Why don't you just tell me what you're after and stop wasting my time."

"No bullshit, cut to the chase?"

"Please."

In all seriousness, he tells me, "I need money." I laugh, and he snaps, "What the fuck is so funny?"

"*You.*" I sit back, cross my legs, and ask, "Why on earth would you be coming to *me,* of all people, for money?"

"Because I trust you to keep that pretty little mouth of yours shut if anyone were to come asking questions."

"What do you need money for?"

"You haven't been watching the news?"

"I've been a little preoccupied to be keeping up with American news."

He shakes his head with an arrogant smirk, and I cross my arms in irritation. "Enlighten me. Please."

"Linq Incorporated is under investigation. I thought you'd know that by now since your lover's father has been sitting in jail for his part in the fraud."

"What?" I question, confused as to what the hell Cal has to do with my husband's business and what was fraudulent about the company. "What fraud?"

"The company's just a front for washing money."

"Money from what?"

Richard then stands and walks across the room. When he's right in front of me, I freeze as he reaches his hand inside his suit jacket. "Guns," he states as he pulls out his own and aims it at me.

Adrenaline flushes through my system as I stare into the barrel of the pistol that's marked me as its target. I try to appear calm, but my staggering breaths are my tell—I'm scared.

"I want what was left to you in Bennett's will. You give me that and I'll disappear. You'll never hear from me again."

"I don't . . . He didn't . . . " I stutter over my words. "I didn't get everything."

"You're lying to me. I know you're the sole heir."

Shaking my head, I try to explain, "I thought I was, but . . . he changed it before he died. I didn't know until I met with the attorney."

He scowls, takes another step closer, and presses the cold steel to my forehead. I gasp in fear, clutching the arms of the chair as my heart beats in erratic terror.

My voice is pitchy when I frantically explain, "Look, if what y-your wanting is m-money to flee, I-I don't have that much for you. I mean . . . it wouldn't be enough."

"Then where is it?"

The desperation in his eyes makes me fear what he would do if I told him the truth. He'd most likely lose his shit and pull that trigger if he knew about his son being Bennett's. But beyond that, what the hell was Bennett doing with his company? Did he even know? My mind warps in confusion, overwhelmed with too many questions, that I begin to lose focus.

"Where is it?" he shouts, scaring the shit out of me with his murderous glare.

The tip of the gun shakes against my head as I look up into his furiously crazed eyes, and I begin trembling. My whole body jittery in fear.

"I-I don't know."

WHACK!

I scream in heated pain as I fall out of my chair and onto the floor. My hand cups the side of my head where he just pummeled his gun. The blunt force sparking a fire of light in my vision as I fight against the sharp agony that pierces through my skull.

He stands over me, pointing the gun at my face, and I wail, "Okay! Okay!" I throw my hands up in surrender.

"Stop fucking around with me!"

"I'm not!"

"Where is it?"

"It's in a trust," I reveal. "He put it in a trust I don't have access to."

Richard kneels down to one knee, hovering over me, gritting between clenched teeth, "Whose trust?"

With nerves crashing, I tell him, "A trust for his son."

"You lying cunt."

"Fuck you. It's the truth," I lash out when my anger grows at his degrading words. My emotions get away from me as my head spins in waves of turbulence. As I stare up at this man I've loathed for years, I see the wretchedness and desperation in his eyes, and I feel a little deranged as I begin to laugh at him.

"What the fuck are you laughing at?"

"He played us both," I say as my laughter intensifies.

"What are you talking about?"

"Bennett," I tell him.

"He doesn't have a son. I've known Bennett since he was a kid. I know everything about him, so I don't know what the fuck you're talking about."

"No?" I question in mockery. "Tell me something then," I start, and pleasure blooms inside of me to be the one to deliver the truth to him. I smile and continue, "How deeply have you looked into Alexander's eyes?"

I watch as his face contorts and add, "Because if you look deep enough, you'll see Bennett staring back at you."

And when realization splays across his face, he takes a step back in shock. I know Richard adores his son. Probably more than he does his wife. So to be the one to stab this dagger of truth through his heart delights me.

I move to stand, and when I do, the giggle that slips from my lips is maniacal as I gloat, "That's right, Richard. Your precious little wife fucked my husband and they had a baby together."

"You're full of shit!"

"Bennett left everything to him. But if you think you can get the money, you're wrong. You see, Bennett was smart enough to not assign Jacqueline as the executor. He assigned his attorney."

His nostrils flare, and I lose myself in utter delirium as I continue to laugh at every fucked up part of this crazy story. The room spins around me, a blurry realm of colors and shadows, as my hearing tunnels in the reverberations of my own laughter.

"Fuck you!" his voice cuts through, but only for a moment before he swings his arm around. It all happens in a flash of slow motion, but too quick for me to stop, as he drives the gun with a force that parallels his anger into my head, knocking me off my feet.

My head clips the corner of an end table before smashing against the floor.

Light flashes behind my eyelids.

Sparks.

Diamond dust.

Clouds.

Blackness.

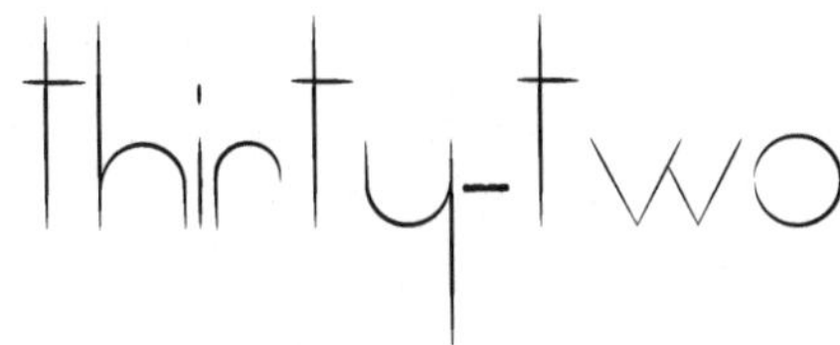

thirty-two

"MMMMM!" I SCREAM from my throat behind the tape over my mouth.

My heart crashes so hard it beats in my head. Sheer panic punctures every organ inside of me, flooding my body in pure fear as I thrash around in the darkness. I jerk and kick, but my wrists are bound behind my back and my ankles are tied together in duct tape.

"MMMMM!" I force my voice as loud as I can as it scratches through my strained cords. I know no one can hear me, but I don't care.

Twisting my hands is useless against the tape that's secured in a tight restraint. Frustration boils over, pricking in tingles along my palms, and I lose control. I release another worthless, muffled scream, squinting my eyes in an attempt to amplify the sound as I flail my body around like a maniac in the trunk of the car I've woken to.

Time wisps past me as the miles collect and my panic dissolves. My body slacks, absorbing the bumps in the road as I'm being taken into the labyrinth of Richard's desperation.

I knew better than to push him over the edge like I did, but I lost it. I was outside of my head and taking joy from my lashings. But now those lashings have me tied up in the trunk of his car, and I have no way to escape.

I fill the drive trying to figure out what the hell Bennett's company was being used as a front for. Richard said guns, but in what capacity? All I can think about is my father's business. He trafficked guns; is it possible that's what Linq is a cover for? Another trafficking scheme? Surely not. But if so, is it in any way linked to my dad? My thoughts aren't logical. I mean, maybe it's coincidental.

Fuck, what's going on? Did Bennett know? I find it so hard to believe that he did. He was such a straight-edge guy, built out of strong values and always following the rules. It was sickening to watch, but that was the core of Bennett.

And how the hell was Cal involved? Maybe Bennett did know. After all,

Bennett and Cal worked in a few business deals together through the years. Does Declan know about his dad? God, he seemed like such an honest guy as well, but maybe he knew.

Irritation swarms the more I think and question, but what's the use? I'm not going to dissect this on my own.

My body alerts as I feel the car slow and then come to a stop. My pulse quickens when I hear the door slam shut.

Are we in a public place? Are people around? Do I risk making noise?

Taking in slow, quiet breaths, I focus on what's going on outside, but I hear nothing. Every muscle in my body is tensed up as I wait, but nothing happens. Time continues to pass, and eventually, I feel myself drifting to sleep. I struggle to stay awake as my eyes fall shut.

I DON'T KNOW how long I've been out when I feel the car halt to a sudden stop. I wonder how far we've traveled. I hear the door shut, and it's only seconds until the trunk pops open.

Light burns my eyes, and I flinch away as Richard's hands grab on to me, yanking me out of the car. I don't even think to take in my surroundings, simply fighting against his hold, jerking my body around.

With his hands on my arms, he slams me against a solid rock wall. He knocks the wind out of me, and I gasp desperately through my nose while my throat strangles against my depleted lungs. Hunched over, I panic and choke when he grabs my hair and pulls my head up. Hairs rip from my scalp as a steel blade meets my cheek.

My eyes widen in horror as my breath finally catches. Whimpering, I close my eyes as he presses the blade into my soft flesh. My cry is muffled by the tape that still covers my mouth when I feel the pop of my skin as he slices me open.

He then presses the flat of the blade to the tape that covers my lips, saying, "If you think I have limits, you're wrong."

Bending down, he uses the knife to cut the duct tape around my ankles, but leaves my wrists bound. The blood from my cheek drips from my jaw, landing on my top.

"Walk," he commands, grabbing my arm and leading me down an alleyway.

I look around, quickly attempting to figure out where we are, but it's too dark, and the alley is too narrow. He leads me down a flight of steps to an underground area, and I remember Lachlan telling me about the vaults under the city. He told me some of them now serve as clubs or restaurants, some for ghost tours, but others simply remain empty. And there's no doubt that's where he's taking me as he moves me through a stone tunnel, damp with water, and into a fairly large room.

Taking in my surroundings, I can tell this used to be used for a business of sorts. There's electricity, built-in counters along one of the walls, a desk, and a couple of chairs. I watch as Richard walks over to the desk and lays his gun down. When he returns to me, he rips off the tape covering my mouth, and my eyes prick with tears against the sting.

"Sit down," he tells me, and I obey.

"What do you think you're doing?" I ask.

"You're all I've got. I need you to help me disappear."

"From what?"

"If the cops find me, I'll spend the rest of my years in prison."

And he's right. Richard is in his late fifties. I don't know the crimes he's committed, but the fact that he's just kidnapped me tells me he's in deep shit.

"But I told you, I don't have what you're looking for," I tell him.

"You may not, but someone who loves you does."

"Who?"

"Declan McKinnon."

I shake my head, saying, "You're wrong. He doesn't love me. He hates me."

"Yet you're living with him? I think you're lying to me."

"I'm not. You have to believe me. He doesn't love me. He keeps me there to punish me."

"Punish you for what?" he questions, but I bite my tongue, not sure how much to say.

I won't incriminate Declan, but do I incriminate myself? If I do, I run the risk of going to jail myself. So, I give him what he already knows from following me back in Chicago, and say, "For the fact that I wouldn't leave Bennett for him."

I tell the lie, but I hate it because Declan is worth so much more than anyone else on this planet.

Richard chuckles in irritation. "I don't know exactly what you were doing with Bennett, but I'm smart enough to know, *Elizabeth Archer,* that you didn't love him. So what was it about for you? What were you after? Money?"

I don't respond to him as he stares down at me. After a moment, he grabs a chair, pulling it in front of me, and takes a seat. He leans in towards me, and my head throbs in beats of aching heat from where he pistol-whipped me.

His eyes bore into me as a sly smirk creeps across his lips. His voice is low when he asks, "Or does it all have something to do with your father?"

My body pricks in chills at the mention of my dad. I tense around my hollowed chest, and wonder why he would even mention my father.

What does he know?

I don't say a word out of utter terror that I've gotten myself mixed up with the wrong people when I started this fucked up game. I've always been in control when it came to my charade in Bennett's life. But now all that control is gone and in the hands of this bastard, and that has me scared beyond belief. I pretend to be strong, but the reality of this situation has all confidence lost. I've been kidnapped and I don't have the first clue how to get myself out of this.

"I don't know what you want from me," I finally say, my voice coming out weakly. "What I told you about Declan was the truth. He hates me; he won't care if you hurt me."

"Then you need to find a way to make him care," he sneers before backhanding me so hard I fall out of the chair and onto the floor.

My vision fades for a moment when my head hits the concrete, and my urge to attack fumes inside, but I'm bound and useless.

"There isn't anything I wouldn't do for my family," he tells me and then steps away.

Staring up at him, my frustration multiplies, and since I can't knock the shit out of him, I attack with my words.

"Even with Bennett's dick inside your wife? Would you have done anything for her in that moment?"

"Your lies are humorous."

I don't acknowledge his denial as I continue antagonizing him, spitting my words, "Did you enjoy fucking her when my husband's cum was still inside her filthy pussy?"

He stomps back over to me, and I laugh to just piss him off even more. He grabs my hair, and immediately shuts me up when he balls his fist and punches the side of my face. Everything turns bright white, and my mouth fills with blood from where my teeth puncture the inside of my cheek.

Writhing in agony, I groan in exploding pain from my head. My skull thumps hard, and I can't open my eyes because it hurts too much. And the next thing I know, he covers my mouth again with tape.

The pain in my head increases as time passes. I've got my body pressed against the wall as I continue to lie here, and I wish he would just knock me unconscious to put me out of my misery.

When Richard walks out of the room and into the corridor, I make an attempt to break the tape as I twist my wrists, but it's not budging. I roll off my side and onto my stomach before I start grazing the side of my face along the floor. When I start to feel the corner of the tape pull away from my mouth, I press my face down harder, rolling it to try and catch more of the tape to pull it off. Once I feel the tape peel off the corner of my lips, I use my tongue to push it off, and when I can move my mouth and speak, I wait for Richard to return.

I can hear him talking to someone on the phone, but I can't make out what's being said. After a while, he returns, and I keep my voice as free from hostility as I can when I say, "It's true."

His eyes meet mine, and I add, "They did a DNA test that Bennett kept in his safety deposit box. Bennett left him everything. I couldn't believe it when I found out, but it's true."

"Tit for tat?" he says, confusing me.

"What does that mean?"

He then pulls his chair around to me and sits as I lie here, staring up at him.

"You hurt me, I hurt you."

My brows pinch together, not understanding his riddled words.

He continues, "I've got nothing to lose, and unless I get my money, you're not walking out of here alive. And from what I remember of your father, he wasn't much of a fighter, so I have a feeling your days are numbered as his were."

"Fuck you!" I snarl at him for speaking shit about my dad. "You don't know what you're talking about."

He laughs at me, revealing, "I know more than you think, little girl. You see, I knew your father."

My chest palpitates anxiously when he says this, and a thousand questions flood.

"Steve and I go way back."

I don't want to believe Richard had anything to do with my dad, or that my dad had anything to do with him. But . . . if he were still alive, he'd be right around Richard's age, so there's possibility in what he claims. But how?

"When Bennett had me following you, I started digging into your past. When all the pieces came together, I couldn't believe the Archer girl had been right in front of my face for years. I should've known you'd turn to pulling cons. At first, I thought I was your target when I was convinced you knew who I was. But when I started thinking back, I realized you didn't. I knew then it was Bennett you were after. But I still don't know why."

"Why would I be after you?" I question in terror, wondering who this guy really is.

"Maybe you blamed me for what happened."

"Tell me how you knew my dad."

"There's a lot I can teach you, you know? You were pretty good at fooling Bennett for all those years, but whatever it was you were trying to do, you moved too slowly and didn't properly assess the people you were surrounding yourself with."

"Tell me," I demand as I struggle to keep my tears back because just talking about my dad has me falling apart. He's my weakness, my softest part, and now I fear Richard has something to do with me losing him. "Tell me!"

"Call Declan."

"What? I don't have his number."

"Then we wait," he says. "I know he's in London and will be returning tomorrow. You'll call his landline then."

"Tell me how you know my father, Richard. You want to hurt me? Is that what you want? Then just tell me, because anything you have to say about him will surely be a dagger."

"That's too easy."

Richard then leaves me to be as he moves to the other side of the room and sits. I struggle to get comfortable with my hands still taped together. I lie on the cold concrete and rest my cut cheek to the ground to help soothe the ache that pulses through the gash. My head weighs heavy in an excruciating headache, and I close my eyes to drown out the cheap fluorescent lighting, but the buzzing from the bulbs keeps me agitated.

Hours pass as I drift in and out, and when the fog from all the high-strung emotions begins to clear, I'm finally able to focus. I run through everything Richard has told me, trying to figure out what the fuck is going on, when I remember his claim.

Guns.

thirty-three

(DECLAN)

MY MEETINGS HAVE been long, sitting around and listening to several architectural firms make their presentations and going over the bids for the job. This will be another boutique hotel that will cater to wealth, and above all, privacy. Lotus was my first solo venture, and it has proven to be a success in the few months it's been open. We maintain an exclusive clientele, which the city of Chicago was in desperate need of. It's full service in every luxury accommodation, selective on who's approved to book a room, and the London property will be the same.

I ring the house as I head back to the hotel for some much needed sleep. It's late, and I'm at my end.

It feels strange to have Elizabeth in my home, as if she's more than just a houseguest. She has me on mental overload. There are times I see her and I want to smash her face against a wall because my anger is too much to contain. And then there are times I look at her and I wish it could be like before with us. In those moments, I want to touch her and inhale her soft scent. I want to feel her, lick her, taste her, fuck her. I want it all, but my heart refuses to get too close to her.

She's the devil's angel.

The moment I start crossing lines, I shut down. It's not even something I consciously realize I'm doing, it just happens. One moment, I want my tongue tasting her sweet mouth, and the next, I want to rip more of her hair out.

Fucking her outside against my house yesterday was a twisted delight I selfishly indulged in. When I saw her from my office window, sitting on the ground, I saw someone so broken that I doubted her malice. In that moment, I let my guard down and got tangled up in the moment. And nothing can deny the solace that consumed me when I sunk my cock inside of her sweet pussy. Having her snug around me, Jesus, no woman has ever felt as good as her. But her warmth and comfort are merely an illusion. She's a magician's ruse that I stupidly fall for repeatedly.

She's evil and duplicitous, and yet a part of me wants her—a very disturbed part of me. Because no one in their right mind would want anything to do with the widow who injects her poison with self-serving motivations. For some reason, in knowing what a con she is, I don't want her to leave. A part of me feels sorry for her. I pity her. I've never seen a person at a lower point than she is at right now. This has to be her rock bottom because I'd hate to see what would happen if she got any lower.

Her body is branded in self-inflicted abuse. She craves the moment that she can hurt herself. I know Elizabeth is a sick woman who needs help, and the dark part of my soul wants to be the one to offer it. It's screwed up, because I also want to punish her.

When I told her to strip down last night, my plan was to humiliate her by having her perched on the ground as I had instructed. I left her to grab some rope because I had every intention of punishing her. I was walking around the house with a hard-on just thinking about it. My mind was consumed with visions of her tied up while I slapped her pussy and tits until they welted up red, picturing my cock shoved down her throat, gagging her, just so I could see tears fall down her rosy cheeks.

Even now that I know about all that she endured as a little girl at the hands of her foster dad, I still wanted to debase her like that. It's wrong; I know it, which is why I didn't return to her. I couldn't allow myself the pleasure that would just solidify the savage I fear I am—the savage she groomed me to be. But I hurt her anyway, and when I went to her room and saw the mortified look on her face, I hated myself in that moment.

There's no answer when I call, so I hang up and dial my home again.

Nothing.

She's probably outside.

I pull up the security app on my phone to log into my home system. Once it's connected, I tap on each camera to view the rooms in the house. From the kitchen to the library, atrium, bedrooms, dining room, office, roof . . . nothing. I then flip over to the outdoor cameras and check the grotto, backyard, and various cameras that overlook most of the grounds. No sign of anyone. When I tap to view the garage, I notice my Mercedes roadster is missing, which explains why she's nowhere to be seen. Irritation scathes me, not knowing what she's up to or where she is.

I hate not knowing details, especially when it comes to her. I know I'm controlling and overbearing, but it's the only way I know how to function without losing my shit.

She no longer has her old cell phone, and I haven't seen a new one, so I don't have a way of contacting her.

I decide to call Lachlan. I told him to stop following her because I didn't like how involved he was getting in her life, but I swallow my pride, and call him anyway.

"McKinnon, how did the meetings go?" he says when he answers.

"Good," I snip. "Look, I'm trying to get ahold of Elizabeth, but she isn't at home and I don't have a cell number for her."

As soon as I have her number, I hang up and dial it.

(ELIZABETH)

A SUBTLE VIBRATION is all it takes to rouse me from my restless exhaustion. My mouth tastes metallic from the blood I consumed when Richard punched my face. I shift off my side and onto my back. The arm I've been lying on tingles and aches painfully. Looking across the room, I see Richard slumped back in a chair with his eyes closed and a hand on his gun.

My body alerts when the vibrations return. My thoughts are hard to grab on to with the multiple strikes to my head and the emotional rollercoaster I've been on since Richard appeared in front of Declan's home. I focus on the faint buzzing sound, and my stomach clenches when I remember my cell phone. My body went numb a while ago, so it's hard to pinpoint, but I know I shoved the phone in the pocket of my pants.

I look back to Richard; his eyes are still closed. My heart begins to race as I shimmy to try and move my arms as quietly as I can. With my eyes locked on Richard, I make attempt after attempt, but it's no use. I can't get my hands to my pocket. I know it's Lachlan calling me because he's the only one I ever gave that number to.

"Richard," I call out to wake him up when I get an idea. "Richard."

"What the hell do you want?" he says on a groggy voice when he opens his eyes.

"I have to go to the bathroom."

"Hold it," he snaps and closes his eyes again.

"I can't, but I have no issues peeing myself if you don't have any issues smelling it," I lash back.

He breathes out in frustration and walks over to me, grabbing my arm and picking me up off the floor. Walking me down one of the corridors, we stop in front of a door.

"Hurry," he demands, and I look at him, reminding, "My wrists."

With a long, distrusting glare, he then says, "Turn around," and I do.

He takes his knife out, and when he slices through the tape, finally releasing my hands, the phone begins to vibrate, and fear crashes inside of me, locking my body up. When I turn to look at Richard, I can tell he hears the phone by the look on his face.

He knowingly cocks his head to the side, and in a moment of fright, I lurch forward and bolt. I'm not even allowed one second of attempted freedom as he immediately catches his arm around my waist, pulling me back.

I fight against him, but the moment his fingers latch around my neck, I freeze. His hand pats my pockets, and he pulls out the cheap disposable phone I've been using since I arrived here in Scotland. He flips it open and holds it out in front of my face while he has me in his chokehold with my back pinned against his chest. He then selects the last number that called and clicks it.

Putting it on speakerphone, he threatens, "Say one word and I'll make you regret feeling like you ever had a chance of one-upping me."

And then the ringing stops when the call is connected. I hold my breath, and Richard remains quiet as we both wait for the contact to reveal themselves.

A few seconds pass, and then my heart pumps hope when I hear the worried voice of the man I never gave this number to.

"Elizabeth?"

His accent wraps around my name, and it feels as if it's wrapping around my body in a soothing hug. I want to speak, to defy Richard and yell out all the details of my surroundings so that Declan can find me, but instead, I hold tightly to my breath.

"Elizabeth, are you there?"

"She's here," Richard answers.

"Who's this?"

"A man that has no conscience or limits," he responds before letting me go and handing me the phone.

In an instant, after taking a couple steps away from Richard, he has his knife to my face as I slowly bring the phone to my ear. Richard then takes my trembling hand as I listen to the gravel in Declan's voice, assuming

Richard still has the phone, threatening, "My word is my mark, and if you lay a hand on her, I'll—"

"AHHHHH!" I cry out in white, blistering pain, dropping the phone to the ground, and stumbling back on my feet. Gripping my wrist, I wail and stare in horror at the palm of my hand that Richard just dug his knife into, slicing it wide open. Blood is everywhere, oozing out as I hunch over and cry. Looking up, Richard now has the phone, but my body is in shock so that I can't hear anything he's saying to Declan.

I fall to my knees, forcing myself to calm down by taking in slow, staggering breaths, but all I'm doing is choking in shallow pants. I ball my hand into a tight fist, wincing through the burning sting as I hold my hand against my chest.

"Let that be a lesson," Richard says as he walks over to me, no longer on the phone. "Don't cross me again."

He then reaches down and starts tugging at my clothes and shoving his hands in my pockets.

"You hiding anything else?"

"No."

"Stand up," he orders, and once I'm up on wobbly legs, he grabs the neckline of my top and slashes his knife through the fabric, cutting it right down the center.

Shoving the fabric away, he runs the flat of the blade over the swell of my left breast, and when he reaches my nipple, he flips the knife to its razor edge. I've lost all control of my body as it shakes violently.

My eyes are closed while he taunts, "Defy me now; I dare you."

His words are an echo of Carl's. He would provoke me the same way, daring me to push his limits, as if it was giving him my consent to hurt me even more.

"What are you doing?"

Flicking my eyes over Richard's shoulder, I see Pike standing behind him.

"You're forgetting everything I ever taught you," he tells me. *"You're so much stronger than this pussy in front of you. Stop letting him think you're weak."*

Shifting my eyes back to Richard, I take Pike's lingering voice and inhale his words in a steady breath and release it slowly from my nose. I let my walls down with Declan, something I felt was right to do, but I forgot to bring them back up the moment Richard showed up. So with calculated intent, I mend the chink in my armor and steel myself to take whatever comes my way.

The knife continues to roam over my tits as I pull my strength together, and once I feel confident in my shield, I move my eyes to meet his.

"Can I take a piss now?"

"That's my Elizabeth," Pike encourages before Richard gives me a snide nod, and I turn to open the door.

(DECLAN)

THE CALL DISCONNECTED but not before I heard her blood-curdling screams. Focusing on the threats coming from the unidentified man on the phone was almost impossible when my only concern lay within the girl whose shrieking cries could be heard in the background. I demanded to know what he had done to her, but his priorities were in the instructions he was giving me.

And now, I fly around my hotel suite, shoving my clothes into my suitcase at the same time I wait impatiently for Lachlan to answer my call.

"Where the fuck is Elizabeth?" I bark when he answers.

"I don't know. Why?"

"She's gone. I need a plane. Now!"

"Slow down, McKinnon," he says. "What's going on?"

Blood courses erratically, like a raging stampede inside of me. Zipping up the luggage, I answer, "Someone's taken her."

"Are you sure?" he says in surprise.

"Yes, I'm fucking sure! I need a plane five minutes ago. Make it happen and call me back."

I don't waste time arranging for a driver, instead rushing down to the lobby and grabbing the first cab I see.

"Biggin Hill Airport," I tell the driver.

"You okay, sir?"

"Get me there as fast as you can."

He nods without further question as I wait impatiently for Lachlan's call, but all I can hear are her screams as they play over and over in my head. So many times I've wanted to inflict a pain so brutal to induce that type of reaction, but knowing her torture is outside of my control has my heart racing to protect her. It's a twisted thought, but if anyone is going to hurt her, it's going to be me.

I think of all the people who would choose to use her to get to me, and I'm drawing blanks. Truth is, I don't know the people she surrounds herself with, if any at all. But this person, whoever it is, was targeting her and knew just where to find her.

Logging back into the security cameras from my phone, I click through the rooms looking for any kind of clue I can because I don't know what else to do in this moment. When I check the camera that looks over the drive, I see my car that's missing from the garage. She must have been taken from the house if the car is there, but how? Why would she let anyone in the gate?

The phone rings, and I quickly answer. "Did you get it?"

"Yes. The plane will be ready to go in half an hour."

"Good."

"What can I do?"

"Have you seen her or spoken to her since I left yesterday?" I ask.

"No. I've been home."

"They want money," I tell him.

"Who?"

"I don't know. After you gave me her cell number, I called, but she didn't answer. I dialed the number a few times, and then a man answered. I could hear Elizabeth in the background."

"What did he say?"

"That we each hold something of value to the other. That he will let her go when I wire money into an offshore account."

"How much?"

"Enough to destroy either my foundation or my business."

"What are you gonna do?"

And when he asks, my answer comes easily and without second thought. "I'll do anything to make sure she's safe."

Once the words are spoken, I catch myself in a revelation I wasn't expecting to come to so effortlessly. I hang up with Lachlan and attempt to convince myself that I shouldn't be wanting this. That I should just turn a blind eye to her and let this situation work itself out. She'll be destroyed, and in return, I won't ever have to deal with Elizabeth again. Because if this man owns up to the promise he made on the phone, he'll kill her if he doesn't get his money. And then the book will be closed, and I can move on.

But I can't do that.

I can't turn away.

Taking the laptop from my briefcase, I log into the security cameras again. This time, to backtrack the footage that was recorded. I load the camera that monitors the gate to get a timestamp on when any cars arrived. It takes a while, but soon, two cars approach, my roadster being one of them. I watch closely and switch cameras when they pull up to the front of the house.

An older man, around the same age as my father, emerges from the one car. They speak and then head inside. I switch cameras again when they walk through the house and down to the library. She grows irritated, and I wish for the life of me there was audio on these cameras.

They sit and talk before the man turns angry, lurching off the couch, moving towards Elizabeth. And what happens next drains all warmth from my bones. I lean in toward the screen while I watch this unknown bastard take a gun out of his suit jacket and aim it right at her face. Her hands are white-knuckled to the chair as he then presses the barrel against her forehead.

Every cell in my body fills with a storm of tumult as I watch my world spin more and more out of control. I watch helplessly when he pistol-whips the side of her head, sending her flying to the floor. They exchange more words, she stands, he slams the gun into the side of her head again, this time, knocking her unconscious. He then goes out to his car and returns to duct tape her lifeless body, binding her ankles and wrists. Anger explodes, erupting in an outburst of seething fire when he hunches over her and spits in her face. Once he's dragged her out of the house and tossed her into the trunk of his car, I slam the computer shut.

My breaths come heavy, loaded with guilt, fury, and an undeniable urge for vengeance.

I want to kill that motherfucker.

"Drive faster, God dammit!" I bark at the driver.

Raking my hands through my hair, I can feel my body shuddering in emotions I need to get in check before I lose all the temperance necessary to keep my shit together. As we continue to drive and the mania begins to dissipate a little, I'm reminded of all the ways this woman has sent my life into an upheaval of disarray—her cunning hypocrisy, her ugly spitefulness hidden underneath her shiny exterior, and the blood that will everlast on my hands because of her malicious and selfish vendetta.

I remind myself of all the reasons why I should let this man kill her, remind myself of all the reasons why I hate her. But no matter how many reasons there are, I can't rid myself of the unyielding need to find her. It tugs on the threads that stitch my heart together, the heart that she ripped from my chest and tore apart. And as much as I want to deny it, as much as the thought repulses me, the fact is, the one that destroys is the one that heals.

I need her.

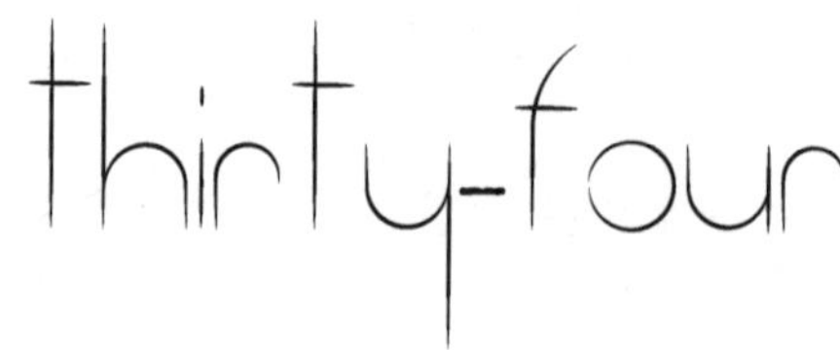

thirty-four

MY STOMACH GROWLS as I sit here on the ground with my hands bound with a plastic zip tie around a pipe that runs down the length of the wall. Since restraining me, Richard has retrieved a bag from the car filled with food and water that will never find its way into my stomach that hungers. So, I sit and watch, having no idea how much time has passed, if it's night or day.

We're underground, and I can tell by the looks of his phone that he's also operating on an untraceable disposable, making me worry that no one will be able to find me. Although Declan called and now knows I've been taken against my will, a part of me doubts that he cares enough to even come looking for me. But he's the only hope I have because there's no one else out there that even knows who I am. No friends. No family. Nothing.

Strength wanes.

Hope fades.

The tired fight inside of me vanishes.

Slowly, I open my fisted hand and wince from the sting of oxygen hitting the gash in my palm. Flesh covered in crusted blood—blood dead—proof that nothing survives forever. Old news to me, but yet I've always chosen to go on.

Why?

What's the point?

Win one battle only to be faced with another, but when will it end?

Will it ever stop?

Cellophane crumpling draws my attention to Richard's hand that holds a wadded chip bag. He stares at me as he throws it my way, but it doesn't reach me as it falls to the ground. I look at the garbage and can't help but compare myself. I sit here, lifeless as well, but marred in swollen bruises, cuts, and scabs. Some are self-inflicted, but others come from my love and this bastard in front of me.

I'm waste.

"What are you waiting for?" my voice cracks.

My words catch Richard's attention, and he looks down at me with question in his expression.

"No one's coming for me," I tell him. "If you think Declan cares about me, you're wrong."

He doesn't respond as we stare at each other, and then I ask what I need clarity on before my time runs out, "How did you know my father?"

His eyes shift to his gun that lies on top of the desk, and when he reaches over and picks it up, he gazes at the steel as if it's his desired beloved.

"You worked together, didn't you?" I ask on a trembled voice that threatens to break. Pieces begin to connect in my theory. "You said you used Bennett's business to wash money from guns."

Keeping his hand around the pistol, he rests it upon his thigh when he leans forward, saying, "You have no clue the tangled web you're caught in. It's almost a privilege to be the one who gets to unwrap this gift for you."

I thought I knew Richard. Thought he was nothing more than an ascot-wearing chauvinist that I didn't have to worry about. But now, I have no idea who this man sitting in front of me really is. I'm wondering if we're more alike in the fact that we mold ourselves in pursuit of self-gratification and manipulation.

"Just tell me," I say, free from revealing the emotions tugging at me.

"Steve worked for me. He worked as the middle man, the eyes and ears on both sides."

"Both sides?"

"Me and the mules."

I can't even attempt to connect the dots that led him to Bennett because all that floods my mind is my dad. Never have I pictured my father other than what he always was to me and still is—my prince with a handful of pink daisies. I can't imagine him working for a man like Richard, a man that dug his knife into my face and hand just to prove a point.

"He was always loyal though," he adds. "Until he took a plea bargain in exchange for names. I guess he thought the Feds would protect him, but Menard is filled with prisoners that are linked to me in one way or another. Although he never gave me up, which I hold great respect for, he did give up names of men who walked the low ladder of the business, and for that, he paid the price."

"You bastard," I breathe in sulfurous hate.

"Me?"

"You knew he gave up names?"

"Yes."

"And out of loyalty to you, he never gave you up?"

"Steve did what the Feds asked of him in exchange for an early release—for *you,*" he says, nodding his head to me for emphasis. "But at the same time, he never turned his back on me."

His words are gloats of pride for his assumed stature, and I grow in rage at the price it cost my father. The gravel in my voice thickens along with my animosity when I say, "But you held power. You knew the danger he was in, and you did nothing to protect him from what you knew would be inevitable!"

"It was out of my hands."

Blood boils, fists clench, and I begin to tug my wrists against the zip ties as I seethe, "But you're the boss! You hold all the power, and you did nothing!"

And then it starts clicking. The pieces now begin snapping together. Twisting my hands even more, the edges of plastic dig into the tender flesh of my wrists, cutting the tissue and releasing the blood my wounded heart pumps.

"You wanted him dead," I state in my revelation. "You were scared, weren't you? You knew he gave up names, and you feared it was only a matter of time before he sold you out too, right?"

His head tilts, and his condescending gesture acknowledging my theory as truth sets me off.

"You fucker!" my screaming voice scratching my throat. "It was you! You put the hit out on him, didn't you, you *motherfucker!*"

His only response is a slow upturn to his lips as he sits there.

I've always put all the blame on Bennett, and even though I hate Bennett for being the catalyst for all this shit, it was Richard who had the say in my father's life, and he took it to save himself.

"You're a fucking coward!" I spit out as I feel the bursts and pops of veins and ventricles—heartbreak over and over and over. My daddy risked his life in giving up names just to get to me.

Blood rolls down my arms like teardrops as my skin rips open as I fight against the zip ties. When my frustration snaps, I release a defeated scream and slump over. My bones tremble, and when I hear Richard chuckling, I turn to him in disgust.

"Does this get you off?"

He stands and walks to me. "Seeing the queen of Chicago society fall apart before my eyes? Yes," he responds and then kneels down in front of me, touching his finger to my face and running it along the cut on my cheek and then down my neck.

His touch is vile, rousing my stomach in putrid disgust, and I just can't take it.

"Tell me something," he starts. "When you found out that Bennett cheated on you, did you wish you'd known before he died so you could've gotten even with him?"

He then takes the knife out of his pocket and pops the blade up. My eyes follow his hand as he moves the blade to the zip tie and holds it against the plastic that's now covered in my blood.

"Did you?" he questions again.

"No." I didn't give a shit about Bennett cheating because I never felt anything for him other than pure hate.

Suddenly, with quick movements, Richard cuts through the restraint and frees my hands. He then moves the blade between my breasts. My top hangs open from when he cut the fabric earlier. I hear the lace snap apart when he presses the blade against the fabric, and I know his intentions. Focus is key, and knowing the process all too well, I protect myself and shut down.

He now knows the truth about his wife and son. I could overhear him when he was down the corridor and on the phone right after he bound me to the pipe. I knew he was talking to Jacqueline. He questioned her, and I could tell from the words he spoke, that she admitted the truth to him. He didn't raise his voice or become irate. It was the opposite. He remained collected, but looking into his eyes right now as he cuts through my bra, I see the fire of betrayal burning, and I brace myself for what I know is coming my way—retaliation.

Richard doesn't know how strong I am when it comes to sex. After all, I made it through four years of fucking the enemy, and I did it so well that he was none-the-wiser of my deep-seated hatred for him. My body is used up and polluted. It always was and always will be. Even Declan desecrated it when he raped me. So when Richard pushes the fabric aside to expose my tits, I feel nothing.

The cold, dank air hardens my nipples, and when this happens, he smiles and gloats, "Eager, huh?"

Fucking idiot.

When he stands up, I notice his erection pressing against his slacks. He walks over to the desk, exchanging his knife for the gun, and returns to me.

My breath catches when he shoves the muzzle underneath my chin.

"Don't get brave on me," he threatens. "One wrong move, I'll put a bullet in you."

Although I now know his true profession, I still want to doubt that he would be a man capable of killing, but his next words disintegrate all doubt.

"But something tells me you won't beg for your life like your little boyfriend's mother did, which is disappointing. I love hearing a woman beg."

My eyes widen is shocked disbelief. "You?" I question, horrified.

"Sometimes in life you have to teach people lessons, and when Callum thought he could screw me over, I made sure he learned I wasn't someone to be fucked with."

He's right—I've gotten myself tangled in the most fucked up cryptogram imaginable.

"What does Cal have to do with any of this?"

He shushes me, running his gun down my belly and shoving it into my pants, the coolness of the metal seeping through the lace of my panties. His grin is scathing when he unzips my pants to earn more room to slip the barrel between my legs. He slides it back and forth along my pussy, all the while smiling. But I'm detached. My mind is in the past with Declan on the afternoon when he opened up to me about his mom being shot in the head.

The pain he hides so well surfaced in his eyes, and just like me, the moment he lost his parent, he was forever maimed with a wound that would never heal. I would do anything for him, and to know that Richard was the one who pulled the trigger that forever fucked up Declan's faith in security and comfort fuels my affinity for revenge.

Richard catches my attention, taking me away from my memories when he begins tugging my bottoms down my legs.

"My wife acted like a cunt," he says. "But she's not here for me to release my anger on, and neither is Bennett. All I have is *you.*"

With my panties gone with my pants, he forces my legs wide open and presses the muzzle of the gun over my clit. My body locks up in horrid fear. I close my eyes, bracing myself for whatever is to come next, and after he makes me wait, I gasp when he forces the barrel of the loaded pistol inside of my pussy. Keeping my eyes pinched shut, I press my lips together and force myself out of this moment while he fucks me with his gun.

I remove my emotions and escape, giving him my body that's proven to be nothing but a piece of garbage. He glides the pistol in and out of me while I dig my fingers into the concrete beneath. Richard lets out a pleasurable groan as he starts fondling my breast in his one hand. I swallow down the puke that burns the back of my throat. My head rings loudly, and when the shield becomes too much for me to keep up, I beg for Pike to come, but he doesn't.

The iron cast cracks, chipping away piece by piece, and behind my closed eyes is Carl. No longer is Richard's gun raping me, but instead, Carl's filthy dick. My body jerks when the numbness wanes, and soon I can feel everything that's being done to me. When my hips buck, my eyes flash open to see the devil above me, and I lose it. With all my strength, I grab his wrist and lurch my hips back, forcing the gun up to my forehead, screaming like a maniac, "PULL THE FUCKING TRIGGER!"

He looks at me bitterly, and with my hands fisted tightly around the barrel of the gun, I shriek, pressing it harder against my head, "Do it, you piece of shit! Pull the trigger!"

He yanks the gun out of my hands and snarls, "What the fuck is wrong with you?"

"What are you waiting for? Declan's not coming, he would've already called by now. So why wait?" I tell him. "Just get it over with. Shoot me."

"Like this?" he questions, cramming the gun into my mouth.

I sit still, tasting the mixture of my pussy and metal. My lips wrap around what I yearn to be my savior. I nod my head and pray for the shot that will end my misery once and for all. But instead, he uses it to degrade me even more. Fisting my hair, he forces my head further down on the gun.

"Suck it," he demands as he bobs me up and down.

I gag, tears springing from my eyes as he makes me deep-throat it. He then pushes me away and stands.

"Put your pants on and shut your fucking mouth."

And as the saliva drips from my chin and I wipe my eyes, the phone rings.

thirty-five

(DECLAN)

"THE CELL NUMBER is coming up blank. It must be a burner phone," Lachlan tells me, and it makes sense that she would be using a disposable under the circumstances of her dead husband and all the lies. "Maybe the police would be able to bypass the blocks. I mean, the calls are going through a cell tower, perhaps they can track that."

"No cops," I order. "The call was choppy, cutting in and out, so they have to be somewhere secluded. I'm almost home though, how far are you?"

"Half an hour."

I hang up, and when I arrive at the house, I take my time heading up the drive, looking around for any clues. My black roadster is parked in front of the fountain, and when I get out of my SUV, I walk over to check the door to find it's still unlocked. The car is empty aside from the suitcase I find when I pop open the trunk.

Once inside, I head straight to the library to see the furniture slightly disheveled from the altercation I witnessed on the surveillance. I look around, stomach twisting, heart thudding, questions brewing. Setting the suitcase onto the couch, I start digging through it and realize that she went back to the Water Lily to retrieve the rest of her belongings.

As I'm rummaging through her clothes, my hand hits something hard. Grabbing the object, I pull it out, and the moment I catch sight of it, a chill takes over me. My fingers shake as I hold the picture frame and stare down into my own eyes looking up at me.

Where did she get this?

Unlatching the back of the frame, I take the photo out to see if anything is written on the back to find there is:

Declan

6 years old

I'm sitting by the small pond that was on the land of the home I grew up in. I'm staring up at the camera, smiling. The water is filled with lotus blooms, the blooms my mum loved so much. I remember how much she enjoyed that pond. She would sit along the bank with her legs hanging over the edge, just as I'm doing in the picture. She'd laugh in the sun's edge of spring, skimming her painted toes on the water's surface, calling out to me, her voice delicate and loving, "*Sit with me, sweetie. Dip your toes in.*" And I did.

The water was cold that day as we sat together among the fragrant lotus flowers. Her face is still so vivid in my head, flawless and milky. She was beautiful, with long brown hair that she would pin up in a bun around the house, but when she was in the gardens or by the pond, she would let it down.

My eyes close to bear the ache in my chest. The memories hurt, and the visions only remind me of what I allowed to be taken from me. I shake the past away, forever weak to let myself think about my mum for too long before I'm reminded of the coward I am.

Reality comes back into play when Lachlan calls from the gate. I let him in and stash the photo back inside Elizabeth's bag, still confused about where she got it and why she has it. But I push the thought aside when Lachlan walks into the room and tosses his jacket over the back of one of the chairs.

"He was in this room with her," I blurt out. "I pulled up the security cameras. He had a gun, smashed it into her head, knocking her out before he taped her up and threw her in the trunk of his car."

"Fuckin' hell," he mutters in disbelief. "Where's the computer? I want to get a look."

Grabbing the laptop, I log in and pull up the footage to show him. He takes the computer and sits at the desk in the corner of the room. I pour two fingers of Scotch and throw it back quickly, not even caring to respect the smoky flavors because I just need it to take the edge off before I completely go ballistic.

"Where's the gate cam?" he asks, and I walk over to show him the particular camera he's wanting.

I watch over his shoulder as he clicks to zoom in on something, which I didn't think to do because I swear to God, I'm losing all sense of focus.

"There it is," he says as he grabs a pen and jots down the license plate number.

"Christ, I'm a fucking idiot."

"Not as much as this fucker," he counters and then grabs his cell. "Try to relax. We'll find her. Let me make a couple calls while I grab a cup of coffee from the kitchen."

I nod and walk over to the couch and take a seat, but the moment I do, I hear a buzzing coming from Lachlan's jacket. Curiosity piques, and I go over to find another cell in one of the pockets. With no name flashing on the screen, I accept the call and stay silent.

"Baby, are you there?" a woman says, and it takes me a few seconds to connect the voice in my head.

"Camilla?"

There's a moment of silence before my father's girlfriend questions in return, "Declan?"

"Why are you calling Lachlan?" I ask, but she quickly pivots, saying, "How have you been? Your father and I haven't heard from you since you—"

"How do you know Lachlan?" I question, cutting her off mid-sentence.

"Umm, well . . . " she stumbles. "Maybe you should . . . you should probably ask Lachlan."

"I'm asking *you.*"

There's no immediate response, but it isn't long before she releases a sigh and reveals, "Your father is in a little trouble. I wanted to call you and tell you this sooner, but your father insisted that I refrain. You know how stubborn he is."

"Stop the shit, Camilla. How do you know Lachlan?"

"It's a rental," Lachlan announces when he rushes back into the room, and in the same second, Camilla hangs up, disconnecting the call.

"What the fuck is this?" I question as I hold up the cell.

He's collected and calm, responding, "My personal cell."

"And that is . . . ?" I question, eyeing the cell in his hand.

"My work phone."

"So tell me then, why is my father's girlfriend calling your personal cell? And why, when I asked her how she knows you, did she choke like a cheap whore giving head?"

"Camilla's an old friend. Don't worry; your father knows that. You probably just caught her off guard when you answered the phone."

His composure makes me second-guess whatever suspicions I have, but she called him *baby,* and I can't ignore that, but I also can't waste time right now. I'll have to deal with this shit later as I draw my attention back to what he said about the car.

"McKinnon," Lachlan adds. "Relax, okay? We're going to find her."

"I'll relax when she's back in this house. Tell me, what did you find out?"

"I'm waiting on a call from the rental company. Seems, whoever this guy is, he wasn't aware that the car has a tracking device in it that the company installs on all the vehicles."

"What about the police?"

"The minimum wage kid who took the call was an easy payoff," he tells me.

Grabbing her bag, I say, "I'm going to check her room. I'll be down shortly."

"Sure thing."

Heading upstairs, I walk into the guest room I put Elizabeth in since bringing her home with me earlier this week. I set the bag down and sit on the edge of the bed. When I look over to the nightstand, I see a pair of pearl earrings along with a necklace that catches my attention. I pick up the thin silver chain and stare at the small charm that hangs from it—a lotus.

How could a woman who is so dead inside be so sentimental?

This girl is incredibly damaged. To wrap my mind around her psychotic thoughts and deranged actions would be a wasted effort because there's no way to make sense of it all. The trauma that a person has to endure to get to the state of mental instability that she's in is gut-wrenching to think about. Everything she's told me about her childhood, everything she went through, is morbidly sickening. If I had to walk around holding on to what she does, I'm not sure I could live with myself.

Her past has molded her into a monster. But to look into her eyes as deeply as I find myself doing, there's something innocent inside of her. She's very much like a child in many ways; I see it in small glimpses. It's almost as if she hit pause and stopped living when she lost her dad. Like she's somehow stuck because the life she was thrown into was too heinous that she never let go of the childlike beliefs that the world is a good place filled with good people. You would never know it unless you found yourself in the core of her. She knows how ugly life is, but there's a little girl inside of her that hasn't given up just yet.

I'm helpless sitting here, not knowing where she is or what that fucker is going to do to her or *has* done to her. Never have I wanted to save someone as much as I did when I believed her to be Nina. I would've done anything for her, and I did. My love for her was so strong that I never thought twice about turning myself into a monster too—for her.

As much as I hate her, as much as I want to hurt her, as much as I wish I'd never met her, I can't walk away from someone I love so deeply that she's in my marrow.

The girl is crazy and out of her mind, and for wanting her, I am too. Nothing can deny the force that pulls me to her, even in my most wretched thoughts, I'm still drawn to her.

"McKinnon!" Lachlan shouts. "Get your ass down here. Let's go!"

Flying down the stairs, I ask, "What is it?"

"She's in Edinburgh. The location of the car isn't a pinpoint, but it's close enough."

"One second," I tell him before rushing up to my bedroom to grab my gun.

Energy powers through me like lightning as I move quickly through the house, and when I make it outside and jump into Lachlan's SUV, my heart races out of control.

"Talk to me. Where is she?"

He hands me the phone with the map open, and suddenly, my surge of optimism that we might know where she is morphs into dread.

"There's no way. It's too populated," I say.

"It's all we have to work off of. That's where the car is."

"That may be where the car is, but there is no way that's where he's got her," I tell him as I look at a map of downtown Edinburgh.

"Who're you calling?" he asks when I pull out my phone.

"Her. He's got her phone."

After one ring, the call connects, but there's nothing but silence.

"Tell me where you are."

My demand is met with a sinister laugh from this dick fuck, before he responds, "Now why would I tell you that?"

"I have the money you asked for," I lie.

"Very good, but I don't want to touch it. I'll give you the account information you're to wire the money into. Once I get verification the money has been transferred, I'll text you the location of wherever I decide to drop the bitch off."

"I want to talk to her first."

"I don't know if she's in the mood to talk right now."

"I don't give a fuck!" I shout. "Put her on the phone or the deal is off. I can take or leave the bitch, so it's up to you!" My words, fallacies.

Silence spans before he responds, "I don't think so. You see, I don't give a shit what you feel for the girl. I mean, I'm not gonna lie, I wanted to use her as leverage, but she isn't the only leverage I have on you."

"And what's that?"

His next words drain my veins and then fill them with icy fear.

"Bennett Vanderwal."

Fuck.

"WHAT DID HE say?" I ask timidly after hearing Richard tell Declan that if he couldn't use me as leverage that he would use Bennett.

"Looks like you were telling me the truth."

"What do you mean?"

"Seems Declan doesn't give a shit about you."

I knew it. I knew that if forced for an answer that I would never be it. And now I sit here, half-naked, beaten, and raped as the last of my heart incinerates into ash.

Go ahead and take a breath now because I'm finally ready to be blown into nothingness.

I now know my lies truly destroyed what I never wanted them to. I knew Declan was conflicted, I felt it in his push and pull, but I hoped there was a piece of him that still wanted me regardless of all my sins.

So I close my eyes, and green meets blue as Declan looks at me the way he did back in Chicago. He will never look at me with adoration as he once did. I ruined it for both of us. Now I'm left with this pain, ripping inside of me. It isn't the pain of heartbreak though, because I've already lost that. My heart no longer exists. And it can't be my soul, because I'm without that too.

But it's real, the pain I feel. It comes from somewhere inside of me, a place I never knew I had, and it hurts deep. Hurts in a way I've never felt before. It's so unbearable my body can't fight it, so it shuts down on me. I'm lifeless, flesh and bone, the weakened muscle inside my chest beating slowly, pumping what I pray is venom into my veins.

I don't want this anymore.

"What if he's lying to you?"

Keeping my eyes closed because just hearing his voice is enough to console me, I lie down with my head in Pike's lap, and he places a soothing hand gently over my swollen face.

"He's not," I whisper to him in response. "My destruction went far beyond the capacity of forgiveness."

"What the fuck are you talking about?" I hear Richard's voice bark, but I shut it out and focus entirely on Pike.

Pike is all I want right now. He's the constant that's always been in my life. He never turns away from me, never stops comforting me, never stops caring for and loving me.

My face scrunches in despair as I try so hard to hold myself together. "I can't stop missing you."

"I can't stop missing you either."

Battling with my emotions causes my body to tremble, and I know Pike feels it when he says, *"You wanna play a game?"*

I nod. "You can pick this time."

"How about breakfast foods?"

"Okay." Pike and I always used to play this word game when we were kids and I was locked up in the closet. It was his way of distracting me from my awful reality. We'd play this game for hours in the middle of the night while he sat on the opposite side of the door. And in this moment, in his death, he never fails to take care of me. "Pancake," I say, playing my first word.

"English muffin."

"NutriGrain bar."

"Rice Krispies."

We continue to play our words while he runs his fingers through my hair, careful to not hurt the tender scab that still remains on the back of my head. I never open my eyes, and eventually, before declaring a winner, I drift to sleep.

COLD METAL PRODDING my face wakes me up. My tired eyes come into focus as I jerk my head away from Richard's gun. I look at him, his face pale and his hair messy, as if he's been anxiously running his hands through it. He's jittery, kneeling beside me, and I have no clue if something happened while I was asleep to cause his shift in demeanor.

"Have I given you the impression that I'm one to be toyed with?" he says with a tight jaw, pissed.

I shake my head, and he snaps, "Then where the fuck is he?"

"I don't know."

"I will put a bullet in your head the same way I did the McKinnon woman. I swear to God, I will."

"I won't fight you," I tell him calmly. "You want to kill me? Then kill me."

He grabs my tattered shirt and shakes me, losing control while he screams in aggravation, "What the fuck is wrong with you?"

"If you wanted me to fight, you picked the wrong girl. There's nothing for me to fight for."

He shakes his head, confounded, and then clues in, saying, "So you don't give a shit what happens to you? I could do whatever I wanted with you, and you'd let me?"

"You can't possibly hurt me; I'm already dead," I tell him, the sound of my own voice creeping me out with its eerie tone. "But first," I add, "Fill in the blanks."

"What do you want to know?"

"Cal. What does he have to do with the guns?"

"He was my washer," he tells me freely, taking a deep breath and sitting next to me with his back against the wall. "Cal used to push the money through a random laundromat he acquired for the sole purpose of covering the money trail. But I later found out he was being greedy and filtering some of the money into an offshore account that was linked to him. That's when I taught him his first lesson in loyalty and killed his precious wife. He never stole from me again."

His words turn the venom of my heart into the blood of life. Just because Declan doesn't give a shit about me doesn't change my love for him, but I hide my shift. I'm like a machine when I continue my quest for clarity. "And Bennett?"

"Bennett was a man who trusted too easily, which made him my perfect asset. His father actually worked with yours."

"What?" I ask in shock.

"I always suspected bad blood between the two, then it became apparent when he put the authorities on Steve. I didn't know this until after Steve was already locked up, but apparently when Bennett came home one day talking some nonsense about how he thought your father was hurting you, that's when he saw his chance to get your dad out of the game."

My hands tingle in fury as I listen to his admissions. I can't even see straight as my desire to kill that piece of shit sparks to life. This man, my fucking father-in-law, was yet another man who had a hand in my father's death and the destruction of my life.

"Later, when Bennett was older and acquired his first production plant, his father convinced him to partner with me. We knew it would serve as a better cover for laundering the money. Bennett trusted me as a longtime family friend, took the advice of his father, and the rest is history, until you came along and fucked everything up with your stupid charade."

I sit in silence, trying with everything I have to control the anger exploding within me as I process what I've just heard, realizing that all of us are linked in one way or another. There was a time I was the one in control and able to manipulate people into my puppets, but I know now I was never in control because I never truly knew the cast of characters I lured my way into.

"But I will admit," he continues, "I'm impressed with your efforts, even though you failed miserably."

"Who says I failed? You're stuck down here with me too. You're not free."

"I will be."

I can't contain my chuckle, and when it grows, Richard fumes, "What's so funny?"

"*You.*"

"Do tell."

"You're so focused on yourself, that you're shadowing the fact that, in a very twisted way, I won."

He cocks back the hammer of his gun, the snick of the metal sounding when he does, and then points it straight at me, but he doesn't intimidate me.

"Don't you see?" I say in total control. "I *want* you to pull that trigger. So no matter what you do, I win." I take a hard swallow before going on, telling him, "It was *you.* You're right, I did get myself tangled up in something that was much bigger than me, but the root of everything, which I thought was Bennett, is actually *you.* And because of my *stupid scheme,* your family is now tainted in Bennett's blood through your son, your whole cartel is falling apart, and your freedom depends on the money of a man who'd rather see me dead than alive."

His eyes narrow in a murderous glare, but I don't stop, adding, "And if you think you have him fooled by threatening to know about his involvement with Bennett's murder, you're wrong. If anyone is to be pegged for that crime, it's you, the leader of one of the largest international gun trafficking rings, using Bennett as your cover."

Richard pulls the gun away from my face, but doesn't disengage the hammer.

"You've got it all figured out, don't you?" he taunts. "You think you have me played, telling me you want to die to take the pleasure away from me? You say I can't hurt you, but I think you're lying."

"Kill me or don't kill me, I don't care."

"I think you do."

I then wrap my hands around the barrel and place it back on my forehead, stating firmly, "I don't."

Agitation streaks in the lines of his face now that I've taken his bargaining chip away from him. He gains nothing from killing me, not even joy because he knows I won't beg for my life.

Richard drags the gun down my face, along the bridge of my nose, over my lips, and then slips it into my mouth.

I knew my sanctuary would be in death, and I was ready to be released into the oasis I'd been longing for. But even though I was ready, it didn't mask the fear of having a loaded gun with the hammer cocked inside my mouth. One slip and that chambered bullet would fire. I can still taste the steel of his pistol on my tongue if I think about it hard enough. Can still feel the way my heart ricocheted off my ribs. I had been close to death before, but it was always in my control. Not this time. This time I was on Richard's watch. He would say when. He would be my executioner.

I remembered hearing the voices—my ballasts. Daddy, Pike, and even Carnegie, they were there with me while I rested on death's lips, waiting for its kiss. Their words of courage to guide me from evil sang in my head like a melody of deliverance, but it wouldn't be enough, and I was about to find out why.

Richard uses the gun to guide me down on my back while he pushes it into my mouth. With his free hand, he rips the buttons to my pants open, demanding, "Take them off. You're not going to rob me from feeling gratified."

Idiot.

He's stupid to think that he can degrade me for his pleasure by fucking me. I do as he instructs, kicking off my pants while he fumbles with his own. I don't offer any fight when he shoves his pants down just far enough to pull out his dick. Nudging my legs open, he sits on his knees while holding himself in his hand and slapping it against my pussy a few times.

"Hands under your ass," he tells me, and I lift my hips to place them beneath me. "Time to even the score."

This man's pride is fucked up, to be concerned about getting even with his wife in this moment. My body slacks when he slams inside of me. I refuse to give him the satisfaction of tensing up. I keep my eyes focused on the pistol in my mouth as the metal rattles against my teeth while he violently pounds into me. He braces all his weight on his one bent elbow, grunting with each thrust. My tits hang out of my ripped clothes, jiggling while he fucks me with barbaric force.

This is my life.

This is all it's ever been.

Light turns dark as my eyes close, silently begging for him to release me to my paradise.

From across the room, I hear my cell ring, and my heart jolts alive.

He's calling.

My eyes pop open when the thought flashes quickly that maybe Richard was lying about Declan. My body jerks the moment the phone goes off, startling Richard in that exact moment, and everything happens in a lightning fast haze when he falters, losing his balance.

The instant the gun slips from my mouth, Pike shouts urgently, *"Elizabeth, FIGHT!"* and without thinking how or why, I automatically react.

Willing my strength, I drive my elbow into his arm, knocking the gun out of his grip. Adrenaline pumps through my system when the gun goes off, firing a bullet into the concrete wall as it skitters across the ground. The blast is deafening, but somehow I'm able to flip onto my stomach, scrambling as fast as I can. I sling my arm out to grab the gun when he locks his hand around my ankle and yanks me back.

My fingertips skim the pistol as I'm being pulled away, and the commotion is a total blur. Ripping out an excruciatingly demented scream, I fight with everything I have in me when I twist around and lurch my shoulders off the ground. With his pants still down, I dig my hands into his thighs, and with all the force in me, bite the ever-living-shit out of his dick, snarling like a wild beast as I do, and his voice erupts in pure acid.

"FUUUUUCK!"

Flesh pops in my mouth as my teeth cut straight through the elasticity of skin and sink into tissue, spurting blood everywhere. I feel the thick heat of it splattering on my face and coating my lips and chin. His screams are deadly as his body falls to the ground, and I jump to my feet, charging for the gun. The moment my hand wraps around the pistol, I turn, aiming it at his head, and scream like a maniac as my body detonates every emotion imaginable, but none of them make sense as they shake me to the bone.

thirty-seven

(DECLAN)

LACHLAN AND I located the rental car a while ago with no traces of where they could be. We're wasting delicate time wandering around the usually busy streets of downtown, but it's the middle of the night, and Lachlan and I are the only ones lurking around.

"This is fucking useless," I gripe in frustration. "Every business is closed and locked up. They could be anywhere."

"What do you want to do?"

Huffing out an angry breath, I let my head fall back as I look up into the dark of night. We've been scouring these streets for hours, and nothing. For all I know, this car could've been ditched for another and they could already be in another country.

Lifting my head, I turn to look down the narrow close that's to my right. There are so many of these alleyways in the city, and we've been walking through them all night it seems.

I'm plagued with an unsettling sense of doom that I'll never find her. The thought grabs ahold of me, twisting my gut as I think about not being able to see her face again or hear her say my name in her sweet American accent. I can't stand the thought of her never knowing the truth of my heart. She deserves to have the peace of knowing that I still care about her. After everything she's been through, and even after all the corruption within her, she still deserves to know.

Pulling out my cell, I begin to walk again and decide to call her phone once more. I dial the number, and after the first ring, I startle when I hear a loud crack that splits the night.

"You hear that?" I ask Lachlan, the words flying out of my mouth.

His eyes are wide, alarmed, saying, "That was a gunshot."

Grabbing my gun from its holster, I fly down the steps of the alley, because that sounded like it came from beneath me. My body surges in a rush of power as I go into overdrive.

"McKinnon!"

Darting down the stairs, I don't stop as I shout over my shoulder, "Keep a lookout!"

A man's torturous screaming fuels me, and I follow the echoes into the underground vaults. My heart has never raced so fast when a woman's screams filter in through the man's. With my gun in my hand, I run as fast as my legs will move through the narrow passageways. In an instant, I kick through a door to find a scene so disturbing, my gun immediately finds it target.

Their screams bounce off the cement of the small vault, piercing my ears. I'm horrified as my eyes flick back and forth between the two of them while my mind tries to grasp what's in front of me.

A man I don't recognize is crumpled on the floor, his face utterly pale as he begins choking on his breath. His pants are down, and his lap is covered in blood, and when I look over to see Elizabeth, I turn sick. She stands there naked with only a cut up shirt and bra hanging off her arms. Her mouth is covered in blood, and when I jerk my head back to the guy, I realize that the blood on her is from that bastard's dick.

Cries slice through her screams as her whole body shakes while she steps towards the man with her arm outstretched, holding a pistol.

"Elizabeth, no!" I shout when she rams the muzzle of the gun into his forehead and keeps it there.

She doesn't respond to me in any way as she stares down at the man.

"Don't pull the trigger!" I order, my words coming out fast while I have my own gun aimed at the man.

Her screams are replaced by staggering breaths hissing through her teeth, and I know that any second, she's going to murder him.

"Elizabeth, look at me," I urge. "Don't kill him."

"Why?" she seethes.

"Because you already know it's not going to make you feel better."

"You MOTHERFUCKER!" she screams hysterically at him like a crazed animal.

I take a couple steps closer to her, but she snaps, "Stay away from me!"

"Please," I beg. "No more killing."

"If not for me, then I'll do it for you," she says cryptically. "Consider this a gift."

"What are you talking about?"

She cocks the hammer back before finally looking over at me, and says, "He's the one that killed your mother."

Looking over to him, I pull back the slide on my gun to chamber a round; the metallic *click* is all I hear in this moment. I can feel the beast inside, digging his claws into the most wounded parts of me. It takes control of me, and without hesitation or question, I squeeze the trigger and put a bullet in his head.

I can't look away from him as blood sprays and chunks of his head fling across the room. His body tips over, still as death takes him instantly, dark blood draining from his mouth.

Elizabeth continues to aim her gun at him, trembling in shock with wide eyes, and I move cautiously over to her. Not taking a moment to process what I just did, my concern goes straight to the distraught girl in front of me.

When I reach out, she snaps, "Don't touch me!" and I immediately recant.

"Let me have the gun."

"No."

"He's dead," I tell her, but she doesn't respond as she keeps her gun pointed at him. "Look at me."

"No."

Her body is battered beyond belief as I scan over her. Added to her self-inflicted bruises is a nasty wound on her cheek covered in crusted blood, swollen contusions on her face, and a black eye. She's not only covered in her own blood, but also the blood from the man who lies dead at her feet.

Her breathing is rigid as I watch her, and eventually, she drops her arms and allows me to take the gun from her hand before falling to her knees. I release the hammer and set the gun down along with my own. As I start unbuttoning my shirt, I kneel down next to her and drape it over her back to cover her up. She keeps her chin tucked down, and I noticed her slashed wrists covered in blood when I take her hand in mine.

"It's going to be okay."

She remains silent as I sit with her. I want to do so much, but all I can manage is to simply observe. Her once-beautiful red hair is dirty, matted in blood. She's a fraction of herself, and I find it painful to look at, but I look anyway. And as sick as it sounds, I've never felt more bonded to her than I do now. Both of us exposed for the evil we are. Killers with mangled souls. No longer can I blame her for my sins because I just murdered of my own free will without her persuasion or seduction. She may have birthed this malignity inside of me, but I'm the one who now embraces it.

"He killed your mom," she says again, and I can barely hear her faint voice when she adds, "He's the reason my dad is dead too."

"Who is he?" I ask in utter confusion to this situation.

"Richard Brooks. He was Bennett's business partner," she answers and then goes on to explain how our fathers worked for him and the hit he put out on her dad. I sit and listen to everything she tells me, the whole time keeping her eyes downcast, almost cowering as if she's afraid of me. But it's when she says, "Cal is in jail," that her eyes finally lift to mine.

"Did Bennett know?"

"No. He thought he was running an honest business. Richard and Cal used him."

Every muscle in my body in tensed up because I know at any minute, I'm liable to break completely. As I ask questions to piece the puzzle together, my heart and mind remain with my mum. The fucker's blood that killed her at point blank pools under my loafers, and I have to swallow down the bile that threatens. I have to get out of here.

"Come on," I say, urging her to stand. "Let's go."

She coils away from me, pulling against my hold on her. "I can't."

"Can't what?"

She looks up at me, tears filling her eyes, blood smeared across her face, and says, "I can't keep pretending that . . . that we . . . "

"Just come home."

"I don't have a home."

Looking past the ugliness, deep into her eyes, into the depths of what's hidden beneath, my heart beats a beat I've never felt before. It comforts all the fears and doubts I have about her and assures me that she's where I belong.

"I know life hasn't been good to you, and I know you've lost a lot, but you haven't lost everything," I tell her. "I still want what I told you back in Chicago; I want to give you a home you can feel safe in. I want us to have a chance to make that happen."

"But . . . you hate me."

"You're right," I confirm. "I do hate you, but I love you and that's not going away."

"Do you forgive me?"

"No," I answer, shaking my head.

"Are you done punishing me?"

"No."

She drops her head, and I immediately cup her cheeks, angling her back to me when I explain, "I don't know if I'm ever going to get over this—if I'm ever going to get to the point where I don't want to punish you for what you've done. But I need you to understand something; I need you to know that even though you may feel pain, I will *never* hurt you. I will do everything to give you what was taken from you. I'm going to make you feel safe, I promise you that. No one will ever lay a hand on you again."

She never allows the tears to fall as I watch her struggle against her emotions, and I know it's a defense mechanism she uses to protect herself from pain, but she needs to feel it.

"Stop fighting yourself," I tell her as I hold her in my hands. "I want to see you cry. Don't hide from me anymore."

"I'm not a person you should love."

"Neither am I, but you do, don't you?"

Nodding her head, she let's go and weeps, "So much."

"And I love you," I say and then gather her in my arms. I hold on to her, listening to her broken breaths before making my selfish request. "Cry, Elizabeth. I want to hear you cry and know that it's for me."

She tucks her head into the crook of my neck, and when I feel the wetness of her warm tears dripping onto my skin, I'm satisfied. She's quiet in her sadness, and her release comforts me. I like knowing that she can hand it over to me and I'm the one getting to soothe her. I know she's right in that fact that she shouldn't be loved. Neither of us deserves it, but I can't help myself when it comes to her. I've never been able to curb my addiction to her, even when I thought she was a married woman. I wanted her regardless, and I want her still.

"McKinnon," Lachlan's voice hollers out.

"In here," I shout as I keep a tight hold on Elizabeth.

When he eventually finds his way to us, his voice is disjointed as he takes in the scene before him, uttering, "Holy fuck."

"Tell me I can trust you," I say to him, and without a second of hesitation, he responds loyally, "You can trust me."

"Call the police."

My arms remains locked around Elizabeth's trembling body while she continues to silently weep, hiding her head against my chest. Without having to even ask, Lachlan hands me her pants before turning around to make the call.

It doesn't take long for the authorities to arrive. Elizabeth plays her part as Nina, explaining her *husband's* murder and the crimes that Richard was conducting through Bennett's company. We twist the story, informing them that Richard murdered Bennett after he'd discovered the money laundering. It takes a while to give our statements that clear me of any involvement in the murder I committed.

The medics offer to take Elizabeth to the hospital, but she refuses, fervent that nobody touches her. Before we go, the detective advises us that we may be called in for additional questioning. He hands us his card with his contact information and we leave.

Arriving at the SUV, we climb into the backseat and I pull her onto my lap, cradling her back in my arms.

"Everything's going to be okay," I try assuring her, confident that we both just got away with our crimes.

She draws back from me, and I can tell she wants to speak, but she doesn't. She simply stares at me, and I'm able to look beyond the blood, dirt, bruises, cuts, and tears to see what I fell in love with when I first saw her in my hotel back in the States. I'll never forget how beautiful she looked at the grand opening of Lotus, standing across the room in a long, midnight-blue gown. She was confident, snarky, and so sure of herself, and in this very moment, I vow to give all those qualities back to her.

Running my hand around the back of her neck and up into her hair, my fingers graze over the scab that remains from when I pulled her hair out. I stop and she turns her head in shame away from me.

"Look at me."

And when she does, I cup her face once again and swallow against the emotional knot in my throat, saying, "You're safe with me," and then move her head to rest against my chest, banding my arms around her.

thirty-eight

SHAME AND EMBARRASSMENT only exist in things you value. I feel none of that as Lachlan drives us back to Galashiels. I know Declan assumes I'm feeling that way after finding me naked, raped, and covered in Richard's blood from where I bit his dick, but I don't. My body trembles and quakes in his arms as he holds me, but I tremble from fear. Declan told me everything I've been longing to hear, but who's to say I can trust him? Who's to say this won't fail like everything else?

Life has taught me that heartache is inevitable, proving over and over that dreams are simply that—dreams. Imaginative figments of our subconscious. Why am I to believe this is anything different? I certainly don't deserve it.

So here I sit with two options: die or trust.

Death seems the safest choice, but I'm also not ready to let go of what I'm starting to get back. Declan's like my heroin; I get one small taste, and I'm stuck, feening for more. But I'm terrified of losing it, knowing I can't survive without him—I don't want to survive without him. So if this is undoubtedly doomed, I'd be smart to just end this all now.

Maybe my true home doesn't really exist in the hills of Scotland, but instead, in the presence of all that was and is no more. They say death is the ultimate paradise, and the idea of being back with my father and Pike is beyond tempting. But I can't deny how good Declan's hands feel on me right now. Holding me and stroking my back. He smells like he always has, and I find comfort in the spicy notes of his cologne the same way I used to find comfort in Pike's clove cigarettes.

So as the uncertainty wracks my body in unquestionable fear, I hold on tightly to the one thing I fear the most—Declan. He's the one who holds all the power here. He could easily destroy me or make all my dreams come true, but in order for me to find out which, I have to let go of my control, something I've never done before. It terrifies me to hand all the parts of me over to him and trust that he'll take care of them.

For now, I selfishly take the affection he's offering me and nuzzle my head more deeply against his chest so that I can hear every sound his heart is making. Allowing its rapid beats to sing to me, I cling more tightly to him. The closer I get, the more senses I open up to him, the more I let the fear consume me. All I want is comfort, but I'm too scared of the pain I'll have to endure when it's gone—and it *will,* one day, be gone.

When we arrive at Brunswickhill, Declan helps me out of the SUV as I wince in pain. The long drive back gave my body time to dissipate the adrenaline, and now my muscles and bones scream angrily at me, causing me to hunch over. Bracing my hand on Declan's arm to steady myself, he moves to pick me up and carries me inside.

Neither of us speaks as he takes me up the stairs, but instead of going into the guest room, he carries me into his. He sets me down on the edge of his bathtub, and I watch him as he wets a washcloth. When he kneels in front of me, he begins wiping my face, and my eyes focus on the terrycloth as it turns from white to pink to red, collecting Richard's blood.

I'm a tomb, sitting in the palace, observing. I couldn't move if I wanted to.

So I sit.

Maybe my body's in shock.

Or maybe it's just numbing itself for departure.

There's no feeling, only sounds as Declan moves about, tending to me. He holds out a toothbrush, but my hand won't move to take it.

"Open," he gently requests, and I do.

Mint touches my tongue as he brushes my teeth, but it doesn't taste right. And when I look up at Declan, he doesn't look right. Sounds don't sound right, as everything begins to vacuum itself into a tunnel of fog. And now, my chest doesn't feel right. Pins prick along my body at the same time my eyes swim out of focus.

"Are you okay?" Declan's lips ask, but his voice is muted and a million miles away as I sway.

My brain tells my mouth to speak, but the wires don't connect the message as Declan's face morphs into a concoction of colored specks.

And then he's gone.

Strong hands press through the pins; one on my chest, and the other on my back, lowering my body down.

"Drop your head," he instructs.

I reach out for him when I let my head fall, and his hands quickly move to mine, and I latch on to him. Everything's disconnected, floating in an abyss, causing my pulse to pick up in a panic.

"I'm here. I've got you. Just close your eyes and take deep breaths."

My tongue is completely numb as I attempt to finally speak, but my words only slur when I say, "I feel sick."

"It's okay. Just focus on breathing."

Soon, I feel the heat of my blood flow, warming my insides, and when my vision comes into focus, I move slowly to sit up.

"Better?"

I nod.

"Let me get you some water," he says before going to fill a glass from the faucet. "Here."

I take a few sips, and Declan turns the water on in the shower. He undresses, and I can't peel my eyes away from him as I watch. Every part of him is smooth and cut in deep, muscular lines. Walking over, he takes the glass from me, and helps me stand up.

With my hands gripped to his shoulders to steady myself, he begins unbuttoning the shirt he put on me. I let go of him, letting the shirt fall to the floor along with my other top and bra that Richard cut with his knife. My body is sore as I help him remove my pants, and he then leads me to the shower.

Hot water rains down on me, washing away exterior grime. If only I could turn myself inside out, I'd do anything to cleanse the grime from inside of me, but I can't. And I wonder if that rot will always remain.

Declan's fingers run along the open wound on my cheek where Richard dug his knife in, and I hiss against the sting.

"Sorry," he whispers, and as I look up into his harrowed eyes, I'm overtaken with guilt, and it becomes too much to hold on to.

Heated tears slip out, merging with the heated water as I let my emotions roll down my cheeks. Declan sees it coming out of me, takes my head in his strong hands, and presses the side of my face tightly against his chest. I curl my arms between our bodies and cuddle into him.

As we stand here under the water, naked and boundless, exposed and vulnerable, I feel the faint line-fracture begin to split. It's a sharp razor, slicing a jagged line through the scar tissue of my deepest pain. A part of me is terrified, but another part of me is ready to end the war inside. But I'm not even given a choice when I feel it taking a life of its own, shredding the fibers of the walls I've spent my whole life erecting.

"It's okay," I hear Pike whisper. *"If you shatter, he'll put you back togeth-*

er."

His voice, his words, they allow the severing to happen, and I rip open.

Tremors quake through me and Declan feels it, banding his arms around me. And when he speaks his next words, "I've got you, darling. If you shatter, I'll put you back together," I bleed it all out.

Dropping to the floor of the shower with me, he tucks me in his arms, and for the first time ever, I cry for everything I've suffered through—I *really* cry. It's ugly and messy, screaming and sobbing, bawling harder in an attempt to drain all the misery out of me. Salt burns, sadness scathes, memories devastate, but somehow, his hands alleviate.

I'm tired of being steely and callous. I'm tired of pretending and always fighting against my own skeletons. I'm tired of the uncertainty and hatred that drives the tenebrific evil in me. My wish is that his arms hold the magic to intenerate my heart—to make me good—to make me worthy—to make me lovable. But I doubt any man's arms are that powerful, and that doubt adds more fuel to my fear of Declan.

So I cry for fear as well.

Because I'm scared.

I'm *so* scared.

It's always been there though—the unease, the worriment. It's lain dormant inside of me since I was five years old, coming to life every now and then, but Pike taught me how to quickly silence it in order to survive. The dormancy is gone now. It's a live wire of unfiltered anguish that pours out of me and into the arms of my prince on earth while my other prince exists only in the nirvana I've yet to become a part of.

Warm breath feathers over my ear with a tender, "I'm so sorry."

"It's me," I blurt out through the unwavering tears, lifting my head to look into his eyes that own responsibility for things he was never responsible for. "I'm the cause of everything, not you. It was all me."

"You were just a kid. You didn't deserve what happened to you."

With his words, I reach out to his chest and run my fingers along the two bullet wounds that mark my deceit and give him *my* words, "And you didn't deserve *this.*"

His hand covers mine, pressing my palm against his scars, saying, "I did. Because without it, I would've never found the truth in you."

"But my truth is so ugly."

"Like I said before, the truest part of a person is always the ugliest. But I'm ugly too, so you're not alone."

As the water cascades over us, I feel weighted down in guilt for what

I've put this man through. Because none of it mattered when all I truly cared about was simply him.

"Tell me how to make you forgive me. I know I'm not worthy of your forgiveness, but I want it."

"I wish I knew, but I don't," he tells me. "We're broken people, Elizabeth. You can't expect me to not have my issues, because I have thousands of them. But just because I hold a hate for you doesn't take away from the love I have for you."

His words might not make sense to most people, but for me they do. I just have to choose whether or not to risk handing myself over to him.

"Come here," he says as he stands to help me up.

I take a seat on the built-in slate bench, and allow him to wash me as I sit here, drained to depletion. Closing my eyes, I relax into his touch while he washes my hair and cleans my body. But it's when he opens my legs and curses under his breath that I open my eyes and tense up.

"What?" I ask, looking down at him as he stares in horror between my thighs.

Shifting his eyes up to mine, his jaw grinds before demanding, "Tell me exactly what happened."

I look down to see the nasty collection of bruises.

"He raped you?"

I nod.

"What else?"

His hands remain on my thighs, spreading me open, when I admit, "He used his gun."

"What do you mean *he used his gun?*" he seethes through his teeth.

"To fuck me with. He used his loaded gun and then forced it in my mouth to suck."

His fingers sink into my skin as he drops his head, and I can see the muscles in his shoulders and back flex in anger as he tightens his grip on me. His words strain when he goes on to ask, "And all the blood on your mouth?"

"He was raping me with his gun in my mouth, but I managed to get away and I bit him."

"His dick?"

"Yes," I whimper, and when he looks up at me, I reveal, "I wanted to die. I begged him to shoot me."

"Don't you dare think about leaving me," he scolds.

"He told me you didn't care what happened to me, that you weren't coming."

"I *did* come for you," he affirms. "All I could think about was finding you. I was going crazy not knowing how to get to you."

Grabbing a washcloth, he runs it between my legs and begins to gently clean me. Once he has me washed, he keeps me naked as he helps me up into his bed. Nestled in his sheets with his scent all around me, I want to smile, but I can't. Regret consumes, hating the darkness I've brought to us, wishing I could erase it and go back in time to do it all over again.

"I need you to know something," he murmurs, wrapping me up in his arms. "I'm not the same as I was."

But I already know that. It's evident in his eyes. From the moment he stepped out of his SUV and I knew he was alive, I saw the corruption inside of him.

"I keep trying to process what I did to Bennett, find reason for allowing myself to lose control, but I can't."

Reaching my hand to his face, I press my palm against his stubble, and all I can manage to get out is a breathless, "I'll love you no matter how dark you turn."

And with that, he finally kisses me, pressing his lips to mine in a fever of emotion that tells me everything that is buried deep within him. His body, heated in bands of roped muscle, rolls on top of me. We're flesh on flesh, transparent, bare. Scars opened wide for each other to see.

His lips move with mine, opening me up to reunite, claim, and control in carnal ustulation. He growls, rolling his tongue with mine, as I tangle my hands in his hair, savoring his taste.

His cock is thick and hard against me, but the moment he grinds himself over my pussy, I wince in pain, crying out as I flinch away from him. He tenses above me, and I try pushing him off of me, but he doesn't budge.

"Are you okay?"

"I'm sorry," I blurt out as he allows me to sit up.

"It's okay," he soothes.

"I just—"

"You don't need to say a word."

Coming in, he takes my breast into his mouth, sucking my nipple, all the while keeping his eyes pinned to mine as I look down at him. He feasts in primal need and I don't deny him of his need for closeness in this limited capacity. With my legs bent and spread, he lowers himself on me, dropping his lips to my pussy.

"Don't let me hurt you," he tells me as I run my hands in his hair, fisting it the moment his tongue dips through the seam of my core.

He keeps his touches soft in a very un-Declan-like way that I'm not used to. Dragging his tongue over my clit and then pressing the flat of it against me in slow circles, sending a chill up my spine. Gently, he sucks the bundle of nerves into his mouth. His deep groans vibrate against me, and I know he's restraining himself, so I grant him permission, saying, "It's okay. You won't hurt me."

As soon as my words are out, he bares his teeth, sinking them into my most tender flesh as I pull his hair. I hiss in a pleasurable pain that only Declan is able to give, and I'm satisfied in knowing he's content to inflict it upon me. I sink down into the bed when his hot tongue begins fucking my pussy, dragging in and out of me in torturous delight.

Grabbing on to my hips, he begins to move me over his tongue, up and down, push and pull, forcing me to now fuck his face. Sparks flicker when I close my eyes, and I give in, grinding down on his face, and his approving growls to selfishly take this pleasure he's offering spurs me on more.

Thighs quiver, hips buck, heart thuds, and I don't deserve this.

"Stop."

I push him away and scoot back.

"No," he barks at me, pulling me back down, wrapping his lips around my clit as he grips his cock and starts jerking himself off.

"Declan, please," I whimper as he draws me closer to my orgasm, but he ignores me.

His tongue laps over me, teasing, sucking, biting, licking. He's fervent in his movements with only one goal in mind, and when he rolls my hips against his mouth, I explode.

Shattering waves of electricity burn and spark through nerves and veins, heating me in a frisson of passion. I come sinfully hard, feeling every pulsing contraction of my pussy gripping Declan's tongue as he moans out his own orgasm. Our sweat-covered bodies writhe together as internal wounds open in vulnerability. Tears spill from the corners of my eyes when he kisses his way up my battered body, over my breasts, along my neck, and up to my lips where he says, "Taste how perfect you are for me," before dipping his tongue in my mouth so I can taste myself on him.

And we kiss.

We kiss like no two humans have ever kissed before.

We're tear-stained savages, sharing a single breath of life, death, and love. Giving, taking, bruising, and reuniting what I thought was forever destroyed.

And for the first time in a very long time, when I tire out and close my eyes, I spend my slumber with Carnegie.

WAKING UP, DECLAN is sitting up in bed next to me, drinking a cup of coffee and watching the world news on the flat screen above the fireplace that's across the bedroom. As the rain falls outside, pelting against the windows, I lie still, allowing my body to wake up slowly as I watch a breaking news segment.

When I stretch out, Declan notices I'm awake, saying, "Morning, darling," and opens his arms up for me to curl into.

"What time is it?" I ask in a groggy voice.

"After one. We slept all day."

Turning my attention back to the television, I listen to the report on an American aircraft that crashed after there was a malfunction with the landing gear. I melt into Declan's hold as I watch the reporter give an update as the passengers are deplaning in the background. He announces everyone's survival and that only a few were injured and are being taken to the hospital. But it's when the camera pans over the passengers that my heart stalls and I immediate sit up.

"What is it?" Declan asks, but I can't speak, and then the segment is over.

"Can you rewind this?"

"What's going on?"

"Just rewind it," I say on a trembled voice and my body goes into high alert.

Declan rewinds the segment, and as soon as the camera zooms in on the passengers, I tell him, "Pause it."

My eyes widen in shocked disbelief as my pulse races out of control.

It can't be.

Crawling to the edge of the bed, Declan's worried voice calls to me in question, "Elizabeth?"

Oh my God.

"He's alive."

from the author

Need to talk to someone about the Black Lotus series? There is a discussion group on Facebook for those who have finished reading.

Discuss the Black Lotus series (https://www.facebook.com/groups/bang-discussion/)

acknowledgements

SOMETIMES IT TAKES a village to make things possible, so let's get straight to it.

My fans, *thank you* will never be enough for all you do for me. You have waited so patiently for me to write this book. You stood by me, supported me, encouraged me, and everything in between. This book would not have been possible if it weren't for each and every one of you. I've said it before, and I'll say it again: E.K. Blair fans are the best fans!

My husband and children, I know the sacrifices you all make to allow me to pour my soul out onto paper for the world to see, and I love you for that. The three of you are the blood my heart pumps, the air I breathe, the fibers of my soul, the salt of my tears, and the icing on the sweet life I've been blessed with.

My editor, therapist, and dear friend, Lisa, what would I do without you? Through tears and laughter and more tears, you've proven to be a steady rock for me. When life gives me lemons, you have a way about you that turns those lemons into a lemon drop martini. Thank you for loving me both professionally and personally.

To my fellow writers who helped me out of the burning flames, Aleatha Romig, K. Bromberg, Corinne Michaels, Adriane Leigh, Pepper Winters, and Kathryn Andrews, your uplifting words and supportive messages, no matter how big or small, provided me with the threads needed to create the rope that helped pull me above the under.

Sally, Bethany, and Teri, the time you girls sacrifice for me is simply unreal! I couldn't ask for a better team to assist me. The three of you make it possible for me to spend more time with my family, and that time is so precious to me. Thank you!

My brave beta readers, Jen, Kiki, Ashley, Jennifer, you girls are amazing! Thank you for giving up months to go with me on this wild ride and for embracing the darkness in my head.

Tarryn Fisher, for supporting me and sharing me with your fans. And also for being my Twilight-Bestie and for loving the series as much as I do! We crazy psychos must stick together.

Thank you, Denise Tung, for always being there to organize all my promotional marketing from cover reveals to reviews. You have been with me from the very beginning, and without you I'd be lost.

Erik Schottstaedt for another beautiful cover photo.

And last but certainly not least, to every blogger and book reviewer who has read my words, reviewed my books, and promoted me, THANK YOU! No, seriously, THANK YOU!!!! Everything you do for me and the lengths some of you go to for me is valued immensely.

NEW YORK TIMES BESTSELLING AUTHOR

e.k. blair

"Addicting and captivating. Filled with enough sexy twists and turns to keep you up all night reading."
-Alessandra Torre, *New York Times bestselling author*

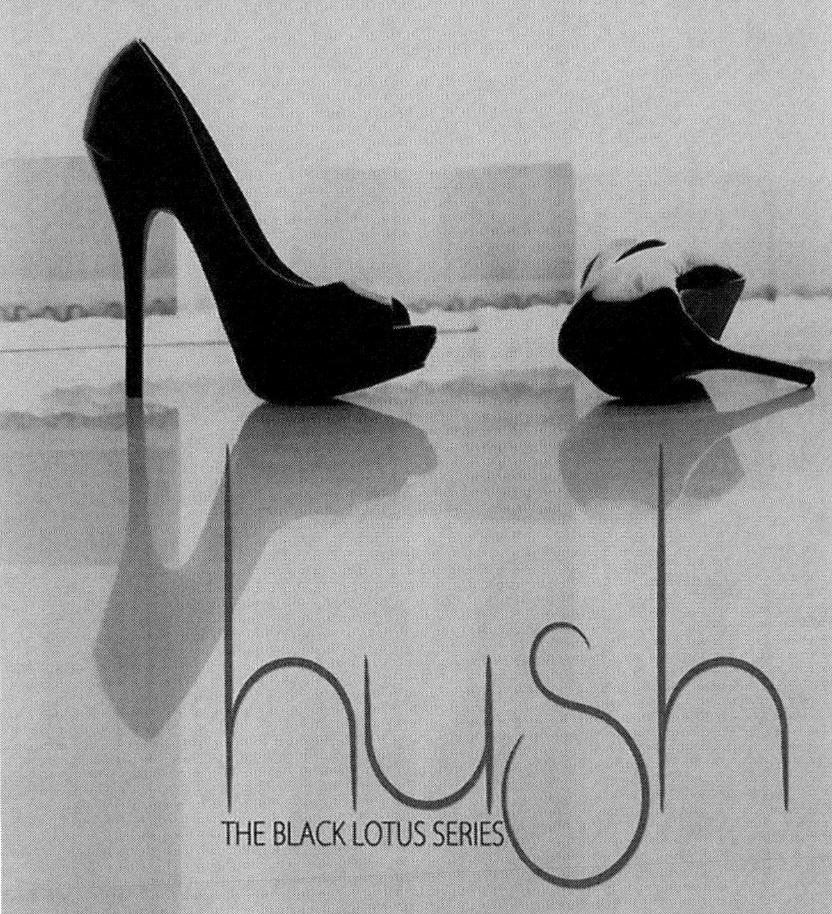

To Sally

Because you love him as I do

“It’s no use going back to yesterday,
because I was a different person then.”
-Lewis Carroll

I'VE COME TO know illusions well. They're the phantasms I cling to because I'm not ready to let go of the comfort they give me. Most of what brings me solace and peace are nothing more than ghosts of my past, yet I hold tightly to keep them with me in the present for fear that without them, I just might disappear too.

I'm scared to be alone, even though in some ways, I always have been.

A jolt of electricity shoots through the thick blood in my veins. It's the one thing that lets me know the difference between reality and delusion. The spark shocks my system into high alert, forcing my heart to leap out of rhythm as my eyes widen in a storm of a thousand questions my mind can't process.

I crawl to the foot of the bed on my hands and knees, staring at the TV above the fireplace. Declan sits behind me, but I no longer feel him as I struggle to breathe.

"He's alive." It's all I can mutter as I stare at the paused screen of the news report.

"Who?" Declan questions from a million miles away as I stumble off the bed and walk in uneven steps across the room, closer to the TV.

I reach out my hand as I near the image that can't be true, but is. I step onto the hearth, my fingers trembling when I slowly press them onto the screen. The moment I touch him, my heart ruptures, and I cry out. Blood from my wounded soul floods my eyes and spills down my cheeks. My breaths fracture and fill the room.

Strong hands grip my shoulders, and I want to collapse, but I can't look away from the one thing I've been searching for my whole life.

"Talk to me," he says, voice panic-stricken.

Pressing my hand more firmly against the screen, I beg to feel the warmth of him on my skin.

"Who is he?"

"This is real, right?" I ask of Declan. "You and me, in this room, it's real, isn't it?"

"Look at me."

But I can't. I'm afraid to look away for fear that I'll lose him. That somehow he'll vanish from the screen.

"Tell me it's real," I cry.

"It's real, darling. I'm here with you."

And with his words, an ugly sob rips out of my chest, but I catch it quickly when Declan steps onto the hearth next to me. As memories swirl inside, a mixture of foggy emotions fight with each other, and when anger claims victory and swells to the surface, I turn my head to look at Declan. His eyes mirror mine in utter confusion.

"He's dead," I say to him, the words like razors slicing my vocal cords, but I speak through the pain as tears stream down my cheeks. "They told me he was dead. Why? Why?"

"Who?"

"I saw his grave. I felt the stone where his name was etched," I go on. "Why would they lie to me? Why did he lie to me? Why didn't he ever come for me?"

Declan pulls me into his arms, pressing me tightly against his chest as I wail over and over, crying out for answers that don't find me, screaming for comfort in all of my whys.

"Who?" he questions again, and when I turn my face and bury it into his bare chest, I sob through shattered dreams, broken hearts, and lost souls.

"My dad."

I fist my hands against Declan's chest as his grip tightens around me. His embrace is unwavering and entirely hard as his muscles constrict around my weakened body.

"Why am I so easy to walk away from?"

"Don't do this," he scolds. "Don't you dare blame yourself."

"Why not?" I scream, jerking my body out of his hold, pissed at the world, and for the first time in my life, pissed at my father. Stepping down and away from Declan, I turn back around and lash out in self-pity at the top of my lungs. "What did I do to deserve this life?"

"Elizabeth, please. Just take a deep breath."

"No."

He moves towards me, saying, "The last time you saw him you were only five years old, right? How can you be sure that's even him?"

I step up to him and seethe between my tears, "Because you don't forget the face of the one man you've spent your whole life aching for. There is no doubt that man is my father."

Returning to the TV, my eyes are stoned to the bright blues I remember so vividly. Eyes I thought loved me beyond anything in this world. Eyes I thought bore black six feet under. But he's here, and I've never felt more alone.

"Elizabeth?"

My hands grip the mantel to keep my legs from failing me.

"Elizabeth, please. Look at me."

"Elizabeth?"

His voice is both poison and wine, and hearing it causes my limbs to go ataxic and I crumple to the floor. The familiar smell of clove cigarettes both soothes me and torments me.

"Is it true?" I ask my brother, Pike, but Declan answers first.

"I'll do whatever I can to find out."

"Yes, it's true."

Looking up, I shift my eyes away from Declan to the corner of the room where Pike stands. We both know I shouldn't be looking at him, because Declan thinks I'm taking the pills that kill my hallucinations, but I'm not. I can't say goodbye to my brother yet. Maybe never.

But there he stands, alive, with his dark hair tucked under his black beanie, and his hands shoved into his pants pockets with his inked arms showing. His eyes send love and strength before he nods his head over to Declan, and I follow his cue, knowing I'll lose him when I do.

My throat swells in torment, painfully blistering as I sit here on my knees. It's every dream come true; I just never knew the dream lived within an unimaginable nightmare. No matter all the anger I feel right now, one thing still remains: you can cut me deeply with lies, you can throw me into the flames of life's evils, but I will never give up on what I've always yearned for.

With tears falling down my face in a steady stream of anguish, I painfully choke out the heartbreak of the little girl lost inside of me. "I want my dad."

In two quick steps, Declan is on the floor with me, holding me, rocking me, soothing me, and vowing to do everything he can to find him.

Clinging to him, I take all the comfort he's giving and attempt to steal more, gripping him tighter and pressing my fingers deeper into his skin. If I'm hurting him, he doesn't show it, so I close my eyes and crawl onto his lap just as a child would.

When I open my eyes again, they sting against the fully risen sun, and my cheeks burn with the bite of salt. I'm still wrapped within Declan's arms, and my body aches not only from being in this position for God knows how long, but also from the torture of the past couple days of being held captive.

"I hurt."

Declan stands and scoops me off the floor before laying me on the bed. He hovers above me, looking over my battered face and body with eyes filled with rage and pity.

His expression irks me. "Don't."

"What?"

"Look at me like that. Like you feel sorry for me."

"I'm worried about you. That's all." He then hands me a painkiller that I slip into my mouth.

"I don't understand. I don't understand any of this."

"I don't either. But you've been through a lot lately, so I don't think your mind is capable of clarity. Mine isn't either. So let's focus on one thing at a time, okay?"

"All I can focus on is why my dad's face is on that screen when it shouldn't be. I don't know if I should be happy or angry," I tell him. "Why didn't he want me?"

Declan doesn't respond as he pulls me against him. I try to fight the haze from the pills that creeps in, but my eyes grow heavy when Declan whispers softly into my ear, lulling me with a comforting, "Shh, darling. I'll take care of you. I'll do what I can to find the answers."

And as I hang on to his words, I give in, releasing a breath before drifting to sleep.

(DECLAN)

ELIZABETH TREMBLES IN her sleep as I hold her. My mind is a goddamn labyrinth as I close my eyes and attempt to process the past forty-eight hours. It's an impossible task as visions race with a hundred new revelations and a thousand new questions. The only thing I do know is that I'm terrified I won't be able to keep Elizabeth from having a full-on mental collapse.

Her face is a canvas of bruises, welts, and lacerations that illustrate the rape and torture she's been through. It pains me to know that I play a part, that some of those wounds were put there by my own hands and the others were put there because I couldn't protect her from that asshole—Richard—the man I murdered.

I didn't even hesitate when I put a bullet in his head after Elizabeth told me he killed my mum. The fact that I could kill so easily scares the shit out of me. It's a grim feeling to be terrified of your own self. I now know I'm capable of anything. I'm a monster created by this woman, whose body is wrapped around mine.

I want an explanation, just as she. Who was Richard? How did he know my mum? Why did he kill her? What part does my father play in all of this? I want to know. I want to understand, but as out of control as I am, she is more volatile than I. She needs strength, so I have to set aside all that haunts me right now and focus on her.

When her breaths even out, I slip out of bed and allow her the rest her body desperately craves. I stop before I walk out of the room and look at Elizabeth lying in my bed as a swell of contentment and anger rushes in a tidal wave under my skin. She's knocked my control off its axis, and I need to steady it back into place to keep her safe—to make sure nothing else happens without my say-so.

(DECLAN)

"CHRIST," LACHLAN SAYS with a startle when I slam the double doors to the library, closing us off from the rest of the house.

With my back facing him, my hands grip tightly around the door handles in a lame attempt to control my turmoil. There's rioting in my bones, rattling me into a cold sweat. Pulling back to open the doors slightly, I slam them once more, grunting, hammering my palm into the aged mahogany.

"What can I do?" Lachlan questions from across the room.

A string of answers fills my head and wraps around my neck in a tightening noose. I can't talk as I think about Elizabeth upstairs in a drug-induced sleep. Visions from when I found her last night flash behind my eyes in vivid detail. Her naked and bloodied body, the bruising and lacerations between her legs from what that dickfuck did to her, it brings up sour bile that I fight to swallow back.

All I wanted to give her when she woke this morning was as much peace as I could, but instead, I watched her world erupt into even more chaos. Chaos she doesn't need. Chaos I'm worried she's not stable enough to handle.

"Declan."

I turn and face my friend, thankful that he stayed the night and is here right now, because there's no way I could sort through my deranged thoughts on my own without smashing my fists through the walls and destroying this house in a blacked out rage.

"How is she?" he questions.

"Sleeping." The word is strangled as it comes out. I walk over to the couch and sit down, lowering my head to meet my clenched fists. My harsh breaths through my nose are audible. I won't allow Elizabeth to see this. She needs to believe I'm in utter control and that she's completely safe with me.

"How is she really?" he pushes for a better answer than the one I just gave him.

I look up and meet his concerned eyes as he takes the seat on the other side of the coffee table.

"She's not good."

I won't go into detail with Lachlan, because what's hers is mine and no one else's.

"Look, what happened last night, what you witnessed—" I start to say but Lachlan cuts in, "It's vaulted."

"It better be," I tell him, my voice glazed in unspoken threats. "You'll never speak of it, not even with her, understand?"

"Without fail," he responds with a nod.

"I need your help," I tell him, shifting the conversation.

"Anything."

"I need you to find someone for me."

"Who?"

"His name is Steve Archer."

With a curious look, he responds, "Why does that name sound familiar?"

"He's Elizabeth's father."

"Her father?" he reacts in surprise. "He's dead. I came across his death certificate when I found her mother."

"I don't know. We were upstairs watching an American news report and she swears she saw him."

"On TV? There's no way."

"She's adamant."

"Declan, her mind has to be a mare's nest right now. I'm sure she's seeing what she wishes to see," he says. "The man is dead."

I shrug my shoulders, releasing a heavy breath. "Pull the news footage and compare the two men."

Lachlan steps over to the desk in the corner of the room, and I follow, directing him to the correct news station webpage. We find the video, play it, and when I see the man who Elizabeth made me pause on, I reach down and stop the video, freezing on his face.

"Him."

It takes a few minutes to find an archived article on his arrest, but Lachlan finally comes across one with a photo.

"There," I say when I see the link. "Click on that."

And with a single click, I know Elizabeth isn't imagining things. It may be an old photo, but there's no way I can argue that it's not the same man.

"Holy shit," Lachlan says as he compares both of the photos.

"That's him. Tell me you're seeing what I'm seeing."

"I'm seeing it."

"Fuck!" Raking my hands through my hair, I pace over to the windows, wishing I never had the goddamn TV turned on this morning. "I can't allow anyone else to hurt her.

"I know."

"Jesus. I mean, she just found out that her piece of shit mother sold her when was just a baby. And now this? I don't think she can take much more."

"Tell me what you want me to do."

She won't let this go. Not that I could expect her to. But I need to keep the upper hand here and remain two steps in front of her.

"Find him. And nothing, not a single piece of information gets past me. Understood?"

"I understand."

"You screwed up once," I berate. "Don't do it again."

He stands, steps over to me, and assures, "You have my word." My glare doesn't waver because what's at stake is too precious to gamble with. Lachlan sees the doubt, grips my shoulder with his hand, and states firmly, "I care about that girl too."

"Then don't fuck this up."

With a curt nod, he squeezes my shoulder before walking away and pulling out his phone.

"I want security too," I call out. "She's not to be alone."

"I'll get on that now."

"You'll do."

"I'm not security, McKinnon."

"You're right. You're a fuckin' dobber when it comes to taking orders. But after last night, you're the only one I trust to keep her safe when I'm not around."

"I'll need to situate a few things in Edinburgh."

"Do it today," I tell him. "You can stay in the cottage next to the grotto."

"The cottage?" He laughs. "You mean the maid's quarters?"

"That's the one, you wanker," I respond with a chuckle. "Oh, one more thing," I add before Lachlan leaves the room, exchanging the banter for seriousness, "Thank you."

"Of course."

I'm willing to go to any length to make sure nothing comes close to touching Elizabeth, but options are limited with the history the two of us carry. Although our time together has been short, it's been riddled with more than enough to land us both in prison. So Lachlan is it for us.

Wandering into the kitchen, I walk over to the security monitor on the wall and check the cameras out front. I flip through them and stop on the gate camera. I'm watching as Lachlan's car drives out onto the main road when my cell rings.

"McKinnon," I answer.

"Good afternoon, Mr. McKinnon. It's Alexander Stanforth from Stanforth and Partners. How are you doing?"

"I'm well," I respond to Alex, the architect that will be working on the London property I recently purchased.

"I hope you don't mind my calling on your cell, but with your interest in expediting the initial meetings, I figured I would bypass your office manager."

"It's why I gave you this number, Alex."

"Good. Well then, I'd like to set up a meeting to discuss the scope of the project, along with schedule and budget. Are you free next week?"

"I can be free. Set it up and call my office to get it on the books, and I'll be there," I tell him.

"Sounds good. I'll get with the team and give your office a call later today."

"Thanks, Alex."

Hanging up the phone, I grab an ice pack from the freezer and make my way up to Elizabeth. She's sound asleep when I enter the room and sit down next to her. The side of her face is swollen; black and blue mar her eye. Gently, I touch the ice to her skin and she flinches.

"Sorry," I whisper when her eyes flutter open. "The swelling is really bad."

Her eyes are dilated dopey black, but she doesn't keep them open long. I watch her lie motionless, soft breaths filling the space around me.

"We used to dance," her hoarse voice murmurs.

"Who?"

"Me and my dad."

I don't say anything when she curls her body over and lifts her head onto my lap.

"Dean Martin was his favorite," she says sleepily, never opening her eyes. "'Volare' . . . that's the song. He'd sing along, and I remember always giggling during the Italian parts."

"He had a good voice?" I ask, keeping the ice on her.

"Mmm hmm," she answers slowly in her listless state. "He'd set me on top of his feet and dance while I hung on to his legs."

She pauses, letting time falter, and I think she's fallen back asleep, but then she begins to blink. When her glassy eyes find me, she whimpers, "Why would he leave me?"

Never in my life have I seen so much heartache in anyone's eyes, and I hate that it's in hers that I see it. She wants answers, but I have none to give her, and it kills me.

"I thought I made him happy."

Setting the ice pack on the bedside table, I turn back to her, and with her face cradled in my hands I assert, "I promise you I'll do everything I can to give you answers. We *will* find him."

"What if he doesn't want me finding him?"

"It doesn't matter what he wants. It's not his choice to make."

This isn't the woman I know. She's something else entirely. She may have been putting on an act to deceive me, but she always had a bold-spirited backbone that a person can't fake. Beneath the lies, that part of her was real, but now it's lost somewhere inside of her violated body.

She takes in a small pain-filled gasp as she shifts her body.

"Why don't you soak in a hot bath?"

"What's the point? Rot is rot."

"That's bullshit," I lash back. "Rot has hurt you, but it hasn't claimed you. And I suggested a bath to help with your pain, not to clean you." My words are half truths; I do want to clean her. Clean all the filth from the sack of shit that did this to her. I want to erase him from her skin because the thought sickens me. I want her covered in me, in my scent, with my hands all over her body. I want her to taste like me, smell like me. It's a feral need to mark her as mine. To own her, every single piece of her.

Pulling her up to me, I press my lips to hers, kissing her softly when I really want to devour her, but she's much too fragile. Her breath on my tongue sparks a shudder through my veins, causing my pulse to race. It takes control not to throw her down, spread her thighs, and bury my cock deep inside her. I want to fuck her so hard she feels me in her bones.

I force myself back, gripping her neck in my hands as I take in a deep breath that I release slowly.

"I've missed having your taste in my mouth," she says, her words not doing much to help me calm myself.

"I want more than just my taste in your mouth, but I can't let myself be that selfish with you right now. I won't be able to control myself, and I'll just hurt you."

Getting out of bed, I go to start the bath before returning to her.

"Give me your hands," I tell her and then help her onto her feet. "Lift your arms."

Moving slowly, I undress her, careful not to hurt her. When I have her naked in front of me, I quickly remove my clothes and then walk her to the bathroom. I step into the tub first and then hold on to her as I help her into the water. She sits between my legs, leaning back against my chest with a grimace of pain.

Her body is hard to look at. The bruises are enough to get my blood boiling. It coils my gut in a retching of turbulent emotions. There's a serrated bite mark on her left breast that I didn't notice last night when I showered her.

"What?" she questions, looking up at me. "What's wrong?"

"What do you mean?"

"Your body tensed up."

"I'm sorry . . . I just . . ." I start, trying for gentle words.

"What?"

But gentle doesn't come easy for me, so I go with honest. "I want to take all these marks away. All the ones that aren't from me."

"I'll always be marked by someone else's touch. I always have been."

"I'd give anything to take them away," I tell her, knowing now that the scars on her back and wrists came at the hands of her foster dad.

"You can't make me into something I'm not, you know?"

"You're not my charity case, if that's what you're inferring," I snap with irritation.

"Was I ever? Even in the beginning?"

"No. You were never a woman I pitied."

"If not pity, then what?"

"There's no easy answer. I don't understand you or your reasoning for all the shit you've done. All I do know is that I must be crazy for loving you, because dammit, I do love you. I've tried not to, I've fought it, but I can't stop."

"But what about what you said last night? You still hate me?"

"Yes."

She drops her eyes, but I bring her back to me, saying, “I love you, Elizabeth.”

“Do you really?”

“Of course I do. I’ve killed for you.”

three

(ELIZABETH)

HIS WORDS, HIS truth, they may haunt some people, but for my decrepit soul, they soothe. It's true—he has killed for me—and I have also killed for him. I murdered Pike when I thought he killed Declan. And it's also a murder that I wish every day I could take back. But I can't. The only way I can have Pike is through my mind's trickery.

But aside from Pike, I was a split second away from killing Richard last night, and it would've been all for Declan. In a sick way, it was going to be my gift to him. To rid the world of the man who took my love's mother. Declan wouldn't let me pull the trigger though—he did it for himself, robbing me of the satisfaction. I wanted it selfishly, but if there was one kill Declan deserved, it was that one.

Declan's eyes dig into mine, and I know I've touched a nerve by questioning his love for me.

"I'm sorry," I tell him, running my hands over his, which are tensed around my neck.

"I've never been anything but honest with you."

"I know. I didn't mean to be dismissive of your words."

His grip loosens as he relaxes, resting his shoulders against the back of the tub.

"I'm having a hard time processing everything," I add.

"Then talk to me. Don't hold it in."

Declan made his feelings known last week when I read the file on my mother. He made it clear he wants me to deal with my feelings instead of hiding them and locking them away the way I've done my whole life. I owe him anything he asks of me because of everything I've done to him, but sometimes it's just easier to go numb.

"Maybe later. I'm still really tired from the pain pill." But there won't be a later. I can't cut myself open like that for him because there's nothing that will stop the blood gushing from the wound. Declan's ability to connect me with my emotions scares the shit out of me. There's too much to feel. There's too much termagant despair inside me. I need it to go away and disappear so I can find relief.

I'm in the arms of the man I love, the man I was so desperate to have again, and here he is. Flesh on flesh—every part of me touching every part of him, and here I am—scared and closed off. He's wrapped around me, and I should be content, but in this moment, I crave another man's arms. It's Pike I wish I had right now. He's the only one who can numb me.

He's safety.

He's constant.

He's my painkiller.

"You'll rest better if you get your thoughts out," he suggests.

Leaning forward, breaking the contact, I lie, "I'm really tired. Can you help me back to bed?"

"Don't shut me out, Elizabeth."

"I'm not. It's just the tub is uncomfortable, and I really am exhausted and not feeling well."

I hate lying to him when I swore to him and to myself that I never would, but the alternative is unbearable to even think about. It's best for the both of us if I don't go down that road.

Declan dries me off, brushes my teeth, and dresses me. I give him these things because he needs them. I know him well enough to see that he needs his hands on me, to control and take care. He's always needed that, and I can't even imagine what these past few days have done to him with not knowing where I was and having that authority taken away by another man.

After he applies the ointment to my cuts, he grabs the prescription bottle and shakes out a pill.

"Here," he says, holding the mood stabilizer that was prescribed to me by the doctor who examined me the first night I arrived here.

It's the pill I've been tossing in the toilet because I don't want to lose Pike, and that pill will vanish him from me. I can't say goodbye though. I don't want to. I need him. His smell, his voice, his presence. I'm not willing to let him go.

I take the pill from his hand, and when he gives me a glass of water, I cheek it instead of swallowing.

Another lie.

Another deception I swore I'd no longer partake in.

Another broken promise.

"Good girl."

He walks me back to the bedroom and helps me get into bed.

"I'm going to run downstairs to get something to drink. Are you thirsty?"

I nod my head and watch him as he strides out of the room. When I hear the creaking on the stairs beneath his feet, I spit out the pill. Being in too much pain to get out of bed to flush it down the toilet, I shove it into my pillowcase until I can throw it away. When he returns, he slips under the covers beside me and pulls me into his arms.

"By the way, Lachlan's going to be staying here," he tells me. "I want security, and with all that he's already seen, he's the only one I trust."

"Okay."

"Are you comfortable with that?"

"Yes," I respond. "From the time I've spent with him, I've come to like him."

"While you were sleeping, I spoke with him about your father. He's working on getting information."

I nod my head against his chest, unable to speak through my tightening throat. I'm sure Declan feels my body tensing up when he bands his arms a little more strongly around me. Closing my eyes, I inhale deeply as he kisses the top of my head.

"I know it's upsetting, but I want to be transparent with you about all of this, okay?"

"You don't think I'm crazy, do you?"

He combs my hair back with his fingers, and I look up at him when he says, "No, darling, I don't. Lachlan was able to retrieve an old photo of your father, and it's the same man from the news."

Declan's face blurs, and I quickly close my eyes before the tears fall. I can't think about this. It's the worst pain I've ever felt, so I focus on armoring myself against all that threatens to completely eviscerate me.

"You're stronger than your emotions," I hear Pike tell me, the timbre of his voice providing me with the strength I need to take control of my heart.

"Are you okay?"

"Yes."

"There's something else I need to talk to you about."

"What's that?"

"When I was in London, I hired an architecture firm for the new property. Meetings start next week, so you're coming with me."

"London?" I question, pushing myself to sit up. "For how long?"

"For the duration of the build . . . a few years."

"I . . . um . . ." I stammer, unsure of what to say. Then, the realization that I have nowhere else to go hits me, and it all becomes so terrifying. If somehow I lost Declan again, that would be it for me. He is the only person I have, and without him, I wouldn't know where to go. Even though I'm now aware that my father is out there somewhere, it's heartbreakingly clear that he doesn't want me, or else he'd have come for me.

"You don't want to go to London?" he questions.

"No, it isn't that. It's just . . . I don't really know."

My voice cracks slightly, and Declan promptly soothes, "You have nothing to be worried about. I'm here. I'm not leaving you. Wherever I go, you go with me."

I don't respond as he holds me close to him. I'm not sure what to say, because even though he says I shouldn't be worried, I am.

"I really need you to talk to me," he urges. "Don't close yourself off again."

There's a desperation in his eyes, a neediness that reminds me of our time in Chicago. I played him well, deceiving him to believe I was locked in a violent marriage that I couldn't escape. He held the same desperation then. He tried so hard to help me, to save me, but I was always careful to keep him at a measured distance. I wanted him to believe he had all of me but none of me at the same time.

The game is over though. No longer do I want to see that look in his eyes. It once gave me pleasure to know I had him fooled, but that absconded the moment he crept into my heart. But in order to keep my soul intact, I need to continue to move in calculated steps.

"I *am* worried," I admit.

"About what?"

"About you. If there's no you . . . there's no me."

"You're scared of losing me?"

I nod.

"You're not going to lose me, you hear? It's not happening."

"I lost you once though. It was my fault. Trust me, I know. But I still lost you. I still know that pain, and it scares me."

"I know that pain too. It wasn't just you who felt it." His words drip with intensity. "I felt it in my marrow. That's how deep you run through me."

"So much has happened. I wanted you the second I lost you, and now that I have you, I feel so . . ."

"What do you feel?"

Reaching my hand up to his face, I run my fingers along his jawline and through his overgrown stubble, listening to it crackle against my palm. "Disconnected," I reveal and then drop my hand along with my head.

"Look at me," he demands, and I do. "It's okay. I'm having a hard time wrapping my head around everything that's been thrown my way these past few weeks, so I understand. I'll take it away, I promise, but it's going to take time. One thing I need you to know is that I'm here. I'll remind you of that every day if I have to. I'm here."

I allow his words to attempt their quieting on my anxiety as I take my hand and cover the bullet wound on his pec, the one Pike inflicted on him with the intent of killing him. My thumb brushes over the raised flesh, and when I look up, his focus is on my hand. Guilt courses its way through my bloodstream. His eyes flick to meet mine, and I ask, "Did it hurt?"

"Not as much as losing you," he responds, wrapping his hand around my wrist while I continue to run my fingers along my betrayal that's now branded on him for eternity.

"I manipulated you. I lied."

"You did. And I hate you for that. I hate you for what your lies turned me into."

"But you missed me?"

"I couldn't unlove you."

Pressing my hand flat against his chest, I feel his heart pumping, and I decide to rip a piece of my own heart off to give to him, exposing a tiny part of what I know I must protect in the fortress of my soul. Declan has always had a way of cutting right through to the core of me. So, I hand over my offering in the form of truth, letting him know, "You scare me."

His heartbeat grows in force, exposing his frustration to my words.

"What about me scares you?"

"The way you break my walls so easily."

"Why do you want walls between us?"

"Because I'm afraid to feel right now. There's so much inside me that I'm fighting off. I'm scared it'll be too much."

He lets go of a hard breath, upset with what I just admitted to him. He drops his head for a moment, and then, with controlled force, he grabs my other wrist and pushes me down onto the bed. I don't resist him when he straddles my legs and sits on top of my thighs. Green eyes scream for obedience, and I give him just that when he rips my top open, tearing the fabric and breaking the buttons to expose my breasts.

The chill of the air hardens my nipples instantly, but it isn't my tits he's after. He quickly gathers both my wrists into his one hand, restraining me, and then takes his other and presses it firmly to the center of my chest.

"This is mine," he professes. "You want me?"

"Yes," I breathe.

"You want to be with me?"

"Yes."

"Then this little heart of yours is mine. It beats for me, and I'll provide its protection. You hear me?"

I nod.

"You need to trust me enough to take care of you. I won't ever let you break."

The rise and fall of my chest hits hard as I take hold of his words, needing them to calm my fears.

"Do you trust me?"

I nod again.

"Tell me."

"I trust you."

Another lie.

four

(DECLAN)

I LEFT ELIZABETH reading in the library. It's been a few days since I found her, and even though bruises are fading and swelling is dissipating, she continues to be distant. I've yet to fuck her, not that I haven't tried, but I also haven't pushed. Taming the beast inside me isn't something I enjoy while I wait impatiently for her fragility to wane.

Having Lachlan here has helped though. Whatever friendship they forged while she was staying at The Water Lily has dulcified the awkwardness for all of us, leaving just minor remnants. Knowing what Lachlan and I saw that night, the state we found Elizabeth in, doesn't seem to bother her as much as one would presume, as much as it bothers me. I figure her lack of shame stems from her childhood and what she was forced to endure. It was just the other day she admitted that she saw herself as nothing more than rot.

"McKinnon," Lachlan announces, redirecting my thoughts when I walk through the door of the guesthouse he's staying in. "Sorry I bailed on breakfast this morning, I hope Elizabeth wasn't offended."

"Not at all. Important call?"

"Yes, actually."

I walk farther into the house and take a seat in the living area.

"I got information about Steve from my contact."

"And?"

He sits in the chair adjacent to me and drops a few papers onto the coffee table. "And . . . he's a dead man."

"What?"

"Everything checks out. Take a look for yourself. All the documents, the funeral information with plot and burial. Even the death certificate is there. It's a dead end from that point on. Steve Archer doesn't exist; he's been dead for sixteen years."

I pick up the papers and flip through them, examining the trail of proof that he is indeed dead.

"What's he hiding from?" I ask aloud, not expecting Lachlan to have an answer for me.

"That's what I'm trying to find out."

I set the papers down, knowing damn well they're nothing but bullshit propaganda to support the prevarication of death, and inquire, "What about the passenger manifest?"

"I'm working on it, but we're talking about breaking some strict federal laws. I have a friend putting in a few calls for me, but it might be a long shot. I don't know if anyone is going to be willing to risk their job or compromise their values."

"Values can be bought for the right price, but we need more people on this," I stress with growing intensity. "I want everything my money can buy. Private investigators, hackers, *everything* we can think of."

"I know, and trust me when I tell you, I'm on it." He takes a pause as I let go of a frustrated breath. "On another note, I got everything lined up at One Hyde Park, so the apartment will be ready by the time you arrive."

"I've never been more thankful for buying that property than I am now."

"You should have no worries with Elizabeth's safety there," Lachlan says about the building that I own an apartment in.

It's one of the most secure properties in the world, if not *the* securest. The moment I started considering building in London, I went ahead a snagged up a dual-floor apartment in One Hyde Park. The privacy measures go above and beyond from bulletproof windows to x-rayed mail.

After being shot in Chicago, I not only transferred Brunswickhill into a private trust, but also moved the London property into one as well. No one will know where Elizabeth and I are except for the people I choose to inform.

"I need to go take care of a few things."

"I'll check in with you as soon as I get an update on the Archer case," he says as I make my way to the front door.

"Don't drag your ass on this one, Lachlan. I need this handled yesterday."

"I'm on it."

On my way into the main house, I peek in the library, but Elizabeth is no longer there. Just the book she was reading, facedown on the sofa.

"Elizabeth," I call out with no answer in return.

I walk down to the atrium where I know she likes to lie on the chaise and enjoy the sun's heat through the glass. The room is empty though. I stand for a moment, looking out the glass, and eventually movement catches my eye. I watch Elizabeth as she walks aimlessly. She loves taking long strolls outside to explore the grounds.

I make my way out to where she is. "What are you doing?"

"I never knew there was a stream over here."

"There's a lot you haven't been able to see because of the snow," I tell her, pulling her into my arms and pressing my lips to hers.

She quietly moans, slipping her hands under my coat and around my waist.

"You're freezing."

"I'm okay," she responds as I bring her in even closer, strengthening my arms firmly around her body. "What are you doing out here?"

"I want to talk to you, but you weren't inside where I left you."

"Where you left me?" she teases, tilting her head back to look up at me. "What am I? A little trinket of yours that you can place wherever you choose?"

"Something like that." I shoot her an amorous wink and watch her beautiful smile creep in. "Come. Sit with me."

We walk over to a bench perched aside the stream coated in ice.

"I just spoke with Lachlan and wanted to let you know where we are in regards to finding your father."

Blithe ease fades into yearning hope rimmed in years of pain.

"Do you want to talk about this right now?" I ask as her body language takes on a sudden shift.

"Yes." Her voice is full of anxiety, eager for answers. "What did you find?"

"Evidence of his death."

"But he isn't dead." Her voice pitches with even more anxiety.

"I know that. Lachlan is doing what he can to get a copy of the list of passengers. When we get that, we can go from there."

"Well, how long is that going to take?"

"He's working as fast as he can, but he doesn't have any straight connections with the airline."

Frustration marks her face as I watch her body tense up and fight back against the puddle of tears in her eyes. She's unmoving, and it's taking all her strength to not lose her composure. I wish I could give her the answers she's so eager for. It's a painful sight to see the one I love ache so badly.

I reach my arm around her shoulders, and coax, "It's okay to cry. It won't hurt as bad if you let go of some of the pain."

"I spent my life crying for my father, and it's never lessened the pain," she says, refusing my words.

"Look at me," I demand, and when she does, I continue, "This is not fine. You holding everything in is not fine."

"Why do you want to see me break so badly?"

"You're breaking right now," I rebut. "You, forcing yourself not to feel the hurt. You, pushing me away. You present a stone exterior, but it's just a façade of all your brokenness inside. You're a fool's paradise, but I'm no fool. I see right through you."

"You're an asshole," she bites, pissed that I'm calling her out on her charade, but I won't back down.

"What are you afraid of? My seeing you in a light you're embarrassed of? I've seen you at your worst. Or are you still worried about feeling too much that you'll break apart and be unable to put the pieces back together? What is it?"

"Why are you pushing so hard?"

"If you can't put yourself back together then I'll do it for you."

"Stop!"

"Is that why you won't let me touch you?"

At that, she jerks away from me, but I grip her arms tightly.

"Let go!"

"Why won't you let me fuck you?" I hiss, losing my control and letting frustration and rejection spew out of me. "Answer me, for Christ's sake!"

My voice strains in temper as she fights against my hold, and I eventually loosen my grip and allow her to break away from me. She stands and stumbles back, fuming in pure anger.

"Is that the problem?" she spits. "Your ego is hurt because you can't get in my pants?"

I stand and walk right up to her, chest to chest. "You know damn well that if I wanted what was in your pants, I'd take it."

"Then take it. I don't give a shit. If that's all you want, then have it." Her words taunt, but they infuriate me even more.

"You're so fucking blind. It's not your pussy I want. It's so much more than just that. I want all of you. Every piece. I want to be inside of you because that's the one place you'll be so weak you'll have no choice but to hand all of yourself over to me."

With a slight shake of her head, she looks deep into my eyes, confessing on a whisper, "I just can't."

My hands clutch her face and I speak with fervency, "You can. I need you to try."

"But you have me," she cries out. "I'm here. I'm not running away."

"Stop avoiding."

"I'm n—"

"You're here," I break in, cutting her off. "But you're not really here. You may lie next to me every night, but you're not really there. You're somewhere else entirely. Somewhere deep inside that body of yours, you're hiding away."

There's no response on her part, only glaring eyes that expose just how furious she is.

"How many times do I have to tell you to convince you that you're safe here? That you're safe with me?"

"Let go of me, please," she requests in an even tone.

I drop my hands from her face, and she immediately turns and walks away from me without another word, without ever looking back. I don't say anything to stop her, I just let her go. And before I allow my aggravation grow any further, I too find my way back to the house and up to the third level where my office is.

Needing to relieve my mind of the stress, I busy myself with work. Between phone calls to the office and checking in on my Chicago property, time passes quickly. Lotus is thriving financially and is proving to be one of the most sought after hotels in the city. Exclusivity is key, and that notion is proving itself.

But I can't think about Chicago without thinking about my father. I haven't spoken to him since Elizabeth told me about his arrest. Honestly, I haven't even delved into his involvement with Richard, Bennett, or even Elizabeth's father for fear of what it might stir up inside me. Elizabeth would deem me a hypocrite, and she'd be right, which is why I haven't broached the topic with her yet.

So for that reason alone, I call Elizabeth up to my office, and it takes her only a few minutes to appear in the doorway.

"What's so urgent?" she asks with a hint of agitation that's leftover from our earlier quarrel.

"Come in."

She does, finding a seat in front of my desk. I get up from my chair and walk around to take the seat next to her.

"First, I won't apologize for earlier, except for one thing—I accused you of being afraid of facing your fears when I've been doing the same thing."

"What do you mean?"

"I've been avoiding my father out of trepidation," I admit to her. "But I'm putting that aside, hoping you'll do the same for me."

Her eyes soften.

"So, can you help me?" I ask and she nods, saying, "Okay."

"The night I found you, you told me that Richard and my father were working together, using Bennett's company as a cover for gun trafficking."

"That's what Richard told me," she says.

"You also said that Richard was the one who killed my mum."

She nods.

With my throat constricting as visions of my mum getting shot in the head flash in my memory, I speak on a strained voice, "I need to know why it happened."

She holds my hand in hers, taking her time before she says anything. "He told me Cal was embezzling money into an offshore account. Richard said he wanted to teach your dad a lesson that would ensure his loyalty."

"So my father knew what Richard was going to do?"

With a hard swallow and eyes full of pity, she nods. "He knew. It was why your dad left town. He didn't want to be there when it happened."

My breathing falters in unsteady breaths as rage explodes in volcanic measures inside my chest. Every muscle in my body indurates in tension, and I let go of Elizabeth's hand for fear I'll crack her delicate bones. I pop out of my chair and it topples over.

"That bastard has spent every day since her death blaming me," I fume. The blades of each word slicing my tongue, filling me with the blood of putrid hate. "He made me believe it was my fault!"

"No matter how it happened, Declan, it wouldn't have been your fault."

I walk over to the window's edge, grip my hands on the sill, and drop my head as I hunch over. It's a battlefield of emotions, to which there is no victor. Outrage and fury fight alongside sadness and longing. I've mourned my mother the way no man should ever have to, but I did. I've allowed the pain to dwell in my heart, embittering it and giving it the power to grow into the man I am today. A man who can't relinquish an ounce of control without being consumed with unsettling fear. God only knows who I'd be if it weren't for this manifestation.

I flinch when I feel Elizabeth's hand on my back. When I turn to look at her, her cheeks are tear-stained, and I wipe them away with my thumbs, asking, "Why are you crying?"

“Because . . . it hurts me to see you in pain.”

“I need you to see it though,” my voice breaks.

She then reaches her hands up to my face, pulls me to her, and kisses me. She swallows up my ragged breaths, pushing her body against mine, and I instantly grow hard. It’s a storm of emotions that begs to be released.

With a growl, I pick her up, and she gasps when I drop her to the couch. She watches intently, trembling as I unbuckle my belt.

“Don’t.”

“Don’t tell me no, Elizabeth,” I command.

She jolts up, lurching off the couch in a panic. “I can’t.”

There’s fear in her eyes as she backs away from me, heading towards the door, as if I’m some monster from her nightmares.

“Bullshit! You can, you just don’t want to.”

She continues to retreat, refusing to connect with me and it’s the last fucking stab to my heart I can take! I fucking love her, but she’s built this wall around herself to keep me away. It pisses the raging shit out of me, and I explode in a thunderous roar when I watch her leave the room, rejecting me.

“Just give me one motherfucking piece of you!” my scathing voice ruptures, reverberating off the walls.

five

(ELIZABETH)

HIS VIOLENT SCREAMS echo through the house as I bolt down the stairs to the bedroom, scared that he will take what I'm terrified to give. Not that I don't want to be close with him, but it's the ramifications I'm not ready for. I shut the door, and try to calm myself down.

"What are you doing?"

I look up, relieved to have Pike here with me right now. "Where have you been?" I say breathlessly as I rush into his arms. "I've missed you."

There's never any temperature to his touch, but there's pressure, and it's enough to soothe.

"Just because you can't see me doesn't mean I'm not always here."

"Don't leave," I beg of him. "Stay with me, just for a while."

He strokes his hands through my hair, cradling me close, and I nuzzle my face against his chest. With a deep breath through my nose, I inhale his scent through the fibers of his shirt.

"I'm worried about you."

An overwhelming neediness consumes me, and I finally let the tears fall that I've been holding in for days now. "I miss you so much, Pike," I cry. "It only gets worse as time passes."

"Is that why you're not taking your meds?"

"I won't ever say goodbye to you, Pike. Don't even think about asking me to because it'll never happen. I'm keeping you for always."

"I want you to get better though."

"You make me better. You always have."

We walk over to the bed and slip in. I rest my head in the center of his chest as we lie together, and even though I'm in the arms of a dead man, I feel at home. For the first time since Declan found me with Richard, I feel at peace, in the arms of my brother. He continues to hold me as time passes and the sun sets, darkening the room.

"Can I ask you something?"

"Sure."

"Why are you shutting Declan out after all you've been through to be with him?"

"You know why," I tell him. "You know me better than anyone else does."

"Why are you letting your fear win?"

"I'm not. I'm only protecting myself the way you taught me."

"I taught you to protect yourself against people who hurt you. Declan's not trying to hurt you, but you're definitely hurting him."

Sitting up, I look down to Pike and take in each and every feature, unable to look away.

"What is it? What do you want to say?" he questions, reading my face and knowing I'm hiding something.

"You'll think I'm crazy."

He smiles, and it's so perfect with the moon casting its glow down upon him. *"I already think you're crazy, Elizabeth. But I'm crazy too. So, tell me what you're thinking about."*

My mind drifts back through our life together. He was always there for me in ways no one else was, giving me what I needed to escape and numb.

"Just say it."

"Take my pain away," I request hesitantly.

He sits up, looking at me as if I've lost my mind by asking him for sex. Maybe I have, but I know what I need, and it's him. He has the power to stop the world from spinning so out of control. If even for just a moment, I crave the reprieve.

"Please, Pike." My voice, filled with so much pain and sadness, pleads as tears drip from my chin.

"I'm not real."

"To me you are."

"Elizabeth," he says cautiously and then repeats, *"I'm not real."*

"But I feel you," I tell him, taking his hand in mine. "I can *feel* you."

"It's not real."

"It is!"

He wraps his arms around me, and I cling to him—desperate for him.

"I'm not crazy. I feel this; I feel your arms holding me. Tell me you feel it too."

"Elizabeth, no. We can't."

"Why not?"

Pike takes my arms in his hands and pushes back to look at me straight on. *"Because of Declan."*

"But he can't give me what you can."

"He can give you something better."

"It's too much though."

"Trust him to know your limits. And trust me when I tell you that he loves you. He'll take better care of you than I did—than I ever could."

"You took perfect care of me."

He takes my face, kissing me softly, and the selfish animal in me moves to wrap my arms around him as tight as I can to keep him close, but my arms slip right through him. My eyes pop open, and I'm all alone. He's gone with a faint shift in the air, whispering, *"I'm never too far from you."*

"Pike!" I cry out, but it's no use.

His scent slowly evaporates as Declan's takes over, replacing the comfort of my past. I'm torn between this polar energy that pulls me from one end to the other—a tug of war. Pike is the easy choice, the safe choice, because with him, there's no pain and no fear. Declan is a different story altogether though. He's a multifaceted enigma with layers, creating an illimitable depth. If I immerse myself in him, I just might fall forever. But if his words are truth, he'll catch me. It's an unknown that's so unsettling it's terrifying.

With every gust of wind from outside, I dart my eyes around the room, hoping Pike comes back, but he doesn't. Unable to sit still, I get out of bed and make my way to the restroom for a drink of water. After downing the tall glass, I set it down with a clink next to the orange prescription bottle. My mood stabilizer, my Pike killer. Shaking out a single pill, I screw the cap back on before walking into the toilet room and flicking it into the water with a tiny *plop*. I watch it disappear after I flush and feel appeased to know that with this deception, I've given another day of "life" to my brother.

Walking back into the bedroom, I notice the door opening and the shadow of Declan as he takes a step in and stops. The room, donned in black, is forgiving on my love's face, casting a muted blue tone to his features. No words are spoken as we both stand and stare at each other while a tornado of words swirls between us.

My earlier conversation with Pike screams the loudest of all. And the possibility of him being right about Declan saws away at the scar tissue of my heart, filling me with sorrow for the way I've treated him. He deserves love, compassion, and obedience, all the things I'm frightened to hand over.

The lines of his face are hard, and when I see his jaw tick, he begins to walk toward me in even steps. My body tenses at the fervor he exudes. In sharp movements, he grabs my face and kisses me with icy control, stealing my breath and marking my tongue with his.

I gasp.

It's desire.

It's sadness.

It's fear.

White-hot fear.

"I won't allow you to be scared of me," he demands when he pulls away.

Breaths hit hard for the both of us, my body trembling as I look into his dilated, lustful eyes.

"I let you build this wall between us because I thought you were too fragile for me to forbid it, but I forbid it now."

His mouth crashes into mine before I can say anything, and he takes my hesitance, swallowing it into his soul, breathing a new life within me. But he leaves a little behind to linger. He leaves it for me to give willingly.

Releasing me from his hold, he steps back and sits in one of the chairs. In full command, he instructs, "Take your clothes off."

The weight of my heart aches painfully in my chest, and the moment I drop my eyes, he takes notice.

"Look at me."

With reluctance, I do.

"Keep your eyes on me."

Every nerve ending is firing inside of me as I unbutton my top and drop it to the floor. I then move to slip my pants off, and watch as Declan grinds his teeth. My stomach turns in anxiety, not knowing what's to come next, but I stand here and try with all I can to believe Pike when he says Declan won't hurt me.

"All of it," he presses as he sits in the night's obscurity, shielding himself in its obsidian.

Cold air trills in goosebumps along my flesh as I unhook my bra and drop my panties to my ankles, exposing the tarnished veneer to my aberration. The bruises have faded, the lacerations are nearly healed scabs, but we both know the garbage I am. I've told him my past in full detail; he knows my life in the closet and in the basement, and yet he grows hard for me as he sits and examines.

He's too good to be a monster like me, too good to be turned on by the grotesque.

"On the bed," he orders. "Lie on your stomach."

"No!" I blurt out at the humiliation that still remains from when he last took me from behind. Although my voice never screamed no, every part of my vitality did as he ripped me apart and violated me beyond boundaries I never thought I had.

"On the bed!" he shouts.

I turn and walk across the room as my eyes prick. Taking a hard swallow, I will the vulnerability away. My back stiffens as I cage my heart in self-preservation.

I can do this.

When I sit on the edge of the bed, he stands, his cock pushing against the fabric of his pants. He walks over to me, taking my knees in his hands and opening me up to stand between my legs.

"Do you trust me?"

"Yes." I'm quick to answer, and he immediately shakes his head.

"I'll punish you for lying, you know I will," he threatens. "Let's try this again. Do you trust me?"

With my neck craned back to look him in the eye, I give him the honesty he deserves. "No."

Declan threads his fingers through my hair, fisting it in clumps, and I wince as it pulls through the scab that's almost healed. The scab he gave me when he ripped my hair out. The scab I kept alive by picking when I thought I'd never have him again.

He keeps his forceful hands on my head, vowing, "I'm going to change that. Right now. Tonight. I won't allow you to fall asleep until I've done so."

His words strangle me.

I panic.

"Take my belt off."

I hesitate.

"Now!"

My fingers fumble as I work quickly to unfasten his belt and pull the leather loose from the loops of his slacks. He then holds his palm open to me, and I hand it over to him.

"Are you scared of me?"

"Yes," I respond with no mask.

With his one hand clutching the belt and the other clutching my hair, he gives his next order, "Take my pants off and suck my cock."

I unhook, unzip, and pull down.

He's raging hard, and when I slide him into my mouth, he releases a guttural moan into the still of the room. My heart races as I suck him deeply.

My hands grip around the backs of his thighs while I run my lips up and down the smooth skin of his cock.

"Fuuuck," he groans, and when I look up to him, his head is tilted back.

His hand squeezes around my hair, pulling it even more, ripping the scab when he bucks his hips suddenly, forcing himself to the back of my mouth. I gag slightly, and reflex with a swallow, the opening of my throat clamping around the head of his dick when I do so.

"Jesus Christ." His words claw through the grit of ecstasy as he pulls out of me. In flashes of seconds, he slings his shirt across the room and kicks off his pants.

We're entirely naked.

He kneels down, draping my legs over his broad shoulders and opens me with his hands. The sound of him inhaling deeply takes over me and becomes too much. I pinch my eyes shut, because the sight of him alone is enough to rip me to shreds.

Why does he do this to me?

Soft, wet heat slides through the core of me. It's a single lick through my folds that throws my pulse off beat and I retract.

"Don't!" he barks, and when I open my eyes and look down at him, he continues, "Don't fight me. Don't push me away." And with our eyes linked together, he moves in and closes his mouth around my clit, sucking me gently. My heavy breaths are loud, staggering in rapture as I twist the sheets in my hands. He continues to watch me as his tongue laps and massages, spurring my body to grind against him.

He's soft and deliberate, and then, in an utter contradiction, he bares his teeth and bites my clit, erupting a euphoric scream from deep inside my gut as the pain rips through my pussy and up my spine. I fall back onto the bed, my body now writhing when his lips replace his teeth. Black and white fill my eyes with grey. I want to scream for him to stop and, at the same time, beg him to do it again. I'm hyperventilating when he shoves his tongue inside me, the prickles of his beard chafing my tender skin.

I'm swept away, floating in the air, unable to escape. I hear whimpering, and I know it has to be coming from me, but it isn't sadness my heart feels. I reach down for him, needy for some sort of anchor, and fumble around before he locks a hand to mine, holding it tightly.

His lips are now on mine as his body hovers over me, and he dips his tongue into my mouth. I slide my tongue along his, tasting myself, tasting him. It's a potent cocktail.

"Turn on your stomach," he tells me, and when my eyes widen, he assures, "I won't fuck you like that, not tonight."

I waver for a moment when he begs of me, "Trust me enough to be powerless. I want you weak and depending on me, to know that I'll keep you safe. Give me that power back."

I wanted Pike in that moment. It was a brief need that rushed through me. Pike was always the safe choice; Declan came with so many uncertainties. I feared becoming too exposed with him, and yet I feared becoming too distant with him. I wondered if I kept pushing him away if he would eventually leave me. I couldn't bear that thought. I'd lost him once before and it was the worst pain of my life. Whatever direction I went with Declan, one thing was inevitable: Fear.

I've been told in the past to never make decisions out of fear, but I was at a road block. Turn left—fear. Turn right—fear. I'd rather be scared with Declan than be scared without him. The choice, was clear. Pike faded in that room as I allowed Declan to fill every vacant space.

Turning onto my stomach, I rest my cheek on the bed and make the decision to let all my fears come to life. He takes my arms and crosses the belt around my wrists then turns me over to bring the two straps around my waist, cinching the loop even tighter as he fastens the belt around my stomach.

Bound with no escape. I'm completely his—en masse.

"Are you scared?" he asks, kicking my thighs open.

"Yes."

"Good," he says chillingly. "I want your eyes on me. I want you watching me as I fuck all that fear away."

Before I can digest his words, he slams into me with intense force, rocking my body backwards and kicking the breath right out of my lungs. I have nothing to grab on to as he rears back and thrusts inside me again. Wadding up a handful of the sheets beneath me, I hold on tightly as he begins to pump his scorching hot cock in and out of me.

I move to wrap my legs around his hips, but he stops me, grabbing my knees and pushing them wide open and down into the mattress. His eyes are on fire, molten black.

"Do you feel that?" he grunts. "You feel me inside of you?"

"Yes."

He then grips his hands around my shoulders and buries his cock so deep in me I whimper in ultimate pleasure. He keeps a tight hold on me, never relenting as he pushes himself as deep as he can. It's a searing pain in the tender flesh of my pussy, but so intoxicating.

"Tell me you feel that," his voice strains.

I nod, unable to catch my breath enough to speak.

His cock begins to throb inside of me as he holds himself still, the pressure becoming too much for me to contain. He keeps pushing, deeper and deeper until I can't take it anymore and I burst out in a breathless sob. It isn't from pain though, it's something else. An unyielding need to touch him, to grab him and pull him even deeper. It's a reckless urge for him to permeate me wholly, to rip me open completely. All of him in all of me. My arms ache to be freed, but he has me restrained.

I begin to scream, tears springing from my eyes, needing more.

More.

More.

When I think the pressure can't go any further, it does, intensifying, blinding my vision. My chest bears a thousand pounds of emotion, and I scream out, begging for more.

"That's it, darling. Cry," he encourages. "I want you crying for *me*."

And I am. Every tear is his as I sob for more of him.

He wanted me weak, and here I am, happily weak and desperate. I'm thrashing and fighting the restraint of his belt, but it only makes my muscles burn even more. My whole body is a raging fire, incinerating all my doubts of his love for me.

"I won't let you go!" he yells over my screams. "So stop fighting."

And when I do finally stop tugging against his belt and quiet myself, he leans down and licks the tears that coat my cheeks.

"Are you done fighting me?"

I nod, unable to stop the maniacal emotions from flooding out of me.

"Say it."

"I won't fight you again." My voice, hoarse and cracked.

He slowly releases the pressure, sliding his cock out of me, my muscles aching as I begin to lose him, but he returns with another forceful thrust, claiming, "I own you."

His words provide solace as he fucks me in long, hard strokes. My vision clears, and his face comes back into focus. His body is covered in sweat, every ridge of every muscle flexes and strains as he takes back the control I had been attempting to steal from him. It belongs to him though, so I freely give it.

I watch him move above me, and he takes my hips when he props up on his knees and pulls my ass off the bed. The roped muscles of his shoulders and arms bulge in swollen heat as he takes my pussy. My whole body begins to climb, tingling, sparking, igniting.

"Ask me for it," he snaps, reaching his hand behind my back to hold my hand, as he always does when I orgasm.

I immediately tense up, tightening my core, and he growls as I constrict around his shaft, fighting my release.

"Let me hear you beg."

And I do, pleading for him to fuck me hard, to make me cum, and he does. I shatter, exploding around his cock in pulsing contractions of passion, love, and trust as he squeezes my hand that remains bound behind my back, reminding me that he's here for me, that I'm not alone in the ache we both share for each other. And just as I reach my ultimate peak, live wires spark through my veins, taking my whole body captive. He pulls out and shoots his cum all over my stomach and tits. His hand continues to pump his cock as he empties himself all over me.

Tears paint my face in a piece of art that embodies a love so powerful it can only be ours. It's ugly and beautiful and painful, but it's ours. We are monsters and lovers, animals and killers, but nothing can extinguish what we have when we're together.

He takes his hand and rubs his semen into my skin all over my stomach, breasts, and neck before unlatching the belt buckle, freeing my arms. I immediately sling them around his neck.

"I'm sorry," I cry, tears falling from my cheeks and rolling down his back. "I'm so sorry."

"Shhh, darling," he consoles, whispering into my ear as he holds me tightly. "I have you. You're safe."

He sliced me wide open, and I cry for a long while until the wound slowly mends back together. He holds me the whole time, patient, whispering to me, calming me down.

I lie in his arms, covered in his feral scent, and when he pulls the sheets over our naked bodies, I take his face in my hands, telling him with absolute certainty, "I love you." My heart weeps as I say the words and fresh tears slip out, but I say it again because I want no doubt. "I love you."

He kisses me, and it's tender. Lips brushing lips, sucking and licking. He isn't taking; it's purely giving.

"I don't want you to ever go a day without knowing how much I adore you," he tells me. "You're life-consuming."

With tangled legs, bleeding hearts, and tethered souls, we claw each other throughout the night—desperate for unsurpassable symbiosis.

Six

KARMA IS OFTEN slow to respond, and because of its intimate relationship with destiny, often waits until a future incarnation. I won't have to wait that long though—it's been long enough. Fate became my divinity today when I got a phone call from an old buddy I hadn't heard from in a while. Seems there's a guy who needs to get his hands on an airline flight manifest—the same airline I've been working at for the past decade.

It's not the first time I've been approached to do something that would entail turning my back on the oath of honesty this job requires. But this is the first time I want to turn my back—and I did.

All it took was one name.

Steve Archer.

I first heard that name sixteen years ago when my brother was arrested for smuggling guns over international lines.

I sought my revenge on that man after I found out he ratted out my brother, but it was too late, he was already dead.

Or so I thought.

I hung up the phone and immediately pulled up the manifest for the flight in question. Since I work for the airline's IT department, retrieving the document took mere minutes to do. Steve Archer wasn't on the list though.

But that's okay, because I have the man's name that's looking for him. Lachlan Stroud—he will serve as my map, leading me to fulfill long overdue retribution.

Seven

WAKING UP THIS morning is surreal. It's what I used to fantasize about back in Chicago when Declan told me about this estate. And although I've been staying here with him for a couple weeks now, this is the first time I've truly felt connected to him. He's made his feelings known; he's made it very clear that he's not leaving. I've had my doubts, but after talking to Pike last night and Declan forcing me to reconnect and trust him, something has shifted between us.

I'm snug in his arms as I watch the sun bathe the walls. Everything around me glows in warmth. My body sinks into the arms of my prince as we wake in our castle. I try to control my elation, because this world is filled with unknowns that lurk behind the corners of life's winding streets. But for now, I'm at peace.

I watch Declan as he sleeps, and for the first time, I see the stress I've inflicted up close. It's in the extra grey hairs that weren't there in Chicago. It's in his beard that's a few weeks overgrown. It's in the deepening lines at the corners of his eyes. I reach out and run my hand along his jaw, through the bristly hair of his beard. It crackles against my palm, and I smile. He begins to rouse, but I don't stop touching, feeling, studying. Every touch, smell, sight, I cement to my memory. Carving everything about him into the delicate flesh of my heart.

Strong fingers comb through my hair as he wakes, opening his eyes—bright emerald green.

"'Morning, darling." His voice is wrapped coarsely in sleepiness.

"Mmm," I hum softly, nuzzling my head against his chest, and I fall deeper into his hold when he tightens his arms around me.

His body is so warm against mine, and I wonder what I was so afraid of. How did I allow my mind to trick me into believing he was the one to fear? So many questions come to life, and I want to punish myself for doubting him so much, for shutting him out, for not trusting his love.

"Tell me how you feel," he requests, and without any hesitation, I respond, "Safe."

He rolls over on top of me, propping himself up on his hands. I push a lock of hair back that's fallen over his eyes and keep my hand fixed in his thick tresses.

"This is all I wanted, you know? You, here with me—safe."

"I'm here," I whisper softly.

He drops tender kisses along my shoulder, across my collarbone, and over the swell of my breasts. I feel his cock harden against my thigh beneath the sheets, and I open my legs for him to settle against me. His lips move down the length of my body, and his soft kisses intensify when he sinks his teeth into my flesh. His greedy hunger punctures, and I scream through the pain, but I don't want him to stop.

Blood trickles along my stomach and legs as he continues to bite me between his gentle kisses.

This is how savages love.

With his scent from last night still dried on my body, he now marks me in a different way.

My legs open wider when he buries his head between my thighs. He's a wild beast, fucking my pussy with his mouth. He leaves my hands free to pull and rip his hair as I mewl loudly in sexual delirium. Time no longer exists in this room as he devours me powerless.

He doesn't stop after my body explodes; he keeps going, sending me into a freefall. Every bone in my body aches, both his hands holding both of mine through every orgasm that pounds through my body. It becomes too much, but I don't deny his appetite.

I let him take me higher as my chest seizes in overwhelming paroxysms love. It's only when I lose my breath and begin to gasp for air that he stops. He moves above me, but I can't make out his face. Everything is drowned behind hazy pops of light as I struggle to fill my lungs with its life source.

My body lies limp on the sheets that are drenched in our arousal, sweat, and blood. There's no doubt that Declan is as raw as they come, but that's what I love about him. This love is shamelessly amaranthine.

He's all over me.

I'm all over him.

There's no doubt we belong to each other.

MY BODY IS sore as I walk down the stairs with Declan. We're showered and dressed and in dire need of food. Walking into the kitchen, Lachlan says goodbye to whomever he's talking to on his cell.

"Afternoon," he greets when we walk in.

Declan starts pulling out food from the fridge, and I eye Lachlan's cup of coffee and the French press on the table, asking, "Is the kettle still hot?"

"Yes."

I take a teacup down from the cabinet and begin to prepare a cup of hot tea.

"Roasted tomatoes and toast?"

"That sounds good," I respond to Declan as I take my tea to the table to join Lachlan.

It's been nice having him around. When Declan is up in his office working, Lachlan will often take walks with me outside. It's a relief that his treatment of me never changed after what he saw the night he and Declan found me. His banter has been a welcome reprieve from the stress of late.

"Are you hungry?"

He takes a sip of his coffee before responding. "I had a bowl of oatmeal already."

I try to hide my laughter, but he catches me, giving me a questioning glare.

"You eat that every morning."

"It's good."

"It's old man food."

He removes his glasses, and sets down the newspaper he's reading, and teases, "Says the old lady who's about to eat toast for a meal."

"Touché," I admit with a smile, and quickly change the direction of conversation, asking eagerly, "Have you found any leads on my dad?"

"I've made calls to all the contacts I have that have links to the airlines. I'm waiting to hear back."

"Well, how long do we just sit and wait?"

"I know you're anxious," he tells me, "but it's only been a day. I promise you I'm doing all I can, love."

"Lachlan," Declan calls out when he shuts the oven door, taking Lachlan's attention. "What did you decide about London?"

"A hotel would be best."

"A hotel?" I ask. "A hotel for what?"

Declan takes a seat next to me at the table. "Lachlan's coming with us to London."

"Why?"

"For protection."

"I don't need a babysitter, Declan."

"Is that so?"

Narrowing my eyes, miffed, I respond, "Richard's dead. What are you worried about?"

"When it comes to you . . . *everything*."

I look to Lachlan and tell him, "No offense, but I don't need you looking over my shoulder."

"I agree with Declan on this one."

"We'll be living in one of the most secure buildings in the world," I argue. "What could possibly happen?"

"What about Jacqueline?"

"Jacqueline? Richard's wife?" I practically laugh. "She's nothing. She's a socialite. A housewife. A whore. A—"

"A widow," Declan interrupts harshly. "She knows we killed her husband."

"She doesn't have it in her. She's too weak."

"I wouldn't be so quick to underestimate. She's lost everything, and now her baby has no father."

"Richard wasn't her baby's father," I reveal. "It's Bennett's child."

Declan's brows cinch together in question, and I explain, "He got her pregnant while I was married to him. I didn't know until after he died. That bomb was laid on me when I went to have the will read. Bennett left the business assets to him."

He quickly looks to Lachlan, saying, "Could you give us a minute?"

"Of course."

Once Lachlan leaves the room, Declan continues, "You took his money?"

His accusing voice has a lick of judgment to it, sparking a tingle of rebellion from me.

"Yes," I bite. "I took it."

"How much?"

"Not as much as his bastard child got, but enough."

His teeth grind before he presses further, stressing his words, "How much, Elizabeth?"

My hands grow tense when I think about the number, but I tell him the truth. "One point two."

Declan releases a relieved sigh, and it's then I realize he's assuming fewer zeros, so I clarify, adding, "Billion."

"Billion?" he blurts out.

"Yes, Declan. One point two billion. Surely you knew how wealthy he was. This shouldn't come as a surprise. The only thing that was surprising was how little I got."

My words are snappy, and it frustrates me to see his indignation.

"What?" I question with vexation. "Stop looking at me like that. If you want to say something, just say it."

"You can't take that money."

"Why not? Do you have any idea the hell I went through to get it?"

"But why? For what purpose, really? Because unless you've left out some important detail, Bennett was, by all accounts, an innocent man."

"Innocent?" I yell as heat creeps up my neck. "His lie took my father from me! His lie put me in that foster home! His lie raped me of the life I deserved!"

"He was a child, for Christ's sake!"

"If you want to rationalize this, do it with someone else."

"I saw the way he looked at you, Elizabeth."

"Stop." My voice is cold and hard and blatantly demanding.

"He loved you."

"Stop." I shake my head, blocking his words and refute, "He loved an illusion. He loved *Nina*, the woman who molded herself to be everything he ever wanted in a wife. It was a con, so don't you make me feel guilty."

"But the con is over."

"It may be over, but my feelings about him haven't changed."

"I see that," he finally concludes. "I understand your need to pin the blame for all this, it's just . . . you're blaming the wrong person."

"What does it matter? He's dead. It's not like I can hurt him anymore even if I wanted to."

His eyes are sternly focused on me when he repeats, "You can't keep that money. I killed him; I don't want that on my hands. You may not see this clearly for what it is, but that doesn't mean I don't."

I shake my head, not wanting to lose everything my brother and I worked so hard for.

"It's just money. Money you don't need because you have me."

"That's not the point," I tell him. "And besides that, how do you suggest getting rid of that amount of money without raising suspicion?"

"What about his parents?"

"Are you kidding me?" I exclaim. "His father took my dad out. They worked together and he used Bennett's claim to ensure my dad would be out of the way so he could move up the chain and make more money. Bennett's father hated him!"

Declan lowers his head and pinches the bridge of his nose. I know he's stressed trying to digest all this information I'm throwing at him. It's generations bound by a twisted web of deception and fraud. Everyone is a con in someone else's agenda.

"If I found a way to get rid of the money, would you do it?"

I look at him as my mind goes to Pike. I think about all he gave up for those few years while I worked the scheme with Bennett. I think about his life in that shithole trailer, about the days, weeks, and sometimes months we'd have to be apart. This is as much his money as it is mine. Am I really going to just toss it away as if everything we sacrificed wasn't worth it?

"Tell me your hesitation."

"Pike," I blurt without thinking first.

"Your brother?"

"He earned that money too."

Declan reaches over and takes my hands in his as his eyes immediately soften. "Elizabeth, you're making decisions based on people that are no longer alive," he tells me as gently as he can, but his words still hurt. "When people die, the world changes whether you want it to or not. Your refusal to change with it is doing nothing but hindering the future. A future you deserve. But I'm telling you now, I can't live in the past where you still are."

He motions for me to come to him, and I do. Pulling me onto his lap, he wraps me up in a strong hug, and I hold him close. I need comfort, because I'm not sure if I can continue to carry the weight of my world anymore.

"I need you to let go of the past. I'm not asking you to do it all at once, but you're with me now. I'm your future. Can you do that? At least try to?"

I loosen my arms and pull back to look in his eyes.

"Start with the money," he tells me.

"Don't hang on to this for me. Let the money go. It isn't worth pushing Declan away."

"Okay," I agree with a boulder of reluctance, but Pike is right. I can't take a step back with Declan when we're finally moving forward.

He smiles, repeating, "Okay."

"I GOT THE address," my buddy tells me when I answer my phone.

I'd be stupid to email, fax, or deliver this manifest in any other electronic way. I don't need my ass getting busted for this breach of security with the FAA. With an address, I can payoff some random Joe to mail this off from any location.

But more importantly, I now have a point of contact.

"Thanks. I'll get this overnighted."

Now, I need to start making a few calls because I need a PI, and quick.

nine

"I'LL GET YOU added to my accounts so you can go shopping. I don't want you touching Bennett's money any more," Declan says when I zip up my luggage.

"What are you talking about?"

He eyes my bag, asking, "Those are all your belongings, right?"

"Yes. Well, most of them. I left everything else behind in Chicago. It felt strange to keep them. Those are all Nina's clothes, not mine."

"That's why you need to go shopping."

I take my luggage off the bed and set it on the floor before taking a seat on the mattress.

"Did I say something wrong?" he questions as he walks over to me.

"No, it's just . . ."

He takes a seat on the bed next to me. "Tell me."

"I've never had money," I begin. "I came from white trash. It was one thing for me to spend Bennett's money, because I hated him and it felt good. But . . . I've never . . ." I stumble over my words, unsure of how to say what I'm attempting to and finally conclude, "I don't come from your world, Declan. I can fake it. I can blend in. But at the end of the day, I'm just a runaway street kid. And you asking me to spend money . . . it doesn't feel right."

"Darling."

"I wouldn't even know what to buy. I don't know what I like and don't like. I've never had the luxury of that choice because I wore whatever scraps we could afford from thrift stores and garage sales. It was easy shopping on Bennett's dime because I simply copied what the other women in his circle were wearing." I pause for a moment before admitting, "I know Nina well, but I have no idea who I am because I've spent my life caged up and detached. And when I was with Bennett, I was simply pretending to be what he wanted."

"You have choices now," Declan says. "And you have time. You take all that you need to find yourself. That's one thing I won't rush you to do. But I don't want you feeling guilty for the things I want to give you. You may not have started in my world, but you're here now."

"A part of me still doesn't feel like I deserve to be. I don't doubt you when you say you love me, but it feels undeserving."

"It's not. If I could give you more, I would. Nobody should ever have to face the nightmare that you did." He takes my chin, angling me to him when he states, "You are not trash."

"Some of those choices were mine though."

"Like what?"

"Pike."

His hand drops as he sighs. "I've tried to make sense of your relationship, and although I hate knowing that side of you two, all I can conclude is that you guys were just two kids trying to survive in a world that was deeper than hell. But you're right, it was a choice you made. Luckily our choices don't define us." He then cradles my face in his hands, saying, "And you, darling, you were never a choice. You were put on this Earth destined to be loved by me."

And with his words, in our continuing need to reclaim each other, he throws me back onto the bed, strips me, ties me up, and fucks me. It's raw and primal and everything else Declan embodies.

LATER THAT DAY, after all our bags are packed and the boys have prepped the property for our vacancy, we are ready to go to London. I feel like a child on her way to Disneyland, and I wear it on my face in an obnoxious smile. Lachlan loads our bags as I sit with Declan in the back seat of his Mercedes SUV.

"You seem mildly excited," Declan teases, giving my hand a gentle squeeze.

I turn my head to him. "Is it that obvious?"

"Insanely obvious. You might as well be skipping instead of walking."

"Skip? I'm not sure I ever learned how to skip. But keep joking with me, and I just might."

"Well, that's everything," Lachlan announces when he gets into the front seat. "Are we ready?"

Declan looks to me, and I give him an approving nod. "I'm ready."

Lachlan drives down the winding road that leads to the gates I used to cling to and cry when I thought Declan was dead. He pulls out onto the main street, and as we get further away, a part of me feels free. Even though I love Brunswickhill, I'm ready for a little distance. So much has happened in the past couple weeks, so many lows, so much anger blended with beatific highs of love and newborn trust. It's a rollercoaster I'm ready to get off because I'm craving the stability of walking with Declan on a solid surface.

Declan never lets go of my hand. It's a simple gesture that reassures I'm safe with him throughout the trip.

"Take her over London," Declan calls out to the pilot who has the cockpit open on his private plane.

The plane's wing dips down as we turn, and Declan kisses me. It's love and avidity, devotion and prurience as he takes ownership of my mouth, forcing me to breathe the air from his lungs. If Lachlan weren't on this plane with us, I'm sure Declan's cock would be buried inside my body right now.

He eventually relents, pulling back, leaving me breathless.

"Look," he says, pointing out my window.

I look down and smile when I see London lit up in the night's darkness, and it's magical. We fly over the River Thames where the Tower Bridge glows brightly above the water. Declan points out the major landmarks as we pass them, and I drink in every word he says. Parliament, Big Ben, and the London Eye are behind us in a blink of a moment as we prepare to land at Biggin Hill Airport.

Once landed, it's another hour drive into Knightsbridge, London. We pass designer store fronts and swanky restaurants that line the brightly lit streets. Everything about this area screams luxury.

"We're here," Declan tells me when Lachlan pulls the car into an underground parking garage that's heavily secured. "You doing okay?"

"Mmm hmm. Just a little tired."

Lachlan finds our designated parking spot and turns the car off. We make our way through the garage, and Declan wasn't lying when he told me how private this place is. I watch as Declan approaches a sleek black box mounted on the wall. He leans his face in, placing his eyes up to the lenses and hits the silver button. A few seconds later, the door clicks and he's able to open it.

"What was that?" I question.

"Iris scanner," he tells me. "It's the only way to get through the first set of doors. We'll get you into the system tomorrow."

I follow him next through the fingerprint sensor that opens another door, and the last door is secured by a key card. Three barriers of security, and we're finally inside the building.

He takes my hand, and with a sexy smile, says, "Welcome home."

"It's practically a fortress."

"Practically," he repeats before stopping at the concierge to drop off the keys to the car and instructing the delivery of all our luggage.

Lachlan stays behind in the lobby as we step onto the elevator. It's one thing for me to be Mrs. Vanderwal, living in the penthouse of The Legacy, but this is on a totally different scale. When Declan told me we'd be living here, I did my research. I knew I'd be living among the world's elite: Ukrainian business moguls, Qatar's former Prime Minister, Russian real estate magnates, among others. We may not be living in the penthouse, but the seventh floor is as intimidating as any penthouse in the United States.

It's a simultaneous finger scan and key card scan to unlock the door.

"After you," Declan says as he motions for me to enter.

I walk through the grand foyer into the impressive living room. Everything is razor sleek lines, clean and simple. Intricate raindrop crystal chandeliers cascade their soft glow over the crisp white walls and white furniture, creating a warmth to the otherwise stark color. The rich mocha woodwork is a pleasant contrast to the white, warming the space even more. It's contemporary design at its most opulent.

"What do you think?"

Turning my head to look over my shoulder at Declan who's still standing in the foyer, I respond with phony condescension, "A bit much, isn't it, McKinnon?"

"You're displeased?"

"It'll do," I tease with an ever-so-slight grin, and he laughs, saying, "Well, it's all yours. Go ahead, darling. Explore."

I look around, opening every door and peeking in every room. The kitchen is outfitted in commercial grade appliances, and the bathrooms are as lavish as those you'd find in upscale spas. Every perimeter is lined with floor to ceiling, wall to wall windows that overlook Knightsbridge. There's an office upstairs that's clearly been furnished by Declan because it's filled with a rich chesterfield couch and chairs, the same as his office in Chicago and his library in Scotland. And both bedrooms, one on each wing of the second floor, have en suites and large, plush beds that stand taller than your average.

"This one is ours," Declan whispers from behind my ear as I stand in one of the bedrooms.

His lips press against my pulse point, sending shivers up my arms.

"It's perfect."

We stand in front of the window, looking down on the lights of the city, and I cannot believe I'm here—in London—with a man who knows my truth and loves me regardless.

"I read an article about this building the other day. They said it was soulless and devoid of life. I know it was referring to the secrecy of its occupants and everything else, but if they only knew what was behind this bulletproof glass."

"And what's that?" he questions, and when I turn around in his arms and look up at him, I respond, "Life."

He leans down, kisses my forehead, and I speak softly to him. "I've never felt so alive as I do with you. Right here, right now. I never thought this was possible, to feel the way I do."

"I never wanted this with anyone else. Even in my darkest days without you, even when I thought I couldn't hate you more, I still wanted you."

Before he can get the chance to kiss me, the ring of the doorbell sounds.

"Bawbags," he fumes in irritation at the interruption, and I can't help but laugh at his Scottish curse.

It really is an ugly language, but the accent is beyond sexy.

I follow him downstairs to the living room, and when Lachlan walks in with two employees with our luggage, I beam with excitement. "Have you seen this place?"

He doesn't respond to me, but instead approaches Declan, asking, "May I?" as I watch in curiosity.

"She's all yours," Declan tells him. "She's about as excited as a lass at her first tea party."

Lachlan laughs, walking straight towards me, and I can't help my own laughter at his demeanor. He grabs me, picking me up as if I were a little girl and gives me a joyous embrace.

"This smile you wear makes dealing with McKinnon's shit-stain moods worth my while."

We laugh as he sets me down, and I'm so thankful for his loyalty to Declan and the friendship he's given me. He's twenty years my elder, and I find comfort in that. As if I can look to him for guidance in a way I can't with Declan. In a way a child might look to a parent. He gives me that feeling, and it's settling.

"Thank you."

"For what, love?"

"Opening my car door the night I first met you."

"Oh yes, our first date," he animates in a shameless attempt to taunt Declan, and Declan doesn't miss a beat when he responds, "Fuck off, Lachlan, and you can get your hands off her now. You got your hug, you're done."

His words are harsh, but they're in jest. These boys go way back to their days at Saint Andrew's, so it's no surprise they fight like brothers, despite their age gap.

"Well, then, if all is in place here, I guess I'll head to my hotel."

"Lachlan, wait."

He takes a step closer to me, and I ask, "Have you heard anything about my dad? Good or bad? Has anyone called you?"

"You've been with me all day," he says, but no matter how content I feel, there's still unsettling anxiety when it comes to my dad.

"I know, I just . . ."

"I promise you I'm doing everything I can, love. We'll find him for you."

I nod as I feel the weight of the unknown swell in my chest, and Declan immediately senses it. He quickly dismisses Lachlan when I wander over to the windows and stare out.

"This is a good day," he tells me when he moves to stand next to me along the window.

"What if he's down there, right under my nose, among all those people?"

"Then he won't be too hard to find."

My eyes skitter over the men and women walking along the sidewalks, enjoying their night, when Declan pulls me away.

"I'm doing everything I can. We have several people at this point that are trying to find him. The manifest is only one angle of the many we are working on. But you heard Lachlan," he stresses. "He'll call us with any updates."

"I know, I'm just—"

"On edge," he interrupts, finishing my thought, and he's right.

I want answers, and these past few days of waiting are eating me alive.

"Not tonight. I want to see that smile again."

"You act like it's the first time you've ever seen me smile."

"It's the first time I've seen you truly smile from your soul. *You*—Elizabeth. You wear it differently than the woman I knew in Chicago, and I want to see it again," he says and then picks me up, hoisting me over his shoulder.

"Declan!" I squeal out in playfulness. "What are you doing?"

"I'm going to get you naked, tie you up, and then order myself dinner," he teases.

"You're such a romantic asshole."

ten

MY FIRST MORNING here at One Hyde Place was a busy one. No time for lounging in bed until the afternoon. Declan was up early yelling on the phone at a hacker he hired to find out more information on my dad. After that call ended, I sat in his office with him as he proceeded to make more calls about my father, growing more and more impatient as his stress amplified. He's been putting himself under so much pressure to find him, but I didn't want him to get any more worked up than he already was, so I convinced him to step away for a while and take a shower with me to calm him down.

After we were dressed, I met with the head of security downstairs to input all my information, along with my iris and fingerprint scans. Declan then introduced me to a few of the employees that I would be seeing on a daily basis before we returned to the apartment. It wasn't but a few minutes later that the woman who works for the butler service arrived with groceries we requested earlier in the morning.

And now I sit in the living room, reading "A Tourist's Guide to London" that I asked Lachlan to bring over from his hotel. He dropped it off earlier along with a new cell phone that Declan insisted on me having instead of the cheap disposable one I was using since I left *Nina's* phone back in the States. Lachlan input his number along with all of Declan's before heading back out to run a few errands for us. But it's now inching closer to one o'clock, and I'm growing hungry.

I rifle through the fridge, looking for something easy, and decide on a simple grilled cheese. It's practically all I know how to cook, but it's comforting and reminds me of my brother.

"Is the fire extinguisher handy?" Declan jokes when he walks into the room.

I flip the sandwich with the spatula and then flip him the middle finger.

"What a lovely gesture. If we're done with the pleasantries, I'd like to make a request."

Turning the burner off, I slide my grilled cheese onto a plate and walk over to the island bar to sit next to Declan. He hands over an invitation engraved on heavy linen paper with an embossed gold seal at the top.

"What's the Caledonian Club?" I ask, setting the invitation down on the cold soapstone countertop.

"A private Members' Club I've been associated with my whole life. Both my father and grandfather were members."

"Is this one of those male-only chauvinist clubs where you all stand around, smoke cigars, and compete with each other to prove who has the biggest dick?" I badger and then take a bite of my food.

"Something like that, but luckily for you, they started to allow women to accompany members at the social events a few years ago."

"How progressive of them."

"Yes, well, if you're done being stabby, I've RSVP'd our *pleasured* acceptance," he informs me with an appeasing smirk.

"When is it?"

"This evening."

"Tonight?" I blurt in surprise. "Declan, I don't have anything to wear. All my formal attire is back in Chicago."

"Harrods is right across the street," he tells me. "Lachlan can take you."

I drop my sandwich onto the plate, huffing in mild irritation. "Lachlan? Really? So, I'm not allowed to walk across the street by myself, something a child is capable of doing?"

"I thought I made my concerns clear before we came."

"You did, but I didn't think he'd be at my side at all times."

He cups my cheek as he stands, saying, "Must you fight me on everything?"

"Fine," I exhaust. "I'll see it your way this time, but you know he's going to be pissed at you when he finds out you're forcing him to do this particular errand."

"That old man is always pissed at me. I can handle him."

I laugh under my breath, enjoying the lightness of our exchange, and then ask, "What's the attire?"

"Black tie." He then gives me a kiss and starts heading back to his office when he calls out over his shoulder, "I'll call for Lachlan."

"Where is he taking me again?"

"Harrods," he shouts from his office.

I grab my tourist book, flip to the shopping section, and read while I finish my lunch. I don't have to wait long for Lachlan to arrive.

He's slightly distracted—quiet—as the day moves forward, but I don't push him to talk. Instead, I gather gowns to try on. I'm not sure what Declan's preferences are the way I knew Bennett's. I had more time to learn about Bennett, to study him. So I spend a good amount of time pulling gowns, second-guessing, and shoving them back on the rack.

Thank God for patient sales associates.

Lachlan sits outside the fitting room as I try on the various dresses. One by one, until I finally make my choice when I slip on the Givenchy in kombu green. I decide to take a step out and show Lachlan, but when I do, he's not there. I walk past the empty chair and then hear his hushed voice.

Peeking around the corner, I spot him a few racks down on his cell and quickly retreat when I see him look my way. I strain to hear what he's saying, hoping that it has something to do with my dad, but when I hear his harsh tone barking, "Calm down, Camilla," under his breath, my mind begins to spin.

Camilla?

I step back into the fitting room and wonder why that name sounds so familiar. I trace back and it finally clicks.

Cal's girlfriend.

I met her a few months ago when I accompanied Bennett on a trip to New York City. It was the night Declan showed up unexpectedly at his father's house. But why the hell is Lachlan talking to her? Whatever the reason, he clearly doesn't want me to know. Declan would have his ass if he knew Lachlan left me alone, so whatever he's talking to her about must outweigh the risk.

After I make my purchases, he walks me back home and leaves after I'm safely inside the building.

"How'd it go?" Declan asks when I enter the apartment, and I hold up the garment bag, saying, "I found a dress."

"Good," he says, and my unease intensifies with the knowledge that Lachlan, a man that Declan highly trusts, is corresponding with his father's girlfriend. "Everything okay? You look worried."

I drape the gown over the back of the couch and approach Declan.

"I heard something strange today, and it has me feeling unnerved," I tell him.

"What happened?" he questions with concern.

"It could be nothing, but did you know that Lachlan knows your father's girlfriend?"

"Camilla?"

"Yeah."

"Why? What happened?"

"I overheard him on the phone with her. He sounded mad or maybe annoyed."

"What did you hear him say?"

"Nothing really, he just snapped at her to calm down, and when I heard him use her name, I went back into the fitting room. Something about the tone he used with her and the fact that he'd been distant the whole time I was shopping made me apprehensive."

I see the unpleasant look on his face and ask, "What is it?"

"When we were scrambling to find you, I answered his phone when he wasn't in the room. It was her and she called him *baby*. When she realized it was me on the line, she quickly ended the call."

"Did you ask Lachlan what was going on?"

"He dismissed it as them being old friends. Honestly my mind was completely fucked at the time."

"Maybe it's nothing," I tell him.

"Maybe, but I'll address it with him before I leave you alone with him again."

"Declan . . ."

"Don't contest me. I'm not willing to risk anything when it comes to you."

"You can't control the world."

"No, but I control you and what happens to you," he tells me as he takes my hand and places it on the side of his neck. "Do you feel that?"

I nod as his pulse beats hard into my palm. It's an exorbitant sign of anxiety that he hides well, but it's clearly at war with him on the inside.

"That's you," he says. "You're my pulse. You're the reason it beats and keeps me alive, so don't defy me when it comes to protecting you, because I refuse to be reckless with my quintessence."

He's strident with his words. I know his desire for ultimate control; he's been that way since the day I met him, and he's explained why he is the way he is. Witnessing the murder of his mother has burdened him into adulthood and has shaped him into the man he is today. His demanding ways with me might be harsh for others, but they stem from a loving place.

"I'm sorry. Truth is, you're the first person who's ever gone to the lengths you do to make sure I'm taken care of. I know I give you a hard time, but the rule you have on me feels good."

Before I know it, he has me in his arms, and I'm quick to wrap my legs around his waist as he carries me over to the couch. Tossing me onto my back, he orders me to take my top and bra off, and I do so in mere seconds at the same time he rips off his pants and shirt.

"Hands under your ass," he commands, and when I have them securely beneath me, he straddles my body, pinning me under him. "Spit in my hand," is his next directive, and again, I obey.

His cock is rock hard, and I watch as he beats himself off above me, using my saliva as lube. He's mean and he knows it, teasing me like this. He gives into his desires while forcing me to withhold my own. He refuses to feed my hunger, leaving me without touch as he pumps the length of himself.

I want to touch him, but he's testing my obedience, so I squeeze my thighs together in a lame attempt to create much needed friction for my throbbing clit. I can't contain myself as I watch him stare down at me while he indulges his craving. His breaths begin to stagger unevenly as a sheen of sweat coats his hairline. Every groan that escapes his throat spurs me farther, and I press my thighs together even harder. The moment my body writhes in utter heat, he catches me.

"Open your legs," he barks, and I do.

He then leans forward and locks his free hand around my neck to keep control of me. My pussy aches painfully for him to fill me up, but I know he has no intentions. When I see the muscles of his abs begin to contract, he's getting close. He chokes on a breath of air, his grip around my neck tightening, and then explodes all over me, scenting me in his semen.

His hand leaves my neck, and he kisses me roughly before getting off the couch. I lie here and look up at him when he says, "Don't clean that off, and don't wear any perfume tonight."

I sit up, and a few drops of his cum roll down between my breasts. "Lucky for me, my dress doesn't have a plunging neckline," I tease with a smile, knowing he gets off leaving his mark on me.

"I'm going to take a hot shower," he says and then kisses my forehead.

I admire his firm ass as I watch him walk to the bedroom.

While he's in the shower, I take my time doing my makeup and hair. The dress may not have a plunging front, but the back does, so I curl my hair and wear it in a ponytail at the base of my neck so that my scars will be covered. I keep my look simple and clean with no jewelry.

I smile when I look over to Declan who's now fastening his kilt. The Caledonian Club is a private Scottish club here in London, which I was pleased to learn because Declan in a kilt is about the hottest thing I've ever seen.

This is the first event we are attending as a couple, and it feels good to be getting ready and sharing this moment together—a moment we had to work so hard to get to—a moment so many probably take for granted. I slip on my gown and smooth down the fabric that contours closely to my body. It boasts a high round neck, concealing the dried cum that's all over my chest, and flows to the floor in a sweeping, fluted hem. The deep green flatters my red hair, and also complements the green in Declan's plaids.

I stand in front of the mirror and look myself over with restless hands.

"Why are you fidgeting?" Declan asks when he steps behind me. "You seem nervous."

"I am," I admit as he runs his hands up and down the length of my arms.

"Why? You must've gone to hundreds of events like this in Chicago. You're an old pro."

"Yeah, but I was always pretending. I'm a good actress, but this is the first time mingling among the upper crust as *me*. I'm not hiding behind a façade anymore."

He plants a kiss on my shoulder. "The real you is so much better than the lie."

"I don't know about that."

"I do," he says and then turns me around. He looks me over from head to toe. "You're incredibly stunning."

I take hold of Declan's hand to quell my nerves when we arrive at the mansion that was built in the early 1900s. He smiles down at me as we walk to the entrance. When we step inside, my eyes take in the ornate ambiance. The walls are painted ivory with rich gold accents, and heavy ruby drapes fall from the ceiling to the floor. Oil paintings hang from the walls and glow beneath the opulent chandeliers.

The wood floors that lie beneath the carpet creak under my feet as Declan leads me through the club that has a wealth of history here in London. I take in the men dressed in their kilts and fly plaids and the women in their elegant gowns. And suddenly, without my mask, I feel like an imposter—garbage wrapped in silk—and my stomach turns. So, I quickly decide that even though I have no clue who I am, I'll do my best to fake it. The last thing I want is to show Declan any more weakness.

As we walk into the party, I stiffen my spine and feign my place in society with my head held high like I've done for years.

"Declan," a gentleman who looks to be in his fifties calls out. "It's been a long time since we've seen you."

The two of them shake hands.

"It's good to see you, Ian. How've you been?"

"Busy as ever," he says before turning his attention to me, asking Declan, "And who's this lovely lady?"

"You're a charmer," I lightly flirt and then introduce myself, "Elizabeth Archer."

"Lucky man," Ian notes, to which Declan responds while looking over to me, "Extremely lucky."

We continue to mingle and Declan introduces me to old friends and a few business men and their wives. He drinks his typical Scotch and I sip champagne, we share a few dances, and when Declan can't help himself, he whispers his obscene thoughts in my ear. "I want to take you to another room and suck on that pretty little clit of yours until you cum in my mouth."

I drop my forehead to his shoulder as he speaks to me, my neck igniting in heat with each of his obscenities.

"Just thinking about the taste of your pussy gets my cock—"

"Declan!" a tall woman with long, dark hair says, interrupting our private moment. "I had no idea you were going to be here!" Annoyance rankles me when she pulls Declan in for a hug.

"Last minute move," he tells her, composed as ever.

"Move? You're living here now?"

"I am."

"So I take it you purchased the land to build on?" she asks, and a trill of jealousy creeps alive in me with how much she knows.

"Davina, this is Elizabeth," he introduces.

"Yes, I remember you. You were at the charity gala in Edinburgh last month, right?"

And then I remember. She was Declan's date that night, hanging on his arm and constantly by his side.

"That's right. And you are . . .?"

"An old family friend," Declan answers for her.

"Practically brother and sister," she adds with a big smile. "Although I do fondly remember our wedding. How old were we?"

"Ten. Eleven, maybe."

Watching them go back and forth with such ease turns that jealousy into full blown spite.

"Sounds charming," I interject with mockery, and when I do, I can feel

Declan's eyes hurling daggers at me, but I don't engage.

Davina continues to wear her pretentious smile, adding, "The shortbread and jam reception wasn't all that elegant, but it still makes for good memories."

"Well, as much as I'd love to hear more about that humble reception of yours, you'll have to excuse me."

As I walk away from the both of them, I wonder if the feelings swarming inside me are anything like what Declan feels, because if I could put my mark on him like a dog claiming ownership, I would. I want to lock him up and pretend he never had a life before me.

And then I have to question how friendly they've been, because it was only a few weeks ago she was on his arm as his date.

Red heat slithers up my neck, and before I explode, I rush out the doors and into the chill of night. Clouds of vapor escape me with my heavy breathing. Never in my life have I felt threatened and jealous over a man, but then again, never in my life have I been in love. I loved my brother, but in a very different way. I knew he fucked other women—lots of other women, but never did I care. And just to know that this woman has had more time with Declan than I have is enough to ignite this thrashing inside me.

"What are you doing out here?" Declan asks from behind me.

"Did you fuck her?" I seethe quietly so passersby won't hear.

He takes me by the arm and nearly drags me around the building to the parking lot in the back, pushing me against a random car. He isn't happy about my question, but I ask it again.

"Did you?"

"Would it make you mad?"

My anger grows.

"Hmm? Answer me."

"Yes," I spit in hostility.

He presses his chest against mine, fury roiling behind his eyes when he asks, "Tell me how it makes you feel to think about my dick in another woman's pussy."

In a sudden flash, I slap him hard across the face, but he barely flinches.

"Go ahead. Hit me again."

"Go to hell."

"That outrage you feel," he says through gritted teeth. "That rage mixed with passion and jealousy could never amount to what you made me feel. You let me fuck you, fall in love with you, all the while knowing you were fucking your husband. And then I find out you were also letting your brother fuck you. And you have the nerve to question me!" He takes a pause, pinching his eyes closed before opening them again and continuing. "Do I need to remind you of all the fucked up ways you destroyed me?"

"No."

"I didn't think so. And to answer your question, no, I've never fucked her. Never wanted to."

"She was your date."

"Yes," he responds. "She was. Like I told you, she's an old friend. Our families were close and we grew up together. She's attended many events with me in the past so I didn't have to go with random women. But now I have you."

Guilt eclipses jealousy.

"I'm sorry."

"There should be no doubt in that heart of yours that you belong to me. Everyone in that room knows it. My cum is all over your skin, and yet you feel threatened by another woman."

"You just . . ."

"You want to know my past? Because it isn't that interesting. I've never been in love. Not once. I've dated less than five women in my life, but I never loved any of them. Did I fuck them? Yes. Have I fucked others? Yes, but not many. Casual sex isn't really my thing. I've spent my life working hard, trying to live up to my father's expectations. Work was always my main focus. And then there was you. You came into my life and turned everything upside down."

"I don't know what I'm doing," I admit. "I hate that you've seen so many of my weaknesses. I love you, there's no question, but I don't know how to do this the right way."

"You don't fool me. You're the strongest woman I know." He cups my face in his hands, dips his head down to my level, and looks deeply into my eyes, adding, "But you're weak too, and when you let me see that part of you, it only makes me love you more. You and I have been through hell and back, and this isn't going to be easy for either one of us."

I slip my arms around his waist and rest my head against his chest.

Declan presses his lips to my head in a tender kiss. "You have nothing to worry about, you hear me?"

"Yes."

"Come on," he says. "Let's go home."

"We can go back in."

"I've had enough socializing for one night. Let's get out of here."

The drive back to the apartment is a short one, and when we walk through the door, I kick off my heels. Declan gets the fireplace going and we simply hold each other as we lie on the couch. We settle into the silence and darkness, too lazy to slip out of our formalwear. I soak in the heat from his body while he runs his fingertips along my spine.

After a while, Declan's phone rings. I'm edging on sleep when he takes the call.

"McKinnon . . . Yes. Let him up." He ends the call and gently brushes my hair back. "Lachlan's here," he tells me, and I groan, not wanting to get up.

A couple minutes later there's an abrupt knock on the door, and when Declan opens it, Lachlan rushes in.

"I've got it," he announces urgently, holding a sheet of paper.

"What is it?" I question, standing and walking towards him.

He comes straight to me, passing Declan, and hands me the paper. "The passenger manifest."

"THIS COULDN'T HAVE gone any better," the PI that I hired a few days ago tells me.

"Were you able to plant the device on him?"

"Even better. I followed Stroud from his hotel to a residential building. It wasn't long before he emerged right out the building's front doors with a woman. I trailed them as they walked to a department store," he recounts as I sit in my derelict cubical and listen. "The woman was in the fitting room when he became distracted with a phone call. As soon as the woman walked out to the shopping racks, I figured her phone would have to do since I didn't see a way to get to Stroud's. It only took thirty seconds to find her cell phone in her purse, pop out the SIM card, and replace it with the tracker SIM."

"Why the fuck do we care about some chick? You were supposed to plant it in Stroud's phone."

"This is when you're going to thank me," he says with a bout of pride. "I pulled the data stored on her phone, and that woman is Archer's daughter."

"He has a daughter?"

"Elizabeth Archer. She is exactly who we need to be following. It has to be her who's looking for Archer. I looked into her, and it seems she went straight into foster care when Archer was arrested."

"Holy shit," I murmur in astonishment.

"I say we keep quiet and allow her to lead us to our point of contact."

"I agree."

"I'm now adjusting my surveillance off Stroud and onto the daughter. I'll call you with any updates."

twelve

HOURS HAVE PASSED since Lachlan delivered the passenger manifest, and I've already completely scoured it. My heart sank a little when I didn't see the name *Steve Archer*. I knew his name wouldn't be on it, but all reasonable thought had vanished in that moment.

Declan immediately pushed Lachlan out when my emotions started getting the best of me. I tried to rein it in as best as I could since Declan is under the impression I'm taking the prescription that's supposed to help these stress-induced meltdowns. But I couldn't deafen myself to the piercing ring in my head. It was painful and sent me into a mild panic.

After I calmed down, Declan suggested I take a break, get a good night's sleep, and revisit the manifest in the morning. But I can't do that. My father is on this sheet of paper, I know it, and I can't sleep until I find which name is his.

Sitting in Declan's office while he's sleeping in the other room, I continue to enter in each name into a people-finder database. I'm not even sure what I'm looking for to guide me in one direction or another, but I jot down any information that pops up for each male passenger. There were one hundred and twenty-two men on that plane. One hundred and twenty-two different paths to follow, but only one will lead me to my dad.

This particular flight was based out of a large hub in Dallas, so the plane is comprised of passengers from all over the States. I star the ones that have a home address in Illinois, but truth is, he's most likely somewhere else if he's hiding out.

My eyes strain against the glow of the laptop in the dark room, but I keep going, entering in the next name: *Dennis Lowery*

"What are you doing?"

Declan's voice startles me, and when he flicks on the lights, I shield my eyes for a moment as they adjust to the brightness.

"I couldn't sleep."

He walks over to me, rounding the desk to see what I'm up to, and when I look up at him, he's annoyed.

"I told you to wait until the morning."

"I know, I—"

"What? Want to give yourself another anxiety attack, because let me tell you something, that episode you experienced earlier . . ." His words falter, and I can tell how much my panic attack affected him. "You can't treat your body like this. You're worn down and sleep deprived."

"Then help me, because I won't be able to sleep knowing that I'm holding his name in my hand. The last time I was this close to him was twenty-three years ago. How am I supposed to sleep? How am I supposed to be patient?"

Raking his hand through his sleep-tousled hair, he releases a heavy breath and succumbs to my eagerness. "Will you start a pot of water for coffee?"

Relieved and grateful for his help, I jump up and let him take a seat, then head to the kitchen to fill the kettle and grind the beans for the French press. I move around the kitchen and gather a few things for the coffee tray. When the kettle whistles, I pour the water into the glass carafe and over the grounds.

I walk back into the office and set the tray down on the desk.

"Come here, darling," Declan says, voice still scratchy with sleep.

He pulls me onto his lap and continues working. I smile down at him, comforted to know his need to be close to me. His fingers type away, entering another name into the search engine, and then he transfers the details into the spreadsheet I've been putting the information in.

"Is there something in particular you've been looking for?" he asks.

"No. I was just getting the addresses and phone numbers and seeing if I recognize any of their listed relatives."

"If he's changed his name and is hiding, I doubt you're going to come across anyone from his past."

"Yeah," I sigh. "You're probably right."

I reach over and pick up a mug from the tray and push the press down to pour his coffee.

"Thanks." He takes a sip and then adds, "There are a few large business-oriented social networking sites for professionals online. We can search all the names through those databases. Most profiles contain pictures."

I grab my phone, anxious to find the man I've been dreaming about my whole life. "Give me the name of one of those sites. I'll search while you're finishing up with the contact information."

Seconds later, I'm on the world's largest business network, punching in the names, starting at the top of the list.

The incessant ticking of the clock greets the sun as it rises behind the cloud-covered sky. I look over from the couch I'm now sitting on to Declan who has just finished the last of his coffee while still at his desk. Sounds of the clock, tapping keys on the laptop, and raindrops plopping against the window are the only noises in the room.

"How are you holding up?"

"There's nothing," I respond in frustration. "Half of these people aren't even on these sites, and the ones that are, half of *those* don't even have a profile picture."

"I'm hitting dead ends myself."

Although I feel defeated, I'm not hopeless, because it's always been my dad who's kept that hope alive when I wanted to give up. Even if it were only a miniscule piece of hope that remained in my heart, I couldn't let it go, and that strength to hang on was always for him.

"I've got to take a break," Declan eventually says, pushing his chair back from his desk. He rubs his eyes, and I can see the reddened fatigue in them. He holds out his hand for me, saying, "Come on. You need a break too."

"I can't."

"Elizabeth, put the phone down. You're going to tire yourself out to the point you'll make yourself sick. If you want to find him, you need to get some rest so your body doesn't give out on you."

"But—"

"It isn't a request, Elizabeth," he states firmly, and it isn't meant to be a test of his authority, but rather a display of concern for me.

It's clear I worry him, so I don't protest again. I take his hand and allow him to lead me back to bed. He curls his body around mine as I lie with my back to his chest, but I never fall asleep. My mind won't quiet down enough for me to relax. Memories flood, playing reels of my past: tea parties, bedtime stories, scratchy beard kisses, and scooter rides around the neighborhood. He's so vivid in my head, his eyes were unnaturally bright, and his smile . . . just the thought pricks my heart in needling pains.

Quiet tears slip out and roll onto the pillow beneath my head, and I wonder if he had been looking for me during the years I wasn't me. Did he just give up when I was living as Nina? Does he know that I devoted so many years of my life to destroying the man who destroyed him? Does he want to find me as much as I want to find him?

"Shh, darling," Declan breathes into my hair, and I'm suddenly aware of my vocal whimpers.

"Do you think we'll find him?" I ask in weak hiccups.

"Yes. It might take time, but I *will* find him for you."

"You know when I was little, after he was taken from me, I spent the first few years being kicked out of every foster home I was placed in," I begin to tell him.

"Why?"

"I would find ways to sneak out in the middle of the night. For the most part, it was me climbing out of my bedroom windows."

"You were only five though. Where did you go?"

"Anywhere. I look back now and feel so bad for the girl I was. A girl so desperate for her dad that she would roam the streets in the middle of the night."

Declan moves to prop up on his side to look down at me and wipes my tears.

"When that foster home realized that I wouldn't stop sneaking out, no matter how much they tried to set up preventions, they'd call my case worker to pick me up and deliver me to the next family who was willing to take me. Eventually, I went through too many homes, and I was sent down to live in Posen, where I wound up staying for good."

"Why didn't you try to leave that house like you did all the others?"

"Because of Pike. Because for the first time since my dad, I had someone who loved me and cared about me," I explain through lamenting pain. "I was more terrified to lose him than being locked away and tortured."

Declan's muscles constrict when he screws his eyes shut. It's an anguished display he can't control, and I suddenly feel guilty for putting that weight upon him.

I reach out to touch his arm and he nearly recoils, causing me to jerk my hand back.

"I'm sorry."

"No," he snaps, blinking his eyes open. "Don't ever be sorry."

"I didn't mean to upset y—"

"I want you to talk to me," he says, cutting me off. "I want you to feel safe enough to unload all your pain, because I want to carry it for you. I want it free from your soul, so I can bury it deep inside mine."

I touch his grief-stricken face and tell him, "I don't want to be your martyrdom. I want to be the thing that makes you happy."

"You do make me happy," he affirms. "You do. I'm happiest when I'm with you—always. Even in our darkness, I'm happier than what I am without you." He drops his head, kissing me, sliding his tongue across my lips. And with my hands tangled in his hair, he looks intently down at me. "You're not my martyrdom. You're my profligacy."

(DECLAN)

I LISTEN TO Elizabeth as she continues to open up to me more. She tells me a story about the time her father let her put makeup on him. She laughs through her tears as I listen, combing her hair with my fingers and licking away the salts that crystallize her heartache. Each granulated fragment, I take for myself, freeing her a tiny piece at a time.

After a while, her guard is down enough that when I suggest a sleeping aid, she takes it without a fight. I lie with her, watching her lull into a peaceful sleep before going to shower and dress. She still remains in bed, in my sheets. Her red hair splayed over the pillow, her milky skin with faint reminders of her kidnapping, her petite body curled into a ball. One could look at her and never believe the titanic life she's endured.

She poises herself as strong, but it's her cracks that cause me to stumble and fall, making me love her even more. I'm a greedy man, and to know that her weaknesses make her more dependent on me feeds my avarice. But at the same time, I get off on her strong-willed feistiness. She's a mélange that appeals to all my facets and allows me to freely indulge in my nefarious needs that other women would take high offense to. But Elizabeth has this unique way of submitting to me without being submissive in nature.

She's enigmatic.

My phone goes off, pulling me away from the room where my love sleeps. When I answer, it's security needing permission to let Lachlan up. I called him as soon as Elizabeth fell asleep because I need to talk to him about why he's been communicating clandestinely with Camilla.

"'Morning," he greets when I open the door.

"We need to talk," I say and then turn to lead him into the office.

I sit at the desk and he takes one of the seats opposite.

"You look like shit, McKinnon."

"Long night, as you can imagine," I respond.

"How's Elizabeth?"

"Anxious. Stressed. Confused," I tell him. "She's sleeping now, which is why I called you over to talk."

"Let's talk."

"Camilla," I state, and when I do, I note a hint of nerves in Lachlan—restless hands.

"Go on."

"Last week, when I answered your phone, she thought I was you. She called you *baby*. When I confronted her about how she knew you, she told me I should ask *you*. So, as a man I hired because of the implicit trust I have in you, tell me why that trust shouldn't be obstructed by this."

"Like I told you before, Camilla and I go way back." He stops his nervous hands and folds them in his lap. "She's actually the reason I stopped working for your father. We had a long relationship and were engaged when I found out she was sleeping with Cal. She didn't have the nerve to tell me, but the close proximity in which I worked with your father, it was bound to surface."

"Jesus," I mumble under my breath, uncomfortable that I'm having him divulge this embarrassment. But if I'm not only going to put my life and trust into his hands but also Elizabeth's, I need to know everything to make sure there are no hidden agendas.

"Without question, I kicked her out of my home, and it came as no surprise that she went from my house to Cal's," he continues. "That was the last day I worked for him. That is, until a lifetime after all that happened, my phone rang. To my surprise, she was still with the bastard, and an even bigger surprise, I find out he never married her."

"Why did she call you?"

"For help. Your dad had just been arrested."

"Wait," I say, stopping him. "You mean recently?"

"A little over a month ago."

Agitation gets me and I lash out at him. "You knew he was in jail this whole time and never told me? What the fuck, Lachlan?"

"He didn't want you to know. Said you two had some pretty harsh words before you moved back to Scotland from Chicago."

"So explain how it goes from a dissolved friendship to him confiding in you from jail?"

"He needed my help. I gave him over a decade of my loyalty. Bad blood or not, he felt I was his last resort for confidentiality."

"And you just gave it to him? That doesn't add up, Lachlan."

"Perhaps it was curiosity," he defends. "I fucking despised your father and Camilla for what they had done right under my nose. So, imagine my shock when I find out he's in jail and she's left high and dry. Karma had done her job, but I wanted to bask in the wake of her achievement. I humored him and lent him the false comfort of an old friendship."

"Baneful."

"Which is why I didn't tell you."

"Because he's my father?" He nods, and I lean back in my chair, clasping my hands in front of me. "He's a piece of shit," I lash out in hate. "He's spent his whole life virulently criticizing my every move in this world."

"He's a narcissistic bastard, but I had been unaware of any discord between the two of you until he told me about the confrontation the two of you had after you'd been shot."

"Our issues go way back," I say. "That doesn't explain why Camilla is calling you."

"She thinks she can run back to me. She calls, sobs her pathetic story, and thinks I'll take grace on her. She's delusional."

"And your loyalty?"

He leans forward with a leaden stare, stating adamantly, "My loyalty is with you and that girl in the next room."

I then lean forward too, resting my forearms on the desk and brutally threaten, "It better be because if I find out otherwise, I promise you, your head will be the next one I put a bullet in."

My words cause him no hesitation, not even a blink—a steady sign of his integrity. This man knows what I'm capable of—he's seen it with his own eyes—so he's fully aware of the repercussions if I find out there's fault in his word.

thirteen

(ELIZABETH)

THE SMELL OF the black pepper tenderloin Declan's preparing fills the apartment, causing my belly to growl. The past few days I've struggled to eat and even sleep. I keep going over that manifest incessantly. Sometimes I think I'm going crazy, but I can't stop myself. Declan practically had to force-feed me a sleeping pill last night just so I could get some rest. I was pissed and lashing out at him.

"Why aren't you trying harder to find him?" I screamed as he fought to hold me down.

"I'm doing everything I can, but I don't know what he's hiding from or the threat we face when we do find him."

He then pinned me to the couch and shoved the sleeping pill down my throat. In the process of gagging on it, I accidentally swallowed it. When he released my arms, I began swinging at him, irate that he would rob me of the time I could've used to get closer to finding my dad.

I woke this morning after allowing sleep to fuel my body with restored energy and a clear head and apologized to Declan. But the moment he left to go attend a meeting with the architecture firm, I was back at it, dissecting the manifest. It's been five days since I received this list of passengers, and I'm no closer to finding a lead. What's even more discouraging is the fact that both Lachlan and Declan are starting to feel like they've exhausted all avenues aside from traveling all over the States to knock on all one hundred and twenty-two doors. And as much as Declan affirms that he will find him, I don't doubt that he would actually go to those lengths to do so.

While Declan is in the other room cooking, I take my time getting ready. As I'm applying a little gloss to my lips, I hear the buzzing of my cell phone. It catches me off guard since no one aside from Declan and Lachlan has the number. When I walk into the bedroom, I spot the phone on top of the dresser and pick it up.

UNKNOWN, reads across the screen.

"Hello?" I question curiously when I answer the call.

"Hey, kitty."

His voice stuns me for a split second.

"Matt?"

"You miss me?"

God, he's so skeevy.

"How did you get this number?" I bite on a quiet voice as I walk into the bathroom and close the door so Declan can't hear.

"Everyone is traceable. Even you, my dear."

"What do you want?" I snap irritably.

"That's no way to greet an old friend."

"Cut the shit, Matt."

"Fine. I need your help."

"Forget it."

"Do I need to remind you of your place in this equation? You owe me."

He's right. I very well could be sitting in prison if he hadn't covered up Pike's murder for me, so I swallow back my hatred for his slimy ways. "What do you need?"

"Well, it seems I'm in a bit of a bad situation with a loan shark."

"What the hell are you doing business with a loan shark for?"

"Pike's murder being the face of my business wasn't a good look, kitty. No one wanted to be associated with me with the threat of cops watching. I needed money."

"What happened to it?"

"It's gone. I gambled it away in hopes of increasing my profits."

"You're an idiot, you know that?"

"The idiot who saved you from a life behind bars," he reminds with growing pique, and then drops the bomb. "They're gonna kill me." He pauses. "I can't buy any more time from them."

I brace my hand on the edge of the sink and drop my head. I could bail him out, sure, but he'll never leave me alone. The threat of this guy will continue to hang over my head, and how do I have a shot in hell of moving forward in this life if my past is forever following me? Matt is nothing but corrosive—he always has been. Unwilling to allow him the opportunity to one day pull me down with him or to risk him turning me in to the cops for all the crimes I've hidden under my belt, I take back the control.

"You want me to bankroll you?"

"I need you to wire the money. My time is up." Panic seeps through his words the more he speaks. "Pretty soon, there's gonna be a bounty on my head."

"If I do this, will you leave me alone?"

"Yes."

I take a moment to let him sweat a little, enjoying the upper hand and listening to him squirm for my help.

"I don't believe you."

"Elizabeth, what the fuck? Come on!"

"Don't call me again."

"You fucking cunt!"

"Let me tell you who the cunt is," I seethe through my teeth, injecting each word with the poison of my rusted heart. "You don't get to fuck with me anymore. I'm not a toy you get to play with. So this cunt is done with you, you little shit. Let them kill you; it'll do me the favor of dispelling you from my life."

Before I give him an opportunity to respond, I disconnect the call and shut my phone off. With both of my hands clutching the countertop, I look at myself in the mirror and greet the monster that stares back at me, but no sooner say goodbye. I take in a few deep breaths and rein in the beast I've been trying to tame—for Declan—for us.

Minutes pass, and my heart settles into a healthy rhythm. I apply a little more gloss before taking the phone and shoving it down in my purse that's in the closet. I turn to the mirror and give myself a lookover, paranoid that Declan will see right through me.

Walking out of the bedroom, I watch Declan for a few seconds. He's barking at someone on his phone while pots are steaming and boiling. He surprised me with the announcement earlier today that Davina, his childhood friend, is joining us for dinner. I'm not exactly happy about it but refuse to let Declan notice my displeasure. He says that he wants me to give her a chance, that it's time I stop secluding myself from people and put myself out there to make friends. The thought doesn't sit well with me though. I've never had friends. The women I socialized with back in Chicago were merely a charade I put on to appease Bennett and play my part in the whole con. Those women weren't my friends though.

The only two people I've ever truly welcomed into my life are Pike and Declan. I never saw the point in having friends; I still don't. But Davina is part of Declan's life and it's important to him that I get to know her. So with my fake smile, I'll do my best to stifle any jealousy that might arise to placate him.

"Is someone in trouble?" I ask when I walk into the room after Declan ends his call, shaking off the residue of Matt's phone call.

"I think I'm going to have to make a trip back to Chicago to deal with some business concerning Lotus."

"Is everything okay?"

"Yes, everything is fine. *Forbes* is going to be doing a feature on me for an upcoming issue and they want to get photos of me at the Lotus property."

"You're kidding. Declan, that's amazing!" I exclaim. "Congratulations!"

He laughs at my reaction, but I can't help myself. Declan's spent his life trying to measure up to his father's success, so to have a feature in *Forbes* is incredible validation.

I take his face in my hands and look up at him with a huge smile. "I am so proud of you."

"You are?" he flirts, hoisting me onto the counter.

"Yes. And you should be more excited."

"I am excited." His voice is low and even, teasing me.

"I'm serious. This is amazing."

"You're amazing."

He takes my hands from his face, pins them down on the countertop beneath his, and moves in to kiss my neck. The whiskers of his freshly trimmed stubble tickle me, and I tilt my head to close my neck off to him. Declan disapproves with a groan and forces my neck open with his head. He continues to kiss and nip, and every now and then sinks his teeth into the sensitive skin. I drop my head back with a pleasurable moan and widen my legs to invite him in closer, but before he presses against me, his phone rings.

"Ignore it," I pant, needing more of him.

"I can't, Davina is here."

He steps away from me and takes the call. Sliding off the counter, I clench my thighs together to help relieve the pulsing ache of arousal that's built up inside of me thanks to Declan.

"You're a tease," I say with a nudge to his ribs when I walk past him. "I'm going to get you back for that."

"Is that a threat?"

"No. It's a guarantee."

Soon there's a knock on the door, and when Declan opens it to let her in, the raven-haired "friend" greets him with a much too affectionate hug. They exchange pleasantries before Declan holds his hand out to me, saying to Davina, "You remember Elizabeth?"

"It's so good to see you again." Her smile is too wide as she hands me a bottle of wine. "I figured you could use this since you're living with the most uptight man I know."

"That's nice," Declan says in mock umbrage as he heads back into the kitchen, leaving me alone with her in the living room.

"Thank you," I tell her, shoving my insecurities away for fictitious assurance. "It's extremely thoughtful."

I used to wine and dine the upper crust of Chicago for the satisfaction of Bennett, so Davina should be as easy as selling age-defying pigeon shit facials to haut monde housewives.

"Please, have a seat. Should I pour you a glass?" I ask, holding up the bottle.

"I never turn down wine."

She's much too perky and much too happy, or maybe it's just me being much too judgy. Either way, I grit my teeth as I walk to the kitchen and open the bottle of Sangiovese.

"Declan," she says as she walks over and takes a seat at the island bar. "How long do we have to wait for your new property?"

"Years. We're building from the ground up," he tells her. "I was in meetings all day today going over budgets and schedules. We haven't even started on the design yet."

"How long do you plan on staying in London?"

"Until completion. Same as the Chicago property. So, three, maybe four years."

I hand her the glass of wine and she holds it up. "Well, cheers to new neighbors," and then she takes a sip. "So, Elizabeth, I know you can't be from around here with that accent of yours."

"No, I'm from the States. Illinois," I tell her.

"Where Declan was? Chicago?"

"Yes."

"So indulge me. Tell me how you two met."

As soon as the question is out of her mouth, I feel the tingling in my palms, but I don't stress for more than a second when Declan begins to answer.

"She was at the grand opening of Lotus," he says, plating the food. "I spotted her immediately in this long navy dress. It didn't take me long to introduce myself, and lucky for me, she needed a place to throw an event, and I offered her the space at the hotel." He picks up two of the plates, adding, "The rest is history."

I pick up the third plate and follow him into the dining room. We all sit to eat, and I listen while the two of them share a few funny stories from their childhood with me. I smile and laugh at all the right places in conversation as I tame the covetousness I feel that she's had more time and shares more memories with Declan than I do. She has a deep-rooted past with him, knows his annoying habits I haven't caught on to yet, and can practically finish his sentences for him.

"Elizabeth," she addresses, exchanging her attention from Declan to me. "What is it that you do?"

I swallow the sip of wine I just took, then clarify, "That I do?"

"Do you work?"

"Oh, um, no. Not at the moment." Not ever, unless helping my brother weigh out and bag the drugs he and Matt used to sell on the streets counts as a job. I feel like such a fraud sitting here with her. As if this is my standard of living.

"That's always nice. Have you been to London before?"

"No. This is the first time I've been out of the States, believe it or not."

"I have a lot to show you then," she says excitedly. "Have you done any exploring yet?"

"Not if you consider walking across the street to Harrods," I joke.

"Declan," she scolds. "Why are you keeping this woman locked up? Take her out!"

"Damn! Why are you jumping my case?" he says, charading indignation the way Pike and I often would with each other—the way most brothers and sisters probably do. "We've been busy trying to settle in."

Turning back to me she continues, "Well, you must let me show you around one day next week. I have a few client meetings, but other than that, I'm free."

"Client meetings?"

"Oh, excuse my bad manners. I'm an interior decorator. I'm working on three homes at the moment. Two I'm finishing so my workload will be lightening up soon."

"That sounds like a fun job."

"Anything that involves shopping on another person's dime is fun," she laughs.

When we finish dinner, I stand and collect the plates, taking them to the kitchen so she and Declan can continue to talk. When I put the kettle on the stove to boil water for tea and coffee, I see Davina's phone on the bar where she was sitting earlier light up and vibrate with an incoming call.

While I wait for the water to heat, I pick up her phone and take it over to her.

"I think someone just tried calling you," I say when I hand it to her.

"Oh, thank you." She takes the phone and looks to see who called, mumbling, "Bawbags."

"What's wrong?" Declan asks as I sit back down.

"It's William."

"I didn't think you two spoke anymore."

"We don't, but apparently I have a piece of jewelry that belonged to his mother that he's demanding. I've told him there's none in the house that belongs to him and to check his safe deposit box, but he claims it isn't in there. He's keeps hounding me about it."

"Tell him to let the attorneys handle it."

"I did, but the cheap bastard refuses," she tells Declan before turning to me to clarify, "Ex-husband."

"Oh."

"We divorced for religious reasons. He thought he was God, and I didn't."

Out of all her jokes she's made, this is the first where I can't help my laughter.

"Have you been married before?" she asks, and my laughter wanes.

I bite my lip and turn to Declan when I nearly blurt out *yes* without thinking. She's caught me off guard, and when Declan sees, he speaks for me.

"No. She's never been married."

Davina looks between Declan and me with a curious expression upon her face, most likely wondering why her question choked me up and why Declan would butt in to answer for me. She knows something is off, and I thank God for the kettle on the stove as it begins to whistle loudly.

"Excuse me," I say, getting up and rushing off to the kitchen.

I take in a deep breath, sick and tired of all the questions. I've lived so many years pretending to be Nina that she feels like a part of me, and when asked questions, I forget that I'm just Elizabeth and I can't be crossing the two lives.

"Are you okay?" Declan asks in a quiet voice when he joins me in the kitchen.

"She knows we're lying. Did you see the look on her face?"

"She doesn't. It's fine," he says. "Stop worrying."

"Here." I hand him the French press. "Take this to the table please."

He does, and I follow with my tea. The evening winds down as we finish our drinks, and when Davina announces she must be going, I pacify her with a few empty pleasantries before thanking her for coming over, and she reminds me to give her a call.

"We'll go shopping or meet up for a nice lunch," she says, and I respond by lying, "That sounds really nice."

"You can get my number from Declan."

We say our goodbyes, and when she's out the door, Declan says, "That wasn't so bad, was it?"

"No," I fib. "She's very lovely."

He eyes me suspiciously.

"What?" I question.

"You're not still jealous, are you?"

"No, I'm not still jealous," I fib again. "You're awfully full of yourself."

"I like it when you're jealous." He reaches for me, but I dodge his touch. "Get your ass back here."

"You wish, McKinnon. You want to touch me?"

"Always."

"Payback's a bitch," I taunt. "You shouldn't have teased me so much earlier."

"You're sadly mistaken if you think you call the shots around here."

He moves towards me again, but with each step forward, I take one step back, keeping the distance between us. He wears a smile almost as big as mine as I try to contain my laughter. I love this side of us together, a side we've yet to explore with one another. It's young and free-spirited and a rare look inside Declan's boyish charm. There's a joyful glint in his eyes that makes me want to run to him.

But where's the fun in that?

Let him catch me!

fourteen

"I HAVE THE plane scheduled to leave tomorrow afternoon," Declan tells me when he walks into the living room. "What are you doing?"

I lift my pencil from the paper and look at the jumbled letters, realizing how crazy it must look to him. "I have to keep trying."

"I'm not accusing, darling. I'm just curious what all those letters mean."

"I don't know," I admit with a shrug of my shoulders. "I guess I wanted to see if there was something to the names. That maybe if I took the letters and rearranged them I would be . . ." I let my words fade when I'm aware of how nutty I sound. "I just . . . I can't give up."

"I would never ask you to give up, but—"

"Let me exhaust this avenue before you tell me I'm wasting my time."

"Okay." Stepping back from the topic he continues, "So tomorrow afternoon . . ."

"I'll be ready. I don't have much to pack, so it shouldn't take me long."

"I was thinking maybe you could get out of here for a while. Go shopping. You have hardly any clothes."

"You mean spend your money?"

"*Our* money," he disputes. "But if you feel awkward spending it, let Davina spend it. It wouldn't be the first time."

"What does that mean?"

"She once stole my piggy bank to buy herself a rickety pair of roller skates."

I laugh at his farcical outrage. "So, she robbed you?"

"Pretty much, that unforgiveable twit. I'd been saving that money for a long time."

My smile dissolves as envy creeps in.

"What's wrong?"

I take a moment, not sure of what to say when I finally speak. "You really had a happy childhood, didn't you?"

His face levels out in emotion when he sees the harbored sadness in my eyes. He doesn't answer me right away until I push him to.

"Yes. I was a happy kid."

There's resentment that festers within me, but not for Declan. It's for all the people who betrayed me and my dad and Pike. I don't hate Declan because he had a good life, but I'd be lying if I said I wasn't jealous, because I am—because it isn't fair.

"You have all these wonderful stories to share with me, and I have none to share with you."

"Come on, you must have some good memories with your brother."

"Honestly," I start and then pause to grip tightly to the sting of tears that threaten, "it hurts too much to think about."

"It's only been a few months since you lost him. Give it time."

I think of the words he chose: *lost him.* As if Pike were a set of keys I misplaced. My gut sinks when I think of the ugly reality.

I didn't lose him.

I killed him.

I doubt that any amount of time will fade away the agony that torments me because of what I did.

"Hey," he says quietly. "This is why you should get out of the house. You need a break from everything. Fresh air and a little distraction will do you well."

"Are you going to let me go by myself?"

"No."

"I didn't think so." I let out a faint laugh. "I'll call Lachlan."

"Why don't you call Davina?"

I set my pencil and notepad down on the coffee table and exhale heavily. "Can I just call Lachlan?"

"Why are you so afraid to make friends?"

"First off, I'm not afraid. And second, why do I need friends when I have you? I'm not one of those girls who has this incessant need to gossip and chit chat about things I find no importance in," I explain with a shard of annoyance. "Women are vicious and catty, everyone knows that."

"If that were true, what does that say about you?"

I squint my eyes at him, but he just smirks.

"I'm vicious, but I'm not catty."

He shakes his head at me. "Do me a favor. Humor me."

"Why should I?"

"Because she's practically the only family I have," he tells me. "She's a good person. A tad on the bubbly side, but she means well and is trustworthy. I also think it would be good for you to start venturing out—make a friend."

"I've never had friends."

"What about when you were a child and in school?"

"All the girls were too busy making fun of me. I was teased every day." I shrug my shoulders as I remember the shame and embarrassment. "I wouldn't even know how to be a friend to someone."

He takes my hands in his, saying, "Just be yourself."

"Well, there's an idea." My voice edges on soreness. "Too bad I don't have a clue who I am."

"You may not see it, but I can. I see parts of you that are brand new and nothing like the girl I met in Chicago. Your laughter, the youthful playfulness that comes out every once in a while, those belong to *you—Elizabeth.*" He's sure of his words. "Nina would have never run around this apartment, laughing and making me chase her the way you did the other night. As more time passes, more of who you are will unfold. But if you need to know who you are because you can't find it within you, then come to me and I'll tell you."

I nod, unable to speak around thick emotion. Staring into his eyes, I'm bewildered by the love he has for me. His patience and reassurance have started to form a solid ground for me. I trust him, but I still suppress so many insecurities, some of which I've yet to share with him. His intentions are good though; he only wants me to thrive and be happy. He'd never intentionally put me in a harmful or unsafe situation.

"So will you give her a call?"

For him, I'll try it his way.

He gives me her number, and when I call, she's thrilled at the mention of shopping and agrees to swing by to pick me up.

After I hang up with Davina, I walk into the office where Declan is. "I wanted to talk to you about something."

"Did you get ahold of her?"

"Yes. She's on her way to pick me up."

"What do you want to talk about?" he asks as he gets up from his desk and motions me over to join him on the leather couch that sits in the corner of the room next to the large windows.

"The penthouse in Chicago. I want to sell it," I tell him. "I'll never live there again. I wish I could erase all of its memories, but I can't, so let's just get rid of it."

"I'll take care it. All of it," he assures without any question.

"I need to go back though. There are a few things I need that were gifts from Pike."

"Okay. I'll put a call into Sotheby's to see what needs to be done to get it on the market," he says, taking all the pressure of having to deal with this off my back. "We can go straight there when we land to get it over with so it won't be weighing on you."

"Are you sure? I mean, you don't have to come with me."

"That place is filled with awful memories for me as well. Memories I too wish I could erase, but I'm not having you go there alone to face it all by yourself."

I sling my arms around him, so thankful because he's right—I know how painful it's going to be to walk through those doors again. It's the tainted sanctuary of ghosts from the past few years. It's Bennett, it's purple roses, it's all the disgusting moments I gave that piece of shit my body, it's where I saw the monster in my brother's eyes for the first time, it's where my baby died, and it's where Declan's spirit forever changed when he murdered Bennett in cold-blooded rage. It's the coffin that holds so many skeletons. I'd burn it to ashes if I could.

"It's one chapter of our past we can close. Just look at it that way." Once again, he is doing what he can to eliminate the pain we both feel about that place, the place he dreaded to send me back to after our time together, thinking Bennett was violently beating me.

So many lies.

So much bloodshed.

But without it, I never would have found Declan. So I'll bear its torture that singes my heart.

THE DAY IS just warm enough to go without a coat. I tilt my head back, looking up to the brilliant blue sky. The sun's rays heat my face while I breathe the crisp air deep into my lungs, and I swear I feel its particles cleansing me.

"Beautiful day, isn't it?" Davina asks as we stand in the middle of Piccadilly Circus.

Declan was right, I needed out of the confines of One Hyde Place. I needed sunshine and fresh air. I needed to feel this breeze whipping through my hair, to see that even though life seems to pause, it doesn't ever truly stop.

The streets are a cascade of people walking in every direction. Davina takes a phone call and I walk up the steps of the Shaftesbury fountain. A swell of freedom erupts when I reach the top step. I've seen grand landmarks in the States, but only with Bennett or because of him. Although he gave me all the freedom I wanted, I wasn't truly free. I was living in *his* life as *his* wife.

But here I stand.

No longer having to pretend.

No longer a prisoner to my own game.

And even though Declan keeps me safely under his thumb, I've never felt more boundless. So much so that if I lifted my arms right now, I bet I could fly.

"It'll only get better from this point."

I scan the throngs of people, searching, and then I spot him.

I gasp.

He isn't thirty-two years old. He's the twelve-year-old boy from our childhood. He stands beneath the colorful lights of the billboards, staring at me. Acutely aware of Davina's presence at the bottom of the fountain, I slip on my sunglasses to shield my heart's ache that puddles in my eyes. Davina's buried in her phone at the moment. I want to run to him, but everyone would think I was crazy.

My heart jumps to life. I'm giving him this, something we were both deprived of as kids, and because I've kept him alive, I can now give him all the joys that come my way. We can share them together.

He looks up at the bright lights, his boyish eyes filled with wonderment, and I smile. Turning to look at me, elation plastered on his face, he waves to me from a distance. In return I give the little boy who did everything he could to save me from the devil in the basement a subtle wave back.

"Sorry about that," Davina says, drawing my attention away from my brother as she shoves her phone down into her purse.

I smile, hiding my grief behind the dark lenses.

"You ready?"

"Yes," I respond, walking down the steps and taking one last look over to Pike, but he's gone. I tell myself he'll come back, because he always does.

Davina and I walk together to Bond Street where she assures me there is amazing shopping, and she's spot on. It's all the designers that still hang in my closet back at The Legacy. Familiar friends greet me as I pass them: Chanel, Jimmy Choo, Hermés. They're all here, reminding me of how I used them to deceive others.

"Here we are," she says, opening the door to Fenwick.

I walk inside the high-end luxury department store that Davina insists has a nice selection of less expensive designers as well. I told her I didn't need anything fancy, just your typical, everyday wear.

I remove my sunglasses and begin to scan the racks and pull items I'm in need of. Davina wanders off to shop a few racks over. I fill my arms with jeans, slacks, casual tops, and soft cashmere sweaters before a sales associate takes them to start a fitting room for me.

We keep the chatter among us light as we try on clothes. She talks to me about one client of hers that's a widow of an aristocrat who she swears is draining the family inheritance on a remodel.

"Her children are going to be bloody mad when they find out she's pissed all the money away," she says.

"How much money do you suspect?" I ask, tossing another top onto the yes pile.

"Around two hundred and fifty thousand pounds!" she exclaims. "The old woman has lost her mind."

Once we're dressed, we make our purchases and head to the second floor where Davina was able to get reservations on short notice at Bond & Brook. The restaurant is glamorous, gleaming in stark whites and silvers. We're seated at a table next to the windows that look down on the street filled with people who are anxious to spend money.

"I could only get us in for the afternoon tea seating, I hope that's okay with you."

"Of course."

Our waiter promptly sets our table with hot tea and Pommery Rosé champagne along with small bites, consisting of crab tartlets, butter pear beignets, and celery-cucumber sorbet.

"This looks amazing," I say. "Thank you for doing this."

"Of course. I'm just happy to see Declan sharing his life with someone. I was starting to worry he'd forever be alone." She gives a whisper of a laugh, but I know she means the words she speaks. "It must have been love at first sight then?"

"Why do you say that?"

"He said the two of you met at the opening of Lotus. That was the beginning of December, wasn't it?"

"Yes," I answer and then take a sip of tea.

"It's April, and he's already moved you in."

"I guess you're right." I'm a bit surprised, but hide it. It feels like so much more time has passed since the night I met him. "I can't believe it's only been four months."

"And I can't believe he's kept you a secret from me," she quips with a smile before biting into one of the tartlets. "Well, I know you're not working here in London, but what was it that you did when you lived abroad?"

"Um . . ." Declan told me to just answer the questions as Elizabeth, but I can't do that. I dab my mouth with my napkin, stalling time, but it moves forward regardless. "I did a little bit of . . ." I think back to how I met Bennett and continue, "I worked in catering for a short period."

I'm not sure if she picks up on my hesitation, but she goes on, saying, "That's so funny. I worked in that realm after university. I was a bartender for a catering company in Edinburgh."

"Really?"

"My parents aren't like most. They paid my way through my studies, but once I graduated, they cut the credit cards, and I was on my own. It took me a while to find work, so in the mean time, I bartended," she explains.

"Did you go to school with Declan?"

"No. Declan was an impeccable student. Me, not so much. I attended the University of Dundee."

"Where's that?"

"Just north of Saint Andrews where Declan went to school. Less than an hour's drive, actually," she tells me. "And what about you? Where did you go to University?"

"Where did I go?" I can't possibly tell her the truth, so I cover my ass and lie. "Kansas State." It's the university I told Declan Nina attended, but I immediately kick myself for lying when Declan made it clear not to, and when I continue, I stumble over my words, knowing I need to right the lie. "Well, I mean . . ." *Fuck!*

"Is everything okay?"

She sees right through me. When she stands, I wonder if somehow she knows I'm a fake. She comes to sit right next to me.

"Let me apologize," she starts, and I don't respond. I just let her continue. "I don't mean to pry. I can see I've made you uncomfortable."

"No," I say, attempting to cover myself. "I'm just a little on the private side."

"I can understand that. It's just, well, after Lillian's death, Declan changed a lot. He isolated himself from nearly all the family. The two of us managed to keep close though, and we've remained that way," she reveals. "I love him dearly, and when I spoke to him after our dinner the other night, he told me that you were an extension of him. So, I can't help but love you as well because of that."

Her words are heartfelt and take me aback. I can see no other motivations on her part aside from genuinely wanting to get to know me. Declan was right when he told me she was a good person, because that's the very impression she's giving me right now.

"I never went to college," I admit to her, needing to erase the lie. "I'm sorry I lied. I guess I was just embarrassed." Airing my truths is not what I'm used to. I'm a liar, a manipulator, an imposter. Or I *was*. But I've always been running from something, a runaway at the age of fourteen. Always dodging the law in one way or another. But today, right now, I'm going to choose to take a step forward as Elizabeth. If Davina believes as Declan does, that I'm an extension of him, she won't judge. "I was a foster kid. I didn't come from money, so college was never an option for me."

She smiles and places her hand on top of mine in a gesture that is both comforting and foreign. "Thank you for trusting me with that."

I nod, and after she gives my hand a light squeeze, she moves back to her seat across from me. She takes a sip of her champagne, smiles, and then adds in jest, "We should order more champagne . . . Declan's treat." She winks and pulls out one of his credit cards and laughs. "He slipped it to me when I picked you up in case you refused to use the other card he gave you."

I shake my head. "That wretch!"

"Well, that wretch is going to pick up our tab."

Conversation is less stressful now that the brick of worry and secrecy has been lifted off my shoulders. She asks about our trip back to the States, and I tell her all about Chicago. I'm not about to tell her my whole life story by any means, but for now, I'm enjoying the light conversation with someone other than Declan or Lachlan. Those two know so much of my darkness, but with Davina, I feel a little . . . de novo—and even a little normal.

fifteen

I STUFF THE manifest along with my notepad and contact list into a manila envelope and zip it up in my suitcase. Last night was another long night of letter scrambling. I know Declan thinks it's nonsense, and maybe it is, but I refuse to sit idle and wait. I'll always find a way to keep moving, because I have to, because I need to find him.

"Do you know where your duffle bag is? I need it for my workout clothes and trainers," Declan asks.

"It's on the top shelf on my side of the closet."

I sit on the bed and wait for him to finish packing. He walks out of the closet with the bag, and I admire him in his fitted button-down that's tucked nicely into his charcoal slacks. Always so polished and refined, even when he's dressed down in jeans and a cotton shirt.

"You want to wipe the drool off your chin and help me?" he heckles when he peers up at me and catches me gawking.

"You're so full of yourself," I shoot back when I hop off the bed to go grab his shoes.

When I return and set the shoes on the bed beside the bag, I watch him pull out a picture frame. He holds it with both of his hands, and I remember it being the picture I found of him in Isla's bedroom at The Water Lily.

"I forgot this was in here," he says.

"You've seen it before?"

"When you were missing, I went through all your belongings, and I came across this," he tells me. His eyes remain on the photo of himself as a little boy, and then he looks to me, asking, "Where did you get this?"

"At the bed and breakfast where I was staying. I found it in the owner's bedroom." I pause for a moment, and when he doesn't speak, I ask, "It's you, isn't it? I mean, your name's written on the back."

"Yes. It's me."

I look at him in confusion and he reflects it back to me.

"Do you know her? Isla?"

"No. Did you ask her about this when you found it?"

"She wasn't there. I found it when you were in London, and I had gone back to pack up the rest of my things. It was the day Richard kidnapped me."

"This photo was taken at my parents' home. This was the pond that was on the property. It would fill with lotus blooms, and my mum would spend hours out there."

"Maybe she was friends with your mother," I suggest.

"She never said anything. I saw her each time I went over there to visit you. If she knew me, why wouldn't she say something?"

"Do you want to call her?"

He hands the picture over to me, saying, "We don't have time. We need to get to the plane. I'll deal with it when we get back."

"Are you sure? You seemed bothered by this."

"I'm not bothered," he states and then throws his clothes and shoes into the bag before zipping it up. "You're probably right. She must've been friends with my mum."

He picks up the bag along with mine, and without another word, he walks out of the room, leaving me alone. Finding that photo has stirred up something inside him. His eyes exposed too much to me, more than he intended. Perhaps it was just the sheer memory of his mom, so I'll respect his request to avoid it until after our trip.

We secure the apartment before leaving to drive to Biggin Hill Airport, where the pilot is already waiting for us. Aside from him, we are the only others on the plane.

"How long have you had this thing?" I ask as I settle into my seat that's next to the window.

"This is more than just a *thing*. It's a G450 Gulfstream jet," he boasts, and I chuckle at him with a shake of my head.

"I see I've offended your toy," I go on to pester.

He takes the seat right next to me instead of across from me.

"Buckle up, because this *toy* is about to takeoff," he says with a sexy smirk and then reaches over to fasten my seatbelt for me, yanking on the strap to tighten it.

The plane is extravagant with its white leather seats and espresso wood finishes that add a masculine contrast. Double seats on the left and single seats on the right with a beverage station in the back next to a decent sized lavatory. There's a flat screen television above the small eating table towards the front of the aircraft next to the cockpit.

"Well, for what it's worth," I say as he fastens his seatbelt, "I like your toy."

"As long as my baby's happy."

The pilot looks over his shoulder from his seat in the cockpit, saying, "We've been cleared for takeoff, sir. Are you ready?"

"We're ready, William."

"Would you like privacy for the flight?"

"Yes."

I look to him, perplexed with a grin, and question, "You didn't want privacy last time?"

"That's because Lachlan was with us."

His flirtations spark the tinder inside me, but he simply winks and takes my hand in his, threading his fingers with mine as the aircraft begins to move.

"Prepare for takeoff," the pilot's voice announces over the speaker.

I grip Declan's hand tighter when the plane speeds up.

"You nervous?"

I look out the window as we lift off and ascend into the sky.

"Elizabeth?"

I roll my head over to him and nod, my fingers fixed around his. He tucks a lock of hair behind my ear, and I close my eyes as I lean into his touch.

"Talk to me."

I blink my eyes open. "It feels weird going back. Everyone there knows me as Nina. I can't be anything but *her* in that city."

"I know," he says, voice drowning in compassion.

"Does that bother you? Because it bothers me."

"It's part of who we are."

"But does it bother you?" I ask again.

Shrugging his shoulders, he admits, "Somewhat. But we're in this together. I'll do what I can to make this trip short and uneventful."

My stomach is in knots, wishing one of my many endless wishes to extinguish memories that are unvanquishable. I want to break out of the cobwebs I've spun that now cling to me like sand to a pearl. I'm no pearl though, more like the goop that embodies the pearl within the oyster. And I have to wonder, if beneath my protective shell, if you dug deep enough through the slime, would there be a morsel of purity?

I remember one of my conversations with Isla—she told me we're all threaded with holy fibers.

Perhaps.

"Come here," Declan says after a span of time.

He raises the armrest between us as I unfasten my seatbelt and then pulls me onto his lap. With my arms around his neck and his around my waist, I rest my head against his.

"We're going to be fine," he whispers deeply.

I nod. His hand slips under my top and trails up my spine, sending a rush of tingles across my skin. With eyes open, we watch each other intently. My hands find their way into his hair, and I grip fistfuls of it as his hand moves to trail across my stomach.

"Tell me what you want," he speaks in a husky breath.

He runs a hand over my breast and pulls the lace of my bra down underneath my top.

"You. Raw and base. Touch me as if I'm unbreakable."

He pinches my nipple hard between his fingers.

I yelp, and my body flinches at the sudden pain that shoots through the nerve endings that maze beneath my skin. "Yes," I breathe.

Black swallows green as lasciviousness fills the air around us, and he clamps down on my nipple again, twisting so hard I have to hold my breath as my fingers claw his shoulders.

"Like that?" he asks, releasing me from his fingers.

"Mmm hmm," I respond behind closed lips as my breast throbs to ebb the pain he's inflicted.

He smiles, but it's filled with imperious satisfaction.

"Good girl."

He slides me off his lap, stands me up, and then joins me. Slowly, he takes the hem of my top and pulls it over my head before removing my bra, my nipples hard from his assault. He removes the rest of my clothes until I'm standing there completely naked and exposed while he remains clothed in his slacks and button-down.

"Turn around, spread your legs, and bend over," he instructs, and I obey his word.

I turn, part my feet wide, and bend over, gripping my hands on to the armrests to steady myself. He then takes one end of the seatbelt and knots it around my left wrist and then does the same to my right with the other end of the seatbelt. He retreats back behind me, and I can feel his eyes on me, but he doesn't touch me. I close my eyes and wait, and after what feels like a few minutes, I hear him shift. Opening my eyes, I look between my legs to see he's on his knees, and then I close them again, startling when he finally touches me.

His fingers dig into my hips, and I feel his hot breath on my pussy seconds before his warm tongue glides along my seam. And then, he dips it between my folds and finds my clit. I whimper when he presses the pad of his tongue against it in a back and forth motion. My breathing picks up and my eyes pop open when my knees begin to buckle. There's so much pressure and so much friction, quickly driving me to an orgasm. He's unrelenting, and then abruptly pulls away, leaving my core needy and begging.

He then strikes my ass cheek hard with his hand, creating a loud *smack*. I immediately feel the abused skin radiate in blazing heat. But before the tingles kick in, he brings his hand down in another ruthless blow.

"Ow!"

Cold air meets the pucker of my ass when he spreads me open. Sweat coats my neck, and my arms begin trembling. His mouth is back on my pussy, lapping his tongue, eating me out like a wild animal. He runs his mouth from my clit all the way back to my asshole. He ravishes me, tasting all of me, and the sensation throws me over, blurring my vision as I mewl in pure ecstasy. He devours me entirely—front to back—back to front, touching me in ways I've never experienced before. He fucks both my openings with his tongue, and it takes all my strength to keep myself standing.

Dragging his mouth to my ass cheek, he sinks his teeth into me, biting me like a barbarian before spanking me once again with a fierce hand.

"On your knees," he demands.

When I lower myself to the floor, he grabs on to me and flips my body around to face him, twisting my arms painfully—one crossed over the other. I scream out, but the pain from the transition dissolves. My ass throbs beneath me as I sit on the battered flesh.

He begins unbuttoning his shirt and stripping down. I admire his body as he stands naked in front of me. Taut muscles wrap around his broad shoulders and rope down his arms. His chest is defined in hard slabs that etch their way down to the deep V that leads to his thick cock. Aside from the bullet wound on his chest, his skin is smooth, but on him, the flaw is flawless; every part of his body is transcendental.

He lowers himself to his knees between my legs and lifts my hips to him, resting my bottom on top of his thighs as my feet are planted flat on either side of him. The head of his cock pushes against me, and he teases me when he drags it up and down between the lips of my pussy, wetting himself with my arousal.

"Tell me who owns you," he says as he holds himself in his hand and tugs my opening with the tip of his cock.

"You do."

"I want more."

"Then take it," I breathe, my whole body screaming in hysteria for him—for all of him. "You have me entirely. I love you, so take it all because it's already yours."

"Fucking Christ, I love you," he growls as he buries himself balls deep inside me.

My tits bounce as he fucks me with powerful thrusts while he holds my hips up. Throbbing flesh and burning arms cease to exist as I allow myself to get lost in this man I've fallen so in love with. I writhe against him every time he enters me, yearning for more. He reaches up and squeezes my one breast roughly before releasing his hand and slapping it. The piercing infliction on such tender skin battles against rhapsodic pleasure, and I cry out in pure carnal heat when he slaps my breast again before leaning down to lick and suck the supple swell of my chest.

The tether of the seatbelts cuts into my wrists as Declan dominates me, doing as he pleases with my body, because he can, because I give him that right.

He slows his pace when he pulls back from kissing me, asking, "Do you trust me?"

"I trust you."

He then takes both of his hands and places them around my frail neck.

"Do you trust me now?"

I nod.

"Give me the words."

"I trust you."

"Don't panic," he says firmly, and when he does, a shudder of fear blazes through me.

His eyes pin to mine, and I feel his fingers clamp down as his hands grow in strength, closing around my throat. He starts to pick up the pace, pumping his cock in and out of me. My hands fist into tight balls as his grip around my neck becomes more intense.

The pressure builds and builds as his hands constrict around me.

I gasp for air when he collapses my trachea.

He's choking me!

His arms strain even more, cutting off my airway completely as he stares into my tear-flooded, wide eyes.

My body lurches as I frantically gurgle, desperate for air.

I panic.

Oh, my God! I can't breathe!!

"This is trust," he grunts as he fucks me wildly, pounding into me. He's brutal. "Don't be scared."

My vision blurs, and I yank ferociously against the seatbelts. My hands and feet begin to prickle, and the sensation creeps through my arms and legs, taking me hostage. Chills wrack my body.

There's no more air.

Everything goes black.

And then . . .

Everything around me explodes in a blazing eruption of every force of nature imaginable when his hands let go of me. Bursts of shattering light impair my vision, blinding me from everything around me as my body contracts viciously, splintering every bone in my body. I spasm in a debilitating orgasm unlike anything that could possibly exist on Earth. I cum violently hard, crying out in an inferno of wild passion. Pleasure rolls in tidal waves through every muscle, every tendon, every cell. It crashes down on me over and over and over, refusing to let go.

I hear Declan moaning deeply in the far distance, I feel his body heat wrap around me. Warmth soaks into my skin, and it feels like medicine when it spreads through my bloodstream. It calms, bringing me back down. I focus on its comfort as my eyes begin to focus. My whole body goes limp, and when I can clearly see Declan, I'm consumed by an overwhelming need for closeness.

"Untie me," I cry out urgently. "Now, Declan. Untie me."

My voice trembles and cracks, and he moves quickly to free me, and with each arm he releases, I wrap it tightly around him. He holds on to me as I straddle his lap, and bury my face into the side of his neck. Our bodies are clammy and we cling to each other.

"I've got you, darling," he whispers again and again. "You're okay; I've got you."

And I know he does. I didn't think it was possible to grow more intimately with Declan, to be even closer to him. But what he just did . . . I swear to God I felt him inside every molecule I'm made of. I've never felt more exposed, more vulnerable, more naked than I do right now in this very moment.

He has me at my weakest.

I finally lift my head and look at him, our bodies still connected, and kiss him, tasting every part of me on his tongue like the savage animal I am.

"Don't ever leave me." I begin to weep. "Promise me you won't ever leave me."

"I'll never leave you," he affirms. "You're the color of my blood."

Sixteen

BY THE TIME we landed and arrived at Lotus last night, I was completely depleted. As soon as we crawled into bed, I fell asleep. We took our time waking up and getting around this morning, but now that we're cleaned up and have had a bite to eat, we're on our way to The Legacy.

Up until this moment, I've been okay. But as Declan drives the familiar streets of the city, I feel sick to my stomach. We pull into the parking garage and park the car next to Bennett's SUV. Declan steps out of the car, but I'm frozen as I stare at the vehicle Baldwin used to drive me around in.

"Let's get this over with," Declan says when he opens my door. He reaches over me and unclicks the seatbelt. "Come on."

I take his hand and hold tightly to him as we make our way into the building and up to the top floor. When the elevator opens and we enter the penthouse, it all comes flooding back. Every smell, every conversation, every sexual encounter I experienced with the enemy.

I look to Declan—he's grinding his teeth. His only memory of this place is when he broke in and shot Bennett, killing him instantly.

"The bedroom is over here," I mutter, knocking him out of his trance.

He roams around while I go into the closet. I climb up on a stepstool to reach the box on the top shelf. When I pull it down, I rip off the tape and see a pile of clothes I used to hide what lies beneath. I dig down and grab the notebook Pike used to always sketch in. Page after page is filled with art created by his own hands. Some are of random strangers, some are visions from his dreams, but most are of me. I reach down and pull out a few other items I snuck in when I moved in here with Bennett. I had to have pieces of Pike with me always.

I dump out the clothes and put all of Pike's possessions back into the box. I try not to think too much. Being in this space is hard enough. When I walk back out into the bedroom I shared with Bennett, Declan is standing in front of the large armoire. As I walk over to him, I see he's holding the framed picture of Bennett and me on our wedding day, and my heart sinks painfully into the deep well of sorrow.

"It wasn't real," I say, keeping my voice soft because he looks like he's about to blow. "I hated that man. I still do."

He doesn't speak, his knuckles are tense and white as his fingers grip the metal frame. I reach out slowly and touch his shoulder.

"Please don't look at that."

"You look so happy," he says, his words dripping acid onto my heart.

"I was happy because I was one step closer to destroying him. That's what's behind my smile," I tell him. "Not love."

"You let him touch you."

"Don't do this."

"He's touched every part of you."

"No."

He sends the photo flying across the room and the frame crashes into a lamp, sending them both falling to the floor, shattering the light bulb.

"Declan, please," I call out. "If you think I gave him what I give you, you're wrong!"

"This is what I hate about you," he seethes as he glares his animosity at me.

It's a painful reminder that he still harbors these feelings for me. He hides it well, but I can't pretend that a part of him doesn't still hate me.

"I look at the fucking bed and all I can see is your naked body fucking him!"

"It wasn't real."

He grabs my arms and slings me around, shoving me against the wall, and spits his venomous words at me. "It was real! What you did was real, so stop lying to yourself!"

He shields his pain in anger, and it tears me apart. I can take his temper, but I can't handle knowing how much he's hurting. That part cuts me deeply.

Capillaries burst beneath my skin under his strenuous grip on my arms that will surely bruise. He jerks me forward and then pushes me back, letting go of me before turning around. His hand rakes angrily through his hair as he storms out of the room and slams the door behind him, leaving me alone in evil's lair.

I don't go after him right away. I allow him time to cool off as I sit by the window and look down over Millennium Park.

"Are you okay?"

I look up to Pike who stands next to me as he leans against the window, and I nod, because I'm scared if I talk, Declan might hear.

"It's only natural for him to feel this way, you know?"

"I know," I faintly whisper.

"Deep down he's hurting. You have to help him carry the weight of that pain." Pike leans down and kisses the top of my head. *"Go talk to him."*

I stand and give my brother a hug, thankful that he's always here with me.

"I love you," I murmur in his ear.

"I love you too."

Picking up the box, I walk over to the door and open it gently. I step out of the room and see Declan sitting on the couch in the living room. His elbows are propped on his knees and he's resting his forehead on his fisted hands, staring at the floor. I set the box down on the coffee table and sit next to it, facing him.

My hands close around his fists, and he looks up at me with shame in his eyes, saying, "I'm sorry I lost it on you."

"No." I refuse his apology with a shake of my head. "You have every right to get your anger out. I'm the one who owes all the apologies, not you."

"I thought those feelings were fading because we've grown so much closer these past couple weeks, but seeing that photo . . ."

"You could hate me forever, and it would be okay. I'll love you regardless."

He unclenches his hands and places them along my jaw while I still hold on to his wrists. I can see his emotions tormenting him when he confesses, "I don't want to hate you."

"It's okay. I'm inherently yours."

I jump when the phone rings loudly, putting an end to our conversation. I rush over to answer it and tell Manuel to send up the agent from Sotheby's.

When I hang up, Declan walks to me and wraps himself around me. I hug him and listen to his heart, hoping I've reassured him enough to take the guilt of his feelings away from him. By the time the knock on the door comes, we're both calm and in a better place since the outburst.

"Good morning," the agent greets, shaking both mine and Declan's hands. "I'm Ray; it's nice to meet you."

"Thank you for coming on such short notice," Declan says. "We're just pressed for time and need to get the ball rolling on this property."

"Of course. If you don't mind, can I take a look around?"

"Please."

Declan waits in the living room while I show Ray around the penthouse as he takes notes and asks a few questions here and there. We then regroup as we sit down at the dining table.

"How many units was this originally?" Ray asks.

"It was four units before it was renovated into one."

After a few more questions, he pulls the amenities sheet out and begins punching numbers on his calculator.

"First, can I ask you what number you had in mind?"

"I didn't have one in mind. I don't even know what my husband bought it for," I respond, nearly wincing at the word *husband*, and it must be gnawing at Declan as well.

"When I combine everything together," Ray begins, "I think a good starting point is looking close to ten point nine million for this unit."

I don't care what this place sells for; I just want to dump it. We won't be keeping the money anyway. "Sounds good. When can we have it listed?"

"That honestly depends on you. As soon as you're ready, I can send the photographer over to take pictures. Once that's taken care of, we can have this property live on our site within twenty-four hours."

"Great."

"We need to make a few arrangements first," Declan adds.

"Of course. Take care of what you need and call me when you're ready to move forward."

We stand, shake hands, and I walk Ray to the door, thanking him for his time.

"What arrangements?" I question after I close the door.

"We need to hire a packing service to clear everything out of here."

"What are we going to do with all of it?"

"What about his parents? Can you give them a call and let them know you're selling the apartment and see if they'd like us to have everything moved to a storage unit?"

"I suppose," I respond, dread sinking in.

"It has to be done."

"I know," I sigh. "What about you?

"What do you mean?"

"They're going to insist on seeing me. I mean, for all intents and purposes, I'm the daughter-in-law, and God only knows what they're thinking about me after I high-tailed it out of the country immediately after Bennett's funeral. If I meet them, you can't come with me."

"You're not going to see them." His edict isn't one I want to argue with.

"Go ahead and call them."

I go to the kitchen and power up Bennett's old phone so I can get his mother's number. Before making the call, I take a deep breath.

"Put it on speakerphone," Declan instructs.

After a few rings, the call's connected.

"Hello?"

"Carol, it's me, Nina."

"Nina!" she exclaims. "My goodness, we've all been so worried about you. Are you okay, dear?"

"Yes, I'm fine."

"Where on Earth have you been?"

"Just traveling," I tell her. "I'm sorry I ran off so quickly without saying anything, I just had to get away."

"Where are you now?"

"Back in Chicago, actually, but only for a short while."

"Can I come see you?"

I look to Declan, and he's shaking his head.

"Um, I don't think that's a good idea, Carol."

"Nina, you're still a part of our family," she says, her voice teetering on tears.

"I know, but it's just easier this way. But listen, I wanted to talk to you about something."

"Yes. What is it?"

"I'm putting the penthouse on the market."

"You're selling it?" The quiver of her voice turns to shock.

"It's too much, and I'm not even here to use the space anyways. I can't live here anymore, it's too painful. Everything here reminds me of *him*," I tell her feigning my sadness as a widow.

"I understand, it's just hard to see something of his go."

"I've packed up a few things to remember him by," I lie. "But everything else, the furniture, his clothes . . . I was wondering if you could help me out."

"Whatever you need," she says. "How can I help?"

"Would it be okay if I had everything boxed up and sent to a storage unit?"

"Are you sure you don't want any of it?"

"I'm sure. I can't look at any of it anymore, it hurts too much," I say with a voice overflowing in sadness. "I have to force myself to move on."

"Move on?" she weeps.

"I'm sorry, but I have to . . . for me."

"Please let me come see you, dear. Let me say goodbye to you properly and not over the phone."

"I'm sorry, Carol. I just can't. I'll text you with the details of the storage unit once I can get everything arranged," I say quickly and then hang up before anything else can be said.

I'm scared to look at Declan, scared to see his reaction to all my deceit. I keep my eyes down when I walk out of the kitchen and into the living room. I pick up my box and head over to the door where he meets me.

"Look at me," he says, and when I do, I respond thickly, "I hate all of them."

"I know you do, but you can breathe now. It's over with and you don't ever have to be a part of those people again."

"I'm ready to go," I tell him as he takes the box from my arms and we leave, locking the door on all the haunting memories that remain in that apartment.

Seventeen

I ONCE SAW a poster that read *Art is an Attempt to Bring Order Out of Chaos*. I don't remember where I saw it, but for some reason, I've always remembered it. Maybe that's why my brother turned to sketching. Our lives were beyond chaotic. He didn't start drawing until he was in his early twenties.

We used to ride the buses. It wasn't because we needed to go somewhere; we rode them to *feel* like we were going somewhere. I'd sit next to him and watch as he sketched random passengers. He was talented. We both knew his talents would never get us out of the slums, but he didn't do it because he had expectations; he did it to escape.

While Declan is with the columnist from *Forbes*, I flip through Pike's sketchpad. I ghost my fingers over his lines, over his shadows, over every inch of paper that his hand would've touched. He drew me more beautiful than what reflects in the mirror. Every picture is amazing, and I wish people could've seen him the way I did. He was so much more than a drug dealer covered in tattoos that parents would shield their children from when they'd see him walking down the sidewalk.

He was a savior.

My savior.

The sound of the door unlocking catches my attention, and I'm happy to see Declan.

"Sorry that took so long," he announces when he walks in and shrugs off his suit jacket.

He loosens his tie that's tucked into the navy vest of the tailored three-piece suit he wore for the photos. Walking over to me, he leans over the couch I'm curled up on and kisses me.

"What's that?"

"Pike's sketchpad."

He takes a seat next to me, asking, "May I?" as he holds his hand out.

I pass him the pad and watch as he looks through a couple of drawings.

"These aren't bad," he notes before turning to the next page that happens to be a sketch of me sleeping on a ratty couch we found at the Goodwill.

He stops and scans the image for a while before saying, "He loved you, didn't he?" When I don't respond, he looks at me and adds, "He's drawn every detail perfectly down to the faint scar you have right under your left eyebrow." He then traces the scar on my skin with his finger. "How did you get it?"

"I was thrown down a flight of stairs and busted my face up."

"Your foster dad?"

"He was mad at me for . . ." I stop as shame builds.

"For what?" he presses, and when I still don't respond, he says, "I don't want you to hold anything back from me."

I've already told him all the filth from my past, so I don't know why this wave of embarrassment has come over me, but I push through it and answer him. "I'd been tied up and locked in the closet for a few days. I had been sick earlier that day and wound up not only defecating on myself but also throwing up. When he let me out, he was furious. He started kicking me in my ribs and then threw me down the basement stairs."

He tosses the sketchpad onto the coffee table and pulls me into his arms quickly. I don't cry, but that doesn't mean the memories don't inflict pain. Declan coddles me like one would a child, and I let him, because it feels good to be nurtured by him. His embrace is hard under his flexed muscles, but I find a way to melt into him anyway. I know he's upset with what I just told him because I can feel the tension in his body, so I keep quiet to allow him to calm himself down, and he eventually does.

"I never got to see where Pike was buried," I say after a good amount of time has passed.

"Why not?"

"I was scared. I was afraid to link myself to him and get busted for my con," I explain. "When Bennett and Pike died, and when I thought you were dead too, I laid low. But since we've been back, I can't stop thinking about where he is."

"Are you sure you want to do this?"

"Yes. He didn't deserve to die like he did and to be left all alone," I tell him through the heavy knot of sadness in my throat. "Do you think you can find out where he was buried?"

He reaches into his vest to pull out his cell, and without wasting a minute, asks, "Where did this happen?"

"He was living in Justice. It's the same county as here."

"What's his full name?"

"Pike Donley," I tell him.

He looks up the number to Cook County and is redirected to the coroner's office. He stands to walk over to grab a piece of paper and a pen as I hear him ask, "Who claimed the body?" He continues to take notes and ask questions as my gut twists and tangles while I listen to one side of this conversation.

Patience escapes me, and I walk over to where he's standing so I can read the notes he's taken. Matt's name is written on the paper. Declan ends the call and tucks his phone away.

"Why did you write down Matt's name?"

"He's the one that claimed the body. Who is he?"

"Um . . . just one of Pike's friends."

"You know him?"

"Yeah, he was Pike's buddy since we were kids," I tell him while still concealing the fact that it wasn't too long ago he was calling me to bail him out of debt.

"Well, since no next of kin claimed the body within the allotted time, Matt was able to do so before cremation. He paid the state fee for an indigent burial."

"What?" I blurt out, upset. "So what does that mean?"

"Nothing. Just that the state was in charge of the burial, that's all."

"Where is he?" My words increase in anxiety as the need to see his gravesite amplifies.

"Mount Olivet here in Chicago."

"I have to go."

"Elizabeth, you're upset. Why don't we take a little time and—"

"No!" I bellow.

"I think you should just—"

"Declan," I say, cutting his words off, refusing to wait any longer to see where my brother's buried. "If this were your mom, and I told you to 'Take some time,' would you be able to do that?"

He doesn't answer me.

"I didn't think so," I tell him and he sees my point when he says, "I'll call the valet to pull the car around."

I throw my jacket on before we head down to the lobby where Declan's Mercedes roadster is already waiting for us out front. I watch as the light drizzle from outside collects on the windshield and then gets wiped away with the wipers, and suddenly, the urgency I was feeling back at Lotus has dissipated. Pike is dead, and I'm not going to the cemetery to say goodbye because he's still with me. But it's a sinking feeling, maybe a part of me is still in denial, but it's the thought of seeing his name on a burial plot that I fear.

Declan begins to speed when we merge onto I-90 E, and I look over to him, asking somberly, "Can you slow down?"

He draws his foot back off the accelerator, slowing the car. "Is everything okay?"

I look out of my window, raindrops skewing my view, and admit, "I'm scared."

He takes my hand, but I keep my head turned away from him.

"We don't have to do this right now if you're not ready."

"Is anybody ever ready?" The question is heavy between us as I turn to face him.

He holds my hand tighter and doesn't respond.

"He needs flowers," I tell him. "Can we stop and get him some flowers?"

"Of course, darling."

I pull out my phone and find a florist not too far from the interstate, and when we arrive, my request is simple. "I need all the pink daisies you have in stock."

"Daisies?" Declan questions when the sales clerk goes to the back cooler.

"They're my favorite."

"I remember," he says with a subtle smile and then kisses the top of my head, resting his lips there for a moment while we wait for the lady to reappear.

"Any shade of pink?" the woman hollers from the back.

"Yes. Mix them," I shout back to her. "All of them."

I wait with Declan's arm wrapped around me, tucking me against his side, and when the clerk reemerges from the back, my eyes widen.

"Christ, that's a lot of flowers," Declan notes in surprise.

"One hundred and sixty-three stems," she tells us. "You wiped me out of inventory."

I watch as she wraps the daisies in huge sheets of brown paper and ties them up with several cords of natural raffia. "It's perfect. Thank you."

Declan pays and takes the flowers in his arms. Popping the trunk, he lays the bouquet down and we both laugh a little when they fill the trunk entirely.

We continue our drive, hitting light patches of traffic, and finally arrive at the gates of Mount Olivet. He parks the car at the funeral home that's right through the entrance.

"I'm going to go grab a map. I'll be right back."

An eerie chill creeps along my arms and it only takes a minute for Declan to reappear with a map in hand.

"Where is he?"

"Block two," he murmurs as he pulls out of the parking space and drives through the cemetery. I look at the gray headstones as we pass them, and before I know it, he's pulling the car along the edge of the grass.

"This is it," he says, turning the car off.

I look out the window and choke up, knowing that somewhere among all these gravestones is my brother. And he's all alone. I battle between not wanting to get out of this car and jumping out of this car to run to him. I'm so scared to see the evidence of what I've done.

Tears spill down my cheeks effortlessly, and Declan reaches his arm over to console me.

"This is all my fault," I strain out on a hoarse voice filled with anguish.

I turn to face Declan, and he doesn't say a word. I know what he's thinking; it's the same thing I'm thinking. No one can argue that this is very much my fault, and Declan isn't a man who will lie to comfort. We both know my part in all of this, and it makes it so much worse when there's no truth out there that can take away any amount of my responsibility.

"Do you want me to come with you?" he asks, and I nod because I know I can't do this alone.

We get out of the car, and he grabs the flowers from the trunk, placing them in my arms. With his arm wrapped around my shoulder, he leads the way. We walk around, looking at the names on the grave markers as my tears drip into the mass of daisies.

We wander for what feels like hours, but is probably only a minute before Declan stops.

"Elizabeth."

I look up at him and he tilts his head over to a flat stone, and when I see it, I gasp in horror. "Oh, my God."

And there it is.

His beautiful name engraved in stone, marking his death.

I step in front of it, my body shuddering in tormenting pain. Every dagger I've ever thrown coming right back to stab me in my chest, and Declan has to step behind me with both of his hands gripping my shoulders.

"How could I have done this?" I cry and then fall to my knees and out of Declan's hands as I clutch the flowers to my chest. "He was my best friend, Declan."

"I know," his tender voice consoles as he now sits behind me.

I lay the flowers on the grass beside me and lean forward on my knees, bracing my hands on top of his name. "I'm so sorry, Pike. I should've just killed myself." My words lose themselves within my agonizing sobs and falter when I can't focus on anything aside from the debilitating guilt and remorse. "It should've been me! It should've been me!" I wail repeatedly.

Declan reaches around my waist and pulls me away, off my knees and onto my bottom, and I fall back into him. I grab ahold of his arms crossing over my chest, and dig my nails into them as I sob, wishing I would've shot myself that day.

"He didn't deserve to die."

"Shh," Declan breathes in my ear. "I know, baby. I know."

"It should've been me," I keep saying as Declan continues to hush and console me.

His hold on me is merciless as I allow every emotion to swallow me up, and when it finally relents and spits me out, I'm utterly spent. The dipping sun measures the hours we've been here. My body aches as I move to sit up on my own, and when I turn back to look at Declan, I notice his bloodshot eyes. He's been crying with me.

"I'm sorry," I say, my throat dry and scratchy.

"Don't be. You needed to get that out. You hold so much inside of you."

"I'm a horrible person."

"You're not," he tells me. "You made horrible choices, but you're not a horrible person."

"I don't believe you."

"Maybe not today, but one day you will. I'm going to make you believe me."

He stands and reaches down to me, helping me up. When I'm steady on my feet, I turn and scoot the flowers to rest over where Pike lies. I take a moment, drained of all my tears, not to say goodbye, but to pay respect to the most selfless person I've ever known.

TIME FREEZES, AND yet, the sun rises and the sun sets, only to rise once again.

I woke yesterday but was unable to get out of bed. Too much guilt. Too much sorrow in a world filled with regrets. So, I hid under the covers and slept, and woke, and slept. Declan checked on me throughout the day, allowing me to wallow in the misery of my wrongdoings. He ordered food from the kitchen, but I couldn't eat. I couldn't risk feeding the pain for fear it would devour me fully.

Emptiness is my companion as I stand here and stare out the window up into the blue sky. It's been two days since I faced Pike's resting place, and although I haven't seen him or heard his voice, I've felt his arms around me ever since.

"You're up," Declan says when he walks into the room, dressed down in dark denim and a plain cotton T-shirt. "How are you feeling?"

"Numb."

He walks over to me, saying, "I'm going to make you feel something today," before kissing me. "Get dressed."

"What are we doing?"

"Whatever we want." He smirks and then shuts the door behind him.

After I shower and pull my hair together, I match his leisurely attire and opt for jeans and a fitted top. When I walk out into the living room, he stands with my jacket already in his hands.

"You're up to no good," I tease.

"You look stunning."

"Yeah," I quip. "You're definitely up to no good."

Once we reach the lobby, he leads me out to the busy streets of The Loop and hails a cab.

"A cab? Where's your car?"

"We're lying low today. Trust me," he says when he opens the door for me. I scoot across the back seat and Declan tells the cabbie, "Navy Pier."

"Navy Pier?"

"You ever been?"

"Oddly, no. You?" I ask.

"No."

"So why are we going?"

"Why not?"

His spontaneity makes me smile, and I make the mindful choice to hand myself over to him today. Because, after all, he's the reason I keep going.

We're among all the tourists when we hop out of the cab. Two people who blend in with all the others. We walk hand in hand into a souvenir shop and look at all the trinkets, and Declan thinks he's cute when he buys me a cheesy Chicago shirt that reads *It's better in the bleachers* across the front.

"Wasted money."

He takes the shirt and slips it over my head, saying, "Then you better wear it and not let it go to waste."

He pulls it down, and when I push my arms out of the sleeves, he takes a step back and smiles.

"Are you happy now?"

He laughs, "You look cute."

With a roll of my eyes, I join in with a light chuckle. He's blithe and lighthearted, and it's refreshing to see this side of him. We've had so many days filled with dark clouds and suffocating emotions, but to see that rays of light can break through those clouds gives me hope for us.

We walk along the water enjoying the spring breeze. He buys me a funnel cake when I tell him I've never tasted one and then licks the powdered sugar off my lips after I inhale the fried treat. When I'm thoroughly buzzed with sweet carbs, he takes me up to the Ferris wheel.

"Come on."

"No way, Declan. That is way too high."

"What are you saying? Tough-as-nails Elizabeth is scared of heights?"

"Umm . . . yeah," I admit with my head craned back, looking up at the enormous wheel.

"It's a *Ferris wheel*!" he exclaims.

"Yes. I know this," I say, and with my arm up towards it, I exasperate, "and it's a deathtrap!"

He shakes his head, laughing, "It's the mildest ride here."

"Don't care. You're not getting me on that thing."

He releases a heavy sigh and succumbs. "All right. No Ferris wheel." Taking my hand, he says, "I've got something better in mind."

We make our way over to a small fishing vendor pavilion on the north dock. With bait and rods in hand, we find a spot to cast our lines.

"Give me your rod and I'll hook the bait for you."

"I'm capable of hooking it myself," I say with a confident air.

"Go for it, darling."

His eyes watch as I dunk my hand into the bait bucket, pull out a shiner, and pierce the hook through it.

Looking up at him holding his rod, I tease, "You need me to help you?"

"I'm impressed."

"I came from the streets, Declan. Baiting a hook is nothing," I tell him with a smirk and then cast my line into the water.

"So, I take it you've fished before."

I watch him cast his line out and respond, "No, not really. Only once with my dad. He would hold the rod for me, and when we would get a bite, he'd let me reel it in. What about you?"

"All the time. When I was living here, I'd take my boat out during my down time, which wasn't often, but I'd get away when I could and toss out a line or two."

"I got something!" I practically squeal when something tugs on my line. I laugh with childish excitement, and then a little fish surfaces.

"It's a perch." He takes the small fish and pulls the hook out, all the while smiling at me.

"I'm winning," I brag, and when he tosses the fish back into the water, he says, "I wasn't aware this was a competition."

"Well, now you are. And you're losing."

I grab another shiner from the bucket and cast my line.

"Tell me a story," I request. "Something good."

"My darling wants a story," he says to himself and then takes a moment, squinting against the sunlight reflecting off the water. "I did my undergrad at the University of Edinburgh and was living at my fraternity house. We used to throw a lot of parties. I was never much of a drinker, but it was the end of exam week, and I'd been under a lot of stress. The girl I was seeing at the time was at the party that night, and I had gotten piss drunk. She told me she was going to call it a night and crash in my room since she had been drinking too. She was nowhere near as drunk as I was, but still drunk enough that she knew better than to drive."

He pauses when his rod dips. Another small perch.

"One to one. It's a tie," he says with a grin, and then continues when he grabs another shiner. "Anyway, I stayed up for a few more hours before stumbling upstairs to my room. I was so wasted, and all I can remember is stripping off my clothes while everything around me was spinning. I pulled the sheets back and slipped in behind what I assumed was my girlfriend."

"It wasn't?"

"Each room housed three guys."

I start laughing and it isn't long before he joins me.

"I spent the whole night in my underpants snuggling with my roommate . . . Bean."

"Bean?"

"Uh, yeah, he had a bit of a flatulence issue."

I burst out laughing.

"Once I realized I wasn't cuddling my girlfriend, it was too late. A few of my frat brothers were standing in the doorway, snapping photos of the supposed indiscretion."

"What did your girlfriend say?"

"Ah, well, she was upset I got drunk and ignored her all night, and that was the end of her."

"You're an ass," I snicker, to which he replies, "So I've been told."

I startle and clutch my fishing rod when it's nearly yanked out of my hands. Grabbing ahold of the reel, I struggle to crank it.

"I need help," I call, and Declan sets his rod down, moves behind me, and grips the rod.

"You've got something big," he says when he puts his hand over mine and helps me reel in the line just like my dad used to.

I let him take control and move my hand with his. The fish fights us for a bit, and when it approaches the water's surface, I see how substantial it is.

"What is that?" I ask excitedly.

He pulls it up, announcing, "It's a big fucking bass." He kneels, pinning the fish down with his foot, and removes the hook. "You want to keep it? We could have the chef in the kitchen prepare it for dinner tonight."

Looking at the fish flopping around, I tell him, "No. Let him live."

"You sure?"

"I'm sure."

Declan drops the bass into the water, looks over the pier's edge, and watches him as he swims down, disappearing into the lake.

I bait my hook and return to our conversation, saying, "A part of me always wanted to do the whole college thing."

"You still could."

With shame, I confess to him, "I never even graduated high school, Declan."

He looks at me and there's a hint of surprise in his eyes. "How far did you get?"

"I never finished the ninth grade. When Pike turned eighteen, I ran away with him, so school was out of the question because I'd get busted by the state. I was always a good student though, made excellent grades. I loved reading and learning, so I had Pike buy me all the materials to get my GED even though it would never be official. Since I was still underage and in the system, I couldn't use my real name for anything."

"And when you were of age?"

"By then, it didn't matter. I knew we'd never have the means for me to ever go to college, so what was the point of going back to get my GED?" I say. "I did what I could though. I'd pick classes that interested me out of the local college class catalog and Pike would buy me the textbooks from a used bookstore. I'd read them, and in a pathetic way, it made me feel like I was making something of myself."

"You were."

"All I did was make a *mess* of myself."

"That too," he responds in light jest. "But you're bright and well-spoken. No one would ever suspect you only made it to the ninth grade. You're an incredible woman who's fighting hard to make things right."

"Things will never be right."

"Maybe the past won't, but right here, in this moment, this is where it all changes," he says. "You can do anything you want to do."

His confidence in me is powerful, making me feel like there's a future to look forward to. That the choices I make won't be for naught. And maybe he's right—maybe it's the here and now that I need to focus on to move forward. I've always been running, and now, for the first time, I no longer have to. I can stand here, in one place, and know that with Declan by my side, I'll be okay.

So with a little bit of optimism, I tell him, "I want to finish high school."

He smiles, pride in his eyes, and says, "We can get all the details on what needs to be done tomorrow. But tonight, I'm taking you out."

"A date?"

"It'll be a first for us."

After catching too many perch to count, we decide I win based on the bass alone. Being able to be out with Declan, free from lies and games in this city where we used to hide, feels great. This is where we fell in love, but that life was always tainted, and now . . . now we can create something new.

WITH THE GOOFY shirt Declan bought me crumpled on the bathroom floor, I finish the last of my makeup after a long shower. Walking into the bedroom, I can see Declan out in the living room sipping Scotch. He looks good as he waits on me, dressed in his usual look—a sleek designer suit, tailored to perfection.

I pick out a flattering navy shift dress that I purchased on my shopping trip with Davina. After I slip it on, I step into a pair of nude heels and join Declan. We then make our way down to the lobby where his roadster is waiting out front.

We drive through the night to Cité, an upscale restaurant that's perched atop Lake Point Tower. We're seated next to the windows, which provide stunning views of the lake and city, and Declan takes the chair right next to me instead of across the table.

He was right—this is a first for us. We've never been on a date, and then it hits me that *I've* never been on a date. Not a real one, not with a man I love. The thought causes me to smile and Declan takes notice.

"What's that grin all about?"

"Nothing," I tell him, feeling a bit juvenile.

"That's not nothing behind those blue eyes of yours. Spill it."

"You're pushy, you know that?"

"I'm aware. And I'm waiting."

"Fine," I exhaust. "I was just sitting here, thinking . . . It's really silly."

"Humor me."

"Aside from fallacies . . . this is my first date."

"Ever?" he says in curiosity.

"Ever."

He slips his hand under the table and places it on my thigh, giving me a gentle squeeze. We order wine and he insists on the Siberian caviar service, promising I'll love it—and I do.

"You're quite divergent, you know that?" I say, setting my wine glass down.

"Why's that?"

"I remember you taking me to breakfast at that diner when I first met you. Stale coffee and pancakes."

"The Over Easy Café does not have stale coffee," he immediately defends, and I laugh, bantering, "Whatever you say. But, now, you have me here, drinking a bottle of wine that's so expensive, it's obscene."

"You don't like it?"

"I never said that; it's just a contrast from the 'not stale' coffee and the hot dog you ate from the street vendor today."

"So what would you prefer?" He leans closer to me and slips his hand back on my thigh.

"I like your contradictions," I admit as he runs his hand under the hem of my dress. My body tenses and I shift my eyes around the room, wondering if anyone knows what's happening under the table linens.

"You nervous?"

Giving him my attention, I ask, "You like making me nervous?"

"Yes."

"Why?" My voice trembles when his fingers hit the lace of my panties and then he nudges against my thigh for me to uncross my legs—and I do.

"Because I like testing you," he confesses, shifting my panties over. "To see how far you'll let me push you."

"When have I ever stopped you?"

"Never," he whispers on a husky voice at the same time he shoves one of his fingers inside my pussy.

I gasp.

He smiles.

Pride and domination color his eyes in heated black.

"You want me to stop?"

"No," I breathe, and he drags his finger out of me and rolls my clit in slow circles.

"Tell me why you yield like this to me."

"Because I love you."

He thrusts his finger back inside of me. "Say it again."

My breath catches, stammering unevenly as I resist the urge to grind down on his hand, nearly whimpering the words, "I love you."

He abruptly pulls out of me, leaving me yearning, and shifts my panties back over to cover me. My chest rises and falls noticeably as I watch him bring his hand up to his mouth and suck my arousal off his finger.

Unsatisfied and aching, I make it through dinner, and when the bill is paid, I'm quick to leave. Declan's cocky smirk should irritate me, but it only makes me want to fuck him more. He takes my hand, and once we're on the elevator, he further tests me by refusing to touch me. My body is on high-alert, sensitive to every element, begging to be touched—but he doesn't engage me.

"Asshole," I mutter under my breath, and he smiles.

The elevator doors open and as soon as we exit the building, my steps halt the moment I see her.

She stops in her steps as soon as she sees me, her eyes narrowing into daggers. It's a look I've never seen her wear, but it's wasted on me.

"You're back," she states.

"It's nice to see you too, Jacqueline," I condescend.

"Jacqueline?" Declan questions to himself, but we all hear.

"You," she accuses, looking at Declan. "You son of a bitch!"

"You're sorely mistaken," I butt in. "Your husband—"

"Is dead! Because of you two," she accuses. Her loud voice grabs the attention of a couple passersby, but they keep moving. She then looks down at my hand linked with Declan's. "And how fast you move on, Nina."

"You've got a lot of nerve. This coming from the woman who not only fucked my husband but was stupid enough to get pregnant. So, don't you dare stand there like you're a goddamn ice princess," I lash out while Declan allows me to handle her on my own.

Tears rise and then fall down her cheeks when she explodes, "You killed my husband! I have nothing because you took it away from me!"

"I didn't take shit from you. I freed you from that asshole. He fucking raped me and tortured me! And look at you," I belittle. "Standing there like *you're* the victim when you should be thanking me for ridding the world of that piece of shit."

Beyond what he did to me, my blood boils when I think of what Richard did to Declan's mother and the part he played in my father's life.

"How dare you tarnish his name with your lies. He'd never—"

"You can't be that ignorant. Surely you know by now the man he was, yet you're so weak that you're still defending him."

"What am I supposed to do? My life is over! My name doesn't mean anything anymore. And because of you, I'm left with nothing. Everything I ever had has been seized. I've been ostracized by everyone and I'm buried in debt."

"And yet you blame me," I say. "I guess you got what you deserved for marrying that asshole and screwing around with a married man. It seems all you have is the hope that your bastard son doesn't grow up to hate you, since he now carries all the wealth." My smile grows. "Must suck to know all that money is within reach, and yet Bennett forbade you from touching it because he hated you."

"You bitch!"

"You're done here," Declan barks, stepping between us. "That man you married was a cold-blooded killer. Accept it or not, I don't really give a fuck, but don't place blame where it doesn't belong."

Not allowing another second to pass, he leads me to his car, leaving her crying, alone, on the sidewalk. Declan closes my door, and I look at her through the window, hating her for the mere fact that she loved and supported such an evil man. A man who left me stripped naked for days while he degraded and humiliated me, beat me, and sodomized me. A man who took so much from both my life and Declan's.

Declan speeds off, and I refuse to let the memories of what Richard did to me come to life.

"Are you okay?"

"I don't want to talk about it," I snap.

I can't talk because all I can do right now is focus on forcing those memories back into the deep cave of my soul. Pinching my eyes closed, battling against myself, I hear the ringing in my head, and it feels like an axe to my skull.

I clamp my hands over my ears, and I don't even notice Declan pulling the car over. He reaches out to me and touches my arm, and when I open my eyes, I see Richard's smug face instead of Declan's. My body coils back, lurching away from him, and I scream, "Don't fucking touch me!"

"Elizabeth, it's okay," he insists, unbuckling my seatbelt and banding his arms around me as I fight against the high-pitched ringing in my head.

I release a wretched scream, my voice bleeding, "Make it stop!"

"Open your eyes and look at me," he demands on a hardened voice. He grabs hold of my head and forces me to focus on him. "Breathe. I need you to breathe with me."

Everything around me and within me is a demented chaos of sounds, voices, visions. A hurricane spinning with inconceivable force, but his eyes remain still and steady. He's the one unwavering element in this maelstrom, and it takes all the effort in me to focus on him—on his words.

"That's it, darling. Just breathe," he encourages when I feel my lungs inflate.

My eyes never waver, and soon everything dulls into a low hum that I'm eventually able to silence. He's managed to chase away the demons I couldn't fight off on my own.

And it's here, in the ink of night, on a deserted side street, that I must face the fact that I undoubtedly need Declan.

nineteen

AFTER MY RUN-IN with Jacqueline, all I want to do is sleep. The stress of my panic attack should've knocked me out, but I've been tossing and turning ever since my head hit the pillow.

When my cell phone lights up, I grab it from the nightstand. The screen reads: *UNKNOWN*, and I know it's Matt calling. I decline the call and turn the phone off. My mind races in a million different directions, stirring up even more memories. Unwilling to lie here in bed any longer, I grab the manifest and my notepad and go to the office to direct all my attention to this list.

I've made it halfway through the names, scrambling the letters around and around and around, not knowing what I'm looking for, but hoping I find something. I get through three more names.

Parker Moore

Dorrance Riley

Quentin Malles

All are dead ends, and before the sun starts to rise, I sneak back into bed without Declan noticing.

I manage to get a couple hours of sleep, and when I wake, Declan has already had breakfast delivered. The smell of his coffee and fresh baked croissants fill the air, and before I'm fully awake, he pours me a cup of steaming water and hands me a tea bag.

"Thanks."

While we sit in bed, Declan reads the newspaper and I watch as bister ribbons through the translucent water in my tea cup. Sleep still fogs my head as I continue to dunk the tea bag up and down until the water turns to a delicate amber, infused with aromatic herbs that help wake me up.

"He's in the paper," Declan murmurs.

"Who?"

He hands the *Chicago Tribune* to me, and there he is—Callum. He stands in his prison-issued orange jumpsuit with the headline "Player in Gun Trafficking Ring Indicted."

I look to Declan as he takes a sip of his coffee, and he says, "You know it's only a matter of time until we're getting wrapped up in this."

"What do you mean?"

"Our involvement. You were married to Bennett, ran in the same circle as Richard, and spent time with my father. That, along with the kidnapping and murder, we'll both be forced to testify," he tells me before tossing the sheets off him and getting out of bed in haste. "This is the last thing I need, that man tarnishing my name," he bites.

He's pissed about the attention this will draw to him and his company.

"Declan," I call out in a panic, my heart beginning to race when it suddenly hits me. "What about me?"

He turns to look at me, becoming aware when he sees the anxiety in my eyes.

"They'll dig into my history and Nina only goes back so far. They'll know I'm a fraud," I blurt out in a pitchy voice. "I'll be charged with identity theft and embezzlement, along with any other crime they can pin on me."

"Fuck," he grits under his breath.

I guess it was inevitable that my con would eventually catch up with me. My mind goes into overdrive, thinking about how I could possibly finagle my way out of this, how I could possibly explain this away, but I can't hone in on anything.

"What do we do?"

"I'll put a call in to my attorney," he tells me. "I don't want you to worry; we have time. It could take up to a year for this to even go to trial."

"What about you?"

"What about me?"

I slip out of bed and walk over to him. "It's you that tells me that I shouldn't hide from the things that hurt me."

"He doesn't hurt me," he immediately defends, but I call his bluff, saying, "He didn't even try to stop the murder of your mom. He stepped aside and just let it happen. So don't tell me that doesn't hurt you, Declan. I know it does." I reach out to him and place my hand over his heart. "You and I share the same soft spot, the same wound—the death of a parent."

He covers my hand with his, and it's full of tension, squeezing me much too hard.

He's in pain.

(DECLAN)

HER BONES ARE fragile in my grip as I fight against the agony that marks my soul in wounds that refuse to heal.

And she's right.

My mum has always been the weak link in my armor. She's the softest part of my heart and anything that comes close to touching it pains me. But that pain is tainted by the fury I hold for my dad now that I know the part he played.

I look down into Elizabeth's eyes and see the sorrow in them. She's called me on my shit, so there's only one option unless I want her to see me as a hypocrite.

"Let's go to New York then."

"You're going to see him?" she asks in surprise.

"Yes. And then I'm done with him."

I leave Elizabeth to drink her tea while I make the call to arrange the flight, and I'm told that we can make it out later tonight. When I return to the bedroom, I see her with that damn notepad. She thinks she's being sneaky and that I don't notice when she leaves my bed at night, but I do. The moment I lose the heat of her body, I wake up. I've chosen not to say anything and to give her the time she feels she needs.

Truth be told, Lachlan and I are hitting roadblock after roadblock. This man clearly doesn't want to be found, but one way or another, I *will* find him—for her.

She sets the notepad and pencil on the bedside table when she sees me.

"The plane will be ready at seven."

I SIT AND wait, looking around the white cinderblock room filled with the city's disgraced and their loved ones. Guards stand and watch the interactions, making sure the rules that were explained in detail are being abided by.

The metal door in the corner of the room opens, and this time it's my father who walks through. Donned in orange, he's escorted into the room, and the guard that's with him removes the shackles as my father's eyes find mine.

He's expressionless.

Once freed from the chains, he makes his way across the room. He looks hard, unshaven, and thinned out.

"Son," he remarks evenly when he approaches the table.

Animosity sparks as I look at this man who sits across from me. Memories of all the disdain he's spit my way throughout my life, only to evade his own wrongdoings, ignites rage inside me.

"How did you find out?"

"You haven't heard?" I respond and he shakes his head. "Your boss?"

"My boss?"

"Keep playing dumb with me," I taunt. "I know everything. I just want to hear you tell the truth for once in your life."

"Stop with the riddles, kid, and just tell me what you *think* you know."

My hands fist; it's a futile attempt to control my fury, and I glare at him. "I know about Mum. I know she died because of you."

"I loved that woman—"

His words—his flagrant lie—set me off, and I punch the table, losing control. "You fucking bastard!"

"Hey!" one guard yells, calling me into check.

"She died because of you," I seethe, lowering my voice. "Because of your greed, she had to pay the consequences."

"You don't know shit, kid."

"Admit it," I say.

He shrugs his shoulders as if he's clueless and guiltless, and I can't stand to look at his smug face any longer, so I speed this up. "You knew Richard was going to kill her. That's why you left the country, because you didn't want to be there when it happened. You were running from the guilt, weren't you?"

"How do you know about Richard?"

"You know he's dead, right?" I ask and he nods. "I killed him." His eyes widen when I tell him this, and I smile proudly. "Don't worry, Dad. Cops already know I did it."

He doesn't respond to what I've just admitted to him. He simply stares at me, dumbfounded.

"Because of him, I know everything you've been hiding from me. *Everything*."

He takes a hard swallow and hangs his head, succumbing to the truth because he has no other choice at this point. He can't bullshit me any longer.

"I know it all, Dad," I whisper harshly, digging the knife into him even deeper, and when he finally gets the balls to lift his head to look me in the eye, he says, "Then you know what I'm facing."

"It's all over the news."

His demeaning voice shifts to that of neediness. "I need your help, son."

"Admit it first. Admit that you were the one responsible for Mum dying."

"I need your help," he deflects, talking quickly in a hushed tone. "Camilla is my only line to the outside, aside from my lawyer, but I haven't talked to her in a week. I need your help to get in touch with Lachlan."

"Why?"

"I can't tell you why, but I *need* to talk to him."

"About Camilla?"

"Camilla? Why would I talk to him about her?" he questions in utter confusion. "What do you know?"

"Only that your girlfriend has conflicting fidelities."

"I'm getting the feeling he does too," he murmurs, jaw clenched in anger.

"What's that supposed to mean?"

"Ask him."

"I'm asking *you*," I say as my irritation grows in sync with suspicions that I'm missing some important details about Lachlan.

"I needed to keep an eye on you when you left Chicago," he says cryptically. "Tell me, because I need to know, who's Elizabeth Archer and what the fuck is she doing at The Water Lily?"

That fucking bastard. I will kill Lachlan when I get back to London, because it's now apparent that whatever involvement he told me he has with my father is a lie. The only way my dad could get that information would be from him. But it's his mention of The Water Lily that has me curious when I think of the photo that Elizabeth found there.

"I'll tell you what you want to know," I say. "But first, tell me what I should know about The Water Lily."

He looks at me suspiciously, saying nothing.

"Why is there a picture of me there?" I ask, giving him a bit of information to try to spur him into an answer.

"Because," he sighs, leaning forward.

"Tell me the truth."

He looks at me for a moment before revealing, "The woman who runs it . . ."

"Isla."

"Yes," he says. "She's your grandmother."

"What?"

"Isla is your mother's mum."

"That doesn't make sense," I mutter. "Why was she never around?"

"Because she never approved of me dating her daughter. It was years of ups and downs, and when I married your mum, that's what finally severed them—the fact that your mother chose me."

"And even when Mum died, you never told me."

"What was there to tell?"

I stand, unable to continue this conversation or look at this man who has filled my life with countless lies.

"Son . . ."

"Stop avoiding and just tell me."

He remains seated, staring up at me. For a beat, I don't think he's going to answer, and my anger burns. Then, he opens his mouth to speak. "Yes, I knew your mother would die, and I did nothing to stop it."

And that's the dagger that spears into what Elizabeth calls "the softest part of me." Blood from the wound that was created the day I watched her die pours out, drowning me, numbing me, debilitating me.

My hands shake when I brace them on the edge of the table and tell him, "You'll never see me again."

"Declan—"

"You're going to die in this shithole all alone, you motherfucker."

I don't look back at him when I walk to the guard who stands at the exit, and I swear I leave a trail of blood in my wake from the wound he ripped wide open. When the guard pulls his keys to unlock the door, I hear my father call out, "Declan, come on. Come back," and then commotion before a guard yells, "Sit down, McKinnon!"

"Declan!"

More commotion.

"Get the fuck off me!"

"Get your ass on the ground, inmate!"

"Declan!"

"ANOTHER," I TELL the bartender in the lounge of the hotel, and he pours me a shot of whiskey.

I can't go back to the room just yet, I'm much too volatile. I've spent my whole life trying to measure up to my father's standards and prove to him that I'm man enough to persevere on my own in this world. And for what? It was all a lie. A lie that claimed my mother's life and mine. I lost a huge part of myself when she died and was left with scars that no man should ever have to bear.

The moment she died, I was blamed. It was me that wasn't man enough to save her, and my father spent his whole life making sure I knew I was the pussy he saw me for. He destroyed everything and has left me in this nightmare of realized deceit.

"How did it go?" Elizabeth asks when I eventually walk through the door of the hotel room.

I'm nothing but knotted up rage and anger and agony that alcohol can't even cure. I'm broken bones and bleeding wounds, empty and missing my mum like never before. My cold stone exterior masks the pansy I feel like. It shields the insecure man in me that wants to fall to his knees and have his girl hold on to him as he cries for all the years he's hidden behind strict control. And at the same time, I want to lash out, punch my fists through the walls, and spew the venom in my veins for all that son of a bitch has done to my life.

"Are you okay?" I hear her say through the static of vehemence rushing under my skin. "Declan?"

I bore my eyes into her, silently pleading to use her to expel my wrath onto. My hands fist, and I feel the vibrations in my flexed muscles when it all becomes too much to hold in.

Her hands touch my clenched jaw and she runs them down my trembling arms, all the while looking up at me so lovingly when I'm pouring out pure fury. She's a goddamn godsend when she perceives my reticence and gives me the permission I'm needing so badly.

"Touch me."

"I'll hurt you."

"It's okay," she says so fucking sweetly. "Give me your pain so you don't have to feel it."

I kiss her with binding brutality, and she allows it. I'm a wolf, devouring her, clawing her, ripping her clothes off in a storm of violence. She stumbles back as I force my body against hers, pushing her to the ground. I stand above her naked body and breathe in broken pants.

She's so small, milky white flesh, and ruby red-hair, and she must be crazy to submit to me right now, but she does, saying, "Don't hold back."

I strip, and she watches, inviting the beast to come out and play. I'm already rock hard, and when she sits up and wraps her delicate hand around my dick, it pulses and leaps in her grip. I slap her arm away. She lies back, and I reach down and flip her over. Kneeling above her, I grab a handful of her hair, yank it back, and strike her ass with my hand. She cries out, eliciting a heady arousal of power in me.

Reaching for my pants, I rip the belt out from the loops and fasten it tightly around her arms, above the elbows. She squirms and emits little ragged gasps, and I raise my hand, letting it drop in a sharp slap across her ass again. It immediately welts as the blood rushes to the surface, making my dick even more thick and hot with need.

She doesn't resist when I reach under her waist and jerk her ass up in the air and shove her knees under her so she's propped up like a fucking beauty. Tangling my hands into her hair, I shove the side of her face into the floor, and when I run the tip of my cock through her slick warmth, I realize she's ready for me, dripping wet.

I slam my dick inside of her with raging force, and without any restraint, I fuck her licentiously hard. I grab ahold of the belt to use for leverage, and with each pounding thrust, I drive her body into the floor.

My skin is covered in a sheen of sweat as I thrust my hips sharply, barraged by a million sensations all at once, blurring the edges of pain and pleasure. Elizabeth's yelps are muffled by the floor as I grunt freely into the air.

I pull out and shove her over onto her back, watching her wince against the pain of lying on top of her arms, but I see her hidden mirth. She then lances her nails into my heart, making me love her even more when her lips lift in a faint smile and she spreads her legs wider for me, inviting me to take more.

I can't *not* be one with her.

I hold my dick and slide into her swollen, ripe pussy. I still myself, and her needy body begins to clench around my shaft. Drawing back, I growl as I fuck her frantically and the room fills with a requiem of moans, gasps, and grunts. Elizabeth bows her lithe body up to mine in an attempt to fuck me back.

She's a fucking paradigm.

My cock begins to swell in her, building in a vigor of ecstasy at the same time I sense Elizabeth's body tensing up, faltering in rhythm. She stares up at me, and I reach underneath her and find her hand. I hold it tightly in mine, needing her to know that she's safe to allow herself to fall apart with me, that we're in this together in our most vulnerable states. Her eyes swim out of focus, and she draws in a tight breath before releasing an intoxicating moan, carnal and raw. Her pussy clamps in spasms around my dick; I buck into her, exploding, shooting my cum deep inside her, groaning in sync with her pleasure. Her hand squeezes mine as we ride out our orgasms together. She writhes under my body, drawing as much pleasure as she can from me, and I love how greedy she gets with me in these moments.

When we're sweaty, sated, and completely out of breath, I roll us onto our sides and unbuckle the belt, and like all the times before, she clings her arms around my neck. My cock twitches as I keep it buried in her and band my arms around her body as she holds on to me.

I'm sure she's unaware that I need her embrace more than she needs mine in this moment. She soothes me in a way no one has been able to, taking the toxins out of my bones and replacing them with her love. She fills me entirely, handing herself over so willingly for me to take whatever it is that I need, and she does it so perfectly.

I pull my head back to look at her, and she nuzzles her forehead against mine, keeping her eyes closed. When I lean in and kiss her, open and deep, I gather her completely in my arms. She becomes desperate, and I meet her urgency to be closer. I bruise her, crashing my lips with hers, and we bleed. Like cannibals, we feed off each other, sharing the blood from our hearts, uniting us even more.

twenty
(ELIZABETH)

DECLAN SITS IN quiet despair as we fly back to Chicago. I knew better than to push him to talk when he returned to the hotel last night. I could see the torment in his eyes, so I kept my mouth shut and handed myself over to him so he could use me for comfort. We spent the whole night on the floor together, naked and wrapped in each other's arms.

He's been quiet all morning, and I've followed suit, returning the silence. I don't know what was said between him and Cal or how it ended, but I doubt it ended well. When I look over to him as he sits next to me, I find him staring at me intently. I want to ask him if he's okay, but I don't. Instead, I simply give him a subtle smile and squeeze his hand that's holding mine. He kisses the top of my head, and I close my eyes, using his shoulder for a pillow for the remainder of the flight.

DECLAN HAS BEEN down in his office on the ground floor of Lotus since we returned from New York while I've stayed up in the penthouse. He's yet to speak to me, and I've been busying myself with the passenger manifest.

Michael Ross
William Baxter
Clint Noor
Ben Wexler

I've spent a couple hours on those names and have come up empty. Deciding to give myself a break, I call down to the kitchen and order some food and then mindlessly flip through a few magazines. Minutes dissolve into hours, and when the sun begins its descent, I sit on the edge of the bed and watch.

When the sun kisses the horizon, the bed dips beside me. We sit together in silence until the day shifts into night.

"She's my grandmother."

His slack voice cuts through the darkness, and when I turn my head to look at him, his eyes are focused on the sky.

"Who?" I gently ask.

"Isla," he reveals. "She's my mum's mother."

"He told you that?"

Declan nods. "I've had a piece of my mum here all along and he never told me."

There's longing in his voice, a feeling I'm no stranger to.

"I'll never speak to that man again," he tells me when he finally looks my way.

His eyes are flooded in pain, and it kills me to see him like this when he's always so pulled together. And in a rare moment, he stands in front of me before lowering to his knees, and then grips my hips and lays his head on my lap.

My undeniably strong Declan, slayed to the core.

Leaning over, I shield his body with mine.

I CAN'T SLEEP. Declan went to bed hours ago, but all I can do is toss and turn. My mind keeps drifting back to the past, and memories of my dad play in my head. Looking over at Declan, he looks so peaceful. I watch him as he sleeps, but it's impossible to ignore my stomach when it growls at me. Slipping out of bed, I pad across the room and shut the door quietly behind me. I head over to the kitchen and pull out a slice of cheesecake that room service delivered earlier. Grabbing my notepad and the list of passengers, I take a seat on the couch in the living room and begin working on the next name.

Asher Corre

Looking at the name, I pick up a strawberry garnish from the plate and eat it, and another memory of my dad finds me again.

"Happy birthday, princess."

"Daddy," I groan as I roll over in bed, rubbing the sleep dust out of my eyes with my hands.

"Wake up, sleepyhead."

I open my eyes to see my daddy sitting on the edge of my bed with a great big bundle of pink balloons and a smile on his face.

"Am I five today?"

"You are. You're getting so big, baby."

"Then you can't call me 'baby' if I'm so big."

"I'll call you 'baby' even when you're my age," he says. "Come on, get out of bed."

I groan again, still sleepy, and he sets the weight that's tied to the bottom of the balloons on the floor and then reaches his hands out in an over-sized gesture. I immediately squeal and throw the covers over my head.

"The tickle monster is gonna get you," he teases in a playful monster voice, and I start laughing before he even gets me.

When his fingers get ahold of me I squeal and squirm with loud giggles.

"Daddy, stop!"

"Say the magic word," he says in a sing-song voice as he continues to tickle me.

"Abracadabra . . . Please . . . Hocus pocus . . ." I ramble off, saying everything I can think of, and then he stops. My belly hurts from all the laughing, and I have to catch my breath.

"Are you getting up?"

"Yes, Daddy."

"Breakfast in ten minutes, princess. Get ready and don't forget to brush your teeth," he tells me as he stands and walks to my bedroom door. "Oh, wait. I forgot something."

I get out of bed as he walks back to me. He lifts me up, and I wrap my arms and legs around him like a monkey when he starts kissing my neck. The prickles from his beard tickle me, and I laugh.

"I love you, Daddy."

"I love you too, birthday girl," he says before setting me back on my feet. "Now get dressed."

Because it's my birthday, I decide to wear as many colors as I can find in my dresser, and when I'm ready and my teeth are brushed, I run out into the kitchen.

"Pancakes!"

"And whipped cream," he adds.

I take a seat at the table in front of a ginormous stack of pancakes, but before he puts the whipped cream on them, he says, "Open up."

He holds the can over my head, so I lean back, open my mouth, and he squirts my mouth full of whipped cream.

"When does my party start?"

"Your friends will be here at noon, so I need to get started on your birth-

day cake as soon as we're finished with breakfast."

"You're making the strawberry cake, right?"

"Of course. It's your favorite, isn't it?"

"Yes! Strawberries are my super duper favorite!" I exclaim.

I begin eating my pancake tower, but it doesn't take long for my belly to get full. I play with my dolls in the living room while Daddy cleans up, and when he's done, he calls me back into the kitchen.

"Did you want to help me with the cake?"

"Yes!" I say excitedly and then drag one of the chairs from the table over to the counter and climb up.

He pulls out all the ingredients from the pantry and fridge and helps me fill measuring cups that I dump into a big bowl. Once the cake batter is made, he lets me lick the spoon and bowl as he puts the pan into the oven.

While it's baking we play a couple games of Go Fish and watch Saturday morning cartoons. The timer goes off and we return to the kitchen.

"Is it time for the strawberry slime?" I ask.

"Yep!"

As Daddy prepares the strawberry gelatin, he lets me stab the holes in the cake with a toothpick. When the gelatin starts to thicken a little, I help him pour it over the cake. He puts it into the fridge to set before we go outside to play in the back yard.

"Will you push me high?" I ask when I run over to the swing set.

"You don't want to do it on your own?"

"Not today."

He pushes me, and when I call out, "Higher!" he says, "What if I push you into the clouds?"

"That's silly, Daddy. That can't happen."

We spend a good amount of time playing outside, and when we're done and the cake is ready, he lets me frost it with strawberry icing.

"You're the best thing that's ever happened to me, you know that?" he tells me as I smear on the icing.

"Am I your favorite?"

"My super duper favorite, but I need you to make me a promise," he says. "I need you to promise me that you'll stop growing up so fast."

"How do I stop growing?"

"Well," he says with animation. "I guess I'll have to stop feeding you."

I giggle, "You can't do that! What if I get hungry?"

"What are we going to do then?"

"I don't wanna be little forever though. I wanna be great big, just like

you."

"Just like me?"

"Yep! Just like you because you're my favorite thing in the whole wide world," I tell him and then lean over to kiss his nose.

"You're my favorite too, princess pie," he tells me and then gives me a kiss on my nose as well. "So I guess I won't starve you. Here," he says, taking the rubber spatula out of my hand. "I always get the first lick."

I laugh when he licks some of the pink frosting.

He hands it back to me, saying, "Enjoy," and I begin licking the strawberry icing.

I take another bite of the strawberry as my heart aches at the memory of the last birthday I had with him, and get back to the next name on the list.

ASHER CORRE

I stare at the letters and begin scrambling them.

SHORE RARE C

HERO CRASER

I take a bite of cheesecake and continue. I know this is nonsense. I'm not even sure what I'm trying to decode, but it makes me feel better than doing nothing.

I continue to stare at the letters.

"My little princess pie," he says again as I lick the frosting. "My little Elizabeth Archer."

_ S _ _ _ _ O _ RE

A H E R C R

"Oh, my God," I murmur and then unscramble the letters.

ARCHER

My pulse picks up as I stare at the letters that spell my last name—his last name. I then look at the remaining letters.

S O R E

Tears prick my eyes and my hands tremble.

I take another lick of the sweet frosting, and he ruffles my hair with his hand, continuing his doting, saying, "My little Elizabeth Rose Archer."

R O S E

ASHER CORRE

ROSE ARCHER

"Oh, my God!" I blurt out as I lurch off the couch, covering my mouth with my two hands. My heart beats rapidly as I stare down in shock at the notepad where my middle and last name look up at me. This can't be a coincidence.

It's him!

And suddenly, I can hear his voice so clearly.

"My little Elizabeth Rose Archer."

"Declan!" I holler, grabbing the notepad and running across the penthouse.

I sling the bedroom door open, waking him up when it slams against the door jamb.

"Declan, it's him! It's him!"

He leaps out of bed, still half asleep. "What's going on?"

"It's my dad!" I cry out. "Look!"

I show him the notepad, and he takes it from my hand.

"What am I looking at?" he questions at the paper that's filled with so many names, and I point to *ASHER CORRE.*

"That's him! The letters in that name spell *ROSE ARCHER.*"

"Who's Rose?"

I look up at him, tears streaming down my cheeks, and I can barely breathe when I tell him, "Me."

He stares at me, confusion etching his face, and I claim without a shred of doubt, "My name is Elizabeth Rose Archer, and that man is my dad."

twenty-one

"THERE'S A LISTING for an A. CORRE in Washington," Declan tells me from behind his laptop. "Gig Harbor, Washington. There's no more information."

"In Washington? Is that him?"

"Only one way to find out," he says. "I had the plane scheduled to take us back to London, so I'll have to wait until morning to call and get it rescheduled."

Adrenaline intoxicates me, putting my body on high alert. My heart pounds, begging me to strap on my shoes and run across the country to get to my dad because waiting seems like an impossible feat. I pace the room, and when that dulls, I pack my bags, and when that's done, I get on Declan's computer and search every social media site and people-finder database to see if anything pops up.

Nothing, aside from what Declan had found. City and state. That's it.

The night drags on, testing every ounce of patience in me. Seconds feel like hours and hours feel like years, and after an eternity, the sun rises. Declan is beyond demanding when he calls to reschedule the plane, and I feel sorry for the poor sap that's on the other end of the line. He barks his orders, and when he hangs up, tells me, "Grab the bags."

"We're leaving now?"

"Yes."

We move at lightning speed as we get all our belongings together, but it's still not fast enough for my growing anxiety. Thank God for his private jet, because the flight takes less than four hours. Once we're settled into our hotel suite in Tacoma, I ask, "Now what?"

"Now we need to find a way to get his address."

"How far is Gig Harbor from here?"

"Twenty minutes or so. Not far," he tells me.

I sit and think, and it doesn't take but a couple minutes for the idea to pop into my head.

"Can you look up the utility companies in that town?" I ask Declan who is already on his laptop.

I walk over and stand behind him while he looks up the information for me. He pulls up the number, and I quickly punch it into my cell phone and send the call.

"City of Gig Harbor," a lady answers.

"Yes, I'm calling on behalf of my brother, Asher Corre. He's been in an accident and is currently in the hospital and unresponsive. We don't know when he's going to pull out of his current state, so I wanted to make sure that his bill is up to date," I lie, and when I look to Declan, he gives me a smirk at my quick thinking.

"What was the name again?"

"Asher Corre."

I hear her typing at her keyboard before saying, "Yes. Our records show that there is currently a zero balance."

"Oh, good," I respond. "In the meantime, would it be possible to have a paper copy of his bill mailed to the house. I know he pays online, but since I don't have access to his passwords, I want to make sure that I can pay via snail mail."

"Of course. Yes. We can definitely have the bill mailed out to you."

"Great. And just to make certain, can you tell me the address you have on file?"

"I'm showing 19203 Fairview Lane with a zip code of 98332."

"That's correct. Thank you so much for your help."

I hang up, and Declan asks, "Did you get it?"

"That was too easy, and that woman was too trusting," I respond and then hand him the paper with the address.

He punches it into his computer. "There it is."

"Let's go!" I blurt with excitement, anxious to see if it's really him.

"Hold on," he says. "We can't just go showing up on his doorstep. He's hiding from something or someone, so we need to be careful for his sake and also yours."

He's right. I need to slow down for a second and think this through.

"I think we should get in the car and drive by. Check the place out. We need to verify that this is indeed your father first."

"Okay." I'll agree to just about anything at this point.

We're back in the car and driving to the address we were given, and soon enough, we're pulling into a nice suburban neighborhood with large,

New England-style coastal houses lining the streets. Children are outside riding bikes and playing, and people are walking their dogs. Everyone looks happy, enjoying the last hours of the afternoon before the sun sets.

Declan slows the car when he turns onto Fairview but doesn't stop as we pass the house.

"It's this one. The two-story colonial," he says.

I look out the windshield at the beautiful house, and my stomach knots when I think about that being my father's home.

"I say we give it a couple hours, let it get darker, and then we come back. Maybe we can catch him coming home from work."

Anxiety mixed with every other emotion swarms in the pit of my gut. How can this possibly be happening when I've spent my whole life mourning his death? And now there's a possibility that I might see him tonight, that he could be alive. It's too much for me to understand and digest.

"Elizabeth?"

My throat restricts like a vice around the sadness inside, and I simply look at him and nod my approval to his plan.

We kill time and head to a local coffee joint. Declan makes a few business calls while I sip a hot tea and read some local Gazette magazine with all the town's happenings. We drove around for a bit before stopping here, and it seems like a quaint place to live. There isn't much, and everything is really spread out, but the neighborhoods are nice.

"We should get going," Declan says, and I quickly order another tea to go.

Very few words have been spoken today; my emotions are much too high to talk, and Declan hasn't pushed for conversation, which I appreciate. I need the silence right now.

Hopping back into the inconspicuous four-door car that Declan rented, we head back over to the house. This time, when we enter the neighborhood, the sidewalks are empty and the streetlights are on. Windows are lit while the families that live inside are probably eating their dinners, and when we pull up to what we think is my dad's home, a few rooms are lit up as well.

We park along the curb on the opposite side of the street, and I stare into the windows, hoping to see something.

"Someone is in there," I whisper.

"I don't see any movement, but I agree. Too many lights are on for nobody to be home."

No cars are in the driveway, but that doesn't mean there aren't any in the garage.

"What do we do?"

"We wait," Declan responds. "See if anyone comes out or if anyone comes home."

So that's what we do.

We sit.

We wait.

My mind doesn't though. It keeps spinning thoughts around, plucking at my heartstrings. They swirl in a kaleidoscope of what-ifs. So many that I can't keep them inside, so I ask Declan, "What if he's married?" My voice trembles in despair. "I mean, this is too big a house for just one person, right?"

Declan looks at me and takes my hand, his face mottled in sorrow, and after a span of silence, he responds, "It's possible."

I look at the clock; it's past eight. We've been sitting out here for hours when bright headlights beam our way.

"Elizabeth," Declan murmurs urgently when the SUV pulls into the driveway.

I hold my breath as my heart pounds rapidly against my chest, the sound filling my ears. Leaning forward, I see the driver's side door open, and when a man steps out, his back is to me. He reaches into the car and pulls out a briefcase at the same time the front door swings open and a young girl comes running out. And when that man turns around, I choke back an audible gasp, gripping Declan's hand tightly.

"That's him," he voices with a look of pure astonishment, but I'm in a state of shock when I see my daddy pull this child into his arms and hug her.

"Dad, why are you so late?" I hear her muffled voice from outside the car ask him, and tears force their way down my cheeks like knives.

"I'm sorry, princess. I got tied up with a client," he says, and I remember his voice like it was just this morning when I heard it last.

But it was *me* that was his princess.

Everything plays in slow motion, and when I look at his face from across the street, there isn't an ounce of uncertainty he's my dad. It's that same face, the same eyes, the same smile that visits me in my dreams. Except now he's older with a head of silver hair. The last I saw him he was in his thirties, and now he's nearing sixty.

But that smile . . .

The smile he gives that girl—his daughter—that was *mine*. It was always mine, and now it's *hers*.

I swore to myself that if I ever found him, I'd run to him, grab him, and never let him go. But when I see a woman and a boy walking out of the house, it's another slap in my face—he's no longer mine to run to. He's *theirs*.

It becomes too much.

I can't believe life would do this to me.

I want to die.

"Drive," I cry, my voice shaky and unrecognizable.

But Declan doesn't start the car.

"Elizabeth . . ."

"Get me out of here," I plead.

He releases my hand and starts the car, and as soon as he begins driving, I split wide open and sob—loud and ugly.

"Oh, my God, Declan. He has a daughter. He has a whole family!"

He reaches over to me and pulls my hand into his lap as all the years of longing burn up in roaring flames. I was disposed of by my dad; I don't exist in his life.

How could he do this?

How could he replace me?

Not only did my mother not want me, but I never thought my dad would feel the same way.

"I thought he loved me," I cry, and the tears feel like hot splashes of acid as they coat my cheeks and drip from my chin. The pain overwhelms like a cleaver to my heart, and everything I thought I knew feels like pure deception. I feel worthless and unloved by the man I've killed for.

I never gave up on life because of *him*.

I kept going because of *him*.

It was all for naught though. He's moved on when twenty-three years later I'm still living for him, dreaming of him, longing for him.

To feel like a nobody to the person who's your everybody is a jagged spike that skewers through the scar tissue of every one of life's blows that mark a permanent wound on my soul.

Suddenly this car is suffocating.

It's too small.

My skin is too tight.

The air is too thick.

I can't breathe.

"Pull over!" I demand, and he does instantly.

Ripping off my seatbelt, I leap out of the car and run.

I don't know where I'm going.

But I run as fast as I can.

I run hard, feet pounding the grass under my feet as I zip across a random field.

"Elizabeth!" Declan's voice echoes behind me, but I don't slow.

My legs begin to burn, my lungs are on fire, but I keep going.

I can hear Declan's feet racing behind me, and I push harder, screaming out my pain. I force it out of my lungs and into the night. The air whips through my hair, and the tears on my face chill against the wind.

"Elizabeth!" he calls again before his hand clutches my arm, sending me tumbling to the ground.

With my hands pressed against Earth's foundation, I tilt my head up to the heavens I can no longer believe in and scream. I scream so hard it hurts, ripping through my vocal cords, searing them, slicing them.

Declan wraps his whole body around mine, every one of his muscles flexing, cocooning me in a steel vice grip. And when my screams strain into an unbearable bleeding agony, I melt and crumple into Declan's warm body.

And I cry.

I cry like I did when I was five years old and watched my daddy as he was being handcuffed and taken from me.

I cry because that's what you do when the person you love most in this world doesn't love you back.

Declan strokes my hair, petting me while he presses his lips to my ear, whispering gently, "Shh, baby."

I allow my mind to focus on his touch, on his smell, and on the sound of his voice. He rocks me in a slow sway, comforting me, and I grip my hands to his back, fisting his shirt with my fingers. And through my cries, I ask, "Why did he do this to me?"

"I don't know, darling," he responds. "But we'll find out. I'll get you answers."

"I don't understand why he never came for me. He's been alive this whole time—my whole life—and he never came for me."

"Maybe it's not what you think," he says, and I look into his eyes and weep, "How could you not come back for your child?"

He doesn't say anything else, he's probably scared he'll dig the knife in deeper. Instead, he stands and scoops me up in his arms, cradling me against his chest. As he walks us back to the car, I rest my head in the crook of his neck and let the tears fall.

He puts me into the car, buckles me in, and not another word is spoken. When we arrive back at our hotel room, he takes over. I'm dead inside, so he bathes me, brushes my teeth, and puts me to bed—all in silence—all while I cling to him.

Because without him, I don't exist—and I need to exist.

twenty-two

I'M WALKING ALONG a busy city street. I'm not sure what city I'm in, but it's filled with noisy cars and too many people to count. I don't know where I'm going, but I go. I follow the crowds. Maybe they know where they're headed.

We all stop at an intersection and wait for the crosswalk sign to light up. Leaning against a large flowerbed that hugs the perimeter of a tall building, I look down to see pink daisies. I grab one of the stems, pluck it from the soil, and watch as a little caterpillar emerges.

I smile when I see my friend.

"There you are, Elizabeth," he greets in his British accent.

"Carnegie!"

I lower my hand for him to crawl onto and then lift him up to my face.

"I've missed you," I tell him.

"It's been much too long."

I stumble on my feet when a bicyclist nearly sideswipes me. Looking back to my hand, Carnegie is no longer there. I scramble, skittering my eyes along the sidewalk, turning in circles.

"Carnegie?" I call out, but he's nowhere to be found.

I'm jostled again, this time by a man as he rushes past me.

"Hey!" I shout, and when the man turns to apologize, I see his face. "Dad?"

"Sorry, miss," my father says as if he doesn't recognize me.

"Dad! It's me!"

He turns, no longer acknowledging me, and I chase after him.

"Dad, wait! It's me!"

He's only walking, but somehow the gap between us widens, and I'm losing him. I whip around a corner and nearly lose my footing. When I right myself, I catch my reflection in the mirrored glass of a building.

I'm five years old and still wearing my glittery princess dress from our last tea party. Turning back in the direction my father was heading, I run while continuing to call out to him. I weave through the crowds of people, dodging elbows, and pushing my way through.

"Daddy!"

I finally catch up to him when he's stuck at a crosswalk.

"Dad," I say when I walk up to him.

He looks down at me with an aged face and silver hair. "Little girl, are you lost?"

"No, Daddy. It's me, your daughter."

He shakes his head. "No, little girl." He then points his finger to a blonde-haired child across the street waving at him. "That's my daughter over there."

I wake with a start.

The room is black.

My heavy breaths are the only sounds I hear.

I roll over, my body numb.

Declan is sound asleep, and when I slide out of bed to get a drink of water, I see that it's five in the morning. I'm rattled by my dream as I sip from a bottle of water while I sit in the living room. I stare out the window at the full moon, and it feels strange to know that only twenty minutes away, the same moon hangs above my dad. Although I doubt I ever cross his mind like he crosses mine.

I think about the girl in my dream—the same girl I saw him call *princess* last night in his driveway. She was young, maybe eight or so. And the more I think about her, the more my hands tingle in acerbic bitterness. Vile thoughts run rampant, thoughts of kidnapping her, thoughts of killing her.

My legs shake erratically, bouncing up and down at a rapid pace. I can't sit still. They're out there—he's out there—and I'm stuck in this hotel room. Thoughts about his new family fester.

I peer at Declan through the bedroom door, and he's still fast asleep. Gently, I close the door after slipping on a pair of pants and a top. Grabbing the keys to the car, I quietly sneak out of the room. He's going to be pissed when he wakes up to find that I'm gone, but if I told him what I'm about to do, he'd refuse. And I can't just sit in that room and drive myself crazy.

Once I'm in the car, I drive back to Gig Harbor and park along the street a few houses down from my dad's. His SUV is no longer in the driveway where he parked it last night. I'm not even sure what I'm doing here.

Time passes, the sun makes her appearance, and eventually the garage door opens. A car begins to back out and then stops halfway down the driveway. I sink down, worried I'll be seen, but keep watching. The driver's side window rolls down and the woman I saw last night hangs her head out and hollers, “Come on, kids!”

A few beats later the blonde girl and the brown-haired boy run out from the garage with backpacks hanging from their shoulders. They hop in the back seat, and when the car starts driving away, I sit up and follow. When we turn out of the neighborhood, I make sure to follow with one car between us.

Hate rises in my soul for these people that my father’s chosen over me. Good or bad, I don’t give a shit—I want to hurt them. I want to take them away from him, then maybe he’ll be so lonely that he’ll finally want me.

My knuckles are white as my hands choke the steering wheel so hard it just might snap. The car pulls off into a strip shopping center, and I follow, parking several spots down from them. The kids hop out of the car, cash in their hands, and run into a smoothie shop while the woman stays in the vehicle.

Without much thought, and honestly, just not caring, I get out of my car. I walk past the woman and see she’s paying no attention as she’s chatting away on her phone. She’s blonde as well and appears many years younger than my dad, and I wish I had a brick to throw through her windshield to smash her pretty little face.

The bell above the door jingles when I step inside the smoothie shop. The two kids are watching the blenders mix up their drinks.

“What can I get for you this morning?” the guy behind the register asks in a much too peppy tone for it being so early in the morning.

I pick a random drink from the menu on the wall and shove him some cash.

“Hailey,” one of the employees calls out, and the girl runs to grab her drink.

Her name’s Hailey. *How fucking precious.*

When I see her walking to the door, I fake clumsiness and bump into her, sending her smoothie to splatter all over the floor.

“Oh, I am so sorry. I wasn’t paying any attention at all.”

“It’s okay,” she says. “Accidents happen.”

I grab a wad of napkins, and with her help, we do our best to clean up the sticky mess

“Let me get you another drink. What flavor did you have?” I offer.

“You don’t have to do that. I can get more money from my mom.”

“I insist.”

She tells me her drink and I place the order.

I reach out my hand and introduce myself. “I’m Erin, by the way.”

She shakes my hand enthusiastically, and giggles, saying, "My name is Hailey."

"I'm going back out to the car," her brother announces as he takes his smoothie with him to the exit. "Hurry up; I don't want to be late to school."

"And that," Hailey says, "Is my annoying older brother, Steve."

Steve. My dad passed his name down to that little fucker.

"You look like you're all ready for school. What grade are you in?" I ask while we wait for her drink.

"Fifth grade."

"Wow. Big girl on campus. So how old does that make you?"

"Eleven."

Her perfect voice, her perfect hair, her perfect clothes all make me want to ball my fist up and slam it through her perfect smile.

"Hailey," the employee calls out, and I fight the overwhelming urge to grab her and run.

"I gotta go. Thanks for the smoothie, Erin." She's so polite it irritates me to the point I want to claw my own skin from my bones.

She practically skips out the door, leaving me to watch their car as it pulls out and drives away.

I snap around when there's a tap on my shoulder.

"I'm sorry, I didn't mean to startle you," the employee says as he holds out a cup. "I called your name, but I guess you didn't hear me."

Without a word, I turn away from him and walk out the door as he stands there like an asshole, still holding my drink.

I hate everyone in this shit town.

Sitting in my car, I can't bring myself to drive just yet. She's eleven years old and has the life I was supposed to have. I was supposed to be the bubbly and polite girl who wore the pretty clothes and grabbed a smoothie before heading off to school. I was supposed to be her. Instead, when I was eleven, I was tied up to a garment rod and locked away in a closet for days on end. I was in the darkness with no food or water, left to piss and shit on myself. And when I wasn't in the closet, I was down in that dank basement being molested, raped, sodomized, pissed on, beaten, and whipped. I wasn't skipping out the goddamn door with my Raspberry Paradise smoothie. Her biggest struggle in life is having an annoying older brother.

I should've grabbed her when I had the chance.

Anger does nothing but ferment in my bones. It aches and pricks from the inside out, and I ball my hands, pounding them against the steering wheel as I growl between my clenched teeth. When I look up, I see an elderly lady staring at me in horror as she walks on by.

She has no idea that she's staring at a monster.

Smoothing my hair back off my forehead, I straighten myself and start the car. It's edging on eight o'clock, and I need to get back to the hotel.

I stand outside of our room and prepare myself for the wrath of Declan before opening the door.

"Where the fuck have you been?" he seethes as soon as I walk in. "Tell me it's not what I'm thinking. Tell me you didn't go back to that house."

Keeping my cool so I don't rile him up any more than he already is, I admit, "I went back to the house."

"Jesus Christ! What were you thinking?" he snaps, grabbing my arms and shaking me.

"I don't know, but I had to go. I knew you wouldn't allow it, so I snuck out."

He shoves me over to the couch and pushes me down, releasing my arms. I watch as he paces the room a couple times before walking back over to me. He takes a seat on the coffee table and faces me. His jaw is locked, a tell to his immense anger. I knew how much my sneaking away would affect him. Declan has to hold all the power for him to feel safe, and I stole that from him this morning.

"It's not what you think." I attempt to mollify him.

"Tell me, since you seem to know everything about me. Tell me what it is I'm thinking." He throws his derisive words in my face.

"I had to see them. I had to know more."

"*Them*?" he questions, growing more irritated. "You mean his kids?"

I nod.

"Christ, Elizabeth," he barks, standing and walking away from me.

"Stop yelling at me!" I snap, getting off the couch and stepping up to him. "You're pissed, I get it! But the expectation you have for me to just sit and be patient is something I can't do."

"You *can't* or you *won't*?"

"I'm not apologizing, if that's what you're after."

I watch him grind his teeth as he glares down at me, and I turn this around on him, saying, "Why don't you tell *me* something . . . If this were reversed, and it were your mother in this situation, tell me you'd be okay just hanging back. Tell me you wouldn't act on every single one of your instincts."

His eyes pierce mine, and I push him even more.

"Tell me you could restrain yourself and stay away."

We meet each other's opposition, neither one of us backing down.

"He's my dad, so don't you dare yell at me and belittle me for acting on my desperation, because you'd do the same thing."

I turn to walk away from him, and when I do, he finally speaks.

"You won't defy me again. Do you understand?"

I look back at him and respond, "Then I need you to bend and trust me. I snuck away because I knew you'd refuse to allow me to go. All I'm asking is for you to at least try to see things my way every once in a while."

"Come here," he orders, and I obey, walking back over to him. He takes my face in his hands, telling me, "I'll try and bend for you."

"Thank you," I respond with an appeased smile.

"You will be punished, so I wouldn't be smiling if I were you," he threatens, and I don't contest.

Declan needs this to feel in control, and I want to give him that because it's what secures him. He depends on it. He can't function without it.

"I want you on the ground on all fours with your pants pulled down to your knees."

He lashes his voice out in anger, and I turn my back to him, positioning myself as instructed. It might be debasing for most, but I understand his need for this. It's how his life has molded him to be, and I'm the perfect one to give him this outlet that he's been deprived of in the past. I'm sure the women he's been with previously have valued their bodies in a way I don't. And because I love him so much, I have no problem handing myself over to him in this way.

I hear him move around the room, and then he kneels down in front of me to tie my wrists together with one of his ties.

"Tell me why I'm punishing you."

I crane my neck to look at him, and answer, "Because I snuck off and took the control away from you."

"Do you know what that did to me?"

"Yes."

He then stands and moves behind me.

"Keep your eyes on the floor," he commands, and I hear something rattling before being set on the ground. "Spread your knees."

I do, and I'm instantly greeted by the piercing pain of an ice cube being shoved into my pussy. And then another and another and another and another.

I cry out in blistering pain and then he begins to spank my ass with a force so great I have to tense my whole body up to keep myself from falling over. The ice feels like I'm being sliced with razors from the inside, and I know I should be focusing on the pain that's radiating from my ass because it's so minimal compared to what's happening inside my pussy.

With each welting blow he delivers, I scream out as the ice begins to melt and the water spills out of me and runs down my thighs.

"Tell me you're my property," he grits, and I instantly respond, "I'm your property."

THWACK!

"Tell me who owns you."

"You own me."

THWACK!

"Tell me you love me."

"I love you, Declan."

THWACK!

"On your elbows," he barks, and the moment I lower myself, his mouth is on my pussy, sucking out the melted ice from inside me.

His hot tongue is an erotic contrast to the freezing shards, and I let go of a heady moan while he buries his face between my legs. My mind rushes in waves of mania at the infliction of a multitude of sensations that I didn't even notice that he's now fucking me with his cock.

I close my eyes when the whole world blurs, and all that matters is this moment—having our two bodies blended as one—and it's only together that we're whole.

twenty-three

THE ICE BUCKET and tie still remain on the floor from earlier. Declan has refused to let me clean myself up, so I sit and wait for him to finish his shower. I decide to log onto the laptop and search to see if Hailey has any social media accounts. When no hits come up, I move on to search her brother, Steve, which brings me to a link for a Steve Corre in Gig Harbor, Washington.

Clicking the link, I pull up his page. His profile picture is of him and a few of his buddies. I start clicking on different tabs on his page, but there's no real information aside from his birthday, which lets me know he's thirteen years old.

It's not until I open one of his photo albums that the vile hate from earlier resurfaces. I scroll through picture after picture of family photos, my dad being in most of them. Photos of family vacations, birthday parties, holidays fill the albums—all the things I never got a chance to experience.

Once I was in Posen with Pike, I never got a birthday party, and most holidays I'd find myself locked in the closet so Carl and Bobbie wouldn't have to deal with me. Pike would always manage to steal or use his drug money to buy me something small, but aside from those private gift exchanges in my bedroom, we never celebrated anything.

I despise these kids for the life my dad has given them, the life I never had. I look at their smiles, and I want to slit their throats. And then there's my dad. Enlarging a photo with him in it, I zoom in on his face. His eyes are still the same, even though the crinkles in the corners from when he smiles have deepened. He no longer has the scruff of a beard, exchanging it for a clean-shaven face. When I close my eyes, I can see the younger him in vivid color. I can hear his laughter. I can smell his cologne.

God, I miss him so much.

Opening my eyes, I'm greeted by this stranger who wears the same face. I don't know this man—Asher Corre. My heart double beats in love and anger. I love my dad, the man who danced with me, sang to me, and laughed with me. But I hate this man on the computer screen. I hate him for wearing the mask of my father, because he's nothing like my dad. My dad loved me beyond love, and *this* man, I don't even exist in his world. I'm nothing but an evaporated memory.

"What are you looking at?" Declan questions when he walks into the room, fresh from the shower dressed in navy slacks, a fitted light blue button-down, and the same black belt he used to restrain me a few days ago.

"Looking at family portraits," I respond, and he tilts his head in curiosity.

When he sits next to me, I can smell the cardamom from his shampoo. Even in the midst of everything going on around us and our quarrel this morning, I feel the need to be close to him.

He is already sliding the computer from my lap when he asks, "Where did you find these?"

"It's his son's social media page."

"His son? How did you even know how to find this?"

"Because I followed them. I got his name from his sister, Hailey."

"I need you to tell me what happened this morning."

"Can you control your anger?" I snark, to which he responds, "You're testing your limits today with that smart mouth of yours. Tell me what happened."

I go through everything that occurred, from following the car to what was said between Hailey and me.

"You shouldn't have ever approached that girl," he scolds. "She's just a kid."

"There are worse monsters out there than me, Declan. If I could handle my life at eleven, then surely she can handle a conversation in a smoothie shop."

"That girl is a part of your dad."

I look at him, angry that he would go there, and snap, "But I'm *all* of him."

"I'm on your side here."

"Then stop defending that family."

"I need you to see things rationally though," he says.

"Nothing about this whole situation is rational, Declan."

He backs off and turns his attention back to the computer, scrolling through the photos. When there's one I want to look at, I tell him to stop. It isn't until a few more photos pass that I realize the kid tags his location when he posts.

"Scroll slowly," I murmur to Declan when I lean in to get a closer look.

"What are you doing?"

"He tags his location in his pictures," I tell him, and we strike gold. "Stop. Click on that one."

Declan enlarges a photo of my dad and his son that has the comment: *Spending my day at work with Dad.*

"Enterprise Brokerage and Realty," Declan reads off.

Declan opens up another window and types the business name into the search bar, and up pops their website with my father's picture on the main page.

"He runs his own firm," he says. "We've got a point of contact now."

"Do we just call him?"

"No. We need to find a way to get him to come to us. But, listen, we have to be careful about this. Whatever he's hiding from is big. I mean, your case worker, a state employee, came to you and told you he died. The man even has a grave site, right?"

"Yes. In Illinois," I say. "I went to the cemetery. He has a gravestone and everything."

"So, this isn't some man who just skipped town. This is a man who needed to kill his identity."

"How do we do this?"

Declan takes a moment to think and then pulls out his phone. "I'll just schedule a meeting with him. There's nothing that links you and me that he would be able to find out about. We've never even been photographed together."

I nod, and when he dials, I tell him, "Put it on speakerphone," because I need to hear his voice.

With each ring, my pulse quickens, and then the line connects.

"Enterprise Brokerage and Realty, how can I help you?"

"Is Asher Corre available?" Declan asks, his accent seeming to catch the woman off guard.

"Oh . . . um, yes. Whom shall I say is calling?" she says, and I roll my eyes at Declan when her whole voice changes in reaction to his voice.

"You can tell him this is Declan McKinnon with McKinnon International Development."

"Just one moment."

I'm practically holding my breath while we wait, and then he picks up the call, his voice crystal clear.

"Asher Corre here."

I bring my hands to cover my mouth when I hear the voice I never thought I'd hear again.

"Good afternoon. This is Declan McKinnon, owner of McKinnon International Development. I have to apologize for the short notice, but I'm in town for a few days and was hoping to discuss a possible land purchase for commercial development."

"What line of commercial development are you in?"

"Hospitality on the high-end scale."

"So I see. I just pulled you up on my computer. McKinnon, is that of Scottish descent?" he asks Declan, and I can't believe he's actually having a conversation with my dad. Declan responds, and then my father continues, "I can start pulling some locations to email you?"

"Call me old-fashioned, but I hope you don't mind my preference to conduct business in person rather than over the phone. I want to establish that you're the right man to be working with. After all, if a purchase is made, you'll be receiving a substantial commission. I want to make sure it's going to someone with integrity."

"I couldn't agree with you more. I'll tell you what, how does your evening look tonight?"

"I have a few emails that need attending to, but other than that, I'm free."

"Would six o'clock work?"

"That works. I've had a tiring couple of days, so why don't we meet at The Pearl's Edge where I'm staying. I'm in the Presidential suite."

He doesn't even hesitate when he responds, "I'll see you at six, Mr. McKinnon."

I watch Declan end the call and set the phone down. "His voice . . ." I start and then lose my words.

"Are you okay?"

I can't speak for a while as I try to digest hearing my father on the phone. It doesn't even feel real, and to know that he'll be here in only a few hours is something I'm unable to process.

"Darling?"

"I never thought I'd hear that voice again. I believed it was gone forever, and now . . ."

"I know. You don't have to try to put it into words."

"I don't even know how to feel. One minute I'm relieved he's alive, and the next I'm so furious. But now, he's coming here, and I'm excited and terrified."

"There's no right way to feel. I think the most important thing is to allow yourself to feel it all," he says.

"I just need you to hold me right now," I tell him.

I curl up in his arms and close my eyes while he runs his hands up and down my back. I open myself up to his comfort and take all I can. It's a myriad of extremities in my heart and head, but somehow, Declan is powerful enough to temper the storm in me.

His warmth is able to relax me enough that eventually I drift off, and when I wake, he's still holding me. I look out the windows and see the sky rippled in waves of pinks and oranges.

"How are you feeling?" Declan asks softly.

My voice is sleepy when I respond, "That's a hard question to answer."

He leans down and kisses me. "Why don't you freshen up before he gets here?"

What does one wear when they meet their dead father for the first time after twenty-three years? After I shower, I dig through my suitcases that I never got around to unpacking yesterday and pull out a pair of black pants and a flowy green top. I busy myself, focusing on making sure I look nice for him; maybe it's me subconsciously distracting myself or maybe it's because I honestly want to look pretty for my dad.

I don't really know.

I dry my hair and fix it with free-flowing waves and then apply my usual light makeup and sweep a little gloss across my lips. I slip on a pair of black flats before giving myself a lookover in the mirror.

My stomach twists in nervousness. I have no idea what I'm going to say to him or how I'm going to react. I've dreamt endlessly about magically getting my dad back, and now that it's here and it's real, I'm suddenly terrified.

"You look perfect."

When I turn to Declan leaning against the threshold, I give him a tight smile. "Are you sure?" I ask, suddenly feeling self-conscious.

"I know you're nervous and worried, but try not to psych yourself out."

"What if I can't do this?"

"And what if you can?" he counters. "Come here."

I walk into his arms and hold on to him.

"You're trembling," he notes. "Why don't I get you a drink to help with your nerves?"

I follow him into the living room and before we make it over to the wet bar, there's a knock on the door.

Stopping dead in my tracks, all the air is sucked out of my lungs, and I'm momentarily paralyzed. Declan looks back to me, and I'm in shock.

"That's him."

twenty-four

MY WHOLE BODY freezes, and I swear my heart skips a beat or two. I'm wide-eyed as Declan looks at me. I can't speak. My skin pricks in goose bumps

Declan places his hands on my cheeks and tells me with sure-fire intensity, "You can do this."

Nodding my head, I speak around the lump lodged in my throat. "Don't let go of me."

"I won't."

Hand in hand, we walk over to the door. Each step I take feels like a marathon's worth of strides. My heart tremors, pumping erratically beneath my bones.

Another knock.

I reach out my jittery hand, and a wave of nausea hits hard when I hold my breath and open the door.

It's him.

His eyes meet mine, and I can't speak. I can literally reach out and touch him, but I don't. I'm too scared he might disappear if I make any sudden movements. He looks at me in confusion. His eyes give a little flick, and I wonder if there's maybe a hint of recognition.

"Dad."

My voice falters and his eyes widen in curiosity, but it's when that very look morphs into astonishment that I know he knows. In one fluid movement, he takes a step towards me and pulls me into his arms.

"Oh, my God," he breathes in disbelief, and I wrap my free arm around him as the tears start falling. "Elizabeth?"

"It's me, Dad," I tell him as my emotions swell to ungodly proportions.

His hold on me is the strongest I've felt in my whole life. And all of a sudden, my fears, my reservations, my hatred, it vanishes. Declan lets go of my other hand, and I cling it around my dad. His back quakes in my hold, and I hear the click of Declan closing the door as the two of us cry.

He cradles my head in his deft hand, the same way he did when I was a little girl, and chokes out, "My baby princess."

He draws back, bracing my head in his hands, and scans my face.

"My God, you're *so* beautiful," he says thickly.

His words mend wounds, and when my face crumples in sobs, I drop my head and he pulls me back against his chest. My body heaves as I release years and years of agony. I want to speak a thousand words, but I can't stop crying. I can't stop clinging. I simply can't let go.

"Let me look at you again," he says when he pulls back and dips his head down to my level.

He's blurry colors and lines, and when I blink, he comes into clarity only to be dissolved all over again. Tears continue to flood and fall as he wipes my cheeks with his thumbs. My hands clutch to his sides, and I painfully weep. "I've missed you so much, Dad."

"Oh, sweetheart, I've missed you even more. The pain of losing you . . . I feel it every second of every day."

"Then why? Why didn't you ever come for me?"

"Oh, princess," he sighs, hanging his head. "I wanted to. So many times I wanted to."

"Then why didn't you?"

Something inside me shifts, and all the pain and anger begins to rise through the enormous joy I feel from being in his arms. It collides and battles, and when he looks up at me, I take a step back and snap, "You just left me!"

Declan takes my hand as my father stares at me, drowning in visible shame.

"Darling . . ."

"I needed you," I sling at him. "I've needed you since the day I lost you!"

"I'm so sorry, sweetheart. Why don't we sit down and talk?"

I turn to Declan, shaking my head, and he encourages, "Nothing you say will be wrong. I won't let you fall apart, okay?"

Leaning my head against his chest, he strokes my hair back and kisses my head before placing his hand on my back. "Let's go sit."

We walk over to the living room, and I take a seat next to my dad on the couch as Declan sits on the other side of me, extending his hand out to my dad, saying, "I'm Declan, by the way."

My father shakes his hand, responding, "Asher."

"That's *not* your name," I accuse, my voice still shuddering through consuming emotions as I look into his eyes. I try with everything I have to pull myself together, but I can't stop the deluge of new tears that fall.

Declan places his hand on my leg, and my dad holds my two hands in his. I watch as he takes in a deep breath before saying, "I'm not sure what to say or where to begin. I never thought I'd ever be sitting next to you, looking into your eyes, holding your hands, hearing your voice."

"You could've been. All these years, you could've had me. But instead, you left me to battle this world on my own."

"You have to believe me when I tell you that's the last thing I ever wanted to do."

"But you did it anyway."

He drops his head again, and I can see his eyes well up.

"I need you to tell me why," I insist. "I need to know why you abandoned me."

"I didn't abandon you, sweetheart."

He blinks and a couple tears skitter down his aged cheeks.

"You did!" I lash out, yanking my hands from his. "You're here! Alive! And living a fucking lie!" I suck in a ragged breath, stand up, and pace across the room before crying out, "You have a whole family! I saw them! A son and a fucking daughter!" Gripping my head with my hands, I stand and face him. "You just . . . you just replaced me as if I never existed. As if I never even mattered."

"No one could *ever* replace you," he asserts, standing up and walking over to me.

"I'm just a forgotten nobody."

"I've never forgotten you," he says as he starts to unbutton the top of his dress shirt. "You've always been with me."

As his collar and shirt begin to fall open, I see the ink of a tattoo, and when he exposes his chest, I stop breathing.

There, across the span of his chest, from shoulder to shoulder, is my name branded on his skin in large script.

"Even if I wanted to, I could never forget about you."

I reach out and run my fingers over the letters of my name. "When did you . . . ?"

"Shortly after I was sent to prison. I had my cellmate do it."

I press my hand to his chest and feel his heart beat into my palm.

"I don't understand. They told me you died in there."

He buttons his shirt back up, asking, "Will you let me explain?"

I nod and he holds my hand as we walk back over to the couch where

Declan is still sitting. My father keeps my hand in his and Declan wraps his arm around my waist as I face my dad.

"They told you why I went to prison, right?"

"Gun trafficking."

He nods. "Seven years into my sentence, the feds came to meet with me. It seems that one of the guns was used to assassinate four government officials from the United States Gun Trafficking Task Force while they were in Argentina to bust one of their bigger drug cartels," he explains. "All the guns that went through me were inspected to ensure the serial numbers had been properly shaved off, but when you're working with the street runners, mistakes are bound to happen. Anyway, the feds offered me a plea deal. I hand over the names in exchange for an immediate release. I knew the risk, but I would've walked through a firing squad to get you back," he says fervently, and I strengthen my hold on his hand.

"So what happened?"

"Turns out, it was a ruse," he reveals. "Once I handed over the names, that was it, I was given two options: go immediately into witness protection, or go back to my cell. If I went back to my cell, I would've been dead in a matter of days; I was a nark and some of those guys I was in there with were in some way affiliated with the names I had just given the feds." He takes my other hand in his and looks at me intently. "They used you to get to me, princess. I knew from that moment that I'd never see you again, and it felt like I was being murdered anyway, because my life didn't exist without you in it."

"And your gravesite?"

"Since the threat level on my life was so great, the feds thought it best to stage my death. I begged them to let me take you into the program with me, but they refused. My hands were tied. A part of me thought it would be better for you that way though. I figured it would give you closure instead of me simply disappearing with no trace." He takes a moment to collect himself before saying, "And here you are. All grown up and so gorgeous."

I continue to shed heartache as memories from the day I was told he died fall from my eyes and down my face. I remember lying in bed with Pike. He held me for hours as I sobbed.

"They assured me you were in a good home and that you even had a foster brother."

Declan's hand suddenly constricts on my leg; he thinks I'm going to tell my dad about my suffering. A part of me wants to because it was a lie—I wasn't in a good home—and the resentment of what could've been festers in me. I want to tell him about the torture I endured so I can slap him in the face with it. I'm furious that I was cheated from the good life he assumed I had.

But I'm not going to tell him—I can't. I have to lie, because telling him the truth would serve no purpose. The past is done, and it can't be changed, it would only hurt him to know, and in the end, I just want his love.

"They told me you were happy and thriving."

I muster up a smile. "Yes, I was happy."

"And your foster parents . . . they were good to you?"

"Mmm hmm," I respond and nod. "I was well taken care of."

The lie is a rusted spike through my veins; it's nearly debilitating to see the relief in his eyes.

"Are you all still close?"

"No. They actually died," I tell him. "And so did my brother." And the tears that puddle in my eyes from the mere mention of Pike are taken by my dad as sorrow for my whole foster family. They aren't—they're solely for Pike. What he doesn't know and will never know is that all three of them died because of me—by my hands.

"I'm so sorry. Do you have other family?"

"Only Declan," I tell him.

"Are you two married?"

"No," Declan answers. "We live together though."

"Close?"

"Declan's home is in Scotland, but we recently moved to London."

"Wow. That sounds amazing," he says with a sullen expression. "Can I ask how you found me?"

"I saw your face on the news," I tell him. "Someone Declan and I know was able to get ahold of the passenger manifest. It took a while for me to discover that Asher Corre was you—was *me*."

"Rose Archer," he murmurs. "Like I said, you've always been with me."

My chin quivers, and I have to ask, "Those are your biological kids, aren't they?"

"Yes."

I look away from my dad. It hurts too much to think they are getting everything I was deprived of.

"I met Gillian shortly after I entered the program. I was so low from losing you, and she helped me stand back up."

"She knows about me?"

"I had to lie to her. She knows I had a daughter named Elizabeth, but I had to tell her that you . . ." His words stall, and I pick them up, positive of what they are and resume for him, "You told her I died, didn't you?"

He nods. "I would've never done so, but the tattoo . . . it's what I was instructed by the government to tell people if anyone were to ask."

"You love her?"

"I do."

"And you gave your son your name—your *real* name."

"I did."

"And your . . . your dau—" I stammer through mounting anguish. "Your daughter . . . you lo—"

"She didn't replace you," he insists.

"But you love her?"

"I do. But don't you dare think for a second that it's the same love I have for you. It isn't. I will *never* love anyone the way I love you."

"You call her princess," I state. "I heard you call her princess."

"You heard me?"

"I was parked across the street from your house last night," I confess. "You were late getting home."

"Sweetheart—" he starts and then stops when I drop my head and start crying.

He wraps his hand behind my head, and I lean against him while Declan rests his reassuring hands on my shoulders. My father's lips press against the top of my head, the same way Declan often does, and I squeeze my dad's hands.

How can I finally be with him and at the same time feel so lost? Feel so excluded?

I want to scream out how unfair this is the way a child would, but I hold it inside.

"You won't be able to tell them about me, will you?"

"No."

I look back up at him, and with a defeated shrug of my shoulders, I ask, "So what now?"

He presses my hands to his chest, affirming, "You are my daughter. Nothing will ever change that. You are the beat of my heart. It's always been you."

Lifting up on my knees, I sling my arms around his neck and latch on to him as he holds me close.

"I love you so much, Dad."

"I love you too, baby girl," he responds. "I love you too."

We embrace each other for as long as it takes for me to cry out all the tears my body has to give, and he never loosens his hold on me. He remains constant, never attempting to pull away from me, all the while repeating how much he loves me, how much he's missed me, and how much he's dreamt about me.

And when nothing else remains except swollen eyes and stinging cheeks, I let go of his neck.

"Can I see you tomorrow?" he asks.

"I'm scared to let you go," I tell him. "What if you don't come back?"

"I'll come back. I put my life on that promise, okay?"

"Okay," I respond, but the fear remains. Terrified that this could possibly be the last time I see him, I grab him and kiss his cheek.

I know all too well how much life can change in an instant.

"I'll be here at nine a.m."

He stands and pulls me up with him, giving me another strong hug. This time, he kisses my forehead and then my cheek and then my forehead again.

"No more tears," he says as he walks to the door with me tucked under his arm.

"Promise me you're coming back."

He lifts my chin, saying, "I promise," and then plants a kiss on top of my head again.

"Declan," my dad acknowledges, "take care of her tonight, will you?"

"Every day of my life, sir."

My father hands me off to Declan, and I trade the warmth of my father for the warmth of my love. I can't stomach the thought of watching him walk out the door, so I bury my head against Declan's chest until I hear the click of the door closing.

twenty-five

WHEN YOU MAKE a wish on a star and it delivers, serving its purpose, then what happens? Does it die? Does it go on to serve someone else's wish? Maybe it rejoices, exploding into a million shimmering, dusting sparkles that flicker down through the stratosphere. It could be that those very particles are what create hope in this world. And maybe that's why I always carried a little piece of that star with me. As much as I wanted to give up on hope, as much as I thought the notion of it was a crock of shit, a miniscule piece of it always lingered in me.

It's a rainy morning as I move about, again full of jittery nerves, and get ready to see my dad—my wish upon a star. Declan has ordered up a tray of food, but I'm too wound up to eat. And I'd be lying if I said I wasn't also scared that he wouldn't show up. I'm all too familiar with Murphy's Law. That law has plagued my life continuously, so why wouldn't it do the same now? Nothing in this world is resistant to change. It can happen in a split second, with no warning at all.

But my mood shifts as soon as I hear the knock on the door.

I look over to Declan, and he wraps up the business call he's on.

This time, I don't feel like passing out. Instead, there's an air of effervescence when I open the door and see my dad standing there with a bouquet of pink daisies. I smile with a wisp of a laugh when he steps inside and closes the door.

"I hope you still like daisies," he says when he hands them to me, and I'm in his arms the next second, responding, "They're my favorite."

Neither of us rushes the embrace. We settle in it and allow ourselves to bask in the comfort we were both robbed of for over twenty years. I inhale, taking in his scent, which reminds me of the past. How is it that I can still remember the way he smelled all those years ago? But I do remember, and it's the same now as it was then. My eyes fall shut as I revel in the moment, a moment that most would fleet through. Yet, when someone has been so deprived, they understand the importance a single touch can hold.

"I couldn't sleep at all last night," he tells me, still holding me in his strong arms, allowing me to decide when to let go, but I'm not ready just yet.

"Me neither."

After another minute or so, I finally loosen my arms and pull back.

His eyes roam my face for a moment before he finally says, "I just can't get over how much you've grown and how much time has actually passed."

"Are you saying I look old?" I quip, making him laugh, and it's such a beautiful sound.

"Old? Are you kidding. Have you seen this gray mop on me?"

I smile big. "You wear silver well."

"Distinguished?"

"Very distinguished."

"Good morning, sir," Declan greets as he approaches us.

"Declan," he responds, shaking Declan's outstretched hand. "Please, call me Asher."

I flick my head to my dad, and he catches my shift immediately, apologizing, "I'm sorry. Habit after nearly fifteen years." He then looks to Declan again and corrects to appease me. "Call me Steve."

"I ordered up some breakfast," Declan says and leads my dad to the dining table that seats eight.

"This room is impressive," he notes as we take our seats next to each other.

I lay the daisies on the table in front of me, suddenly feeling nervous. My dad senses my unease right away, takes my hand in his, and smiles at me. "I'm nervous too."

"You are?"

"Yes," he says through an awkward laugh.

"Steve, would you like some coffee?"

"Sounds great, Declan. Thank you."

Declan pours a mug of coffee for my dad, a tea cup of hot water for me, and then takes a seat across the table from us.

I pluck a buttery croissant from the platter in front of us and then dunk a bag of tea into my cup. The silence between us is thick, and when I look up, my dad is staring at me over the rim of his mug, which makes me pause.

"What?"

With a grin on his face, he shakes his head and answers, "The last time I saw you, you were sipping make-believe tea, and now here you are, all grown up, drinking the real thing."

I smile through the heartbreaking memories of that day. "And I remember you licking imaginary frosting from your imaginary cupcake. You didn't even use a napkin."

"You remember that?"

I nod as the ache inflames. "I remember every detail from that day."

My eyes brim with tears, and I fight hard to keep them from falling.

"I'm so sorry that had to happen in front of you. It killed me to know that was your last image of me."

"You're here now." I need to steer away from what will ultimately break me if I think about it too much. "And oddly enough," I add with a smirk, "this kind of reminds me of that last tea party. I mean, I don't have a sparkly princess dress on, but I've got my pink daisies, tea, snacks, and you."

"True," he says. "But back then, I was your prince. And it seems that position is no longer available."

I turn to Declan who comically lifts his coffee cup in accomplished pride and exaggerated dignity, and I laugh.

"He's seems like a suitable replacement, right?" my dad jokes.

"He fits the role perfectly."

"Since that's the case, an interrogation is in order, don't you think?" my dad says.

"I'm up for the challenge, Steve."

I take a sip of my tea, thoroughly enjoying the fact that the three of us can make light of the situation at hand, and at the same time, knowing I can share this huge piece of my past with Declan.

"So, I did indeed look you up on the Internet. You're quite accomplished for being in your early thirties."

"I'm a hard worker."

"What took you from Scotland to Chicago?"

"My father had done a few developments in the States before I graduated with my master's degree. I had always been interested in the business, so I moved here and worked with him for a little while before going out on my own. I found a great location in Chicago and decided to go for it."

"Lotus, right?"

"That's right," Declan says.

"It's an exquisite hotel," I note to my dad.

"But now you're in London?"

Declan takes a sip of his coffee before answering. "Yes. The build won't begin for another year or so. I just bought the property and am currently working with the architects on the scope and concept for what I'm wanting out of the building."

"You enjoy what you do?"

"I love it. I'm a hands-on man and the job lends itself to fulfill that capability. It's also a great feeling to see the process from beginning to end."

"I can only imagine the pride you must feel to see your ideas come to life," he says before asking, "Tell me, how did the two of you meet?"

"I met him at the grand opening gala," I tell him.

Seeming satisfied after grilling Declan, he then turns to me. "What about you? What is it that you do? Did you go to college?"

I've already lied to him and allowed him to believe I had a good childhood and lived in a loving foster home, which he naïvely took for truth, but I need him to believe it. I refuse to punish him with my reality, since he's not to blame for his absence in my life. We were both robbed from each other and lied to, but I keep the lies alive and tell him some half-truths.

"My foster parents died before I was old enough to attend college. I lived with my brother for most of my life because of the financial situation we both found ourselves in. I did take a few classes here and there, but ultimately never got the chance to seriously pursue anything that would lead to a career."

"Well, you must have done something right to be in the midst of people who were attending this gala. Doesn't seem like something anyone off the streets could just attend; the hotel seems quite exclusive and private," my dad says.

"I had a few friends in that circle," I lie—sort of.

"So, how long ago was that?"

"A little over four months," Declan responds.

"That's quick."

"Maybe for some," Declan tells him. "But look at her—I'd be a fool not to snatch her up."

"You make it sound almost like a hostage situation," I tease.

"It's love, darling," he says and then adds, feigning an evil grin, "It takes everyone hostage."

We continue to talk, and my dad and I do our best not to dwell on all that was stolen from us and enjoy that we have each other now. I suggest getting out and going for a walk, and he informs me that, even after all these years, he is still at risk and has random surveillance as a safeguard—a service provided by witness protection for those whom the government sees fit.

"Even after all these years?" I ask him.

"People in the circle I was working in don't take what I did lightly. Lives were lost after I gave the feds what they wanted. I turned my back on them, and now I'm marked in vendetta for life. Those affected will seek out their revenge until one of us is dead."

I don't doubt him, because I'm one of them. I will forever carry the torch of vengeance for those who wronged me and stole from me. Even though I have my father right here in flesh and bone, I'll still seek revenge from those who took him from me in the first place.

His phone rings, and when he pulls it from his pocket, he looks up at me with an apologetic expression. "I'm sorry. I have to take this."

At the same time, Declan also receives a call and excuses himself to the bedroom. My father walks to the other room when he accepts the call, but it isn't far enough to keep me from hearing parts of his conversation.

"I'm with a client . . . I won't be . . . I know . . . I love you too."

"Was that your wife?" I question with a tinge of disdain leaking through after he hangs up.

When he looks at me from across the room, he's visibly uncomfortable. "Umm . . . yes."

I stand and don't say anything. The light mood from earlier is now vexatious as real life intrudes on our clandestine gathering.

"I'm going to have to leave soon."

"Why?" My chest sizzles in irritation when jealousy rears its ugly head.

"Hailey has a recital today."

How fucking lovely.

"You've missed a million things in my life, you can't miss one of hers?"

His forehead creases in confliction, but my resentment spares no lenience.

"It isn't fair," I say thickly.

"I agree, but it's what we have to deal with."

"So . . ." I begin and then pause when Declan walks back into the room.

"Is everything okay?" he asks, sensing the tension, and my father responds, "I have to leave."

"It seems his other daughter has a recital that he can't miss," I tell Declan while keeping my eyes on my dad.

Declan places a supporting hand on the small of my back, and I continue what I was saying. "So, how does this all work then? I mean, if you can't tell them about me . . ."

"I don't really know, sweetheart."

"I mean, when I leave, I won't be able to call you unless you get yourself a burner phone, but then it's only a matter of time before your wife will accuse you of an affair, and then what happens? You'll resent me?" I sputter off, allowing my thoughts to get the better of me.

"We don't have to figure this all out today," Declan says, trying to reassure me, but I'm well aware how sensitive time is and blurt, "Come back with us."

"Princess . . ."

"When we leave, get on the plane with us. Declan owns the plane; no one would even know you were on it."

He moves towards me, saying gently, "I can't leave my family."

His words burn like acid, and I snap. "I'm your family!"

"You are," he says quickly. "But so are they, and I can't just disappear."

"Like you did with me?"

"It's not the same."

My body heats with rage and jealousy. I'm giving him a choice, and he's choosing wrong.

"They've had you!" I cry out. "They've had more years with you than I ever got!"

"Hey," Declan says softly, trying to get my attention, but I ignore him and lash out at my dad.

"So is this what I'm left with? Scraps? That's all I get of you, whatever time you can manage to sneak away from your precious little family?"

"Elizabeth," Declan says in another attempt to get my attention as my dad stands there speechless.

"You used to be mine," I tell my father on a quivering voice. "It was you and me, and we didn't have to share with anyone."

"And now we do." The sorrow in his eyes is reflected in his voice.

"But they get you first."

"I know it isn't fair. I want as much time as I can get with you, but I have three other people who love me and depend on me, and I can't walk away from them and cause even more people the pain I've caused you."

"Why not? It's okay for me to suffer but not them?"

"It's not okay for you to suffer. It was *never* okay, but I wasn't given a choice. No matter what I did, it was inevitable that you would suffer. It didn't matter if I went into the program and lived or if I went back to prison and died."

As I look at him, I can feel the neediness expand in my soul. Its growth makes me feel like I have so much empty space that needs to be filled. I'm hollow and starved for the one thing I've been deprived of, and it's a horrible feeling I'm forced to withstand.

"Can I come back tonight? Around ten or so?"

I nod, because I'll start crying if I speak. I refuse to cry, but the blades of despair are slaughtering me from the inside.

"Declan?" My father turns from me, seeking permission from the man I love.

"Of course. Come as late as you need."

With his hands on my shoulders, he looks in my eyes with sincerity, saying, "I'm sorry."

And I nod again before he pulls me to him and hugs me. I take his embrace, and with a deep breath, I take in his scent once again, because the same fear remains that he just might not come back.

"I love you."

"I'm sorry," is my response.

"Look at me. You have nothing in this world to be sorry for. It's okay to be angry; I'm angry too. I'm pissed and bitter. I want to grab you and steal you away, do everything in my power to make up for all the time we lost. But do you understand why I can't?"

"I do."

I don't.

"I know it doesn't make it easier, and I'm so sorry. If I'd known that there was a chance in this lifetime that I'd be seeing you again, I would've waited alone so that nothing could stand in the way of me disappearing with you. I need you to believe that. Tell me you believe that."

Taking a hard swallow, I force the words out through all the pain that's suffocating me. "I believe you, Dad."

twenty-six

MY DAD DID come back later last night just as he promised. He and Declan talked business and politics while drinking Scotch. I enjoyed watching the two of them together, debating and laughing as if they'd been friends for years. Dad wanted to know what life was like for us in Scotland and now in London, and although our time there has been plagued by so much darkness, Declan did well to veer around all that. When Dad asked about the house in Scotland, I told him all about my time at Brunswickhill: the history of the estate, all the amazing parts of the land surrounding it, the clinker grotto, the atrium, the library. I went on and on, because truthfully, I love the house so much; it's what most little girls dream a palace to be like.

The more we are around each other, the more comfortable we become. The ease of last night felt so natural and so promising. Having the two men that I love so much in the same room with me is amazing. I try not to focus on the nuts and bolts of how this is all going to work moving forward. Declan told me after my father left last night to just enjoy this time we're able to share in the here and now, and that we will figure out the details later. I accepted his suggestion to live in the moment.

My father returned a couple hours ago with another bouquet of pink daisies. We've been hanging out on the couch, watching an old James Bond movie that my dad claims is one of his favorites. Once the movie ends, we order up some lunch, and are now eating our food as we sit in the living room together.

"Declan, tell me, are your mother and father still living in Scotland?"

Now, it's my turn to give Declan a preemptive squeeze like he had when my father asked me about my childhood. I'm not sure what Declan will say, but I need to let him know that I'm here.

"No. My mother actually passed away when I was a teenager."

He doesn't say anything about his father, and when he turns away from my dad, I know he won't. Before my dad can ask another question, I turn my father's attention to me.

"Dad, I umm . . . I thought you should know that I had a friend of mine look into finding my mother."

He looks at me nervously. "You did?"

"Yes," I tell him and then add, "I know what she did."

"Sweetheart, I'm so sorry. I never wanted you to know about her because I didn't want you to think—"

"That she didn't love me?" I cut in. "Dad, she didn't love me. The thing is, her being sick and depressed when she sold me is one thing, but she's been a free woman for a very long time and still has yet to contact me."

"I don't want to make excuses for that woman and what she did. It was a rough period in our lives—one I had to move on from—which is why when you were little and would ask me if you had a mom, I would always deflect. And since you were so young, it was easy to do."

I can talk about that woman without getting worked-up because I've closed myself off from that facet of my life even though it goes against Declan's word. He's made it clear that he no longer wants me to avoid that which hurts me. But my mother's truth about what she did to me when I was a baby is too painful for me to think about, and with everything else going on, Declan hasn't broached the subject of my mother since.

"Do you think you'll ever see her or talk to her?"

"No," I state firmly. "She's never been a part of my life and I don't see a need for it now."

"I don't want to tell you what to do in this situation, but I think staying away is the best choice. I'd be afraid she'd only hurt you."

"Have you spoken to her since all that?"

"No. As soon as I had you back in my arms, I was done with her and, aside from the day I had to testify at her trial, I never spoke to her or saw her again."

When there's nothing else to be said, we sit in a short span of silence before my dad attempts to lighten the mood. "Tell me something good. Something funny from your childhood."

He has no idea that there's nothing funny about my childhood, but Declan catches the conversation before it drops and says to my dad, "Better yet, why don't you tell me more about Elizabeth. What was she like as a little girl?"

Thank you, Declan.

My father's face instantly lights up with a smile as he reflects on the past. "She was a spitfire of a girl, but in the most endearing way possible."

"So I see that part of her hasn't swayed." Declan's voice is full of humor, but I keep my attention on my father as he goes on.

"She didn't have any women in her life, it was only me and a couple of my good friends that surrounded her," he says and then turns to look at me. "But, somehow, you were so soft and pink and everything a little girl should be."

He says this with a doting smile, which makes me smile as well.

He turns back to Declan and tells him, "I used to have a short beard, almost the same length as yours, and one thing she would always do was rub her tiny hands over it. She'd giggle and tell me she liked the way it felt as it crackled against her palms."

I look over to Declan when my dad says this because I do the exact same thing to Declan's beard every single day. And I do it because it's always reminded me of my dad, and it simply makes me feel good. Declan gazes into my eyes and gives me a hint of a smile when he puts those two puzzle pieces together.

"But as girly as she was, she still wanted to be my right-hand man," he continues with a chuckle. "I can remember when we moved into the Northbrook house . . ."

"We didn't always live there?"

"No. After everything with your mom, I decided it would be best that you and I had a fresh start together. I bought that house for us."

"I never knew that," I murmur.

"You were only three years old at the time, but you insisted on having a little tool belt of your own so you could help me hang the window treatments and artwork on the walls. I wound up tracking one down at a nearby toy store, and you wore it proudly as you followed me around the house."

I laugh when he tells me this, saying, "I don't remember that."

"Well, you were so young, but, yeah, you'd pull out your plastic hammer and tap it against the wall every time I would hammer in a nail." He stops for a moment and smiles at me before continuing, "There was one time when I had a couple buddies of mine over, Danny and Garrett. Do you remember them?"

I do my best to think back and vaguely recall, "You mean Uncle Danny?"

"You *do* remember," he says happily. "Danny was a good friend of mine and he insisted that since you didn't have any aunts or uncles, that you should call him Uncle Danny."

"I don't remember his face or anything, but I do remember an Uncle

Danny," I tell him.

He turns to Declan and explains, "Danny and I had known each other since our twenties, and when it was just Elizabeth and me, he'd started to come around more often to spend time with her. But anyway," he says, shifting his attention back to the story. "I was in the attic, laying insulation because it was unfinished, and I wanted to turn it into a storage space. You were downstairs playing with Uncle Danny, and I had stumbled and my foot slipped off the rafter I was standing on and my one leg fell right through the floor." He starts laughing. "I hollered down to you two, and instead of Danny coming to help me, he took you out to the garage where my leg was hanging through the ceiling. He picked you up so you could reach me and encouraged you to take my shoe off and tickle my foot."

Declan and I join in my father's laughter as he tells this story I have no memory of.

"The more I laughed, the more you tickled, and the more I started to slip through. But I could hear you giggling, and you were having the time of your life."

"Well, it looks like your leg survived that ordeal," I tease.

"It did," he says and then faces Declan. "But if you really want to know what she was like as a child, she was perfect. She had the softest heart and always wanted to please people. If I told her to do something, she always did it and never fought me. She was kind and she was sensitive," he says and then looks at me, finishing, "and she was my every dream come true."

He goes on to tell a couple more funny stories, and when we finish our lunch and clean up, he turns to me and asks, "You feel like getting out of here?"

"I thought you couldn't . . ."

"Forget what I said. You want to go for a walk?"

"Um . . . yeah. That sounds great, Dad."

"It's a little cold outside, but why don't I take you over to Owen Beach?"

With a smile, I respond, "Okay. Let me go change my clothes, and I'll be ready." I give Declan a smile when I walk past him and into the bedroom. Closing the door, I rush into the closet like a kid about to go to her favorite candy store. I slip off my dress pants and pull on a pair of jeans before grabbing a hooded raincoat. I dig through Declan's clothes, looking for his jacket, and when I find it, I make a quick stop in front of the mirror to wrap my hair up in a bun on top of my head.

As I walk out of the bedroom, I notice the two of them standing off by the door talking in hushed tones with one another.

"What are you two talking about?" I announce as I approach, and when Declan turns to me, I hold his coat out and wait for his answer.

"You, of course."

I narrow my eyes at him in mock annoyance and then laugh when he kisses me.

"I don't have a whole lot of time before I have to leave, so why don't we take two cars for time's sake, and I'll just leave from the beach?"

"Not a problem, Steve. We'll just follow you there."

The drive is a short one, and pretty soon, we're driving among fresh blooming buds of spring. The sky may be dank and gray, but the pink cherry blossoms make the gloom beautiful. I press my hand on to the window, absorbing its bitter chill as Declan pulls into a parking spot that looks over the desolate beach.

My dad opens his door next to our car, and when he opens my door and takes my hand, Declan says, "I'll wait here."

I look over my shoulder. "You sure?"

"I need to make a few calls," he says. "Go share a walk with your dad."

Hand in hand we walk over the mounds of driftwood on the beach and down to the water's edge. The wind gusts, creating a mist of sea spray that mingles with the cloud's sprinkles that fall from the sky. I reach back with my free hand and pop the hood of my raincoat over my head as we stroll leisurely across the dense, water-puddled sand.

"Is this where you came when you left prison or have you lived other places?"

"Only here. I love it. The mountains, the water, the gray. I love the cold."

"I do too. Winter has always been my favorite for some reason. Maybe it's because it hides the truth of Earth's death under a blanket of false purity."

"False purity?"

"The white fluffy snow seems so innocent, but in actuality, it's the weapon that kills what lies beneath."

He looks down at me, asking with slight humor, "You always think this much?"

"Sometimes."

"I do too."

I stop and turn to face him, and the wind kicks against us when I ask, "What about?"

"You, mostly."

He drapes his arm around me, tucking me against his side as we look out over the water.

With his eyes cast out, he says, "I've always had a lost soul."

We don't look at each other as we speak, my arm now slung around his waist.

"Me too."

"Sometimes when I see a little girl with red hair, for a split second, I feel hopeful that it's you, but then I realize that you wouldn't be that little girl anymore."

"I used to sneak out of windows in the middle of the night when I went into foster care. You told me about Carnegie the last day we were together. I used to think that if I walked far enough to find a forest, you'd be there."

My tears blend with the mist that collects on my face and trickles down my cheeks as we speak.

He turns to me, his hands running down my arms, and his eyes fill with years of inconsolable pain that I know too well.

"I am so sorry, princess. I have so many regrets in my life, but none bigger than losing you."

I see his tears too.

"I was careless."

"No, Dad."

"I was. I should've never gotten involved with the people I worked for."

I look into my father's reddened eyes as blades nick my heartstrings.

"I will never be able to make up for all my wrongs, for leaving you fatherless, for causing you so much heartache," he chokes out in shame.

"I don't blame you, Dad."

"You should."

"But I don't," I tell him, and he pulls me into his loving arms that I've craved since I was five years old. "All I ever wanted was this. You holding me. I've needed your arms so badly," I say, the words wrapping around my throat, making it hard to speak.

"I need you to listen to me," he says insistently, and I look up at him. "I need you to know how much I love you. I need you to know that without you, my heart is incapable of ever being complete. You . . . you are the very fibers of my being."

I rest my head against his chest and listen to his heartbeat as he continues, "I remember the day you were born. The nurse placed you in my arms, and I was forever changed. You softened my heart instantly, and I knew I would never be the same. I've never been so in love like I've been with you. I need you to never forget that."

"I won't."

"Let me look at you," he requests when he takes my face and cranes it up to him. He shakes his head, saying, "I just can't believe how beautiful you are. My baby, you're all grown up."

Reaching my hand up, I run it along his jaw where his beard used to be. "I can't believe I found you."

"You did. And I will forever be thankful for that. To see you, and to know you're okay."

He leans down, pushes the hood of my raincoat back, and kisses the top of my head. His back shudders against my hands in sadness as he continues to plant kisses in my hair.

"You and I," he eventually says. "We're unbreakable even when we've been broken."

"I've never let you die, even when I believed you were dead."

We stand here, together in the misty rain, and we're tear-stained souls who've finally united when the world has kept us apart for so long.

"I can't believe I have you back," I weep.

He wipes my face with his hands. "No more tears, okay?"

I nod and inhale deeply to soothe myself.

When he turns his head to look up where our cars are parked, he says, "That man up there . . . He's a good one."

I watch Declan, who's talking on the phone, and smile. "He's really good to me, Dad. I don't deserve him."

"You do. You deserve each other. I see how he looks at you, as if it's the last time he'll ever look at you." He moves to stand in front of my view of Declan. "That's the look of a man who's desperately in love," he says. "Even though I love you in a very different way, it's the same way I look at you."

His words comfort in ways I can't explain, and I smile up at him.

"There's that gorgeous light," he adulates, and then kisses my forehead. "I love your smile."

"I love you, Dad. So much."

"I love you too, princess."

When he looks at his watch, he groans. "I've gotta run."

He takes my hand and leads me back up to the car, and when he opens my door, he leans down and looks to Declan, giving him a nod. Declan returns the gesture without any words spoken.

"Thanks, Dad," I tell him. "I needed this."

"I did too, sweetheart."

He leans in and kisses my cheek, and I kiss his before he runs his hand down the length of my face.

"Drive safe, okay?"

"You too."

"I will never love anyone the way I love you," he tells me before he closes my door.

Declan then takes my hand and pulls it into his lap after we pull out of the parking lot and start heading back to the hotel. I reflect on the words my dad said to me, words I've been longing to hear, to know that I was never disposed of. To know that he's hurt for me like I've hurt for him dissolves all resentment. And he's right, even when we were apart, we were still together as one because neither of us let the other fade from our souls. No one can break us.

Walking through the door of our hotel room, a wave of unease hits me out of the blue.

We forgot to make plans to see each other again.

"Declan, did my dad say when he was coming back?"

He shrugs his jacket off and tosses it over a chair, saying, "No."

I watch Declan as he moves aimlessly around the suite as worriment nags me.

"Declan?"

"Yeah," he calls out when he wanders into the bedroom, and I follow him.

"Something doesn't feel right."

"What do you mean?"

"He's never not said when he'd be coming back."

"Maybe he just forgot."

"No. This doesn't feel right to me."

He runs his hands down my arms and scoops my hands up in his. "Darling . . ."

"Declan, something is wrong here, and I don't trust it," I say as a surge of fear takes over me. My hands start shaking. "Can you drive me by his house?"

"Why?"

"I don't know, but my gut is telling me that something is happening here that I don't know about," I tell him in a tremoring voice, panging in terror.

"I don't think that's a good idea."

"Either you take me or I'll go on my own. You can't stop me and you know it."

"Elizabeth, no."

"Why are you fighting me on this?"

"I just don't think it's safe," he says, and I plead, "You promised me you would bend. I need you to bend."

He releases a deep breath. "Okay."

Declan grabs the keys, and I rush out the door.

He drives with a white-knuckled grip on the steering wheel.

"Why are you so tense?"

He doesn't speak, only reaches over to hold my hand, which does nothing for my anxiety. I stare at him as we pull into the neighborhood, and there's a look in his eyes I've never seen before. My stomach holds the weight of a thousand pounds, and I want to scream at the top of my lungs to drive faster!

The moment he pulls onto Fairview, I see the sign.

I never knew the twist of fate that day held for me. But when I look back, I should've known. It was too much. Too much freedom. The words were too strong. The feelings were too intense. The truth was all around me, but I was too consumed with my dream come true to realize the evil nemesis that couldn't just let me be. If I would've paid better attention, I would've said more to him. I would've made sure he knew every beat of my heart, the depths in which I've always loved him, and how utterly perfect I've always thought he was. He was selfish though, and I can't blame him. Because looking back, I know he wanted to see my smile, pure and true, for one last time. There's no way I could've given him that if I knew what was coming.

I sling open the door before Declan stops the car and run up to the now vacant house. In an utter panic, I yank on the front door, and when that doesn't budge, I peer into the windows. My heart snaps loose inside of my chest and falls into the depths of fiery hell. Once again, I'm faced with the stench of tragedy.

"Where is he?" I scream out as Declan walks up the circle drive. "Where is he?"

"Baby, please."

He reaches for me, but it isn't his touch I want so I slap his hand away, seething, "Don't fucking touch me!"

He reeks of guilt.

"Tell me where he is!"

He stares at me with pity. "He's gone."

"Where?"

"Let's get back in the car."

"NO!"

I can't move.

I can't breathe.

All I can do is stand here, a bleeding mess as every part of what makes me human blisters in monumental agony. They grow, filling with the acid of heartache only to pop and sear me from the inside out.

"You knew," I accuse bitterly, my hands fisting at my sides. "You knew, didn't you?"

"Yes."

"You unimaginable bastard!" I shriek, slapping him across his face, and he takes it. I slap him again, and then hammer my fists against his chest, causing him to stumble back.

He doesn't fight me as I yell at him through my tears, "How could you?"

Another searing slap.

"Are you done hitting me?"

"No!" I spit out as I ram my palm into his shoulder, and that's when he grabs ahold of my wrist.

"How could you not tell me?"

He jerks my wrist, forcing me into his arms, but I don't want his embrace—I want my dad.

I fight against his hold, but he dominates my strength and forces me back down the driveway and into the car. Shock riddles my system as I stare at the *For Sale* sign in the front yard.

Declan gets into the car and speaks in an even and controlled tone. "I am so sorry, baby."

The salt of my pain eats away at my flesh when I turn to face him. "I need answers."

"He got caught," he confesses.

"No, he didn't," I cry, unwilling to believe him.

"They allowed him to have this one last day with you while they emptied the house."

"No."

"He's gone."

"NO!"

And it was in that moment the world fell from its axis and tumbled into nothingness. I only existed in a realm of blank space. I don't know what happened next. I don't remember the drive back to the hotel. I don't remember going to bed. Nothing existed that night. I suppose the pain must've been so incredibly excruciating that I couldn't tolerate it and all my senses seized. Maybe it was something greater that was sparing me of having to carry that memory around with me for a lifetime. Whatever it was that saved me from the horror of that night—thank you.

twenty-seven

I SIT IN my car with my gun and watch Archer and his daughter on the beach. I'm far enough away from their cars, so they don't take notice of me, but my eyes never leave them.

I've been anxious ever since I got the phone call on their new whereabouts, and that anxiety is at an all-time high now that I'm here. When someone does you wrong, it doesn't simply disappear. It festers and marinates, growing like wildfire. I think of my brother who lost his freedom. He's been sitting in prison for over a decade. His wife lost her husband. His children lost their father. My parents lost their son. It's a ripple of destruction, and Archer will pay for all that he's destroyed. But this isn't my payback—it's my brother's.

As this little family reunion wraps up, I go ahead and pull my car out and wait down the street for Steve's car to pass. It doesn't take long for him to leave, and I cautiously trail behind him. Once we make it over to Gig Harbor, the traffic thins out. Winding through the heavily wooded backstreets, it's go time.

I hammer my foot on the accelerator, and swerve across the double-lines. When my car evens up to his, I jerk the wheel and run him off the road into a ditch. In rapid-fire movements, I'm over to his car with my gun aimed on him.

"Open the fucking door."

He does, begging, "Take whatever you want, but pl—"

"No talking." I shove the muzzle to his forehead as he looks at me in horror. "This is vengeance for my brother. You ratted Carlos Montego out to the feds, and now he's spending the rest of his life behind bars." His eyes flinch when I mention my brother's name. "He told me to kill you, but I'm going to give you a choice," I tell him, fucking with him, because no matter what he says, he's dying. "I know your daughter is here and staying at The Pearl's Edge."

"No, please don't—"

"Choose. You die or she dies. You have five seconds."

I pull the slide back and chamber a round when he pleads urgently, "Kill me. Don't hurt my—"

BANG.

BANG.

I fire two shots into his head, and he falls lifelessly to the ground, maroon blood oozing out of him. Quickly holstering my gun, I look around, but there's still not a car in sight. I grab him under his arms and drag his body out into the woods. The adrenaline pumping through my veins helps me move at a velocious rate. Tossing this fucker behind a pile of brush, I run back to my car and high-tail it out of there with the thrill of vengeance roiling through me.

It's finished.

twenty-eight

RAIN FALLS AGAINST the window, its particles alone and bleak, waiting to be joined by other raindrops. And once mended, they fall, trickling their way down the glass. I lie in bed on my side and watch this endless pattern repeat itself again and again. I've been up for a while—I don't know how long, but long enough to notice the storm intensifying every few minutes or so.

The somber clouds hang like a veil—cloaked in the darkness of dysphoria. I know the sun is out there somewhere far, far away. She refuses to shine her light on me, but that's okay. I don't want it anyway. I'd rather drown in my misery than be ridiculed by resplendent radiance.

The weight of Declan's arm as he drapes it over my hip alerts me to his rousing. A part of me is angry that he knew and didn't tell me that yesterday would be the last time I saw my dad. But at the same time, I need him close and for there to be no animosity between us. He continues to prove to be the one man I can count on. He's all I have left—again.

I roll onto my back, snug up against him, and watch him watching me.

"I'm sorry," I rasp against the strain of my throat, an attestation of how much I probably screamed and cried last night.

"You slap hard." His lips tick in a subtle grin, and then he shifts, saying more seriously, "Don't you ever be sorry for how you feel. It's okay."

I don't say anything else, exchanging words for reticence. I close my eyes and seek solitude in the warmth of Declan's body. We remain in bed for most of the morning, drifting in and out of sleep, because sleep is much more appealing than having to face the truth. Reality can go fuck itself for all I care; I'd rather frolic among the fantasy of dreams.

Eventually, Declan decides it's time to wake. I remain under the sheets as he calls up for coffee and tea. He then goes into my toiletry bag and finds my prescription bottle. I take the pill he hands me, and again, cheek it. Once he's in the bathroom and I hear the faucet running, I drop the pill behind the headboard.

"He'll be furious if he ever finds out."

"He won't."

Pike stands and leans against the fog-covered window, looking out at the storm.

"Everything they told me about my dad was a lie, you know?" I whisper, keeping my voice low so Declan won't hear.

Pike walks over to me, kneels beside the bed, and holds my hand. *"I know."*

"He was everything I thought he would be after all these years."

"Are you hungry at all?" Declan asks when he walks back into the room, and suddenly Pike is gone.

I shake my head when I look at him from over my shoulder and then turn back to the window. Declan encourages me to get out of bed and freshen up, and like a machine, I do it—all the while numb.

Did last night really happen or was it a mirage?

When I slip back into bed and sit against the headboard, Declan hands me the teacup. I cradle it in my hands as the steam ribbons into the air, eventually evaporating in a metaphoric display.

Declan sits next to me with his coffee in hand. He takes a sip and then punctures the silence. "Talk to me."

I keep my eyes on my tea. "What's there to say?"

"Tell me how you're feeling?"

"I don't know how to feel right now," I respond despondently.

"Do you want to know how I feel?"

When I look at him, his face is marred in suffering.

"I feel like I failed you." His words weigh heavy in the air between us. "I promised you I'd never let you fall. And when your father pulled me aside and told me it was his last day with you, I knew the best thing for you would result in you falling in the worst way possible." He sets his coffee mug on the bedside table and then turns to me. "I was powerless to save you, and it kills me to know I couldn't protect you from this pain. I was put in the worst position last night, and I am so sorry."

Declan isn't a man who ever apologizes, so to hear the sincerity in it is a blatant reflection of his grief. I want to say something, tell him I understand, tell him it's okay, but it hurts too much to speak.

He leans over and opens the drawer to the bedside table, pulls out an envelope, and hands it to me. "Your dad gave this to me yesterday."

I hold it in my hands for a moment before breaking the seal and opening it. His written words cover the paper entirely, and agony conquers numbness and takes over.

"I don't know if I can do this, Declan."

"It might help," he suggests.

Taking a deep breath, I release it slowly before lowering my eyes to his words. Declan wraps his arms around my shoulders and holds me against him when I start reading the letter to myself.

My beautiful girl,

I know you must be hurting, because I'm dying inside. I wish I could be there to comfort you and wipe your tears, but I also know that you're in good hands with Declan. I don't want you to be upset with him. I told him not to tell you I'd be leaving. If I told you, I knew I'd never be able to leave you. I couldn't have our last day together with you in tears. I hope you can understand that.

The thing is, the government found out that you and I had made contact. They stepped in, and as much as I hate it, I have to agree with them. Your association with me puts you at an unbelievable risk, and if anything happened to you, I'd never be able to live with myself. You are too precious for me to put you in harm's way. Selfishly, I want you, but because of the mistakes I made in my past, this is how it has to be.

I don't know where I'm relocating or what my new identity will be, but I need you to let me go. Please don't try to find me. I don't say this because I don't love you. I'm saying it to save you. After you read this letter, I need you to destroy it because no one can ever know that I'm alive.

These past few days were a gift. It was never supposed to happen, but it did, and I will forever be thankful that I have a daughter that fought her way to find me. You are strong and beautiful and smart, and you are destined to do great things. Promise me, you won't let my mistakes stand in your way.

I don't want you to ever forget how much I love you. There hasn't been a single second that you haven't been in my heart. You are irreplaceable and unforgettable. I need you to believe that.

I'm going to take you to the beach tomorrow. I'm going to hold your hand. I'm going to make you smile. And whatever I wind up saying to you, I need you to hold on tightly to those words and carry them with you through your life.

You're my forever princess.

I love you,

Dad

I drop the paper that's covered in my tears and fall against Declan. He envelops me and I sob. There's nothing for me to say, so I let pain devour me. It strangulates and paralyzes, cutting fresh wounds in my soul, marking me with this pain for life.

I want to drown in it.

I want to escape from it.

I'm all over the place.

The vacancy inside of me is about to surpass my body's elasticity, and I grow desperate to fill the void I fear will be the death of me.

I cling to Declan, slinging my leg over his hip and pulling him against me as we slip down in the bed. Drawing my head back, I look through my tears at his blurred face.

"Breathe." His hushed voice lulls, and while he wipes the tears that continue to fall, I give myself the time I need to settle myself down.

The pounding of my heart transitions into neediness, I pull Declan's head to mine and kiss him. He lets me control it, and I keep it soft and move slow. My lips meld with his, and he brings my body in even closer.

I feel a few lingering tears as they slip out and fall down the sides of my face and into my hair.

He rolls on top of me, parting my lips with his tongue and dipping it into my mouth. With my hands getting lost in his hair, I pull him down on me, needing to feel his weight on top of me. We continue to kiss in this new way. There's no urgency or need for control. Declan drags his lips from mine and runs them down my neck before he breaks the kiss and looks down at me.

I gaze up at him, desperate for this closeness, and make my request.

"Show me how tender you can be."

I know I'm asking a lot. Declan isn't one who feels safe when he opens himself up to vulnerability, but I need this. For this moment, I need him to love me in this way—stripped down and free from the barriers he likes to keep on me.

I watch as his eyes soften, and when he gives me a nod, he drops his lips back down to mine. My hands roam freely, something he never allows because I'm always restrained. I slip them under his shirt and feel his abs flex from my touch. We undress each other slowly and soon our clothes are on the floor.

Flesh against flesh, his skin heats mine. He keeps his touches soft, taking my breasts in his hands. His breath ghosts over them and over my puckered nipples before taking one of them between his lips. He sucks lovingly and the sensation causes my back to bow off the bed and into him. My eyes fall shut, and with my hands running along the dips of his muscular arms, I release a breathy moan.

He moves to my other nipple, showing it the same affection before dragging his hot tongue down my stomach. When he reaches the curve of my pussy, he puts his hands on each thigh and spreads my legs.

"God, I love this part of you," he whispers in a husky voice.

I move my eyes down to him and watch as he stares at my pussy. I reach both of my hands down to him and he takes them in his, lacing his fingers through mine. And before he makes his move, he lifts his eyes and fixes them to mine. We watch each other as he holds my hands and dips his tongue into the slit of my pussy. He sends a sizzling current through my whole body.

He moves painfully slow.

I spread my legs wider as he laps and kisses and sucks. Every movement softer than the one before. He groans from deep inside his chest, and when his tongue slides inside of my body, I can't hold on. I mewl in pure ecstasy and grind myself over his face, clutching my fingers around his hands. I grow hotter as he sparks the live wire in my soul, the one that incessantly aches for him.

He moves his lips to my thighs, dropping whispery kisses over every inch of my skin as he lets go of my one hand and drags the wet arousal out from inside of me with his finger and uses it to rub my clit.

Our bodies move together and we're unrushed, unmasked, and completely exposed.

When he finds his way back up to me, I hold his face in mine and kiss him deeply, fusing my lips with his as I glide my tongue along his. He settles himself between my legs, his hard cock pressing against me.

"I want it real slow," I tell him.

"How slow, baby?"

"So slow I can feel you entering my soul."

He reaches down and holds himself in his hand.

Never has the sensation been more intense than in this very moment as he pushes inside me.

It's exquisite.

It's torturous.

It's effervescent bliss.

And when he's fully immersed in me, I'm saved. Free from my cankering misery, I hold on to Declan as he fucks me in slow agonizing strokes. His moans blend with mine, our bodies coalesced like never before. Our souls tethered into one.

He flips us over and I roll my hips over his cock. He sits up and kisses my neck, my tits, my mouth while I fist my hands in his hair and rock into him. When he leans his head back, I stare into his eye as I ride his cock.

"I love you." My words resting on broken pants.

He groans through rictus lips before reaching his hands around the backs of my shoulders and pushing me farther down on his cock. I can feel him throbbing inside of me and then he lifts me off him. Lying on my side with him behind me, he pulls my leg up and buries himself deep inside of me.

He slips his one arm under my head, and I hold his hand while he uses his other to turn my head to him. We kiss, and I reach down between my legs to feel his cock as he fucks me.

"Touch yourself."

Taking my wetness from his dick, I move to rub my clit in slow circles, and my hips buck when I do. He drapes my hair behind my shoulder and kisses the veins on my neck, sending my body into shivers. It doesn't take long before my pussy grows wetter and the onslaught of an orgasm begins to build inside of me.

Declan shifts to his back with me on top of him, my legs bent and feet planted on the bed, and he thrusts into me from behind. My back lies against his chest, and he's now massaging my clit alongside my fingers. Our hands grow wet as he continues sliding himself in and out of me.

"Oh, God, Declan."

"That's it, baby. I want to feel you all over me."

With my hand locked to his, I rock my hips down on him, unable to still myself and greedy for him to fill me with his cum.

"Fuck me," I tell him, and with our fingers mingled in my pussy, he pumps his hips up into me.

My eyes fall shut as my ass slides back and forth over the top of him. Nerves begin to fissure, limbs begin to tingle. He presses his fingers down on my clit, and I rupture. He pounds his thick cock into me, driving my orgasm out of me. I writhe against him, pulling every bit of pleasure he has to give, and then I feel him cum. He groans heavily, spurting his life source inside of my body, grabbing my pussy with his hand and grinding me roughly against him.

We ride each other, taking every piece from one another that we can. My head slips off the back of his shoulder, and he kisses me deeply, our tongues tasting and licking. When he rolls us back to our sides, he pulls himself out of me, cum dripping onto my thighs as I turn over to face him.

He plants his lips on my sweaty forehead.

"Thank you."

"I love you," he tells me. "If this is what you need, I'll give it to you as many times as you need it."

We stay in bed for most of the day, naked and wrapped in each other's arms. If I'm not sleeping, then I'm crying.

If I'm not crying, then we're kissing and touching.

And if we're not kissing and touching, then I'm sleeping.

The cycle laps as the hours pass. Eventually Declan takes a shower, leaving me alone with the rain that has yet to let up. With the blankets tucked around me, I feel at peace here in the hotel room with Declan and away from anything that could have the potential to hurt me.

A buzzing sound alerts me. I sit up and look around the room, unsure of what the noise is. Then, when I spot my purse on the floor next to the closet, it hits me. I slip out of the bed and dig my hand down past my wallet and grab my cell phone.

UNKNOWN reads across the screen.

I accept the call.

"Hello?"

"Hey, kitty."

twenty-nine

“I THOUGHT I told you not to call me.” My voice is razor sharp, but I keep it low because Declan is in the shower.

“I wouldn’t call you if I weren’t desperate. I need your help, so it’s time you got off your high horse and remember where you came from and the people that took care of you.”

As I kneel by the wall next to the closet, I respond, “Took care of me?”

“Who helped Pike save you from your foster parents? Who drove the car? Who let you live with them?”

“Let’s get one thing straight, you were Pike’s friend, not mine.”

“Are you going to help me or not?”

“Not. Like I said, you die and I have the guarantee that I can move forward without having to look over my shoulder.”

“You’re gonna die too,” he says, his words catching me off guard.

“What are you talking about?”

“It was the only way to ensure I stay alive.”

“What the hell are you talking about?” I grit as I stand.

“You think you’re running this show? Think again. You might not value my life, but I’m not willing to lose it over an uptight cunt like you.”

I try to keep my voice from quivering. “What did you do?”

“I gave them your name. Told them you had the money. So you have no choice but to help me. After all, your life is on the line too now.”

The shock and fury that surge through my veins is rampant fuel, and I’m not even thinking about keeping a hushed tone when I spit my fury. “You motherfucker!”

He laughs, saying, “Next time don’t fuck with me when I ask for help, kitty.”

I start when the bathroom door busts open and Declan rushes out with only a towel slung around his waist.

“Are you okay?” His words shoot out quickly. “Who’s on the phone?”

He doesn't wait for me to respond when he takes it right out of my hand. "Who the fuck is this?" He pauses and then holds the phone out and clicks it onto speakerphone.

"Can she hear me?" Matt questions.

"She can hear you."

"They know you're in Washington."

As soon as he says those words, I reach over and end the call.

"What the fuck is going on, Elizabeth?" Declan ferociously demands.

I tell him about Matt, about his calling me when we were back in London, and about the loan shark. And then I tell him that Matt traded me in to save his life.

"There's a bounty on my head now."

Rage takes over Declan in a deadly way that scares the shit out of me. He stands in utter silence as he bores his eyes down on me, and when his nostrils flare angrily, he fumes in an even tone, "Why didn't you tell me about this sooner?"

"I thought I handled it. I thought it was under control."

"You thought wrong, goddammit! And now you have a hit out on you!" His voice ricochets off the walls, his neck blotching the color red in white-hot anger.

"I'll just pay them off, Declan,"

"You think that'll solve this Matt situation? The ease at which he was able to dispose of your life is not something to fuck with. And what happens when he finds himself in trouble down the road? You really trust him when he says he's going to leave you alone after this?"

Declan rips his hand through his wet hair and paces off across the room. I watch as frustration and fiery anger boil over, and I'm quick to make my resolve.

"I'll kill him," I say too fast and too eager.

Declan snaps his head over to me with a look of horror on his face. Maybe I should be worried about how he'll respond or how he'll think of me to know I can rid someone of their life so easily, but I'm not. Declan knows I have three kills under my belt. Hell, he has two himself. He knows the tar my black heart pumps. And when he speaks, I know we're one and the same—two monsters bound by one soul.

"No," he states. "I'll kill him."

"Declan, no. I can't let you do that. Matt's my problem."

He strides over to me in quick steps. "I won't let you kill anyone else, you hear me? I don't want your hands branded by any more blood. I'll take care of it."

"Declan—"

"I'm not arguing with you about this. My word is final," he states adamantly. "Pack your suitcase. They know where we are, so we're getting the fuck out of here."

"Are we going back to Chicago?"

"Yes. We're taking care of this issue now and then going back to London," he says. "But listen to me . . . Bennett's money . . . we're dumping it on the loan shark. Not only will we finally be rid of it, but it'll be enough to make these people forget you ever existed."

Taking a hard swallow, I know this is ultimately the best resolution for us. And now, once again, I'm plagued by my past, which is now forcing the man I love to take another life.

Declan's able to schedule the plane to go out today, and with the vicissitude we now face, there's no time for me to mourn the loss of my dad. We move with urgency, making sure our belongings are packed and ready to go before we head out.

We sit hand in hand during the plane ride.

"Declan, you don't have to do this."

"It's not up for discussion."

The plane lands and we drive straight back to Lotus. Every step Declan takes is purposeful, wasting not a second.

Tension is ghastly as I watch Declan take out the pistol he always travels with. He releases the cylinder and gives it a look before spinning it and locking it back in place.

"Declan?"

Laying it flat on the table in front of where I sit on the couch, he looks down at me. "You're going to call him from your phone."

"It's an unknown number he's calling from."

"There's an identification service I had Lachlan install on your phone. It traps the numbers from any restricted calls your phone receives."

I pull out my phone so Declan can show me where to retrieve the number, and with a few simple clicks, it pops up.

"What do I say?"

"You tell him you're here in Chicago and want to get this over with tonight."

It's after two a.m. and my heart rate picks up. "It's the middle of the night."

Disregarding my hesitation, he goes on to instruct me on everything I need to say.

"You got all that?"

Taking a deep breath, knowing what's about to go down, I steel myself for the inevitable as I dial Matt's number.

"Hello?" Matt says after two rings.

"It's me."

"How'd you get this number?"

"Everyone is traceable. Even you, asshole," I tell him, slinging his words back at him from when he first made contact with me. "I'm here in Chicago."

"You move fast."

"You want to live, don't you?"

"Yes."

"I'm here to save your life, so I need you to do this my way." I'm firm in my tone and a tad shocked when he keeps his mouth shut and listens. "I don't want any fuck-ups or you getting greedy on me. We're meeting tonight. You're to call the shark to meet us. I'll make the transfer from my phone and wait until we get the verification from the shark's account that the money has been successfully transferred."

"Come alone. The last thing I need is your boyfriend fucking shit up because he can't keep his cool."

"Don't worry. I'll be alone," I lie. "You have ten minutes to call me back to tell me the location of our meeting place."

I hang up before he can respond and look to Declan. He smiles. "Good girl."

He takes a seat next to me as we wait in the darkened room, the only light coming from the glow of a lamp on the entryway table. Declan drapes his arm around my shoulder, and when I turn my head to him, he peers at me through dilated eyes, exposing the devil inside. He's the creation of my monstrosity.

I touch his face, and he kisses me with venomous passion before ripping away from me when my cell vibrates against the wooden table.

"Yes?" I answer.

"Twenty minutes. Metra railroad yard. Meet under the Roosevelt overpass."

"How many are coming?"

"Just me and Marco, the shark."

"Twenty minutes."

I disconnect the call and tell Declan where we're meeting. He grabs his gun and then goes to the entry closet where the safe is. I can hear the beeps of the keypad as he enters the code, and when the steel door slams shut, he returns with another revolver.

"Just in case," he says when he hands me the gun.

It's heavy and cold in my hand, and when I release the cylinder, I see that every chamber is loaded.

"You know the plan?"

I nod.

"Tell me."

"I know the plan."

"You're not to draw your gun unless absolutely necessary, okay?"

Blood swims rapidly through my body, and when I slip the gun into the back waistband of my pants, I lower my top and shrug my coat on to conceal it.

"Ready?"

"Yes," I tell him and then walk into his arms for comfort and strength. He holds me, kisses the top of my head, and assures, "We stick to the plan and then it'll all be over and we can go back home, okay?"

"Let's get this over with."

Declan goes first, leaving me behind until I get his call. I wait anxiously as he goes to switch off the security cameras. After a few minutes of pacing the room, my phone rings.

"I'm in my office," he states.

I move quickly, making my way down to him, and we exit the building through the back corridors that lead into the parking garage. Before I know it, we're zipping through the streets of Chicago on our way to the river.

The drive is tense. No words are spoken at all. We both know our parts and what we have to do.

Turning into the train yard, Declan hits the lights. Everything goes black as we weave through lines of train cars. When we edge closer to the water, I spot Matt with a tall man, thick with bulky muscles.

"That's him," I whisper.

Declan stops the car and shuts it off. "You ready?"

Our eyes lock. "Yes."

The moment Declan opens his door, Matt draws his gun and fires. It's a botched shot, but sends me into instant defense mode. Without sparing a second, all guns are drawn in an outburst of chaos.

"What the fuck, Elizabeth?" Matt shouts, but my focus is on the automatic Marco has aimed at me while Declan claims Matt as his target.

So many words are being thrown around at the same time as sparks of fear ignite within me.

"On your fucking knees," Declan yells.

"Fuck you!" Matt throws back.

It's a frenzy all around me, but my only point of concentration is right in front of me—Marco and his gun.

"Elizabeth," Declan's voice calls from behind in worriment, to which I respond in a steady voice, "I'm okay."

"What the fuck is wrong with you?" The shark snaps at Matt, berating him as he keeps his gun pointed at me.

"Marco," I greet in a strong voice, needing him to see me as nothing other than a woman in complete control. He stands a good one foot taller than me and the moon reflects off his shiny bald head. He's intimidating as hell, but I refuse to let it show. "I'm not looking to bullshit around tonight. The fact that my pistol is on you is a mere result of your client firing his gun. Clearly he's as dumb as he looks because without us, you don't get your money and he's a dead man." With Marco's gun targeted on me, I instruct, "You need money from this ass wipe, and I intend on covering his part along with enough to make you forget this night ever happened. But I'm going to need you to holster your gun. You do that, and mine is down as well. But you need to get that little shit under control too."

"You're my kind of girl. Elizabeth, right?"

"It's whatever you want it to be; I'm not here to make friends."

"I like you," he says before taking his aim off of me and swinging his arm around to Matt.

"You're a fucking idiot!" he scolds and then pulls the trigger, sending a bullet straight into Matt's leg, collapsing him down to the ground in an instant. Marco doesn't bat an eye when he holsters his gun and turns back to me while Matt screams in agony.

I watch as Declan picks up Matt's gun before I look back to Marco and shove my pistol into the waist of my pants. "I give you my word that we have no intention of doing you any wrong. That man right there," I tell him, nodding my head to Declan. "He's not too happy that your client has put me in harm's way. So, let me tell you how this night is going to go. You give me the account number you want me to wire the money into. I suggest it be whatever offshore account you no doubt hold, because I intend on dumping a lot of fucking cash into it. Then we wait. When the money is transferred, my friend holding the gun is going to teach Matt a lesson. You're more than welcome to watch, but I'll leave that choice to you. Then I plan on going home and getting some sleep."

My orders are to the point.

"You're good," he compliments.

"I've dabbled in enough cons for one life."

"Elizabeth!" Matt's voice is terror-stricken. "What the fuck is going on here?"

"Shut the fuck up, dickfuck!" Declan shouts, and when I look at Matt over my shoulder, I tell him with a smile, "Who's the cunt now?"

"Please, man. Don't kill me!"

Declan steps closer and presses the muzzle of the gun against Matt's forehead. "I told you to shut the fuck up."

Matt continues to flap his pathetic mouth, begging Declan to spare his life, but I turn back to Marco. "Let's speed this up; I've had a long day."

"My phone is in my pocket," he tells me so I don't assume he's reaching for a weapon.

"I'll get it." I trust no one.

I pull it out and hand it to him before retrieving my own phone. I wait as he pulls up the bank account he wants to use for the transfer. He proceeds to provide all the information that I need to conduct the wire, and once the country code and numbers are all entered, we wait for the delivery. It takes about fifteen minutes for Marco's bank account to update and reflect the deposit.

"Fuck me." His face grows in satisfaction when he sees the amount of zeros in the transaction.

"Are we done here?"

His eyes meet mine, and he shoves his phone back into his pocket. "Done and forgotten."

"Marco, come on, man! Don't leave me here," Matt begs through the pain of his bloody leg.

"I'm not leaving. Not yet anyways." Marco backs up, and when I turn over my shoulder to look at him, he straightens out his coat and says, "Can't be getting my new coat dirty," with a wink.

When I focus back on Matt, his eyes spiral out of control as he continues to plead. "Come on! I swear to you, I'll leave you alone, Elizabeth. Don't shoot me."

"You threw my life away to keep yours, and now you're begging me to save you? You're unsaveable, Matt. You always have been."

"It's me, Elizabeth! Come on!" His body tremors in inexorable fear. It coats his face in a layer of sweat.

"The only thing I owe you before you die is a *thank you*."

"What the fuck?"

"Thank you for handing me the match the night we burned Carl and Bobbi. It's the best gift you ever gave me."

"You fucked up the moment you put her life in danger." Declan's voice is guttural, his eyes merciless.

"Don't do this, man. Plea—"

BANG.

Matt's blood sprays across the side of my face and clothes as the crack of gunfire echoes through the night. His body collapses as dark blood pours out of the hole in his head. Clumps of his brain litter the gravel surrounding us. Declan stands above his unmoving body, aims the gun down, and ensures his death.

BANG.

BANG.

Behind the ringing in my ears, I hear Marco's distant voice, "That's gonna be a bitch to clean up," followed by stones crunching under his feet and the slam of his car door. The tires of his SUV roll over the rocks of the train yard, and then he's gone.

Declan remains fixed above Matt's dead body; he's a cold-blooded phoenix, no longer the man he once was when I met him in Chicago. He's the creation of my monstrosity, forever changed as a result of my demented soul. He fell in love with the devil when he fell in love with me.

When his eyes shift to me, I go to him, grab his blood-streaked face, and affirm, "I love you," before kissing him through the metallic taste of death.

"AT LEAST YOU got to see him. You always said you'd do anything to have him back for just one more second. You got that and more."

"It still hurts."

"I know."

Pike tightens his arms around me as I lay my head on his chest. He's been with me ever since Declan left earlier to pay Lachlan a visit. I haven't been able to get out of bed since we returned to London yesterday. Everything came to a standstill when we boarded the plane in Chicago. All of a sudden, there were no more distractions, and the weight of the past few days came crashing down on me.

I'm sad.

I miss my dad.

"He's alive though."

"Is that supposed to be a good thing?"

His fingers comb through my hair while I grip a wad of his white shirt that embodies the scent of his clove cigarettes. *"What do you mean?"*

"I mean, if his life is plagued with the agony he told me he carries with him every day, wouldn't death be better? This world forces people to endure incredible pain. It's like we're all a bunch of masochists because we continue to choose life over death."

"That's a morbid thought."

"But it's true, right?" I tilt my head back to look at his beautiful face—young and free from stress. "Do you feel anything now that you're . . ."

"Dead?" he says, picking up the word that hurts too much to say. *"I miss you, but it doesn't feel like it did when I was alive. It's hard to describe. Somehow, I'm always at peace even though I miss you."*

"Missing you is excruciating."

"I wish I could take it away from you, but you have so much to live for. You have a life with Declan. He's good to you. He protects you. There are no

boundaries for him when it comes to protecting you—he'll do anything."

I move to sit up in bed, and when Pike does the same, we face each other. "Are you mad about what we did to Matt?"

"No. I agree with Declan; all bets were off the moment that fucker put your life on the line."

I gaze into his eyes and release a deep breath before telling him, "I don't know what I would ever do without you."

His hand comes to meet my face, and I notice his eyes morph into a laden expression. *"Do you think I took advantage of you?"*

"What?"

He drops his head for a beat before returning to me, and he finally voices for the first time what I've always known. *"I was in love with you my whole life."* His eyes glaze over, tear-filled, and he tells me, *"All I wanted was to make you happy. No matter what you asked of me, I gave it to you—even when I knew it was wrong."*

"You didn't take advantage of me, Pike." I take his hand from my cheek and hold it in my own. "It was me. I took advantage of *you*. I knew you were in love with me, and I used that to steal from you. I took your love, and I used it to comfort my pain. And I am *so sorry* I played with your emotions the way I did."

"Don't be sorry."

He takes me into his arms, and as we hold each other, I ask, "Do you still feel that way about me?"

"No."

"Does it hurt you to see me with Declan?"

Relaxing his grip, he pulls away and runs his hands down my arms. *"No."* He holds both of my hands and we sit face to face on the bed. *"I love you, I always will and nothing will ever change that. But something happened when I died. The way I loved you changed. I know Declan is good for you. He's able to love you and care for you in a way I wouldn't have ever been capable of. Seeing you two together settles me. I know you're going to be okay in this life because of him."*

"You and Declan are the best things that ever happened to me in this shitty life."

"And you are the best thing that ever happened to me when I was alive. And Declan is the best thing that's happened to me in my death, because he's giving you everything I wanted to but couldn't. You're the best part of me, you know?"

I look into the eyes of my savior, and although I wish I could turn back the hands of time and not have pulled that trigger, at least I know he's moved on to a better place. And now, in his death, he goes on to serve as my orenda in this vicious world. He claims that it's only Declan who provides my safety and comfort, but it's the both of them together that blend the elixir that just might be my saving grace.

(DECLAN)

I HATE THAT I had to leave Elizabeth back at the apartment, but I don't feel safe handling this situation with Lachlan around her. Between his calls to Camilla and the insinuations from my father that Lachlan is withholding information from me, trust is now riddled with uncertainty.

I'm a sparking fuse dangling over gasoline as I make my way to his hotel. Hot off the kill from the other day, I've been unable to quell the viperous animal inside me. It's spitting at me to fix my own unresolved issue—the way I handled Elizabeth's for her. But I will go to any length possible to ensure Elizabeth's safety. I failed to protect her from Matt putting a hit on her—I won't fail again.

With my pistol holstered under my suit jacket, I step off the elevator and make my way down to his room. After a couple swift knocks, the door opens, and I whip out my gun, barreling the muzzle into Lachlan's forehead. I use the force of the gun to push him into the room and then kick the door closed.

"What the hell?" His wide eyes are consumed with sheer horror and fear.

I back him up as he lifts his hands in surrender, and when he falls back into a chair, I hiss venomously, "I'm going to give you one more chance to tell me what the fuck you are doing talking to Camilla and my father before I put a bullet in your head. You've seen me do it before, so make no mistake, I *will* do it again."

"What I told you was the truth." His words tremble just as his hands do.

"And now I'm demanding the *whole* truth."

I bring my thumb up and engage the hammer, chambering a round, and he gives in to the fear like a whore's pussy.

"Jesus! Okay! Okay!"

"I'm not fucking around!"

"Shit, okay. Please, relax with the gun, man," he blurts out in a panic.

"I'll tell you everything, just . . ."

"Start talking!" My bark is pure sulfur, and he's terrified as he squirms, slipping down into the chair. "Now!"

"I'm stealing from Cal," he jabbers out instantly.

"What the fuck are you talking about?"

"I'm . . . It's . . . The thing is—"

"Goddammit!"

"I can't fucking think with a gun to my head!" he hollers from his slouched position in the chair, and I draw the gun back, keeping it targeted on him. His eyes never stray from my weapon. I stand a few feet back and watch as he clumsily sits up.

"Start talking."

"Camilla called me when your father was arrested. When she realized the evidence was stacked against him, she knew she'd be left out to dry without a penny. She called me, told me her crazy scheme to embezzle his money. She had it all planned out. Told me to reach out to him. She figured he'd be desperate to have someone in his corner, and aside from the fallout we had when I found out about the two of them, I was, in fact, a man he had thoroughly trusted for years."

"Speed it up."

"I reached out to him with the help of Camilla, and before I knew it, he was wanting me to keep an eye on you, which was when I started reporting to him about you," he confesses.

"You told him about Elizabeth?"

"Yes."

"Get to the part that's going to save your life and spare me the headache of cleaning up your murder," I threaten.

"Camilla convinced him to trust me to launder his hidden assets through your charity foundation. She vowed we'd split it fifty-fifty, but I had my own plans. I promise you I never filtered any of that money through any of your businesses."

"Where is it?"

"With a junket in Macau."

I disengage the hammer and lower my pistol, and Lachlan drops his hands and releases a heavy breath of relief.

"I never lied when I assured you have my loyalty. You and Elizabeth, but never your father, and if that's an issue with us then—"

"It's not an issue. He's done," I tell him and then take a moment to process the fact that this man has taken it upon himself to undermine my father and his girlfriend for financial gain in the name of revenge.

"This is why Camilla keeps calling. I had to keep her believing that we were on the mend and working together, but I just got word the other day that he's been indicted. It's only a matter of time before he confesses. He knows he's safer in prison than out. If he allows this to go to trial, it won't matter if he wins or loses—he's a dead man."

He's right. I know him admitting his guilt to forego a trial will be inevitable. A trial would mean witnesses and handing over names. It would be him turning his back on those only a man with a death wish would do. Which is why I refuse to allow Elizabeth to get worked up about her crimes being uncovered.

"I need you to go back. You said the money was with a junket?" I ask. "I'm not skilled in the world of embezzling, so I need you to tell me what's going on. No more bullshitting me."

"Working in the world of finance all my life, I've come to know a handful of shifty people. One of them was able to hire me a junket in China. For a twenty percent fee, he exchanges my cash for poker chips. With Macau being the casino capital of the world and Hong Kong having so many intermediaries that are willing to transfer funds to anywhere without asking too many questions, it was my safest option."

"What happens with the chips?"

"My junket gambles a little and then cashes them in along with other gamblers' legitimate chips. The casino accountant then books my money as paid-out winnings."

"Where does the money go?"

"The funds are wire-transferred in such a way that the money crosses multiple borders to frustrate detection."

"Explain," I demand needing to know exactly how he plans on transferring what I assume to be millions.

"For instance," he continues, "the money might end up in a US trust managed by a shell company in Grand Cayman, owned by another trust in Guernsey with an account in Luxembourg, managed by a Swiss or Singaporean or Caribbean banker who doesn't know who the owner is. It's a whirlwind, basically."

"Were you ever going to tell me?"

He leans forward, resting his elbows on his knees, and then looks up to me. "There's no way to answer that. If I say yes, you'll think I'm a liar. If I say no, you'll think I'm a liar for the mere fact I never told you. But, if you need confirmation of where my interests lie, then I'll give you the accounts. You see, the money was simply a bonus to Camilla landing on her ass, dirt poor and alone. The latter was the capstone."

Testing him, I click the barrel open and dump the bullets. I walk over to him, lay the gun on the desk, and tell him, "I want all the accounts."

"Now?"

"Now."

He gets up and steps to his laptop next to my unloaded pistol. I follow, and when he sits in the desk chair, I stand over his shoulder. I watch as he bypasses the Internet and accesses the deep web through Tor, which is an anonymity network that ensures nothing he does will be indexed.

In a few quick swipes of the keyboard, numbers and codes begin to filter in. "There you go," he says and then points to the screen, explaining, "This column lists the country codes, this one here lists account and routing numbers, and this column here is—"

"Close it down."

He looks at me in confusion but does as I instruct and proceeds to logoff. I'm satisfied that without the threat of force, he handed over all the information without an inkling of hesitation.

"I don't want his money. You can do whatever you want with it."

Lachlan closes the lid to his laptop, picks up the gun, takes one bullet from the floor, and slides it into one of the cylinders. He then gives it a spin before locking it into place.

"Here," he says in an even tone as he hands me the gun. "I'd take a bullet for Elizabeth. You on the other hand . . . I need to come down from you shoving that muzzle into my head, but I'd take a bullet for you as well. You want me to prove my loyalty to you?" He takes a couple steps back. "Pull the trigger."

A sane man would take his word for it, but the gesture isn't enough for me, not after everything that has compromised my life and Elizabeth's. She's much too precious to take anyone's word at face value. So I stretch my arm out in front of me, but with a slight adjustment, one that Lachlan won't be able to detect, I mark his right arm as my target.

He offered this test of integrity, and when I cock back the hammer, I slip my finger over the trigger, and follow through.

I squeeze and fire, but all that sounds is the *snick* from the chamber rounding.

Lachlan's face drops, stunned that I pulled the trigger and then relieved when he realizes his game of Russian roulette just played out in his favor. He falls back into the chair as I holster my gun. And now that I have the confirmation that the only reason he withheld information from me was to fuck over Camilla and my father, I turn and walk to the door.

"Stop by later this afternoon. Elizabeth would enjoy seeing you now that we're back," I say without turning around.

And then I leave.

thirty-one

ELIZABETH IS STILL in bed sleeping when I get home from a long day of meetings. It's been days of the same. She's heartbroken and trying to cope with losing her father for the second time in her life, so I haven't wanted to push her too much. I'm worried though. She's been living in shades of darkness since we returned from the States. It's more than the moping around that concerns me though. After my talk with Lachlan the other day, I came home and heard her voice coming from the bedroom. But she was in there alone. When I opened the door, I could tell she had been crying, so I decided not to question her.

I have to remind myself how fragile she still is. It wasn't that long ago when she completely broke down after she found out about her mother and had to be medicated. She's experienced only a handful of episodes since that night, but none that measure in magnitude.

Walking over to the edge of the bed, I watch her as she sleeps peacefully. Her face is soft and her breathing is steady. I run the backs of my fingers along her cheek, feeling her smooth skin warm against mine. I can finally look at her without the past fueling my hate for her. No longer do I want to cause her pain and suffering. No longer do I want to punish her.

Seeing her with her father helped stitch the wounds she inflicted with her deceitful ways. For the first time, I saw through all the walls she's spent her whole life building and into the very core of who she is. Watching her with him, hearing their stories, and learning about who she was as a little girl suddenly made her transparent, and I could finally see the purity and softness that's shrouded beneath years that have hardened her.

I let her sleep while I go into the closet to hang up my suit jacket, and when I go into the bathroom to splash my face with cold water, I realize I forgot to grab a hand towel. Turning off the faucet, I walk into the toilet room and pull a towel from the linen cabinet. That's when I look down and notice something sitting in the bottom of the toilet bowl. I flick the light on to find it's a tiny blue pill, half-dissolved in the water.

I go to her sink top and pick up her prescription bottle to confirm it's the same pill.

She's been lying to me.

I have to wonder why she'd flush the pill instead of taking it because she *needs* to be taking them every day.

Going back in the bedroom, I sit on the edge of the bed where she's still sleeping. The dip of the mattress beneath me causes her to stir awake. Her eyes flutter open, and I handle her delicately. "You've been sleeping long?"

She looks at the clock on the bedside table and responds, "Not too long. How was your day?"

"Busy. What about yours?"

She sighs when she sits up and leans back again the headboard. "Same as the day before."

"Did you remember to take your pill today?"

"Yes," she answers with a curious look on her face. "Why?"

"You know how important it is that you take them every day, don't you?"

Annoyance paints her eyes. "Yes, Declan. I know. Why are you telling me this?"

"Because I want you taking care of yourself."

"I am."

"Then tell me why your pill is in the bottom of the toilet."

Her eyes tick, widening for a fleeting second, but I catch it.

"Do you want to explain to me why?"

Her throat constricts when she takes a hard swallow, and she shakes her head slowly. She's scared.

"How long have you been doing this?"

"I can take care of myself. I don't need you parenting me," she snaps.

I harden my voice, demanding, "How long?"

"I'm fine. I don't need them."

"How long, Elizabeth?"

She takes a deep breath, steadying herself to take me on when she admits, "Since I got them."

My teeth grit in an attempt to temper my anger, and when she notices my mood shift, she tries coaxing me. "Declan, I'm fine."

"You're not fine."

"I am."

"I heard you talking to someone the other night, but nobody was here,"

I say, calling her out.

"What are you talking about?"

I stand and pace back a few steps as my irritation grows. "You were in this room with the door closed. You were talking to someone. Who was it? And don't you dare feed me a lie."

Her eyes dart to the corner of the room, and when I look over to the window where she's focusing, the truth hits me.

Pike.

I turn back and take a few steps towards her. "What are you looking at?"

Her eyes, now rimming with tears, shift back to me.

"I need you to talk to me," I plead as I sit back down on the bed next to her. "Is it your brother? Are you seeing him again?"

(ELIZABETH)

"DON'T LIE TO him."

I'm completely caught. He's going to run now that he knows I'm crazy and that I've been lying to him. Panic pangs through my body as Declan stares at me.

"Trust me, Elizabeth. Trust me enough to tell me."

He scoops my hands into his, and I can see the worry pouring out of him.

"Is that who you're looking at? Is he here?"

I close my eyes, scared of what his reaction will be, but I can't hide from the truth he now knows. My hands tremble in his when I finally nod my head yes.

"He's here?"

I nod again, and when I get the courage to open my eyes, I confess, "I need him."

"Baby," he breathes, cupping my cheek with his one hand. "You can't do this to yourself. It's not healthy, and I need you healthy."

"But . . . he's my brother."

"He's dead."

I blink and the tears fall. "I know that. But I still need him."

"Need me more."

His words expose an insecurity I wasn't aware of. I look into his eyes—

really look—and I see what I've never seen before—self-doubt. The green in his eyes brightens in vibrancy, the effect of unshed tears that threaten to fall.

"I do need you," I tell him.

"It's not enough."

"Don't you dare choose me over him."

I turn back to Pike as Declan keeps his eyes on me.

"This has to end, Elizabeth. You have to start taking your pills. I need you well."

I don't look at him when he says this, instead I stay focused on Pike as my tears fall.

"He's right."

"No."

Pike walks over to me and crawls onto the bed, sitting on the other side of me, across from Declan.

"No!" I repeat fervently as I feel the fibers of my soul shredding apart.

"You can't keep hanging on to me like this."

"But I need you."

"I can't let you do this to yourself anymore," Declan says, and when I look back to him, I cry, "But I need him."

"And I need *you*. You have to let him go," he insists. "You have to take your pills and get better."

I turn to Pike again, and when I do, Declan adds on a severed voice, "As much as you need him, I need you more."

"I don't want to lose you, Pike."

"It'll be okay."

"It's not okay. None of this is okay."

"It's time to let me go."

His request burns pieces of my heart into ash. I can feel it—scorching hot and blistering inside me, and I can't seem to cry hard enough to temper the flames. How do I let go when I don't know a day of survival without him?

"Don't leave me!" I sob frantically.

"Baby, this is killing me to see you like this," Declan says, breaking by my side.

"Say goodbye to me, Elizabeth."

My face crumples as the agony of losing my brother for good strangles my heart, paralyzing the ventricles. Tears force their way down my cheeks, cutting me like shards of ice.

"Don't leave me."

"You're the best sister anyone could ever have, and I was so lucky that

you were mine.”

“Don’t you dare say your goodbyes, Pike.”

“Look at Declan. Look at what we’re doing to him.”

I turn to my other side and see Declan’s head in his one hand while his other is holding on to me, and he’s crying.

Oh, my God, he’s crying.

“Declan, please don’t cr—”

“I need you,” he beseeches desperately.

“We can’t continue this.”

I watch as tears fall down Declan’s face, and it’s a punch to my gut to see how much pain he’s in. A man who never cracks is now crumbling before me—because of me. Every tear of his is a fissure in my breaking heart, cutting its way deeper into the delicate tissues.

I can’t do this to him.

I love Pike. He’s sacrificed himself again and again, my whole life, just to protect me, and no words exist to express how much he means to me. But now it’s my turn to protect. And it’s Declan that I need to take care of, because I need him strong so he can care for me in return.

As much as this kills me, I dig deep inside all my rotted wounds to grab on to the strength I need to say goodbye. “I never would’ve survived this world without you, Pike.”

“But you did survive. And you’re going to be okay without me.”

“I love you.”

“I need you to promise me that you’ll listen to Declan, that you’ll start taking your pills and get yourself healthy.”

He’s adamant, and I give him my word through the strain of my throat. “I promise.”

I watch as his solid form ghosts into opacity, and I cry harder.

“I love you.”

“Pike!”

Opacity transfuses into a cloudiness.

“I’m going to miss you.”

“I’m gonna miss you too.”

Cloudiness disappears into nothingness.

And when the lingering vapors of his scent fade away, I fall into Declan.

“He’s gone,” I wail amidst the trauma of freshly crenelated wounds that bleed inside me.

“I’m going to take care of you. I need you to believe in me.”

“I do believe in you. It just hurts to let go of him.”

"Look at me," he demands, and when I do, his face is streaked in tears shed. "I love you to the point it hurts, but I relish the pain of it because it reminds me that what we have runs so deep within me. And I swear to you, I will *never* stop loving you."

I wipe the trail of tears from his face.

"Tell me it hurts you to love me too."

Bracing my hands along his jaw to feel his stubble against my palms, I give him the purest part of me. "There's nobody in this world I could possibly hurt for more. Pike helped me survive, but it's you who helps me live. I was never able to do that until you."

And in the madness of heartache and profound love, Declan takes me as his, holding me, fucking me, healing me. Tears never stop falling from my swollen eyes as I open my heart and allow Declan the freedom to climb inside and take full ownership of all that I'm made of.

I no longer know where I end and he begins as we cement the amorphous lines between us.

We're serpents who feed off one another for sole survivorship.

We're everything love is meant to be.

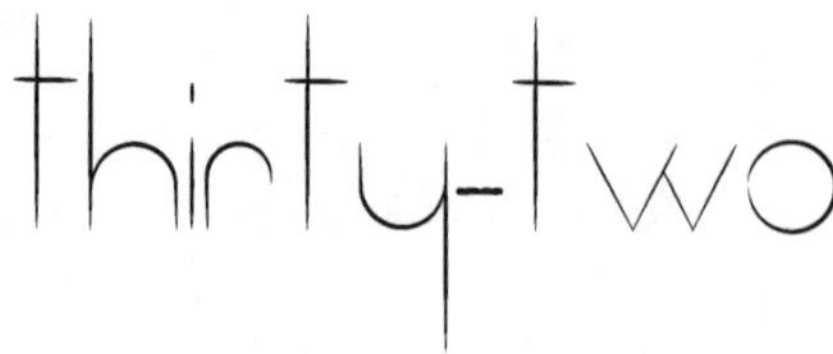

TEARS CRYSTALIZE INTO salts, salts flake into dust, and dust gets swept away into the endless sky. And in the end we are left with a choice: swim or drown. The right choice is often the hardest. Drowning is so easy to do and takes no effort—you simply go weak and float deeper in the despair that consumes. But Pike wouldn't want that for me, and I need to fight for Declan.

So I took my love's hand and started to kick, trusting that together I would find my way to the surface. That was two weeks ago, and today I feel hopeful.

It was four days ago that I laughed for the first time since I said goodbye to my brother. A part of me thought I'd never laugh again, but I did, and oddly, it was Davina that pulled it out of me. Declan thought it would be good to have her over for dinner. He didn't tell her anything we had been dealing with, but she knew something was wrong when I walked into the living room a disheveled mess. One would think a guest would be somewhat reserved, but not Davina. She called me out, telling me I looked like shit. It wasn't just her crass honesty, it was the appalling look on her face and in her tone of voice, which she somehow managed to deliver in a caring way.

And I laughed.

That was all it took.

For a couple weeks Declan has postponed all his meetings and has given Lachlan time off. Declan and I need this time for us to be together and to mend. I feel myself healing little by little.

Declan has been showing me around the city. We've dined everywhere from The Tipperary to the Michelin-awarded Le Gavroche. I fed the ducks at St. James Park, and Declan couldn't hold in his laughter when two geese started chasing after me. The next day, we opted for Hyde Park where we were able to lay under the sun, wrapped in each other's arms. We kissed and talked for hours that afternoon. And then there was the London Eye. Despite my fear of heights and Ferris wheels, I threw caution to the wind and got on. Although I never got off the bench in the center of the glass capsule, Declan appreciated my effort.

We've been desperate for this time together, and now that we have it, we want more.

"If you could go anywhere in the world, where would you go?" Declan asks as we lie in bed, bodies naked and sticky with the smell of our sex in the air.

"Back to Brunswickhill."

"Of all places, you choose our home in Scotland?"

"I love it there."

Running his fingers lazily through my hair, he comments, "You love it that much?"

With my head tucked under his chin, I nod and then kiss his neck as I drape my leg over his hip. Declan grabs my ass and pulls me closer to him, forcing my pussy to grind against his hardening cock. Eager for him to fill me again, I reach down, take him in my hand, and guide him inside of me.

"Fuck me, baby," he growls in need, and when he rolls onto his back, I reach my hands behind me to grab his thighs. Opening my body up to him even more in this position, I fuck him as his hands touch every part of me—caressing, squeezing, pinching. He drives me wild, making me cum all over him, the whole time reaffirming my place in his world—in his heart.

"Let's go there," he says in a heavy breath as our hearts slow.

"Where?"

"Your fairytale castle." He gives me a sexy smirk, and I release a soft laugh when excitement swells at the thought of going back to Scotland.

SOMETHING HAPPENS TO me physically as we drive through the gates of Brunswickhill. I can't fully explain it, but maybe this is what home feels like. It's just the two of us, hand in hand, and for the first time in a very long time, my heart doesn't feel so heavy.

When we get to the top of the winding drive, I hop out of the car, drop my head back, take in a deep breath, and smile.

"What are you doing?"

Declan wraps his arms around my waist, pulling me in close, and with my lips still painted in joy, I tell him, "It feels good to be back."

"This house is your home now."

"I've never had this before. I've never known home until right now—right here with you."

"It's a first for me too, darling, but I wouldn't want this with anyone but you."

His lips land on mine, taking me in a claiming kiss as my hands get lost in his hair. I taste his happiness when he dips his tongue inside my mouth and glides it along mine. This foreign feeling that swirls inside me takes me over and laughter slips out. He doesn't stop dropping kisses on me though, and it's only a matter of seconds when he begins to laugh too.

"What's so funny?" he mumbles against my mouth.

I pull back and look up at him. "I'm just happy."

Declan walks back to the Mercedes and pops open the hatchback to the SUV to grab our luggage, and as he does, I turn to look at the large, tiered fountain.

"Declan, look!" Amazed by the blooms, I walk over to the massive fountain and inhale the earthy scent.

"They've always bloomed in there," he tells me as I look in wonderment at all the lotus flowers.

White mixed with every hue of pink, each one flawless despite the murky water they rose from. They glow as they bask in the sunshine.

"They're so beautiful."

"Come here," he says. "I want to show you a part of the house you've never seen."

We walk inside the double doors, and he drops our luggage in the foyer, taking my hand and leading me up the stairs all the way to the third floor and into his office.

"What are you doing?" I question as he runs his hand along the wall.

When he stops moving, he casts his eyes to me and, with a smile, gives the wall a push.

"Are you kidding me?" I laugh in surprise when it's revealed that a portion of the wall is a hidden spring-loaded partition that opens up to a secret spiral staircase.

"Come on."

I follow him up the narrow stairs, and when we reach the top, there's another door that he opens. My eyes widen in amazement when I step out onto the rooftop, exposing a panoramic view of all of Galashiels. Declan reaches out for me, knowing my fear of heights, and walks me to the wall's edge.

"You see that river?" he asks as he points out.

"Yes."

"That's the River Tweed. It divides Galashiels from Abbottsford. And you see that castle-like estate down there?"

"Yes."

"That's Sir Walter Scott's home."

"The poet?"

"Yes."

"That's no home," I note as I look at the majestic estate that's nestled down below from where Declan's estate sits perched high on this hill. "That's a palace!"

He chuckles. "It's a museum now. There's also a quaint restaurant that's known for their shortcakes in there."

We walk the border of the rooftop, and I look down to the grounds below, admiring all the colorful blooms that are coming to life as the weather warms. The past couple months of spring have done wonders, exposing more pebbled creeks that stream down various hills. There are too many flowers to count, along with a few stone benches—some that rest under trees and some that are out in the open. From up here, I can see the grassy paths that lead from one garden nook to the next, to the next, and to the next. A part of me feels like I'm cheating myself of the wanderlust of exploring and getting lost in the maze down there.

My very own Wonderland.

"It's stunning, isn't it?"

"It's breathtaking," I say and then turn to face him, pressing my body against his with my arms wrapped around his waist. "I never thought anything like this could exist in this world."

"I feel the same when I look at you."

We stand here, on the rooftop of our own personal castle, and wrap ourselves around each other. Declan cradles my head to his chest as he plants kisses down on me. We hug; it's all we need to do in this moment of much-needed peace, and finally, I can breathe. The weight of the world's afflictions are becoming less and less suffocating as I continue to move along this path Declan is providing me. Of course a part of me still aches for my dad and for my brother, but that's a sadness I'll have to brave for the rest of my life. There's simply no cure for heartbreaks that surpass unfathomable agony. Some wounds run so deep that there's no possibility of healing. But here, with Declan, I'm hoping one day the pain will become more tolerable.

"I was thinking about something on the plane ride here," Declan says, breaking the silence between us. "We should go to The Water Lily."

I smile when I think about Isla. Staying with her when I was at my ultimate lowest, thinking Declan had died at the hands of Pike, was probably the best place I could've wound up. We had so many great conversations, and I realize now that I know so much about his grandmother when he's never really spoken to her.

"Isla has a beautiful heart," I tell him. "I miss her."

"Why do you think she never said anything to me? She has a photo of me in her room and she knows who I am."

I see the little boy lost deep within his eyes as I look at him. "Maybe she was scared. Maybe she didn't know what to say."

"Maybe," he responds. "How about we pay her a visit tomorrow? Let's take the rest of the day for us." He leans down and kisses me before saying, "Take a walk with me."

We head back down the hidden staircase and then down to main floor of the house. Walking through the atrium, we make our way outside.

"Everything looks so different than it did when we left a couple months ago," I say as we stroll aimlessly through the flowers.

We make our way up a stone pathway that runs alongside the clinker grotto and then wander along another grassy path, weaving through trees and stepping over a narrow babbling brook. I look down at the house, and laugh to myself when I see the huge gaps that still remain in the now-flowering bushes that rim around the exterior wall.

"What's so funny?"

"I still can't believe you ripped out all the purple bushes," I tell him, and when he looks down to the house to see the gaps, he shrugs. "My darling hates purple," he says nonchalantly and continues to walk.

"Sit with me," he says when we find ourselves surrounded by bright yellow daffodils.

I settle myself between Declan's legs and back against his chest as he sits behind me. We both look out among the flowers as I sink into his hold.

"Tell me you're happy," he says, and I answer honestly, "I'm happy."

"You know, the first time I ever saw you, I knew I had to have you." I rest my head against him as I listen to him speak. "I'd never felt that intensely about anyone before. I can still remember how beautiful you looked that night in your navy silk dress and long red hair. I was beyond fascinated by you."

"And I remember you, not even wearing a bow tie to your own black tie affair," I tease.

"I know our start was fucked up, but I wouldn't change it. Because without it, we wouldn't have *this*."

"I'll never forgive myself though."

"I need you to know something." The seriousness in his tone makes me sit up and turn to face him. "I need you to know that I've forgiven you, and that hate I used to feel towards you . . . it's no longer there."

His words soothe, and when he begins to kaleidoscope, I blink him into clarity. But these tears don't hurt—they heal. He places his hands on my cheeks and kisses me again.

"You give yourself to me in a way no other woman could. And even if they could, I wouldn't want them to. I'm not perfect—you've even called me out on my flaws a few times, but you've never thrown them in my face with ridicule," he says with gratitude. "And when I tell you that I need you, I mean it. I can't battle this world without you by my side. You're the bravest woman I know."

"I'm not."

"You are. My God, the life you've been dealt, everything you've had to endure, and here you are, still fighting. Still trying."

"Because of you," I tell him. "Every breath is a choice, and I choose to keep taking them for you."

"I'm going to give you a long life filled with breaths then," he affirms before he takes my face in his hands and looks steadfastly into my eyes. "I once told you that the truest part of a person is the ugliest."

"I remember that night."

"The ugliest parts of you are your darkest. And trust me when I tell you that I want to love all of your darkest parts." He reaches into his pocket, and my heart beats a beat I've never felt before as he pulls out a ring. "And I promise you that I will love all of your darkness if you promise to love mine too."

"Declan . . ."

"Marry me."

And that was the moment all my dreams came true. We sat there in the garden of daffodils as he held that ring, which embodied exactly what we were between his fingers—two people who harbored so much darkness. The cushion-cut diamond was brilliant and so very black with intricate facets, encircled with tiny, sparkling white diamonds that also adorned the delicately thin platinum band.

But it wasn't the ring, it was him. It was always him. The only one who was strong enough to love me for me. He took all my rot and all my scars and somehow made me feel like a true princess.

My whole life, I was waiting for someone to save me, and he did. I knew in that moment that I would never be unloved, I would never be abandoned, and I would never be left to fight the monsters alone.

"Yes!"

My eyes never leave his beautiful face as he slips the ring on to my finger, and once in place, I throw myself into his arms, knocking him back to the ground. And we kiss like no two people have ever kissed. I pour my soul into his mouth as his hands grip me tightly—we're so needy for closeness.

But that closeness is severed the moment I hear the *snick.*

I jump back and turn in an instant to find myself staring down the barrel of a pistol.

"You move, I shoot her," the man snarls to Declan. But I know Declan isn't armed right now.

We're helpless.

I'm frozen in place. I can't even feel my heart beating anymore.

"This is vengeance. Your father fucked with the wrong family the moment he handed my brother's name over to the feds sixteen years ago. But because I'm sadistic, I'm going to give you the choice. Either you die or your father dies. You have five seconds."

I turn to Declan, already knowing my choice as I mouth *I love you* through razor-sharp tears.

"Elizabeth, no!"

"Don't hurt my dad. Kill me."

"Eliz—"

BANG.

epilogue

I LOOK UP into the brilliant, rich blue sky. There isn't a cloud in sight as the sun shines down in rays of glittering warmth. I look around to find I'm surrounded by gigantic, lime-green canopies, but when I take a closer look, I realize they aren't canopies, but instead, blades of grass.

Carnegie?

My eyes dart down to reveal my bright pink accordion body.

I'm back.

"Hello?" I call out, wondering why I'm all alone, and when I hear a rustling in the distance, I call out again, "Carnegie? Is that you?"

"Elizabeth!" he hollers back, but his accent isn't right. "Elizabeth!"

No. It can't be.

"Declan?" I scoot around to see a blue caterpillar emerge from behind a blade of grass.

"Elizabeth," he exclaims in his unmistakable Scottish brogue as he inches over to me.

"What are you doing in my dream?"

"Dream?" His beady eyes drop in dread.

"What's wrong?"

"Darling . . ."

"What's going on?" I question in fear.

"You died."

Horror fires off inside me as I look at him. "Then . . . Then what are you doing here?"

"Don't panic."

"Oh, my God!"

"We're together, Elizabeth. That's all that matters."

"If I'm dead, then . . ."

"I am too," he tells me. "He shot me right after he shot you."

"NO!" I cry out, and he's right here next to me, comforting, "It's okay, darling. We're still together. Nothing can hurt us now."

"But you're . . . you're dead because of me!"

"No, baby. You made the right choice. That guy was there for revenge, and no matter what you said, he would've killed us anyway," he tells me. "But look around you. This place is incredible."

I stare at him in utter shock and ask, "How are you so calm?"

"We've both been here for a while, a few days or so, but you've been sleeping. I've had time to digest it all, but this place doesn't allow stress to last very long." He slinks his way closer, running his body along mine, and the moment I feel his touch, my heart settles peacefully.

"We're okay?"

He nods and then tells me, "We're not alone either."

"You mean Carnegie? Did you meet him?"

"I did, but there's someone else you're going to want to see."

"Who?"

"Your brother."

"Pike?" I perk up in astonishment. "He's here?"

"He's out with Carnegie right now gathering berries."

"You talked to him?"

"Yes, but don't worry. We've had a lot of time to reach an understanding with one another."

"He's not a bad guy," I immediately defend, and he stops me.

"I know that now. Come on. Let's go find them."

We maze around enormous flower stems and even more gigantic tree trunks as we scoot together, side by side. Every now and then Declan looks over to me and smiles, which makes me giggle. He's right, the stress doesn't last long. As I frolic along, I feel weightless, I feel exuberant, I feel . . . free.

"This way," Declan tells me before we turn and weave our way through the wooden vines of a berry bush. "It's a shortcut."

I look up at the pink berries that are as big as basketballs, and when we come to an opening and make our way out, I see Carnegie. And next to him is a bright red caterpillar.

"Pike?"

"You're awake!"

"Pike!"

I slink as quickly as I can to him, and he does the same.

"I never thought I'd see you again," I tell him.

"You can't get rid of me," he jokes as he nudges his stumpy head into the side of my tubular body. "You know, when you promised you'd do anything to get us a better life, I didn't think we'd have to be fucking caterpillars to get it."

We both laugh and Declan joins in as he sidles up next to me.

"Language, young man," Carnegie nags in his dapper British accent.

I worm my way closer to my lifelong friend. "Carnegie . . ."

"It's been far too long, my dear."

"What is all this?"

"Why, this is your afterlife. Nothing will ever hurt you again, because pain no longer exists. This is where dreams are reality."

"I told you it would all be okay, darling," Declan reaffirms.

I release a pleased sigh and lean my head against Declan.

Carnegie looks to us, asking, "So, this is love?"

Gazing into Declan's eyes, I respond, "This is love."

Declan and I continue to nuzzle each other tenderly while Carnegie and Pike are off by the pond's edge. Movement catches my eye, and when I turn to a tall bush next to me, an orange caterpillar appears. It stops and looks at me curiously, and then the beady eyes widen.

"Princess?"

My body sparks in bewilderment. "Dad?"

He rushes over to me, his tiny mouth fighting for the biggest smile.

"What are you doing h—"

Oh, my God. He's dead.

And suddenly, I see his smile drop when realization hits him that I'm dead too.

He stops moving, and when his eyes slip away from mine, he looks to Declan. "What happened to you two?"

I hold my breath, not wanting my father to feel any guilt that I chose to pay the pay the price for his past—that Declan did too. "You tell me first."

He scoots a little closer before saying, "The brother of one of the guys I handed over to the feds ran me off the road right after I left the beach the last day we were together. He gave me a choice. He told me I could live and that he would kill you instead or he could just kill me." My mouth gapes in shock. "Obviously, I gave up my own life."

"There was never a choice," Declan tells him.

"What do you mean?"

"That same man paid me and your daughter a visit with the same ultimatum."

My dad's eyes dart back to me, and I tell him, "I told him not to hurt you and to kill me instead."

"You sacrificed your life for me?"

I nod.

"Sweetheart . . ."

"It's okay, Dad," I assure him. "Can I ask you something though?"

"Anything."

"What was your biggest wish when you were living?"

The corners of his mouth lift. "You," he says. "I always wished to have you in my life."

My heart floats like a feather. "And my wish was always you, Dad." My eyes mist over in pure delight. "Our wishes came true." I turn to face Declan and tell him in amazement, "This is my every wish come true."

The three of us look at one another as the truth crystallizes. We are a web of wishes come true. We no longer have to creep in the shadows of those who wish us harm. We are finally free from all that has ever haunted us. I know Declan and I would have never been able to find this kind of freedom among the living. It only exists here.

I look around at the magnificently colored flowers that wisp in the breeze above us, I see Pike riding on the back of a dragonfly—happy and whimsical, and then there's Carnegie, who never has to be alone again because he has us now. I laugh as he watches in merriment at my brother flying around. And my dad, overflowing with boundless mirth as he kisses the top of my head.

"This is all I ever wanted," he tells me.

I then turn to face Declan—amazed that our love was so powerful that not even death could part us. And then we kiss a kiss that's never existed until now. It's serene and vivacious and loving and entirely magical.

This is everything dreams are made of.

This is my fairytale.

from the author

Want to join other E.K. Blair fans for book talk, giveaways, and inside peeks into Blair's upcoming books?

Join The Little Black Hearts fan group!
EK BLAIR'S LITTLE BLACK HEARTS
(https://www.facebook.com/groups/bangdiscussion/)

acknowledgements

THIS SERIES WAS a labor of love, and this book in particular! It took many people who love and support me to help me see this story come to fruition. I wouldn't be able to do what I do if it weren't for the following people.

To my fans, I cannot thank you enough for continuing to love my characters and support my stories. Your loyalty means the world to me. The greatest joy is being able to cut my heart open, pour my blood on the pages, and hand it over to you.

Sally Gillespie, you are one of my biggest blessings! The time you sacrifice for me is simply incredible. Thank you for helping me in the creation of this story. I had a blast working with you on the book. We've blushed, we've laughed, and we've cried more times than I can count, but we did it! You are my backbone, and I'd fall to pieces without you.

Bethany Castaneda, thank you for all the little things you do that are huge things for me! You save me so much time and so many headaches. Whenever I call, you are always there for me. And no matter what, I can always count on you for a good laugh. You keep this boat afloat, and I am so grateful to have you as part of my team.

Jennifer Juers, thank you for your honesty and time. I love that you don't sugarcoat anything! You never try to appease me; you only want to help me even if it means telling me the cold, hard truth. The time you put in to making this book the best it can be is invaluable! You are my secret weapon.

Mary Elizabeth, damn Daniel! Thank you for inspiring me to be a better writer. Your support, guidance, and friendship are so precious to me.

Ashley Williams, wow! Just WOW! How do I even thank you properly? The hours upon hours you have devoted to this book are downright incredible! You make my words strong, even though you bust my balls to do so. From the early mornings to the late nights, and everything in between, you have been there with me every step of the way through this book. I am looking forward to sharing this experience with you for many books to come.

You are an amazing editor and friend!

Lisa Lisa Lisa, my partner in crime, there's no one I'd rather fight with than you! I cannot say it enough, you are truly a gem. Thank you for always believing in me, for always pushing me to be a better writer, and for not beating around the bush. You give it to me honestly, and even though I dig my heels in the ground because I'm stubborn, I really appreciate all that you do for me. I love you, and I miss you, and you should totally move next door to me so we can always be together!

Thank you, Denise Tung, for working your magic and organizing all the promos and reviews. I couldn't do this without you!

Erik Schottstaedt, once again, you've crafted another beautiful photo for my cover. Thank you for creating the whole look of this series.

Bloggers, there are too many of you to name, but each and every one of you are equally important. Thank you for your undying support.

To my husband, none of this would be possible without you. You're the best Mr. Mom I know. Thank you for taking care of the children, the house, the laundry, the dinners, and so much more to allow me the time and privacy I need to write. I love you, babes!

And finally, thank you to Elizabeth, Declan, and Pike. Living inside of your souls for the past two years has been an amazing experience. We've been on quite a journey together. I'm heartbroken to say goodbye and to put you up on my bookshelf after all we have been through. I will miss each of you in very different ways the way each of you have touched my heart in different ways. You have allowed me to discover pieces of myself I never knew were inside me, pieces that I needed to know were there. I'm going to miss you. I'll look for you all in my dreams when I find my way into the forest—into the fairytale.

Ways to Connect

www.ekblair.com

Facebook: www.facebook.com/EKBlairAuthor

Twitter: @EK_Blair_Author

Instagram: instagram.com/authorekblair

New York Times Bestseller

THE FADING SERIES

"Heart-wrenching, jaw-dropping, and absolutely beautiful."
-Aleatha Romig, *New York Times* bestselling author

"One of the most incredible, breathtaking stories I have ever read."
-Word

"Beautifully written and emotionally charged."
-Vilma Gonzalez, *USA Today* HEA blog

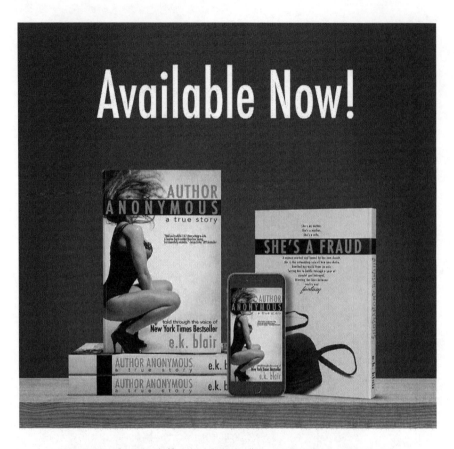